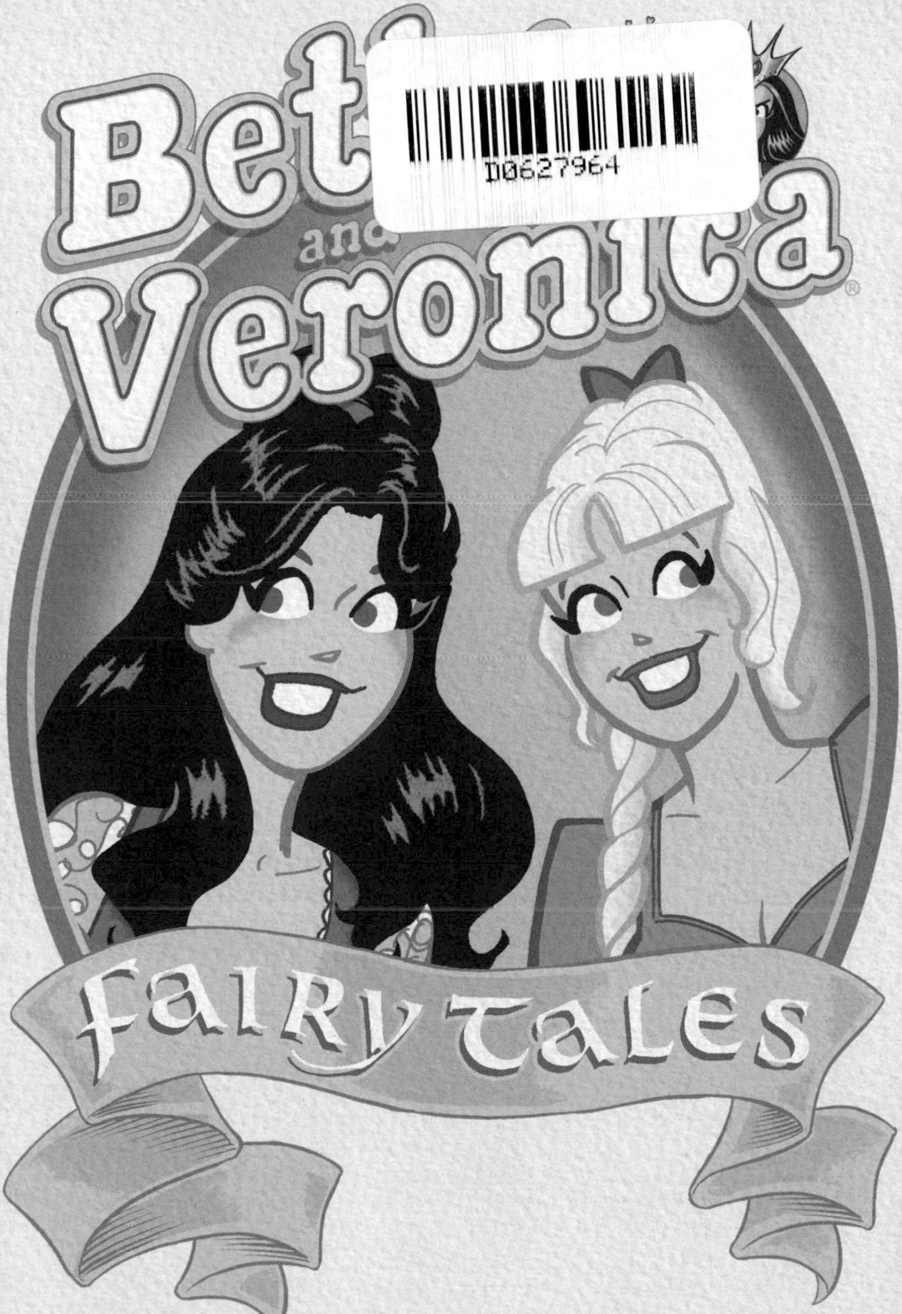
Bet
and
Veronica
Fairy Tales

✳✳✳✳✳✳ CREDITS ✳

STORY ADAPTATIONS BY:
Dan Parent

ART BY:
Dan Parent, Jeff Shultz, Rich Koslowski,
Jim Amash, Bob Smith, Jack Morelli, Janice Chiang,
Teresa Davidson, Barry Grossman & Digikore Studios

VARIANT COVERS BY:
Fiona Staples, Alitha Martinez, Renae De Liz,
Jill Thompson & Stephanie Buscema

PUBLISHER/CO-CEO: Jon Goldwater
CO-CEO: Nancy Silberkleit
PRESIDENT: Mike Pellerito
CO-PRESIDENT/EDITOR-IN-CHIEF: Victor Gorelick
CHIEF CREATIVE OFFICER: Roberto Aguirre-Sacasa
CHIEF OPERATING OFFICER: William Mooar
CHIEF FINANCIAL OFFICER: Robert Wintle
SVP, PUBLICITY & MARKETING: Alex Segura
DIRECTOR, BOOK SALES & OPERATIONS: Jonathan Betancourt
LEAD DESIGNER: Kari McLachlan
PRODUCTION MANAGER: Stephen Oswald
EDITORIAL ASSISTANT/PROOFREADER: Jamie Lee Rotante

Archie & Friends All-Stars Series: Volume 27
Betty & Veronica: Fairy Tales Published by Archie Comic Publications, Inc. 629 Fifth Avenue, Suite
100, Pelham, New York 10803-1242. www.ArchieComics.com

Contents

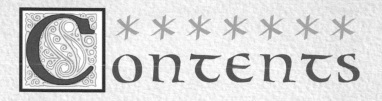

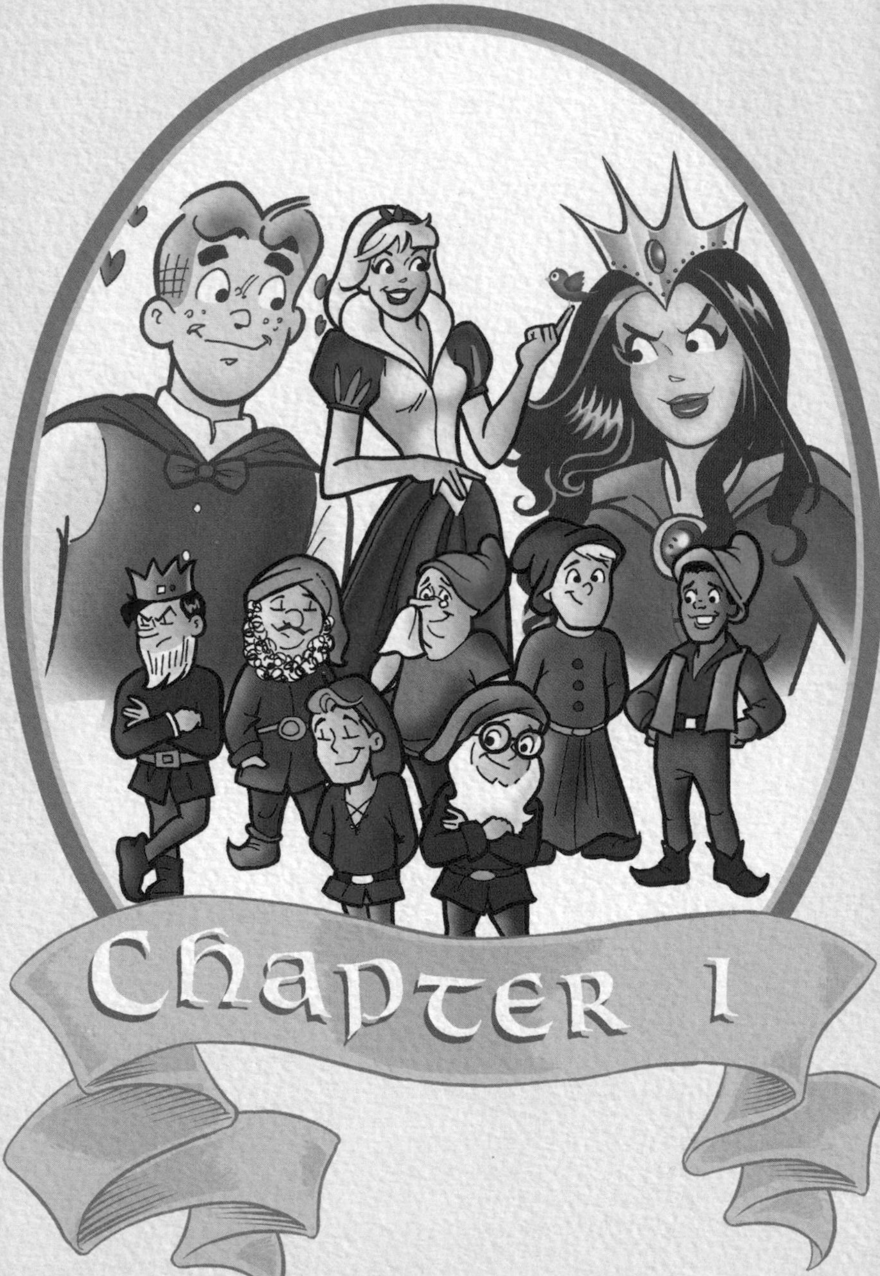
Chapter 1

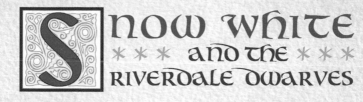 Snow White
* * * and the * * *
Riverdale Dwarves

"Mirror, mirror on the wall, who's the hottest of them all?" asks the evil queen Veronica as she gazes at her own reflection. When the answer is "Snow White," the vain queen makes it her top priority to eliminate the beautiful Betty, unable to live in a world where she's #2 to her blonde rival.

Can Snow White dodge the queen's dastardly efforts with some help from the strangely familiar seven dwarfs and find her prince?

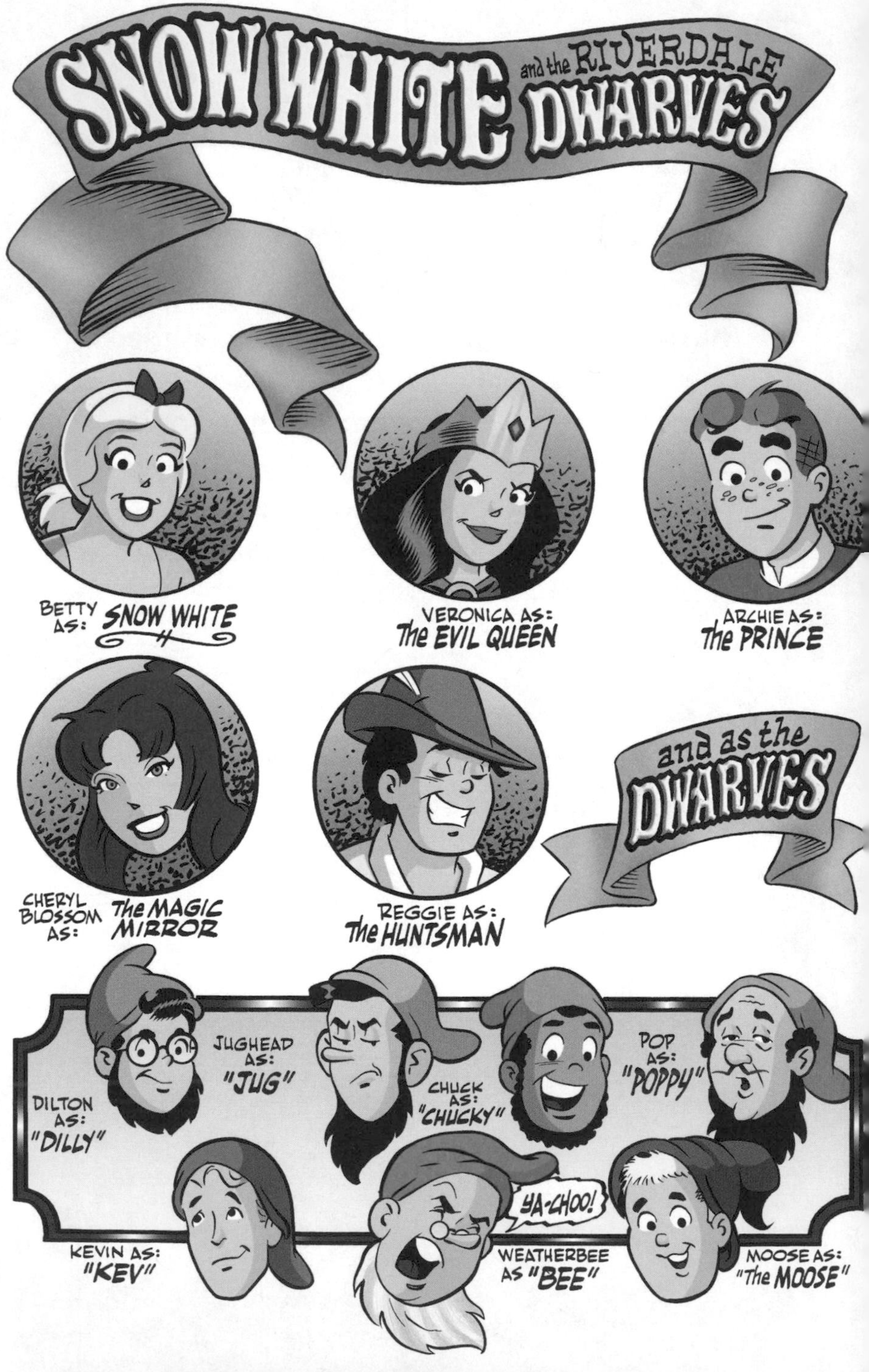
SNOW WHITE and the RIVERDALE DWARVES
BETTY AS: SNOW WHITE
VERONICA AS: The EVIL QUEEN
ARCHIE AS: The PRINCE
CHERYL BLOSSOM AS: The MAGIC MIRROR
REGGIE AS: The HUNTSMAN
and as the DWARVES
DILTON AS: "DILLY"
JUGHEAD AS: "JUG"
CHUCK AS: "CHUCKY"
POP AS: "POPPY"
KEVIN AS: "KEV"
YA-CHOO!
WEATHERBEE AS "BEE"
MOOSE AS: "The MOOSE"

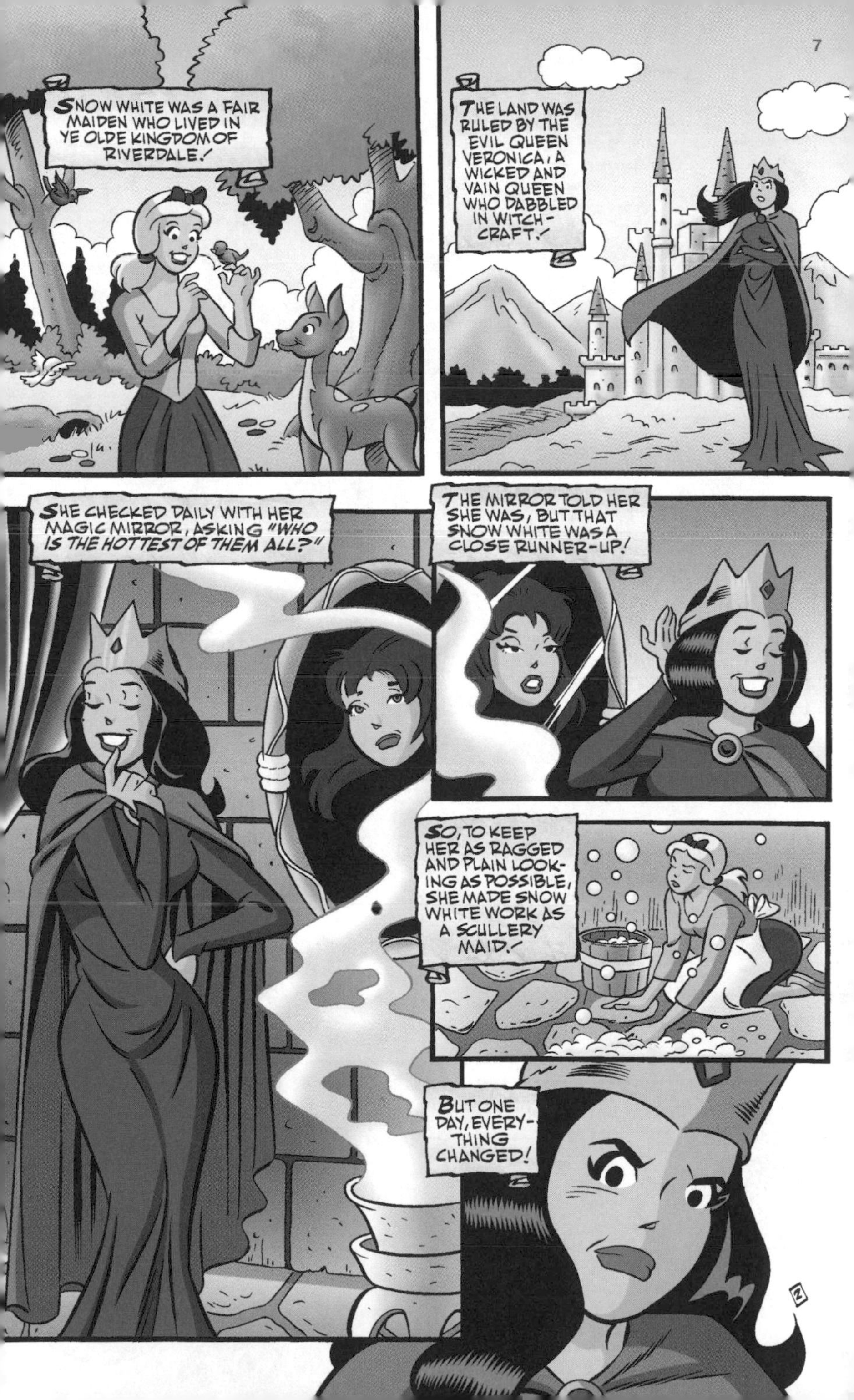
SNOW WHITE WAS A FAIR MAIDEN WHO LIVED IN YE OLDE KINGDOM OF RIVERDALE!
THE LAND WAS RULED BY THE EVIL QUEEN VERONICA, A WICKED AND VAIN QUEEN WHO DABBLED IN WITCH-CRAFT!
SHE CHECKED DAILY WITH HER MAGIC MIRROR, ASKING "WHO IS THE HOTTEST OF THEM ALL?"
THE MIRROR TOLD HER SHE WAS, BUT THAT SNOW WHITE WAS A CLOSE RUNNER-UP!
SO, TO KEEP HER AS RAGGED AND PLAIN LOOKING AS POSSIBLE, SHE MADE SNOW WHITE WORK AS A SCULLERY MAID!
BUT ONE DAY, EVERYTHING CHANGED!

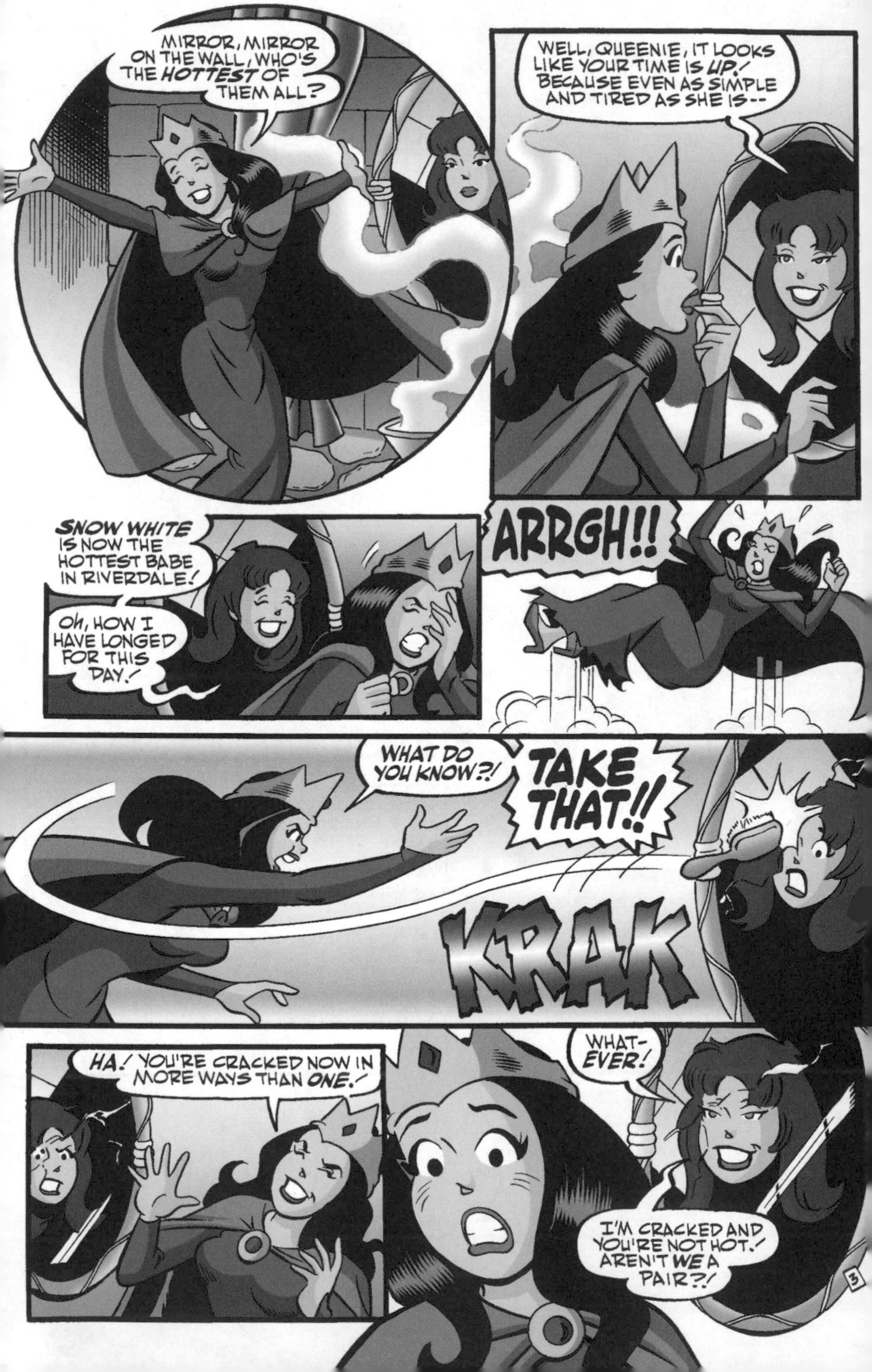
MIRROR, MIRROR ON THE WALL, WHO'S THE HOTTEST OF THEM ALL?
WELL, QUEENIE, IT LOOKS LIKE YOUR TIME IS UP! BECAUSE EVEN AS SIMPLE AND TIRED AS SHE IS--
SNOW WHITE IS NOW THE HOTTEST BABE IN RIVERDALE!
OH, HOW I HAVE LONGED FOR THIS DAY!
ARRGH!!
WHAT DO YOU KNOW?!
TAKE THAT!!
KRAK
HA! YOU'RE CRACKED NOW IN MORE WAYS THAN ONE!
WHAT-EVER!
I'M CRACKED AND YOU'RE NOT HOT! AREN'T WE A PAIR?!
3

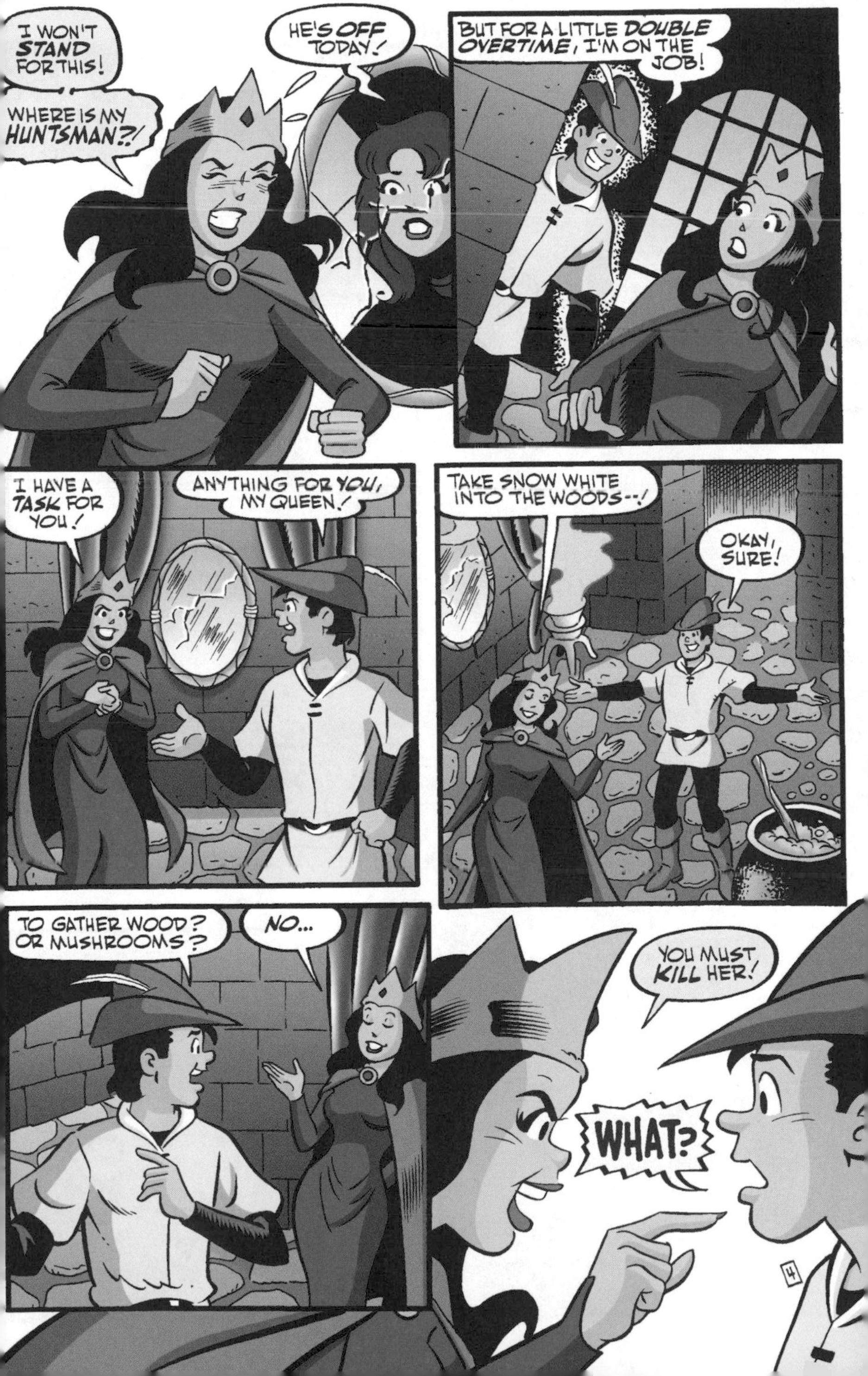
I WON'T STAND FOR THIS!
WHERE IS MY HUNTSMAN?!
HE'S OFF TODAY!
BUT FOR A LITTLE DOUBLE OVERTIME, I'M ON THE JOB!
I HAVE A TASK FOR YOU!
ANYTHING FOR YOU, MY QUEEN!
TAKE SNOW WHITE INTO THE WOODS--!
OKAY, SURE!
TO GATHER WOOD? OR MUSHROOMS?
NO...
YOU MUST KILL HER!
WHAT?
4

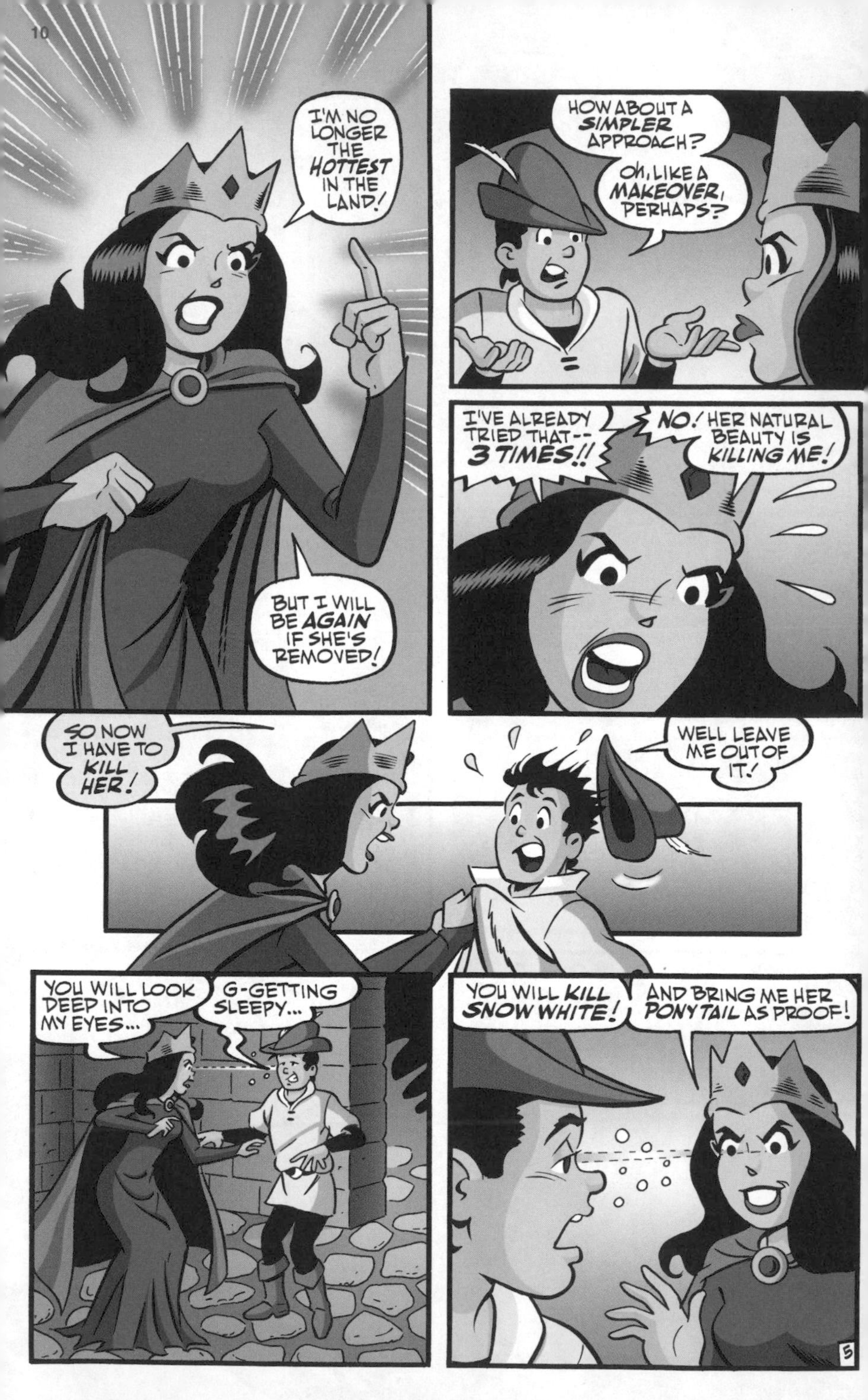
I'M NO LONGER THE HOTTEST IN THE LAND!
BUT I WILL BE AGAIN IF SHE'S REMOVED!
HOW ABOUT A SIMPLER APPROACH?
OH, LIKE A MAKEOVER, PERHAPS?
I'VE ALREADY TRIED THAT-- 3 TIMES!!
NO! HER NATURAL BEAUTY IS KILLING ME!
SO NOW I HAVE TO KILL HER!
WELL LEAVE ME OUT OF IT!
YOU WILL LOOK DEEP INTO MY EYES...
G-GETTING SLEEPY...
YOU WILL KILL SNOW WHITE!
AND BRING ME HER PONYTAIL AS PROOF!
5

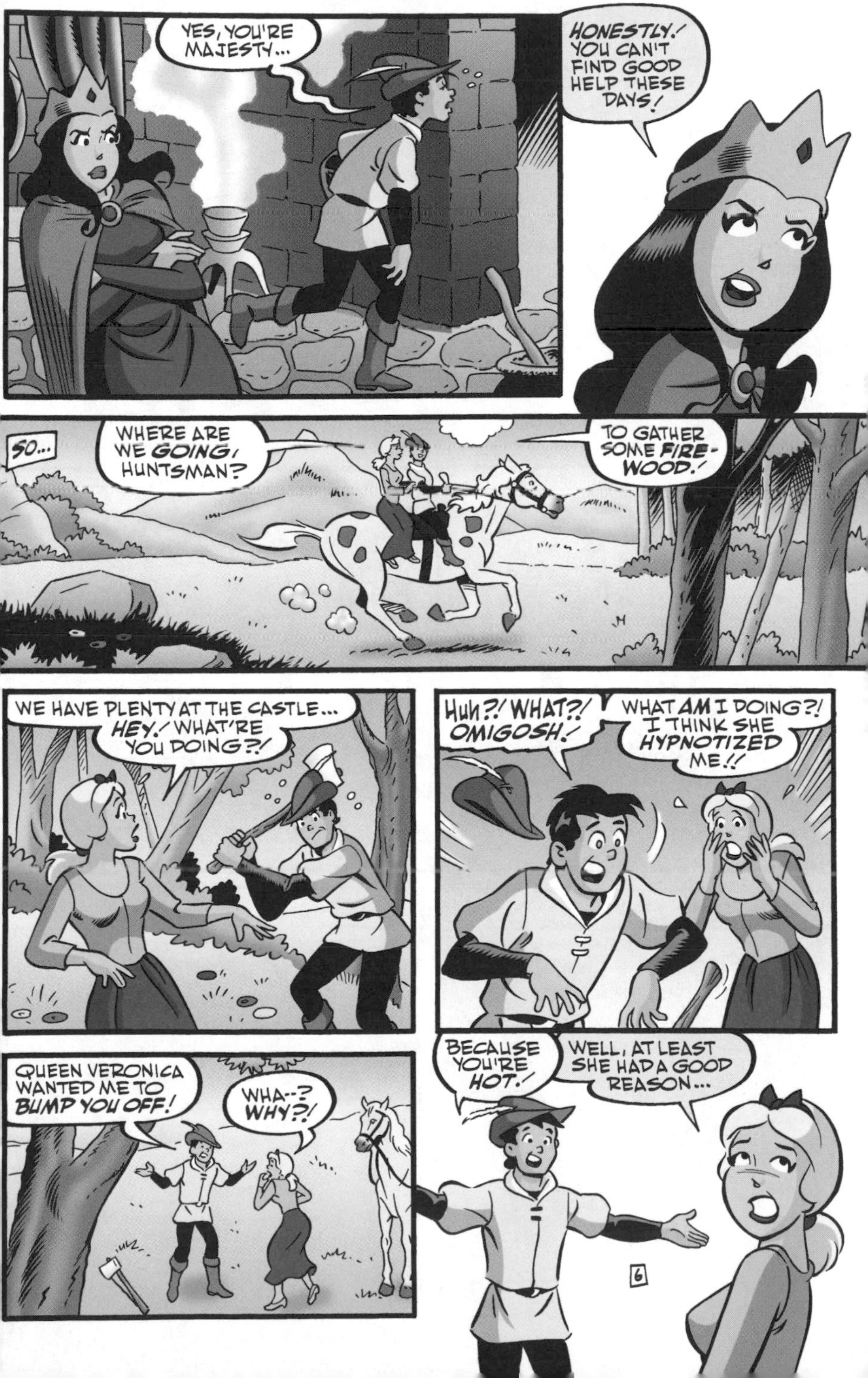
YES, YOU'RE MAJESTY...
HONESTLY! YOU CAN'T FIND GOOD HELP THESE DAYS!
SO...
WHERE ARE WE GOING, HUNTSMAN?
TO GATHER SOME FIRE-WOOD!
WE HAVE PLENTY AT THE CASTLE... HEY! WHAT'RE YOU DOING?!
HUH?! WHAT?! OMIGOSH!
WHAT AM I DOING?! I THINK SHE HYPNOTIZED ME!!
QUEEN VERONICA WANTED ME TO BUMP YOU OFF!
WHA--? WHY?!
BECAUSE YOU'RE HOT!
WELL, AT LEAST SHE HAD A GOOD REASON...
6

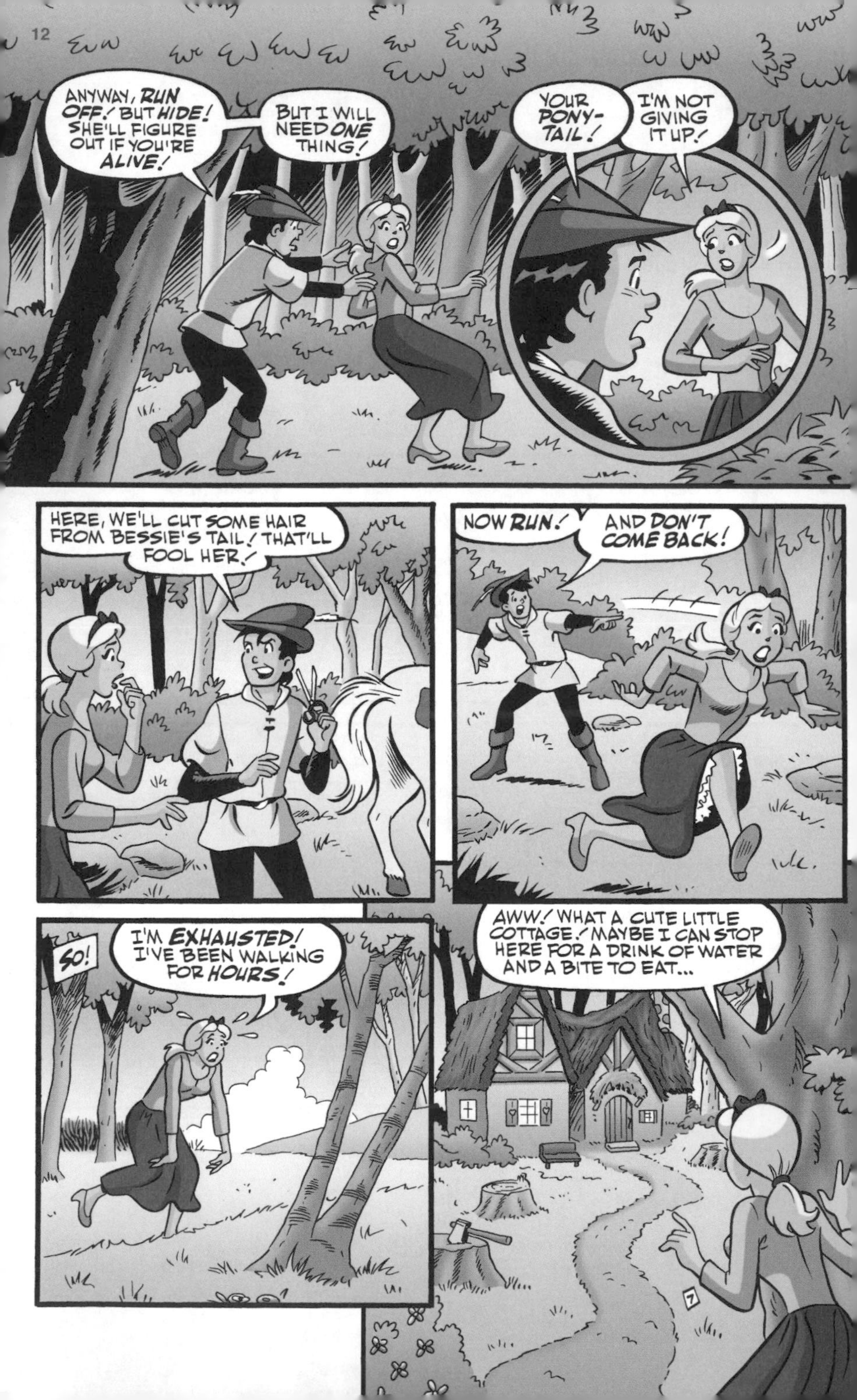
ANYWAY, RUN OFF! BUT HIDE! SHE'LL FIGURE OUT IF YOU'RE ALIVE!
BUT I WILL NEED ONE THING!
YOUR PONY-TAIL!
I'M NOT GIVING IT UP!
HERE, WE'LL CUT SOME HAIR FROM BESSIE'S TAIL! THAT'LL FOOL HER!
NOW RUN!
AND DON'T COME BACK!
SO!
I'M EXHAUSTED! I'VE BEEN WALKING FOR HOURS!
AWW! WHAT A CUTE LITTLE COTTAGE! MAYBE I CAN STOP HERE FOR A DRINK OF WATER AND A BITE TO EAT...
7

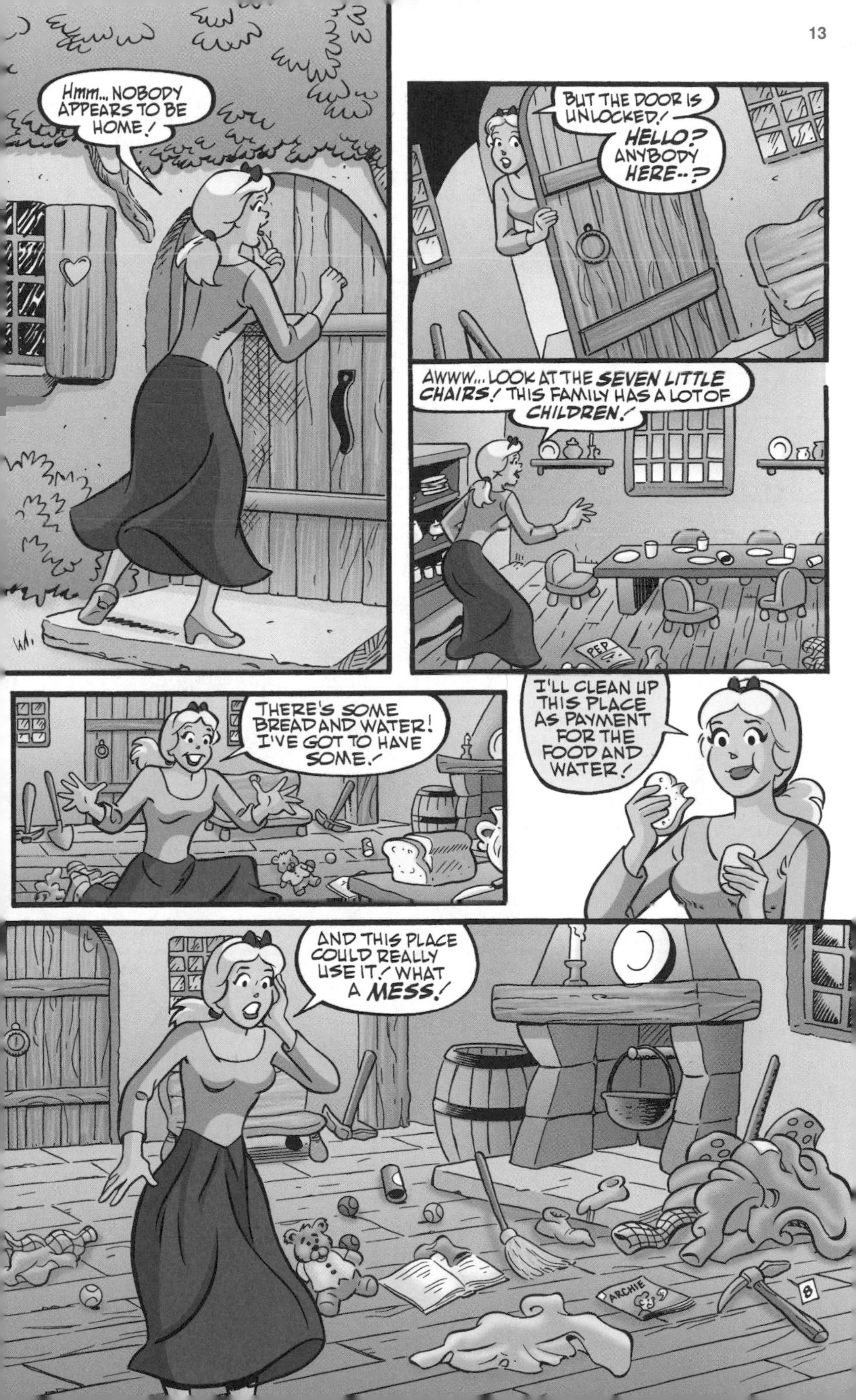
Hmm... NOBODY APPEARS TO BE HOME!
BUT THE DOOR IS UNLOCKED! HELLO? ANYBODY HERE..?
AWWW... LOOK AT THE SEVEN LITTLE CHAIRS! THIS FAMILY HAS A LOT OF CHILDREN!
PEP
THERE'S SOME BREAD AND WATER! I'VE GOT TO HAVE SOME!
I'LL CLEAN UP THIS PLACE AS PAYMENT FOR THE FOOD AND WATER!
AND THIS PLACE COULD REALLY USE IT! WHAT A MESS!
ARCHIE
8

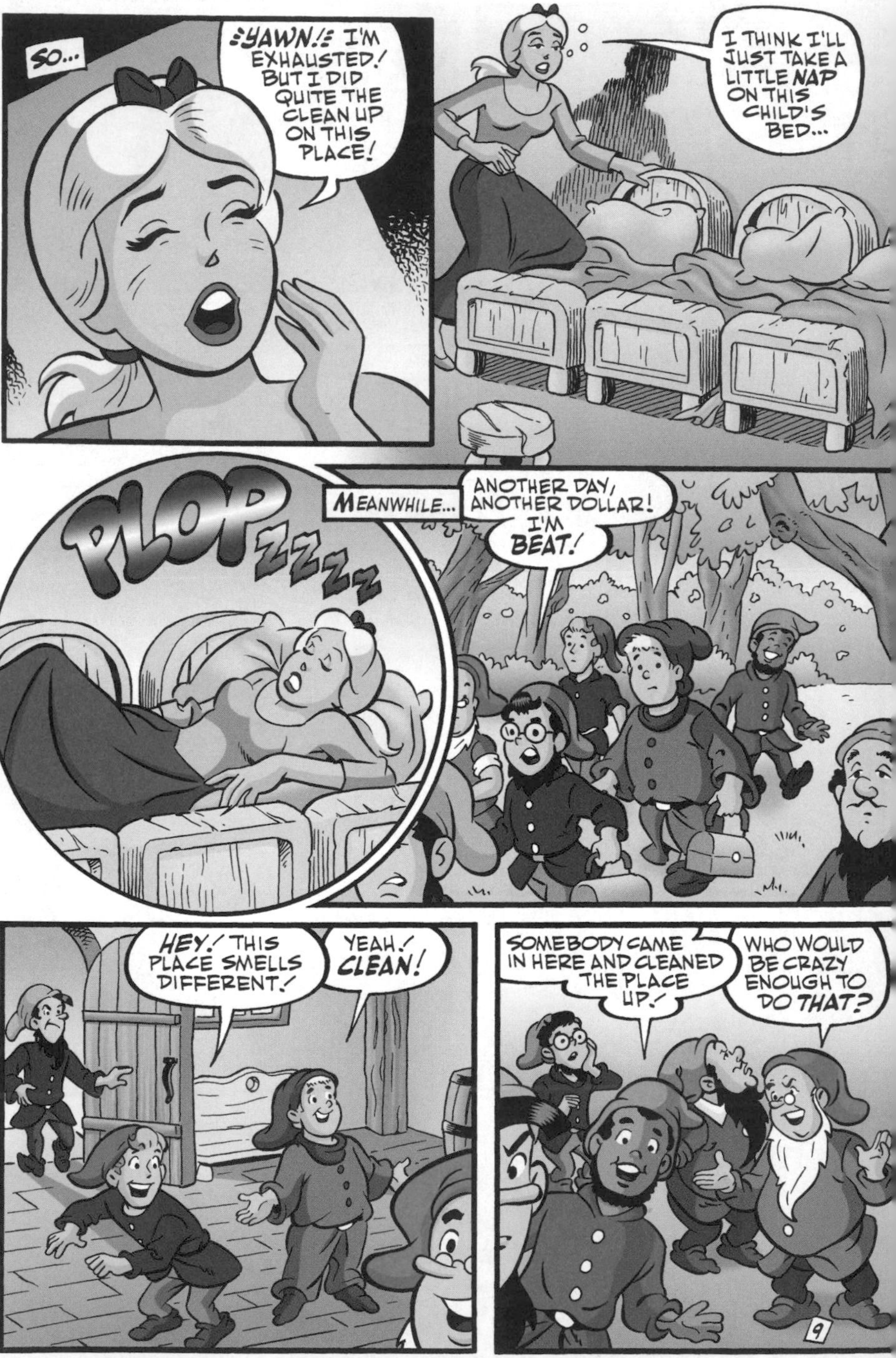
SO...
:YAWN!: I'M EXHAUSTED! BUT I DID QUITE THE CLEAN UP ON THIS PLACE!
I THINK I'LL JUST TAKE A LITTLE NAP ON THIS CHILD'S BED...
PLOP ZZZZ
MEANWHILE...
ANOTHER DAY, ANOTHER DOLLAR! I'M BEAT!
HEY! THIS PLACE SMELLS DIFFERENT!
YEAH! CLEAN!
SOMEBODY CAME IN HERE AND CLEANED THE PLACE UP!
WHO WOULD BE CRAZY ENOUGH TO DO THAT?
9

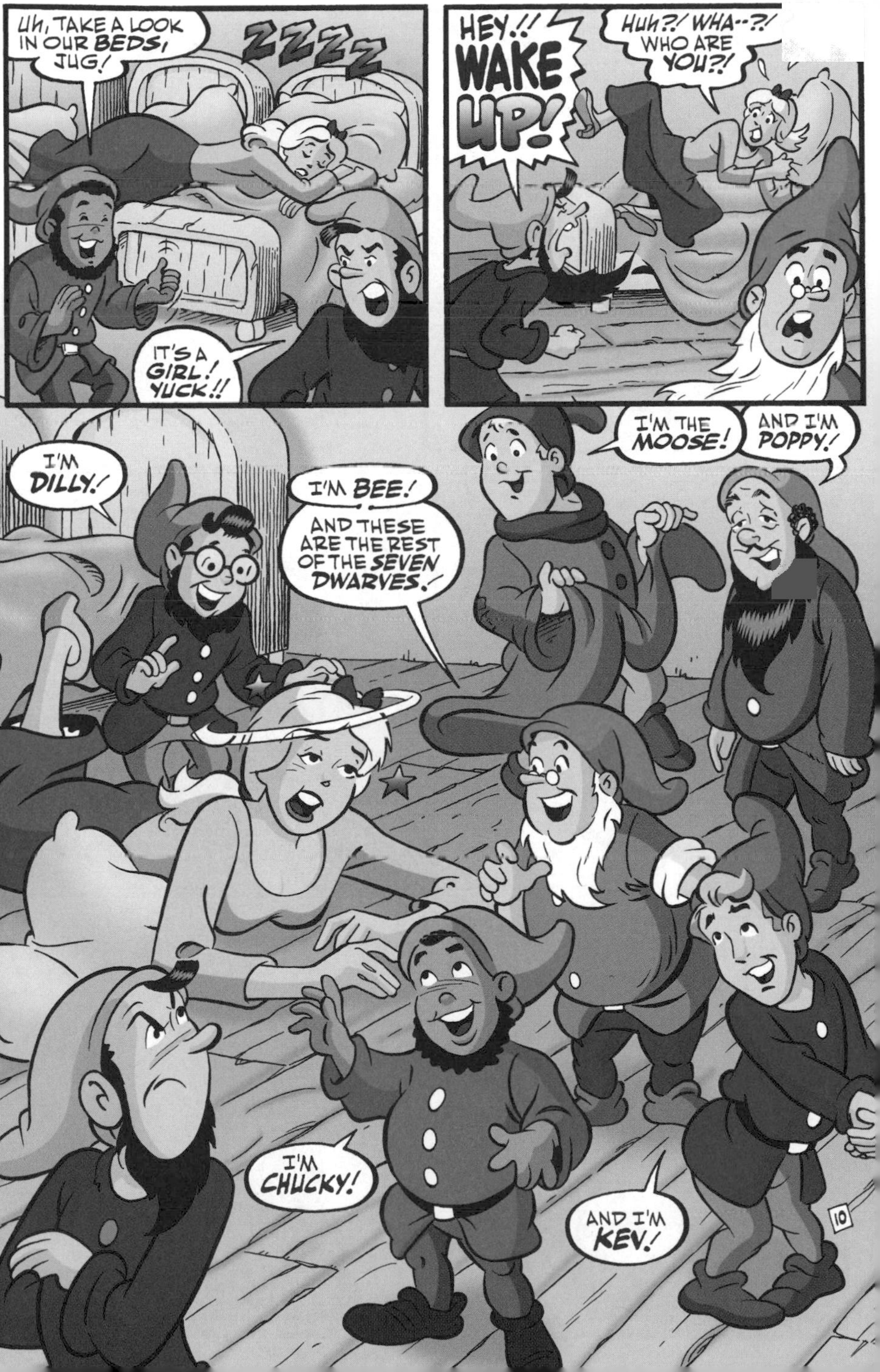
Uh, TAKE A LOOK IN OUR BEDS, JUG!
ZZZZ
IT'S A GIRL! YUCK!!
HEY!! WAKE UP!
Huh?! WHA--?! WHO ARE YOU?!
I'M DILLY!
I'M BEE!
AND THESE ARE THE REST OF THE SEVEN DWARVES!
I'M THE MOOSE!
AND I'M POPPY!
I'M CHUCKY!
AND I'M KEV!

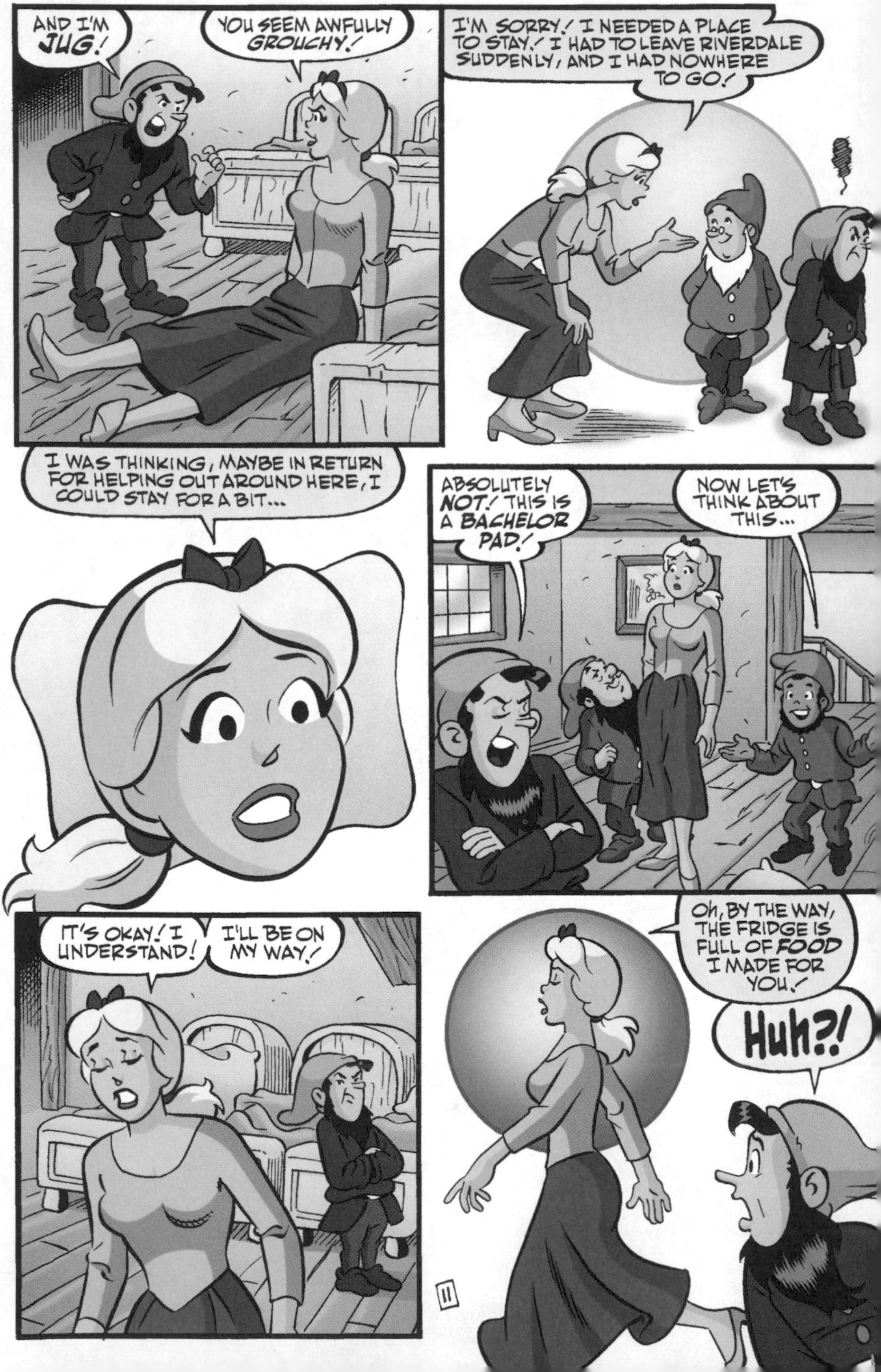
AND I'M JUG!
YOU SEEM AWFULLY GROUCHY!
I'M SORRY! I NEEDED A PLACE TO STAY! I HAD TO LEAVE RIVERDALE SUDDENLY, AND I HAD NOWHERE TO GO!
I WAS THINKING, MAYBE IN RETURN FOR HELPING OUT AROUND HERE, I COULD STAY FOR A BIT...
ABSOLUTELY NOT! THIS IS A BACHELOR PAD!
NOW LET'S THINK ABOUT THIS...
IT'S OKAY! I UNDERSTAND!
I'LL BE ON MY WAY!
Oh, BY THE WAY, THE FRIDGE IS FULL OF FOOD I MADE FOR YOU!
Huh?!
11

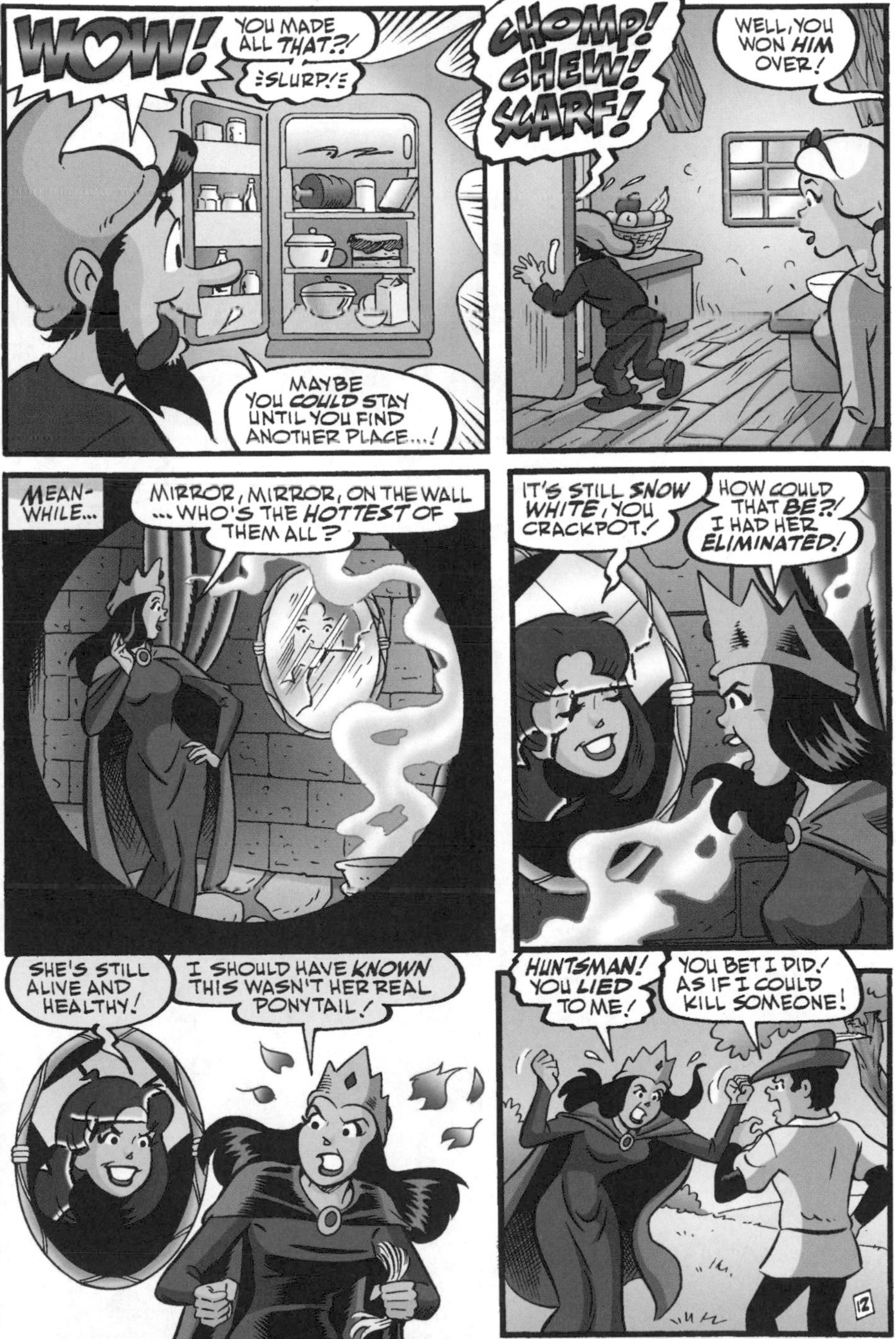
WOW!
YOU MADE ALL THAT?!
SLURP!
MAYBE YOU COULD STAY UNTIL YOU FIND ANOTHER PLACE...!
CHOMP! CHEW! SCARF!
WELL, YOU WON HIM OVER!
MEAN-WHILE...
MIRROR, MIRROR, ON THE WALL ... WHO'S THE HOTTEST OF THEM ALL?
IT'S STILL SNOW WHITE, YOU CRACKPOT!
HOW COULD THAT BE?! I HAD HER ELIMINATED!
SHE'S STILL ALIVE AND HEALTHY!
I SHOULD HAVE KNOWN THIS WASN'T HER REAL PONYTAIL!
HUNTSMAN! YOU LIED TO ME!
YOU BET I DID! AS IF I COULD KILL SOMEONE!
12

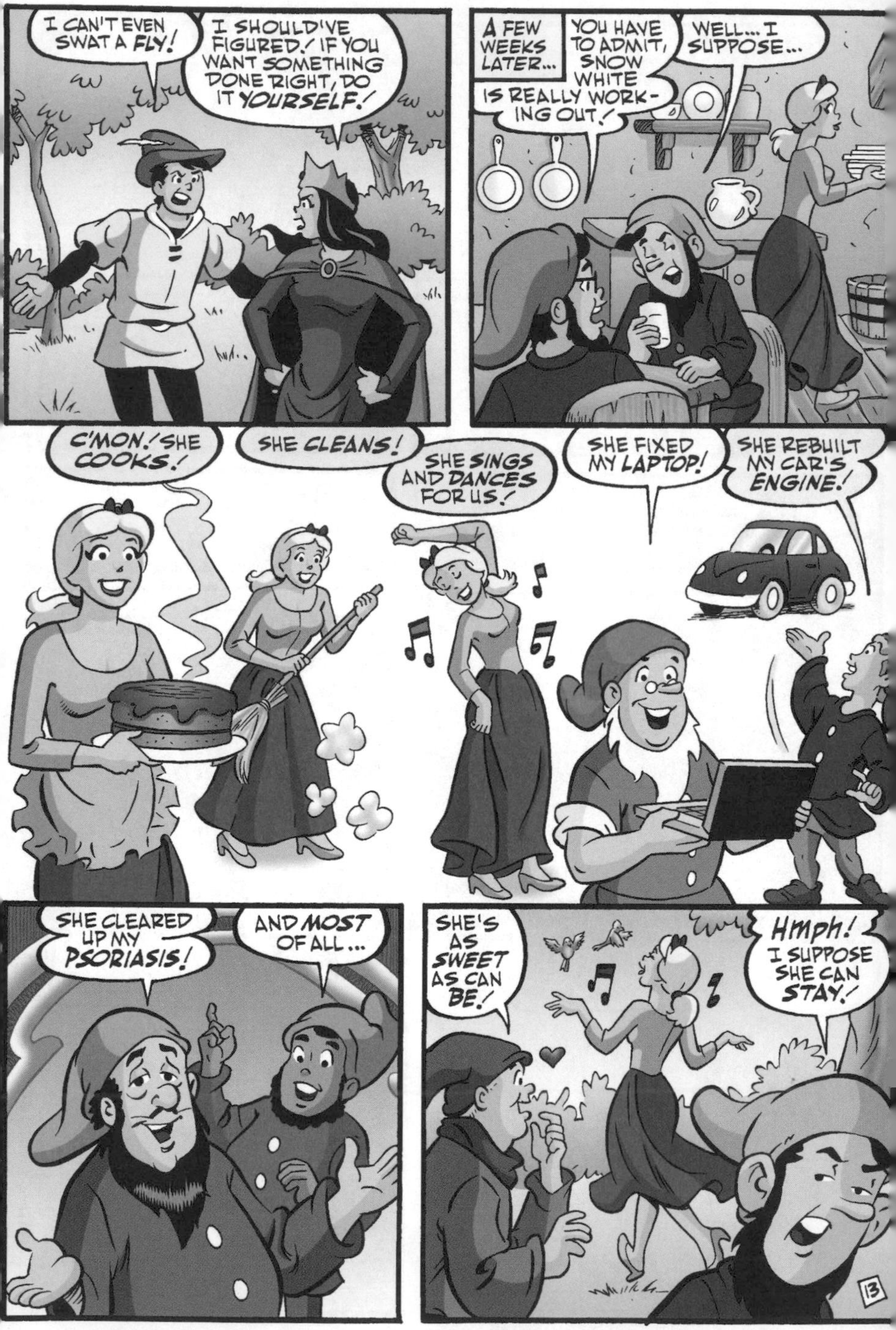
I CAN'T EVEN SWAT A FLY!
I SHOULD'VE FIGURED! IF YOU WANT SOMETHING DONE RIGHT, DO IT YOURSELF!
A FEW WEEKS LATER...
YOU HAVE TO ADMIT, SNOW WHITE IS REALLY WORKING OUT!
WELL... I SUPPOSE...
C'MON! SHE COOKS!
SHE CLEANS!
SHE SINGS AND DANCES FOR US!
SHE FIXED MY LAPTOP!
SHE REBUILT MY CAR'S ENGINE!
SHE CLEARED UP MY PSORIASIS!
AND MOST OF ALL...
SHE'S AS SWEET AS CAN BE!
Hmph! I SUPPOSE SHE CAN STAY!
13

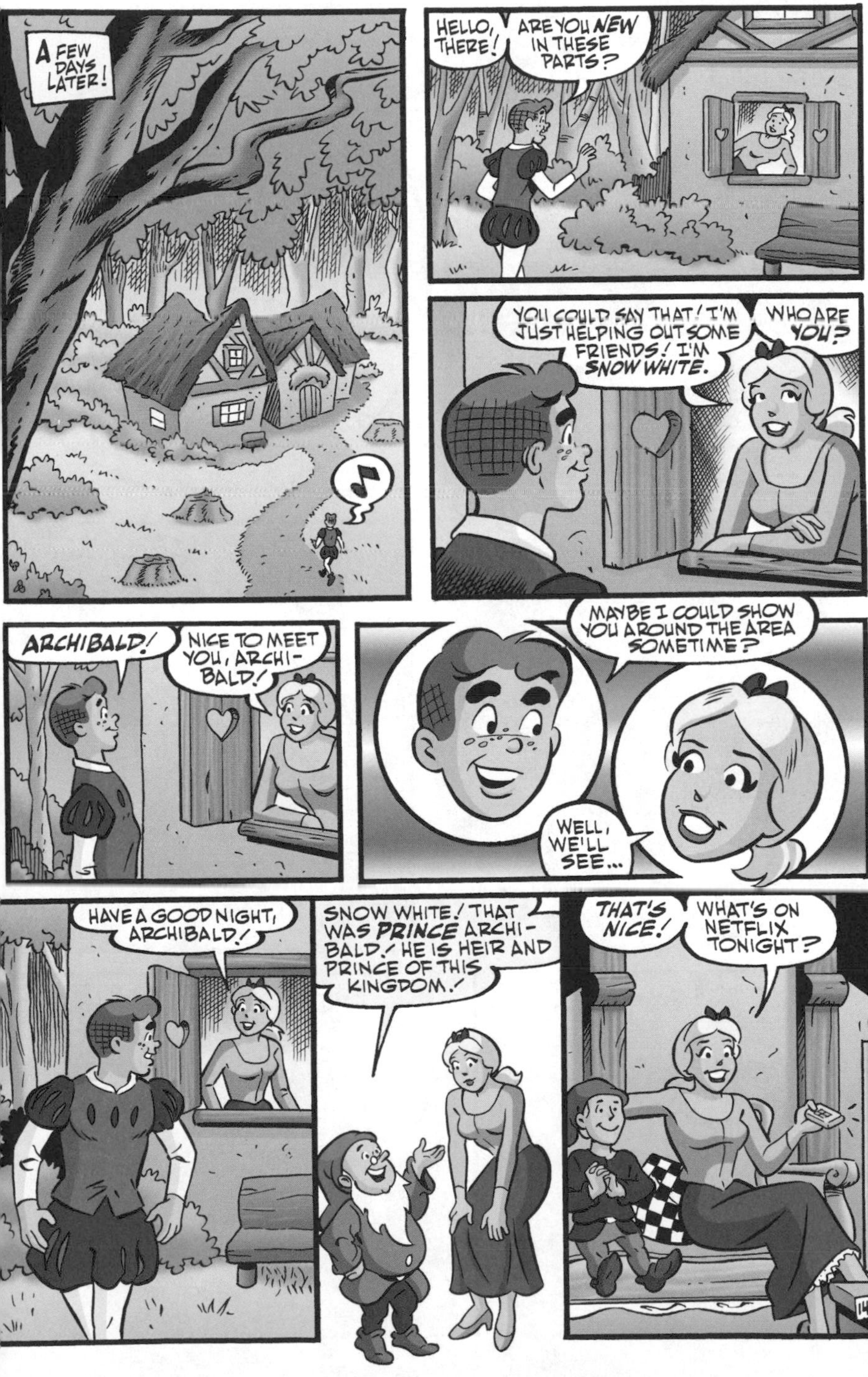
A FEW DAYS LATER!
HELLO, THERE!
ARE YOU NEW IN THESE PARTS?
YOU COULD SAY THAT! I'M JUST HELPING OUT SOME FRIENDS! I'M SNOW WHITE.
WHO ARE YOU?
ARCHIBALD!
NICE TO MEET YOU, ARCHI-BALD!
MAYBE I COULD SHOW YOU AROUND THE AREA SOMETIME?
WELL, WE'LL SEE...
HAVE A GOOD NIGHT, ARCHIBALD!
SNOW WHITE! THAT WAS PRINCE ARCHI-BALD! HE IS HEIR AND PRINCE OF THIS KINGDOM!
THAT'S NICE!
WHAT'S ON NETFLIX TONIGHT?
14

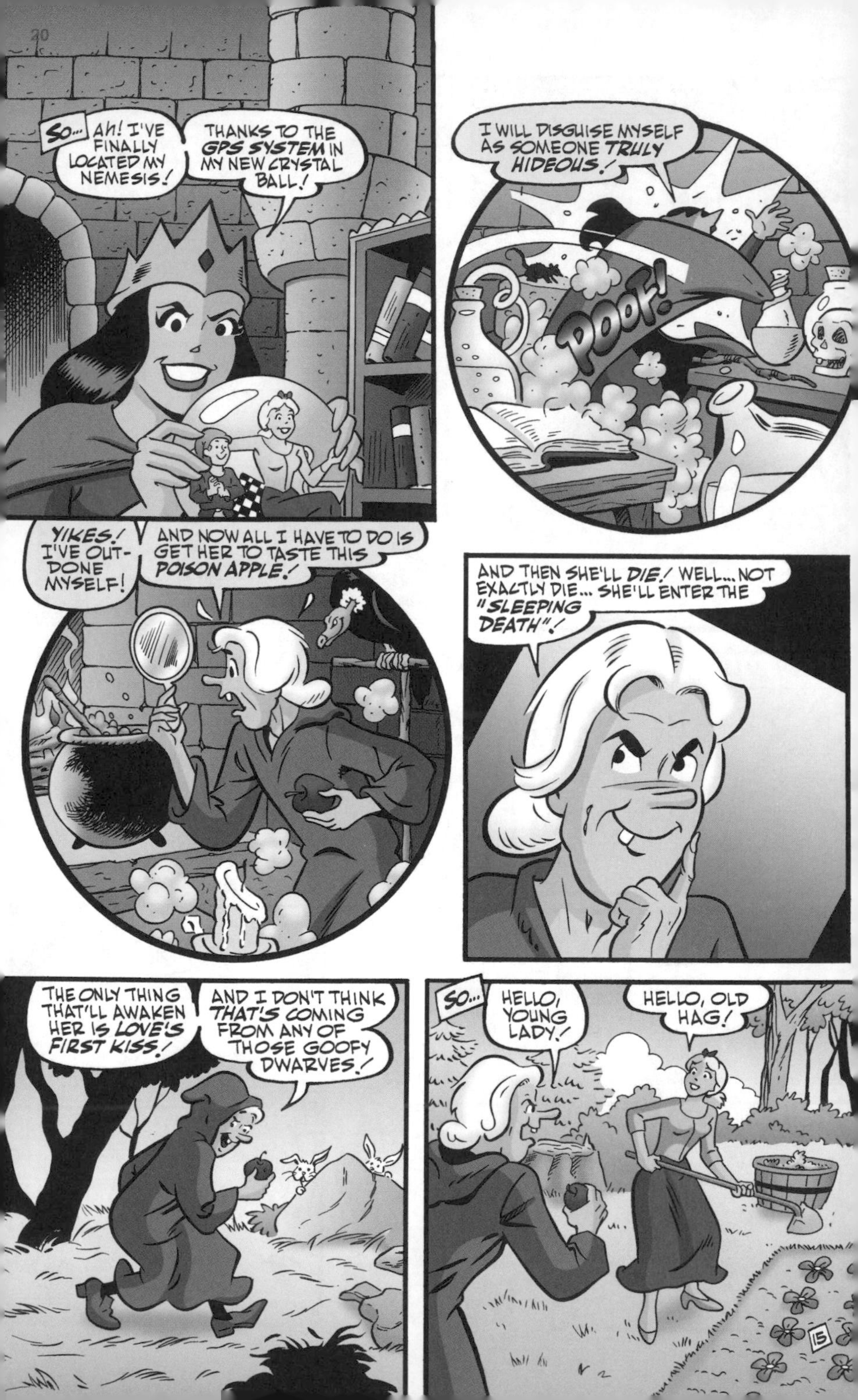
SO...
AH! I'VE FINALLY LOCATED MY NEMESIS!
THANKS TO THE GPS SYSTEM IN MY NEW CRYSTAL BALL!
I WILL DISGUISE MYSELF AS SOMEONE TRULY HIDEOUS!
POOF!
YIKES! I'VE OUT-DONE MYSELF!
AND NOW ALL I HAVE TO DO IS GET HER TO TASTE THIS POISON APPLE!
AND THEN SHE'LL DIE! WELL... NOT EXACTLY DIE... SHE'LL ENTER THE "SLEEPING DEATH"!
THE ONLY THING THAT'LL AWAKEN HER IS LOVE'S FIRST KISS!
AND I DON'T THINK THAT'S COMING FROM ANY OF THOSE GOOFY DWARVES!
SO...
HELLO, YOUNG LADY!
HELLO, OLD HAG!
15

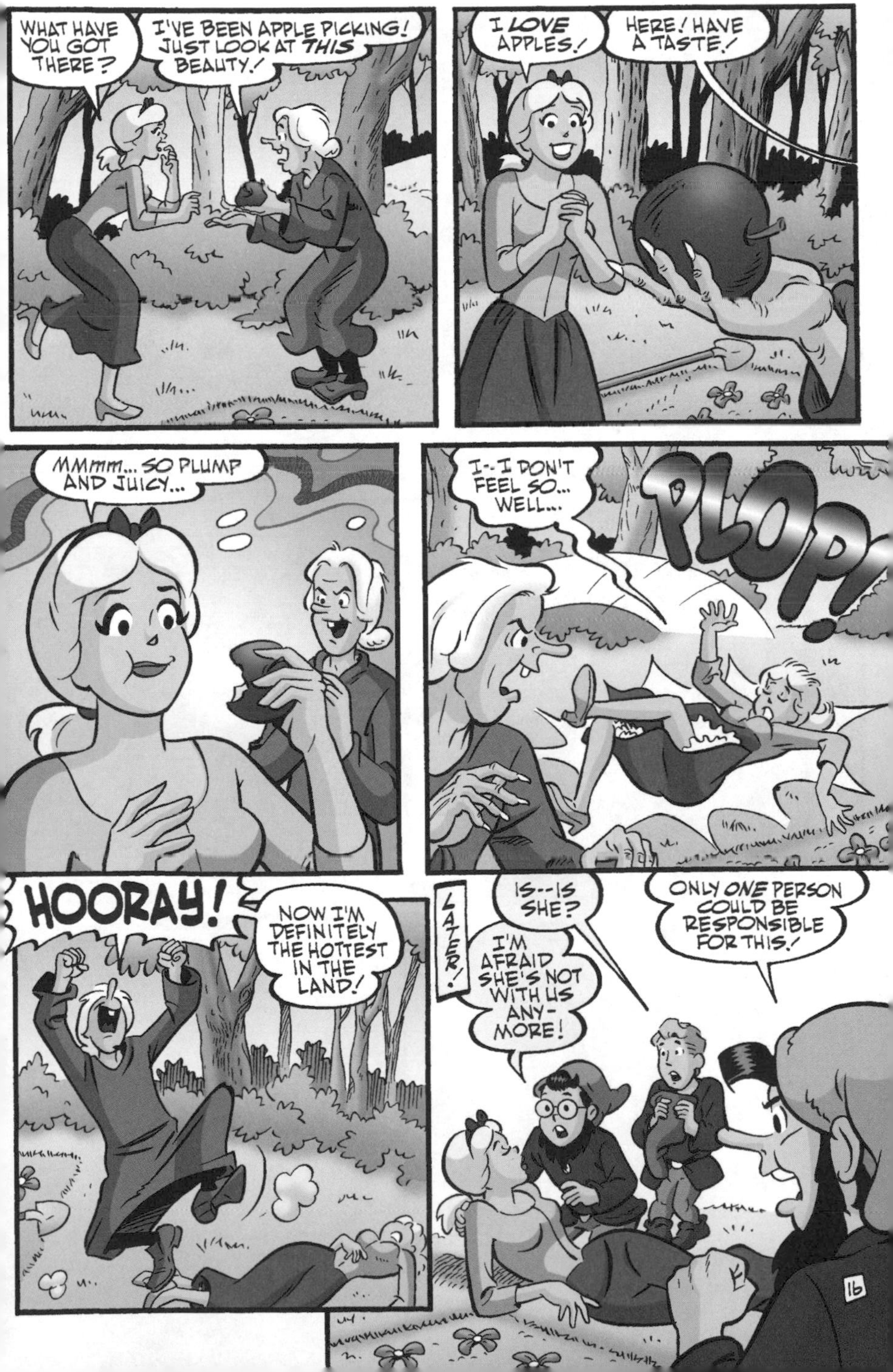
WHAT HAVE YOU GOT THERE?
I'VE BEEN APPLE PICKING! JUST LOOK AT THIS BEAUTY!
I LOVE APPLES!
HERE! HAVE A TASTE!
MMMMM... SO PLUMP AND JUICY...
I-- I DON'T FEEL SO... WELL...
PLOP!
HOORAY!
NOW I'M DEFINITELY THE HOTTEST IN THE LAND!
LATER!
IS--IS SHE?
I'M AFRAID SHE'S NOT WITH US ANY-MORE!
ONLY ONE PERSON COULD BE RESPONSIBLE FOR THIS!
16

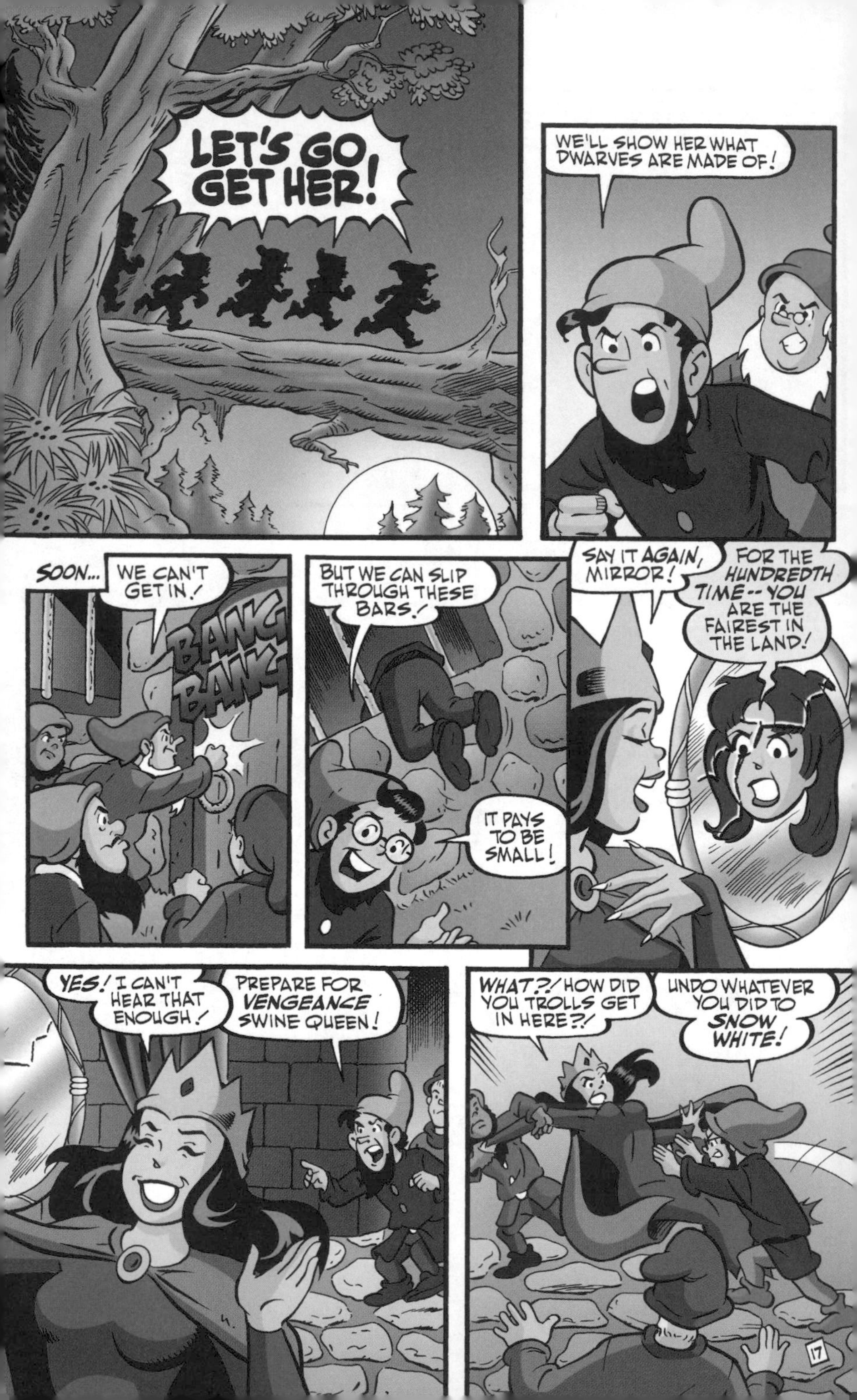
LET'S GO GET HER!
WE'LL SHOW HER WHAT DWARVES ARE MADE OF!
SOON...
WE CAN'T GET IN!
BANG BANG
BUT WE CAN SLIP THROUGH THESE BARS!
IT PAYS TO BE SMALL!
SAY IT AGAIN, MIRROR!
FOR THE HUNDREDTH TIME-- YOU ARE THE FAIREST IN THE LAND!
YES! I CAN'T HEAR THAT ENOUGH!
PREPARE FOR VENGEANCE SWINE QUEEN!
WHAT?! HOW DID YOU TROLLS GET IN HERE?!
UNDO WHATEVER YOU DID TO SNOW WHITE!
17

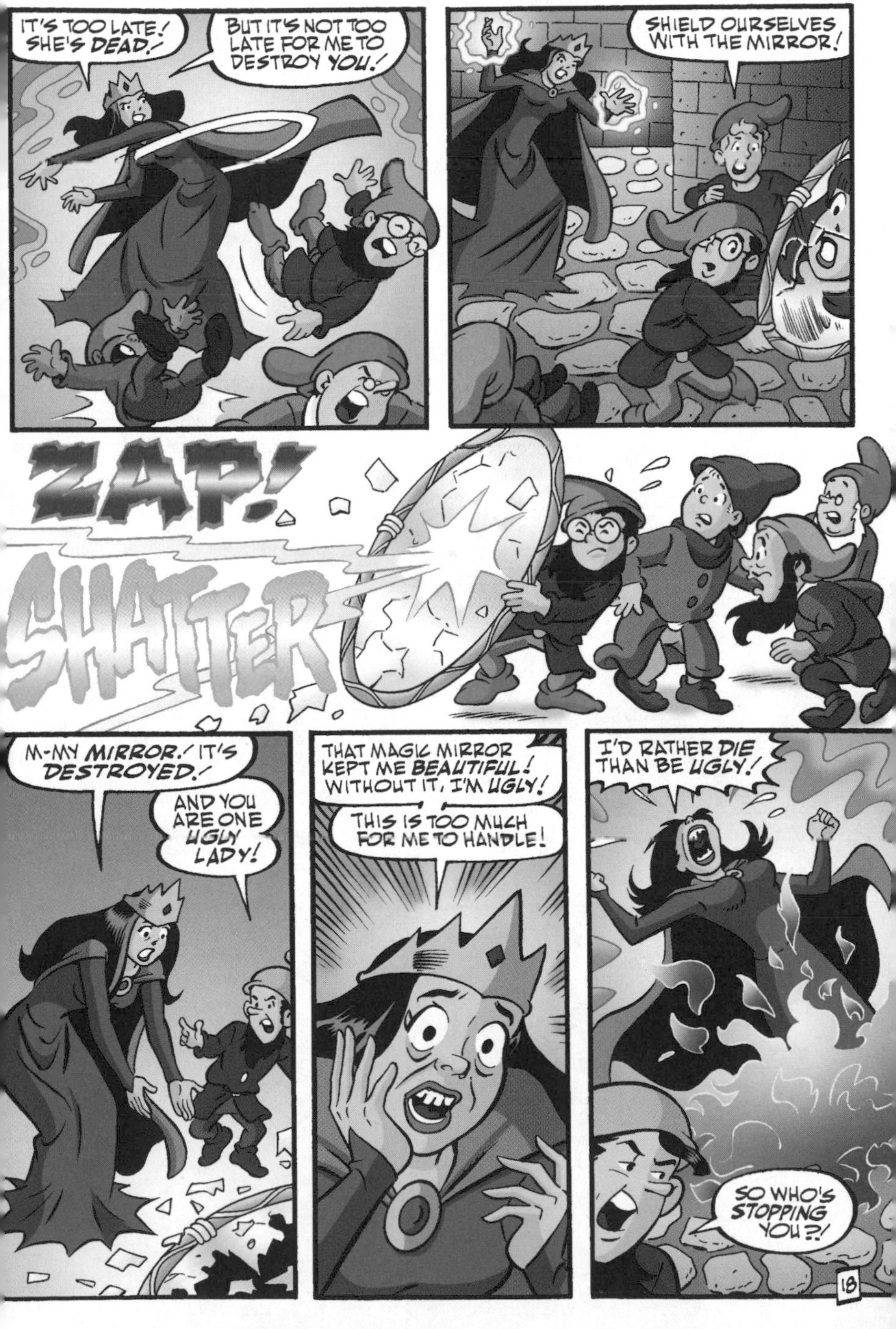
IT'S TOO LATE! SHE'S DEAD!
BUT IT'S NOT TOO LATE FOR ME TO DESTROY YOU!
SHIELD OURSELVES WITH THE MIRROR!
ZAP!
SHATTER
M-MY MIRROR! IT'S DESTROYED!
AND YOU ARE ONE UGLY LADY!
THAT MAGIC MIRROR KEPT ME BEAUTIFUL! WITHOUT IT, I'M UGLY!
THIS IS TOO MUCH FOR ME TO HANDLE!
I'D RATHER DIE THAN BE UGLY!
SO WHO'S STOPPING YOU?!
18

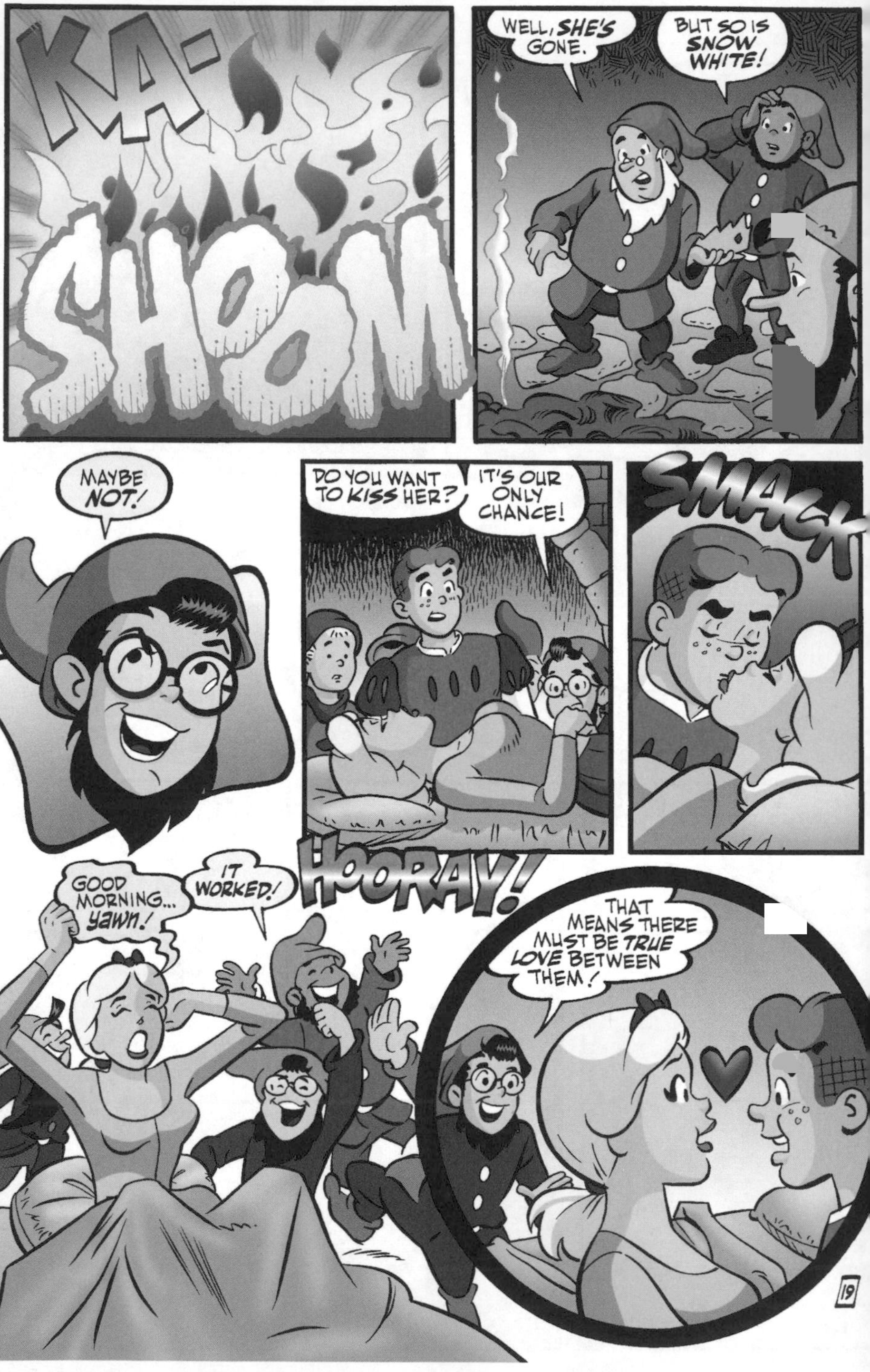
KA-SHOOM
WELL, SHE'S GONE.
BUT SO IS SNOW WHITE!
MAYBE NOT!
DO YOU WANT TO KISS HER?
IT'S OUR ONLY CHANCE!
SMACK
HOORAY!
GOOD MORNING... yawn!
IT WORKED!
THAT MEANS THERE MUST BE TRUE LOVE BETWEEN THEM!

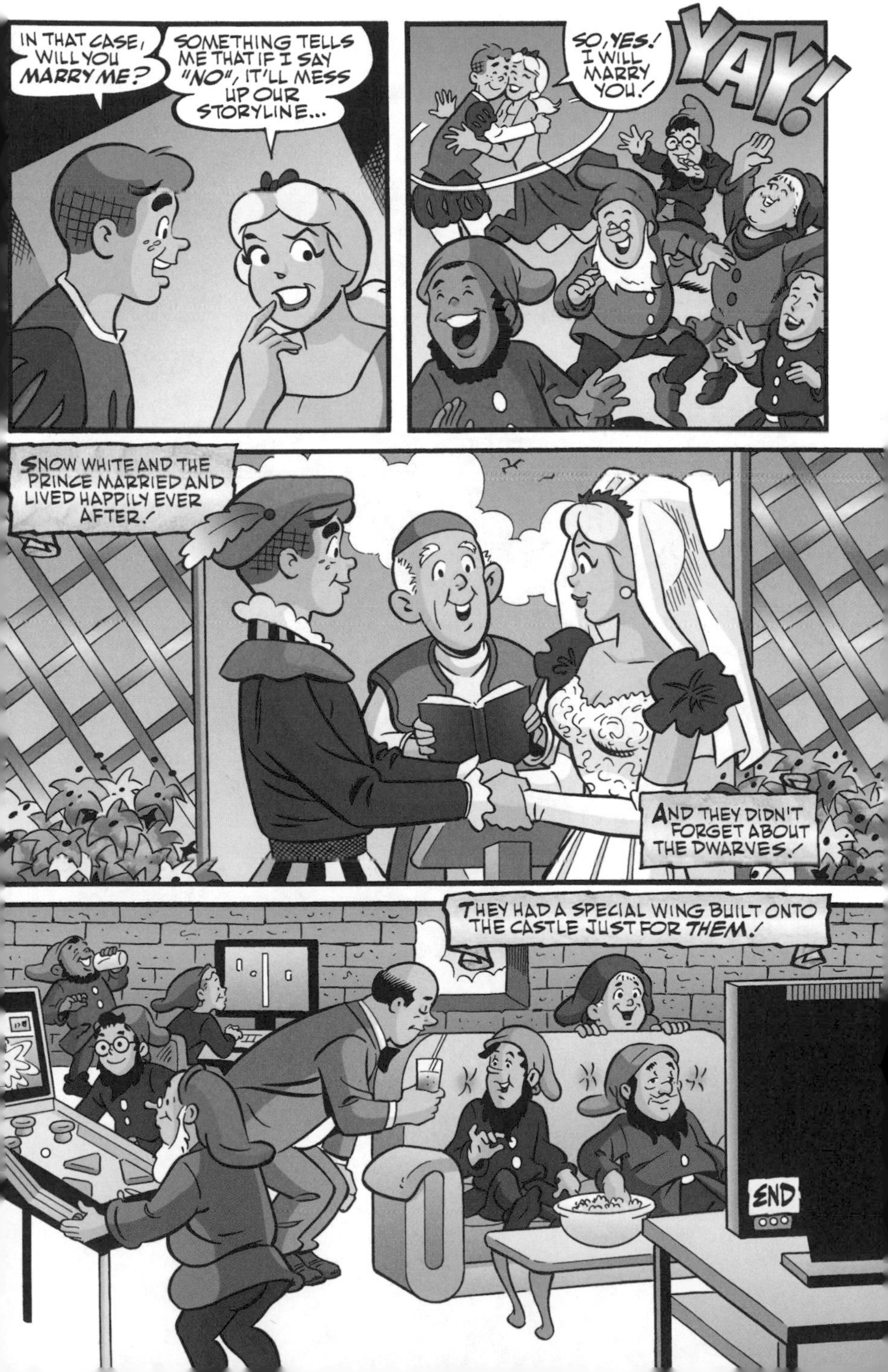
IN THAT CASE, WILL YOU MARRY ME?
SOMETHING TELLS ME THAT IF I SAY "NO", IT'LL MESS UP OUR STORYLINE...
SO, YES! I WILL MARRY YOU!
YAY!
SNOW WHITE AND THE PRINCE MARRIED AND LIVED HAPPILY EVER AFTER!
AND THEY DIDN'T FORGET ABOUT THE DWARVES!
THEY HAD A SPECIAL WING BUILT ONTO THE CASTLE JUST FOR THEM!
END

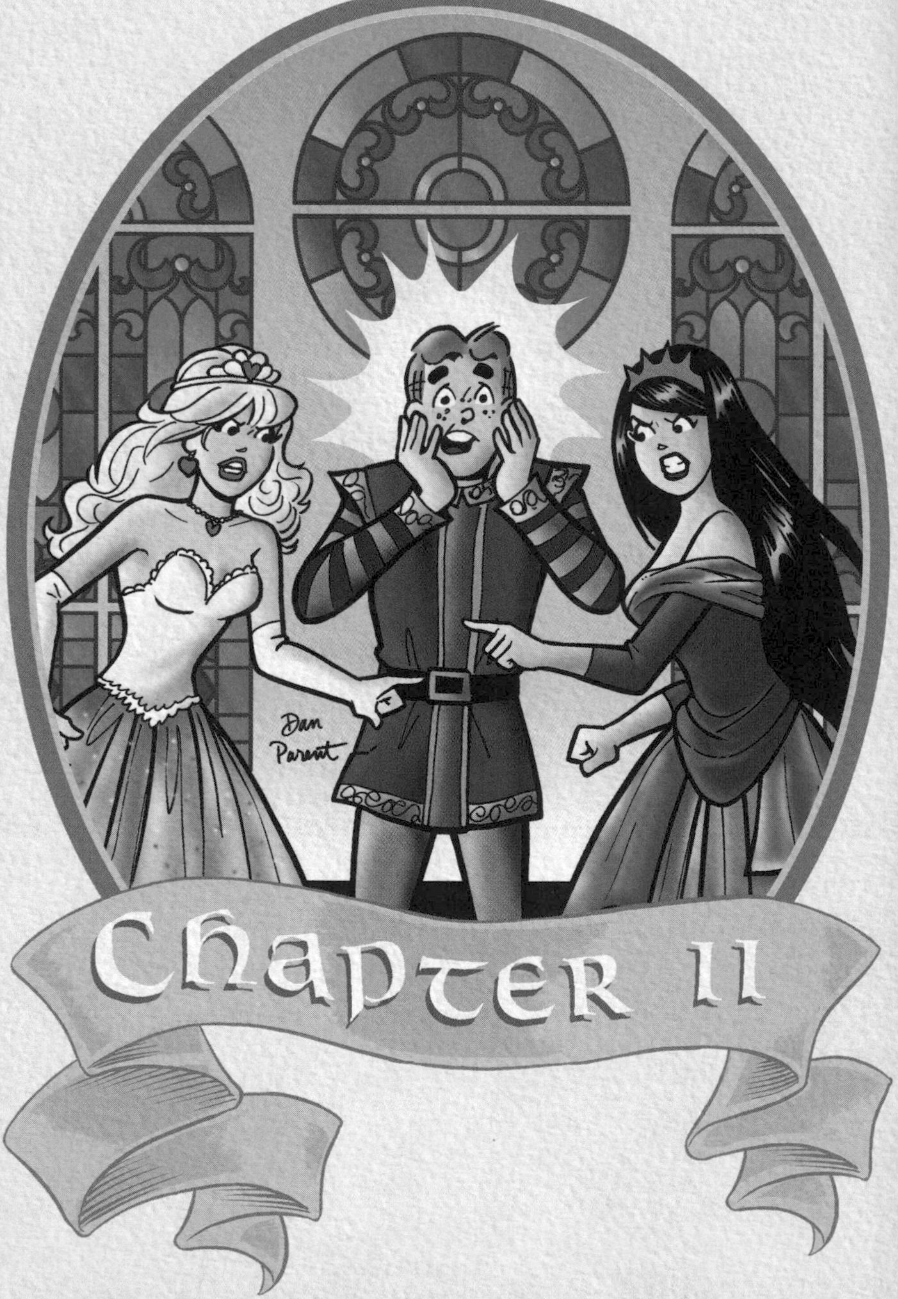
Dan Parent
Chapter II

 A TALE OF TWO CINDERELLAS

It's Cinderella squared in "A Tale of Two Cinderellas," which features Betty and Veronica both taking on the role of the poor but beautiful Cinderella!

Locked away and forced to wear tacky clothing by their evil stepmother and her annoying stepdaughter, the girls must join forces to escape her clutches. With the help of a hip fairy godmother, the girls get glammed up just in time for the great ball.

Will they be able to win Prince Archie's heart when their evil stepmother wants to ensure he marries her daughter? The key lies in a glass slipper that is decidedly not "one size fits all."

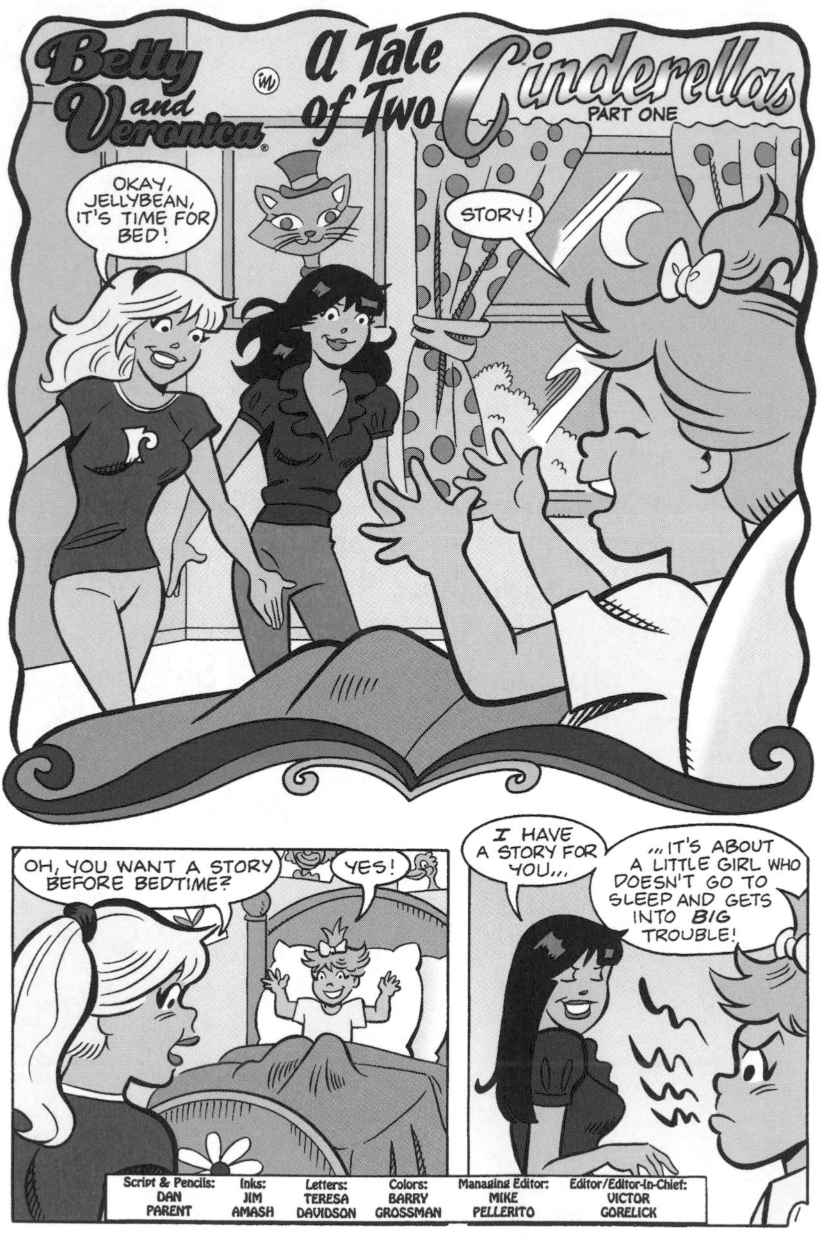
Betty and Veronica in A Tale of Two Cinderellas
PART ONE
OKAY, JELLYBEAN, IT'S TIME FOR BED!
STORY!
OH, YOU WANT A STORY BEFORE BEDTIME?
YES!
I HAVE A STORY FOR YOU...
...IT'S ABOUT A LITTLE GIRL WHO DOESN'T GO TO SLEEP AND GETS INTO BIG TROUBLE!
Script & Pencils: DAN PARENT
Inks: JIM AMASH
Letters: TERESA DAVIDSON
Colors: BARRY GROSSMAN
Managing Editor: MIKE PELLERITO
Editor/Editor-In-Chief: VICTOR GORELICK

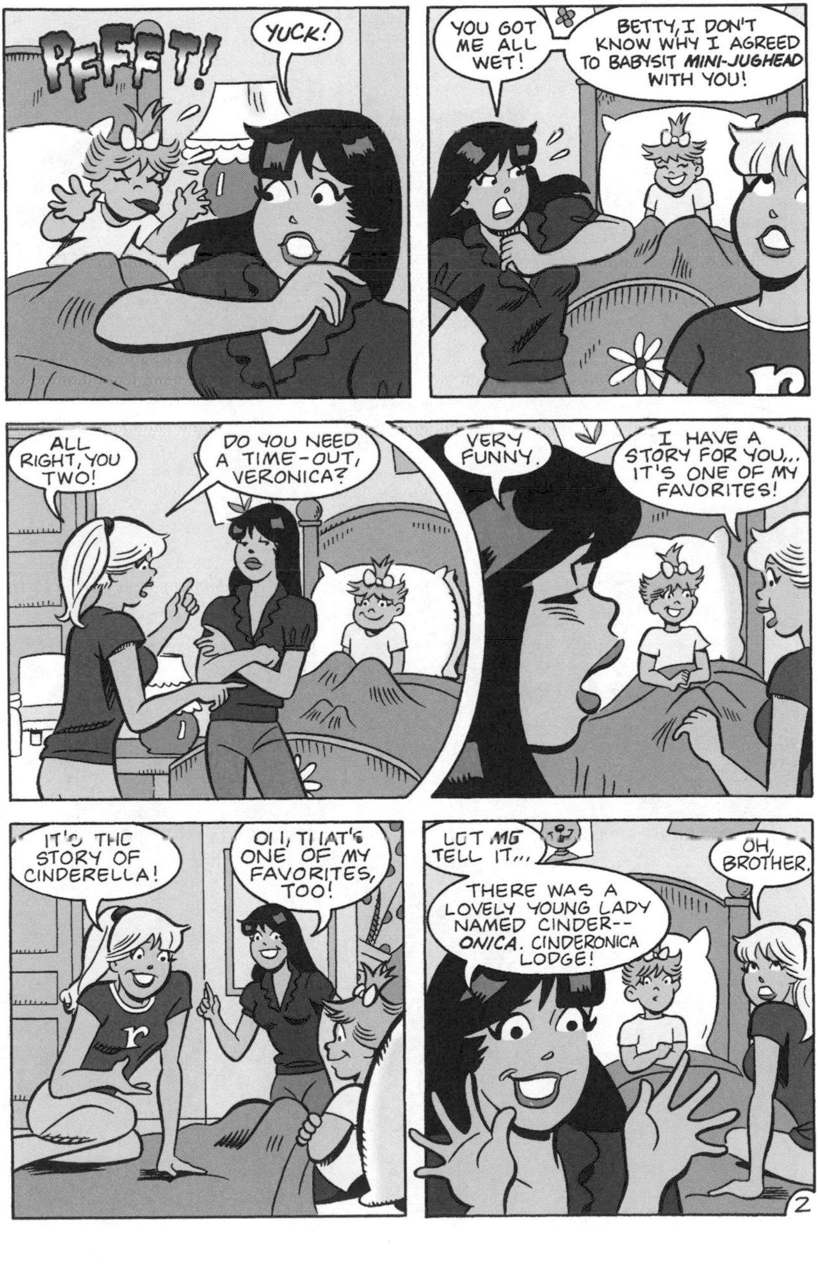
PFFFT!
YUCK!
YOU GOT ME ALL WET!
BETTY, I DON'T KNOW WHY I AGREED TO BABYSIT MINI-JUGHEAD WITH YOU!
ALL RIGHT, YOU TWO!
DO YOU NEED A TIME-OUT, VERONICA?
VERY FUNNY.
I HAVE A STORY FOR YOU... IT'S ONE OF MY FAVORITES!
IT'S THE STORY OF CINDERELLA!
OH, THAT'S ONE OF MY FAVORITES, TOO!
LET ME TELL IT...
THERE WAS A LOVELY YOUNG LADY NAMED CINDER-- ONICA. CINDERONICA LODGE!
OH, BROTHER.
2

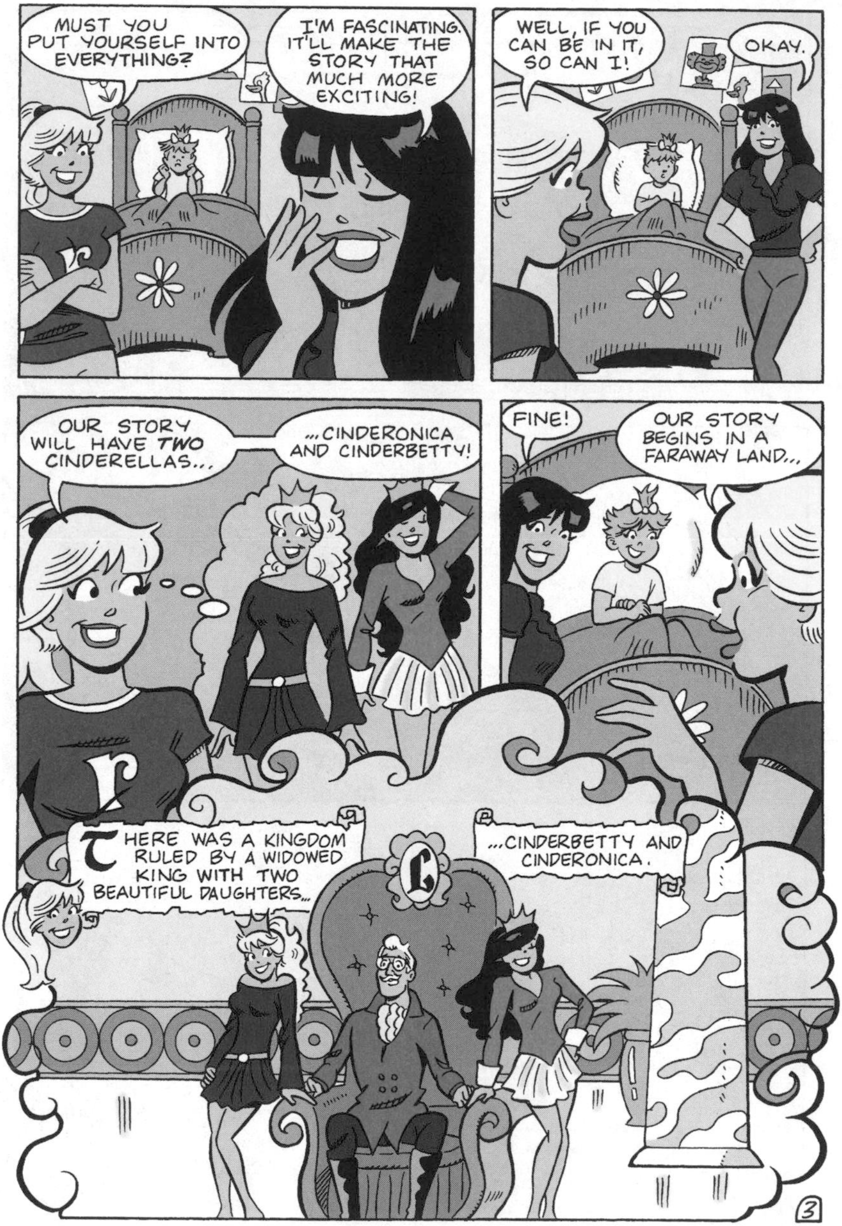
MUST YOU PUT YOURSELF INTO EVERYTHING?
I'M FASCINATING. IT'LL MAKE THE STORY THAT MUCH MORE EXCITING!
WELL, IF YOU CAN BE IN IT, SO CAN I!
OKAY.
OUR STORY WILL HAVE TWO CINDERELLAS...
...CINDERONICA AND CINDERBETTY!
FINE!
OUR STORY BEGINS IN A FARAWAY LAND...
THERE WAS A KINGDOM RULED BY A WIDOWED KING WITH TWO BEAUTIFUL DAUGHTERS...
...CINDERBETTY AND CINDERONICA.
3

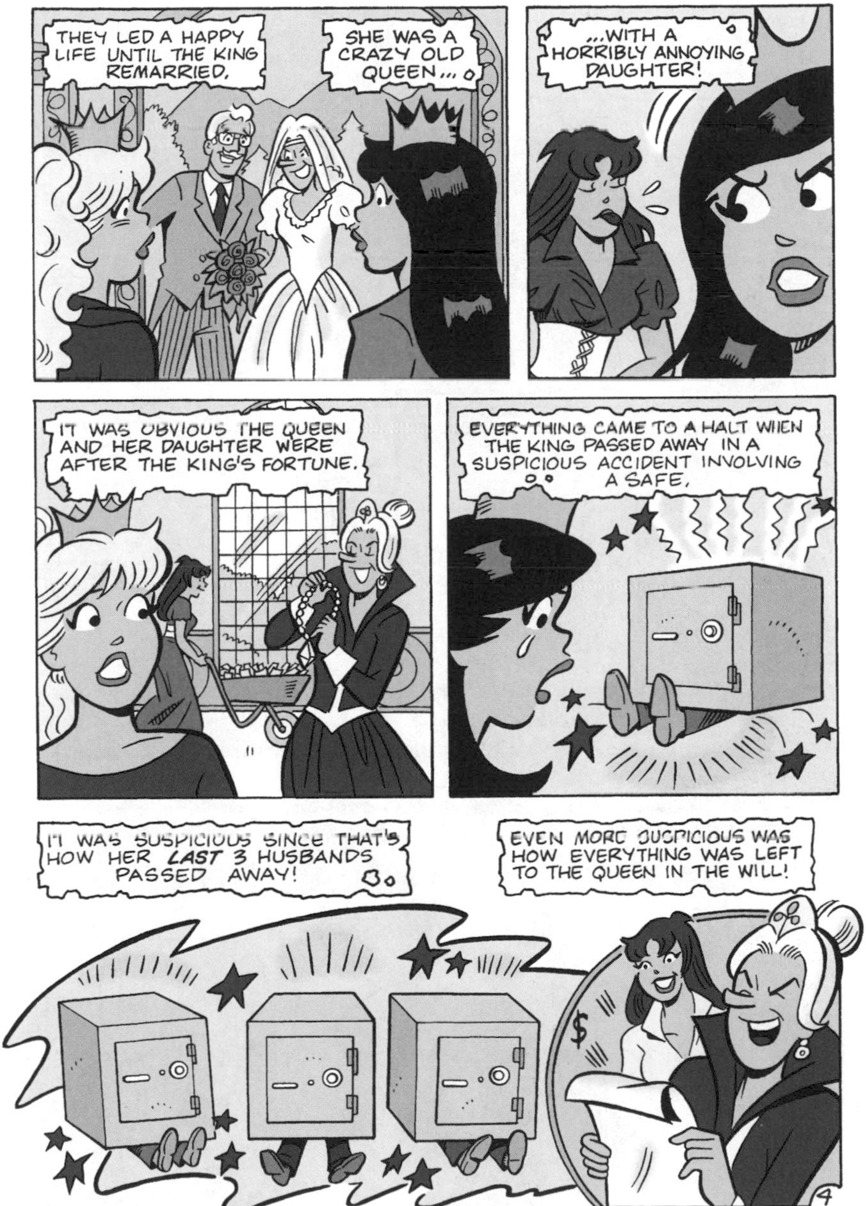
THEY LED A HAPPY LIFE UNTIL THE KING REMARRIED.
SHE WAS A CRAZY OLD QUEEN...
...WITH A HORRIBLY ANNOYING DAUGHTER!
IT WAS OBVIOUS THE QUEEN AND HER DAUGHTER WERE AFTER THE KING'S FORTUNE.
EVERYTHING CAME TO A HALT WHEN THE KING PASSED AWAY IN A SUSPICIOUS ACCIDENT INVOLVING A SAFE.
IT WAS SUSPICIOUS SINCE THAT'S HOW HER LAST 3 HUSBANDS PASSED AWAY!
EVEN MORE SUSPICIOUS WAS HOW EVERYTHING WAS LEFT TO THE QUEEN IN THE WILL!
$
4

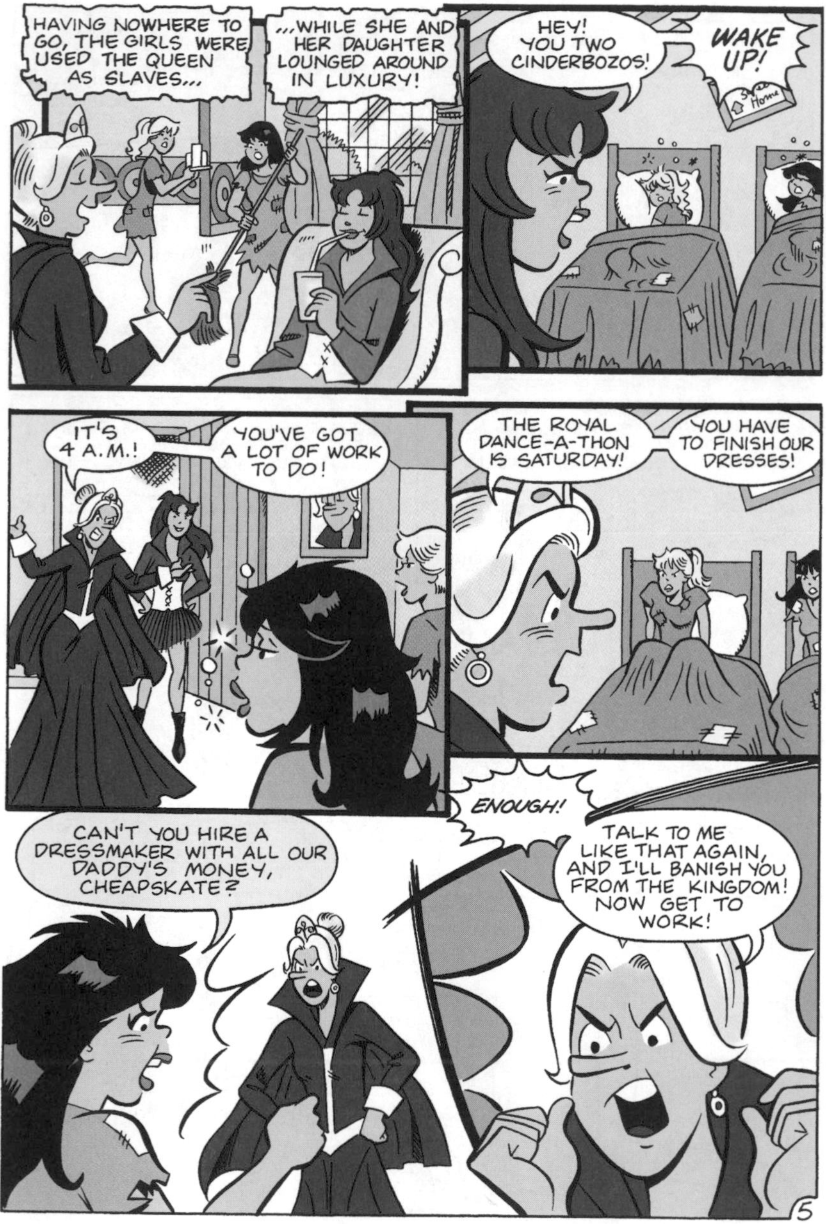
HAVING NOWHERE TO GO, THE GIRLS WERE USED THE QUEEN AS SLAVES...
...WHILE SHE AND HER DAUGHTER LOUNGED AROUND IN LUXURY!
HEY! YOU TWO CINDERBOZOS!
WAKE UP!
IT'S 4 A.M.!
YOU'VE GOT A LOT OF WORK TO DO!
THE ROYAL DANCE-A-THON IS SATURDAY!
YOU HAVE TO FINISH OUR DRESSES!
CAN'T YOU HIRE A DRESSMAKER WITH ALL OUR DADDY'S MONEY, CHEAPSKATE?
ENOUGH!
TALK TO ME LIKE THAT AGAIN, AND I'LL BANISH YOU FROM THE KINGDOM! NOW GET TO WORK!
5

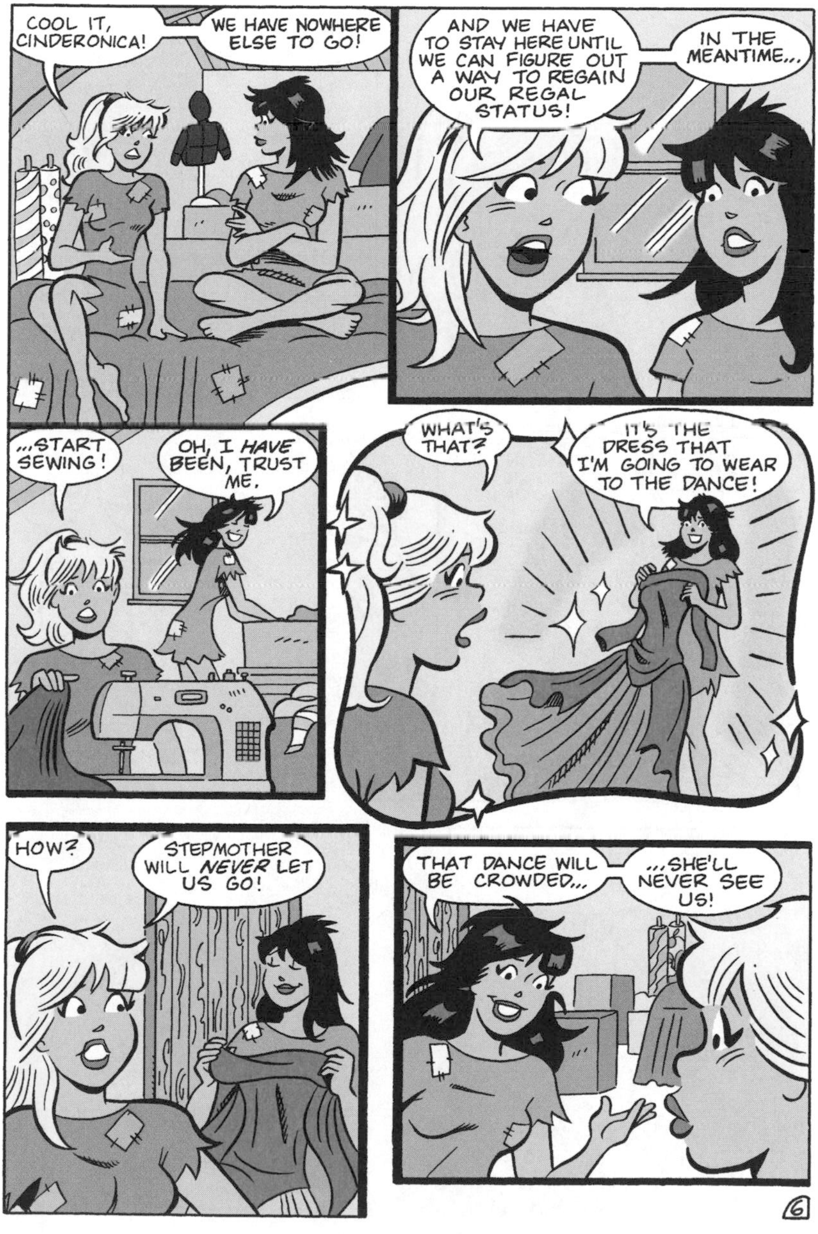
COOL IT, CINDERONICA!
WE HAVE NOWHERE ELSE TO GO!
AND WE HAVE TO STAY HERE UNTIL WE CAN FIGURE OUT A WAY TO REGAIN OUR REGAL STATUS!
IN THE MEANTIME...
...START SEWING!
OH, I *HAVE* BEEN, TRUST ME.
WHAT'S THAT?
IT'S THE DRESS THAT I'M GOING TO WEAR TO THE DANCE!
HOW?
STEPMOTHER WILL *NEVER* LET US GO!
THAT DANCE WILL BE CROWDED...
...SHE'LL NEVER SEE US!
6

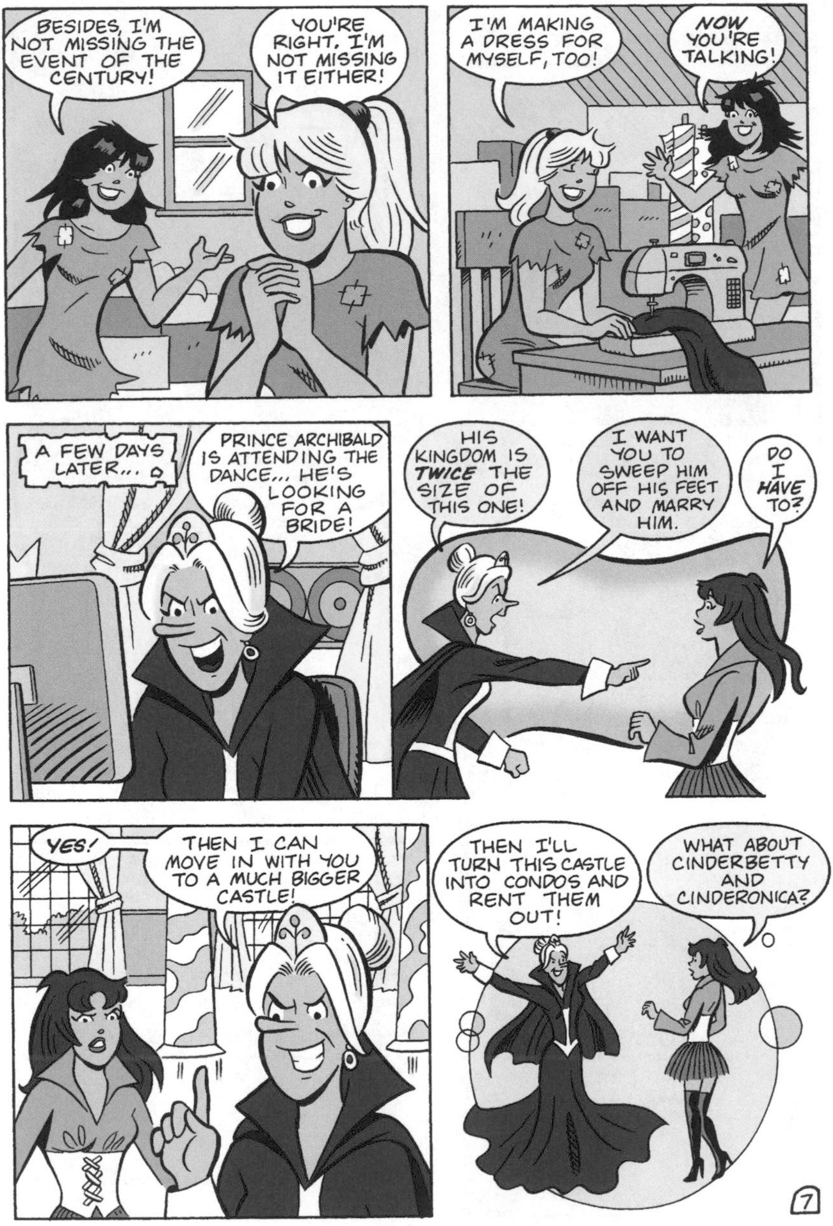
BESIDES, I'M NOT MISSING THE EVENT OF THE CENTURY!
YOU'RE RIGHT. I'M NOT MISSING IT EITHER!
I'M MAKING A DRESS FOR MYSELF, TOO!
NOW YOU'RE TALKING!
A FEW DAYS LATER...
PRINCE ARCHIBALD IS ATTENDING THE DANCE... HE'S LOOKING FOR A BRIDE!
HIS KINGDOM IS TWICE THE SIZE OF THIS ONE!
I WANT YOU TO SWEEP HIM OFF HIS FEET AND MARRY HIM.
DO I HAVE TO?
YES!
THEN I CAN MOVE IN WITH YOU TO A MUCH BIGGER CASTLE!
THEN I'LL TURN THIS CASTLE INTO CONDOS AND RENT THEM OUT!
WHAT ABOUT CINDERBETTY AND CINDERONICA?
7

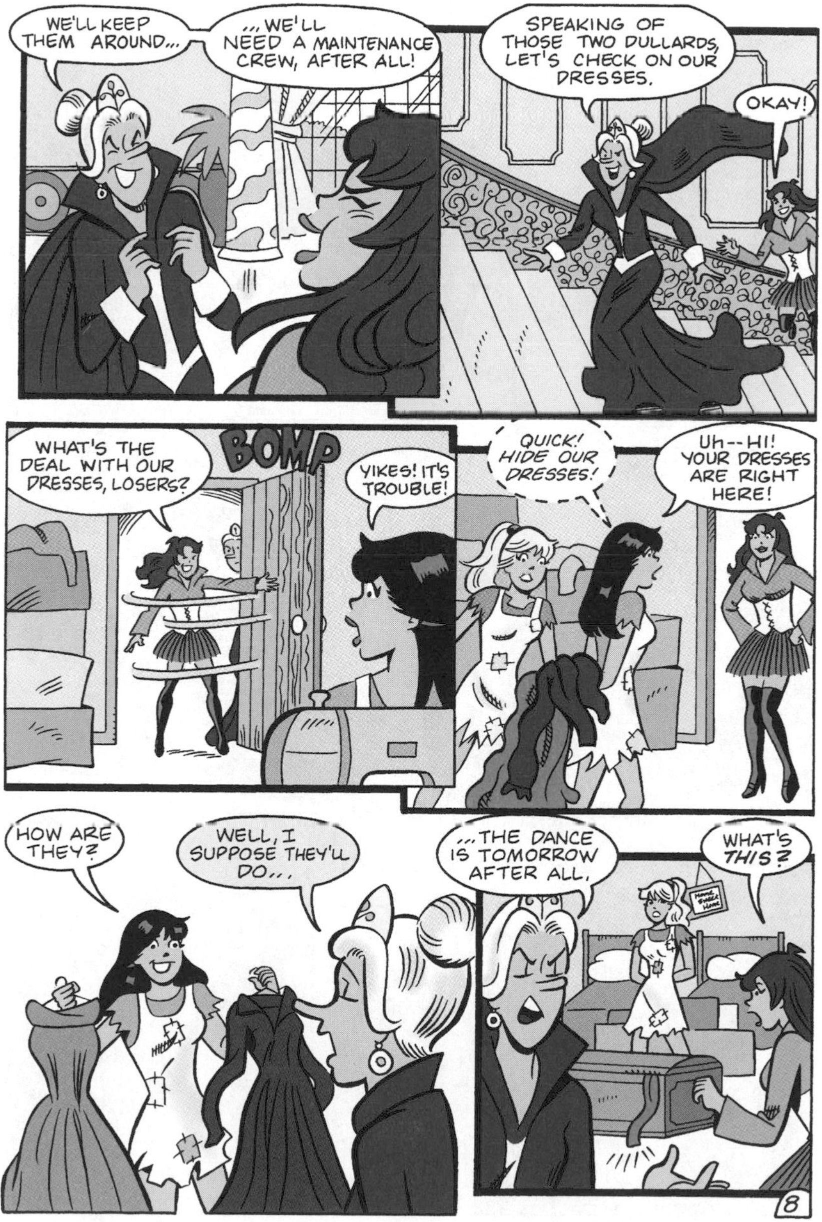
WE'LL KEEP THEM AROUND...
...WE'LL NEED A MAINTENANCE CREW, AFTER ALL!
SPEAKING OF THOSE TWO DULLARDS, LET'S CHECK ON OUR DRESSES.
OKAY!
WHAT'S THE DEAL WITH OUR DRESSES, LOSERS?
BOMP
YIKES! IT'S TROUBLE!
QUICK! HIDE OUR DRESSES!
Uh--HI! YOUR DRESSES ARE RIGHT HERE!
HOW ARE THEY?
WELL, I SUPPOSE THEY'LL DO...
...THE DANCE IS TOMORROW AFTER ALL.
WHAT'S THIS?
8

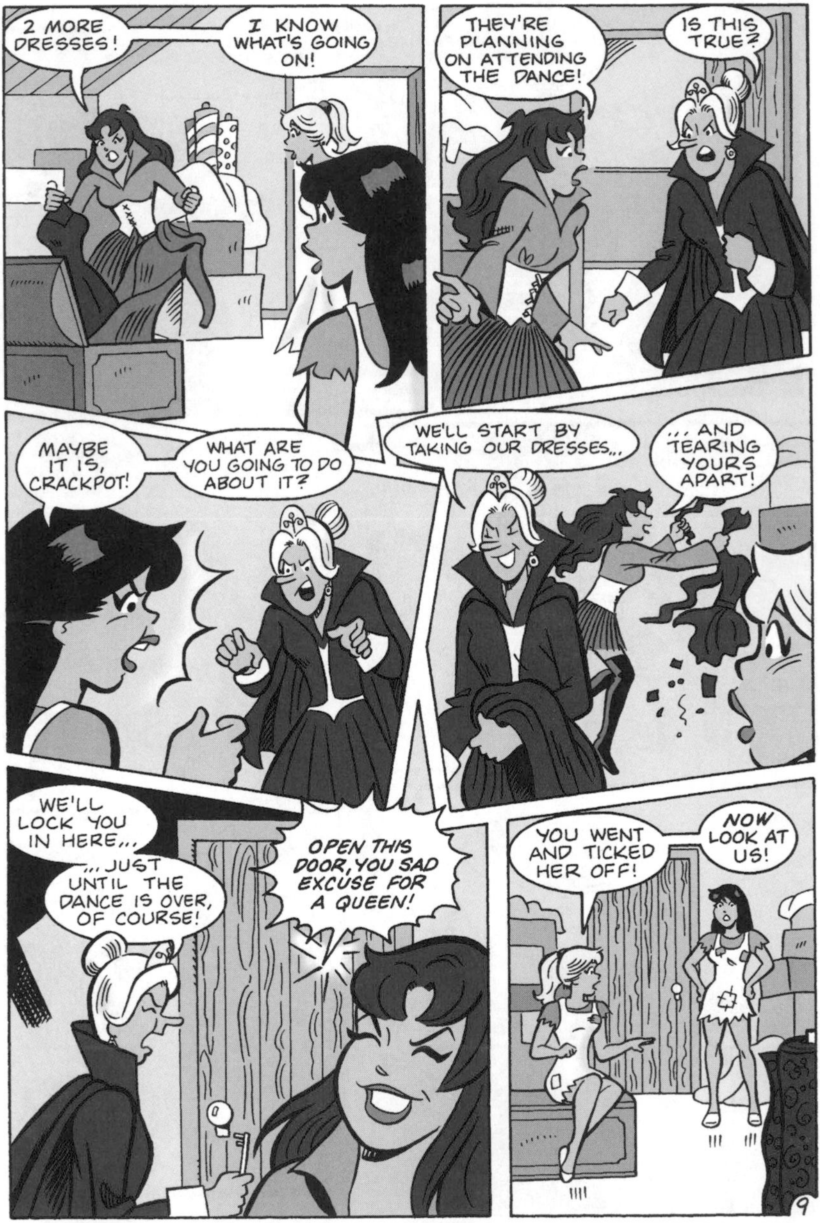
2 MORE DRESSES!
I KNOW WHAT'S GOING ON!
THEY'RE PLANNING ON ATTENDING THE DANCE!
IS THIS TRUE?
MAYBE IT IS, CRACKPOT!
WHAT ARE YOU GOING TO DO ABOUT IT?
WE'LL START BY TAKING OUR DRESSES...
... AND TEARING YOURS APART!
WE'LL LOCK YOU IN HERE...
... JUST UNTIL THE DANCE IS OVER, OF COURSE!
OPEN THIS DOOR, YOU SAD EXCUSE FOR A QUEEN!
YOU WENT AND TICKED HER OFF!
NOW LOOK AT US!
9

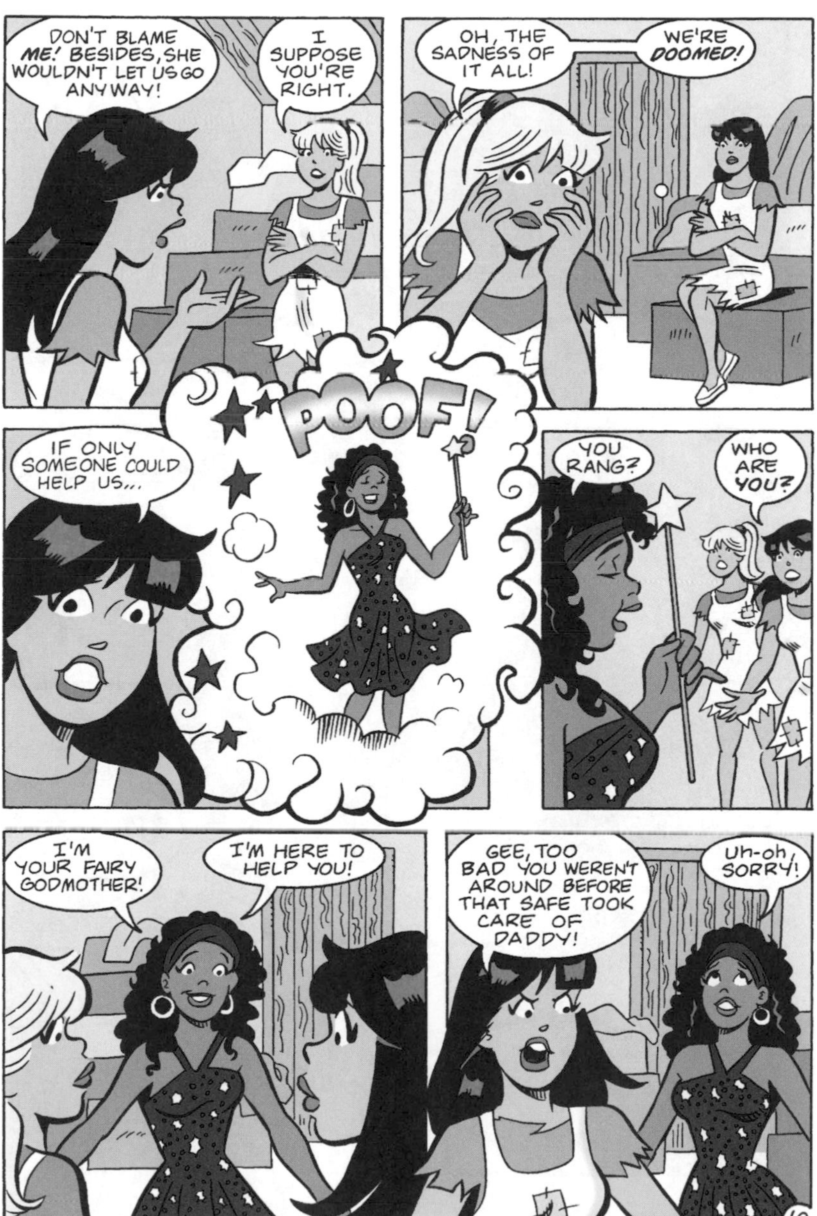
DON'T BLAME ME! BESIDES, SHE WOULDN'T LET US GO ANYWAY!
I SUPPOSE YOU'RE RIGHT.
OH, THE SADNESS OF IT ALL!
WE'RE DOOMED!
IF ONLY SOMEONE COULD HELP US...
POOF!
YOU RANG?
WHO ARE YOU?
I'M YOUR FAIRY GODMOTHER!
I'M HERE TO HELP YOU!
GEE, TOO BAD YOU WEREN'T AROUND BEFORE THAT SAFE TOOK CARE OF DADDY!
Uh-oh, SORRY!
10

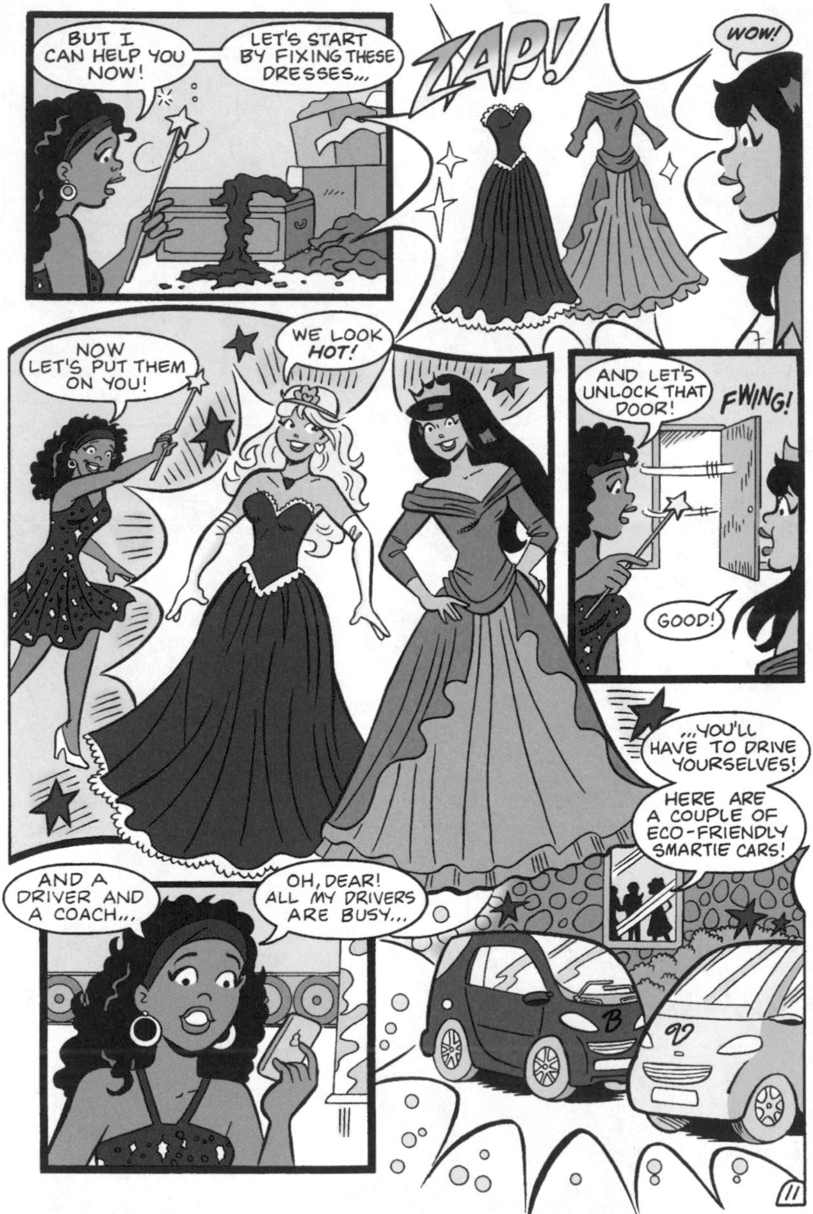
BUT I CAN HELP YOU NOW!
LET'S START BY FIXING THESE DRESSES...
ZAP!
WOW!
NOW LET'S PUT THEM ON YOU!
WE LOOK HOT!
AND LET'S UNLOCK THAT DOOR!
FWING!
GOOD!
AND A DRIVER AND A COACH...
OH, DEAR! ALL MY DRIVERS ARE BUSY...
...YOU'LL HAVE TO DRIVE YOURSELVES!
HERE ARE A COUPLE OF ECO-FRIENDLY SMARTIE CARS!
11

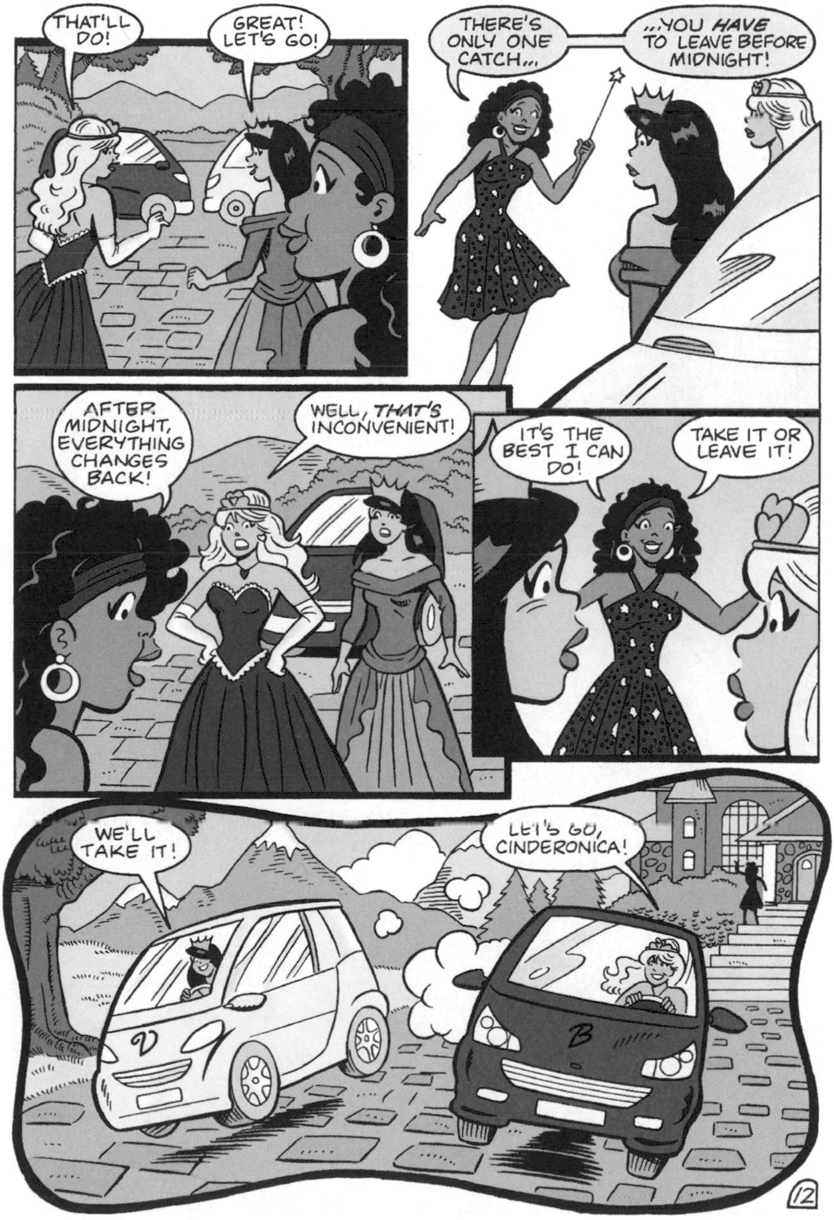
THAT'LL DO!
GREAT! LET'S GO!
THERE'S ONLY ONE CATCH...
...YOU *HAVE* TO LEAVE BEFORE MIDNIGHT!
AFTER MIDNIGHT, EVERYTHING CHANGES BACK!
WELL, *THAT'S* INCONVENIENT!
IT'S THE BEST I CAN DO!
TAKE IT OR LEAVE IT!
WE'LL TAKE IT!
LET'S GO, CINDERONICA!
12

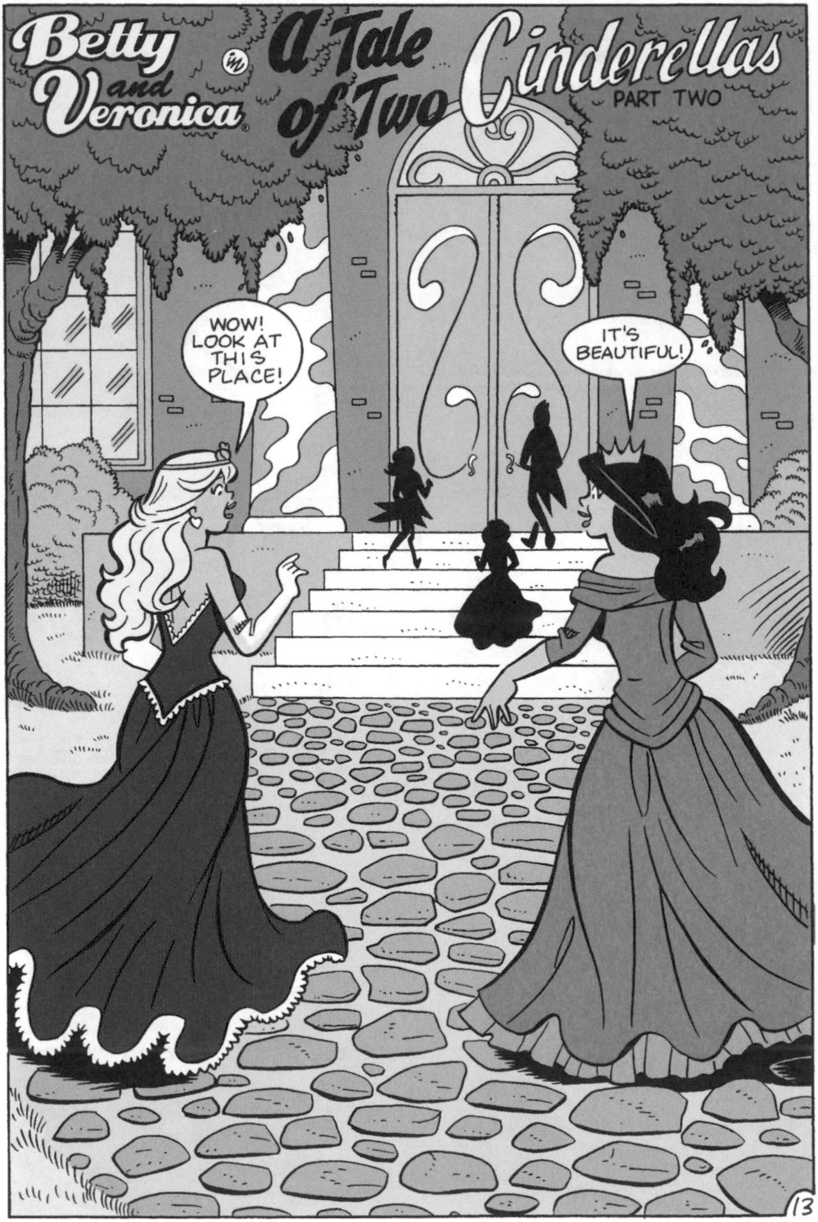
Betty and Veronica
in
A Tale of Two Cinderellas
PART TWO
WOW! LOOK AT THIS PLACE!
IT'S BEAUTIFUL!
13

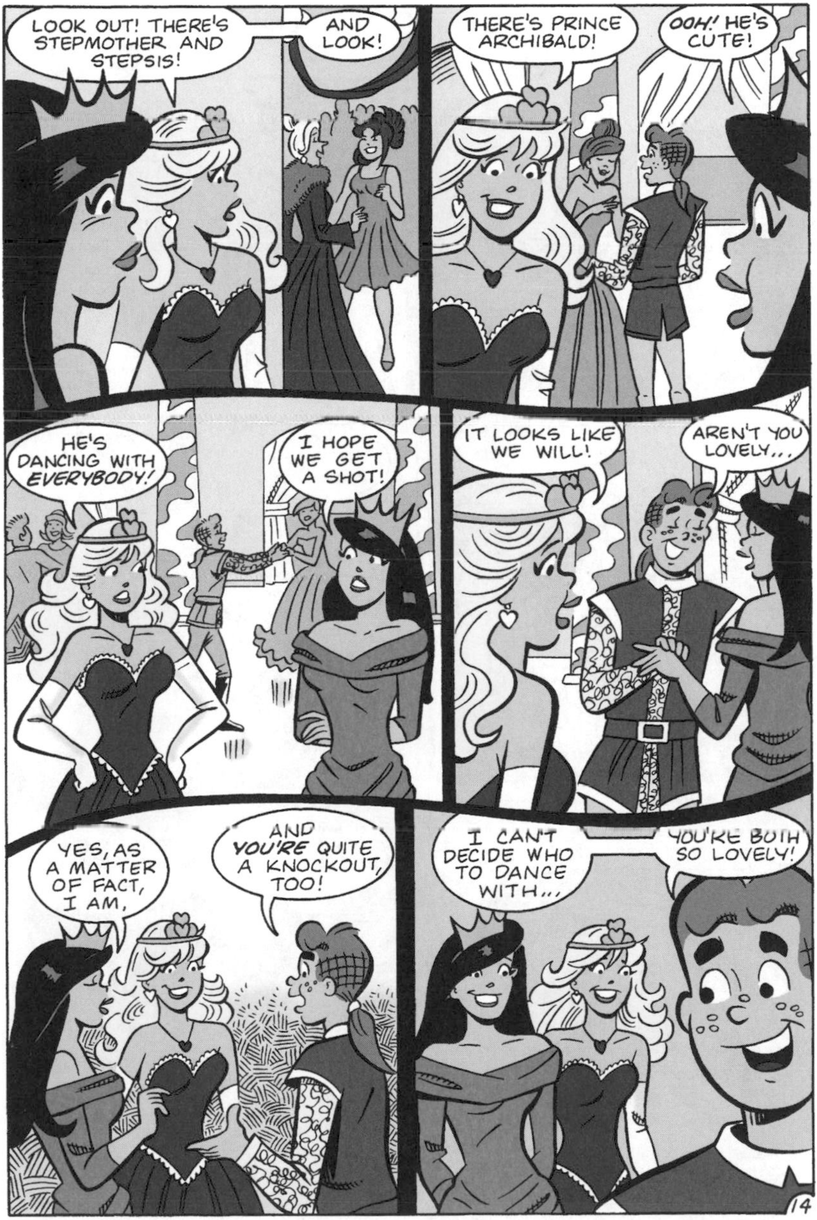
LOOK OUT! THERE'S STEPMOTHER AND STEPSIS!
AND LOOK!
THERE'S PRINCE ARCHIBALD!
OOH! HE'S CUTE!
HE'S DANCING WITH EVERYBODY!
I HOPE WE GET A SHOT!
IT LOOKS LIKE WE WILL!
AREN'T YOU LOVELY...
YES, AS A MATTER OF FACT, I AM.
AND YOU'RE QUITE A KNOCKOUT, TOO!
I CAN'T DECIDE WHO TO DANCE WITH...
YOU'RE BOTH SO LOVELY!
14

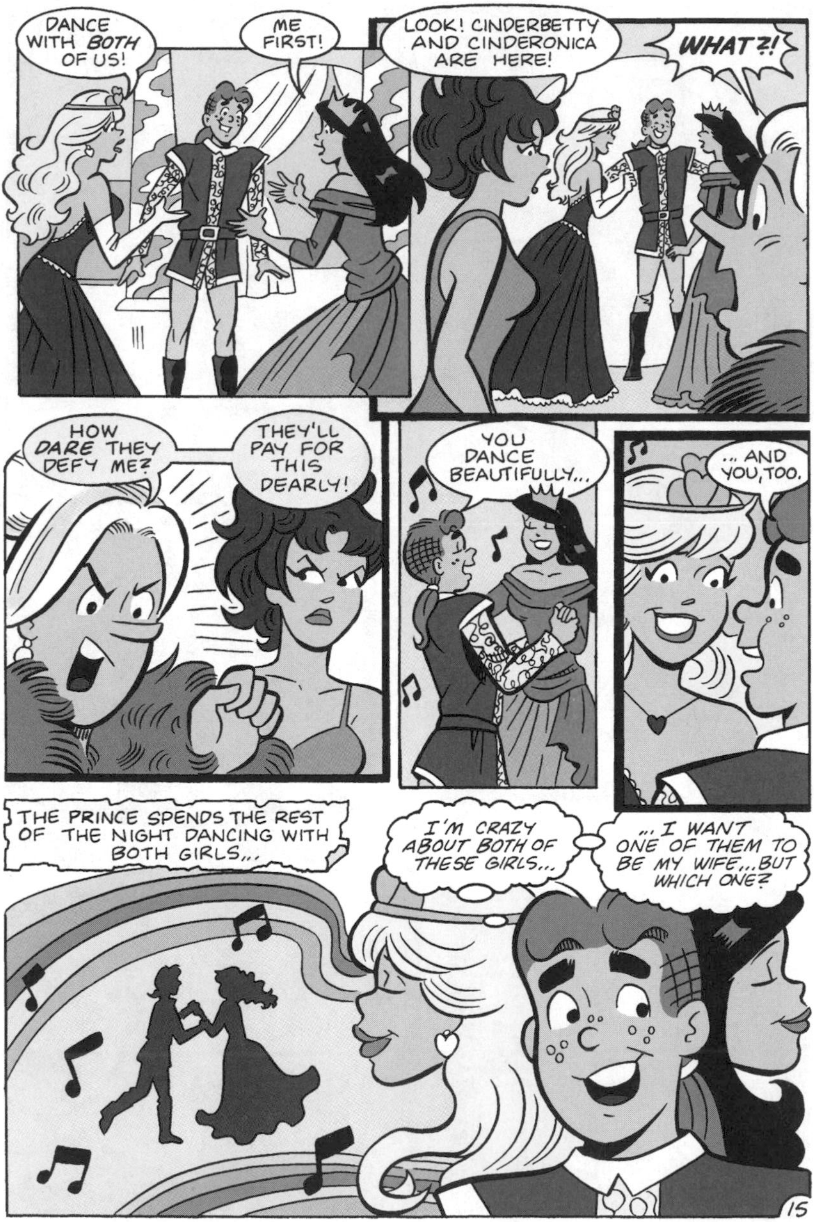
DANCE WITH BOTH OF US!
ME FIRST!
LOOK! CINDERBETTY AND CINDERONICA ARE HERE!
WHAT?!
HOW DARE THEY DEFY ME?
THEY'LL PAY FOR THIS DEARLY!
YOU DANCE BEAUTIFULLY...
... AND YOU, TOO.
THE PRINCE SPENDS THE REST OF THE NIGHT DANCING WITH BOTH GIRLS...
I'M CRAZY ABOUT BOTH OF THESE GIRLS...
... I WANT ONE OF THEM TO BE MY WIFE... BUT WHICH ONE?
15

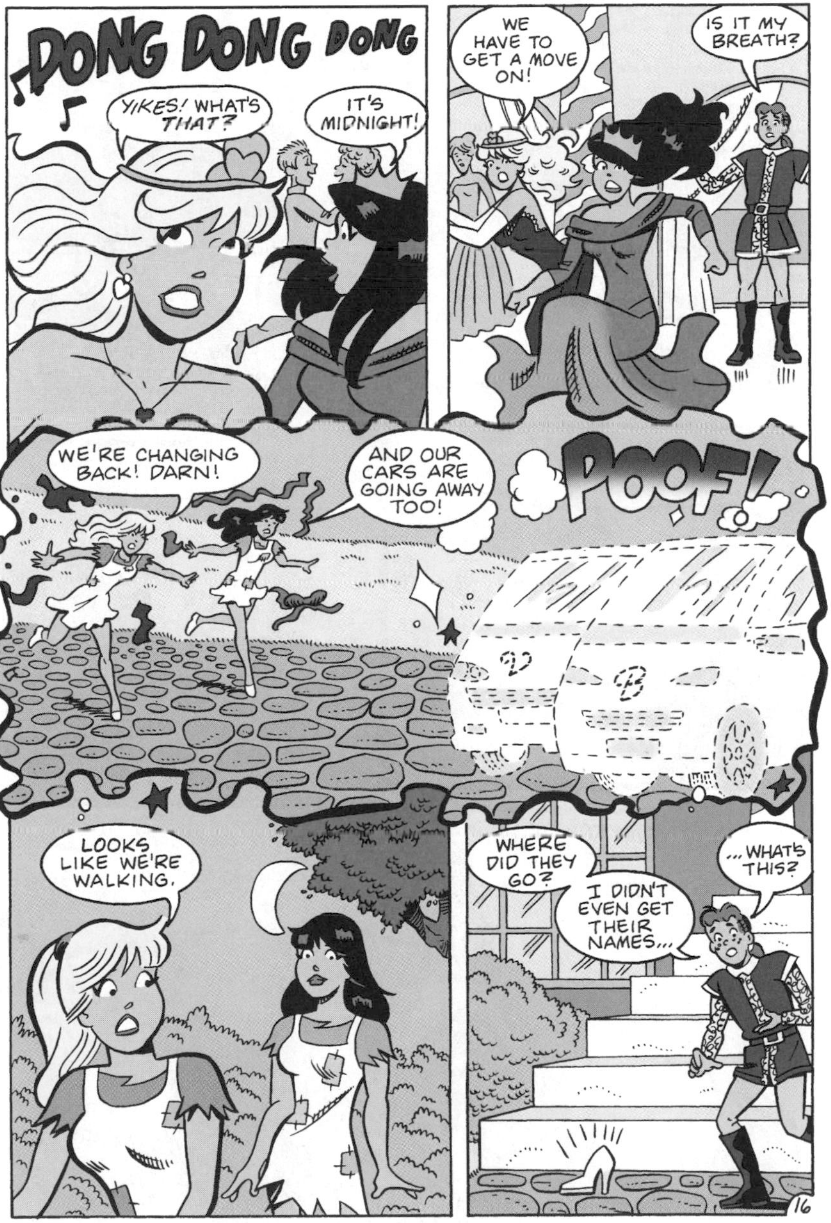
DONG DONG DONG
YIKES! WHAT'S THAT?
IT'S MIDNIGHT!
WE HAVE TO GET A MOVE ON!
IS IT MY BREATH?
WE'RE CHANGING BACK! DARN!
AND OUR CARS ARE GOING AWAY TOO!
POOF!
LOOKS LIKE WE'RE WALKING.
WHERE DID THEY GO?
I DIDN'T EVEN GET THEIR NAMES...
...WHAT'S THIS?
16

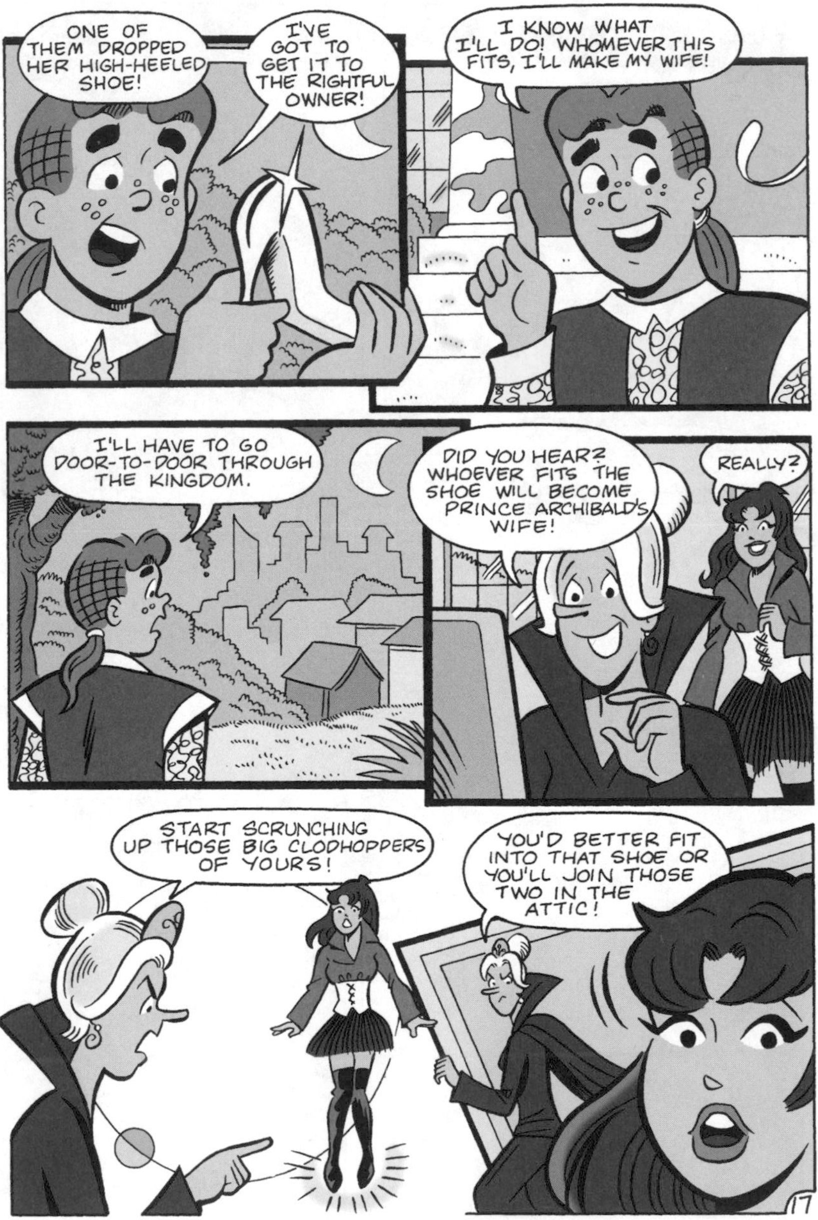
ONE OF THEM DROPPED HER HIGH-HEELED SHOE!
I'VE GOT TO GET IT TO THE RIGHTFUL OWNER!
I KNOW WHAT I'LL DO! WHOMEVER THIS FITS, I'LL MAKE MY WIFE!
I'LL HAVE TO GO DOOR-TO-DOOR THROUGH THE KINGDOM.
DID YOU HEAR? WHOEVER FITS THE SHOE WILL BECOME PRINCE ARCHIBALD'S WIFE!
REALLY?
START SCRUNCHING UP THOSE BIG CLODHOPPERS OF YOURS!
YOU'D BETTER FIT INTO THAT SHOE OR YOU'LL JOIN THOSE TWO IN THE ATTIC!
17

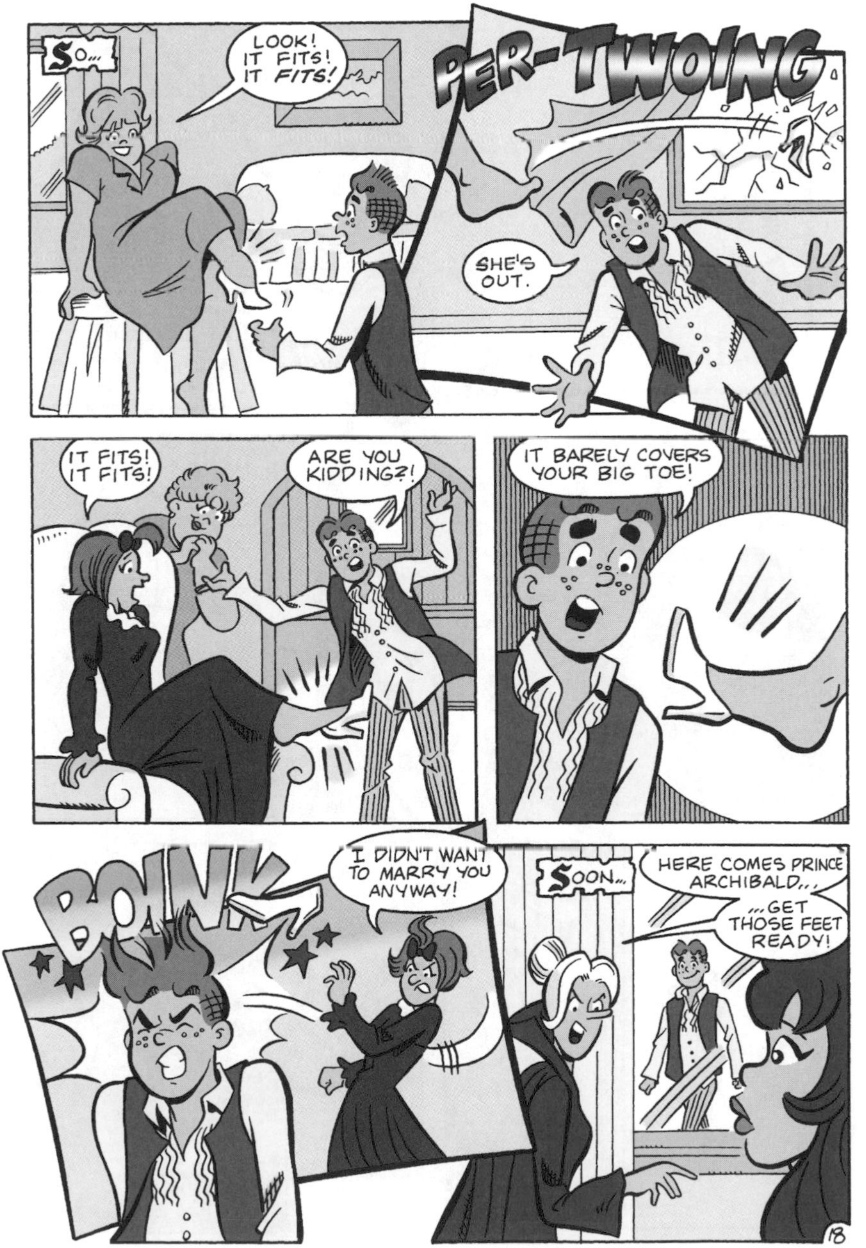
SO...
LOOK! IT FITS! IT FITS!
PER-TWOING
SHE'S OUT.
IT FITS! IT FITS!
ARE YOU KIDDING?!
IT BARELY COVERS YOUR BIG TOE!
BOINK
I DIDN'T WANT TO MARRY YOU ANYWAY!
SOON...
HERE COMES PRINCE ARCHIBALD...
...GET THOSE FEET READY!
18

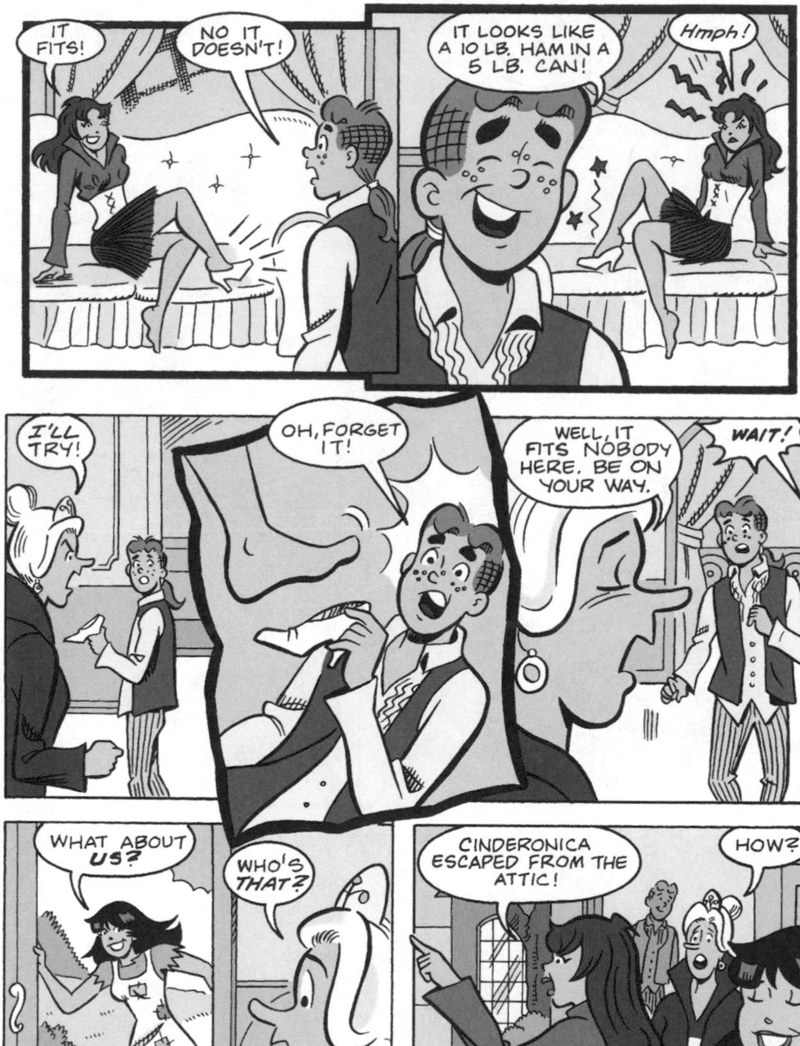
IT FITS!
NO IT DOESN'T!
IT LOOKS LIKE A 10 LB. HAM IN A 5 LB. CAN!
Hmph!
I'LL TRY!
OH, FORGET IT!
WELL, IT FITS NOBODY HERE. BE ON YOUR WAY.
WAIT!
WHAT ABOUT US?
WHO'S THAT?
CINDERONICA ESCAPED FROM THE ATTIC!
HOW?
19

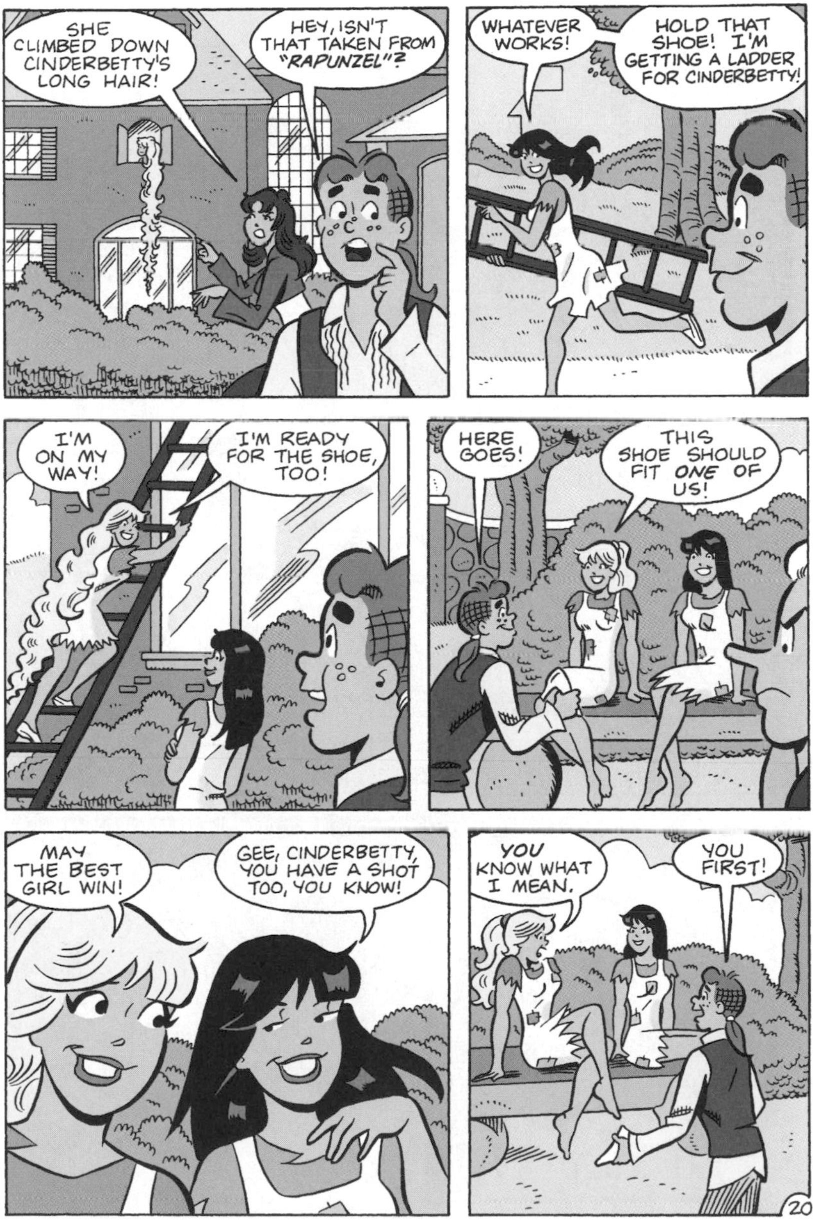
SHE CLIMBED DOWN CINDERBETTY'S LONG HAIR!
HEY, ISN'T THAT TAKEN FROM "RAPUNZEL"?
WHATEVER WORKS!
HOLD THAT SHOE! I'M GETTING A LADDER FOR CINDERBETTY!
I'M ON MY WAY!
I'M READY FOR THE SHOE, TOO!
HERE GOES!
THIS SHOE SHOULD FIT ONE OF US!
MAY THE BEST GIRL WIN!
GEE, CINDERBETTY, YOU HAVE A SHOT TOO, YOU KNOW!
YOU KNOW WHAT I MEAN.
YOU FIRST!
20

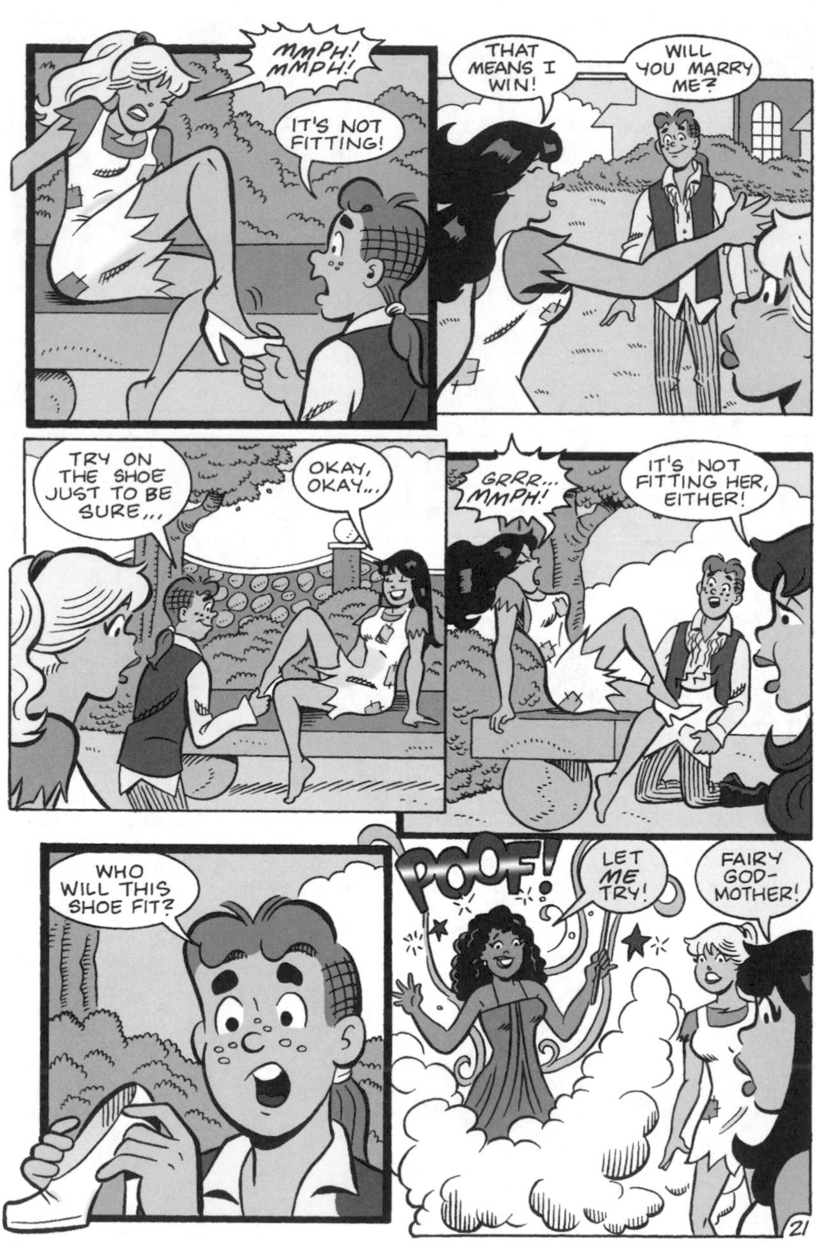
MMPH! MMPH!
IT'S NOT FITTING!
THAT MEANS I WIN!
WILL YOU MARRY ME?
TRY ON THE SHOE JUST TO BE SURE...
OKAY, OKAY...
GRRR... MMPH!
IT'S NOT FITTING HER, EITHER!
WHO WILL THIS SHOE FIT?
POOF!
LET ME TRY!
FAIRY GOD-MOTHER!
21

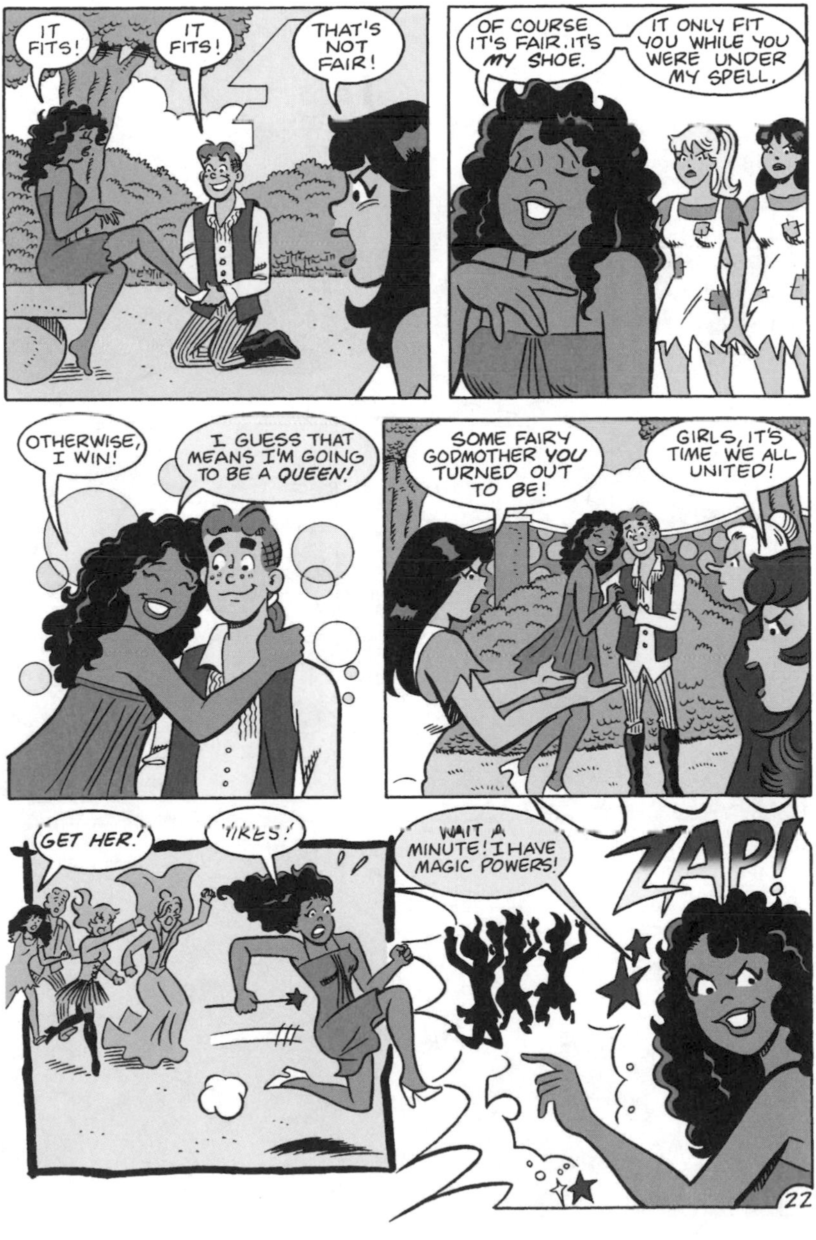
IT FITS!
IT FITS!
THAT'S NOT FAIR!
OF COURSE IT'S FAIR. IT'S *MY* SHOE.
IT ONLY FIT YOU WHILE YOU WERE UNDER MY SPELL.
OTHERWISE, I WIN!
I GUESS THAT MEANS I'M GOING TO BE A *QUEEN!*
SOME FAIRY GODMOTHER *YOU* TURNED OUT TO BE!
GIRLS, IT'S TIME WE ALL UNITED!
GET HER!
YIKES!
WAIT A MINUTE! I HAVE MAGIC POWERS!
ZAP!
22

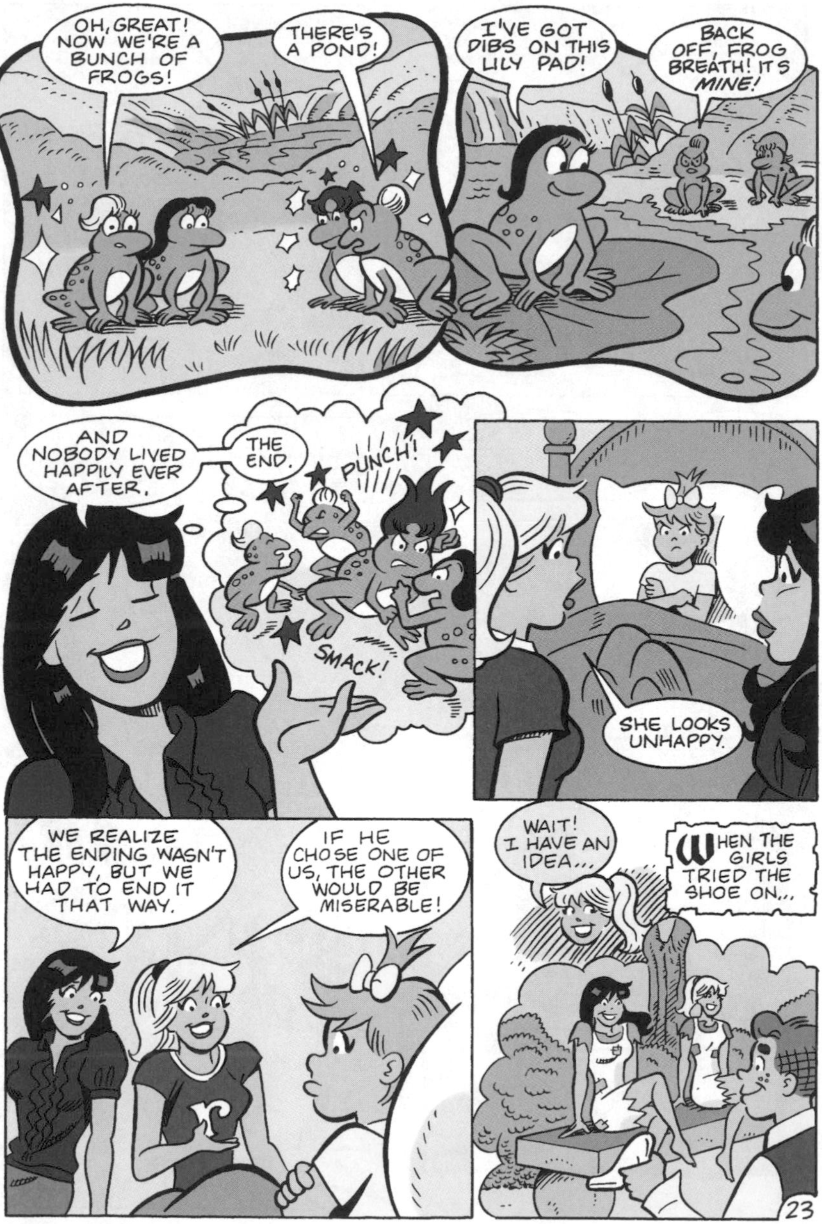
OH, GREAT! NOW WE'RE A BUNCH OF FROGS!
THERE'S A POND!
I'VE GOT DIBS ON THIS LILY PAD!
BACK OFF, FROG BREATH! ITS MINE!
AND NOBODY LIVED HAPPILY EVER AFTER.
THE END.
PUNCH!
SMACK!
SHE LOOKS UNHAPPY.
WE REALIZE THE ENDING WASN'T HAPPY, BUT WE HAD TO END IT THAT WAY.
IF HE CHOSE ONE OF US, THE OTHER WOULD BE MISERABLE!
WAIT! I HAVE AN IDEA...
WHEN THE GIRLS TRIED THE SHOE ON...
23

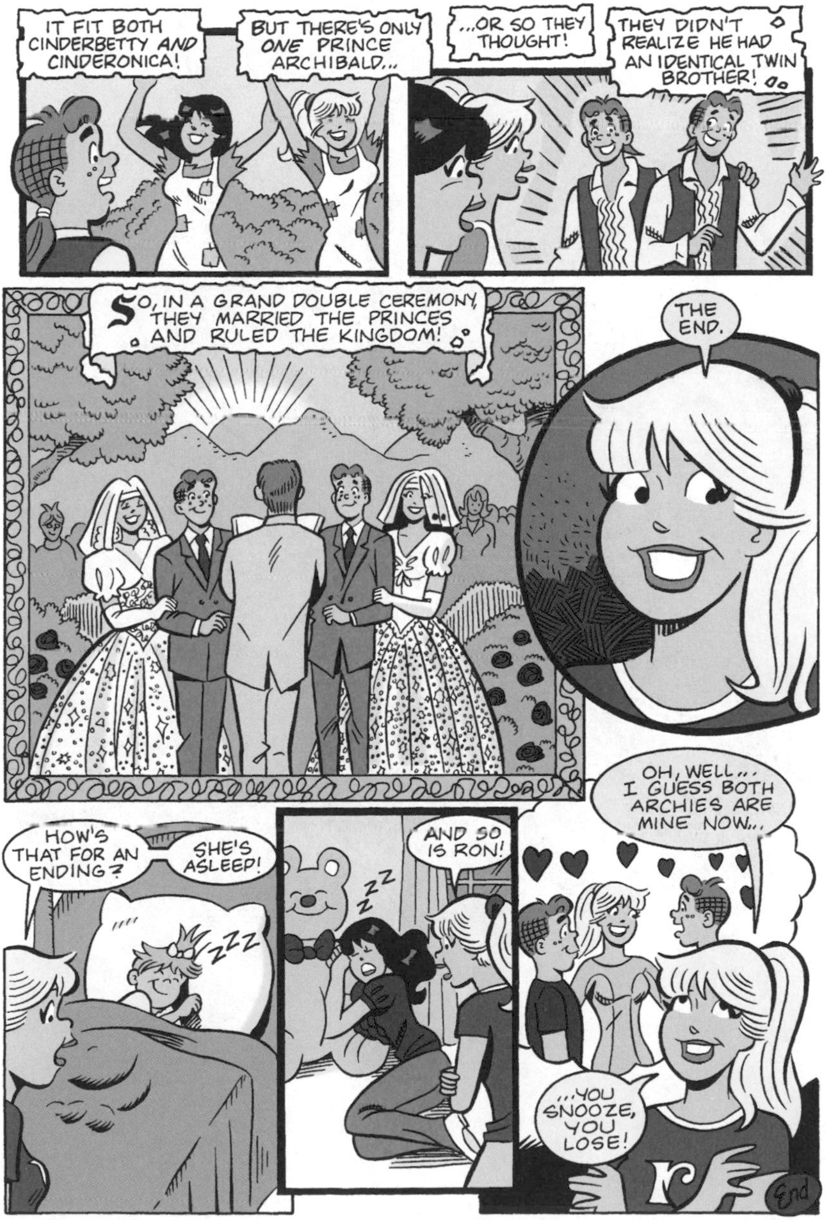
IT FIT BOTH CINDERBETTY AND CINDERONICA!
BUT THERE'S ONLY ONE PRINCE ARCHIBALD...
...OR SO THEY THOUGHT!
THEY DIDN'T REALIZE HE HAD AN IDENTICAL TWIN BROTHER!
SO, IN A GRAND DOUBLE CEREMONY, THEY MARRIED THE PRINCES AND RULED THE KINGDOM!
THE END.
HOW'S THAT FOR AN ENDING?
SHE'S ASLEEP!
ZZZ
AND SO IS RON!
ZZZ
OH, WELL... I GUESS BOTH ARCHIES ARE MINE NOW...
...YOU SNOOZE, YOU LOSE!
End

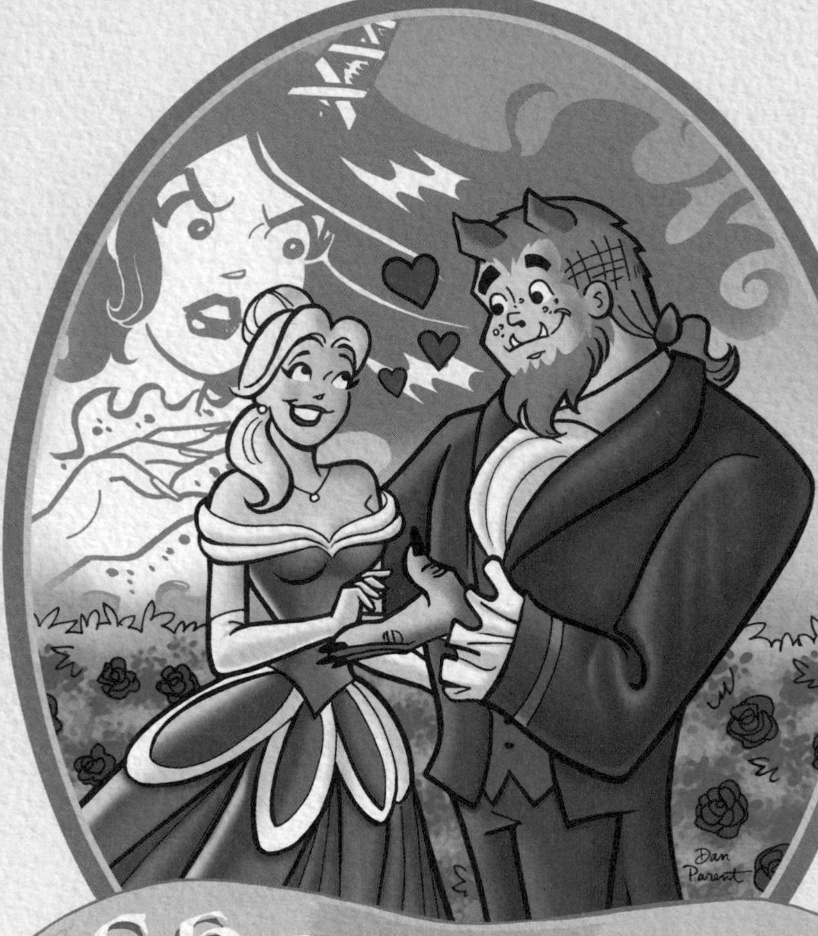
Dan Parent

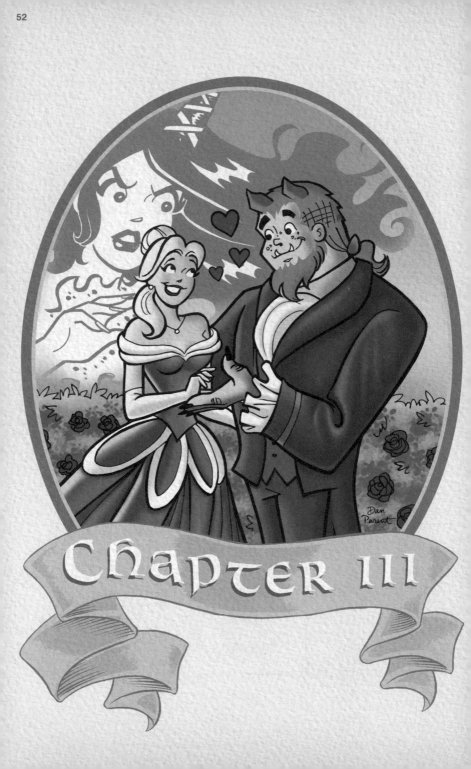

Chapter III

 Betty *and* the Beast

The evil enchantress Veronica usually gets what she wants. But when she finds that Prince Archie holds no love for her in his heart, the solution is simple: turn him into a slobbering man-beast.

There's still some hope for the creature, though. If someone falls in love with the former Prince Archie before his 21st birthday, the curse will be lifted. Could Betty be the one? Not if Veronica has a say in it!

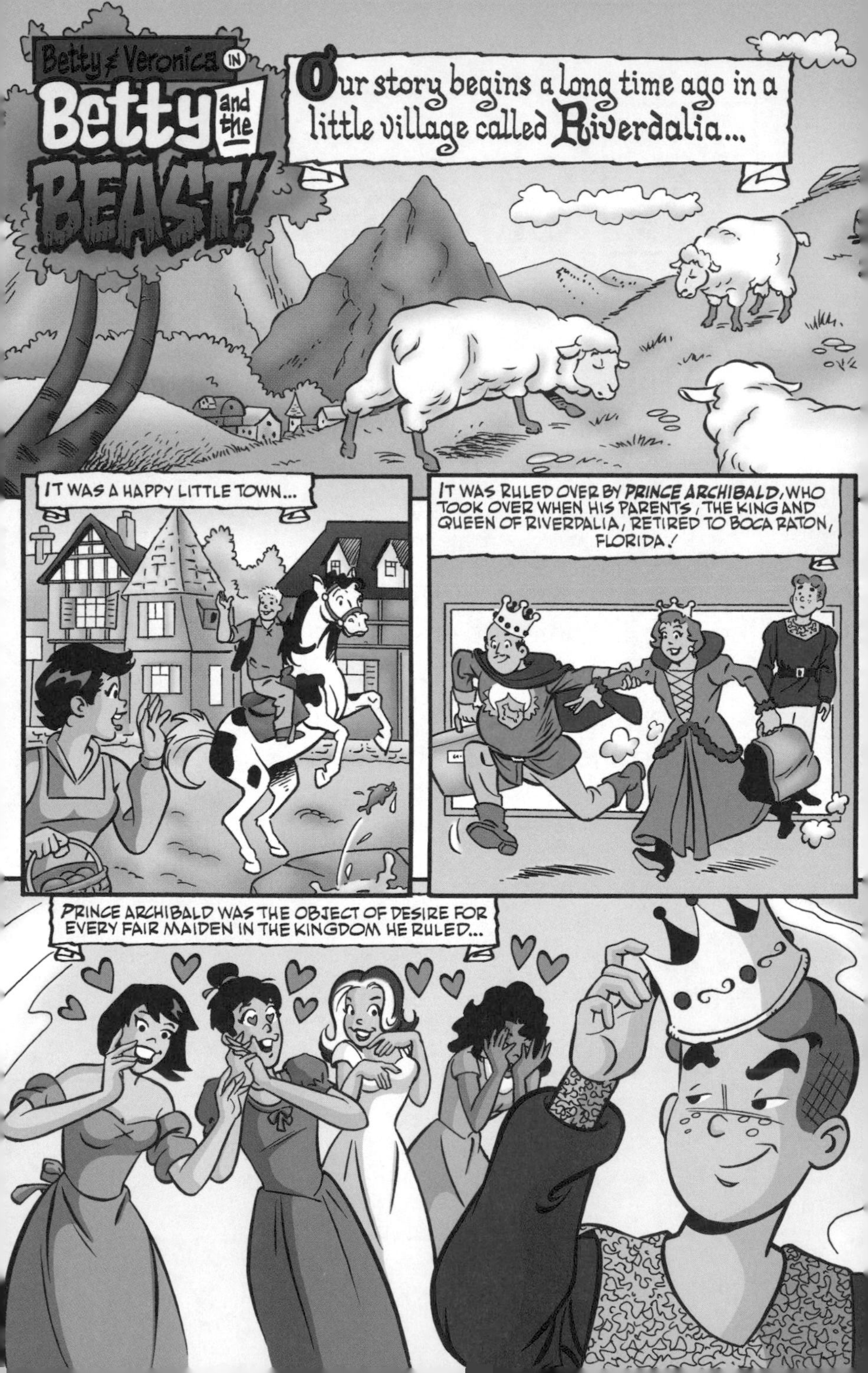
Betty & Veronica IN
Betty and the BEAST!
Our story begins a long time ago in a little village called Riverdalia...
IT WAS A HAPPY LITTLE TOWN...
IT WAS RULED OVER BY PRINCE ARCHIBALD, WHO TOOK OVER WHEN HIS PARENTS, THE KING AND QUEEN OF RIVERDALIA, RETIRED TO BOCA RATON, FLORIDA!
PRINCE ARCHIBALD WAS THE OBJECT OF DESIRE FOR EVERY FAIR MAIDEN IN THE KINGDOM HE RULED...

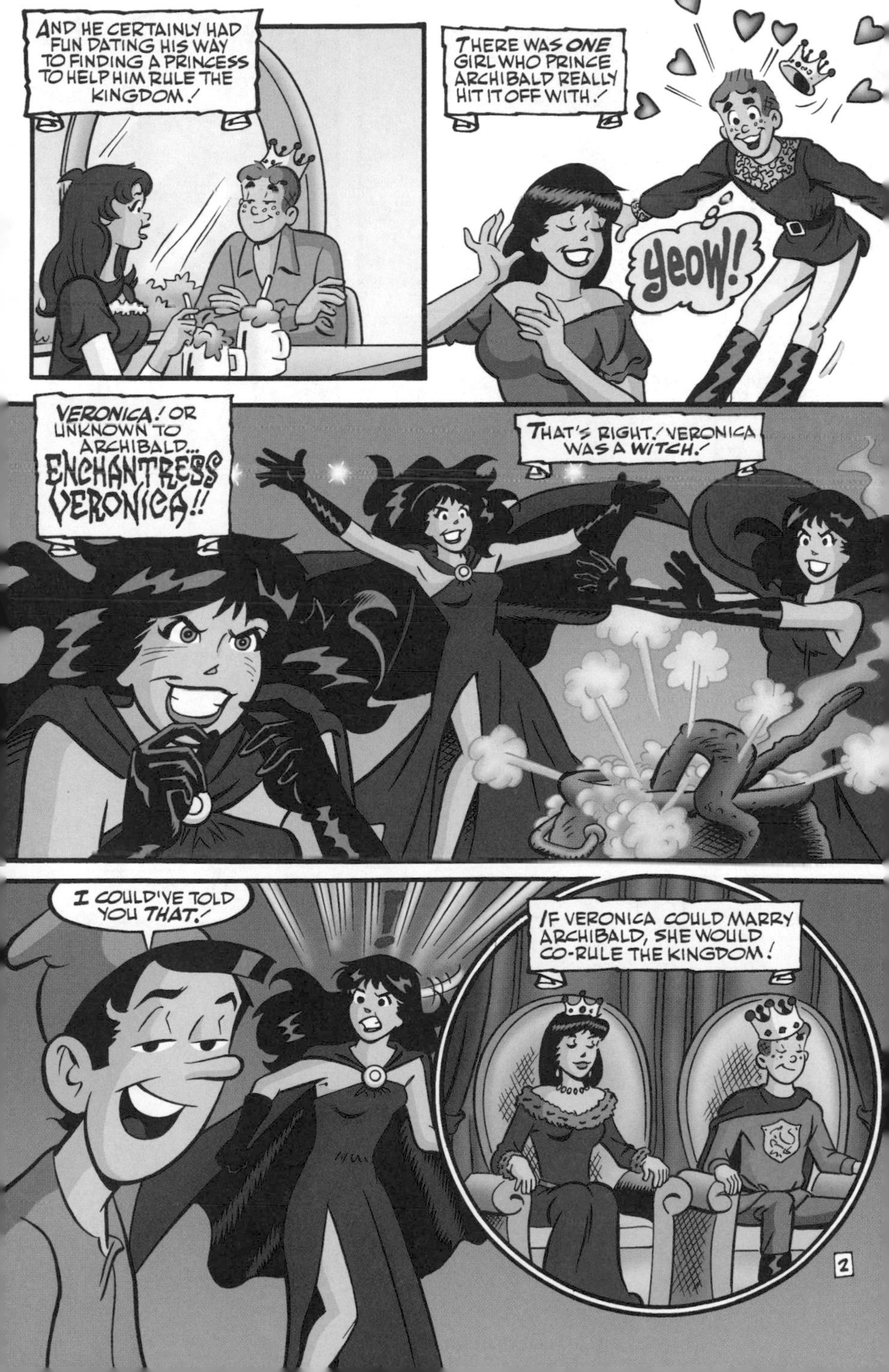
AND HE CERTAINLY HAD FUN DATING HIS WAY TO FINDING A PRINCESS TO HELP HIM RULE THE KINGDOM!
THERE WAS ONE GIRL WHO PRINCE ARCHIBALD REALLY HIT IT OFF WITH!
YEOW!
VERONICA! OR UNKNOWN TO ARCHIBALD... ENCHANTRESS VERONICA!!
THAT'S RIGHT! VERONICA WAS A WITCH!
I COULD'VE TOLD YOU THAT!
IF VERONICA COULD MARRY ARCHIBALD, SHE WOULD CO-RULE THE KINGDOM!
2

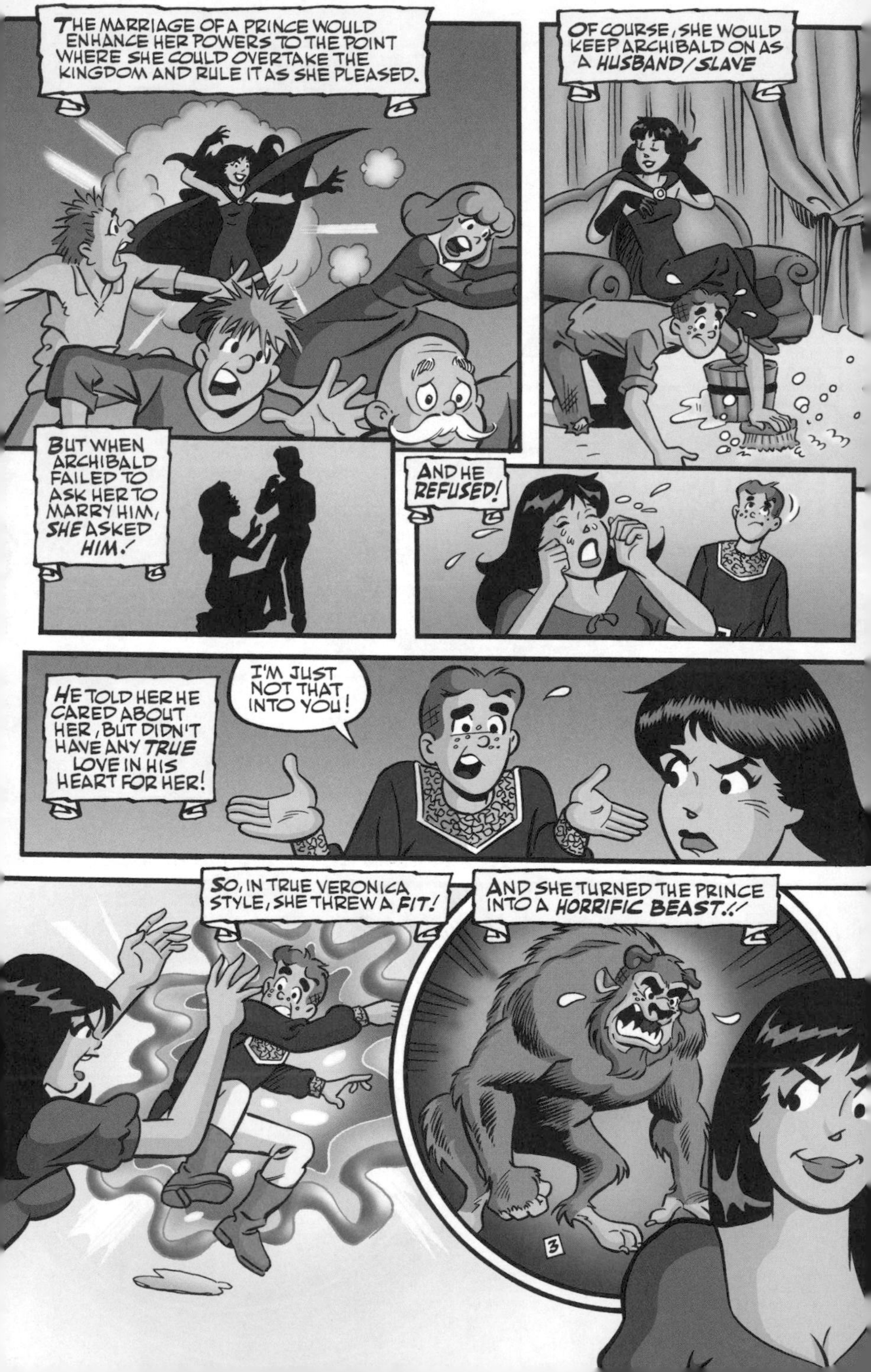
THE MARRIAGE OF A PRINCE WOULD ENHANCE HER POWERS TO THE POINT WHERE SHE COULD OVERTAKE THE KINGDOM AND RULE IT AS SHE PLEASED.
OF COURSE, SHE WOULD KEEP ARCHIBALD ON AS A HUSBAND/SLAVE
BUT WHEN ARCHIBALD FAILED TO ASK HER TO MARRY HIM, SHE ASKED HIM.!
AND HE REFUSED!
HE TOLD HER HE CARED ABOUT HER, BUT DIDN'T HAVE ANY TRUE LOVE IN HIS HEART FOR HER!
I'M JUST NOT THAT INTO YOU!
SO, IN TRUE VERONICA STYLE, SHE THREW A FIT!
AND SHE TURNED THE PRINCE INTO A HORRIFIC BEAST.!!
3

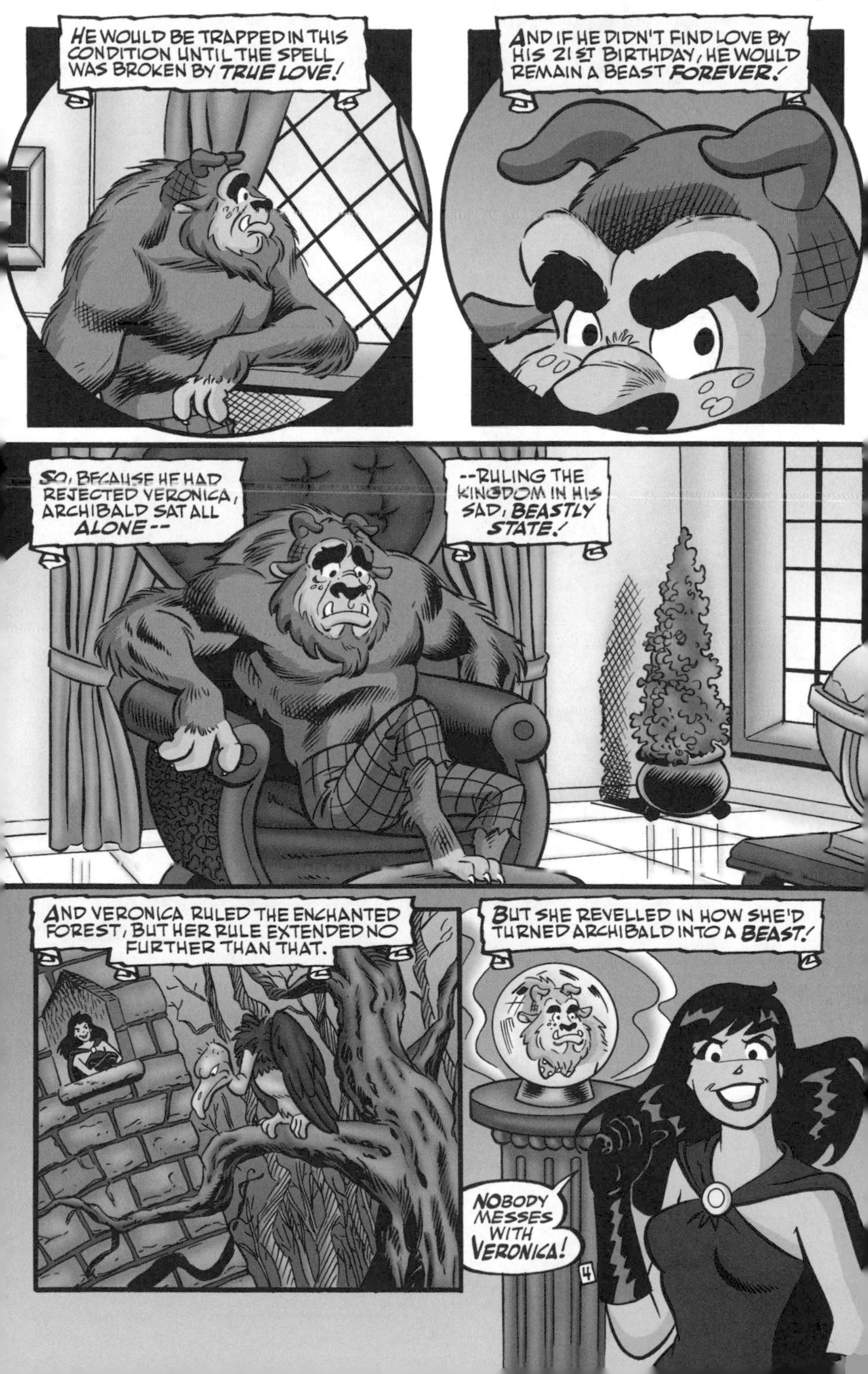
HE WOULD BE TRAPPED IN THIS CONDITION UNTIL THE SPELL WAS BROKEN BY TRUE LOVE!
AND IF HE DIDN'T FIND LOVE BY HIS 21ST BIRTHDAY, HE WOULD REMAIN A BEAST FOREVER!
SO, BECAUSE HE HAD REJECTED VERONICA, ARCHIBALD SAT ALL ALONE--
--RULING THE KINGDOM IN HIS SAD, BEASTLY STATE!
AND VERONICA RULED THE ENCHANTED FOREST, BUT HER RULE EXTENDED NO FURTHER THAN THAT.
BUT SHE REVELLED IN HOW SHE'D TURNED ARCHIBALD INTO A BEAST!
NOBODY MESSES WITH VERONICA!
4

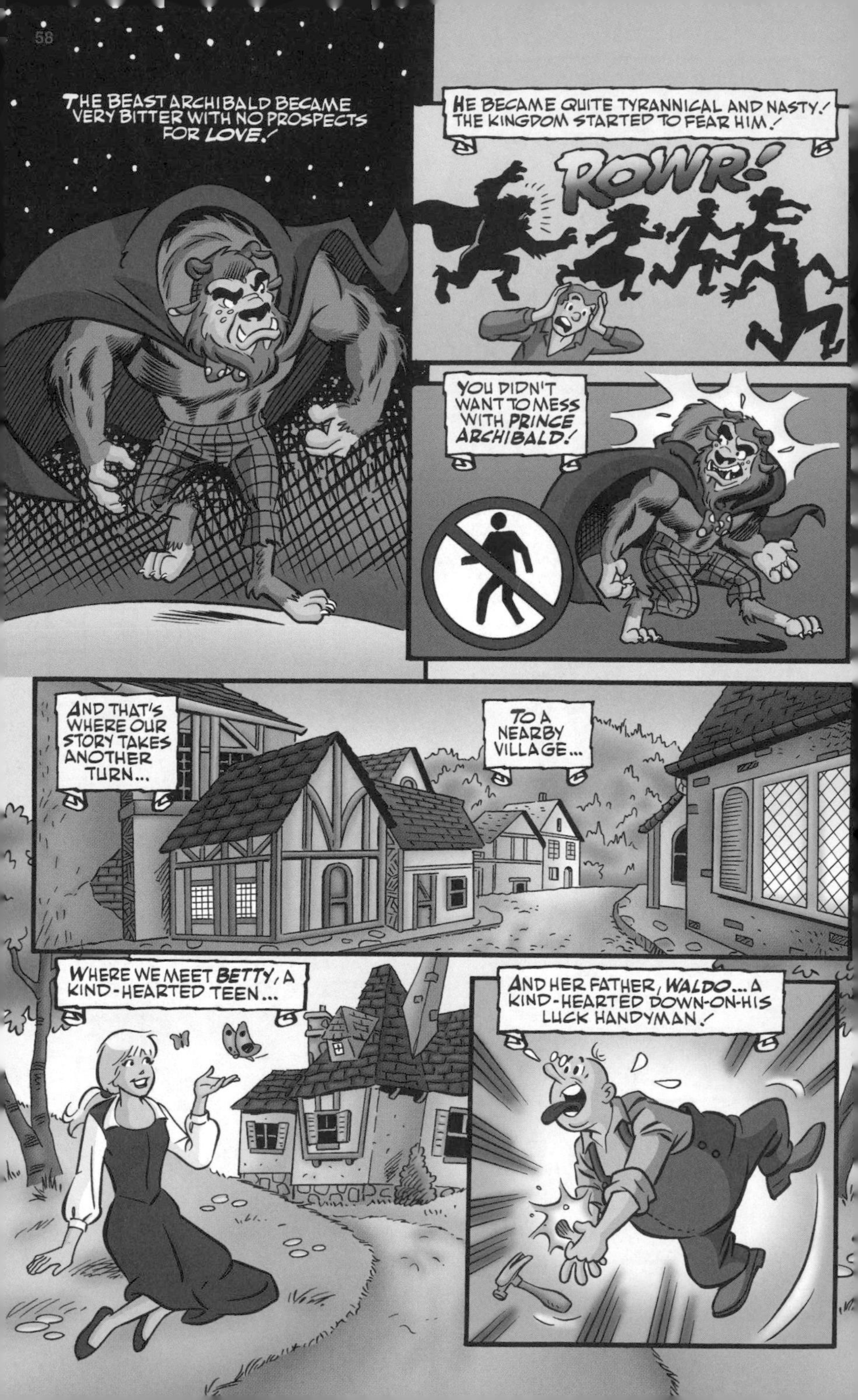
THE BEAST ARCHIBALD BECAME VERY BITTER WITH NO PROSPECTS FOR LOVE!
HE BECAME QUITE TYRANNICAL AND NASTY! THE KINGDOM STARTED TO FEAR HIM!
ROWR!
YOU DIDN'T WANT TO MESS WITH PRINCE ARCHIBALD!
AND THAT'S WHERE OUR STORY TAKES ANOTHER TURN...
TO A NEARBY VILLAGE...
WHERE WE MEET BETTY, A KIND-HEARTED TEEN...
AND HER FATHER, WALDO... A KIND-HEARTED DOWN-ON-HIS LUCK HANDYMAN!

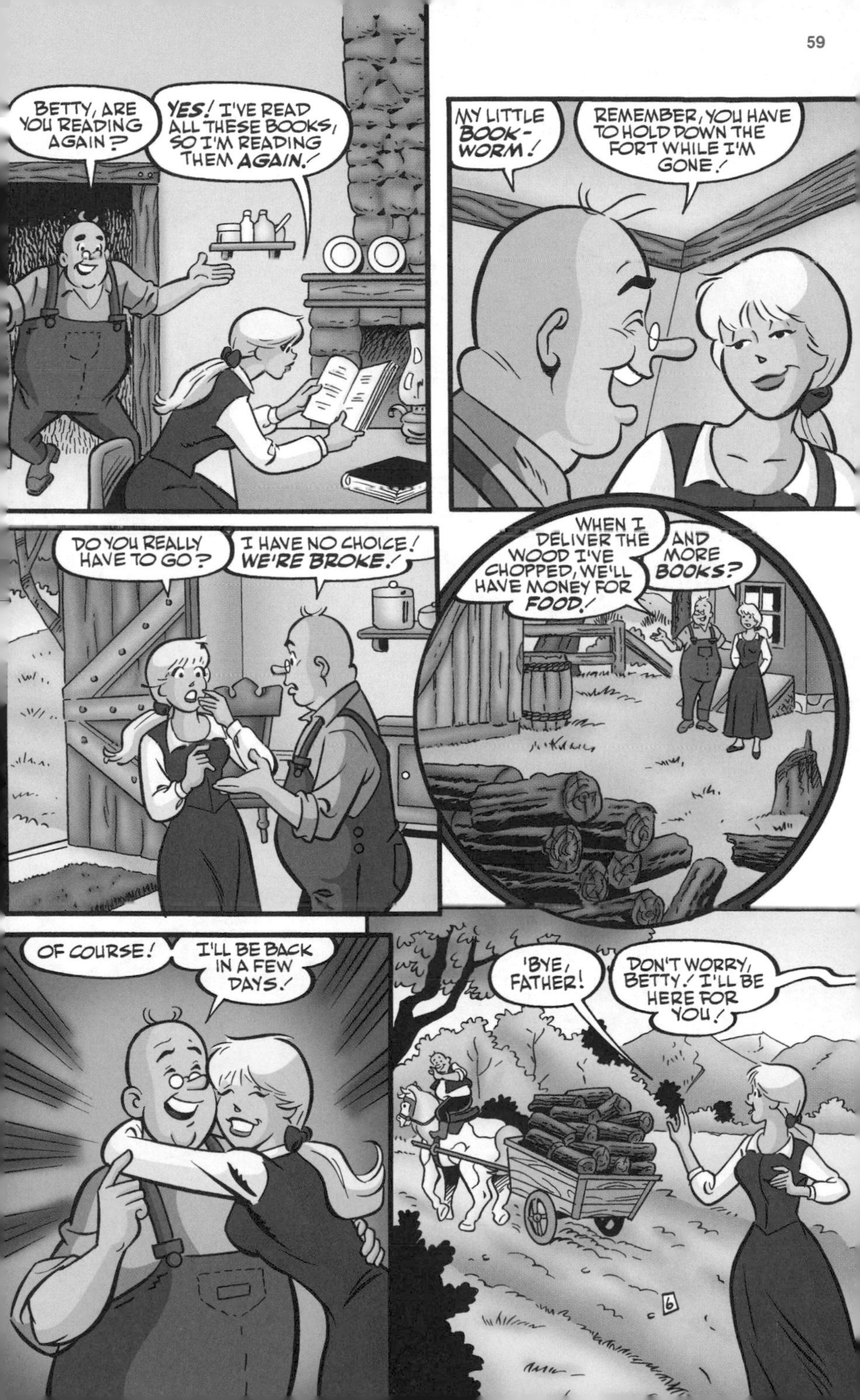
BETTY, ARE YOU READING AGAIN?
YES! I'VE READ ALL THESE BOOKS, SO I'M READING THEM AGAIN!
MY LITTLE BOOK-WORM!
REMEMBER, YOU HAVE TO HOLD DOWN THE FORT WHILE I'M GONE!
DO YOU REALLY HAVE TO GO?
I HAVE NO CHOICE! WE'RE BROKE!
WHEN I DELIVER THE WOOD I'VE CHOPPED, WE'LL HAVE MONEY FOR FOOD!
AND MORE BOOKS?
OF COURSE!
I'LL BE BACK IN A FEW DAYS!
'BYE, FATHER!
DON'T WORRY, BETTY! I'LL BE HERE FOR YOU!
6

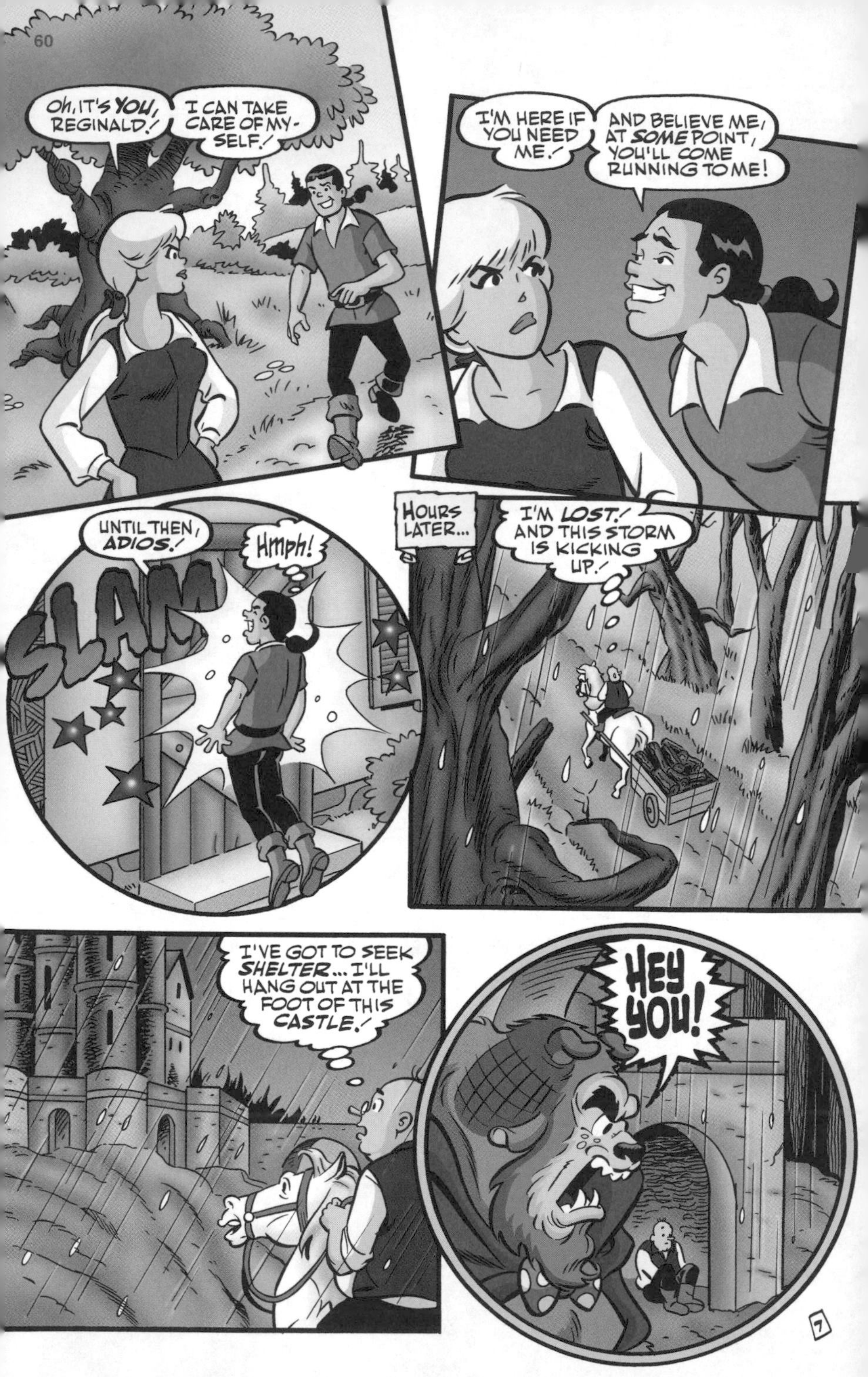

Oh, IT'S YOU, REGINALD!
I CAN TAKE CARE OF MY-SELF!
I'M HERE IF YOU NEED ME!
AND BELIEVE ME, AT SOME POINT, YOU'LL COME RUNNING TO ME!
UNTIL THEN, ADIOS!
Hmph!
SLAM
HOURS LATER...
I'M LOST! AND THIS STORM IS KICKING UP!
I'VE GOT TO SEEK SHELTER... I'LL HANG OUT AT THE FOOT OF THIS CASTLE!
HEY YOU!
7

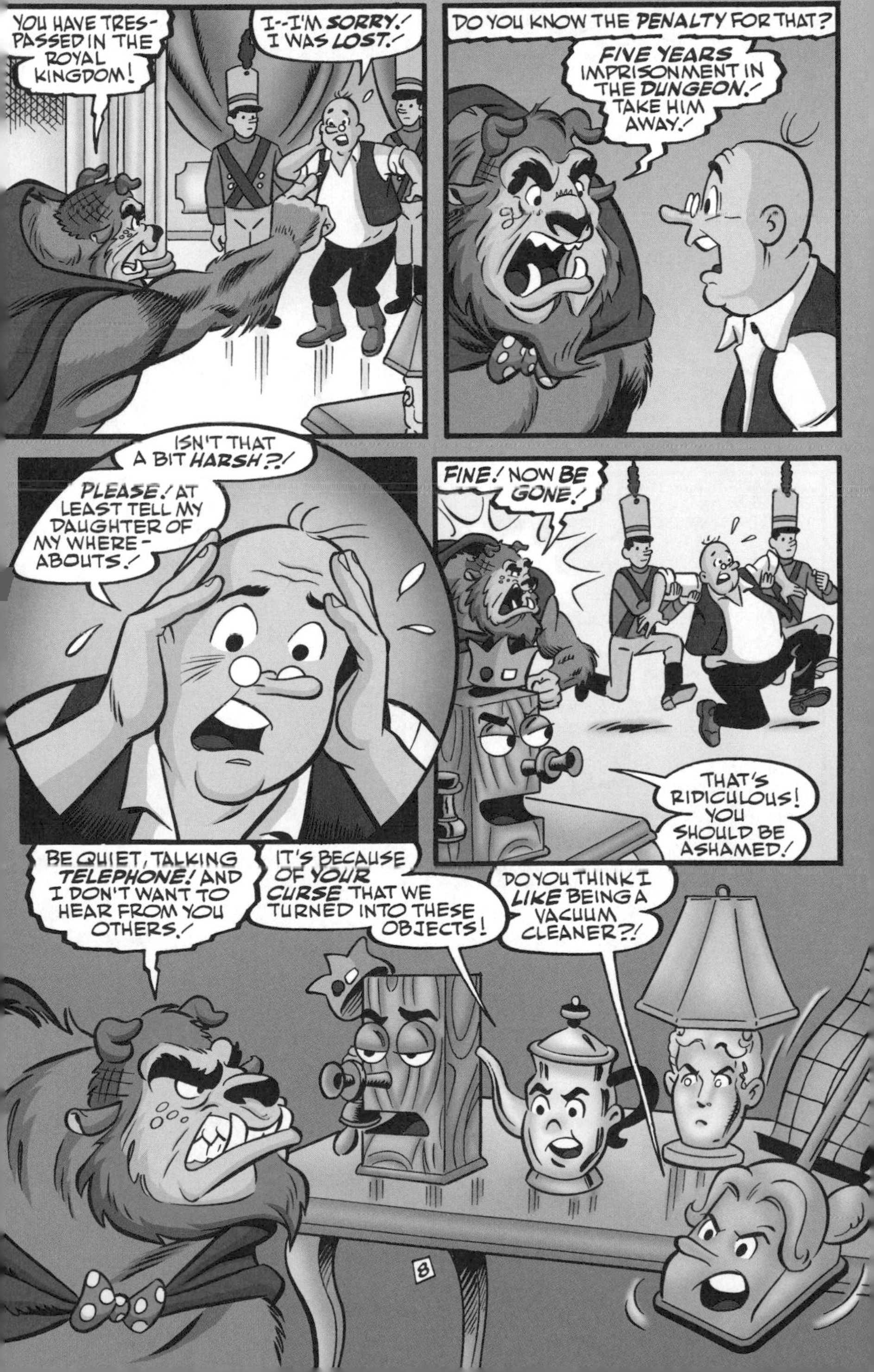
YOU HAVE TRES-PASSED IN THE ROYAL KINGDOM!
I--I'M SORRY! I WAS LOST!
DO YOU KNOW THE PENALTY FOR THAT?
FIVE YEARS IMPRISONMENT IN THE DUNGEON! TAKE HIM AWAY!
ISN'T THAT A BIT HARSH?!
PLEASE! AT LEAST TELL MY DAUGHTER OF MY WHERE-ABOUTS!
FINE! NOW BE GONE!
THAT'S RIDICULOUS! YOU SHOULD BE ASHAMED!
BE QUIET, TALKING TELEPHONE! AND I DON'T WANT TO HEAR FROM YOU OTHERS!
IT'S BECAUSE OF YOUR CURSE THAT WE TURNED INTO THESE OBJECTS!
DO YOU THINK I LIKE BEING A VACUUM CLEANER?!
8

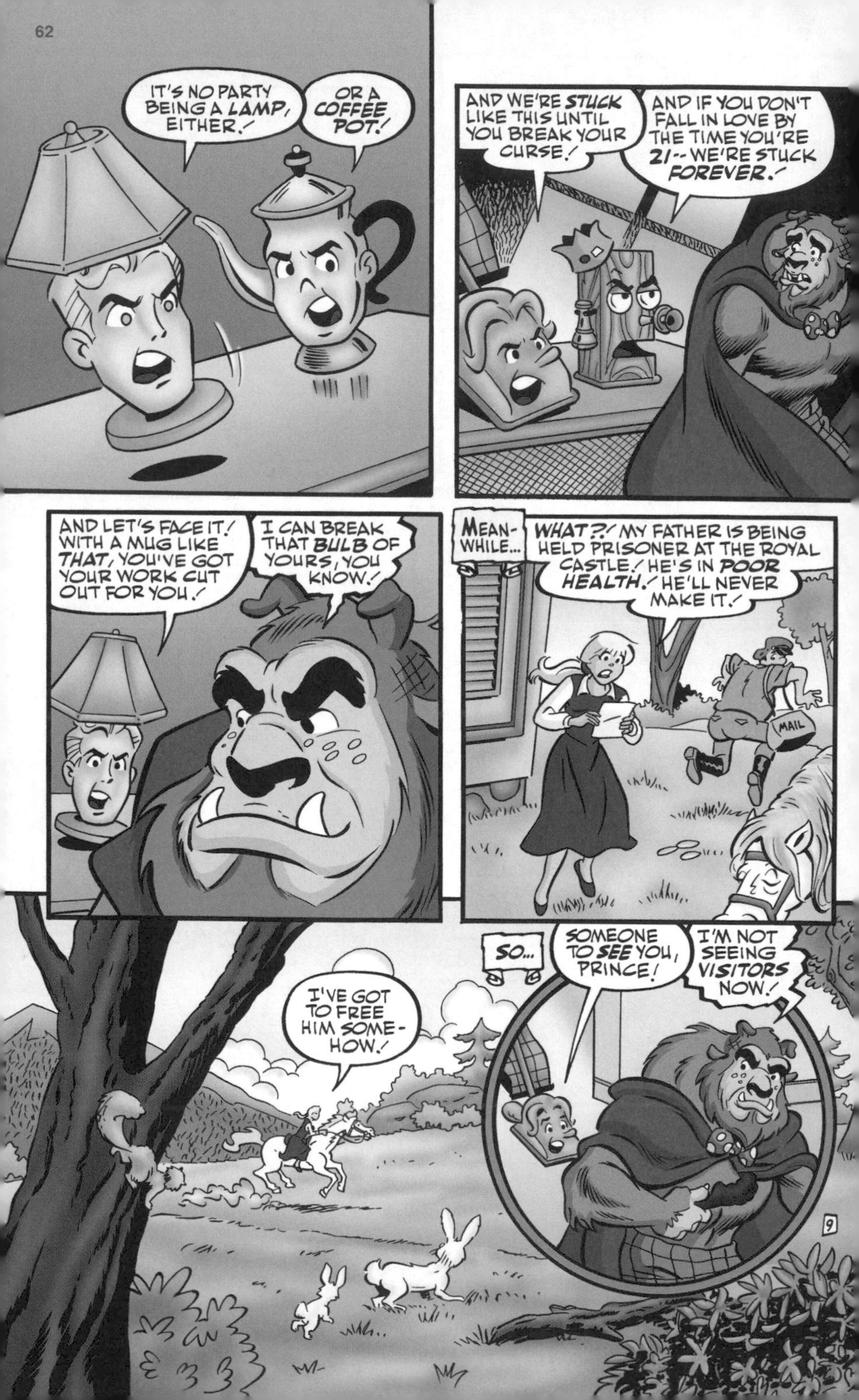
IT'S NO PARTY BEING A LAMP, EITHER.!
OR A COFFEE POT!
AND WE'RE STUCK LIKE THIS UNTIL YOU BREAK YOUR CURSE!
AND IF YOU DON'T FALL IN LOVE BY THE TIME YOU'RE 21-- WE'RE STUCK FOREVER.!
AND LET'S FACE IT! WITH A MUG LIKE THAT, YOU'VE GOT YOUR WORK CUT OUT FOR YOU!
I CAN BREAK THAT BULB OF YOURS, YOU KNOW!
MEAN-WHILE...
WHAT?!! MY FATHER IS BEING HELD PRISONER AT THE ROYAL CASTLE! HE'S IN POOR HEALTH! HE'LL NEVER MAKE IT!
MAIL
I'VE GOT TO FREE HIM SOME-HOW!
SO...
SOMEONE TO SEE YOU, PRINCE!
I'M NOT SEEING VISITORS NOW!
9

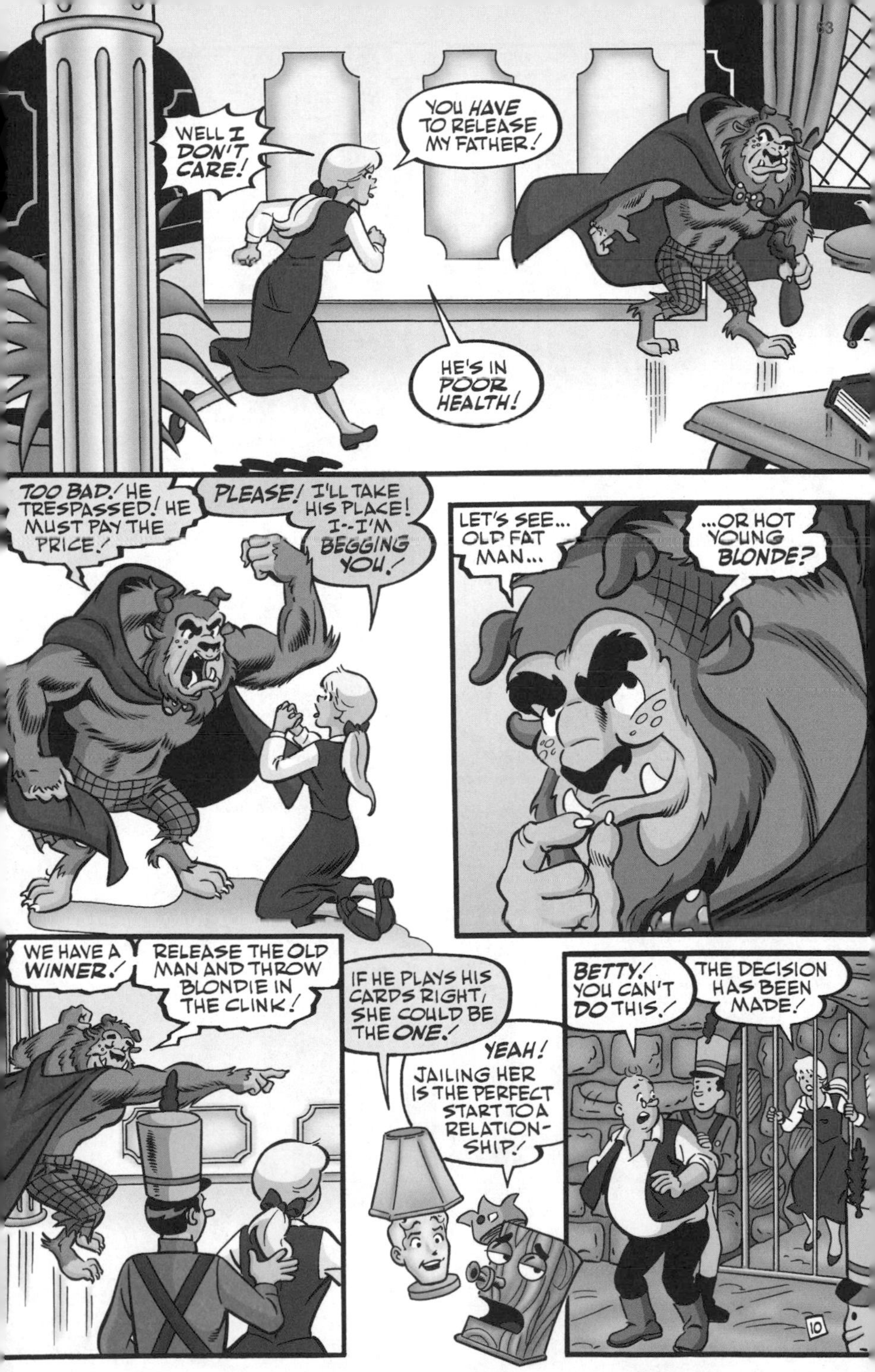
WELL I DON'T CARE!
YOU HAVE TO RELEASE MY FATHER!
HE'S IN POOR HEALTH!
TOO BAD! HE TRESPASSED! HE MUST PAY THE PRICE!
PLEASE! I'LL TAKE HIS PLACE! I--I'M BEGGING YOU!
LET'S SEE... OLD FAT MAN...
...OR HOT YOUNG BLONDE?
WE HAVE A WINNER!
RELEASE THE OLD MAN AND THROW BLONDIE IN THE CLINK!
IF HE PLAYS HIS CARDS RIGHT, SHE COULD BE THE ONE!
YEAH! JAILING HER IS THE PERFECT START TO A RELATION-SHIP!
BETTY! YOU CAN'T DO THIS!
THE DECISION HAS BEEN MADE!
10

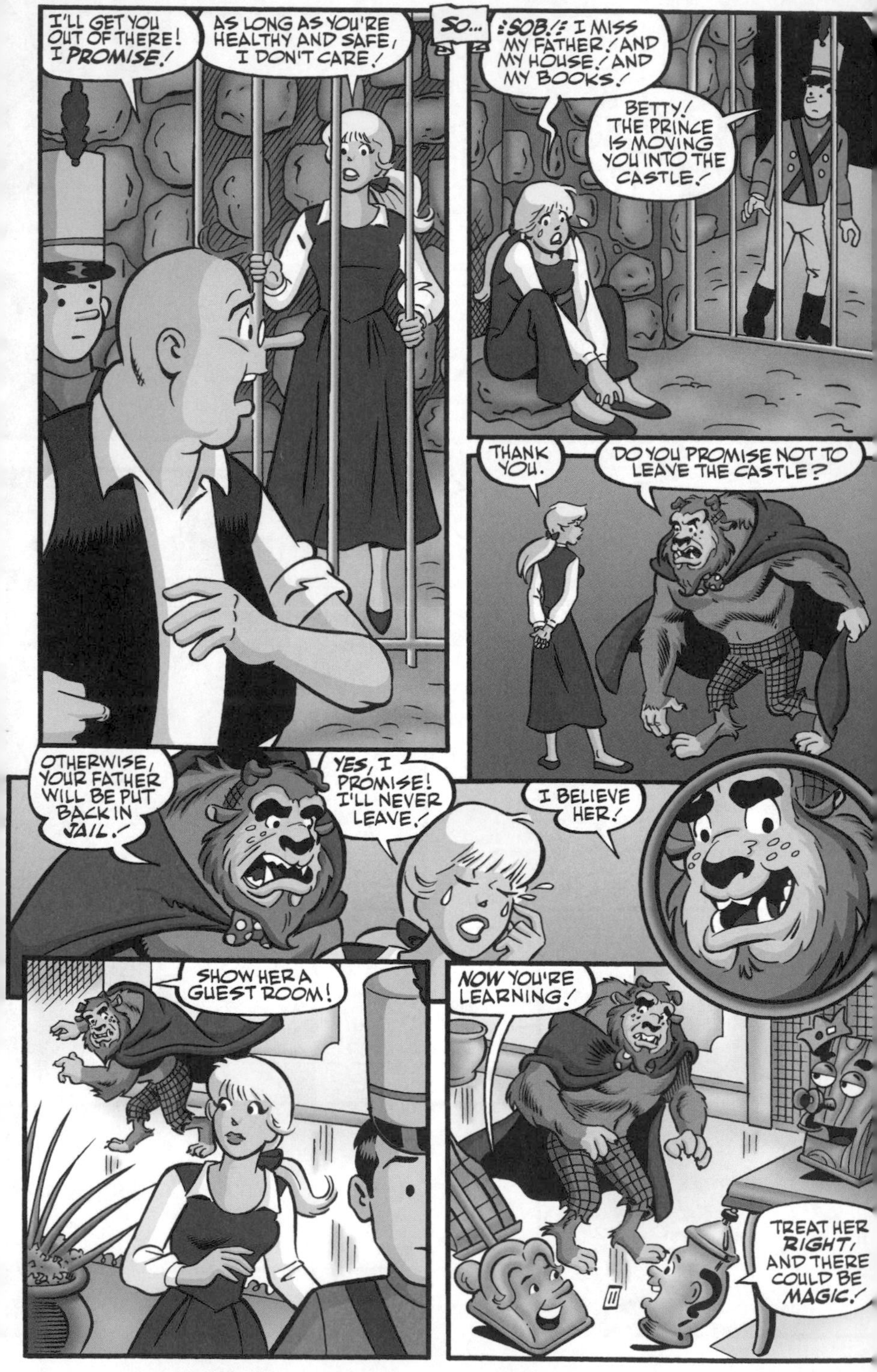
I'LL GET YOU OUT OF THERE! I PROMISE!
AS LONG AS YOU'RE HEALTHY AND SAFE, I DON'T CARE!
SO...
SOB! I MISS MY FATHER! AND MY HOUSE! AND MY BOOKS!
BETTY! THE PRINCE IS MOVING YOU INTO THE CASTLE!
THANK YOU.
DO YOU PROMISE NOT TO LEAVE THE CASTLE?
OTHERWISE, YOUR FATHER WILL BE PUT BACK IN JAIL!
YES, I PROMISE! I'LL NEVER LEAVE!
I BELIEVE HER!
SHOW HER A GUEST ROOM!
NOW YOU'RE LEARNING!
TREAT HER RIGHT, AND THERE COULD BE MAGIC!

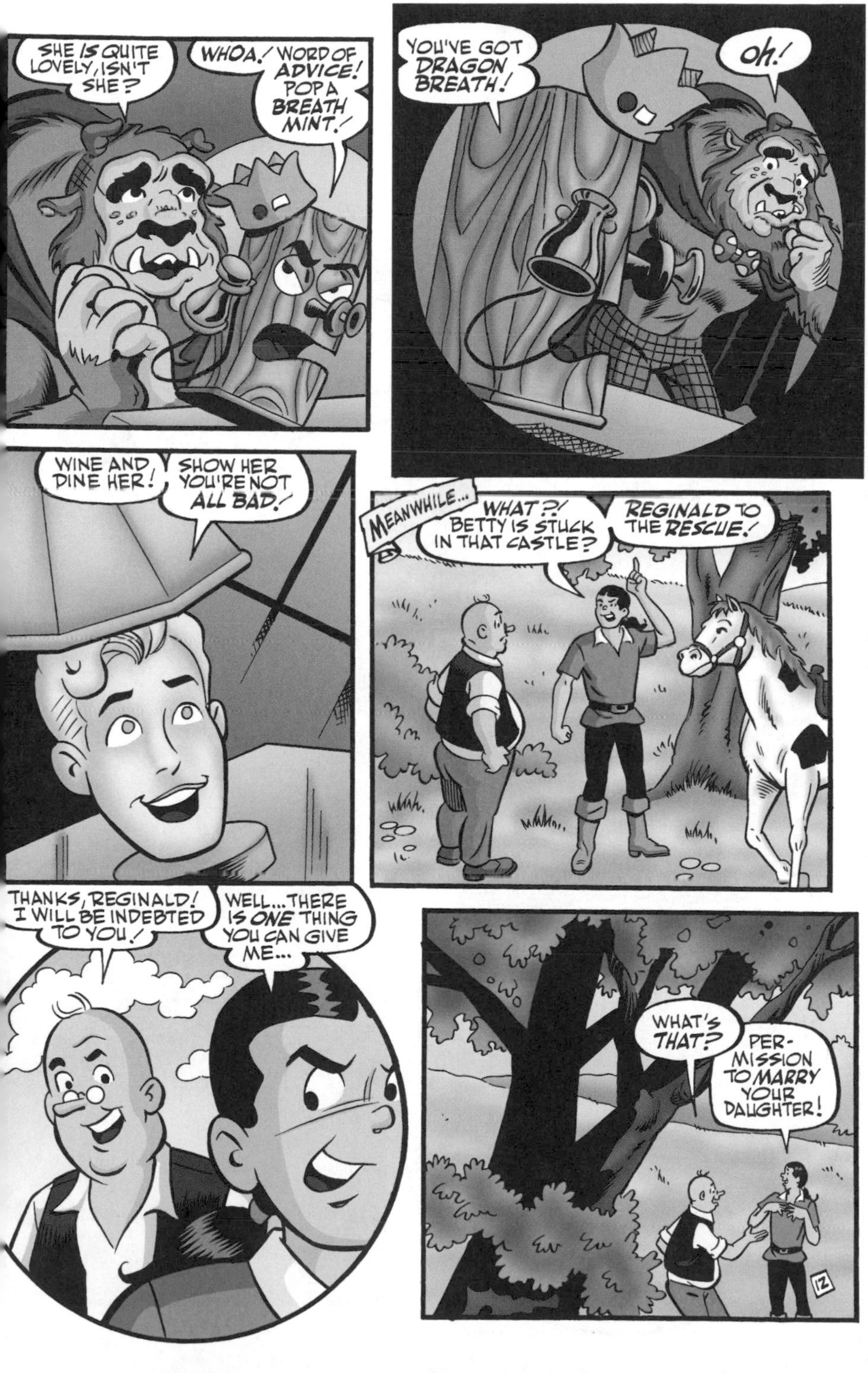
SHE IS QUITE LOVELY, ISN'T SHE?
WHOA! WORD OF ADVICE! POP A BREATH MINT!
YOU'VE GOT DRAGON BREATH!
oh!
WINE AND DINE HER!
SHOW HER YOU'RE NOT ALL BAD!
MEANWHILE...
WHAT?! BETTY IS STUCK IN THAT CASTLE?
REGINALD TO THE RESCUE!
THANKS, REGINALD! I WILL BE INDEBTED TO YOU!
WELL... THERE IS ONE THING YOU CAN GIVE ME...
WHAT'S THAT?
PER-MISSION TO MARRY YOUR DAUGHTER!
12

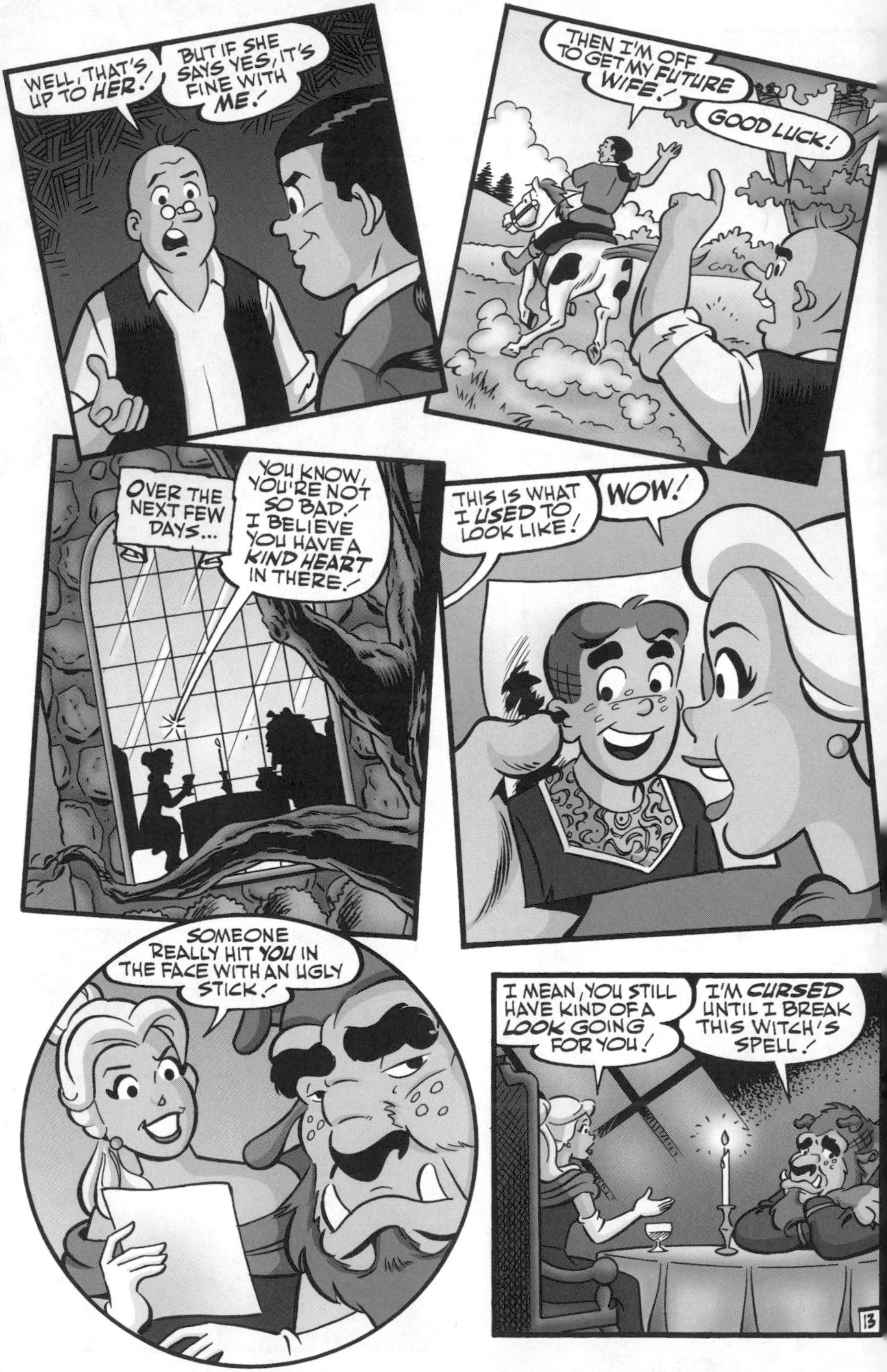
WELL, THAT'S UP TO HER!
BUT IF SHE SAYS YES, IT'S FINE WITH ME!
THEN I'M OFF TO GET MY FUTURE WIFE!
GOOD LUCK!
OVER THE NEXT FEW DAYS...
YOU KNOW, YOU'RE NOT SO BAD! I BELIEVE YOU HAVE A KIND HEART IN THERE!
THIS IS WHAT I USED TO LOOK LIKE!
WOW!
SOMEONE REALLY HIT YOU IN THE FACE WITH AN UGLY STICK!
I MEAN, YOU STILL HAVE KIND OF A LOOK GOING FOR YOU!
I'M CURSED UNTIL I BREAK THIS WITCH'S SPELL!
13

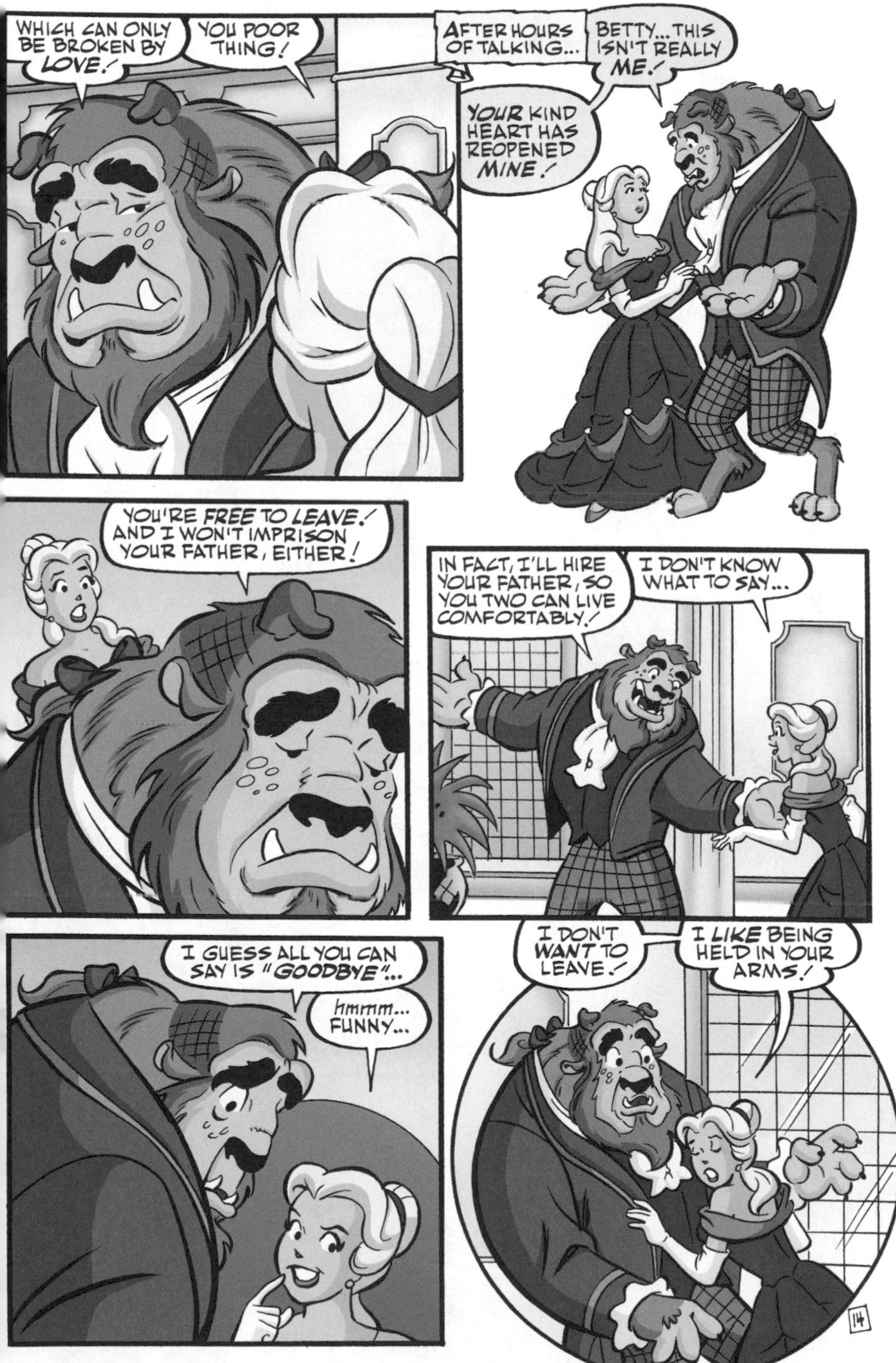

WHICH CAN ONLY BE BROKEN BY LOVE!
YOU POOR THING!
AFTER HOURS OF TALKING...
BETTY... THIS ISN'T REALLY ME!
YOUR KIND HEART HAS REOPENED MINE!
YOU'RE FREE TO LEAVE! AND I WON'T IMPRISON YOUR FATHER, EITHER!
IN FACT, I'LL HIRE YOUR FATHER, SO YOU TWO CAN LIVE COMFORTABLY!
I DON'T KNOW WHAT TO SAY...
I GUESS ALL YOU CAN SAY IS "GOODBYE"...
hmmm... FUNNY...
I DON'T WANT TO LEAVE!
I LIKE BEING HELD IN YOUR ARMS!
14

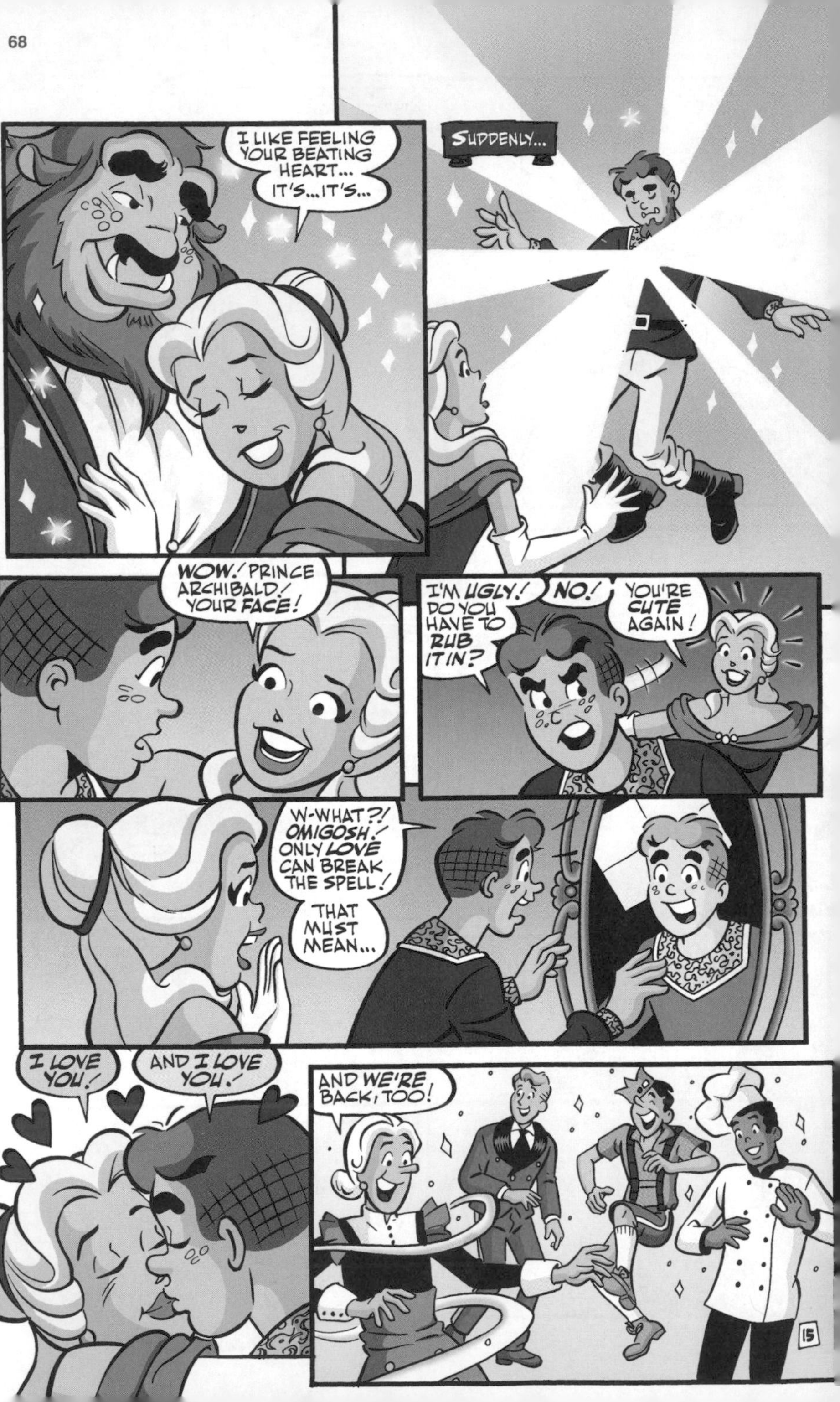
I LIKE FEELING YOUR BEATING HEART... IT'S...IT'S...
SUDDENLY...
WOW! PRINCE ARCHIBALD! YOUR FACE!
I'M UGLY! DO YOU HAVE TO RUB IT IN?
NO!
YOU'RE CUTE AGAIN!
W-WHAT?! OMIGOSH! ONLY LOVE CAN BREAK THE SPELL!
THAT MUST MEAN...
I LOVE YOU!
AND I LOVE YOU!
AND WE'RE BACK, TOO!
15

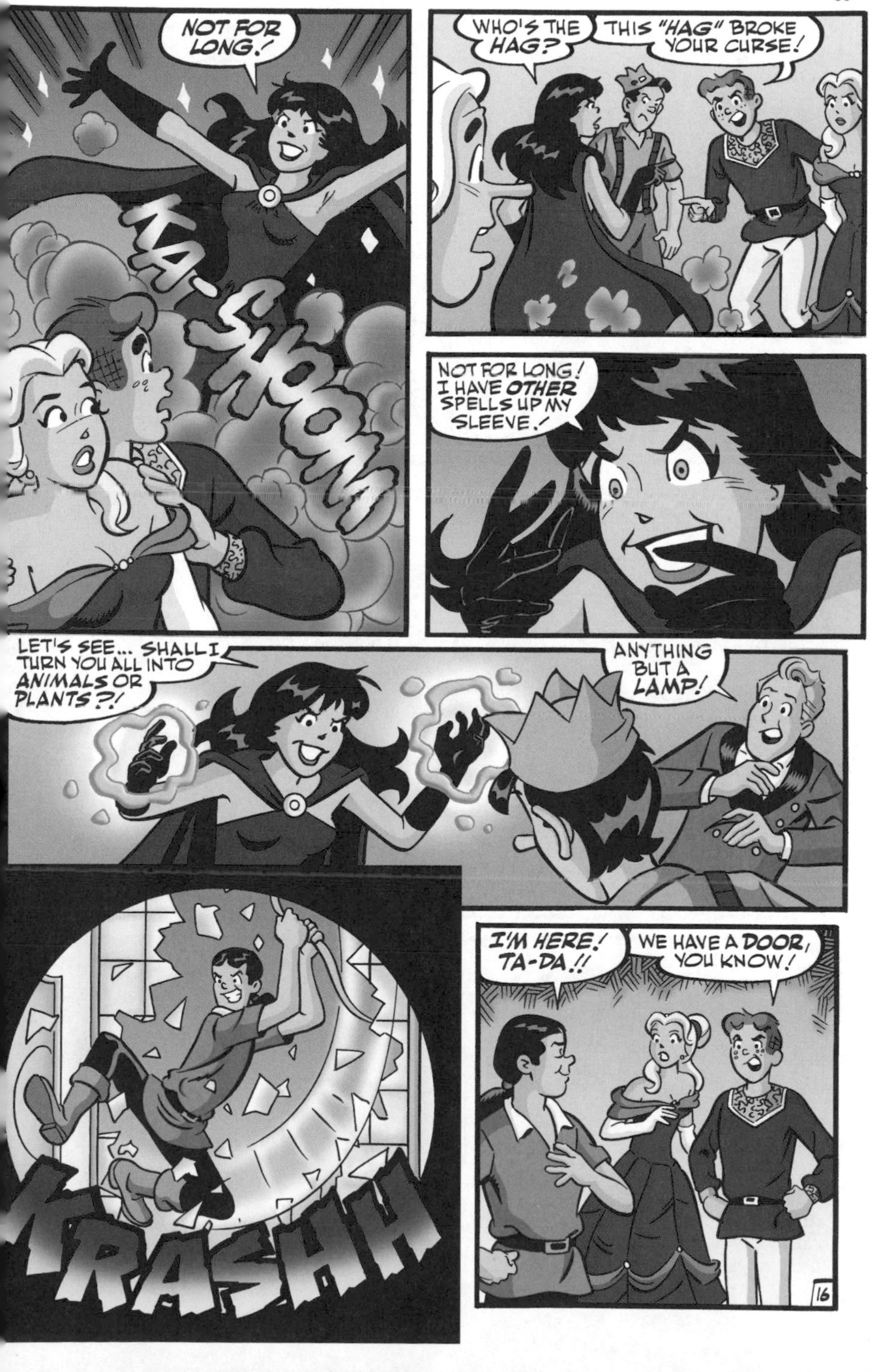
NOT FOR LONG.!
KA-SHOOM
WHO'S THE HAG?
THIS "HAG" BROKE YOUR CURSE!
NOT FOR LONG! I HAVE OTHER SPELLS UP MY SLEEVE.!
LET'S SEE... SHALL I TURN YOU ALL INTO ANIMALS OR PLANTS?!
ANYTHING BUT A LAMP!
KRASHH
I'M HERE! TA-DA!!
WE HAVE A DOOR, YOU KNOW!
16

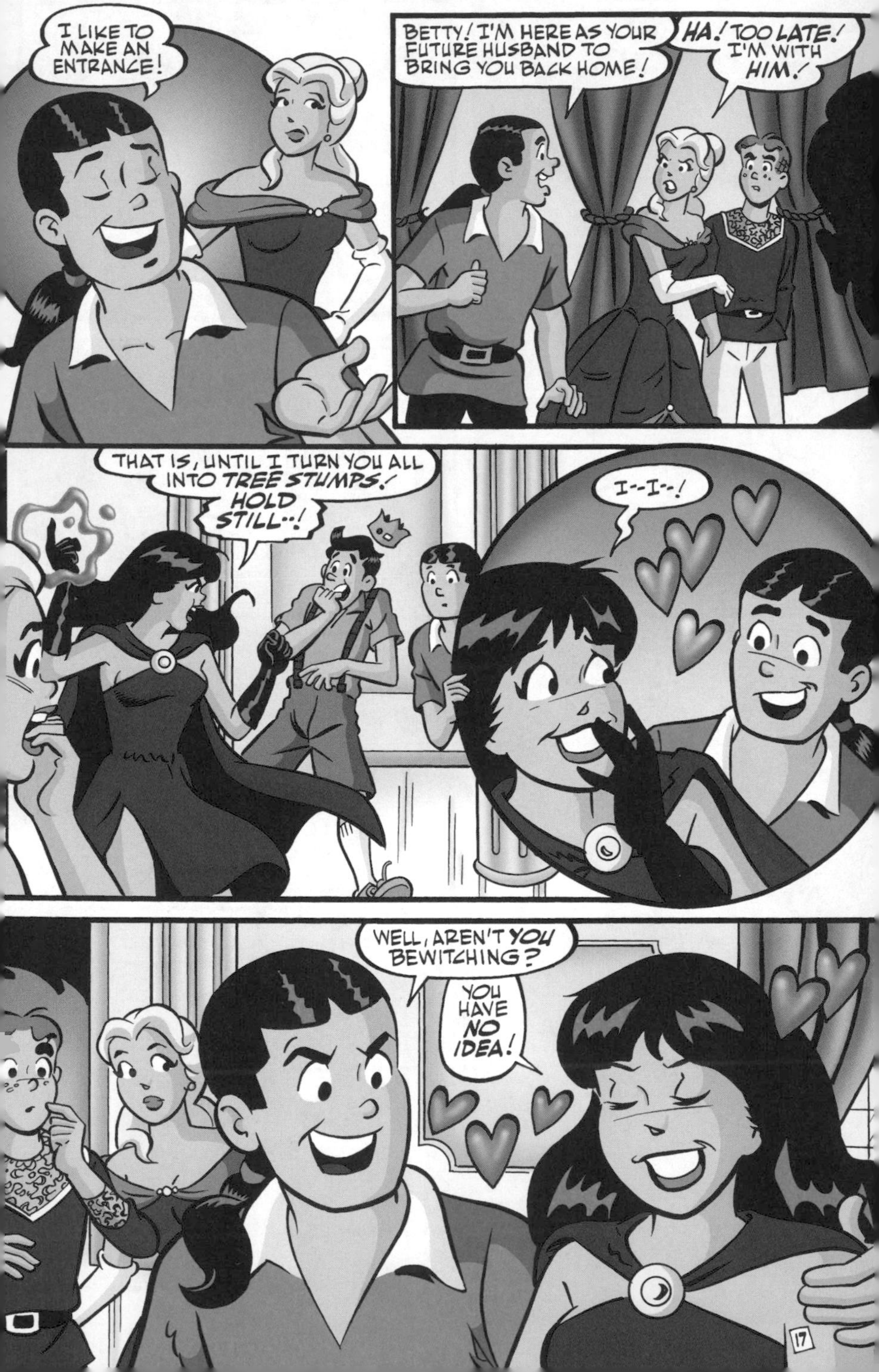
I LIKE TO MAKE AN ENTRANCE!
BETTY! I'M HERE AS YOUR FUTURE HUSBAND TO BRING YOU BACK HOME!
HA! TOO LATE! I'M WITH HIM!
THAT IS, UNTIL I TURN YOU ALL INTO TREE STUMPS! HOLD STILL--!
I--I--!
WELL, AREN'T YOU BEWITCHING?
YOU HAVE NO IDEA!
17

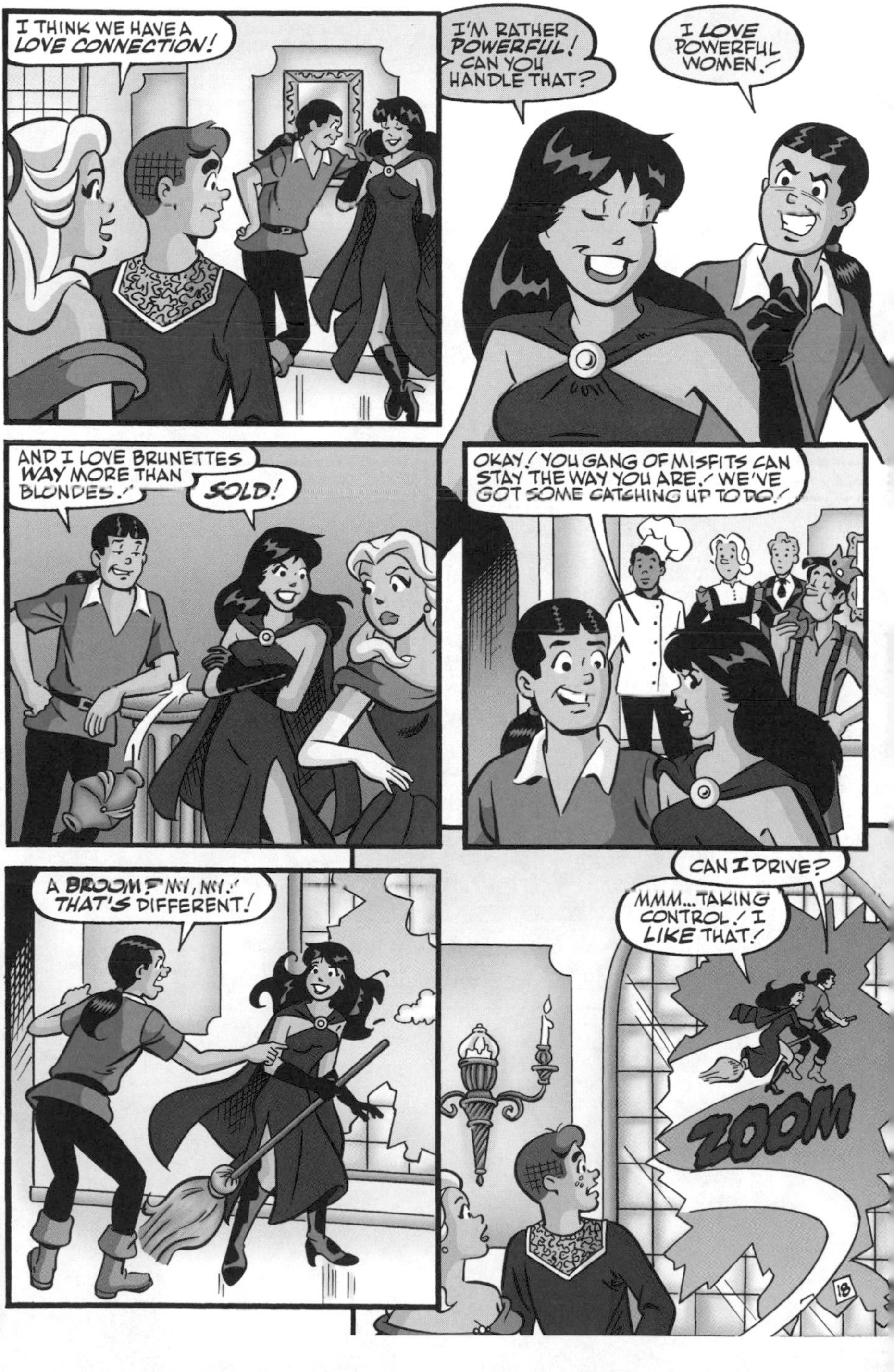
I THINK WE HAVE A LOVE CONNECTION!
I'M RATHER POWERFUL! CAN YOU HANDLE THAT?
I LOVE POWERFUL WOMEN.
AND I LOVE BRUNETTES WAY MORE THAN BLONDES.
SOLD!
OKAY! YOU GANG OF MISFITS CAN STAY THE WAY YOU ARE. WE'VE GOT SOME CATCHING UP TO DO!
A BROOM? MY, MY... THAT'S DIFFERENT!
CAN I DRIVE?
MMM... TAKING CONTROL! I LIKE THAT!
ZOOM
18

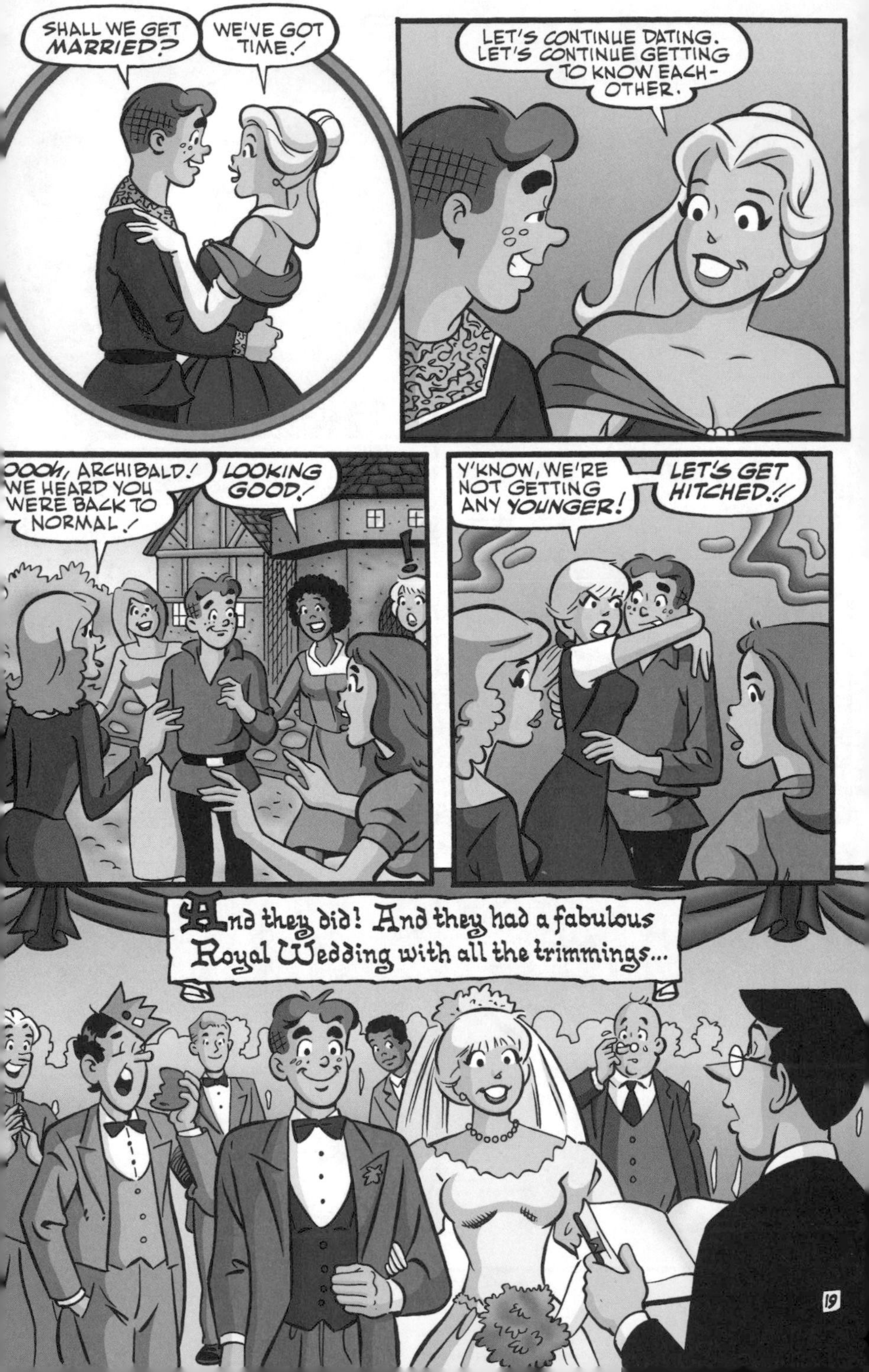
SHALL WE GET MARRIED?
WE'VE GOT TIME.!
LET'S CONTINUE DATING. LET'S CONTINUE GETTING TO KNOW EACH-OTHER.
OOOH, ARCHIBALD! WE HEARD YOU WERE BACK TO NORMAL.!
LOOKING GOOD.!
!
Y'KNOW, WE'RE NOT GETTING ANY YOUNGER!
LET'S GET HITCHED.!!
And they did! And they had a fabulous Royal Wedding with all the trimmings...
19

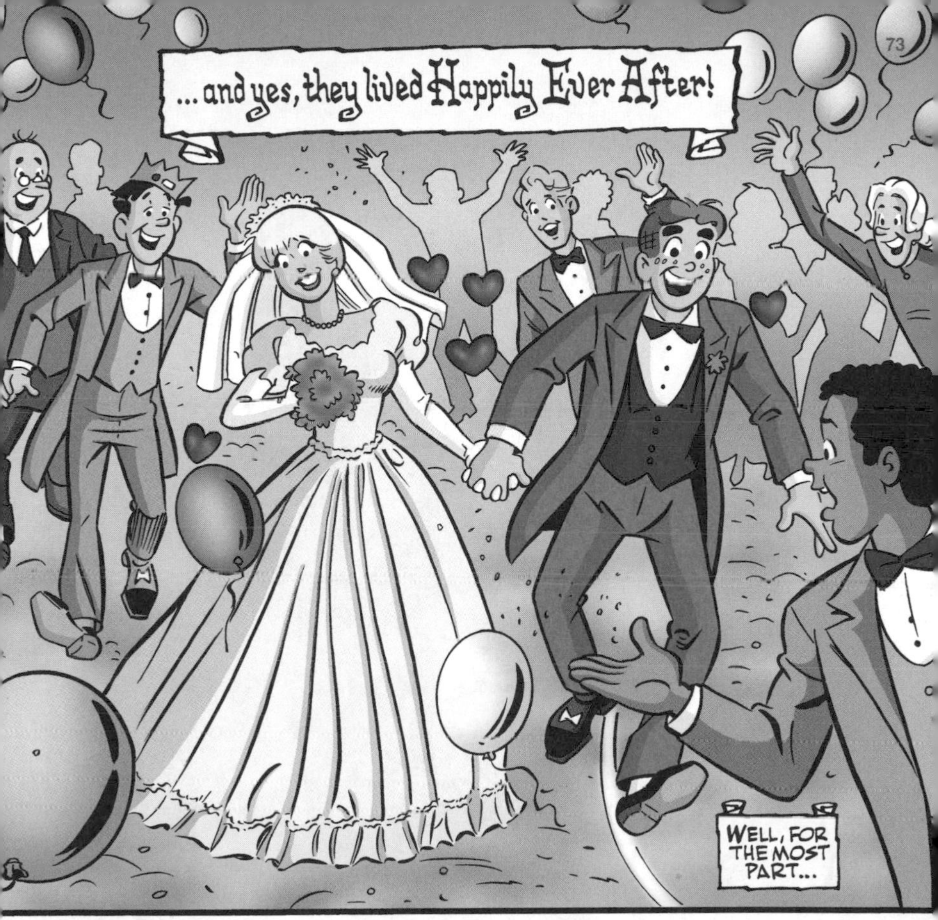
...and yes, they lived Happily Ever After!
WELL, FOR THE MOST PART...

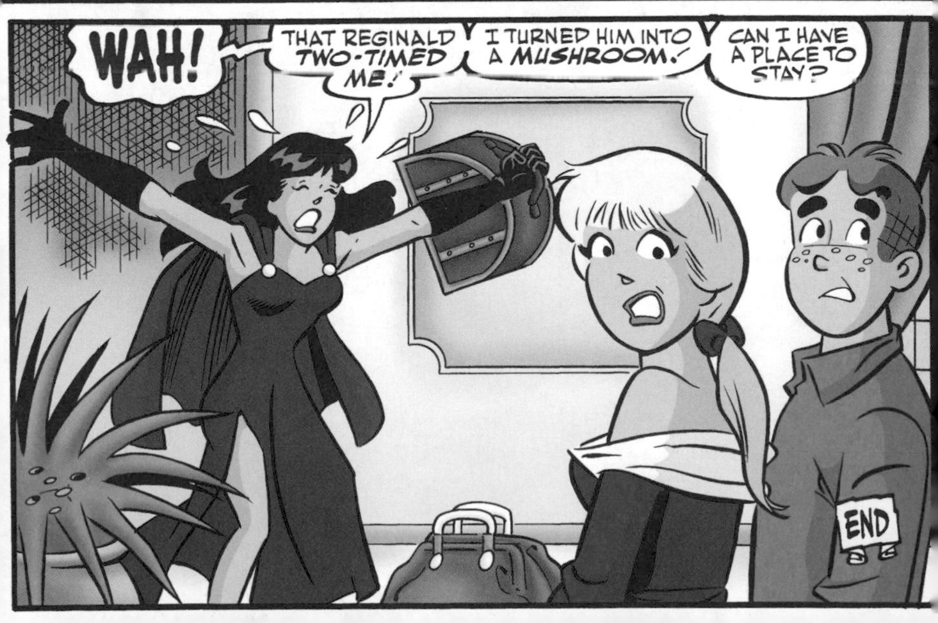
WAH!
THAT REGINALD TWO-TIMED ME!
I TURNED HIM INTO A MUSHROOM!
CAN I HAVE A PLACE TO STAY?
END

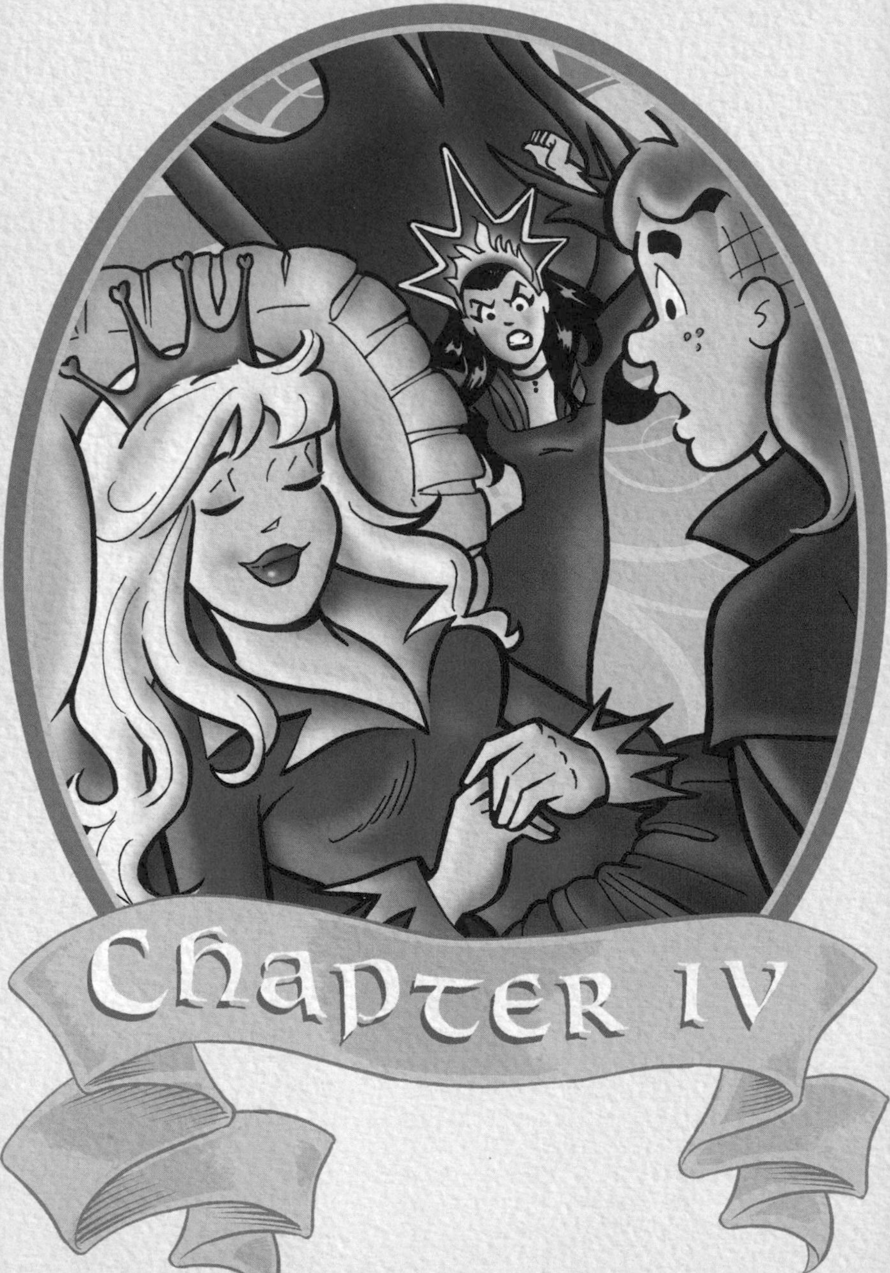

Chapter IV

 SLEEPING ******** ****** BETTY

The newborn Princess Betty receives three enchanted gifts from her magical sisters Ethel, Ginger and Nancy. But she also gets one not-so-great present: a wicked sleep spell courtesy of the evil Veronica!

Doomed to take an endless doze on her sixteenth birthday, Betty's sister hide their special sibling. But things get complicated when Betty discovers she's betrothed to a neighboring prince.

Not only does Betty have to stay undercover, but she must find a way out of her arranged marriage to be with the boy she really loves! Talk about complicated…

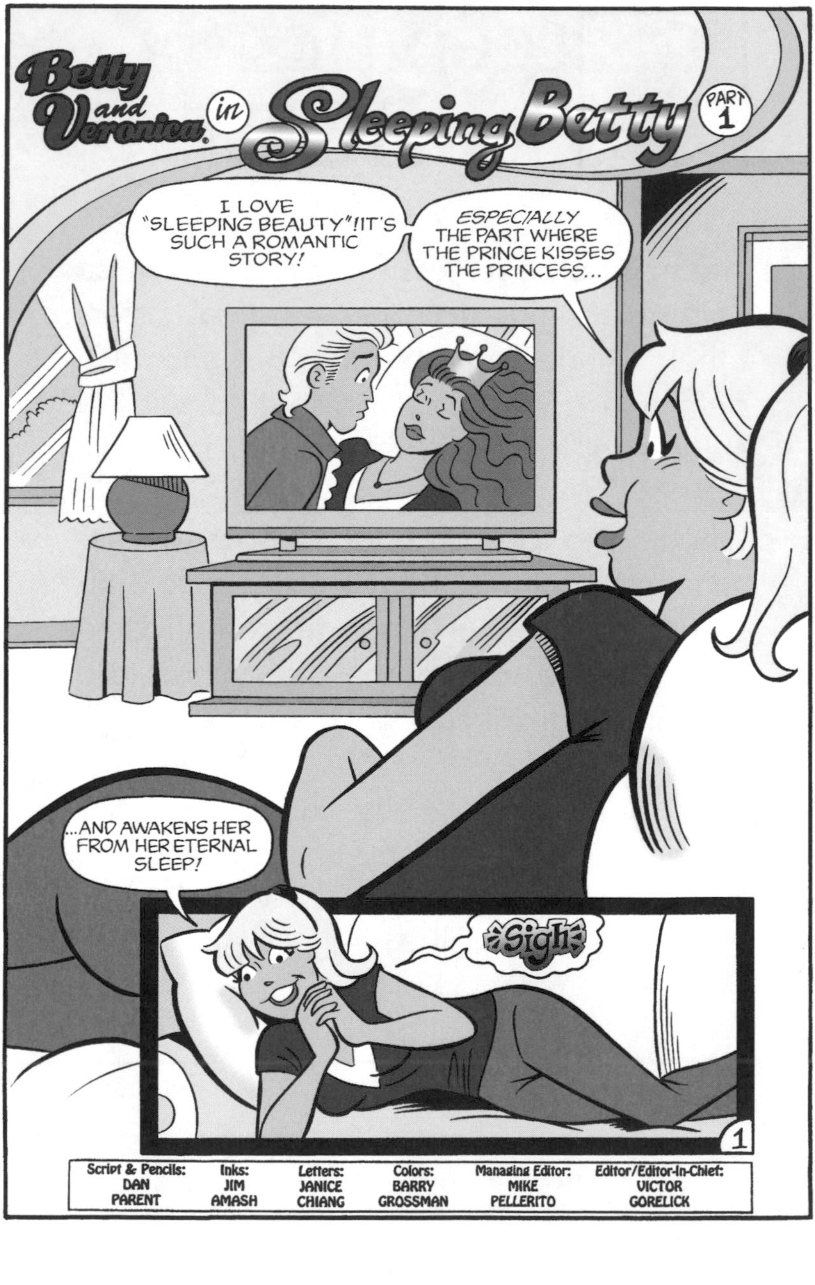
Betty and Veronica in Sleeping Betty PART 1
I LOVE "SLEEPING BEAUTY"! IT'S SUCH A ROMANTIC STORY!
ESPECIALLY THE PART WHERE THE PRINCE KISSES THE PRINCESS...
...AND AWAKENS HER FROM HER ETERNAL SLEEP!
Sigh
1
Script & Pencils: DAN PARENT
Inks: JIM AMASH
Letters: JANICE CHIANG
Colors: BARRY GROSSMAN
Managing Editor: MIKE PELLERITO
Editor/Editor-In-Chief: VICTOR GORELICK

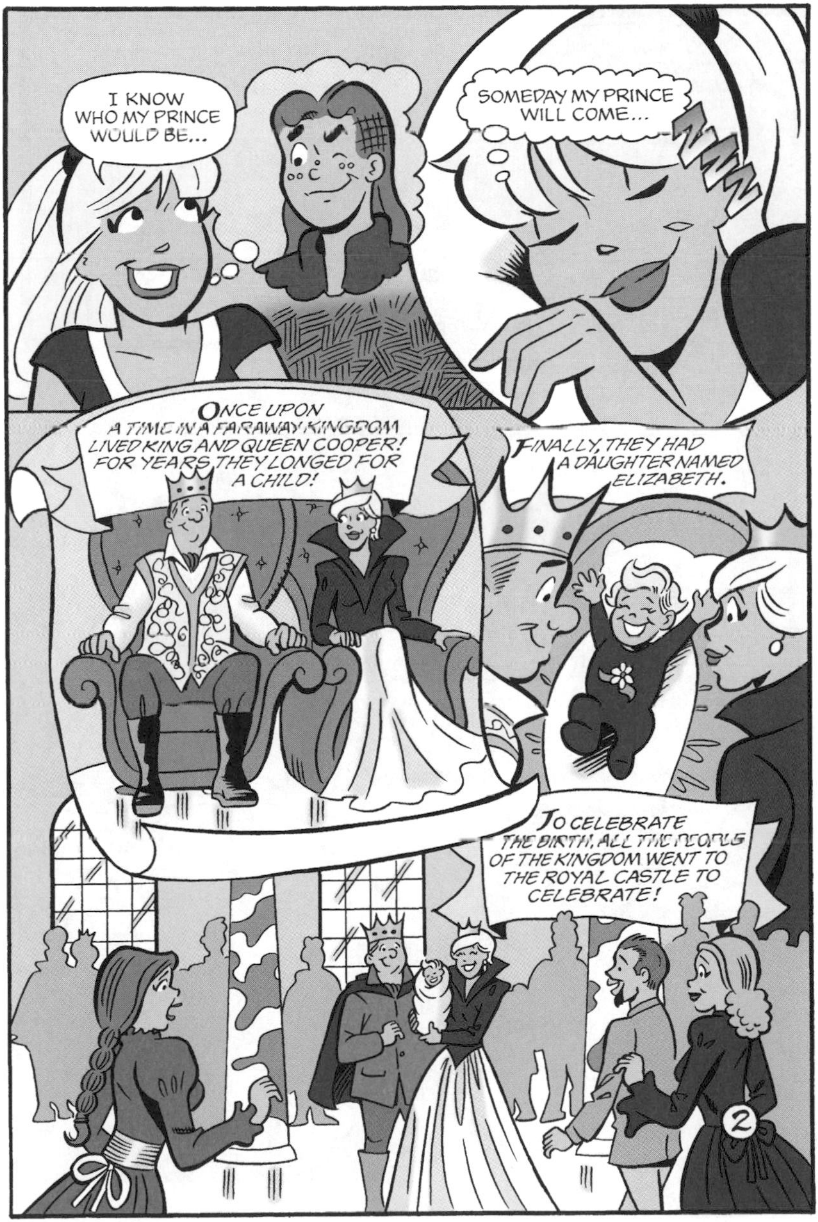
I KNOW WHO MY PRINCE WOULD BE...
SOMEDAY MY PRINCE WILL COME...
ONCE UPON A TIME IN A FARAWAY KINGDOM LIVED KING AND QUEEN COOPER! FOR YEARS THEY LONGED FOR A CHILD!
FINALLY, THEY HAD A DAUGHTER NAMED ELIZABETH.
TO CELEBRATE THE BIRTH, ALL THE PEOPLE OF THE KINGDOM WENT TO THE ROYAL CASTLE TO CELEBRATE!
2

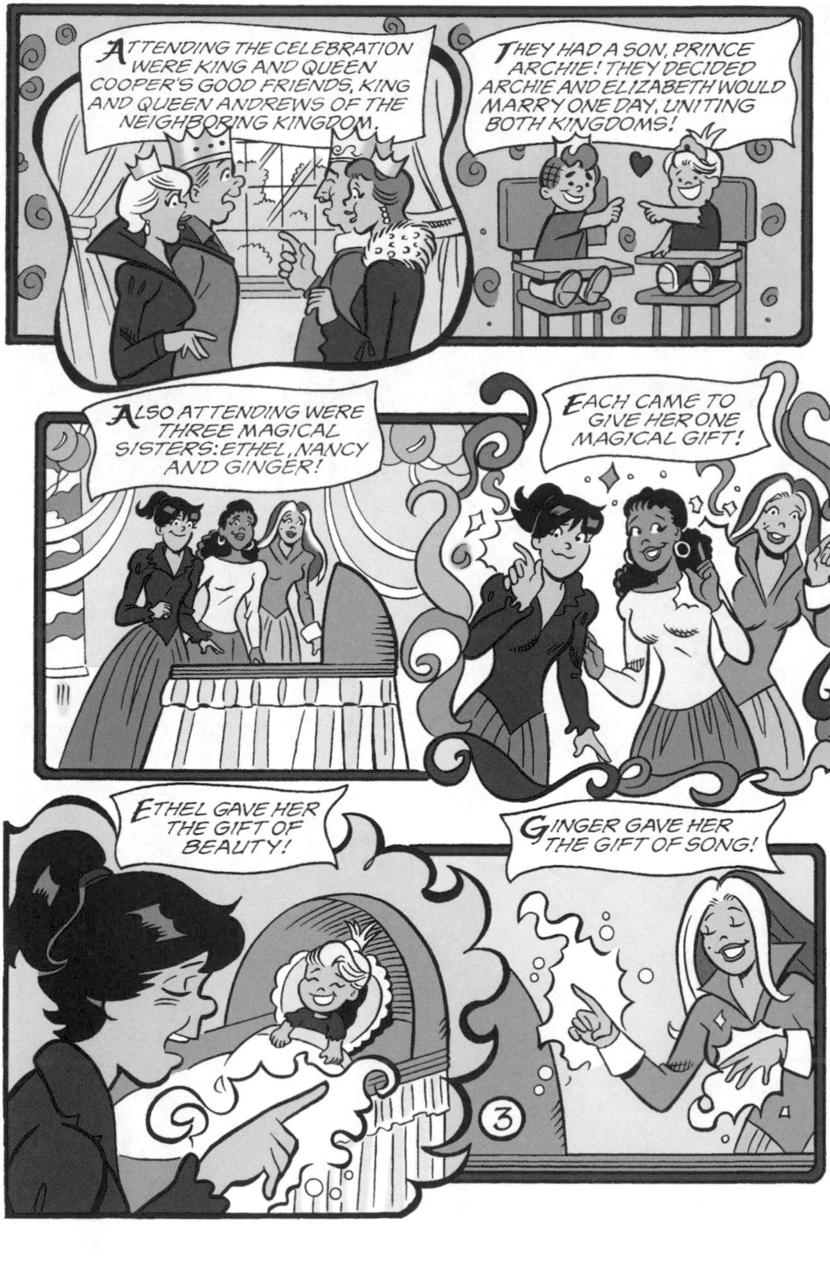
ATTENDING THE CELEBRATION WERE KING AND QUEEN COOPER'S GOOD FRIENDS, KING AND QUEEN ANDREWS OF THE NEIGHBORING KINGDOM.
THEY HAD A SON, PRINCE ARCHIE! THEY DECIDED ARCHIE AND ELIZABETH WOULD MARRY ONE DAY, UNITING BOTH KINGDOMS!
ALSO ATTENDING WERE THREE MAGICAL SISTERS: ETHEL, NANCY AND GINGER!
EACH CAME TO GIVE HER ONE MAGICAL GIFT!
ETHEL GAVE HER THE GIFT OF BEAUTY!
GINGER GAVE HER THE GIFT OF SONG!
3

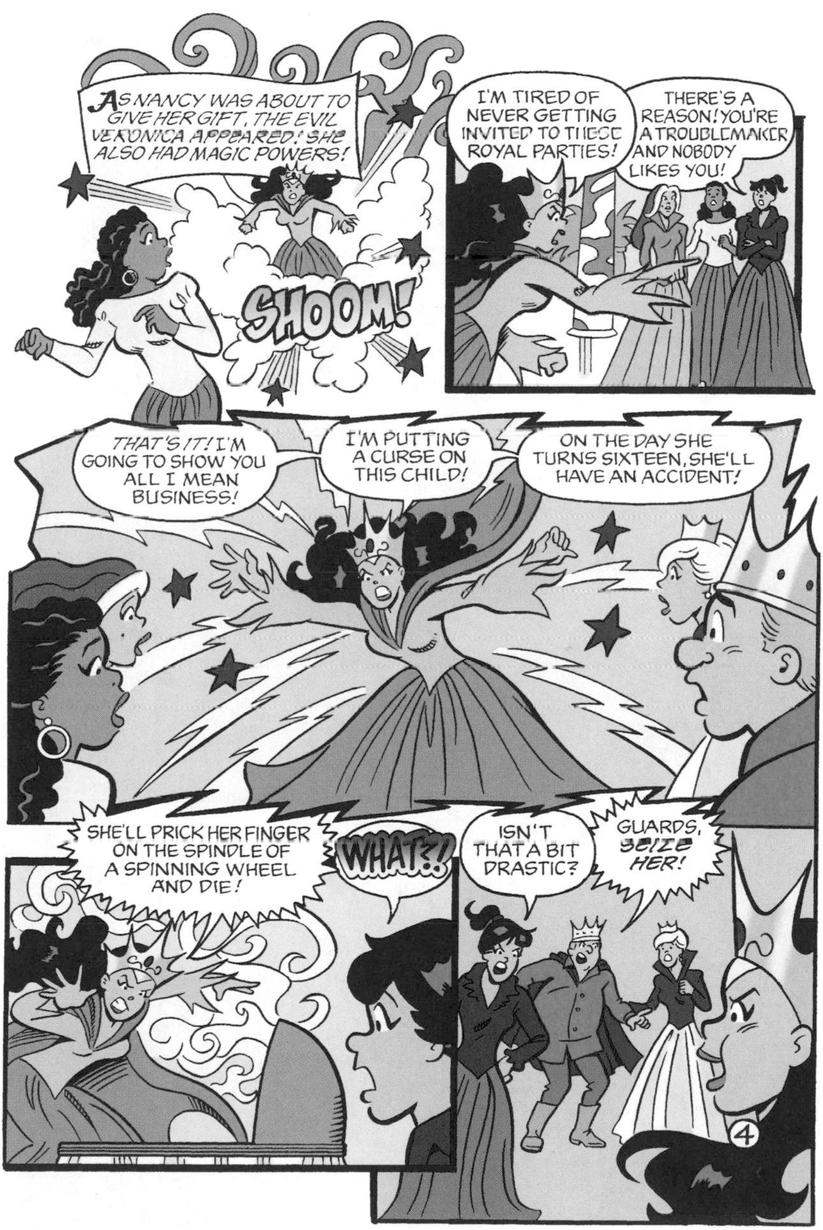
AS NANCY WAS ABOUT TO GIVE HER GIFT, THE EVIL VERONICA APPEARED! SHE ALSO HAD MAGIC POWERS!
SHOOM!
I'M TIRED OF NEVER GETTING INVITED TO THESE ROYAL PARTIES!
THERE'S A REASON! YOU'RE A TROUBLEMAKER AND NOBODY LIKES YOU!
THAT'S IT! I'M GOING TO SHOW YOU ALL I MEAN BUSINESS!
I'M PUTTING A CURSE ON THIS CHILD!
ON THE DAY SHE TURNS SIXTEEN, SHE'LL HAVE AN ACCIDENT!
SHE'LL PRICK HER FINGER ON THE SPINDLE OF A SPINNING WHEEL AND DIE!
WHAT?!
ISN'T THAT A BIT DRASTIC?
GUARDS, SEIZE HER!
4

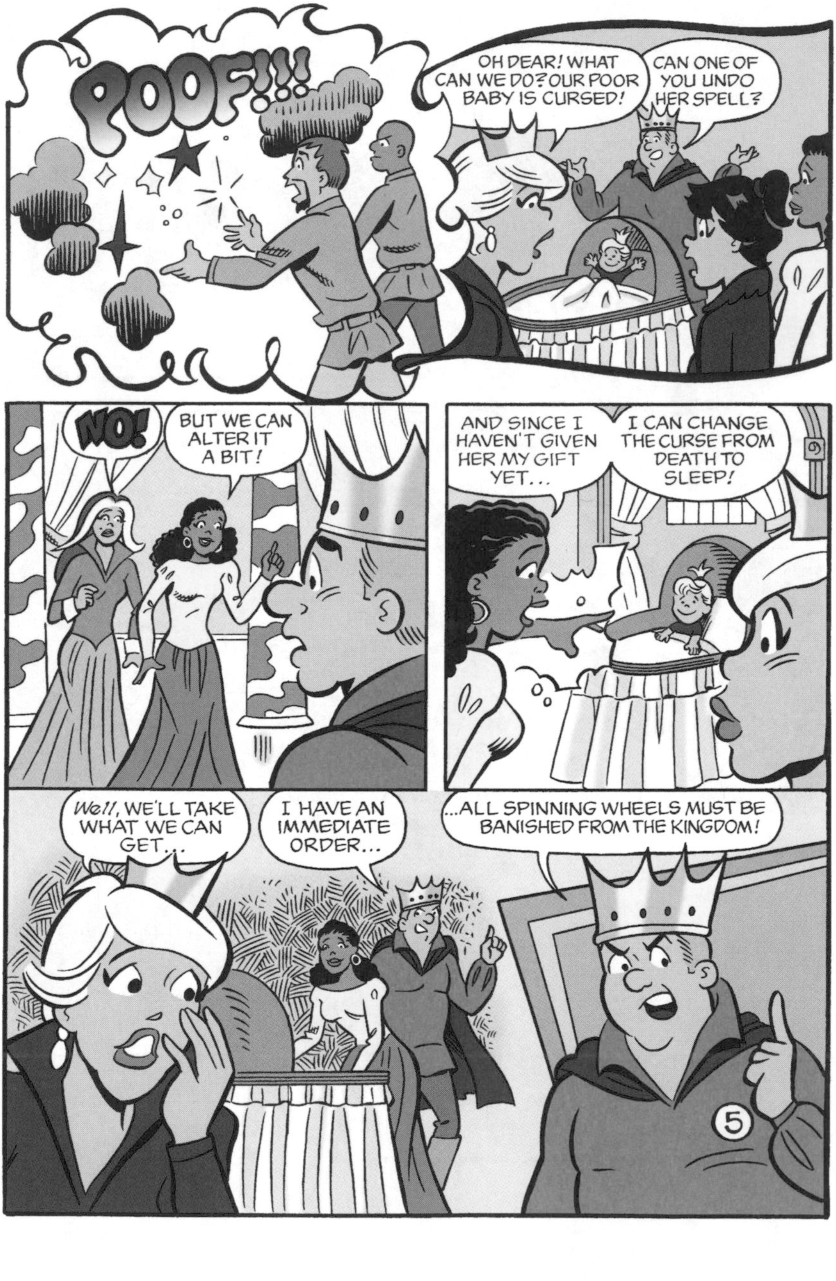
POOF!!!
OH DEAR! WHAT CAN WE DO? OUR POOR BABY IS CURSED!
CAN ONE OF YOU UNDO HER SPELL?
NO!
BUT WE CAN ALTER IT A BIT!
AND SINCE I HAVEN'T GIVEN HER MY GIFT YET...
I CAN CHANGE THE CURSE FROM DEATH TO SLEEP!
Well, WE'LL TAKE WHAT WE CAN GET...
I HAVE AN IMMEDIATE ORDER...
...ALL SPINNING WHEELS MUST BE BANISHED FROM THE KINGDOM!
5

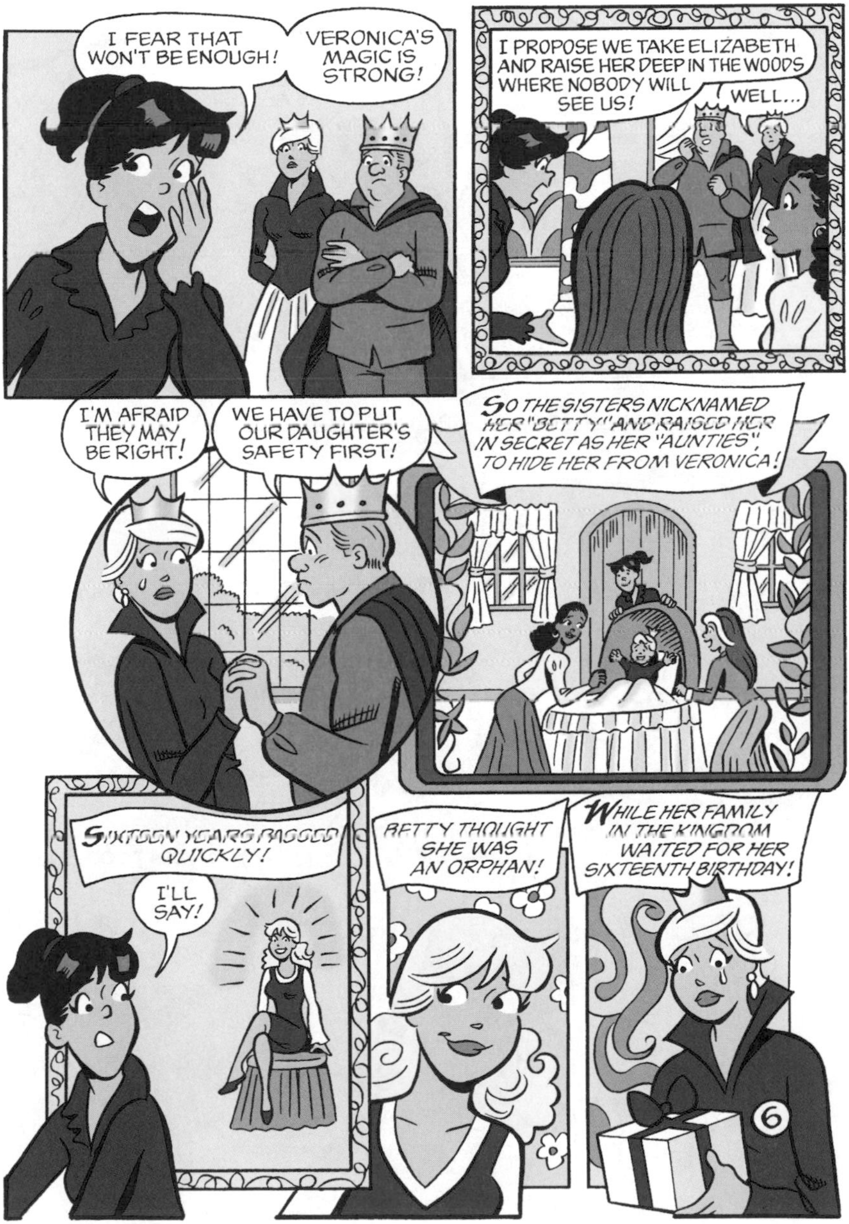
I FEAR THAT WON'T BE ENOUGH!
VERONICA'S MAGIC IS STRONG!
I PROPOSE WE TAKE ELIZABETH AND RAISE HER DEEP IN THE WOODS WHERE NOBODY WILL SEE US!
WELL...
I'M AFRAID THEY MAY BE RIGHT!
WE HAVE TO PUT OUR DAUGHTER'S SAFETY FIRST!
SO THE SISTERS NICKNAMED HER "BETTY" AND RAISED HER IN SECRET AS HER "AUNTIES", TO HIDE HER FROM VERONICA!
SIXTEEN YEARS PASSED QUICKLY!
I'LL SAY!
BETTY THOUGHT SHE WAS AN ORPHAN!
WHILE HER FAMILY IN THE KINGDOM WAITED FOR HER SIXTEENTH BIRTHDAY!

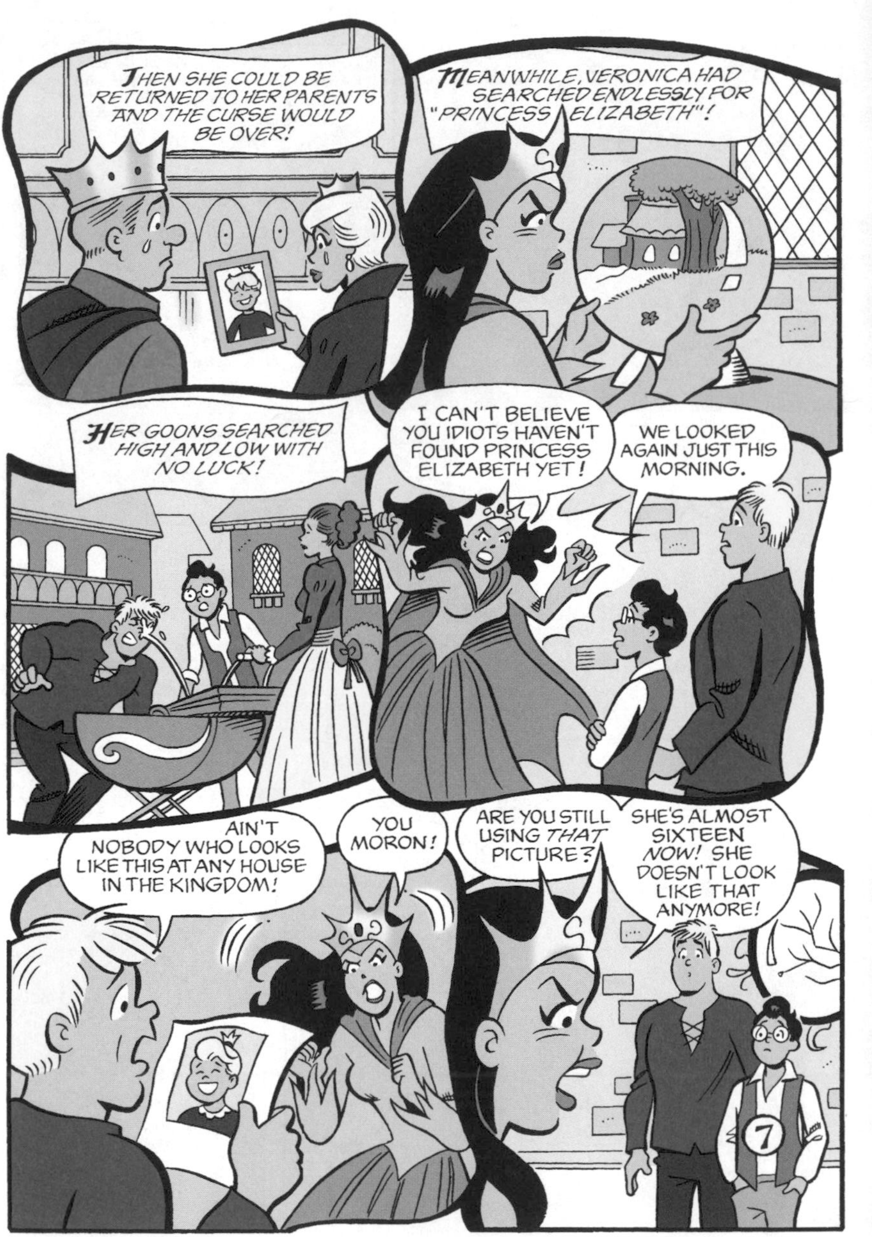
THEN SHE COULD BE RETURNED TO HER PARENTS AND THE CURSE WOULD BE OVER!
MEANWHILE, VERONICA HAD SEARCHED ENDLESSLY FOR "PRINCESS ELIZABETH"!
HER GOONS SEARCHED HIGH AND LOW WITH NO LUCK!
I CAN'T BELIEVE YOU IDIOTS HAVEN'T FOUND PRINCESS ELIZABETH YET!
WE LOOKED AGAIN JUST THIS MORNING.
AIN'T NOBODY WHO LOOKS LIKE THIS AT ANY HOUSE IN THE KINGDOM!
YOU MORON!
ARE YOU STILL USING THAT PICTURE?
SHE'S ALMOST SIXTEEN NOW! SHE DOESN'T LOOK LIKE THAT ANYMORE!
7

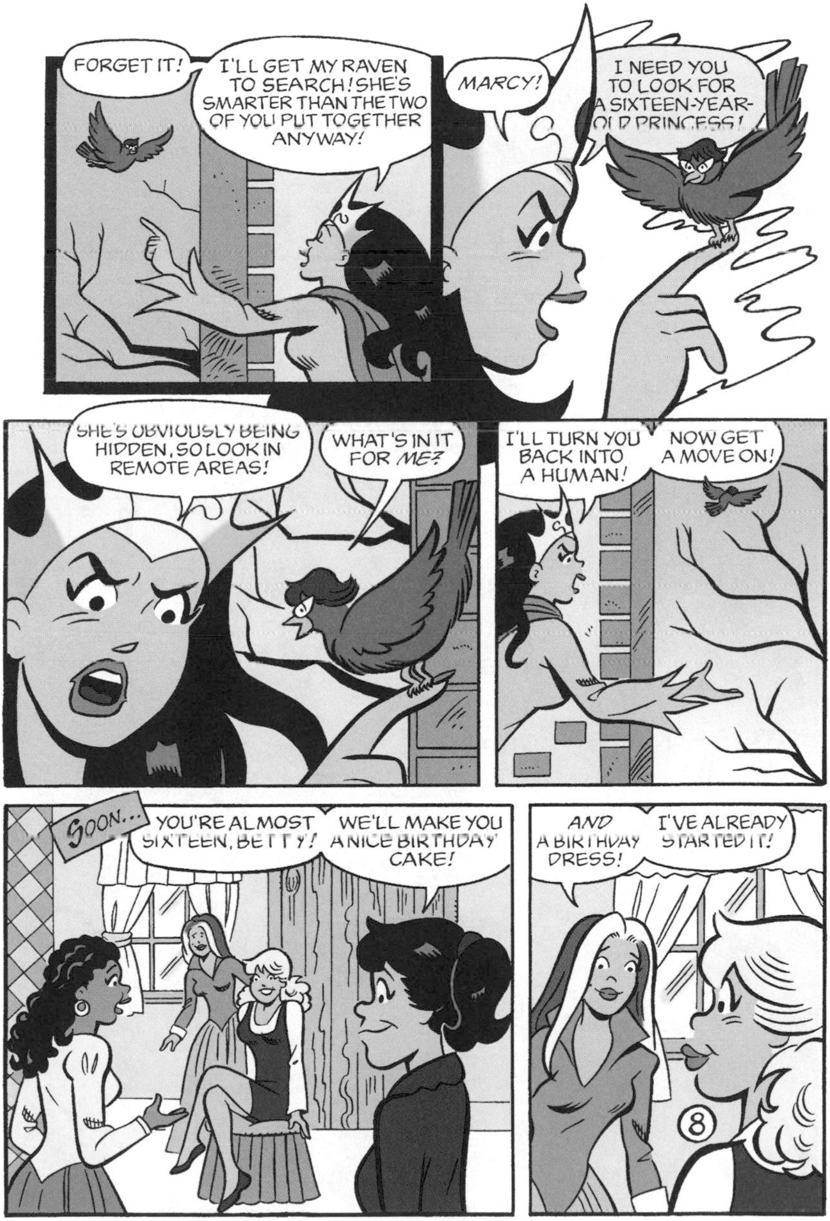
FORGET IT!
I'LL GET MY RAVEN TO SEARCH! SHE'S SMARTER THAN THE TWO OF YOU PUT TOGETHER ANYWAY!
MARCY!
I NEED YOU TO LOOK FOR A SIXTEEN-YEAR-OLD PRINCESS!
SHE'S OBVIOUSLY BEING HIDDEN, SO LOOK IN REMOTE AREAS!
WHAT'S IN IT FOR ME?
I'LL TURN YOU BACK INTO A HUMAN!
NOW GET A MOVE ON!
SOON...
YOU'RE ALMOST SIXTEEN, BETTY!
WE'LL MAKE YOU A NICE BIRTHDAY CAKE!
AND A BIRTHDAY DRESS!
I'VE ALREADY STARTED IT!
8

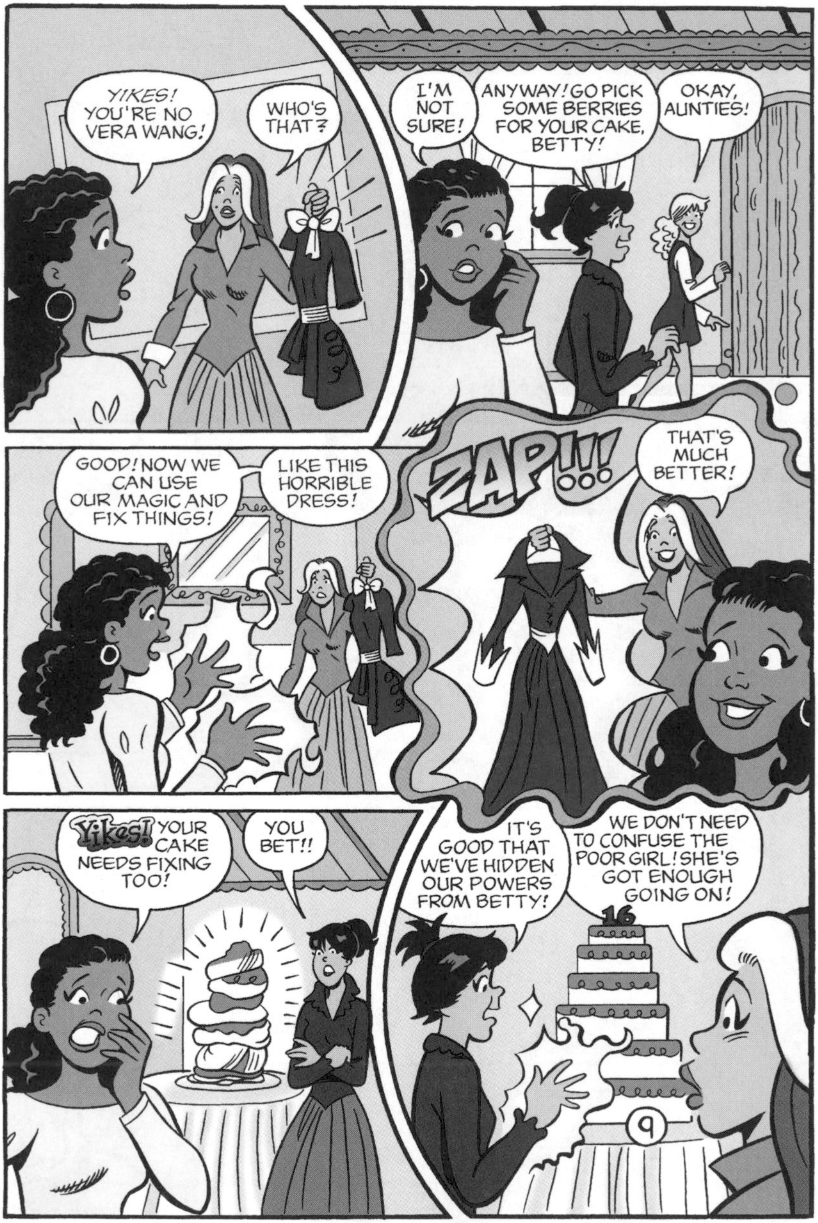
YIKES! YOU'RE NO VERA WANG!
WHO'S THAT?
I'M NOT SURE!
ANYWAY! GO PICK SOME BERRIES FOR YOUR CAKE, BETTY!
OKAY, AUNTIES!
GOOD! NOW WE CAN USE OUR MAGIC AND FIX THINGS!
LIKE THIS HORRIBLE DRESS!
ZAP!!!
THAT'S MUCH BETTER!
YIKES! YOUR CAKE NEEDS FIXING TOO!
YOU BET!!
IT'S GOOD THAT WE'VE HIDDEN OUR POWERS FROM BETTY!
WE DON'T NEED TO CONFUSE THE POOR GIRL! SHE'S GOT ENOUGH GOING ON!
16
9

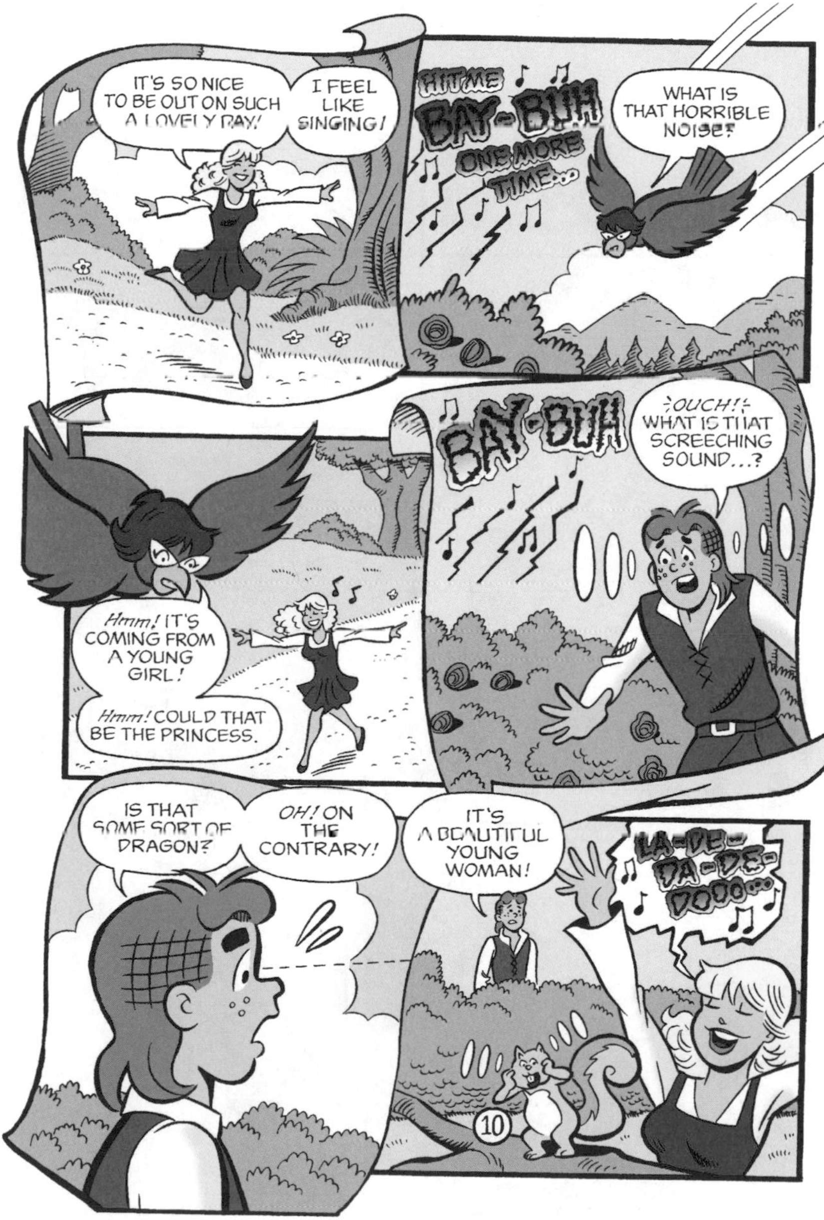
IT'S SO NICE TO BE OUT ON SUCH A LOVELY DAY!
I FEEL LIKE SINGING!
HIT ME BAY-BUH ONE MORE TIME...
WHAT IS THAT HORRIBLE NOISE?
Hmm! IT'S COMING FROM A YOUNG GIRL!
Hmm! COULD THAT BE THE PRINCESS.
BAY-BUH
OUCH! WHAT IS THAT SCREECHING SOUND...?
IS THAT SOME SORT OF DRAGON?
OH! ON THE CONTRARY!
IT'S A BEAUTIFUL YOUNG WOMAN!
LA-DE-DA-DE-DOOO...
10

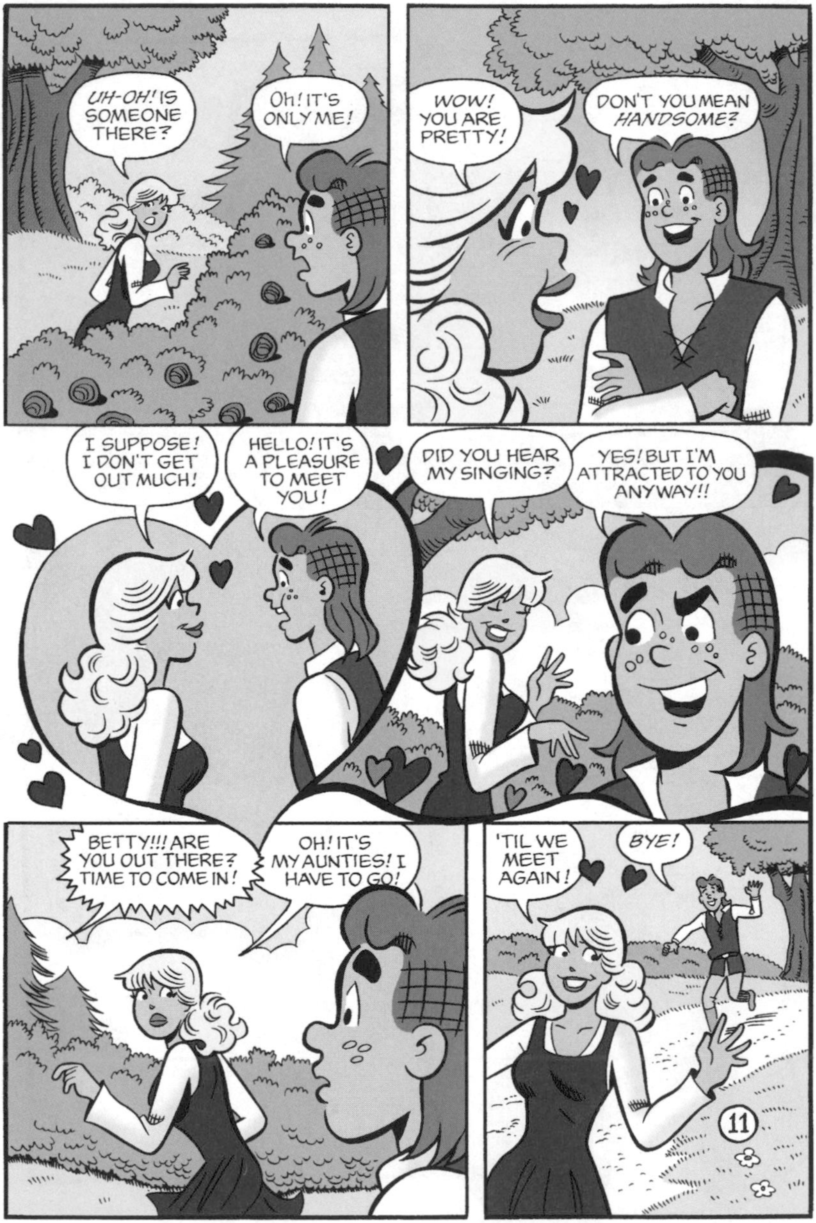
UH-OH! IS SOMEONE THERE?
Oh! IT'S ONLY ME!
WOW! YOU ARE PRETTY!
DON'T YOU MEAN HANDSOME?
I SUPPOSE! I DON'T GET OUT MUCH!
HELLO! IT'S A PLEASURE TO MEET YOU!
DID YOU HEAR MY SINGING?
YES! BUT I'M ATTRACTED TO YOU ANYWAY!!
BETTY!!! ARE YOU OUT THERE? TIME TO COME IN!
OH! IT'S MY AUNTIES! I HAVE TO GO!
'TIL WE MEET AGAIN!
BYE!
11

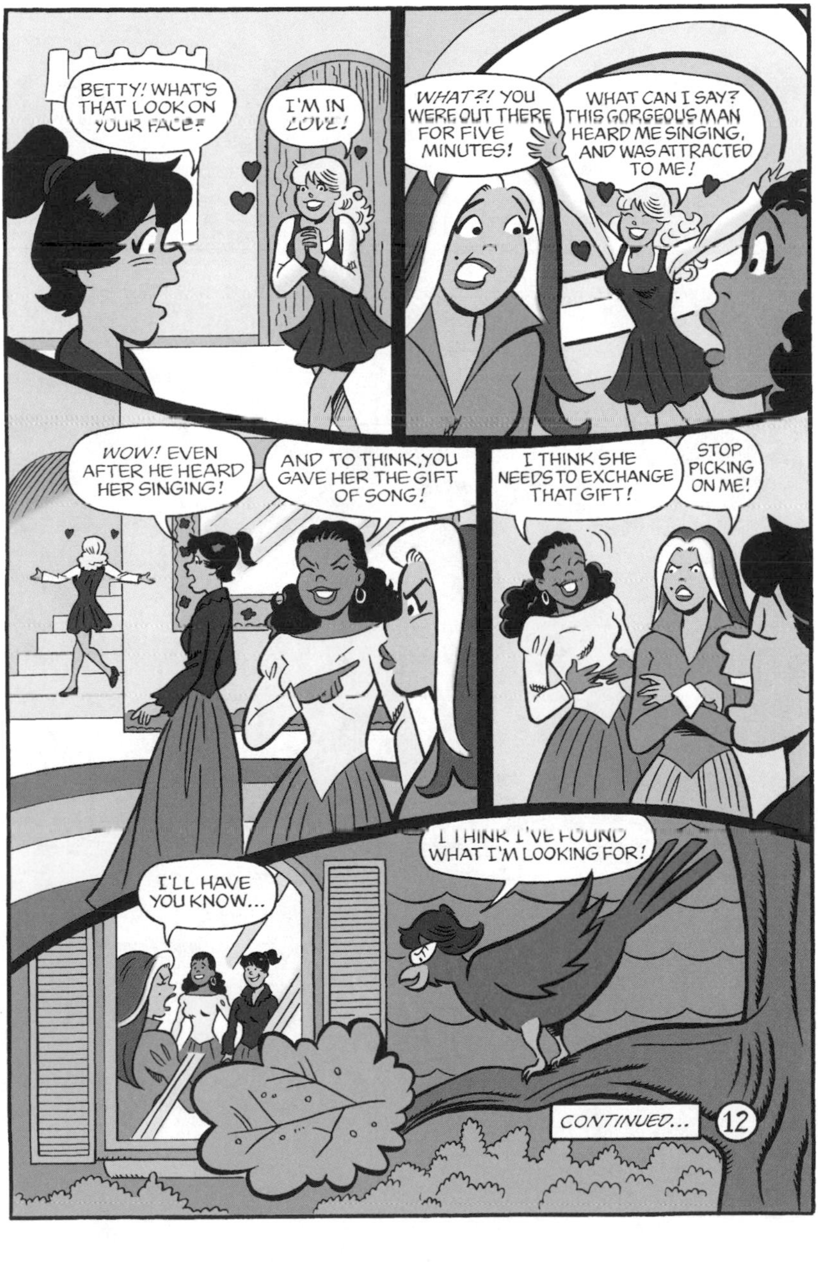
BETTY! WHAT'S THAT LOOK ON YOUR FACE?
I'M IN LOVE!
WHAT?! YOU WERE OUT THERE FOR FIVE MINUTES!
WHAT CAN I SAY? THIS GORGEOUS MAN HEARD ME SINGING, AND WAS ATTRACTED TO ME!
WOW! EVEN AFTER HE HEARD HER SINGING!
AND TO THINK, YOU GAVE HER THE GIFT OF SONG!
I THINK SHE NEEDS TO EXCHANGE THAT GIFT!
STOP PICKING ON ME!
I'LL HAVE YOU KNOW...
I THINK I'VE FOUND WHAT I'M LOOKING FOR!
CONTINUED...
12

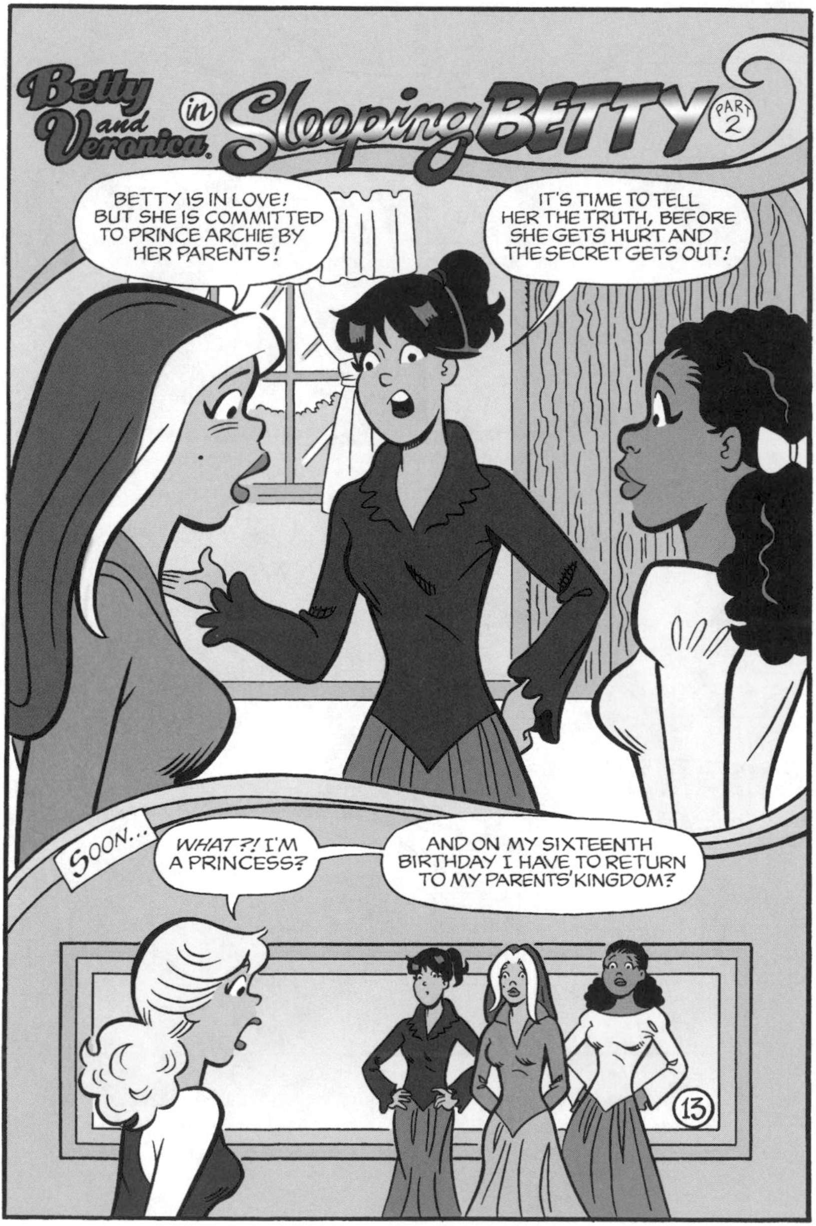
Betty and Veronica
in
Sleeping BETTY
PART 2
BETTY IS IN LOVE! BUT SHE IS COMMITTED TO PRINCE ARCHIE BY HER PARENTS!
IT'S TIME TO TELL HER THE TRUTH, BEFORE SHE GETS HURT AND THE SECRET GETS OUT!
SOON...
WHAT?! I'M A PRINCESS?
AND ON MY SIXTEENTH BIRTHDAY I HAVE TO RETURN TO MY PARENTS' KINGDOM?
13

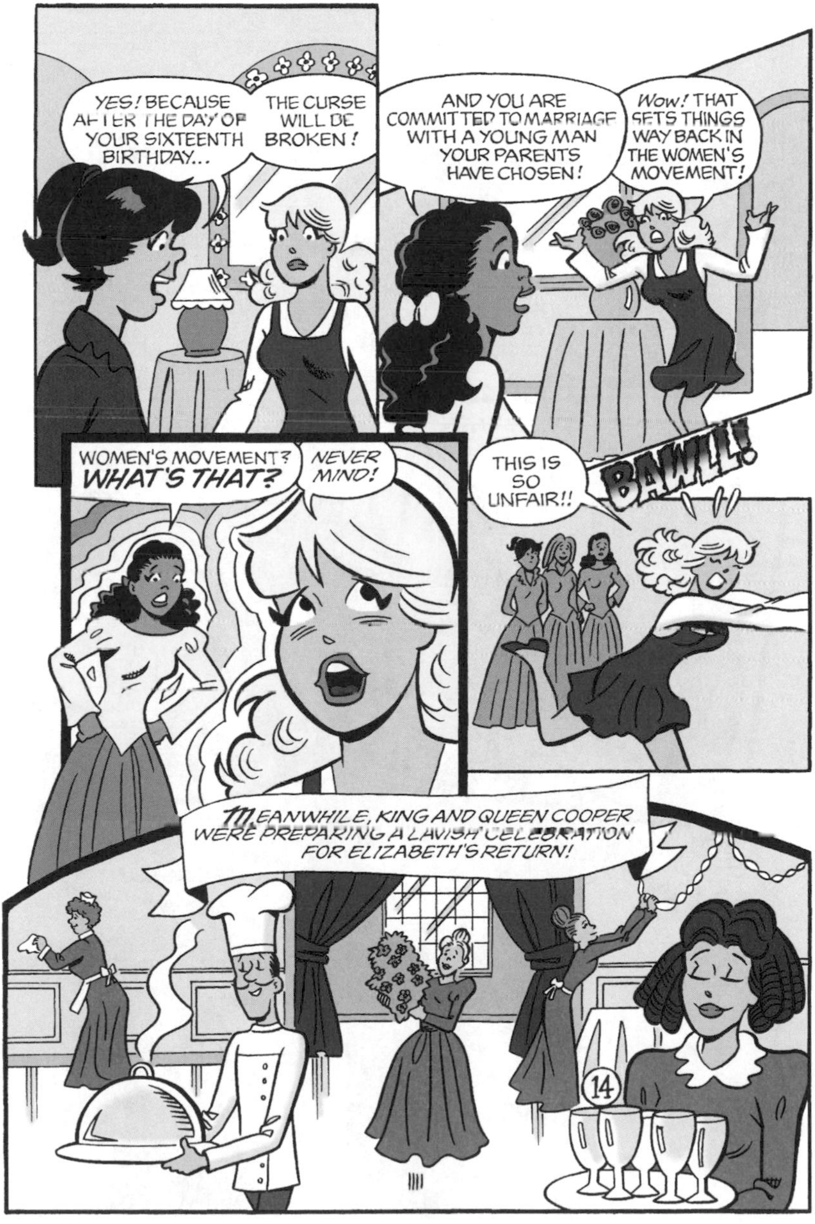
YES! BECAUSE AFTER THE DAY OF YOUR SIXTEENTH BIRTHDAY...
THE CURSE WILL BE BROKEN!
AND YOU ARE COMMITTED TO MARRIAGE WITH A YOUNG MAN YOUR PARENTS HAVE CHOSEN!
WOW! THAT SETS THINGS WAY BACK IN THE WOMEN'S MOVEMENT!
WOMEN'S MOVEMENT? WHAT'S THAT?
NEVER MIND!
THIS IS SO UNFAIR!!
BAWL!
MEANWHILE, KING AND QUEEN COOPER WERE PREPARING A LAVISH CELEBRATION FOR ELIZABETH'S RETURN!
14

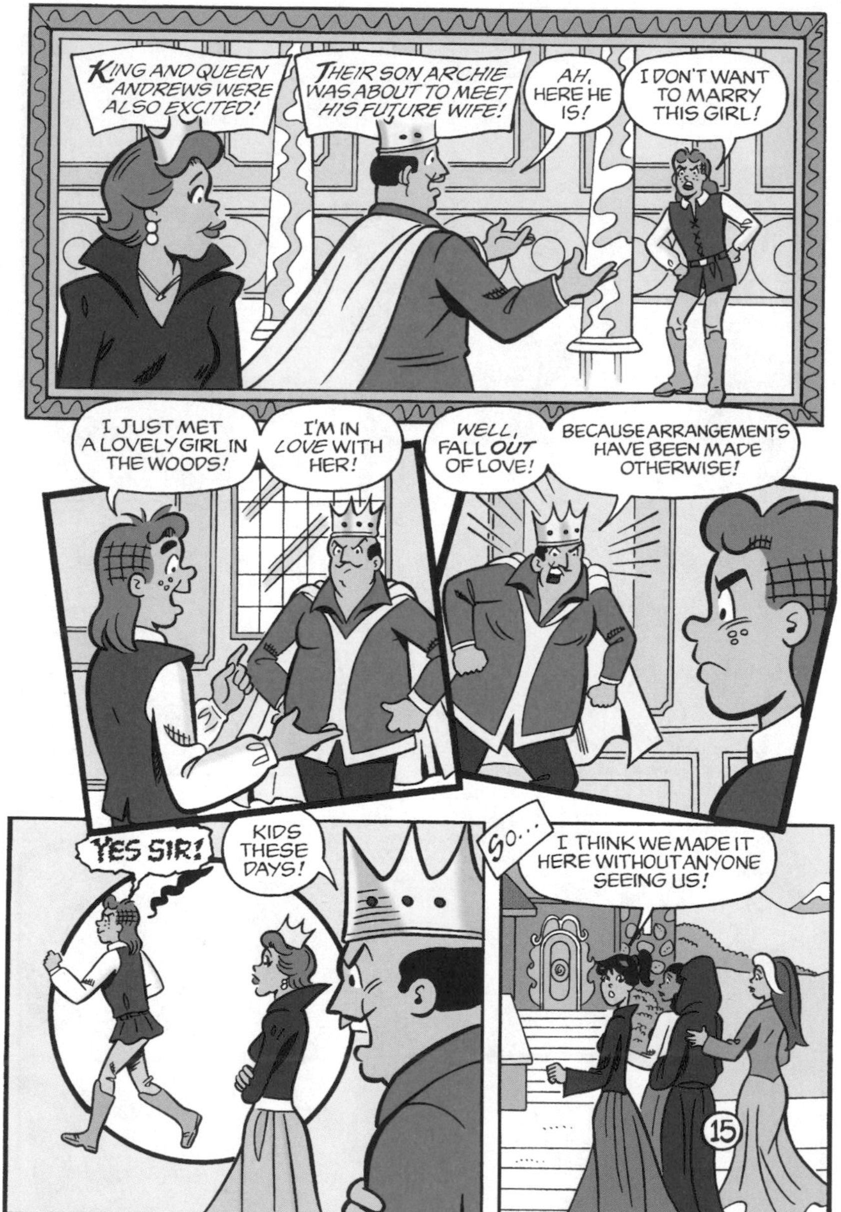
KING AND QUEEN ANDREWS WERE ALSO EXCITED!
THEIR SON ARCHIE WAS ABOUT TO MEET HIS FUTURE WIFE!
AH, HERE HE IS!
I DON'T WANT TO MARRY THIS GIRL!
I JUST MET A LOVELY GIRL IN THE WOODS!
I'M IN LOVE WITH HER!
WELL, FALL OUT OF LOVE!
BECAUSE ARRANGEMENTS HAVE BEEN MADE OTHERWISE!
YES SIR!
KIDS THESE DAYS!
SO...
I THINK WE MADE IT HERE WITHOUT ANYONE SEEING US!
15

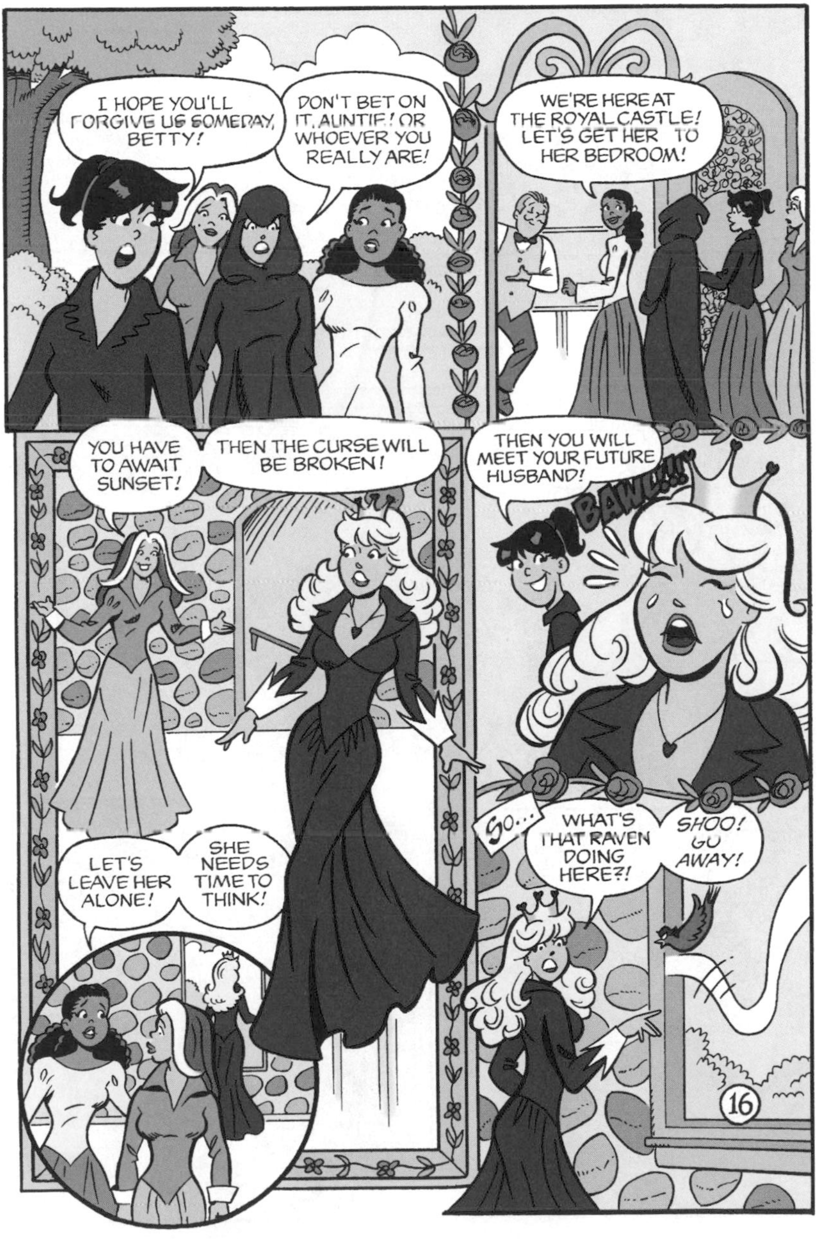
I HOPE YOU'LL FORGIVE US SOMEDAY, BETTY!
DON'T BET ON IT, AUNTIE! OR WHOEVER YOU REALLY ARE!
WE'RE HERE AT THE ROYAL CASTLE! LET'S GET HER TO HER BEDROOM!
YOU HAVE TO AWAIT SUNSET!
THEN THE CURSE WILL BE BROKEN!
THEN YOU WILL MEET YOUR FUTURE HUSBAND!
BAWL!!!
LET'S LEAVE HER ALONE!
SHE NEEDS TIME TO THINK!
SO...
WHAT'S THAT RAVEN DOING HERE?!
SHOO! GO AWAY!
16

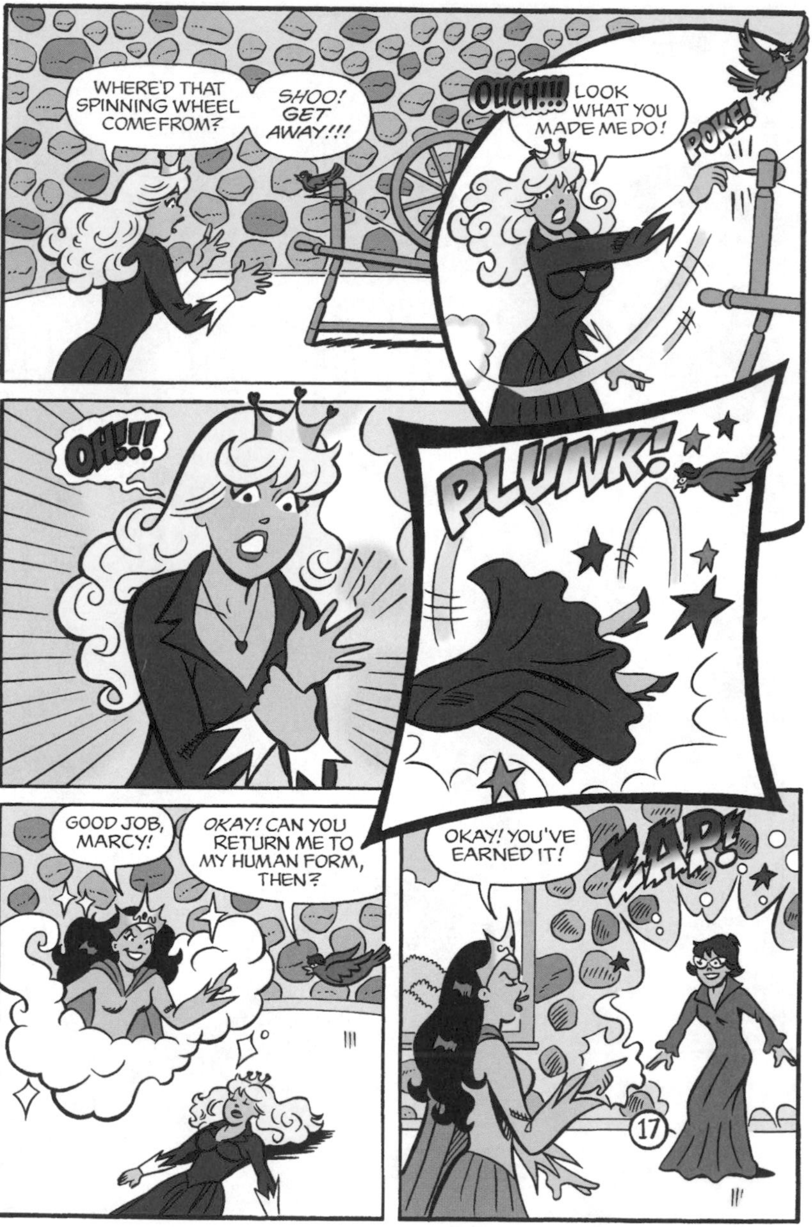
WHERE'D THAT SPINNING WHEEL COME FROM?
SHOO! GET AWAY!!!
OUCH!!!
LOOK WHAT YOU MADE ME DO!
POKE!
OH!!!
PLUNK!
GOOD JOB, MARCY!
OKAY! CAN YOU RETURN ME TO MY HUMAN FORM, THEN?
OKAY! YOU'VE EARNED IT!
ZAP!
17

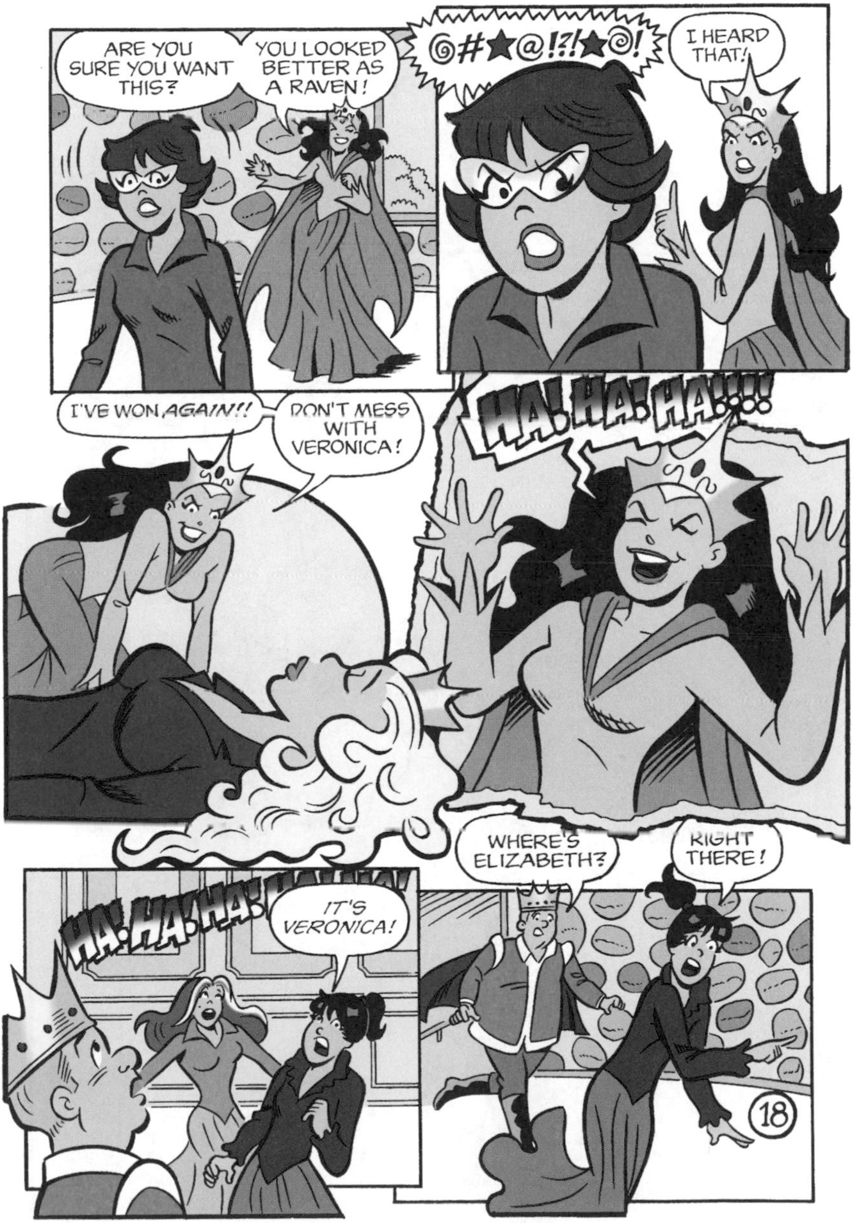
ARE YOU SURE YOU WANT THIS?
YOU LOOKED BETTER AS A RAVEN!
@#★@!?!★@!
I HEARD THAT!
I'VE WON AGAIN!!
DON'T MESS WITH VERONICA!
HA! HA! HA!!!!
HA! HA! HA!
IT'S VERONICA!
WHERE'S ELIZABETH?
RIGHT THERE!
18

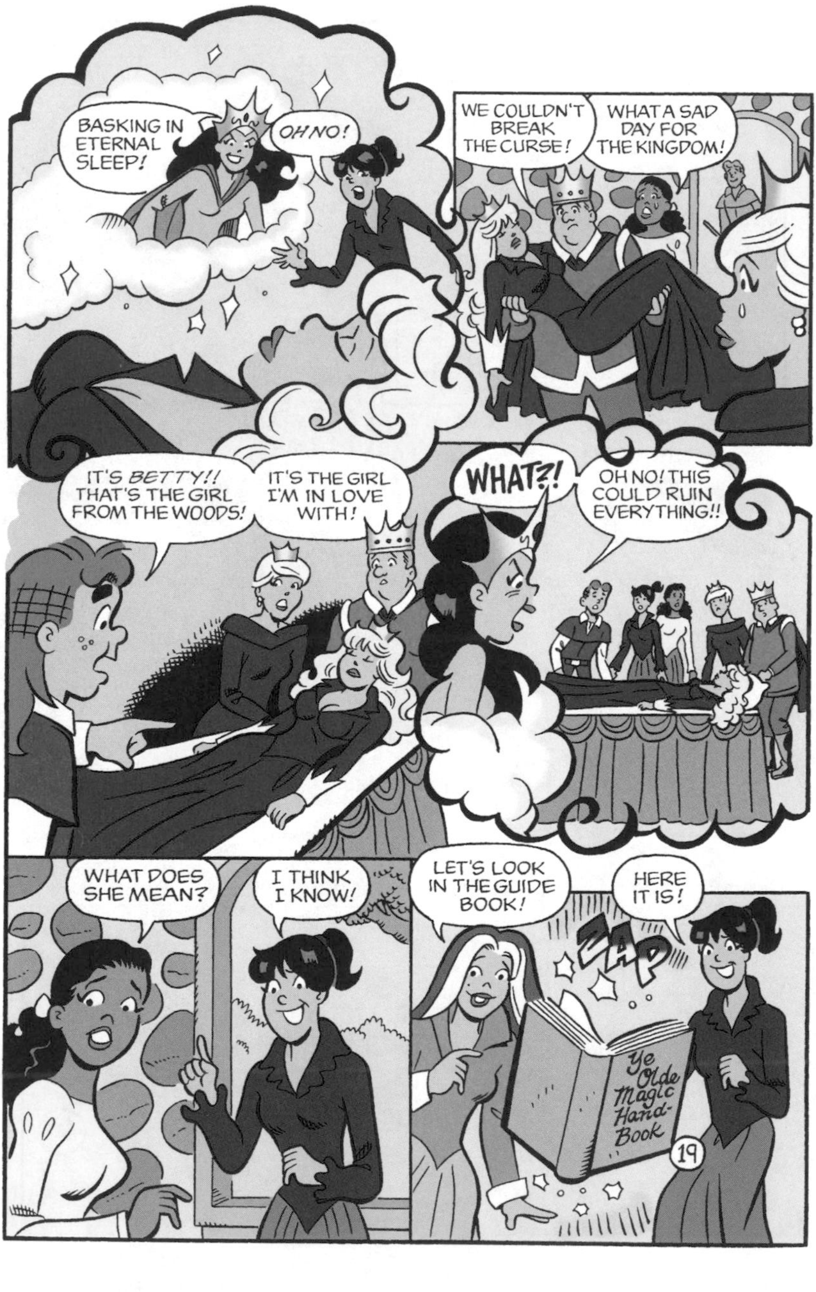
BASKING IN ETERNAL SLEEP!
OH NO!
WE COULDN'T BREAK THE CURSE!
WHAT A SAD DAY FOR THE KINGDOM!
IT'S *BETTY!!* THAT'S THE GIRL FROM THE WOODS!
IT'S THE GIRL I'M IN LOVE WITH!
WHAT?!
OH NO! THIS COULD RUIN EVERYTHING!!
WHAT DOES SHE MEAN?
I THINK I KNOW!
LET'S LOOK IN THE GUIDE BOOK!
HERE IT IS!
ZAP
Ye Olde Magic Hand-Book
19

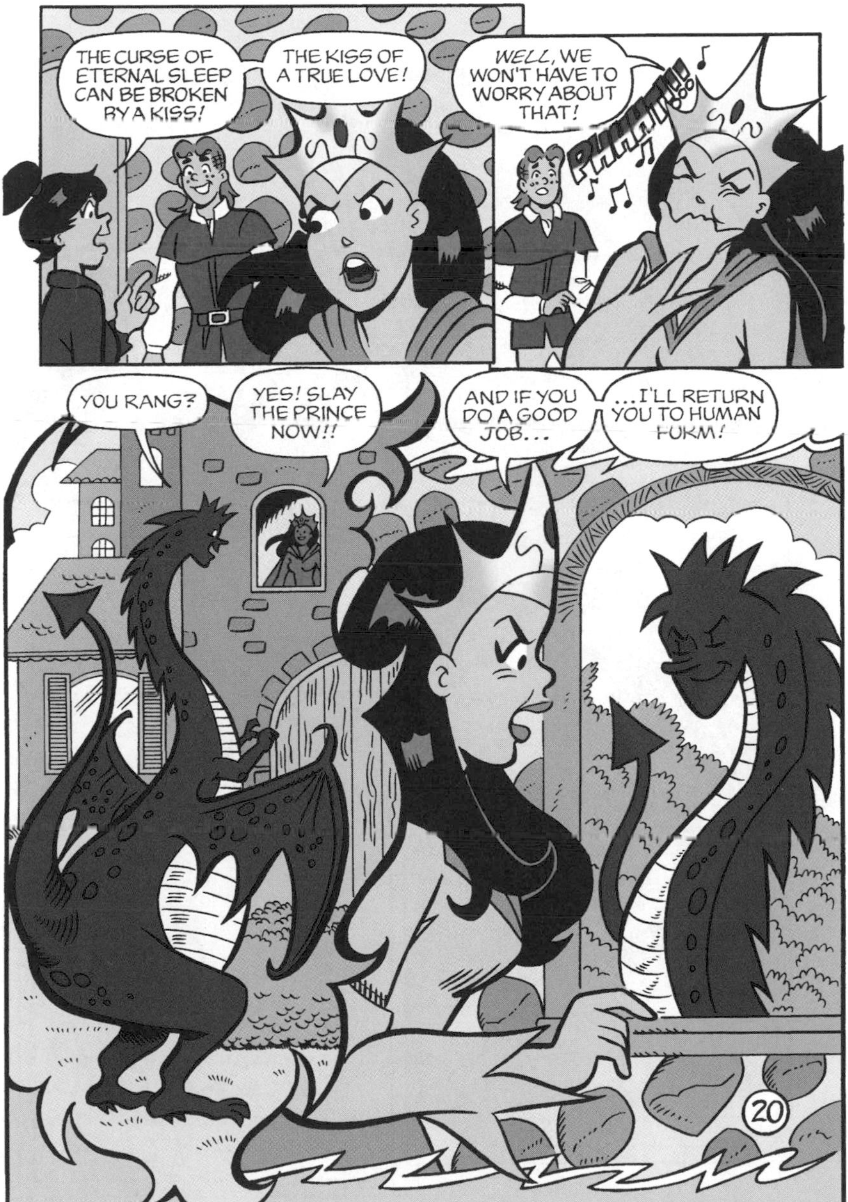
THE CURSE OF ETERNAL SLEEP CAN BE BROKEN BY A KISS!
THE KISS OF A TRUE LOVE!
WELL, WE WON'T HAVE TO WORRY ABOUT THAT!
YOU RANG?
YES! SLAY THE PRINCE NOW!!
AND IF YOU DO A GOOD JOB...
...I'LL RETURN YOU TO HUMAN FORM!
20

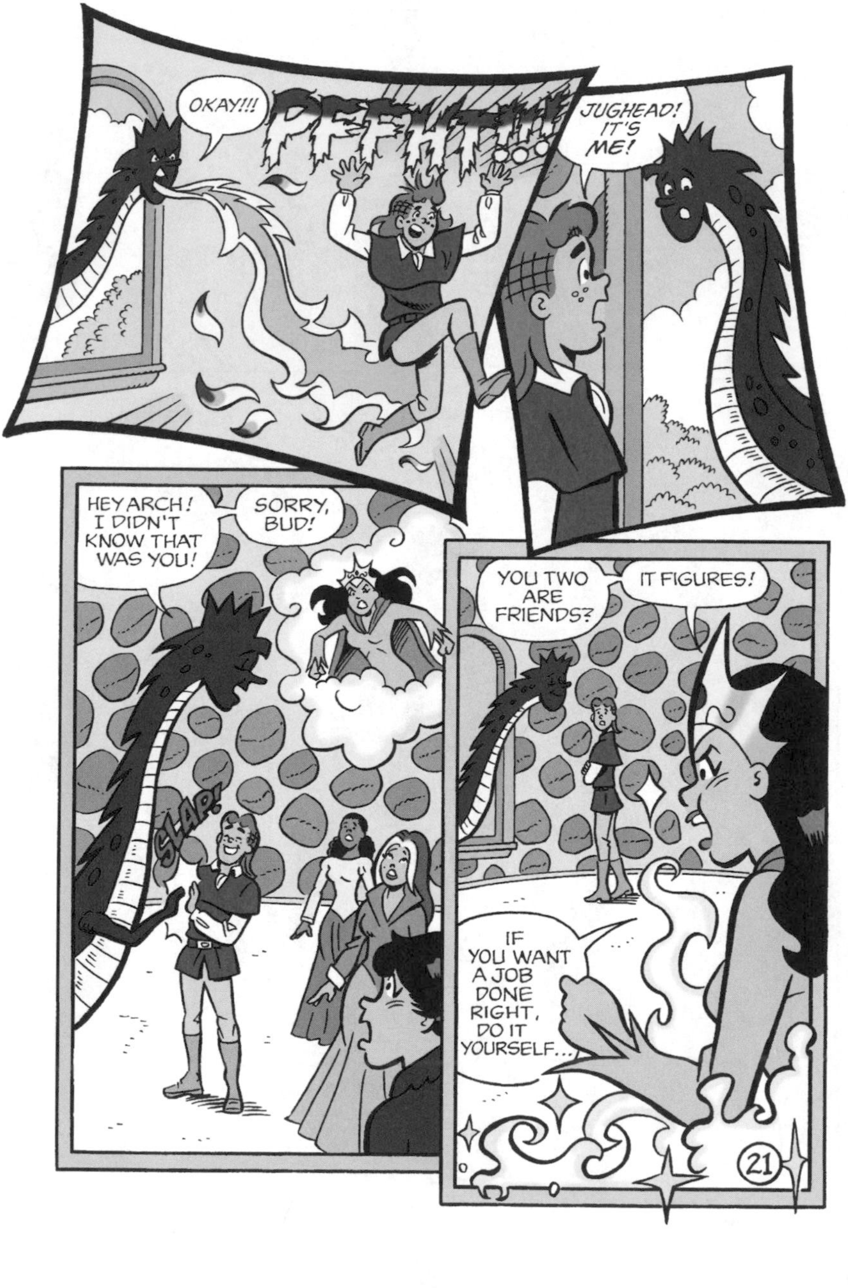
OKAY!!!
PFFHT!!!
JUGHEAD! IT'S ME!
HEY ARCH! I DIDN'T KNOW THAT WAS YOU!
SORRY, BUD!
SLAP!
YOU TWO ARE FRIENDS?
IT FIGURES!
IF YOU WANT A JOB DONE RIGHT, DO IT YOURSELF...
21

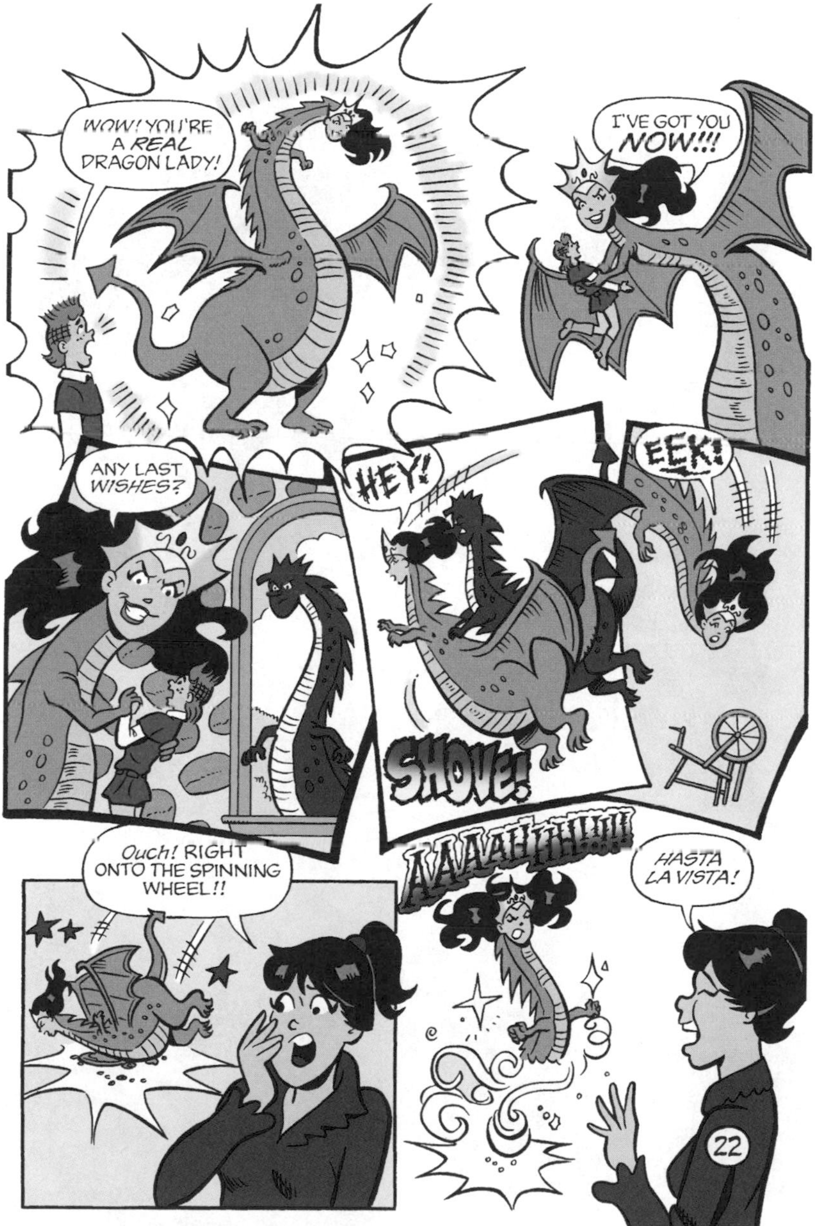
WOW! YOU'RE A REAL DRAGON LADY!
I'VE GOT YOU NOW!!!
ANY LAST WISHES?
HEY!
SHOVE!
EEK!
AAAAHHH!!!!
Ouch! RIGHT ONTO THE SPINNING WHEEL!!
HASTA LA VISTA!
22

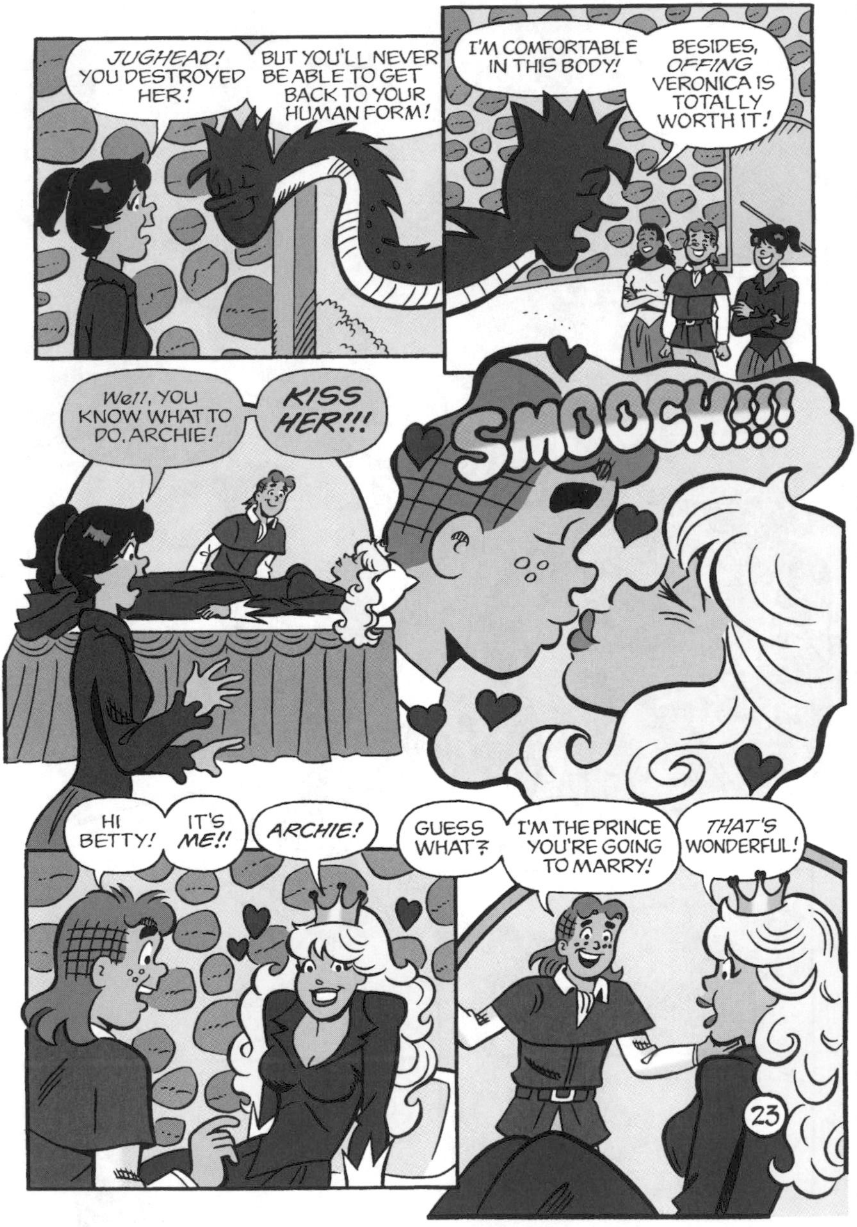
JUGHEAD! YOU DESTROYED HER!
BUT YOU'LL NEVER BE ABLE TO GET BACK TO YOUR HUMAN FORM!
I'M COMFORTABLE IN THIS BODY!
BESIDES, OFFING VERONICA IS TOTALLY WORTH IT!
Well, YOU KNOW WHAT TO DO, ARCHIE!
KISS HER!!!
SMOOCH!!!
HI BETTY!
IT'S ME!!
ARCHIE!
GUESS WHAT?
I'M THE PRINCE YOU'RE GOING TO MARRY!
THAT'S WONDERFUL!
23

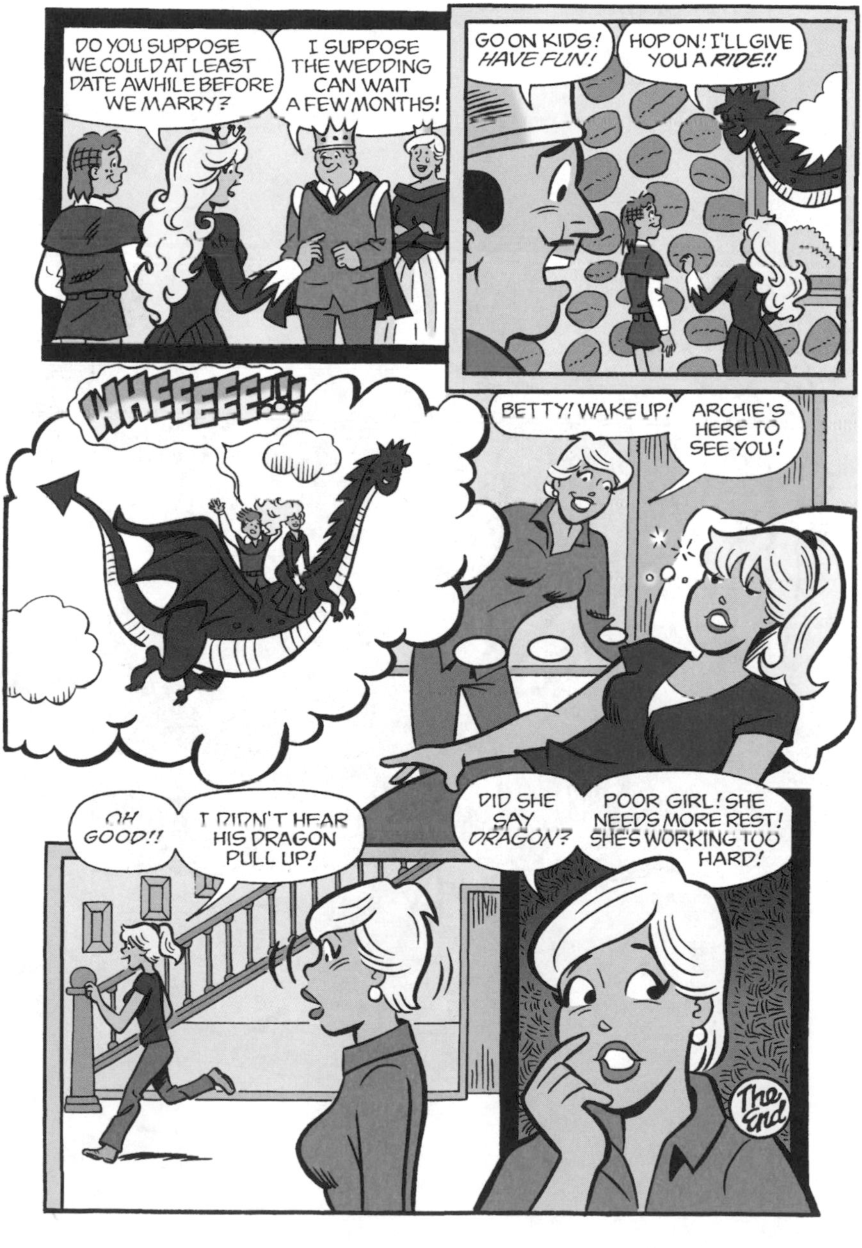
DO YOU SUPPOSE WE COULD AT LEAST DATE AWHILE BEFORE WE MARRY?
I SUPPOSE THE WEDDING CAN WAIT A FEW MONTHS!
GO ON KIDS! HAVE FUN!
HOP ON! I'LL GIVE YOU A RIDE!!
WHEEEEEE!!!
BETTY! WAKE UP!
ARCHIE'S HERE TO SEE YOU!
OH GOOD!!
I DIDN'T HEAR HIS DRAGON PULL UP!
DID SHE SAY DRAGON?
POOR GIRL! SHE NEEDS MORE REST! SHE'S WORKING TOO HARD!
The End

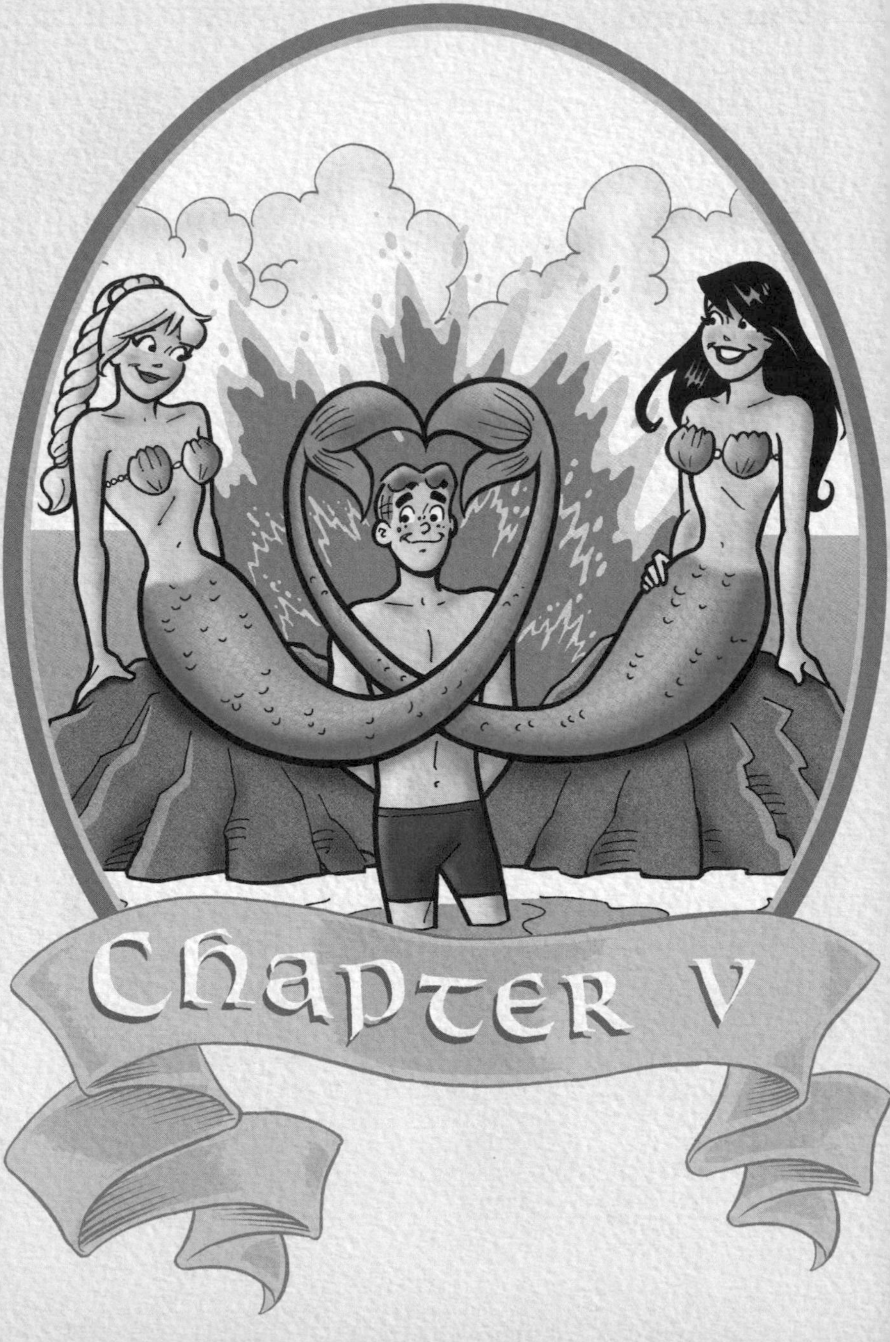
Chapter V

THE LITTLE ✳✳ MERMAIDS

Life under the sea isn't all waves and bubbles. Though Betty and Veronica are mermaid princesses of their aquatic kingdom, they're a bit bored.

Betty, in particular, wants to be part of the human world, much to the chagrin of her father, King Tritonkins, and her step-sister Veronica. Things get more complicated when B&V swim to the surface and save the life of the human prince Archie—and proceed to both fall in love with him!

But the only way to keep their connection to Archie going is by making a dangerous sacrifice—one that sea-witch Cheryl is more than happy to help with. But are they willing to risk all they've ever known for a shot at love?

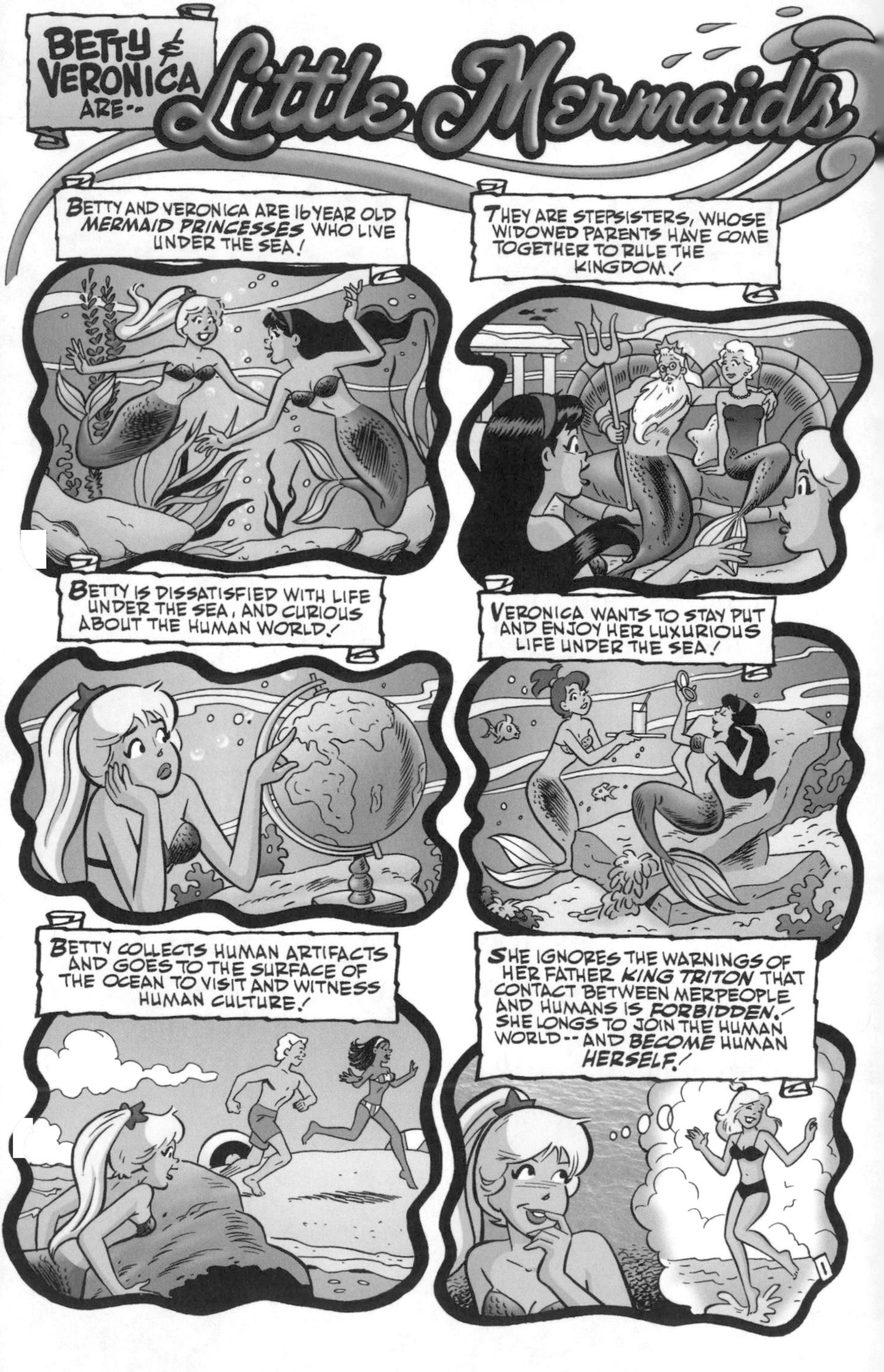
BETTY & VERONICA ARE--
Little Mermaids
BETTY AND VERONICA ARE 16 YEAR OLD MERMAID PRINCESSES WHO LIVE UNDER THE SEA!
THEY ARE STEPSISTERS, WHOSE WIDOWED PARENTS HAVE COME TOGETHER TO RULE THE KINGDOM!
BETTY IS DISSATISFIED WITH LIFE UNDER THE SEA, AND CURIOUS ABOUT THE HUMAN WORLD!
VERONICA WANTS TO STAY PUT AND ENJOY HER LUXURIOUS LIFE UNDER THE SEA!
BETTY COLLECTS HUMAN ARTIFACTS AND GOES TO THE SURFACE OF THE OCEAN TO VISIT AND WITNESS HUMAN CULTURE!
SHE IGNORES THE WARNINGS OF HER FATHER KING TRITON THAT CONTACT BETWEEN MERPEOPLE AND HUMANS IS FORBIDDEN! SHE LONGS TO JOIN THE HUMAN WORLD-- AND BECOME HUMAN HERSELF!

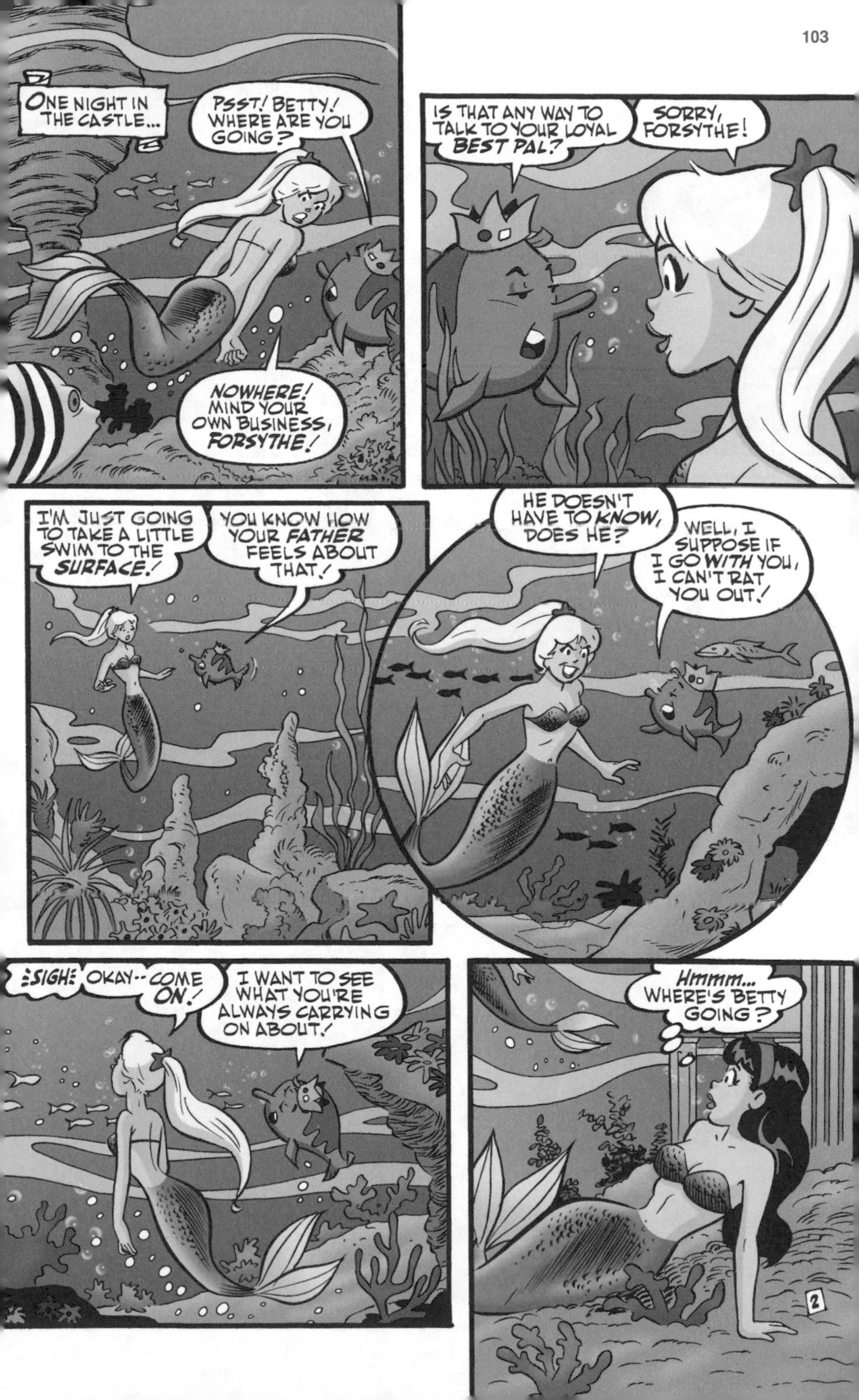
ONE NIGHT IN THE CASTLE...
PSST! BETTY! WHERE ARE YOU GOING?
NOWHERE! MIND YOUR OWN BUSINESS, FORSYTHE!
IS THAT ANY WAY TO TALK TO YOUR LOYAL BEST PAL?
SORRY, FORSYTHE!
I'M JUST GOING TO TAKE A LITTLE SWIM TO THE SURFACE!
YOU KNOW HOW YOUR FATHER FEELS ABOUT THAT!
HE DOESN'T HAVE TO KNOW, DOES HE?
WELL, I SUPPOSE IF I GO WITH YOU, I CAN'T RAT YOU OUT!
SIGH OKAY-- COME ON!
I WANT TO SEE WHAT YOU'RE ALWAYS CARRYING ON ABOUT!
Hmmm... WHERE'S BETTY GOING?
2

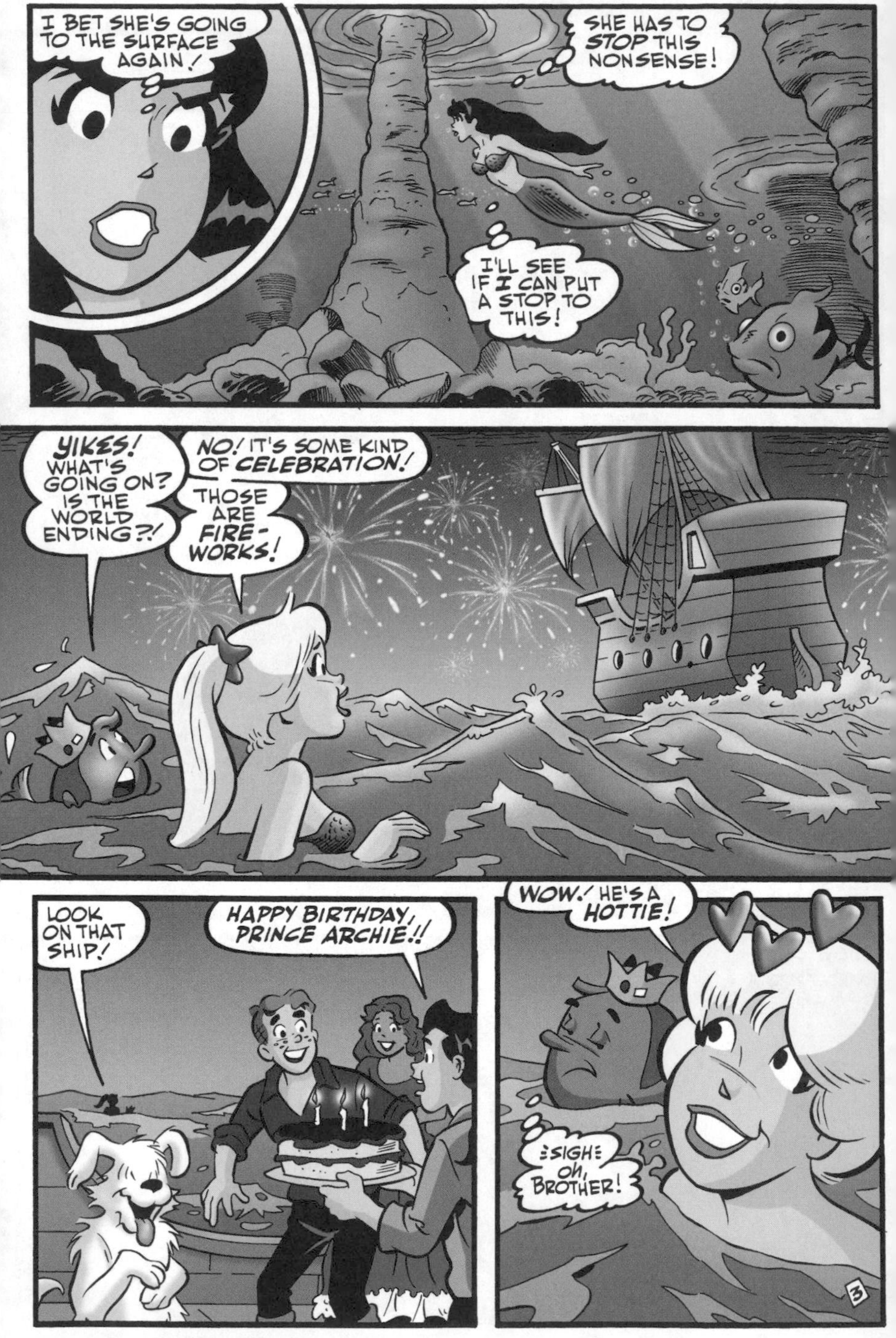
I BET SHE'S GOING TO THE SURFACE AGAIN!
SHE HAS TO STOP THIS NONSENSE!
I'LL SEE IF I CAN PUT A STOP TO THIS!
YIKES! WHAT'S GOING ON? IS THE WORLD ENDING?!
NO! IT'S SOME KIND OF CELEBRATION!
THOSE ARE FIRE-WORKS!
LOOK ON THAT SHIP!
HAPPY BIRTHDAY, PRINCE ARCHIE!!
WOW! HE'S A HOTTIE!
SIGH oh, BROTHER!
3

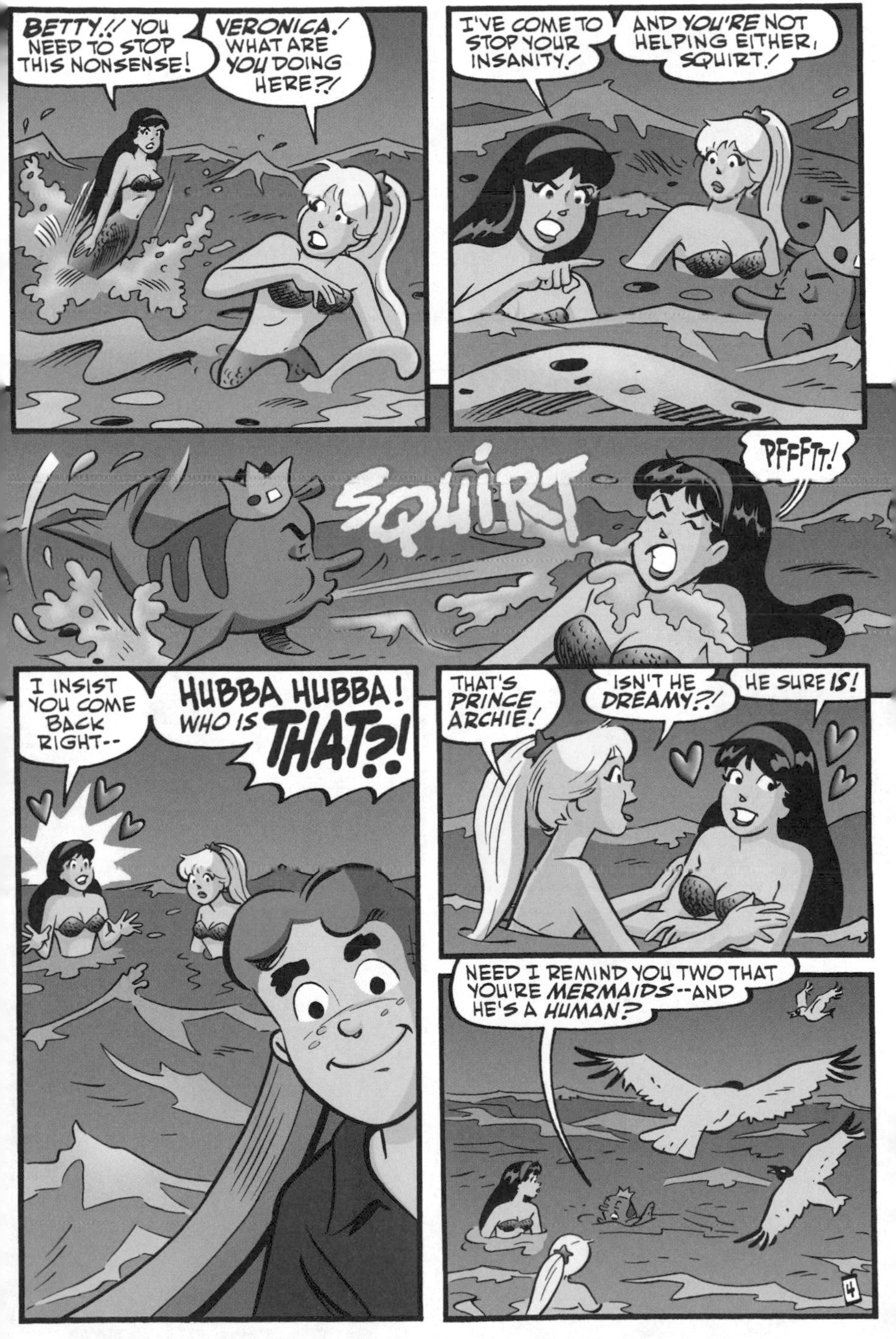
BETTY!! YOU NEED TO STOP THIS NONSENSE!
VERONICA! WHAT ARE YOU DOING HERE?!
I'VE COME TO STOP YOUR INSANITY!
AND YOU'RE NOT HELPING EITHER, SQUIRT!
SQUIRT
PFFFTT!
I INSIST YOU COME BACK RIGHT--
HUBBA HUBBA! WHO IS THAT?!
THAT'S PRINCE ARCHIE!
ISN'T HE DREAMY?!
HE SURE IS!
NEED I REMIND YOU TWO THAT YOU'RE MERMAIDS--AND HE'S A HUMAN?
4

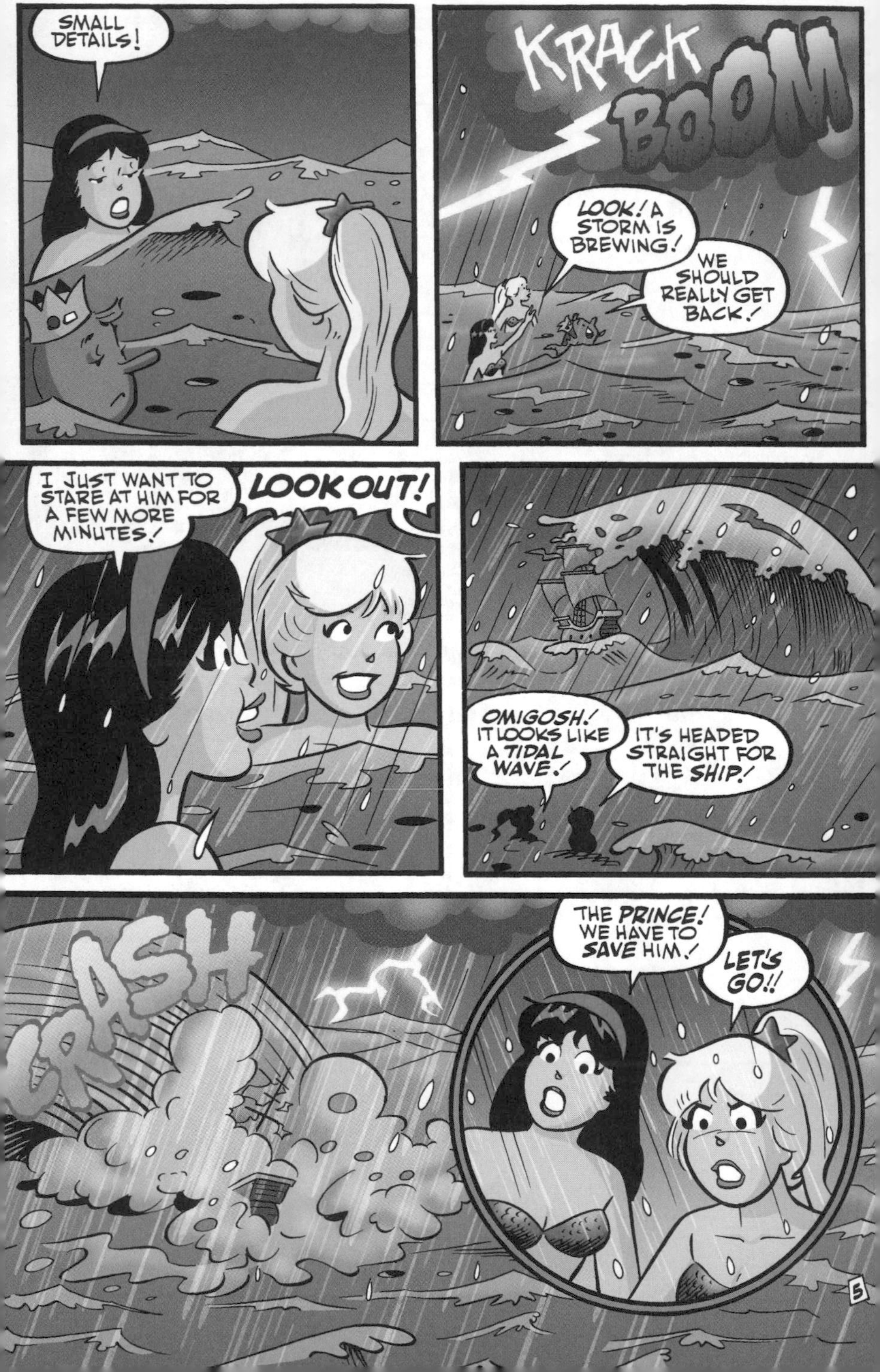
SMALL DETAILS!
KRACK
BOOM
LOOK! A STORM IS BREWING!
WE SHOULD REALLY GET BACK!
I JUST WANT TO STARE AT HIM FOR A FEW MORE MINUTES!
LOOK OUT!
OMIGOSH! IT LOOKS LIKE A TIDAL WAVE!
IT'S HEADED STRAIGHT FOR THE SHIP!
CRASH
THE PRINCE! WE HAVE TO SAVE HIM!
LET'S GO!!
5

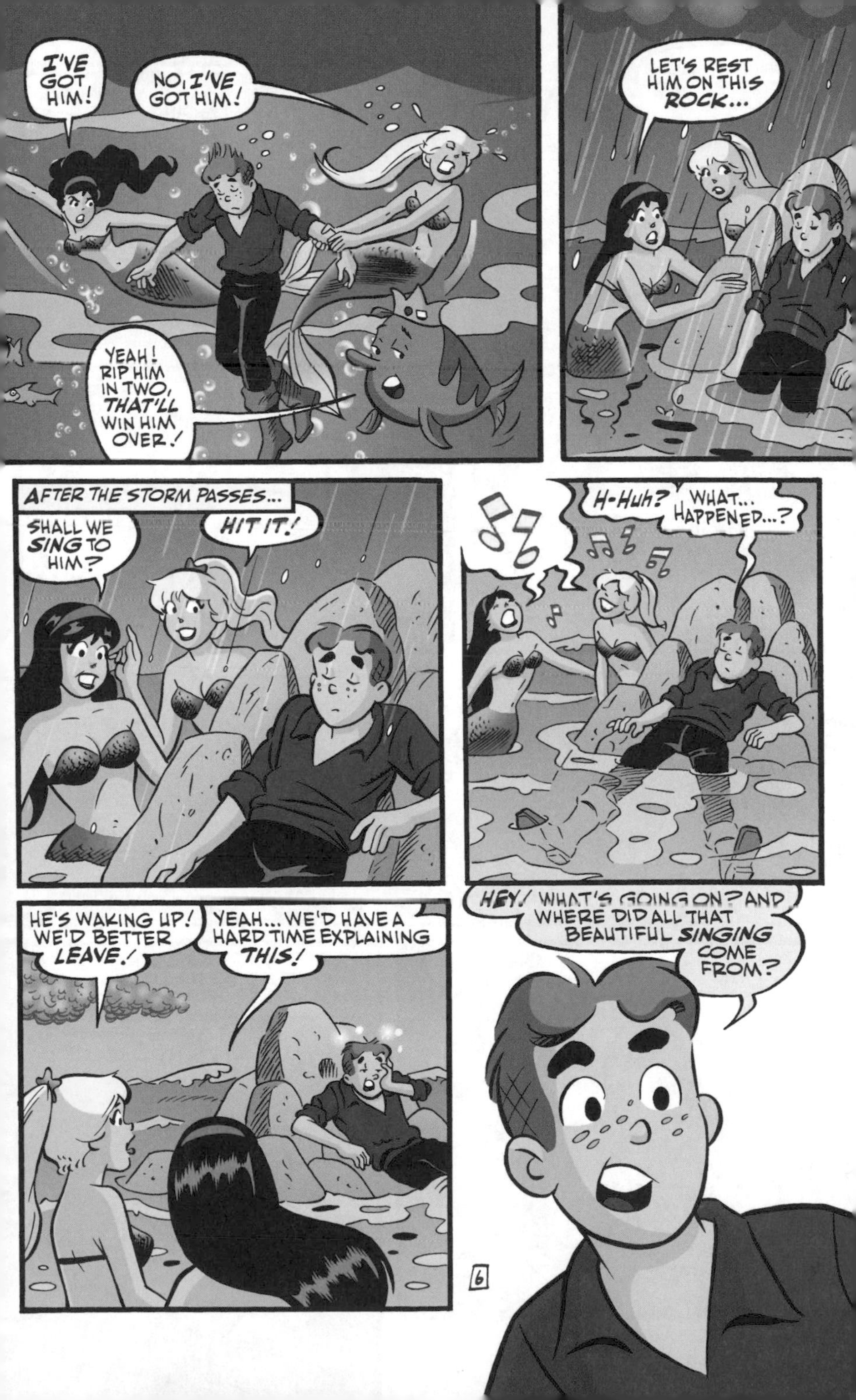
I'VE GOT HIM!
NO, I'VE GOT HIM!
YEAH! RIP HIM IN TWO, THAT'LL WIN HIM OVER!
LET'S REST HIM ON THIS ROCK...
AFTER THE STORM PASSES...
SHALL WE SING TO HIM?
HIT IT!
H-Huh?
WHAT... HAPPENED...?
HE'S WAKING UP! WE'D BETTER LEAVE!
YEAH... WE'D HAVE A HARD TIME EXPLAINING THIS!
HEY! WHAT'S GOING ON? AND WHERE DID ALL THAT BEAUTIFUL SINGING COME FROM?
6

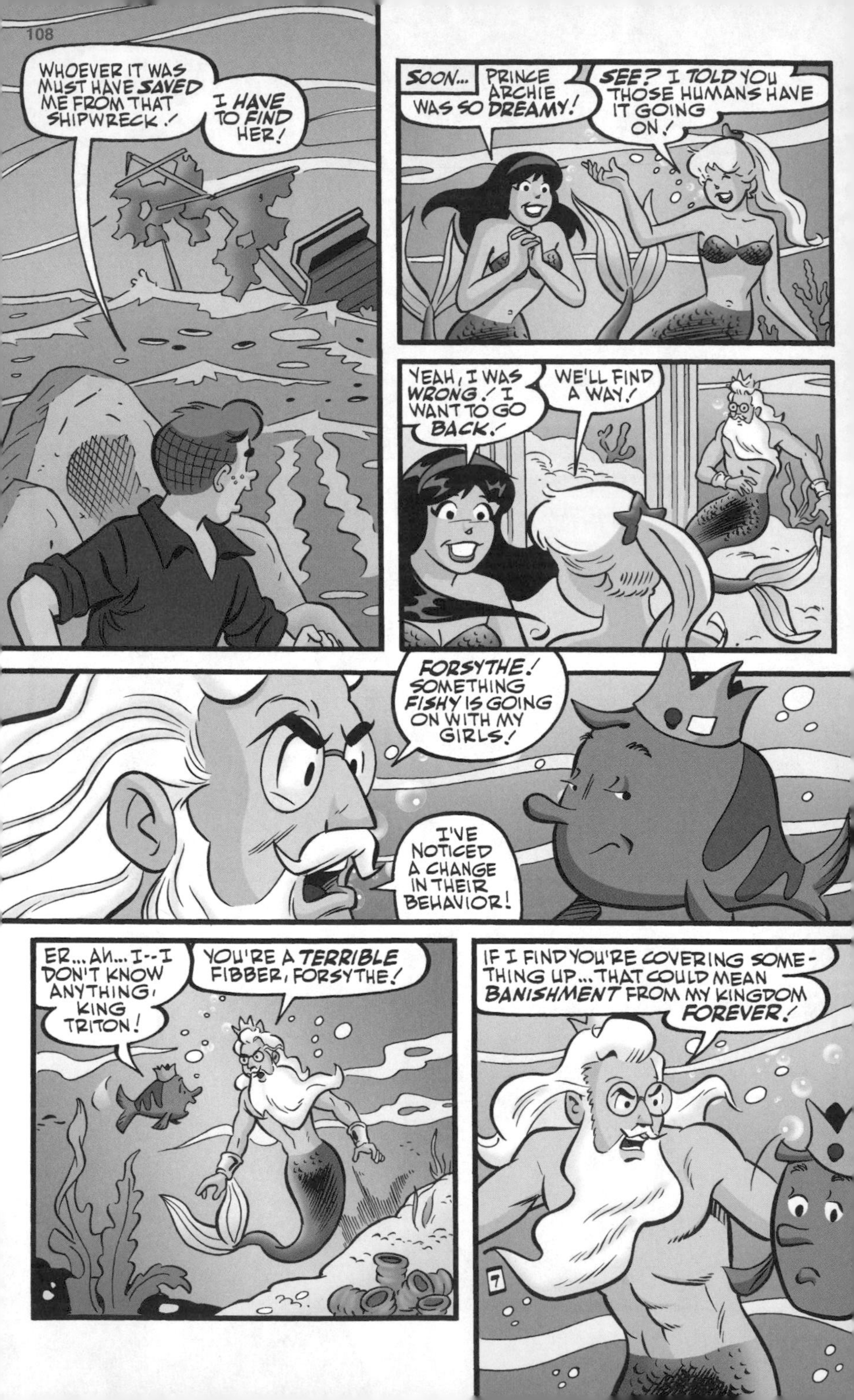
WHOEVER IT WAS MUST HAVE SAVED ME FROM THAT SHIPWRECK!
I HAVE TO FIND HER!
SOON...
PRINCE ARCHIE WAS SO DREAMY!
SEE? I TOLD YOU THOSE HUMANS HAVE IT GOING ON!
YEAH, I WAS WRONG! I WANT TO GO BACK!
WE'LL FIND A WAY!
FORSYTHE! SOMETHING FISHY IS GOING ON WITH MY GIRLS!
I'VE NOTICED A CHANGE IN THEIR BEHAVIOR!
ER... AH... I--I DON'T KNOW ANYTHING, KING TRITON!
YOU'RE A TERRIBLE FIBBER, FORSYTHE!
IF I FIND YOU'RE COVERING SOMETHING UP... THAT COULD MEAN BANISHMENT FROM MY KINGDOM FOREVER!
7

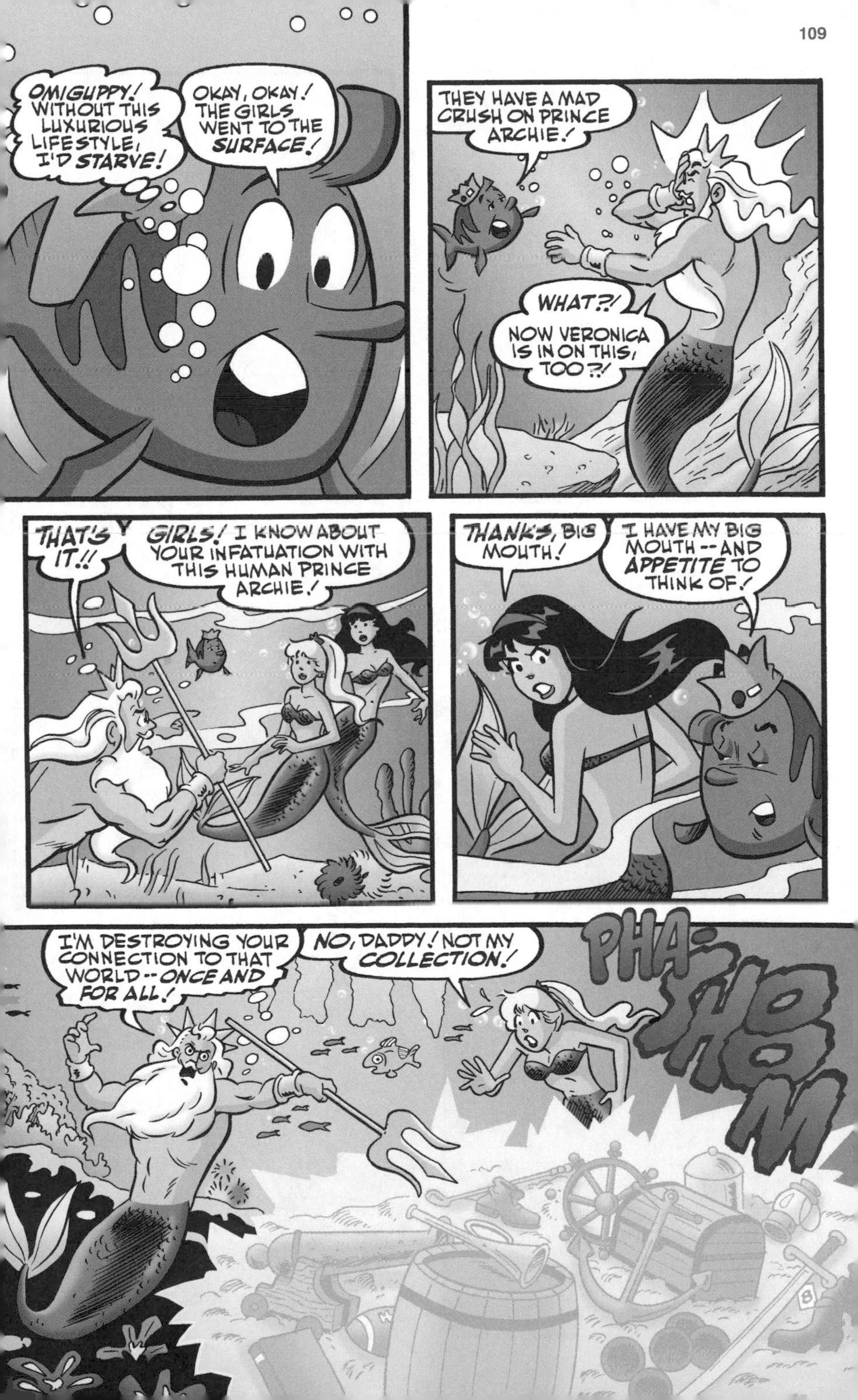
OMIGUPPY! WITHOUT THIS LUXURIOUS LIFESTYLE, I'D STARVE!
OKAY, OKAY! THE GIRLS WENT TO THE SURFACE!
THEY HAVE A MAD CRUSH ON PRINCE ARCHIE!
WHAT?!
NOW VERONICA IS IN ON THIS, TOO?!
THAT'S IT!!
GIRLS! I KNOW ABOUT YOUR INFATUATION WITH THIS HUMAN PRINCE ARCHIE!
THANKS, BIG MOUTH!
I HAVE MY BIG MOUTH -- AND APPETITE TO THINK OF!
I'M DESTROYING YOUR CONNECTION TO THAT WORLD -- ONCE AND FOR ALL!
NO, DADDY! NOT MY COLLECTION!
PHA-SHOOM

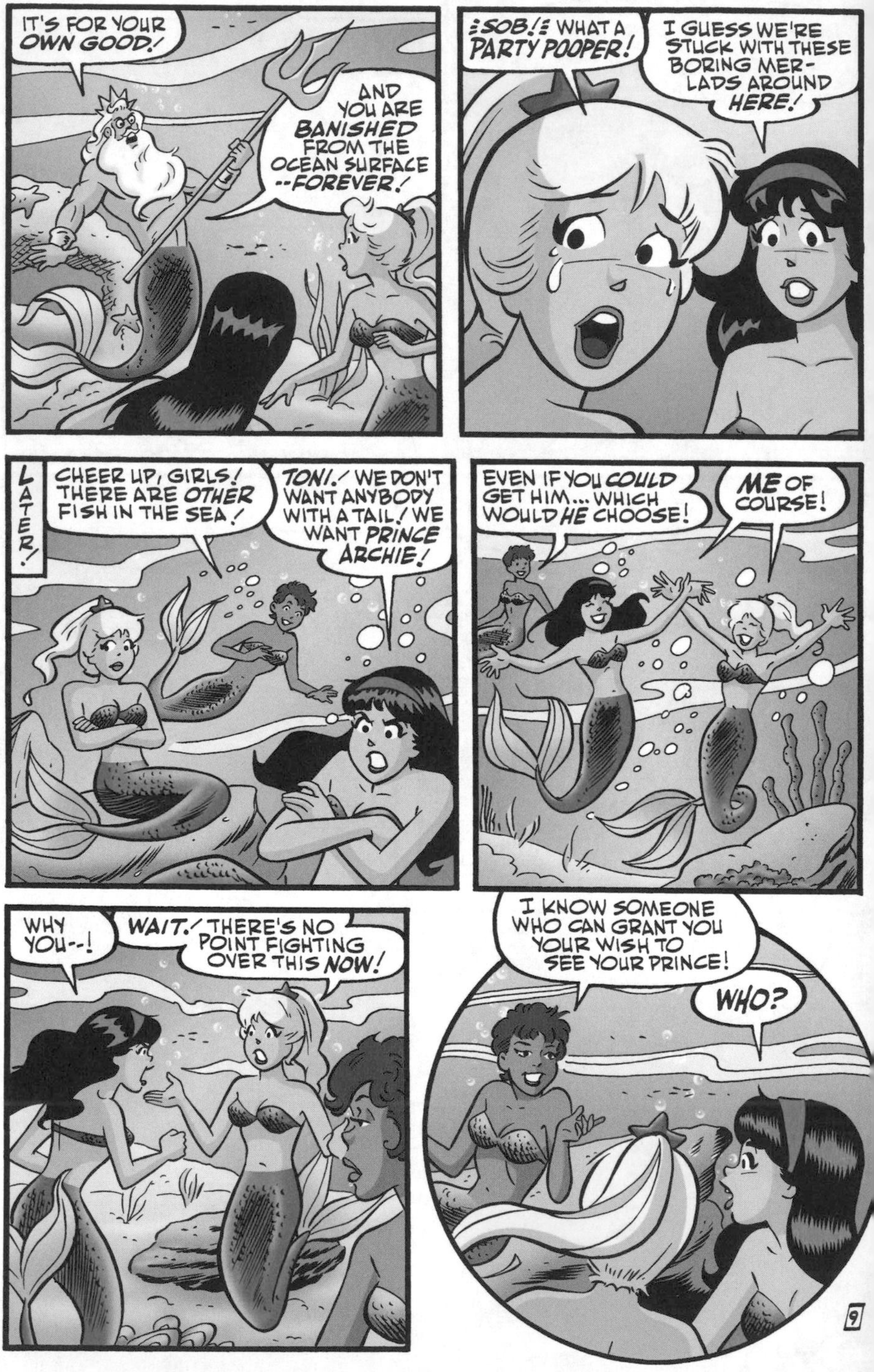
IT'S FOR YOUR OWN GOOD!
AND YOU ARE BANISHED FROM THE OCEAN SURFACE --FOREVER!
:SOB!: WHAT A PARTY POOPER!
I GUESS WE'RE STUCK WITH THESE BORING MER-LADS AROUND HERE!
LATER!
CHEER UP, GIRLS! THERE ARE OTHER FISH IN THE SEA!
TONI! WE DON'T WANT ANYBODY WITH A TAIL! WE WANT PRINCE ARCHIE!
EVEN IF YOU COULD GET HIM... WHICH WOULD HE CHOOSE!
ME OF COURSE!
WHY YOU--!
WAIT! THERE'S NO POINT FIGHTING OVER THIS NOW!
I KNOW SOMEONE WHO CAN GRANT YOU YOUR WISH TO SEE YOUR PRINCE!
WHO?
9

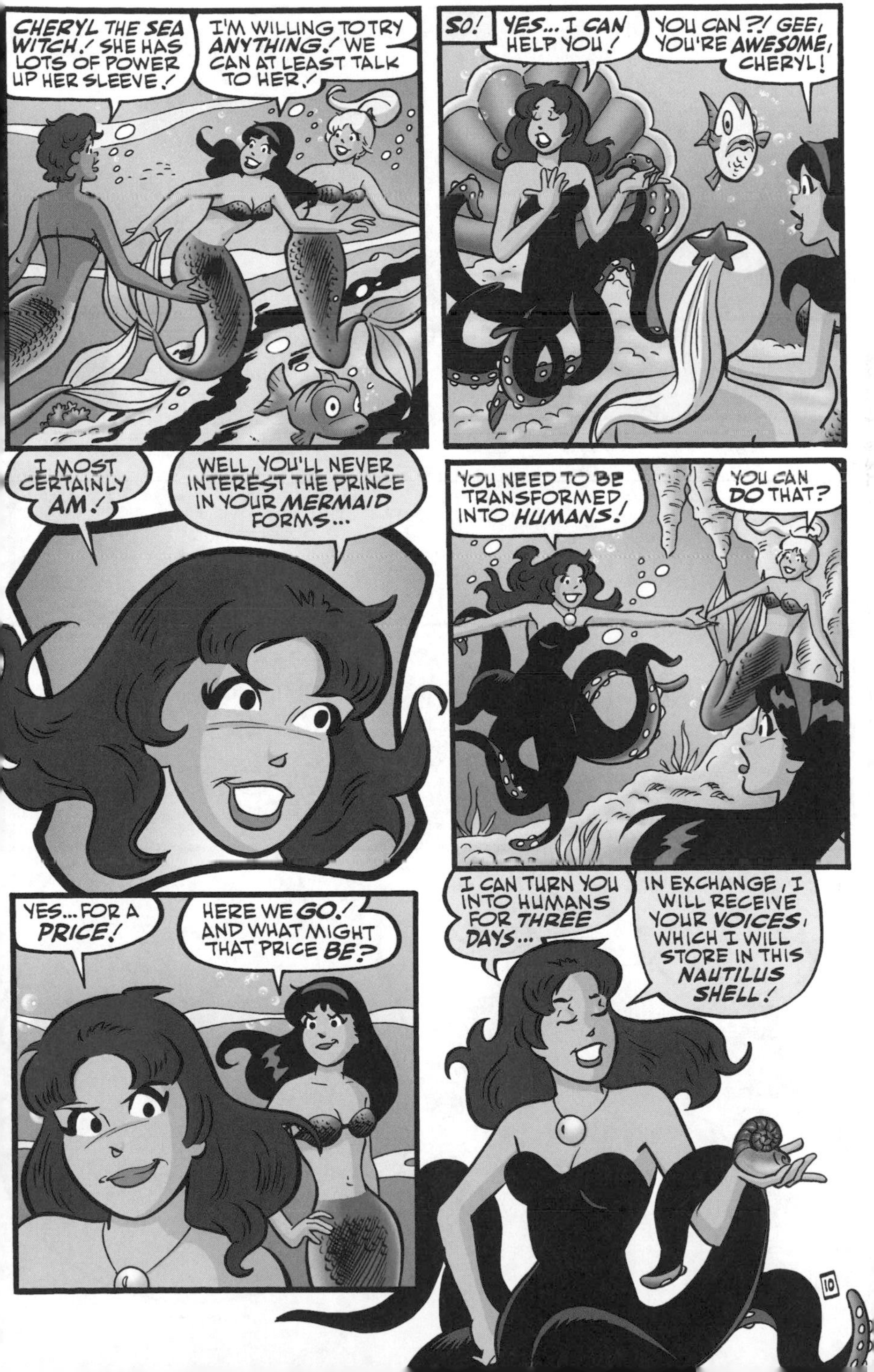
CHERYL THE SEA WITCH! SHE HAS LOTS OF POWER UP HER SLEEVE!
I'M WILLING TO TRY ANYTHING! WE CAN AT LEAST TALK TO HER!
SO!
YES... I CAN HELP YOU!
YOU CAN?! GEE, YOU'RE AWESOME, CHERYL!
I MOST CERTAINLY AM!
WELL, YOU'LL NEVER INTEREST THE PRINCE IN YOUR MERMAID FORMS...
YOU NEED TO BE TRANSFORMED INTO HUMANS!
YOU CAN DO THAT?
YES... FOR A PRICE!
HERE WE GO! AND WHAT MIGHT THAT PRICE BE?
I CAN TURN YOU INTO HUMANS FOR THREE DAYS...
IN EXCHANGE, I WILL RECEIVE YOUR VOICES, WHICH I WILL STORE IN THIS NAUTILUS SHELL!
10

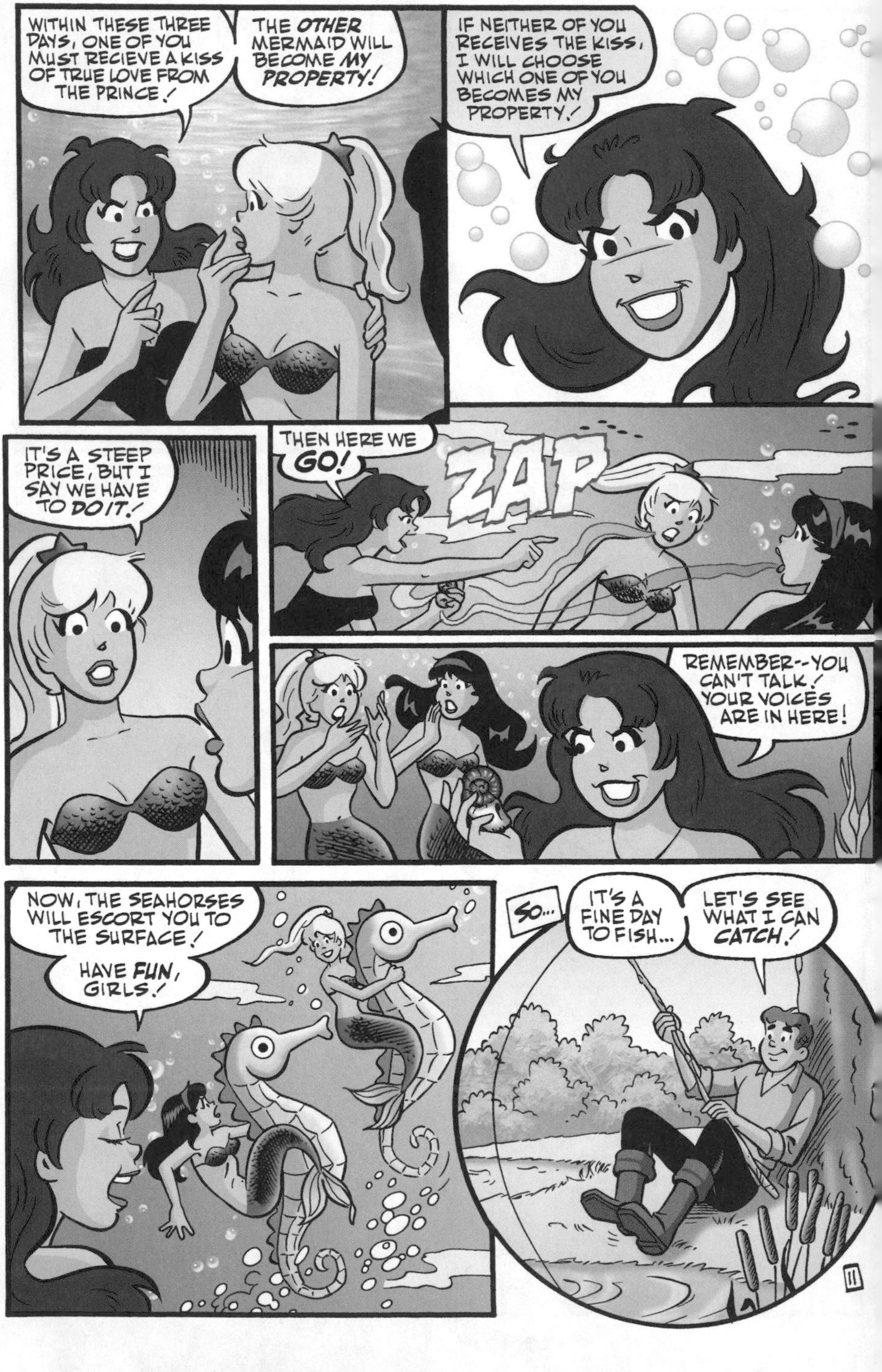
WITHIN THESE THREE DAYS, ONE OF YOU MUST RECIEVE A KISS OF TRUE LOVE FROM THE PRINCE!
THE *OTHER* MERMAID WILL BECOME *MY PROPERTY*!
IF NEITHER OF YOU RECEIVES THE KISS, I WILL CHOOSE WHICH ONE OF YOU BECOMES MY PROPERTY!
IT'S A STEEP PRICE, BUT I SAY WE HAVE TO *DO IT*!
THEN HERE WE *GO*!
ZAP
REMEMBER--YOU CAN'T TALK! YOUR VOICES ARE IN HERE!
NOW, THE SEAHORSES WILL ESCORT YOU TO THE SURFACE!
HAVE *FUN*, GIRLS!
SO...
IT'S A FINE DAY TO FISH...
LET'S SEE WHAT I CAN *CATCH*!
11

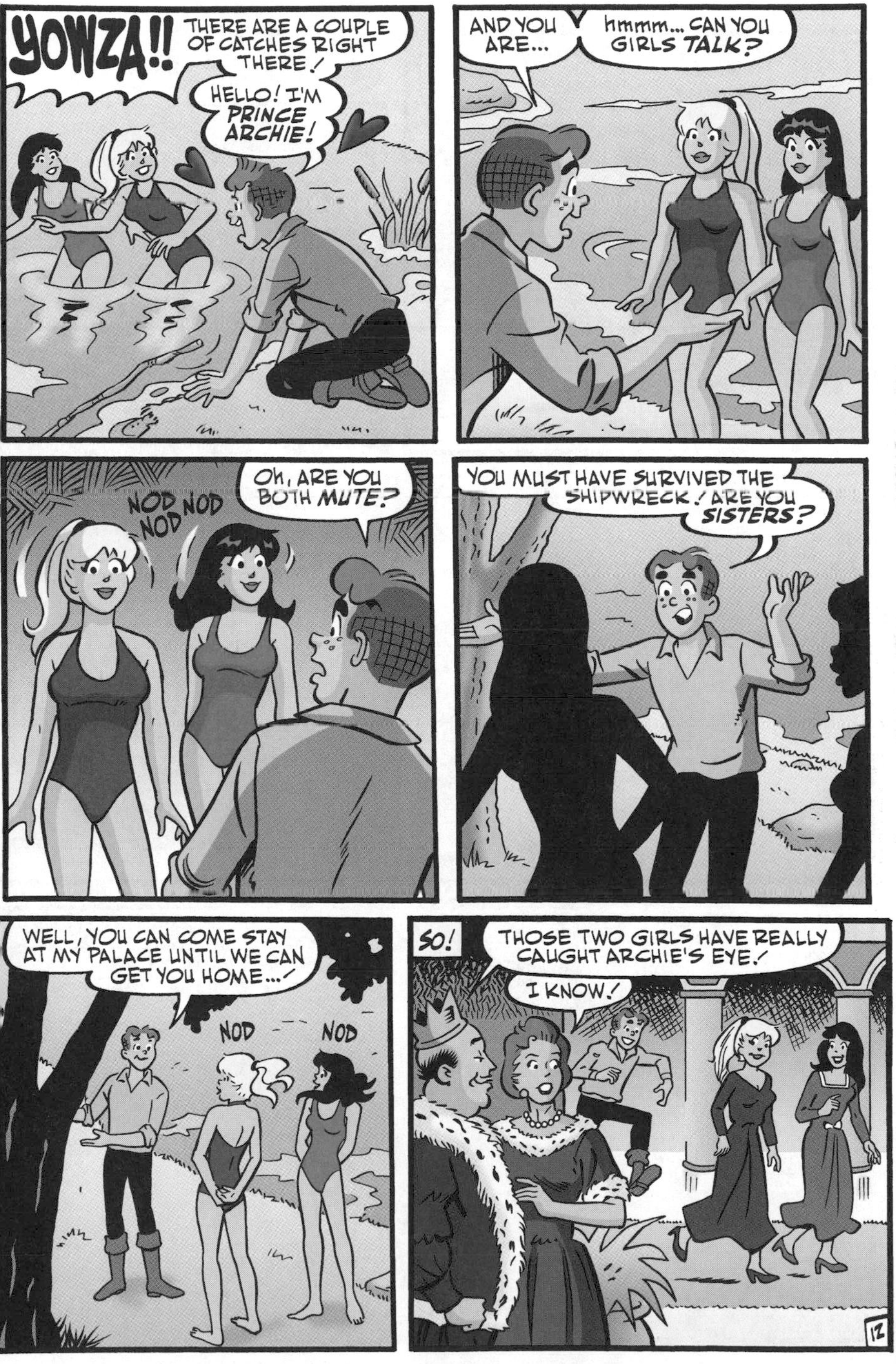
YOWZA!!
THERE ARE A COUPLE OF CATCHES RIGHT THERE!
HELLO! I'M PRINCE ARCHIE!
AND YOU ARE...
hmmm... CAN YOU GIRLS TALK?
NOD NOD NOD
Oh, ARE YOU BOTH MUTE?
YOU MUST HAVE SURVIVED THE SHIPWRECK! ARE YOU SISTERS?
WELL, YOU CAN COME STAY AT MY PALACE UNTIL WE CAN GET YOU HOME...!
NOD
NOD
SO!
THOSE TWO GIRLS HAVE REALLY CAUGHT ARCHIE'S EYE!
I KNOW!
12

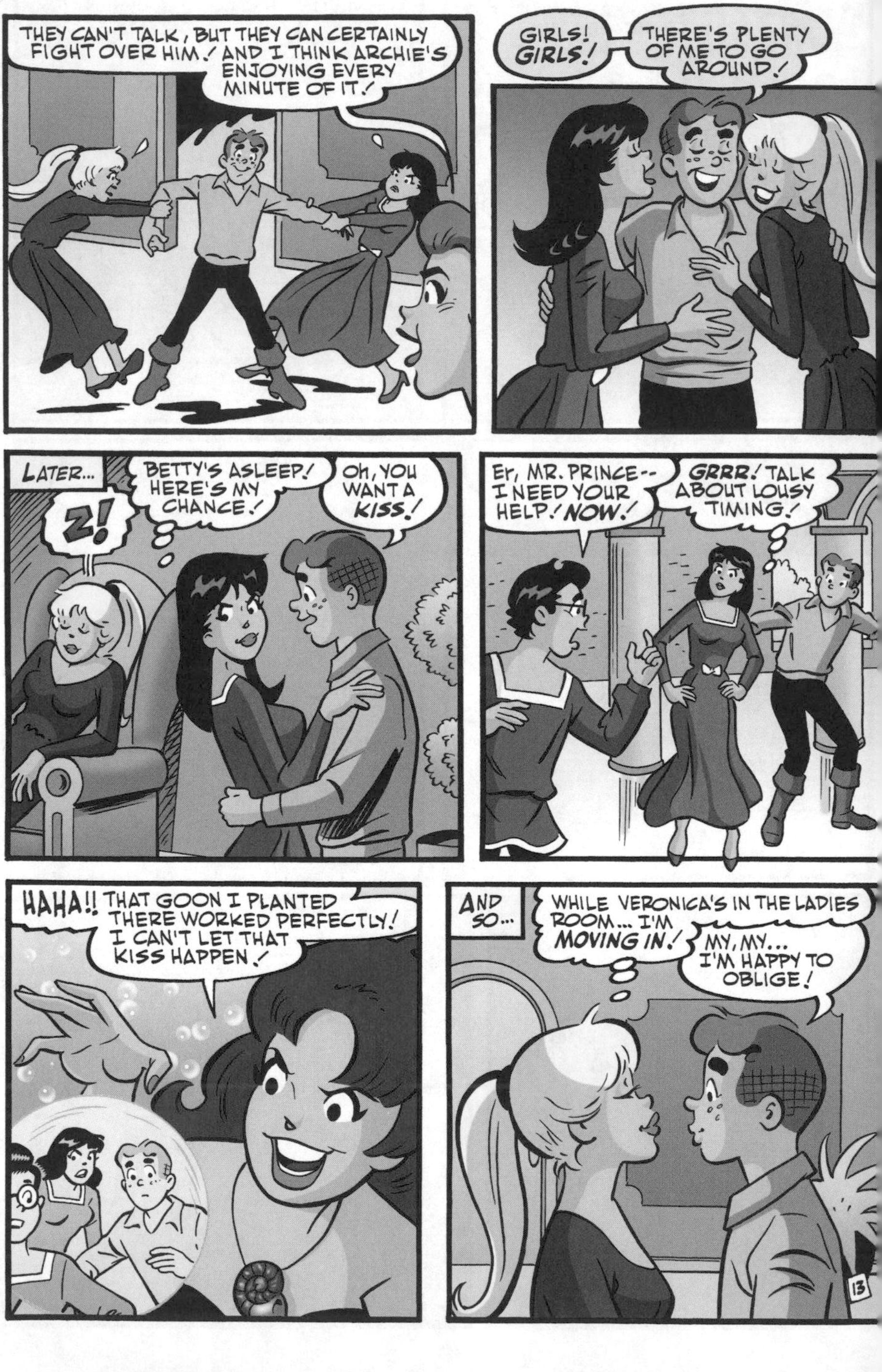
THEY CAN'T TALK, BUT THEY CAN CERTAINLY FIGHT OVER HIM! AND I THINK ARCHIE'S ENJOYING EVERY MINUTE OF IT!
GIRLS! GIRLS!
THERE'S PLENTY OF ME TO GO AROUND!
LATER...
Z!
BETTY'S ASLEEP! HERE'S MY CHANCE!
OH, YOU WANT A KISS!
ER, MR. PRINCE-- I NEED YOUR HELP! NOW!
GRRR! TALK ABOUT LOUSY TIMING!
HAHA!! THAT GOON I PLANTED THERE WORKED PERFECTLY! I CAN'T LET THAT KISS HAPPEN!
AND SO...
WHILE VERONICA'S IN THE LADIES ROOM... I'M MOVING IN!
MY, MY... I'M HAPPY TO OBLIGE!
13

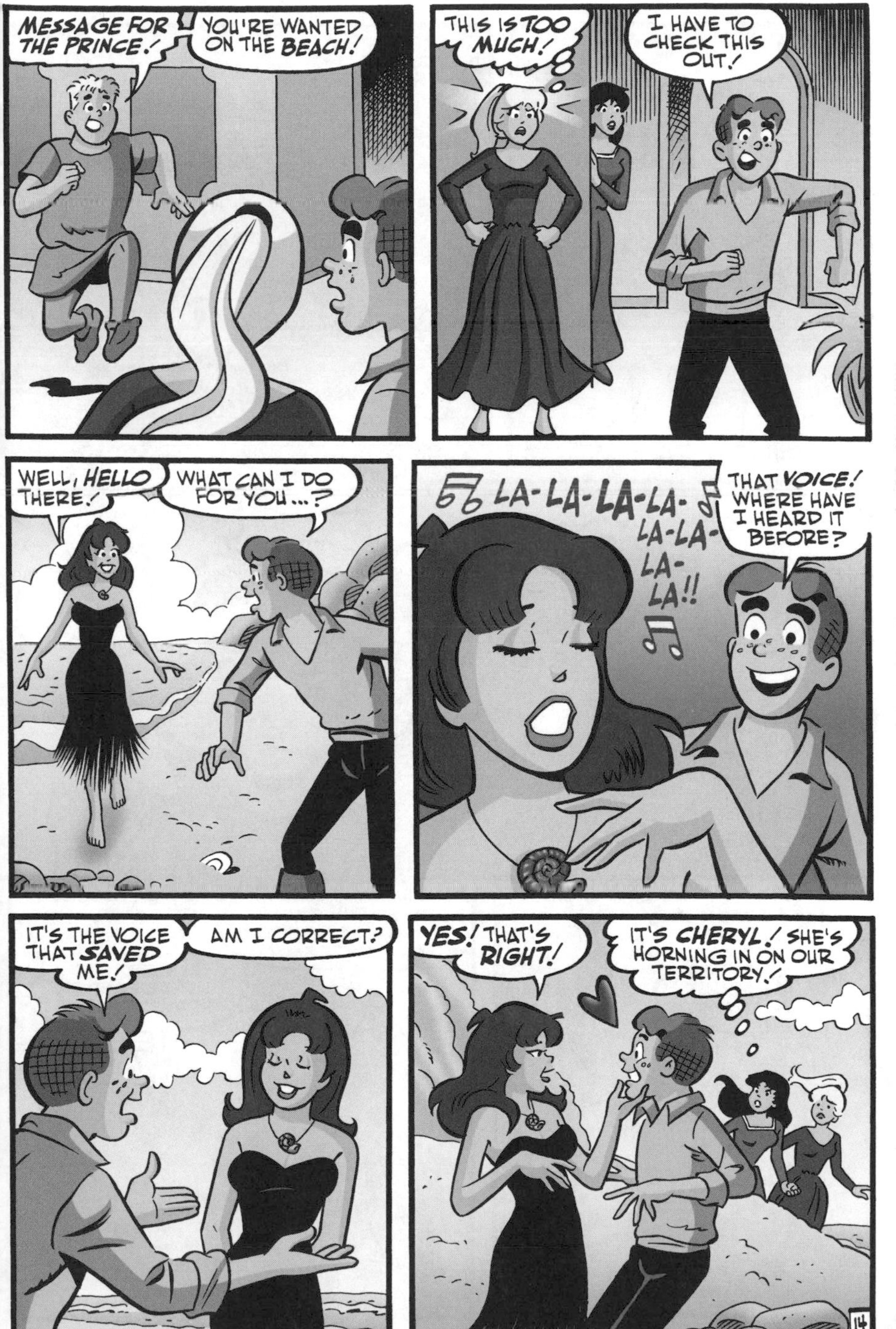
MESSAGE FOR THE PRINCE!
YOU'RE WANTED ON THE BEACH!
THIS IS TOO MUCH!
I HAVE TO CHECK THIS OUT!
WELL, HELLO THERE!
WHAT CAN I DO FOR YOU...?
LA-LA-LA-LA-LA-LA-LA-LA!!
THAT VOICE! WHERE HAVE I HEARD IT BEFORE?
IT'S THE VOICE THAT SAVED ME!
AM I CORRECT?
YES! THAT'S RIGHT!
IT'S CHERYL! SHE'S HORNING IN ON OUR TERRITORY!
14

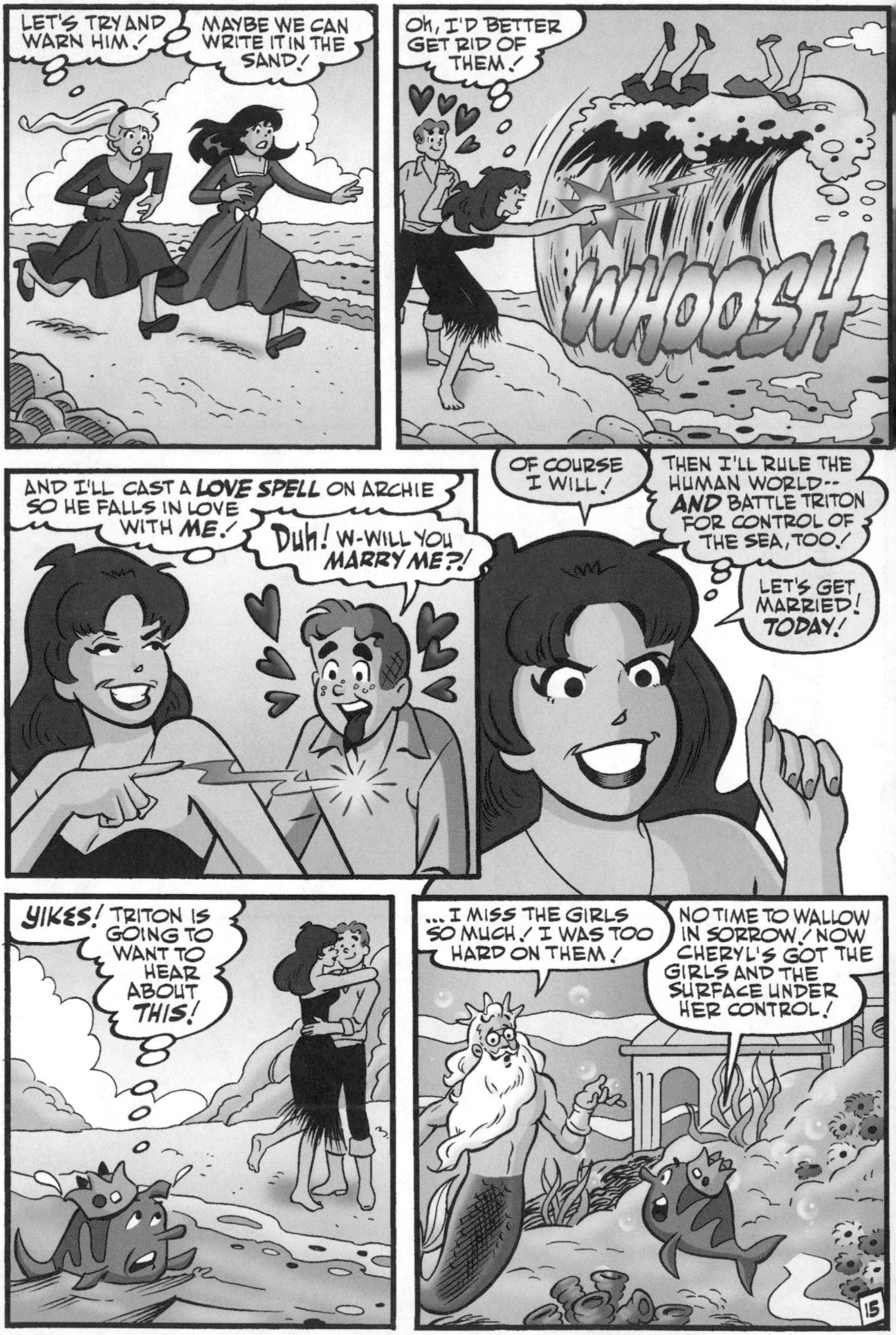
LET'S TRY AND WARN HIM!
MAYBE WE CAN WRITE IT IN THE SAND!
Oh, I'D BETTER GET RID OF THEM!
WHOOSH
AND I'LL CAST A LOVE SPELL ON ARCHIE SO HE FALLS IN LOVE WITH ME!
DUH! W-WILL YOU MARRY ME?!
OF COURSE I WILL!
THEN I'LL RULE THE HUMAN WORLD-- AND BATTLE TRITON FOR CONTROL OF THE SEA, TOO!
LET'S GET MARRIED! TODAY!
YIKES! TRITON IS GOING TO WANT TO HEAR ABOUT THIS!
...I MISS THE GIRLS SO MUCH! I WAS TOO HARD ON THEM!
NO TIME TO WALLOW IN SORROW! NOW CHERYL'S GOT THE GIRLS AND THE SURFACE UNDER HER CONTROL!
15

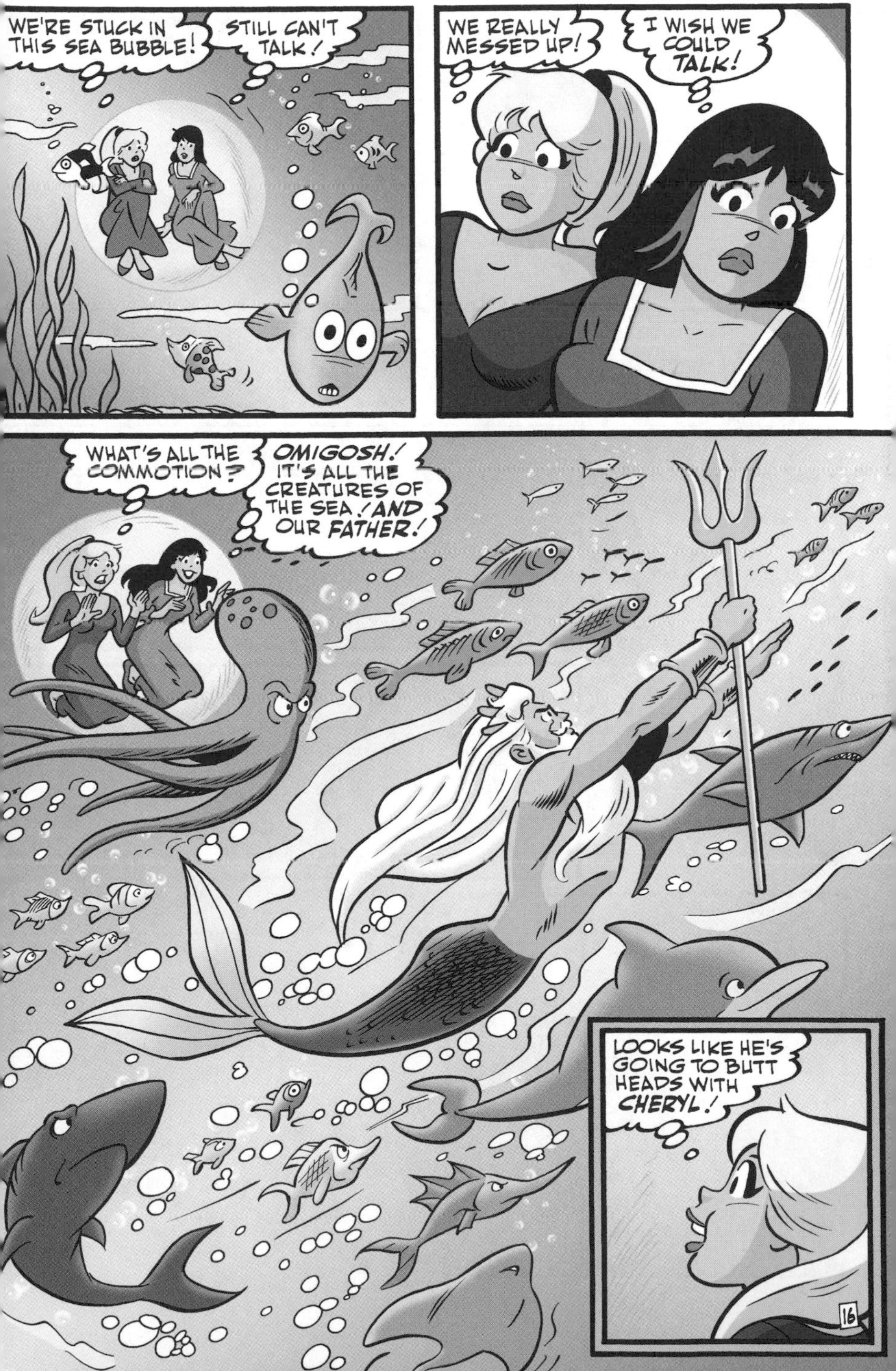
WE'RE STUCK IN THIS SEA BUBBLE!
STILL CAN'T TALK!
WE REALLY MESSED UP!
I WISH WE COULD TALK!
WHAT'S ALL THE COMMOTION?
OMIGOSH! IT'S ALL THE CREATURES OF THE SEA! AND OUR FATHER!
LOOKS LIKE HE'S GOING TO BUTT HEADS WITH CHERYL!
16

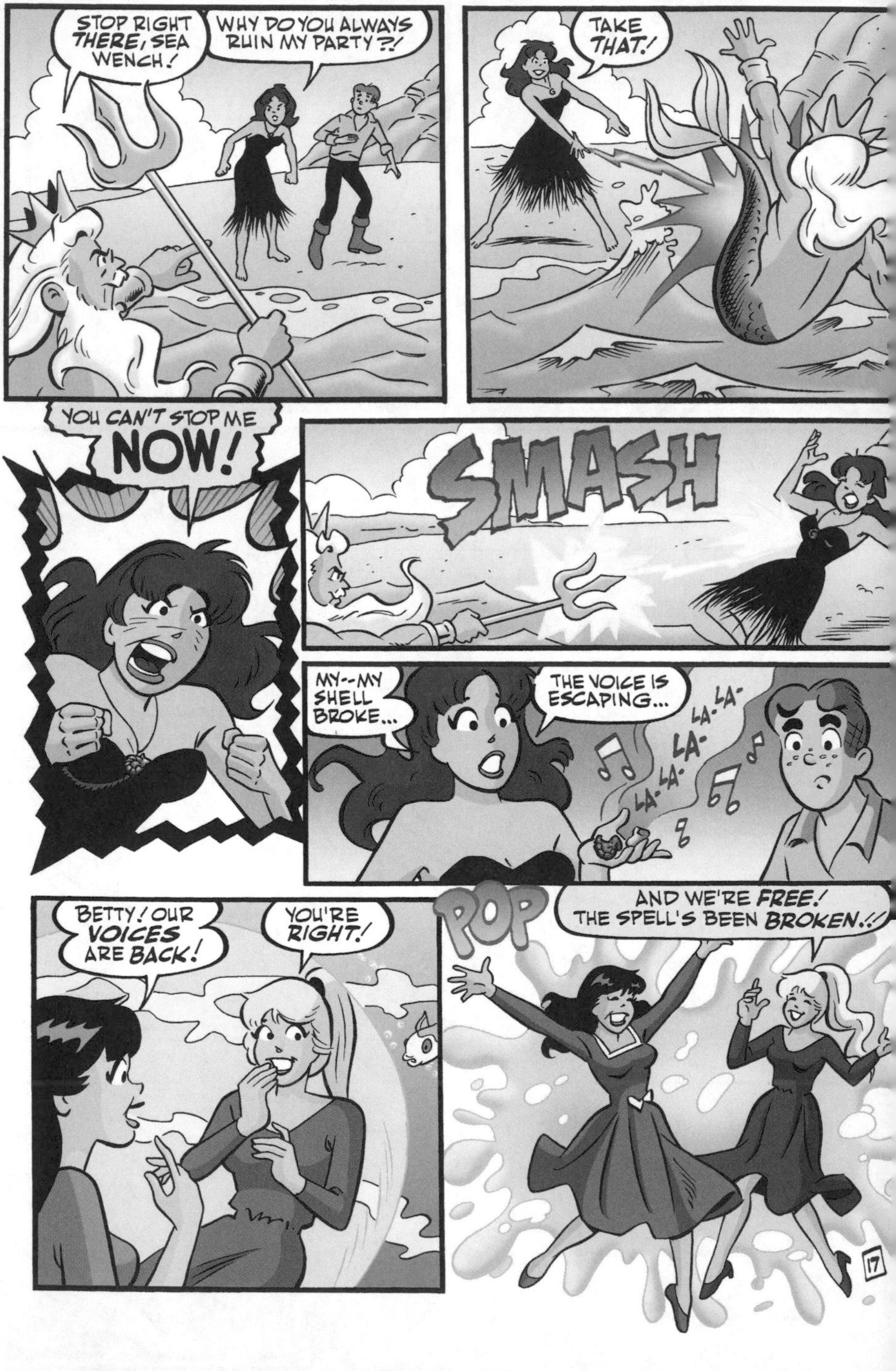
STOP RIGHT THERE, SEA WENCH!
WHY DO YOU ALWAYS RUIN MY PARTY?!
TAKE THAT!
YOU CAN'T STOP ME NOW!
SMASH
MY--MY SHELL BROKE...
THE VOICE IS ESCAPING...
LA-LA-LA-LA-LA-
BETTY! OUR VOICES ARE BACK!
YOU'RE RIGHT!
POP
AND WE'RE FREE! THE SPELL'S BEEN BROKEN!!
17

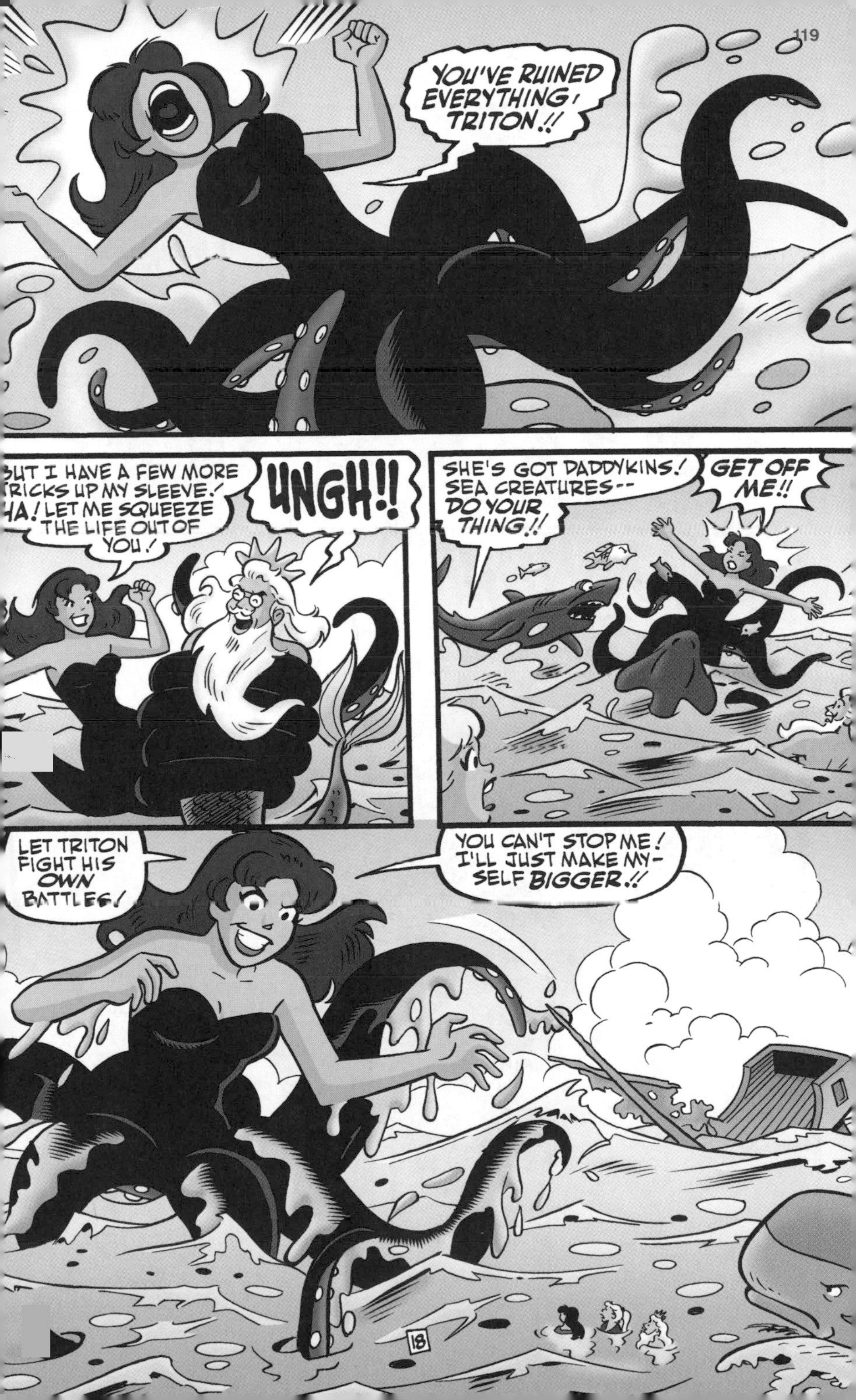
YOU'VE RUINED EVERYTHING, TRITON.!!
BUT I HAVE A FEW MORE TRICKS UP MY SLEEVE.! HA! LET ME SQUEEZE THE LIFE OUT OF YOU.!
UNGH!!
SHE'S GOT DADDYKINS! SEA CREATURES-- DO YOUR THING.!!
GET OFF ME!!
LET TRITON FIGHT HIS OWN BATTLES!
YOU CAN'T STOP ME! I'LL JUST MAKE MY-SELF BIGGER.!!

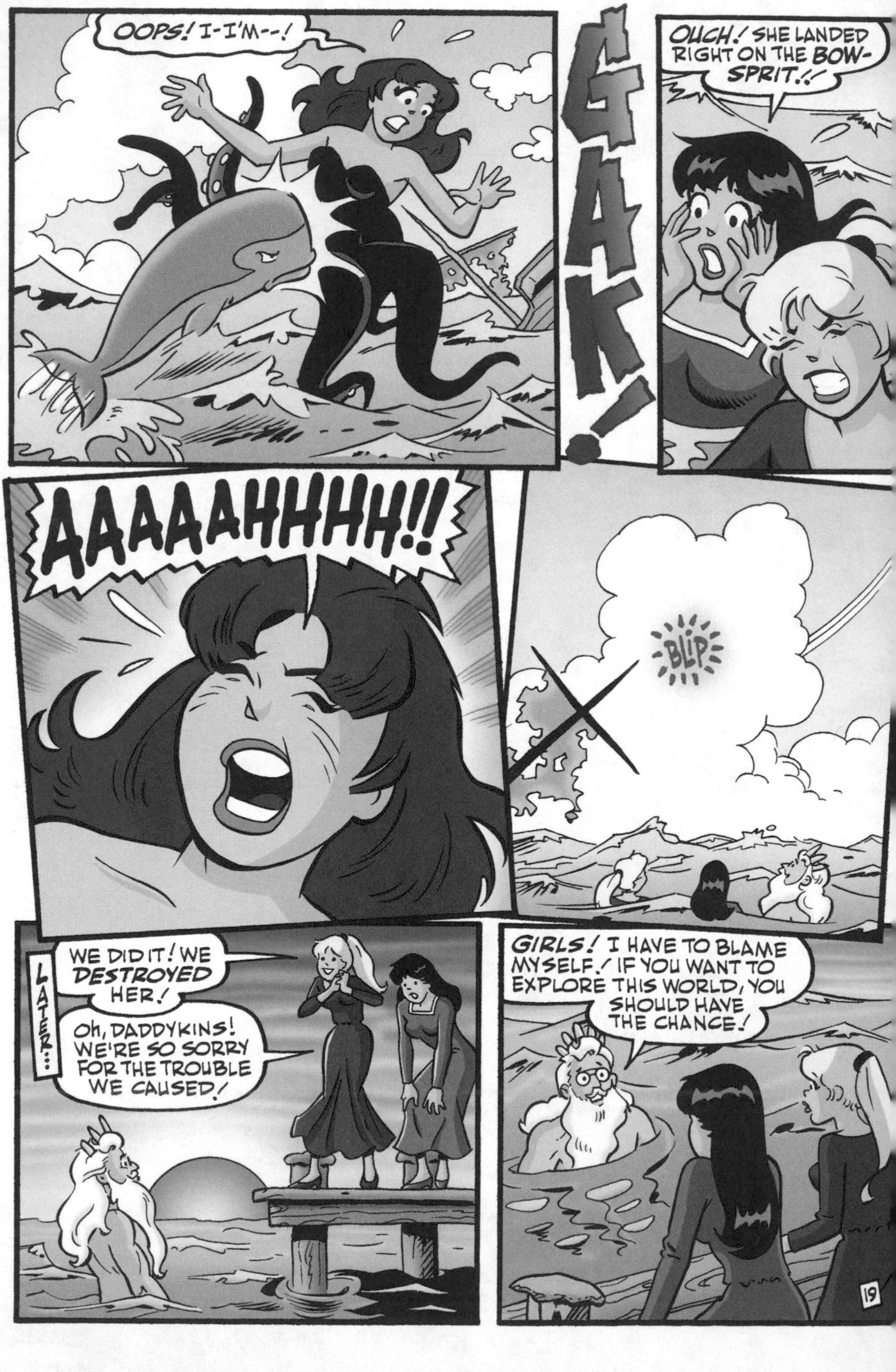
OOPS! I-I'M--!
GAK!
OUCH! SHE LANDED RIGHT ON THE BOW-SPRIT!!
AAAAAHHHH!!
BLIP
LATER...
WE DID IT! WE DESTROYED HER!
Oh, DADDYKINS! WE'RE SO SORRY FOR THE TROUBLE WE CAUSED!
GIRLS! I HAVE TO BLAME MYSELF! IF YOU WANT TO EXPLORE THIS WORLD, YOU SHOULD HAVE THE CHANCE!
19

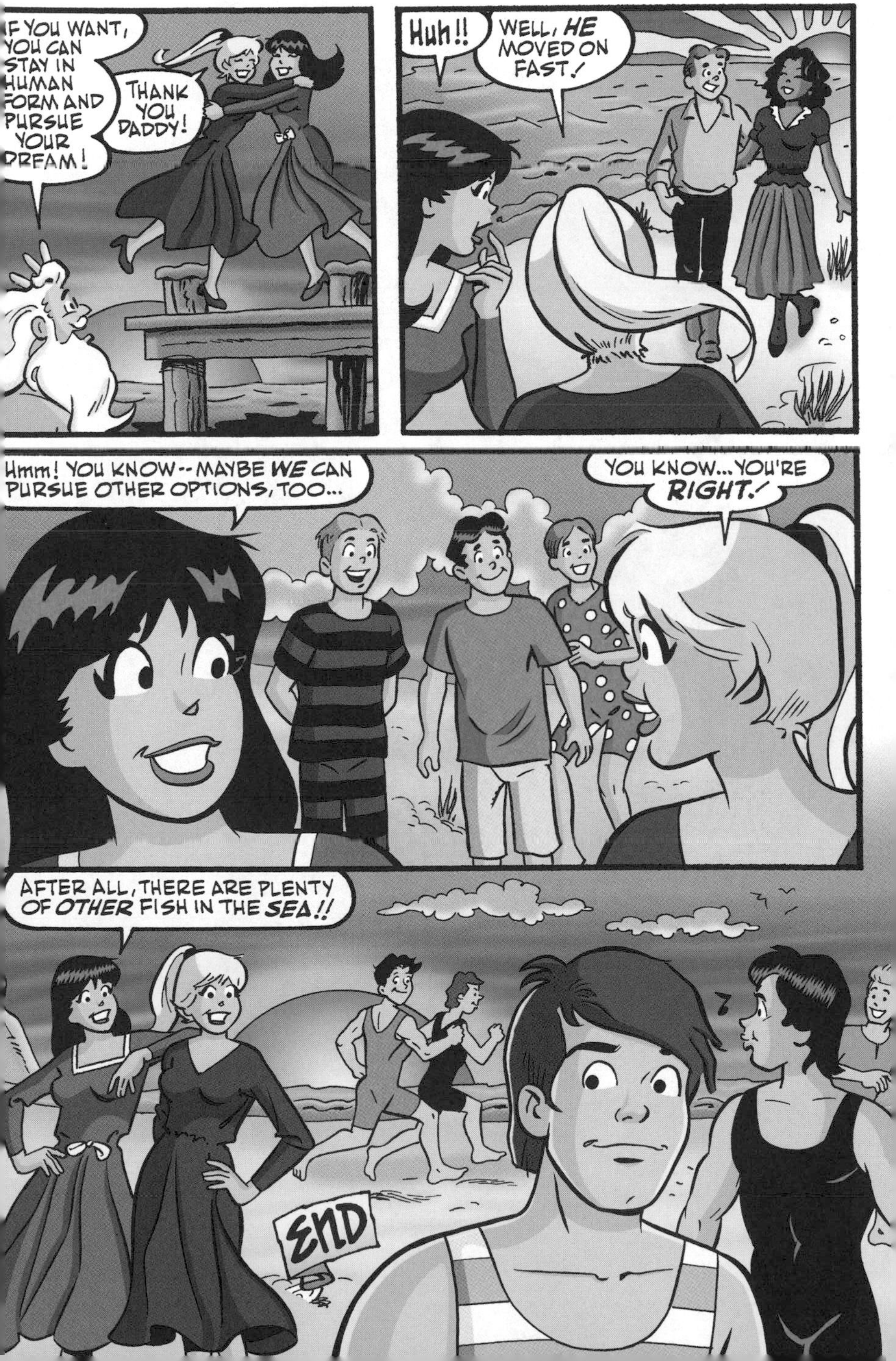
IF YOU WANT, YOU CAN STAY IN HUMAN FORM AND PURSUE YOUR DREAM!
THANK YOU DADDY!
Huh!!
WELL, HE MOVED ON FAST!
Hmm! YOU KNOW--MAYBE WE CAN PURSUE OTHER OPTIONS, TOO...
YOU KNOW... YOU'RE RIGHT!
AFTER ALL, THERE ARE PLENTY OF OTHER FISH IN THE SEA!!
END

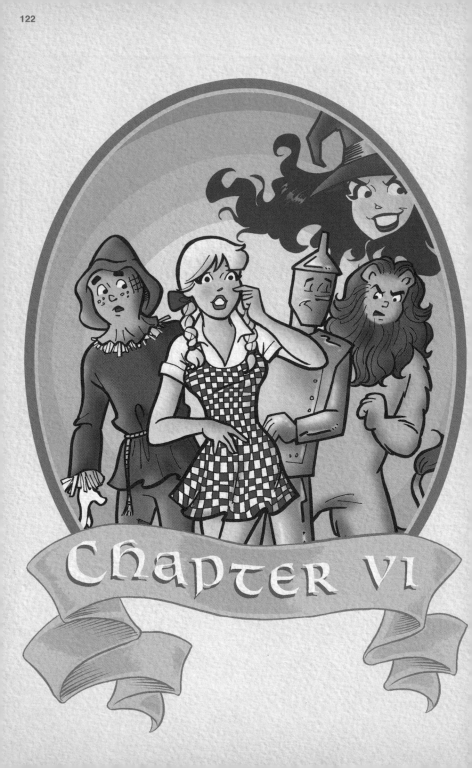

CHAPTER VI

THERES NO PLACE * * * * LIKE * * * * RIVERDALE

In "There's No Place Like Riverdale," a bump on the head sends Betty into a literal tornado of excitement, as she and her faithful feline Caramel skip down the yellow-brick road and run into a host of odd characters, including a munchkin, a brainless scarecrow, a pizza-loving tin man and an egotistical lion.

It's all part of Betty's journey to find the wizard of the strange land of Oz and figure out how to get back to Riverdale. It's made all the trickier by the Wicked Witch of the East, Veronica, who has her sights set on Betty and her band of heroes.

Will Betty ever find her way home, or is she stuck in Oz forever?

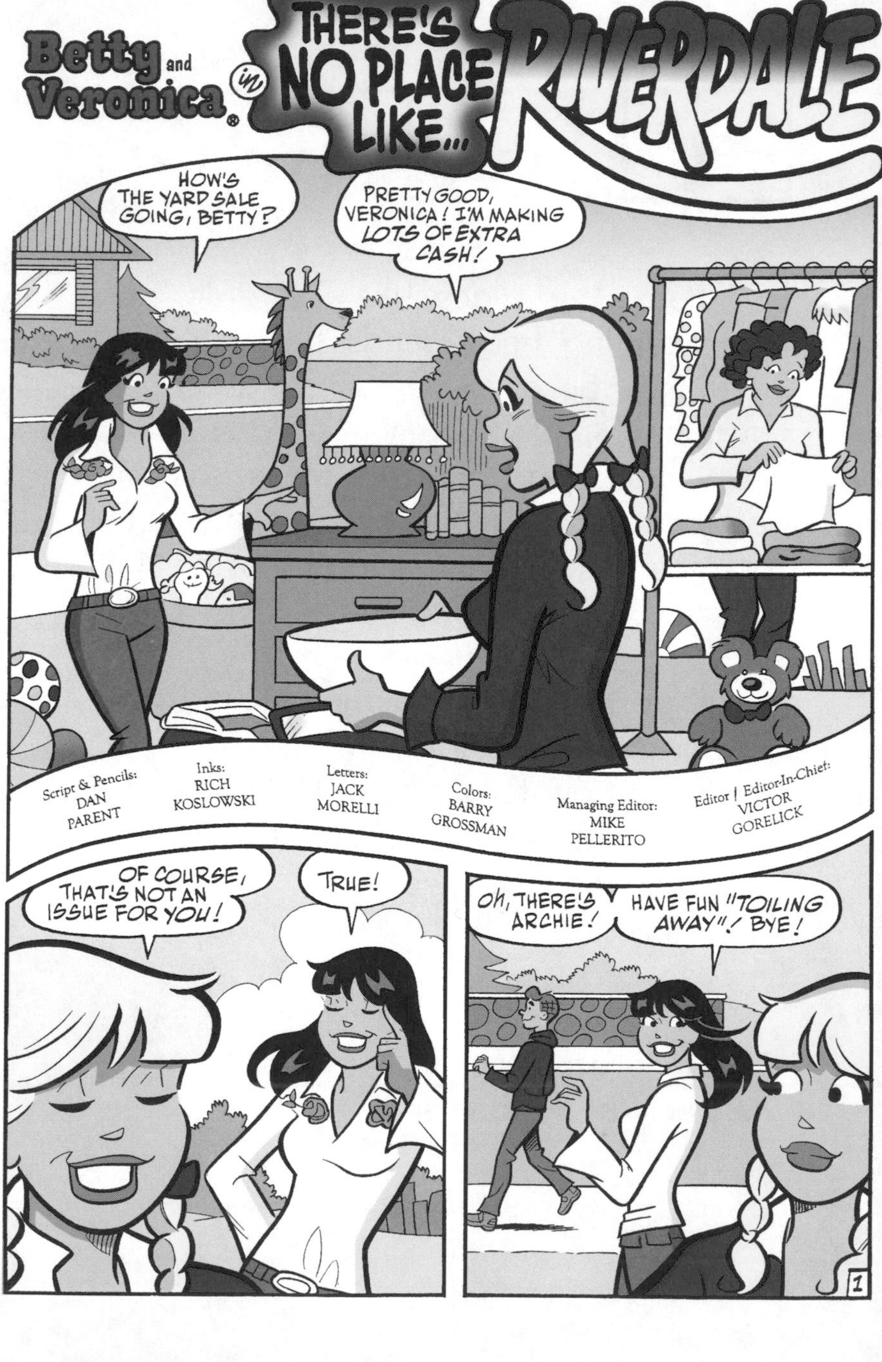
Betty and Veronica
in
THERE'S NO PLACE LIKE... RIVERDALE
HOW'S THE YARD SALE GOING, BETTY?
PRETTY GOOD, VERONICA! I'M MAKING LOTS OF EXTRA CASH!
Script & Pencils: DAN PARENT
Inks: RICH KOSLOWSKI
Letters: JACK MORELLI
Colors: BARRY GROSSMAN
Managing Editor: MIKE PELLERITO
Editor / Editor-In-Chief: VICTOR GORELICK
OF COURSE, THAT'S NOT AN ISSUE FOR YOU!
TRUE!
OH, THERE'S ARCHIE!
HAVE FUN "TOILING AWAY"! BYE!
1

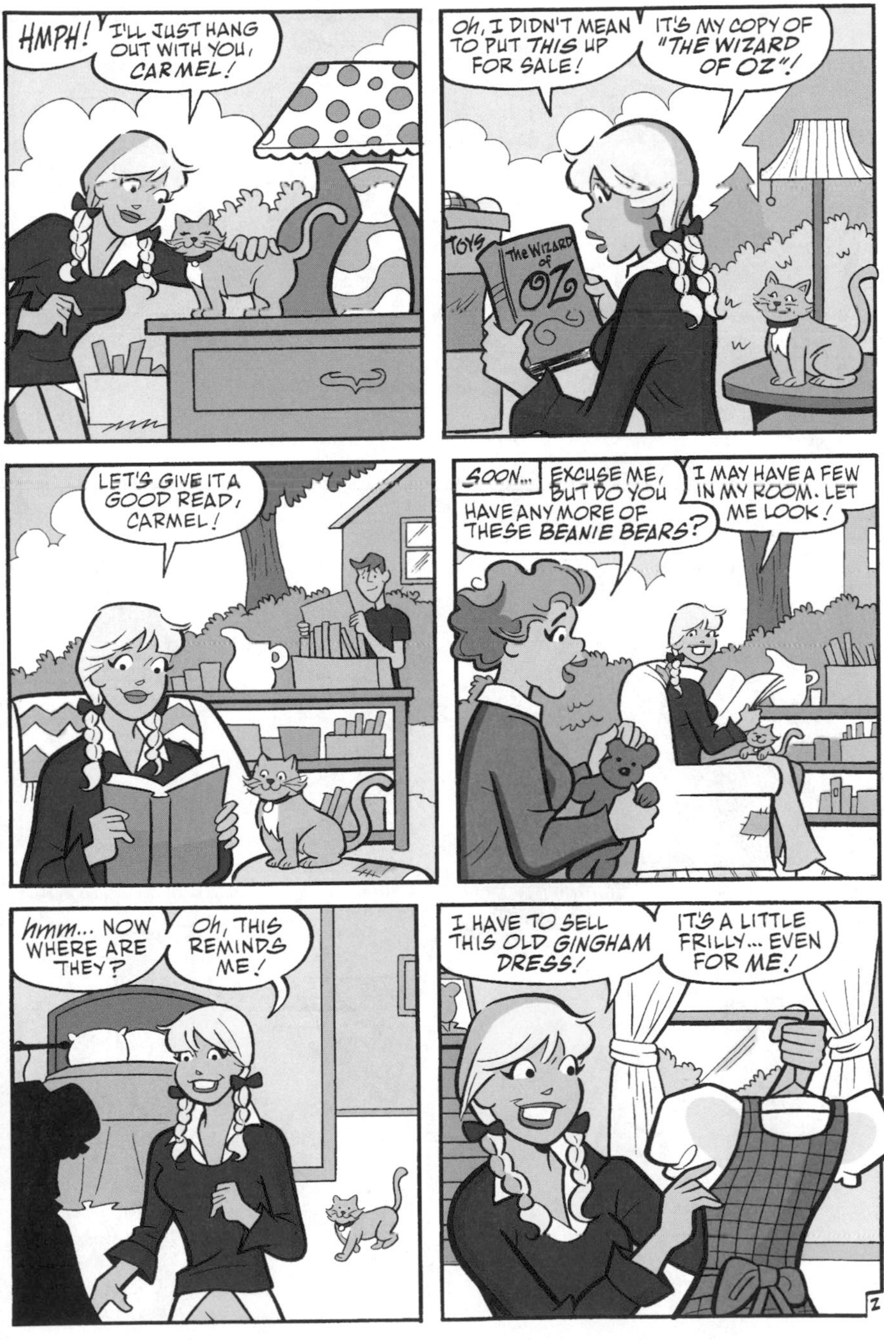
HMPH!
I'LL JUST HANG OUT WITH YOU, CARMEL!
Oh, I DIDN'T MEAN TO PUT THIS UP FOR SALE!
IT'S MY COPY OF "THE WIZARD OF OZ"!
TOYS
The Wizard of OZ
LET'S GIVE IT A GOOD READ, CARMEL!
SOON...
EXCUSE ME, BUT DO YOU HAVE ANY MORE OF THESE BEANIE BEARS?
I MAY HAVE A FEW IN MY ROOM. LET ME LOOK!
hmm... NOW WHERE ARE THEY?
Oh, THIS REMINDS ME!
I HAVE TO SELL THIS OLD GINGHAM DRESS!
IT'S A LITTLE FRILLY... EVEN FOR ME!
2

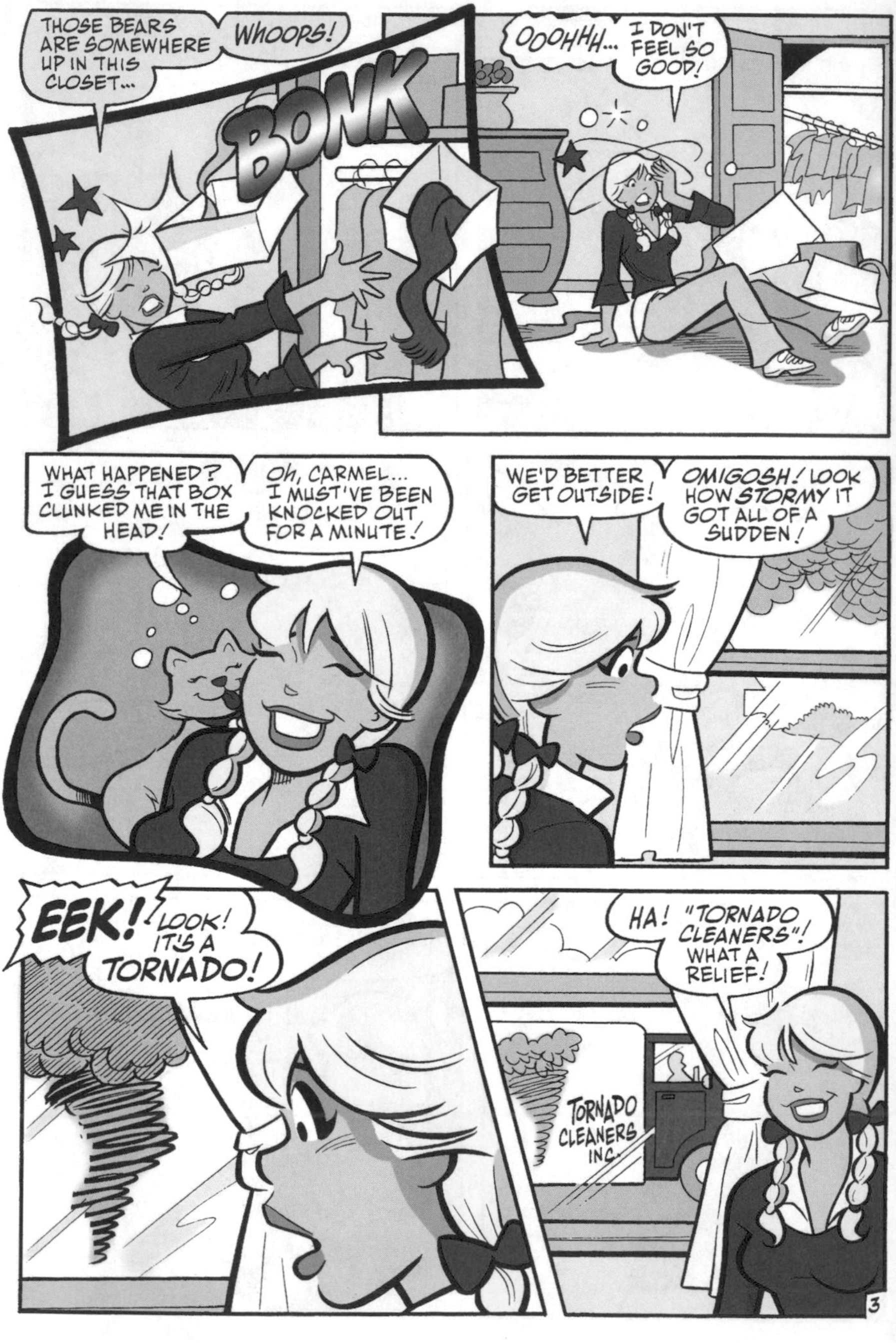
THOSE BEARS ARE SOMEWHERE UP IN THIS CLOSET...
WHOOPS!
BONK
OOOHHH... I DON'T FEEL SO GOOD!
WHAT HAPPENED? I GUESS THAT BOX CLUNKED ME IN THE HEAD!
Oh, CARMEL... I MUST'VE BEEN KNOCKED OUT FOR A MINUTE!
WE'D BETTER GET OUTSIDE!
OMIGOSH! LOOK HOW STORMY IT GOT ALL OF A SUDDEN!
EEK! LOOK! IT'S A TORNADO!
HA! "TORNADO CLEANERS"! WHAT A RELIEF!
TORNADO CLEANERS INC.
3

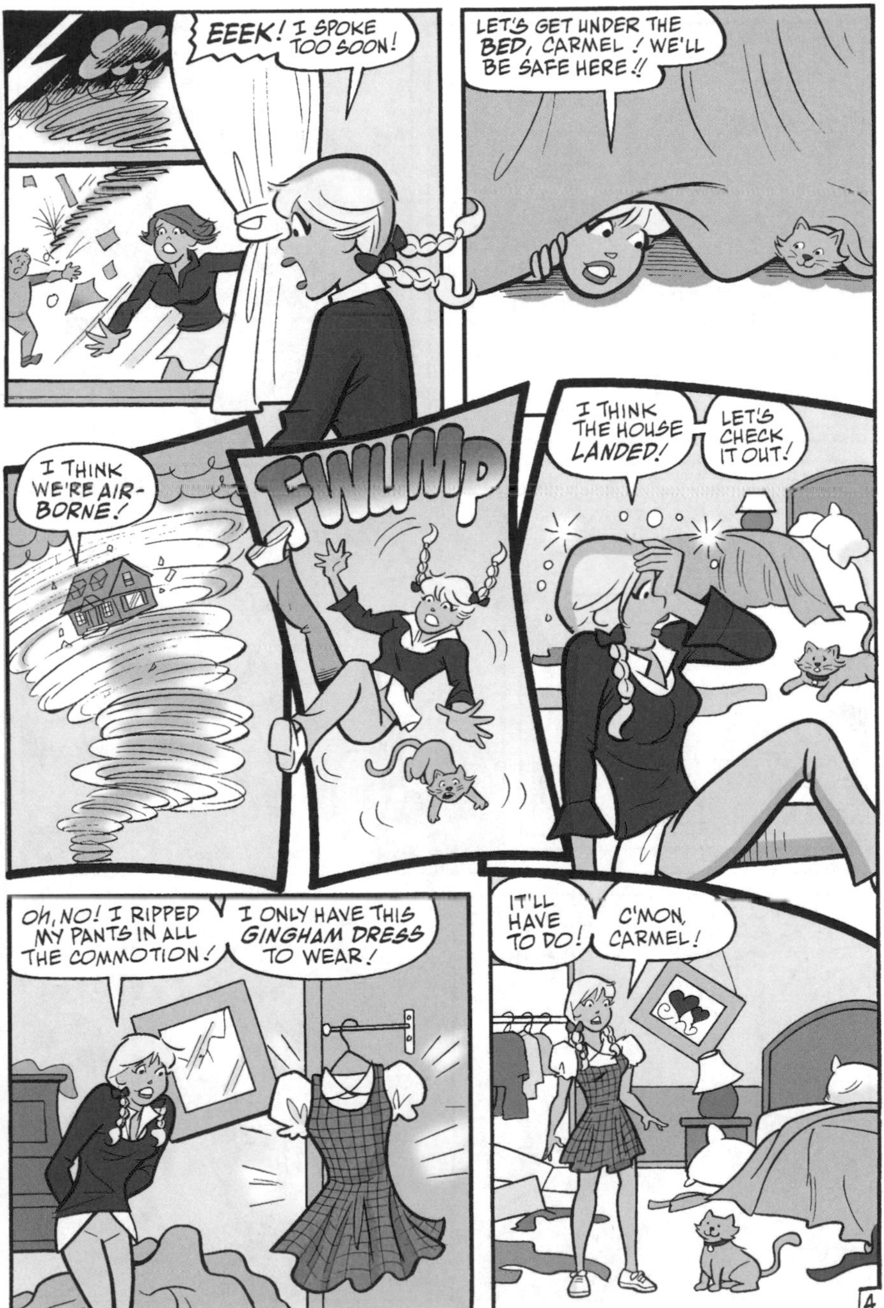
EEEK! I SPOKE TOO SOON!
LET'S GET UNDER THE BED, CARMEL! WE'LL BE SAFE HERE!!
I THINK WE'RE AIR-BORNE!
FWUMP
I THINK THE HOUSE LANDED!
LET'S CHECK IT OUT!
Oh, NO! I RIPPED MY PANTS IN ALL THE COMMOTION!
I ONLY HAVE THIS GINGHAM DRESS TO WEAR!
IT'LL HAVE TO DO!
C'MON, CARMEL!
4

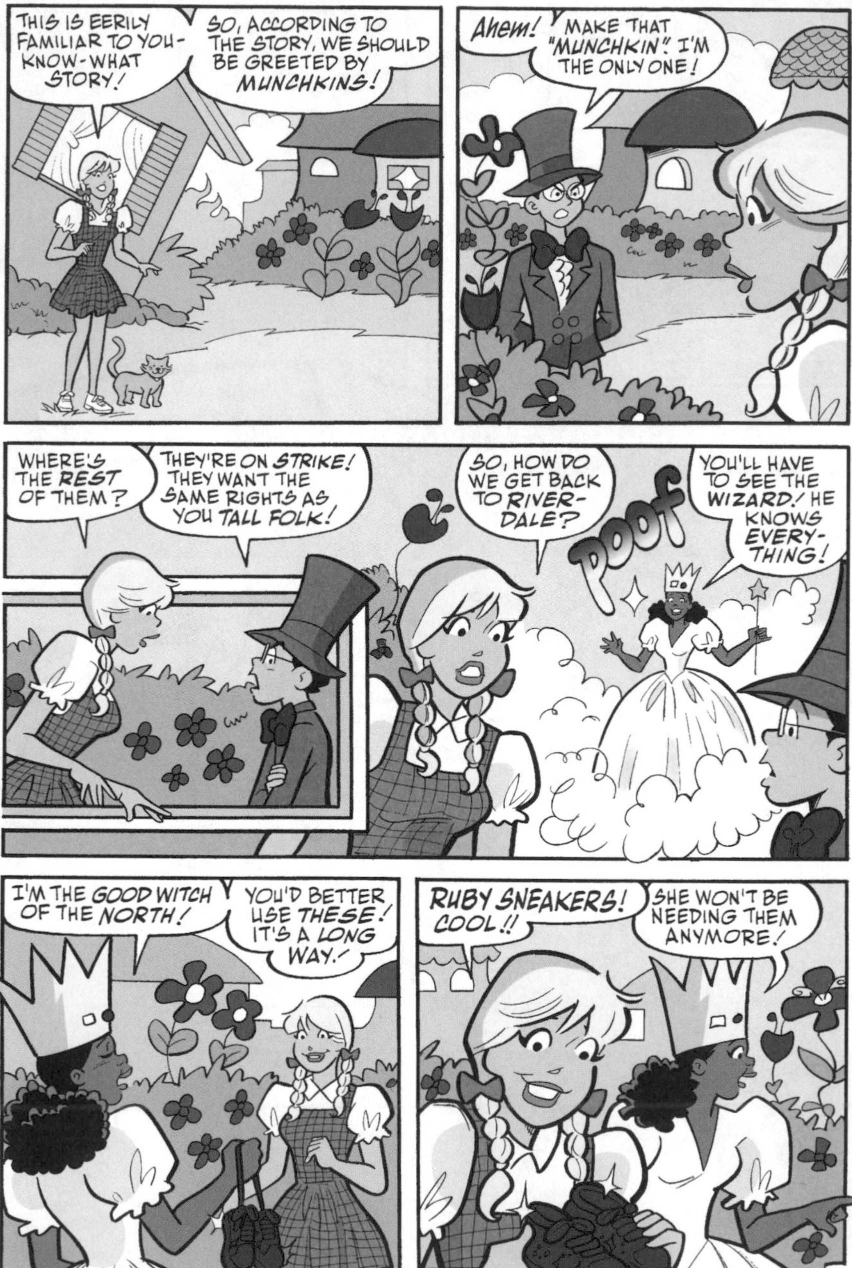
THIS IS EERILY FAMILIAR TO YOU-KNOW-WHAT STORY!
SO, ACCORDING TO THE STORY, WE SHOULD BE GREETED BY MUNCHKINS!
Ahem!
MAKE THAT "MUNCHKIN"! I'M THE ONLY ONE!
WHERE'S THE REST OF THEM?
THEY'RE ON STRIKE! THEY WANT THE SAME RIGHTS AS YOU TALL FOLK!
SO, HOW DO WE GET BACK TO RIVER-DALE?
POOF
YOU'LL HAVE TO SEE THE WIZARD! HE KNOWS EVERY-THING!
I'M THE GOOD WITCH OF THE NORTH!
YOU'D BETTER USE THESE! IT'S A LONG WAY!
RUBY SNEAKERS! COOL!!
SHE WON'T BE NEEDING THEM ANYMORE!
5

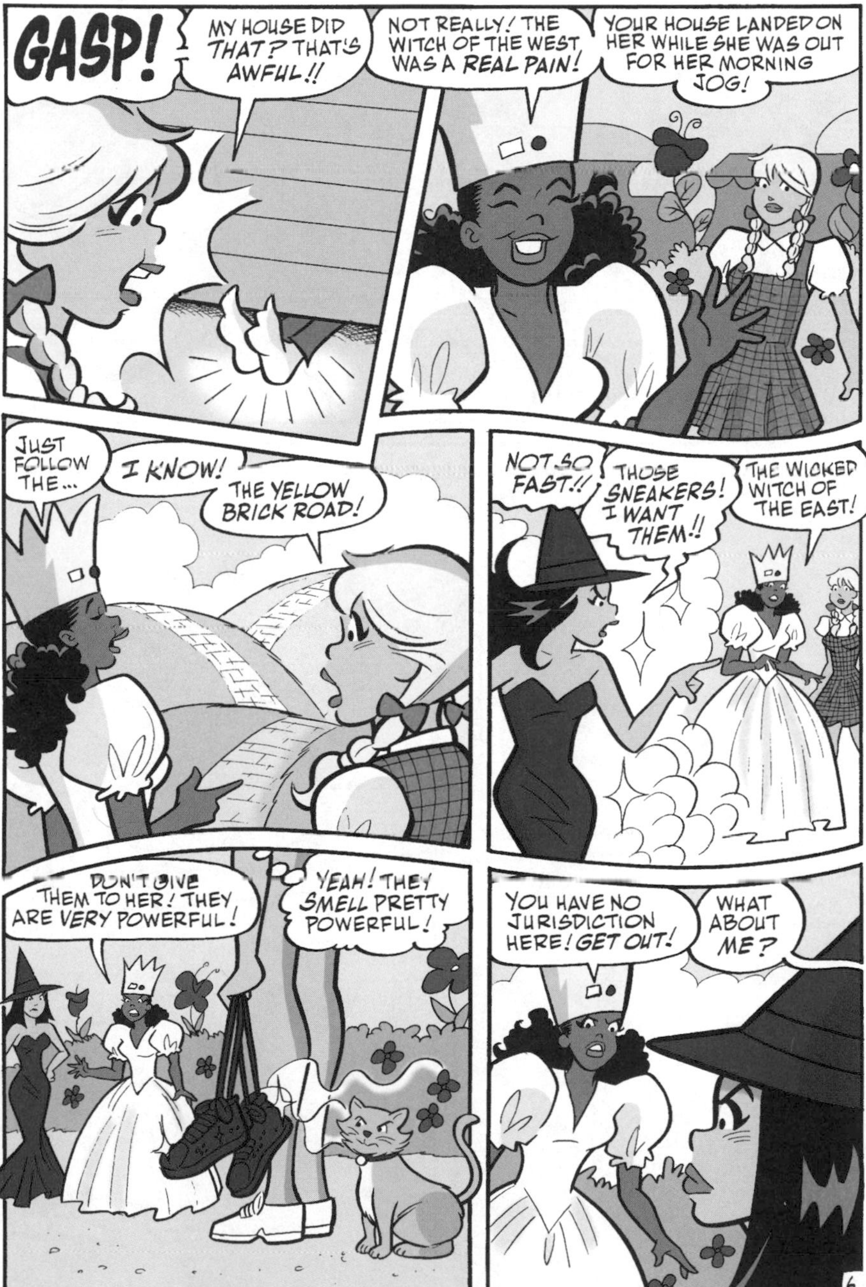
GASP!
MY HOUSE DID THAT? THAT'S AWFUL!!
NOT REALLY! THE WITCH OF THE WEST WAS A REAL PAIN!
YOUR HOUSE LANDED ON HER WHILE SHE WAS OUT FOR HER MORNING JOG!
JUST FOLLOW THE...
I KNOW!
THE YELLOW BRICK ROAD!
NOT SO FAST!!
THOSE SNEAKERS! I WANT THEM!!
THE WICKED WITCH OF THE EAST!
DON'T GIVE THEM TO HER! THEY ARE VERY POWERFUL!
YEAH! THEY SMELL PRETTY POWERFUL!
YOU HAVE NO JURISDICTION HERE! GET OUT!
WHAT ABOUT ME?
6

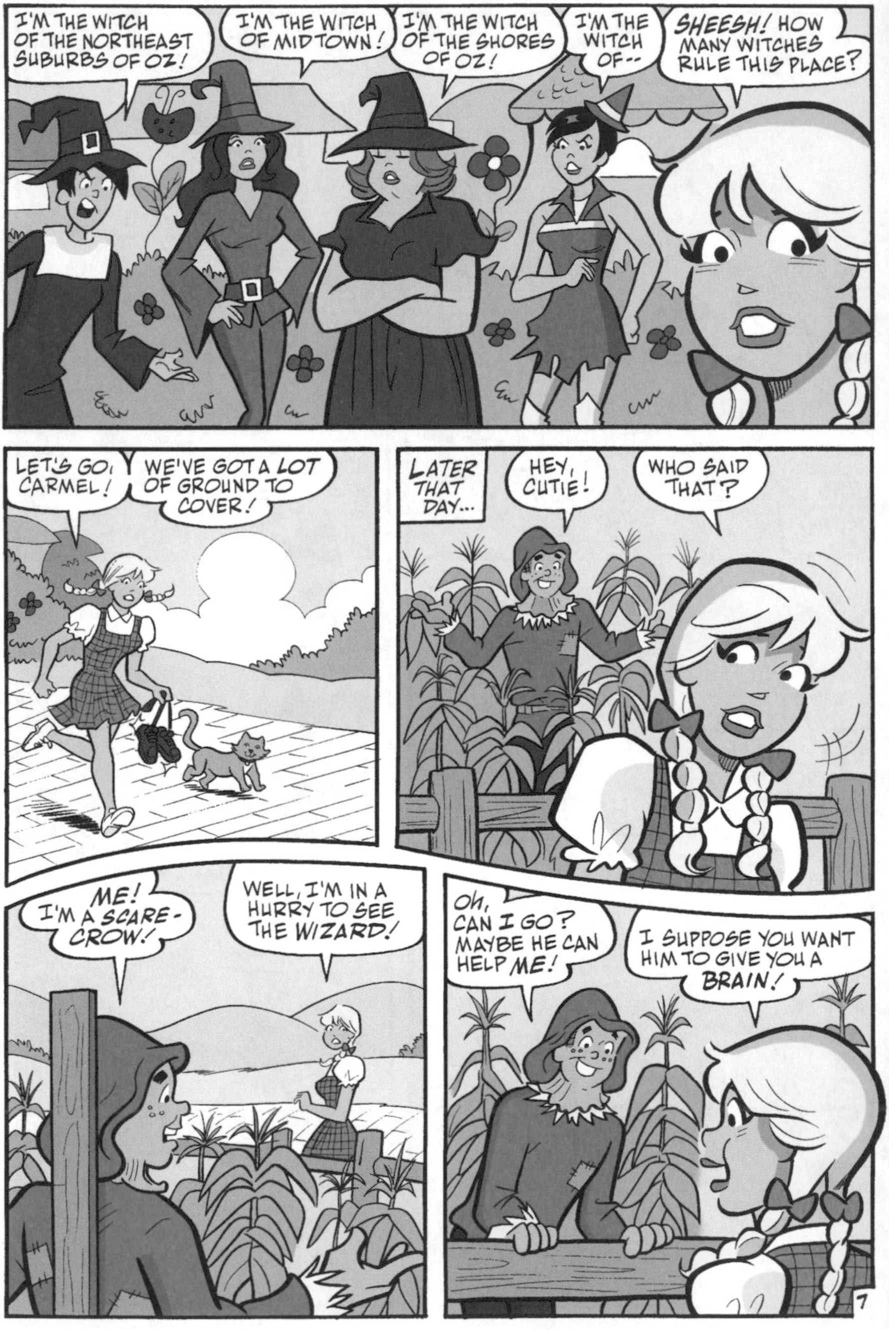
I'M THE WITCH OF THE NORTHEAST SUBURBS OF OZ!
I'M THE WITCH OF MIDTOWN!
I'M THE WITCH OF THE SHORES OF OZ!
I'M THE WITCH OF--
SHEESH! HOW MANY WITCHES RULE THIS PLACE?
LET'S GO, CARMEL!
WE'VE GOT A LOT OF GROUND TO COVER!
LATER THAT DAY...
HEY, CUTIE!
WHO SAID THAT?
ME! I'M A SCARE-CROW!
WELL, I'M IN A HURRY TO SEE THE WIZARD!
Oh, CAN I GO? MAYBE HE CAN HELP ME!
I SUPPOSE YOU WANT HIM TO GIVE YOU A BRAIN!
7

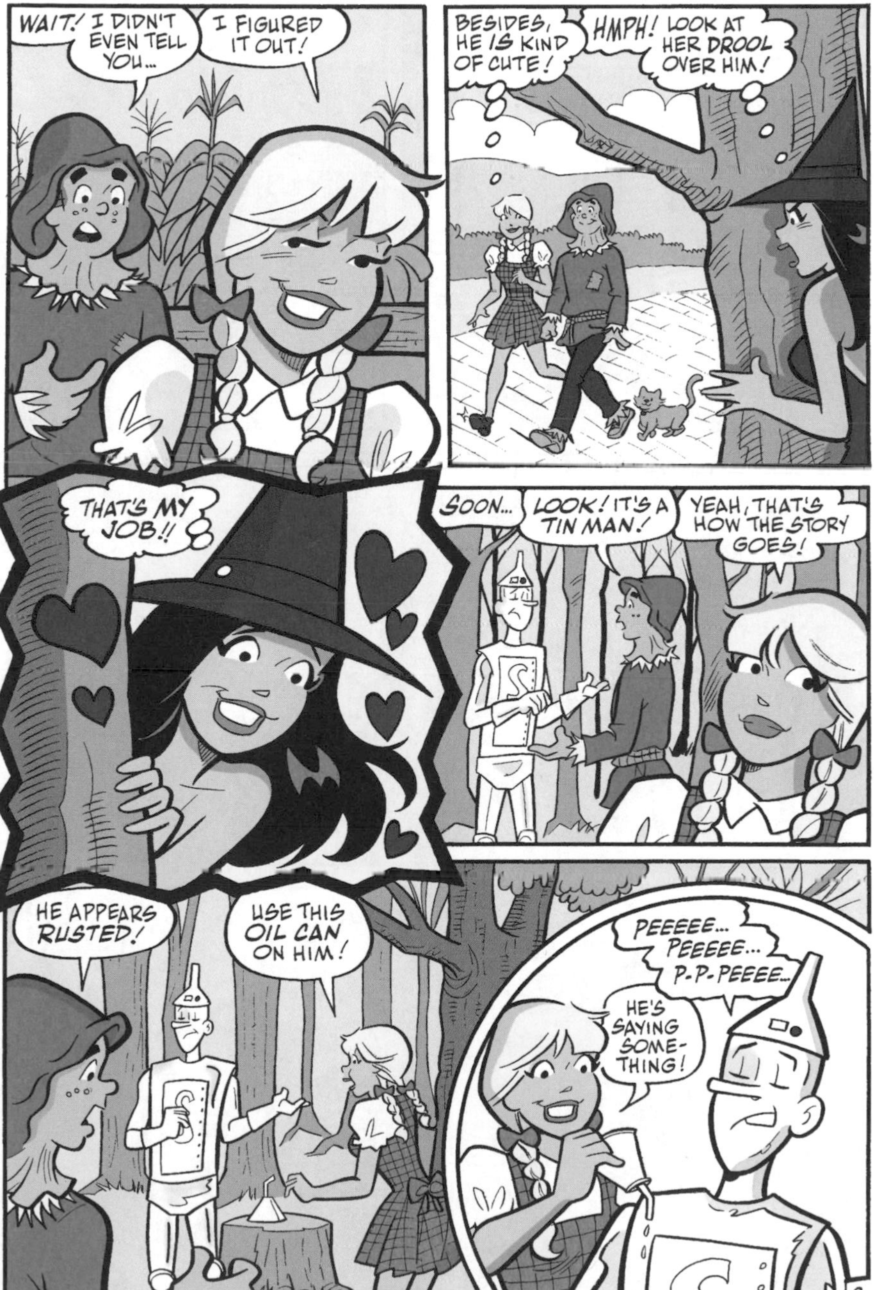
WAIT! I DIDN'T EVEN TELL YOU...
I FIGURED IT OUT!
BESIDES, HE IS KIND OF CUTE!
HMPH! LOOK AT HER DROOL OVER HIM!
THAT'S MY JOB!!
SOON...
LOOK! IT'S A TIN MAN!
YEAH, THAT'S HOW THE STORY GOES!
HE APPEARS RUSTED!
USE THIS OIL CAN ON HIM!
PEEEEE... PEEEEE... P-P-PEEEE...
HE'S SAYING SOME-THING!
8

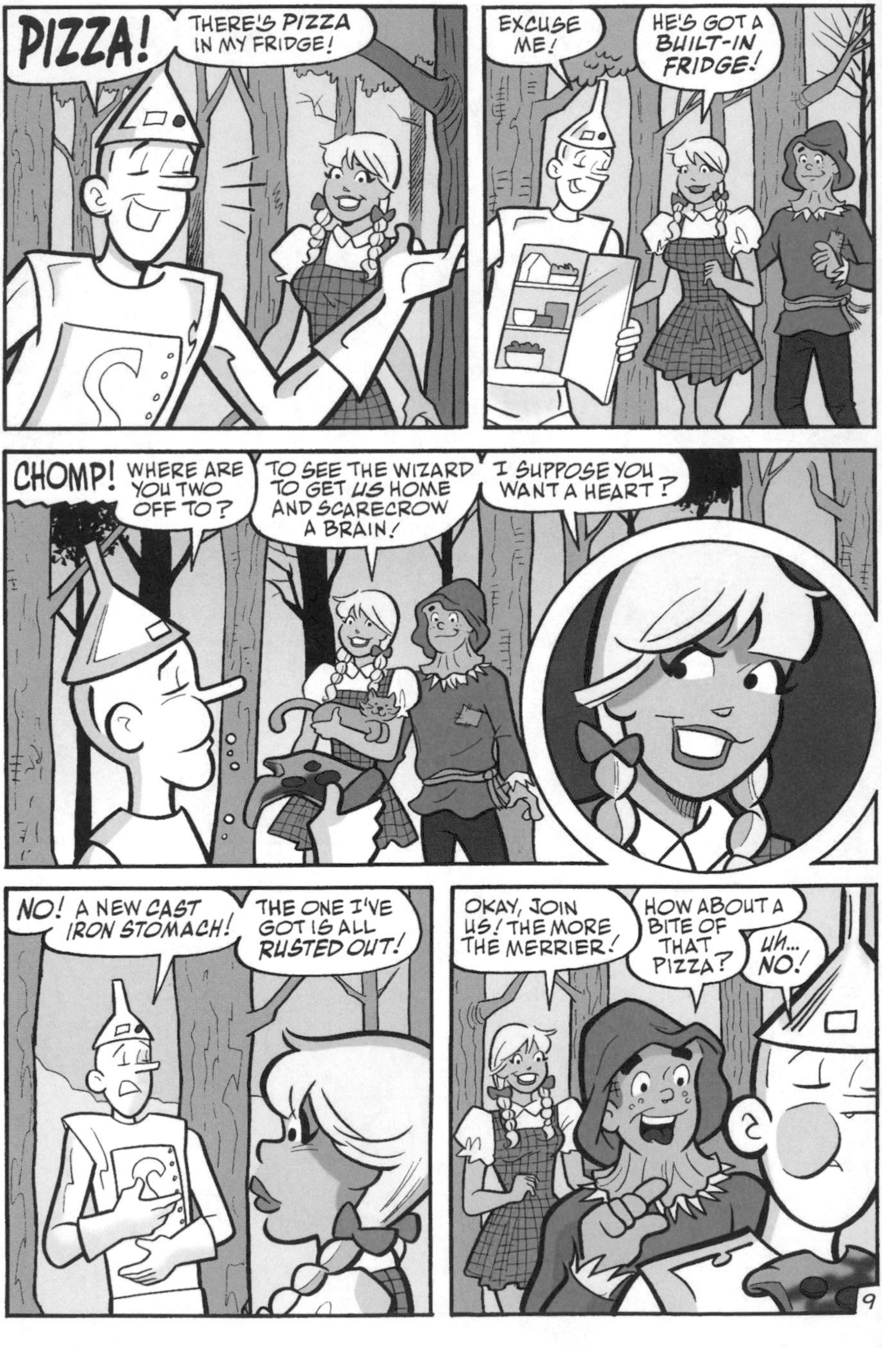
PIZZA!
THERE'S PIZZA IN MY FRIDGE!
EXCUSE ME!
HE'S GOT A BUILT-IN FRIDGE!
CHOMP!
WHERE ARE YOU TWO OFF TO?
TO SEE THE WIZARD TO GET US HOME AND SCARECROW A BRAIN!
I SUPPOSE YOU WANT A HEART?
NO! A NEW CAST IRON STOMACH!
THE ONE I'VE GOT IS ALL RUSTED OUT!
OKAY, JOIN US! THE MORE THE MERRIER!
HOW ABOUT A BITE OF THAT PIZZA?
UH... NO!
9

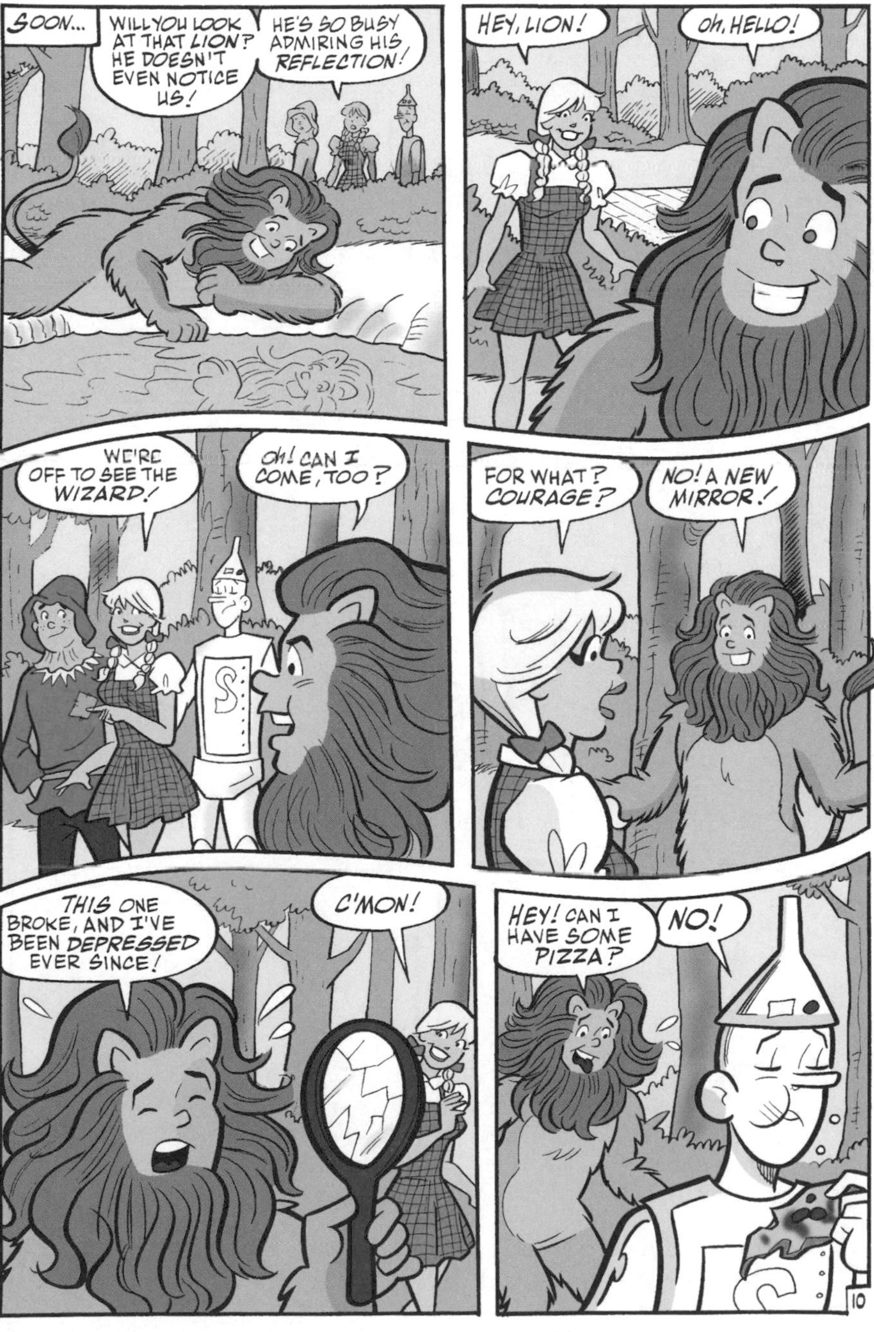
SOON...
WILL YOU LOOK AT THAT LION? HE DOESN'T EVEN NOTICE US!
HE'S SO BUSY ADMIRING HIS REFLECTION!
HEY, LION!
OH, HELLO!
WE'RE OFF TO SEE THE WIZARD!
OH! CAN I COME, TOO?
FOR WHAT? COURAGE?
NO! A NEW MIRROR!
THIS ONE BROKE, AND I'VE BEEN DEPRESSED EVER SINCE!
C'MON!
HEY! CAN I HAVE SOME PIZZA?
NO!
10

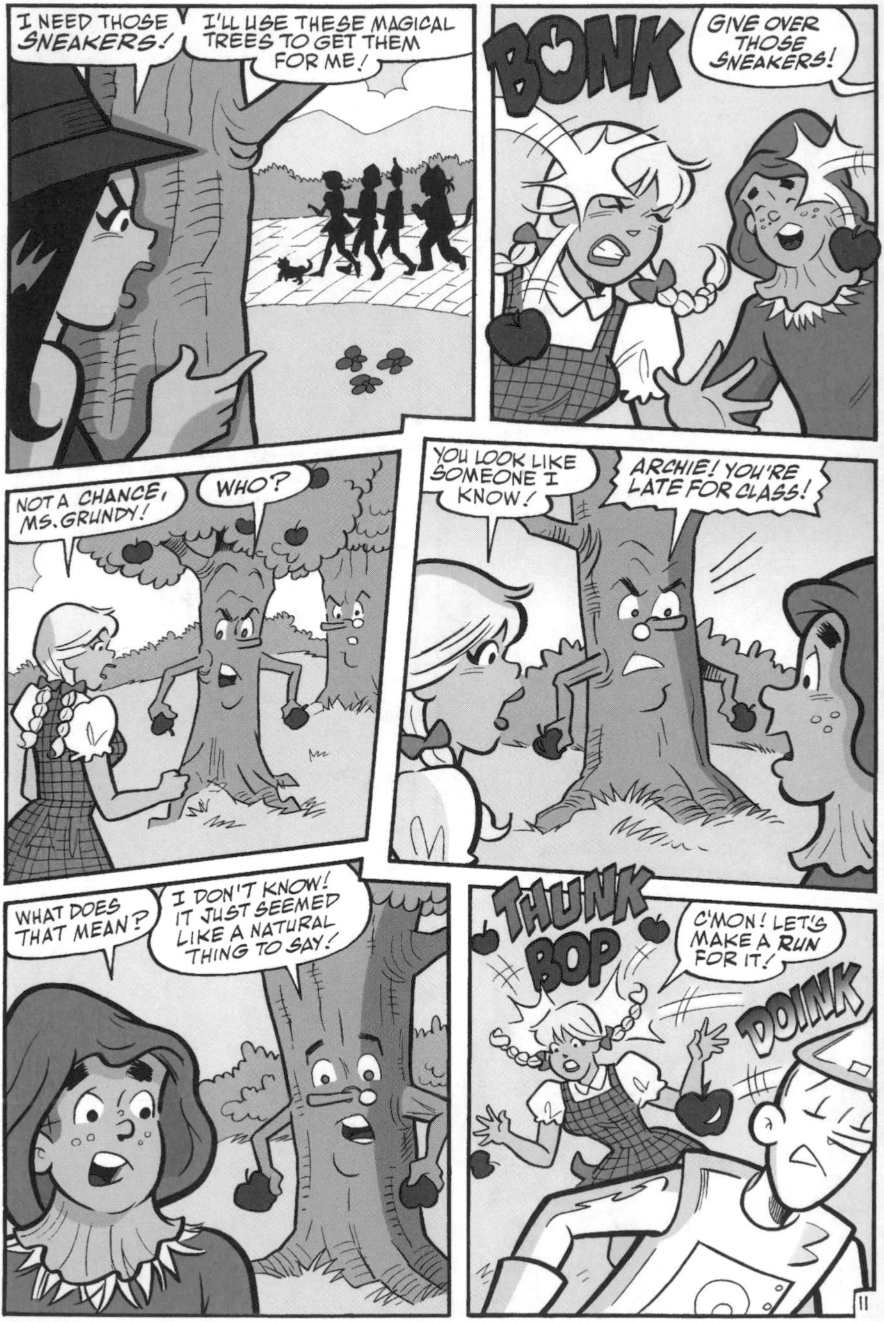
I NEED THOSE SNEAKERS!
I'LL USE THESE MAGICAL TREES TO GET THEM FOR ME!
BONK
GIVE OVER THOSE SNEAKERS!
NOT A CHANCE, MS. GRUNDY!
WHO?
YOU LOOK LIKE SOMEONE I KNOW!
ARCHIE! YOU'RE LATE FOR CLASS!
WHAT DOES THAT MEAN?
I DON'T KNOW! IT JUST SEEMED LIKE A NATURAL THING TO SAY!
THUNK
BOP
C'MON! LET'S MAKE A RUN FOR IT!
DOINK
11

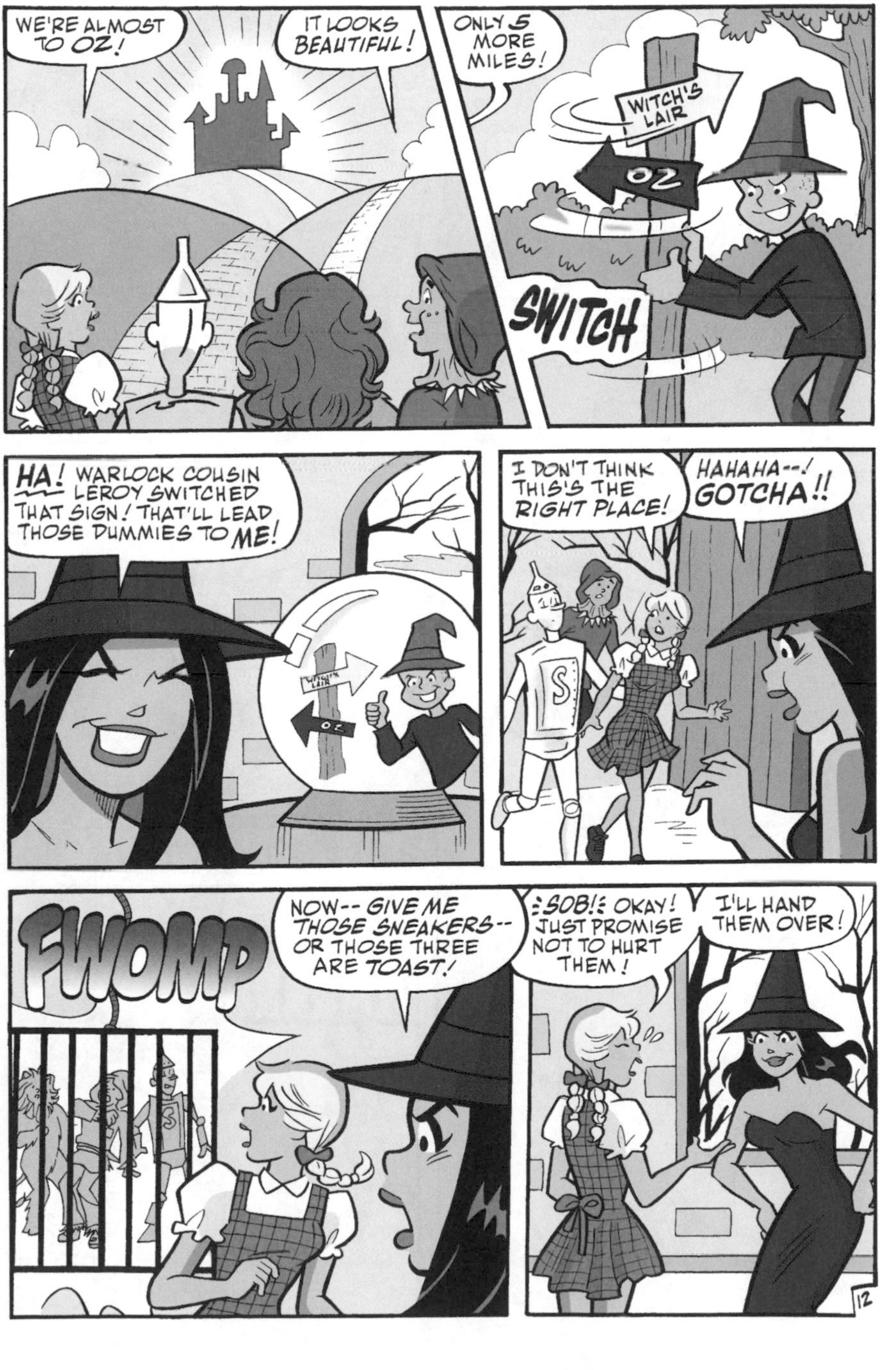
WE'RE ALMOST TO OZ!
IT LOOKS BEAUTIFUL!
ONLY 5 MORE MILES!
WITCH'S LAIR
OZ
SWITCH
HA! WARLOCK COUSIN LEROY SWITCHED THAT SIGN! THAT'LL LEAD THOSE DUMMIES TO ME!
I DON'T THINK THIS'S THE RIGHT PLACE!
HAHAHA--! GOTCHA!!
FWOMP
NOW-- GIVE ME THOSE SNEAKERS-- OR THOSE THREE ARE TOAST!
SOB! OKAY! JUST PROMISE NOT TO HURT THEM!
I'LL HAND THEM OVER!
12

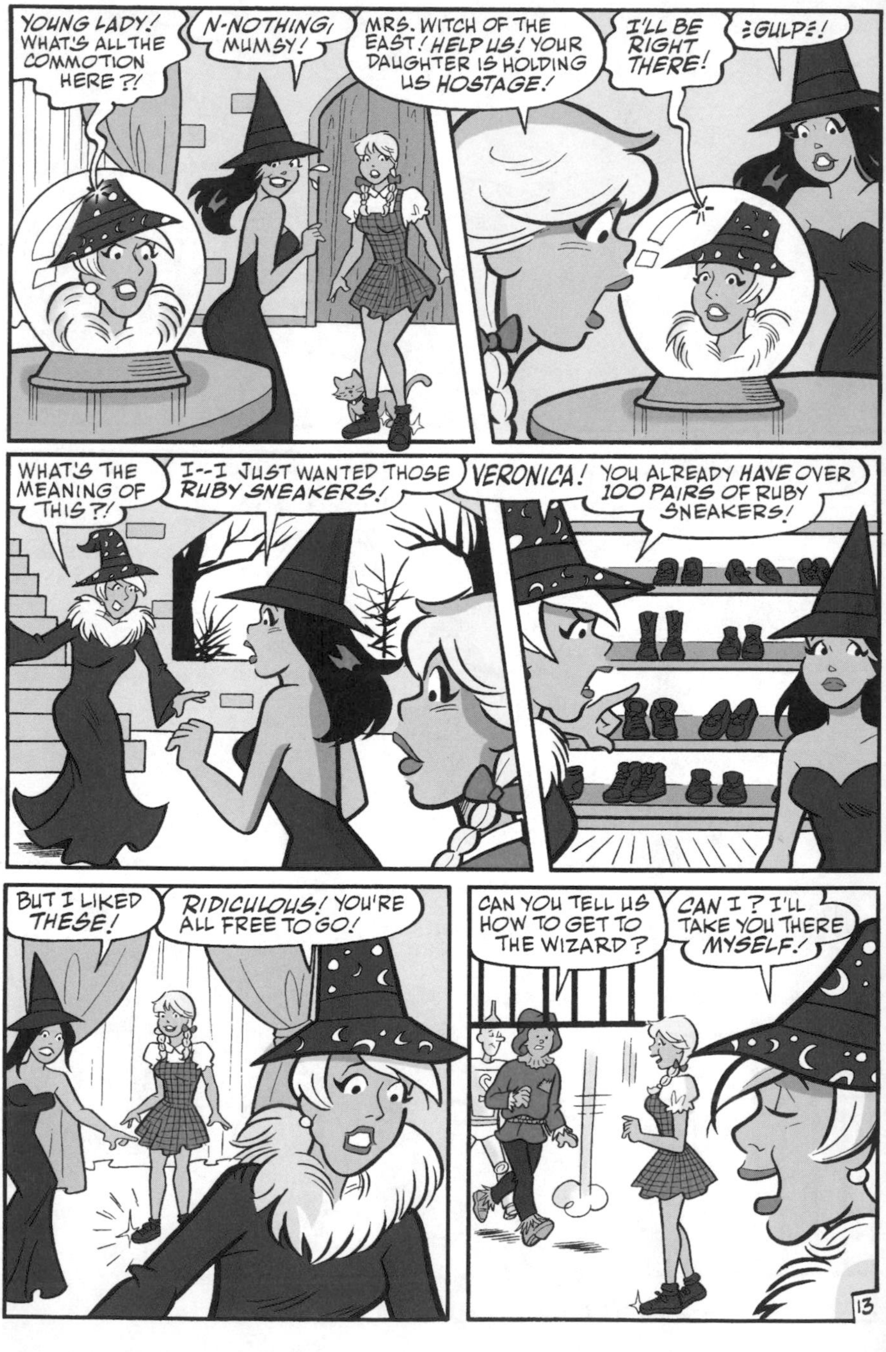
YOUNG LADY! WHAT'S ALL THE COMMOTION HERE?!
N-NOTHING, MUMSY!
MRS. WITCH OF THE EAST! HELP US! YOUR DAUGHTER IS HOLDING US HOSTAGE!
I'LL BE RIGHT THERE!
GULP!
WHAT'S THE MEANING OF THIS?!
I--I JUST WANTED THOSE RUBY SNEAKERS!
VERONICA!
YOU ALREADY HAVE OVER 100 PAIRS OF RUBY SNEAKERS!
BUT I LIKED THESE!
RIDICULOUS! YOU'RE ALL FREE TO GO!
CAN YOU TELL US HOW TO GET TO THE WIZARD?
CAN I? I'LL TAKE YOU THERE MYSELF!
13

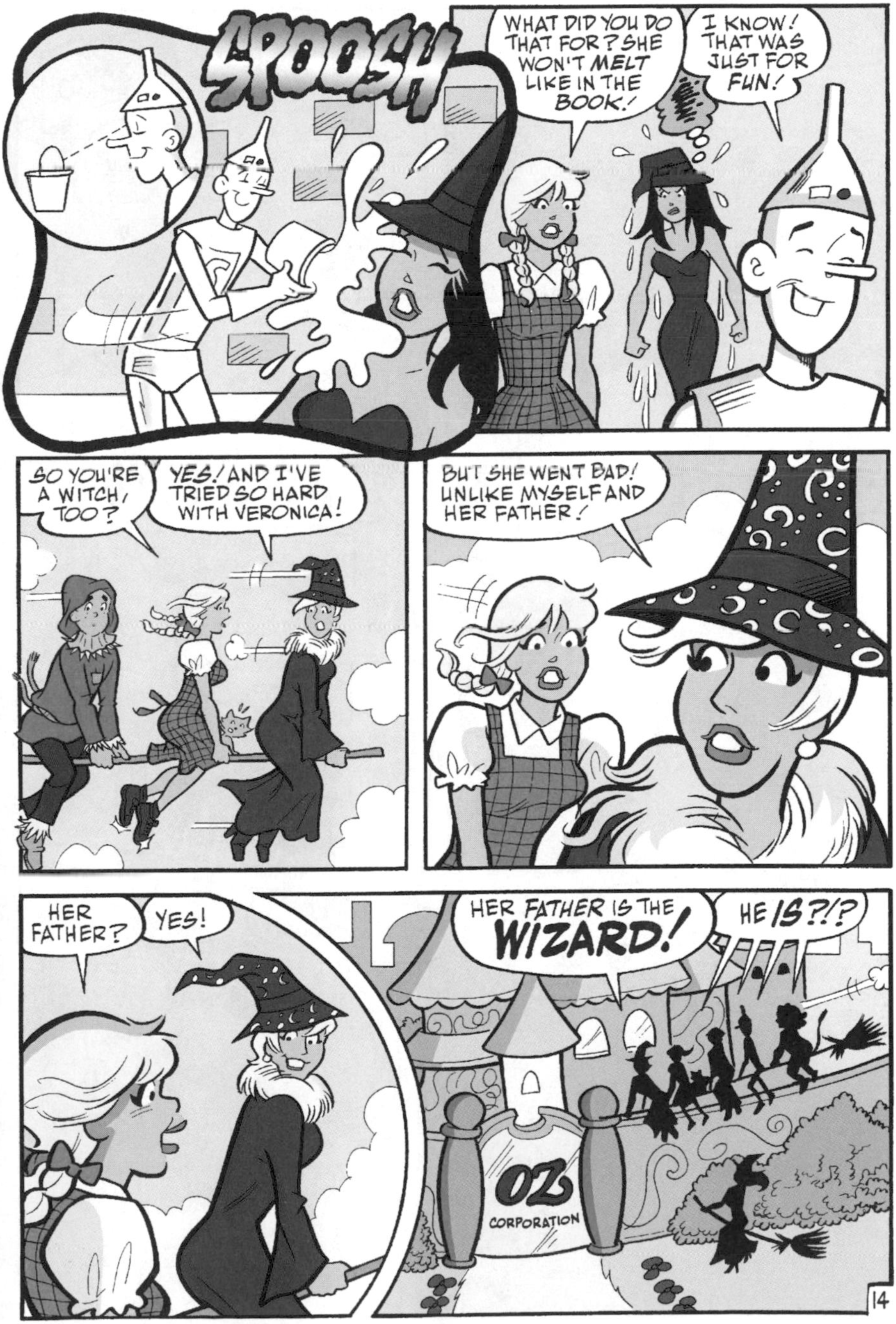
SPOOSH
WHAT DID YOU DO THAT FOR? SHE WON'T MELT LIKE IN THE BOOK!
I KNOW! THAT WAS JUST FOR FUN!
SO YOU'RE A WITCH, TOO?
YES! AND I'VE TRIED SO HARD WITH VERONICA!
BUT SHE WENT BAD! UNLIKE MYSELF AND HER FATHER!
HER FATHER?
YES!
HER FATHER IS THE WIZARD!
HE IS?!?
OZ CORPORATION
14

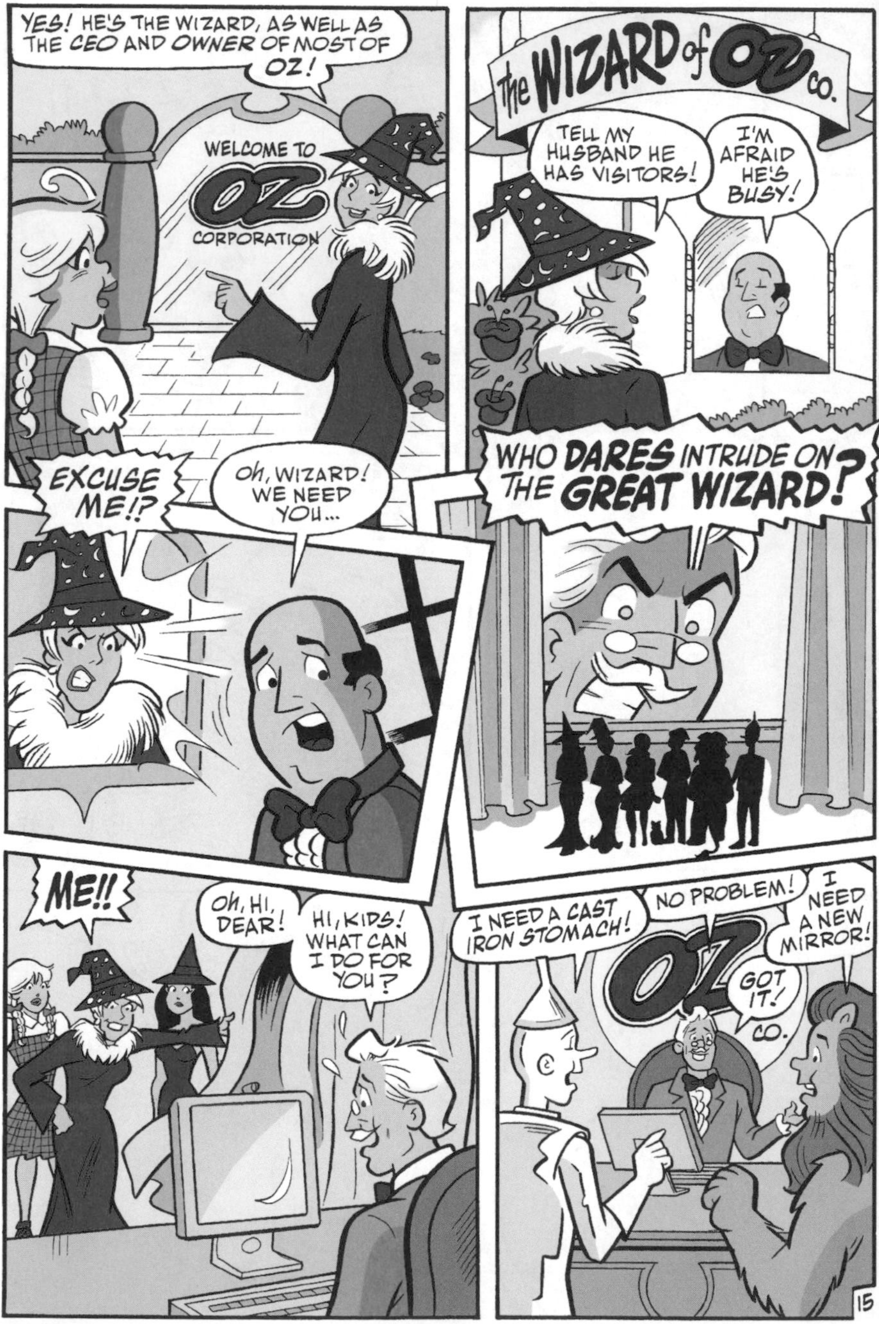
YES! HE'S THE WIZARD, AS WELL AS THE CEO AND OWNER OF MOST OF OZ!
WELCOME TO OZ CORPORATION
the WIZARD of OZ co.
TELL MY HUSBAND HE HAS VISITORS!
I'M AFRAID HE'S BUSY!
EXCUSE ME!?
Oh, WIZARD! WE NEED YOU...
WHO DARES INTRUDE ON THE GREAT WIZARD?
ME!!
Oh, HI, DEAR!
HI, KIDS! WHAT CAN I DO FOR YOU?
I NEED A CAST IRON STOMACH!
NO PROBLEM!
I NEED A NEW MIRROR!
GOT IT!
OZ CO.
15

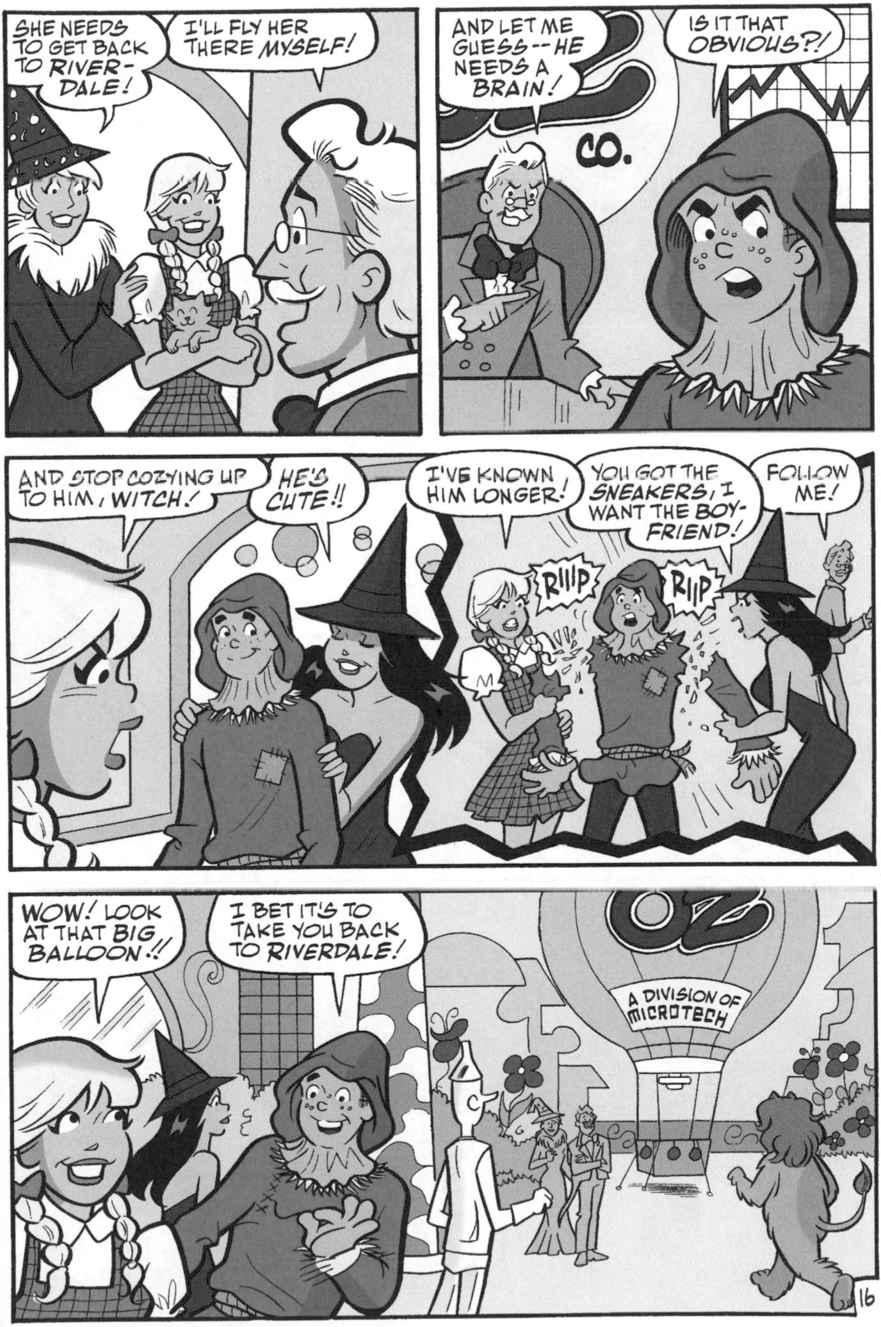
SHE NEEDS TO GET BACK TO RIVER-DALE!
I'LL FLY HER THERE MYSELF!
AND LET ME GUESS -- HE NEEDS A BRAIN!
IS IT THAT OBVIOUS?!
CO.
AND STOP COZYING UP TO HIM, WITCH!
HE'S CUTE!!
I'VE KNOWN HIM LONGER!
YOU GOT THE SNEAKERS, I WANT THE BOY-FRIEND!
RIIP
RIIP
FOLLOW ME!
WOW! LOOK AT THAT BIG BALLOON!!
I BET IT'S TO TAKE YOU BACK TO RIVERDALE!
OZ
A DIVISION OF MICROTECH
16

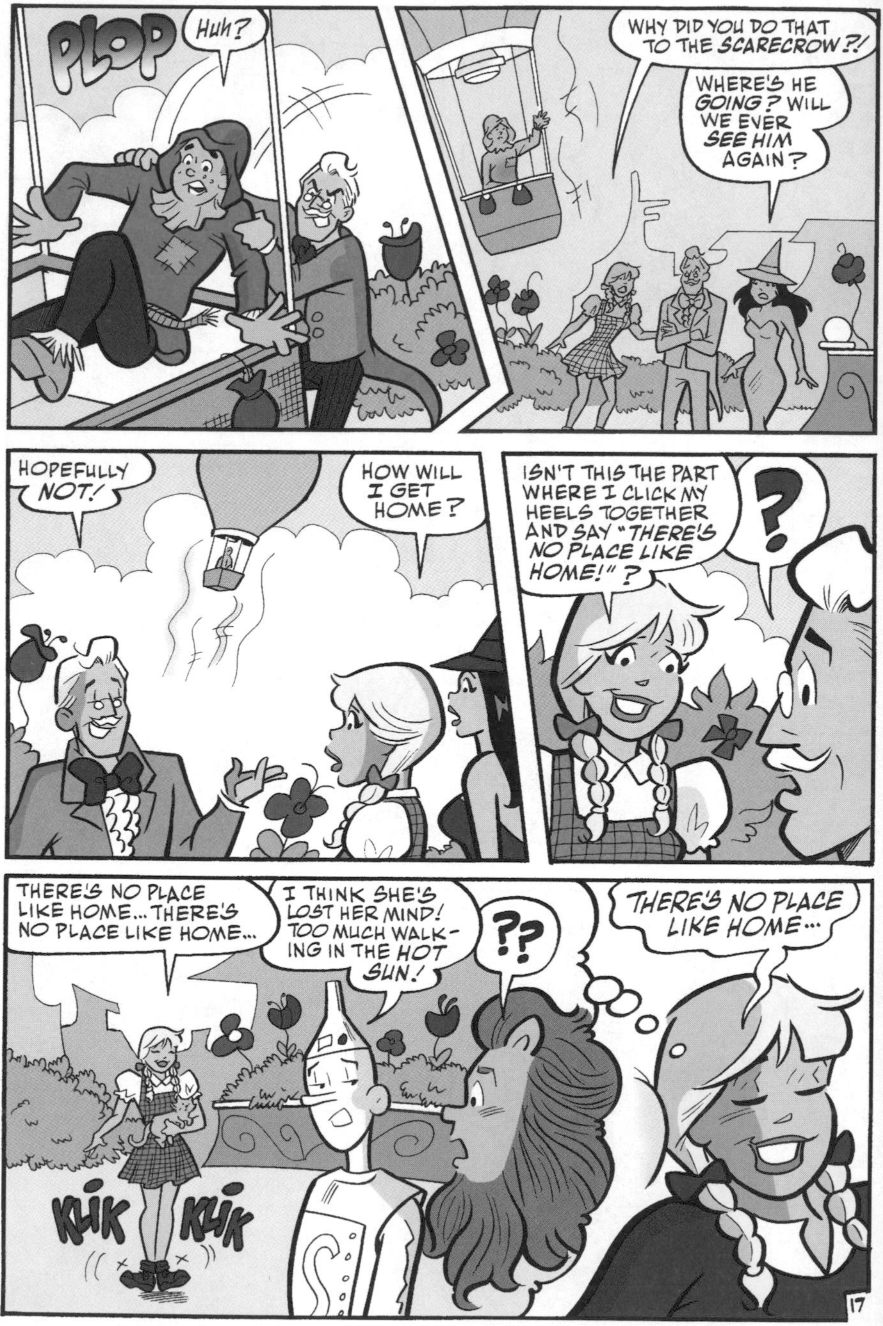
PLOP
Huh?
WHY DID YOU DO THAT TO THE SCARECROW?!
WHERE'S HE GOING? WILL WE EVER SEE HIM AGAIN?
HOPEFULLY NOT!
HOW WILL I GET HOME?
ISN'T THIS THE PART WHERE I CLICK MY HEELS TOGETHER AND SAY "THERE'S NO PLACE LIKE HOME!"?
?
THERE'S NO PLACE LIKE HOME... THERE'S NO PLACE LIKE HOME...
KLIK KLIK
I THINK SHE'S LOST HER MIND! TOO MUCH WALKING IN THE HOT SUN!
??
THERE'S NO PLACE LIKE HOME...
17

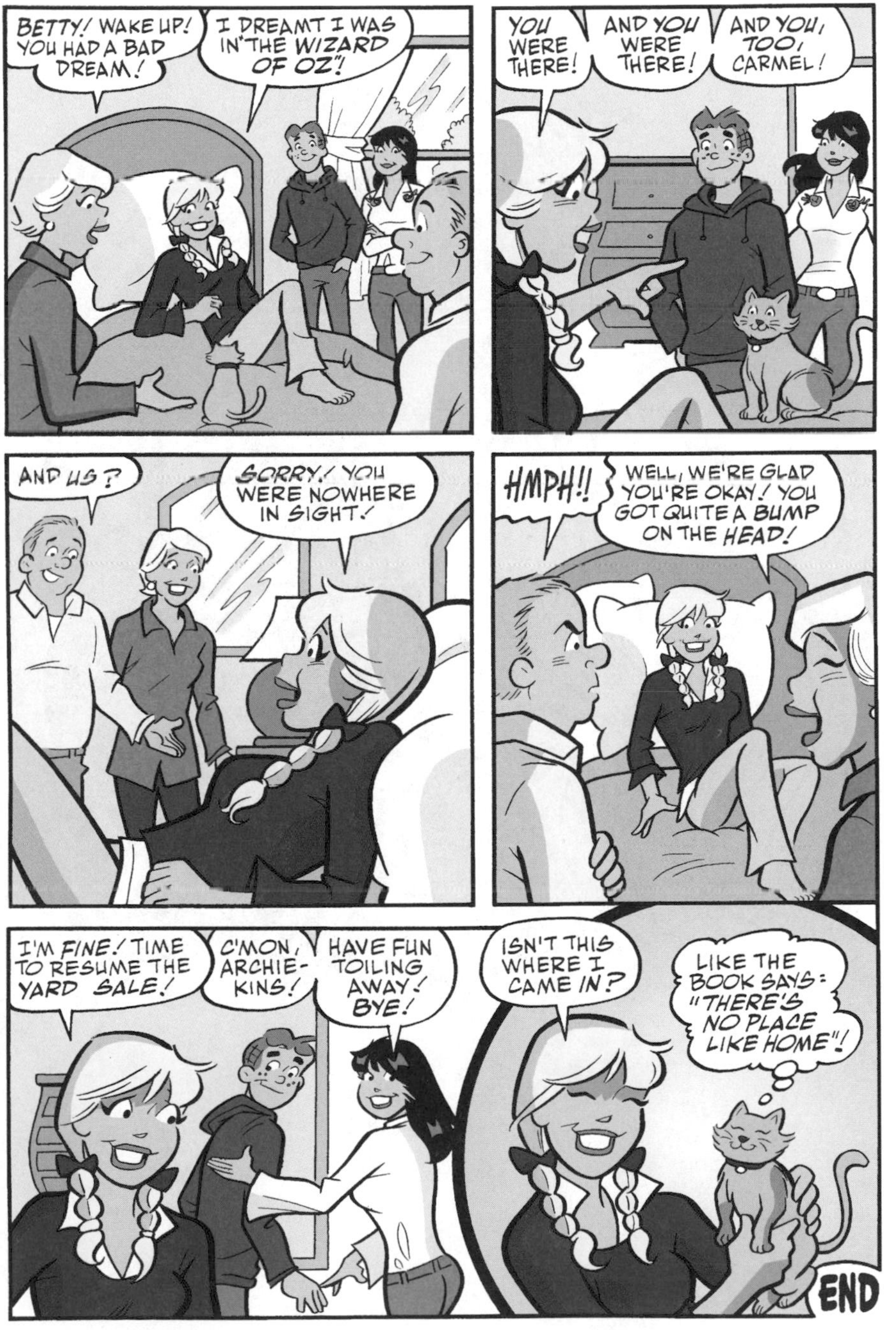
BETTY! WAKE UP! YOU HAD A BAD DREAM!
I DREAMT I WAS IN "THE WIZARD OF OZ"!
YOU WERE THERE!
AND YOU WERE THERE!
AND YOU, TOO, CARMEL!
AND US?
SORRY! YOU WERE NOWHERE IN SIGHT!
HMPH!!
WELL, WE'RE GLAD YOU'RE OKAY! YOU GOT QUITE A BUMP ON THE HEAD!
I'M FINE! TIME TO RESUME THE YARD SALE!
C'MON, ARCHIE-KINS!
HAVE FUN TOILING AWAY! BYE!
ISN'T THIS WHERE I CAME IN?
LIKE THE BOOK SAYS: "THERE'S NO PLACE LIKE HOME"!
END

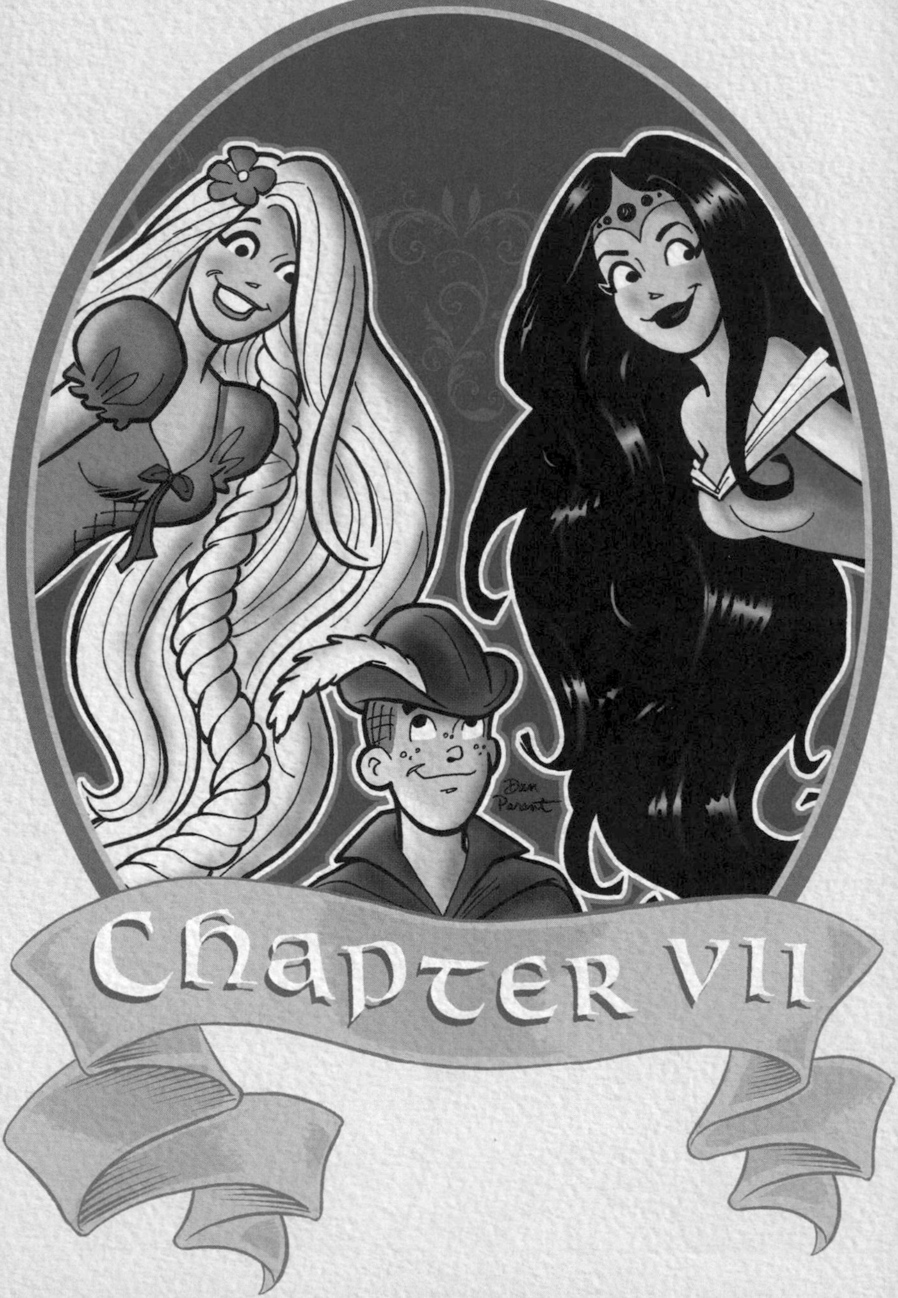
Dan Parent
Chapter VII

The story of Rapunzels

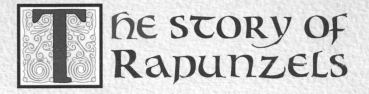

In this retelling of the classic "Rapunzel," teen princesses Betty and Veronica are cursed to live their lives in a giant tower until they're married off. But there's no express elevator to the top, and any suitor must climb the long locks of hair Betty and Veronica have been cursed with.

But the girls get impatient waiting for a prince to arrive and decide to escape their tower, running into a lowly commoner named Archie. Naturally, both girls fall for the charming everyman. But leaving the tower comes with a price, and it could put their royal status at risk.

Will one of them win his love before the sorceress who banished them figures it out?

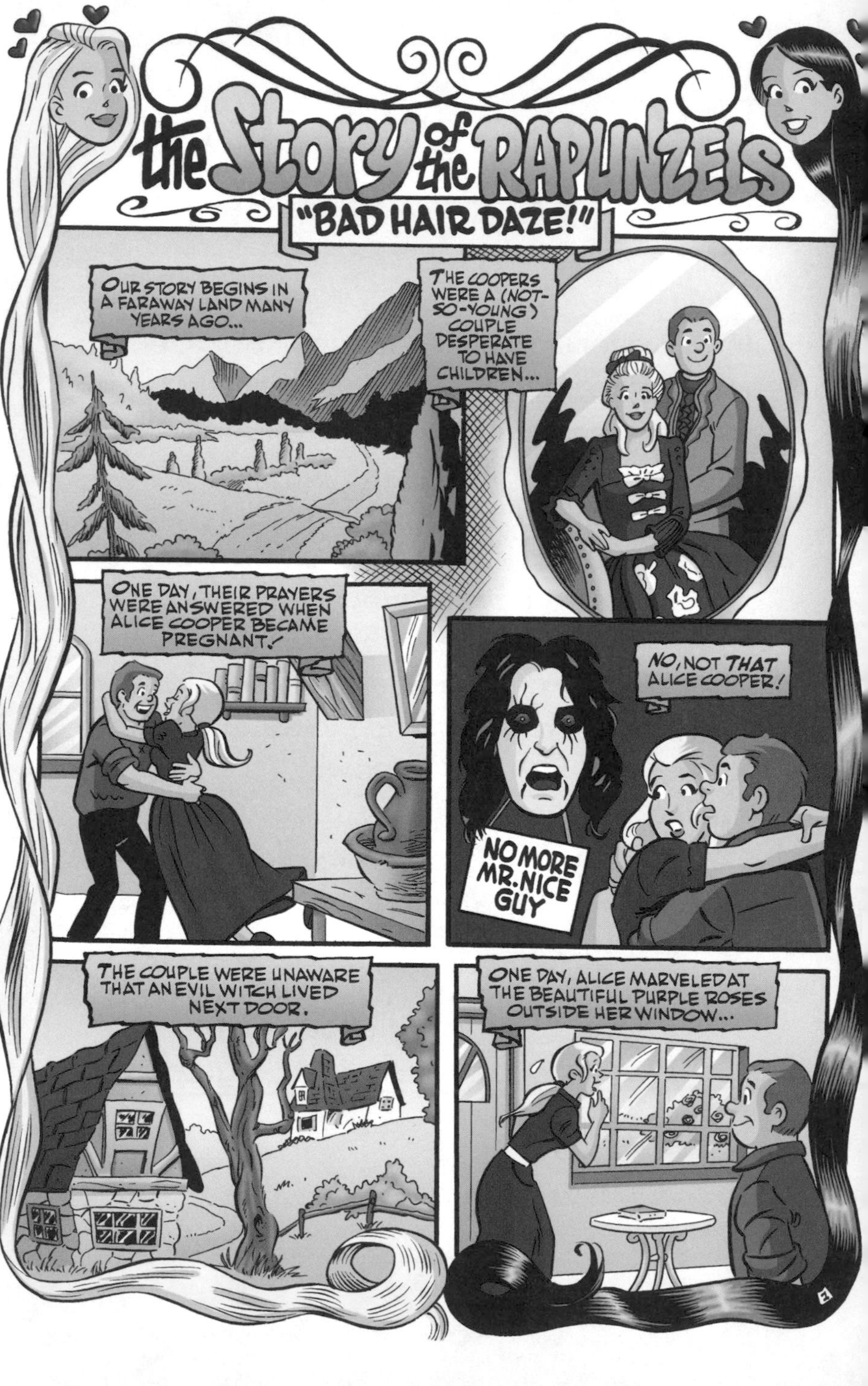
the Story of the RAPUNZELS
"BAD HAIR DAZE!"
OUR STORY BEGINS IN A FARAWAY LAND MANY YEARS AGO...
THE COOPERS WERE A (NOT-SO-YOUNG) COUPLE DESPERATE TO HAVE CHILDREN...
ONE DAY, THEIR PRAYERS WERE ANSWERED WHEN ALICE COOPER BECAME PREGNANT!
NO, NOT THAT ALICE COOPER!
NO MORE MR. NICE GUY
THE COUPLE WERE UNAWARE THAT AN EVIL WITCH LIVED NEXT DOOR.
ONE DAY, ALICE MARVELED AT THE BEAUTIFUL PURPLE ROSES OUTSIDE HER WINDOW...
1

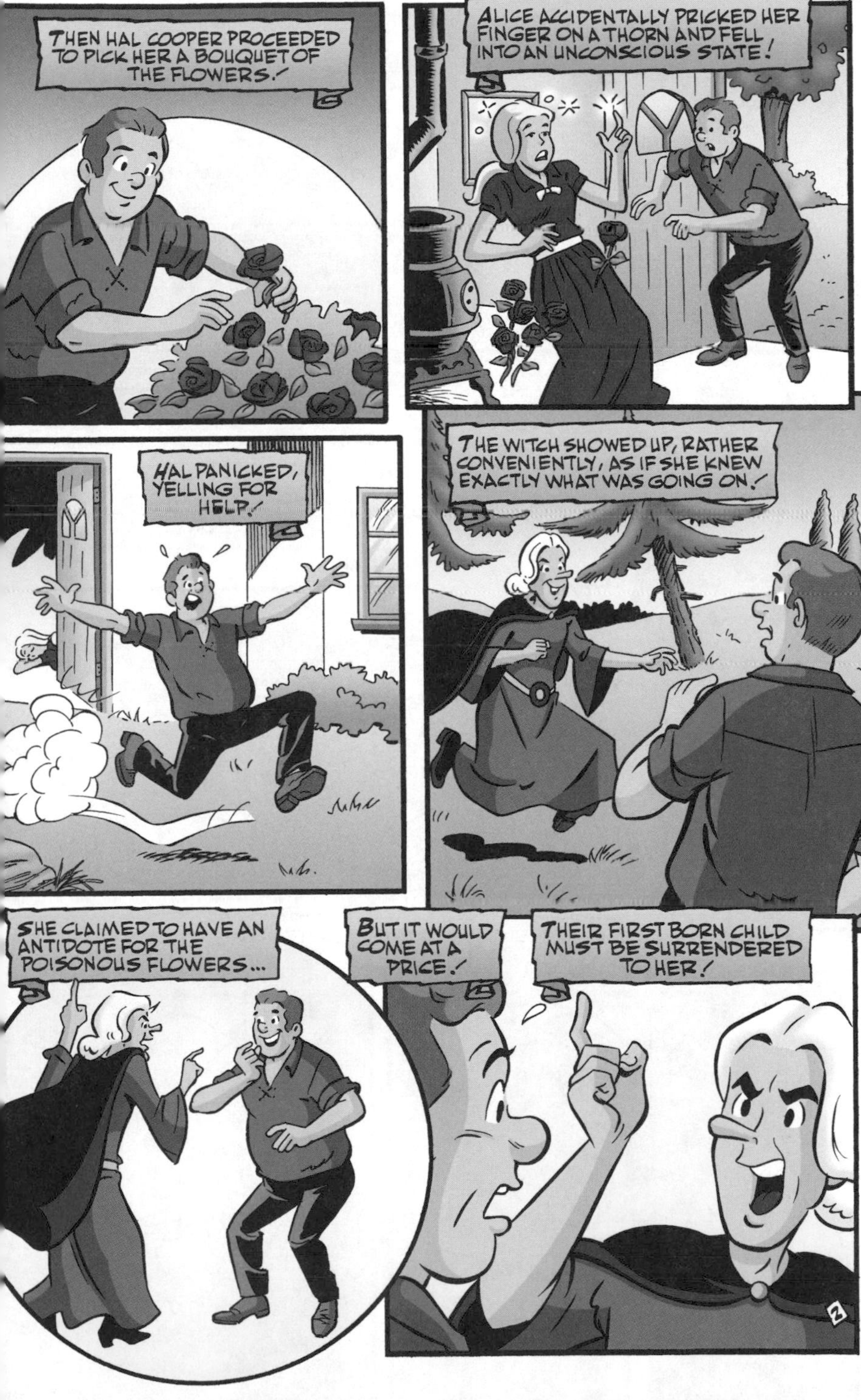
THEN HAL COOPER PROCEEDED TO PICK HER A BOUQUET OF THE FLOWERS!
ALICE ACCIDENTALLY PRICKED HER FINGER ON A THORN AND FELL INTO AN UNCONSCIOUS STATE!
HAL PANICKED, YELLING FOR HELP!
THE WITCH SHOWED UP, RATHER CONVENIENTLY, AS IF SHE KNEW EXACTLY WHAT WAS GOING ON!
SHE CLAIMED TO HAVE AN ANTIDOTE FOR THE POISONOUS FLOWERS...
BUT IT WOULD COME AT A PRICE!
THEIR FIRST BORN CHILD MUST BE SURRENDERED TO HER!
2

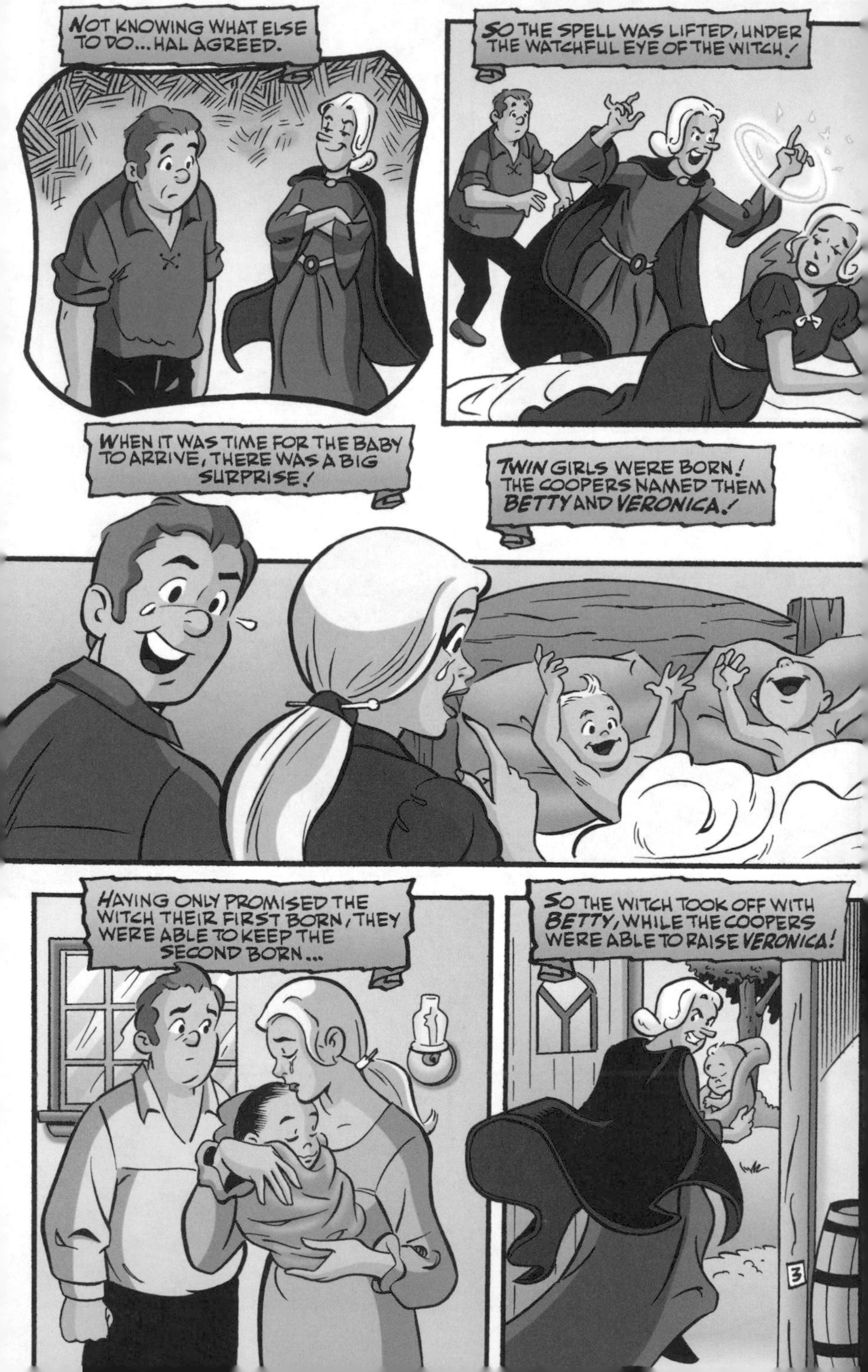
NOT KNOWING WHAT ELSE TO DO... HAL AGREED.
SO THE SPELL WAS LIFTED, UNDER THE WATCHFUL EYE OF THE WITCH!
WHEN IT WAS TIME FOR THE BABY TO ARRIVE, THERE WAS A BIG SURPRISE!
TWIN GIRLS WERE BORN! THE COOPERS NAMED THEM BETTY AND VERONICA!
HAVING ONLY PROMISED THE WITCH THEIR FIRST BORN, THEY WERE ABLE TO KEEP THE SECOND BORN...
SO THE WITCH TOOK OFF WITH BETTY, WHILE THE COOPERS WERE ABLE TO RAISE VERONICA!
3

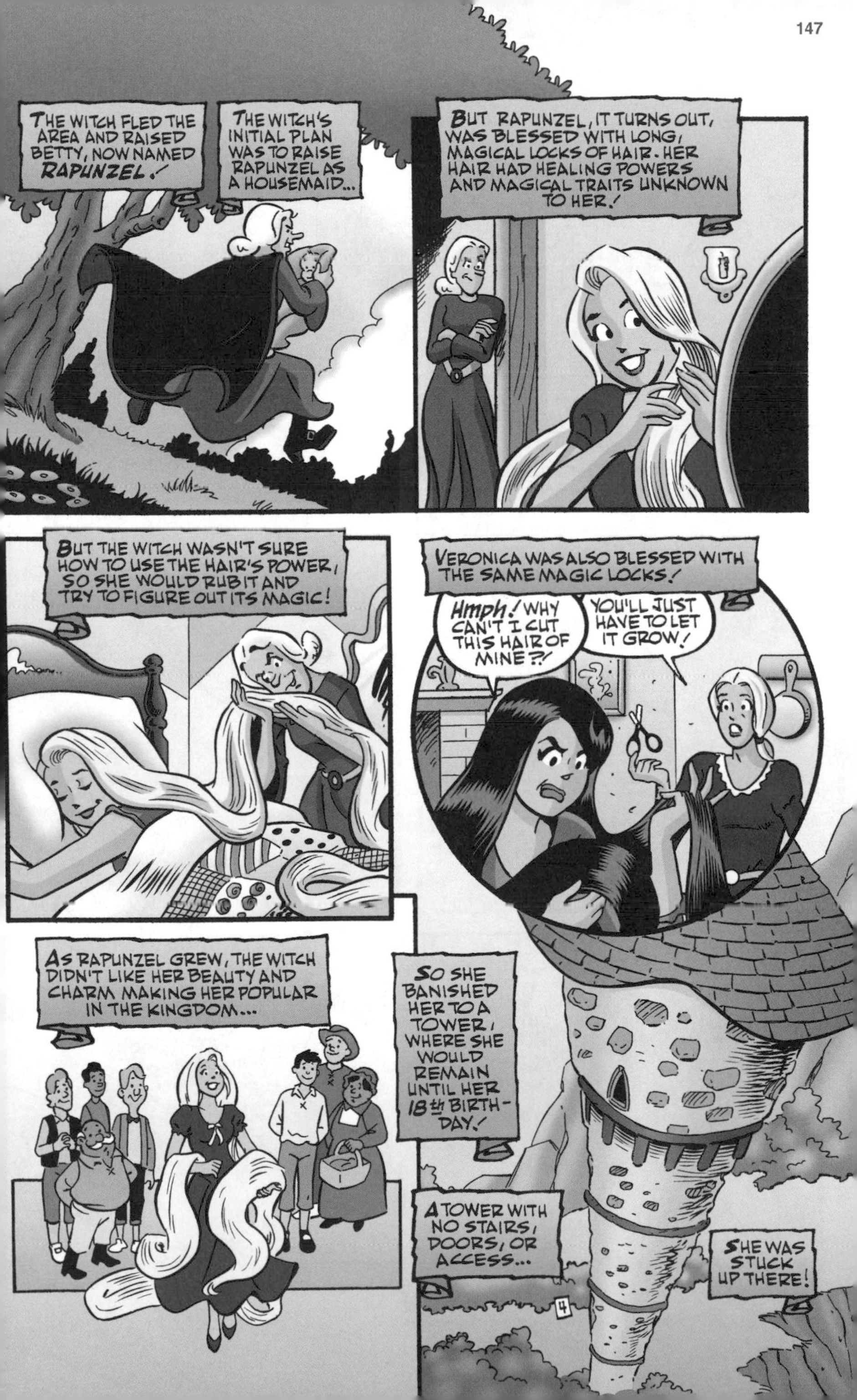
THE WITCH FLED THE AREA AND RAISED BETTY, NOW NAMED RAPUNZEL!
THE WITCH'S INITIAL PLAN WAS TO RAISE RAPUNZEL AS A HOUSEMAID...
BUT RAPUNZEL, IT TURNS OUT, WAS BLESSED WITH LONG, MAGICAL LOCKS OF HAIR. HER HAIR HAD HEALING POWERS AND MAGICAL TRAITS UNKNOWN TO HER!
BUT THE WITCH WASN'T SURE HOW TO USE THE HAIR'S POWER, SO SHE WOULD RUB IT AND TRY TO FIGURE OUT ITS MAGIC!
VERONICA WAS ALSO BLESSED WITH THE SAME MAGIC LOCKS!
Hmph! WHY CAN'T I CUT THIS HAIR OF MINE?!
YOU'LL JUST HAVE TO LET IT GROW!
AS RAPUNZEL GREW, THE WITCH DIDN'T LIKE HER BEAUTY AND CHARM MAKING HER POPULAR IN THE KINGDOM...
SO SHE BANISHED HER TO A TOWER, WHERE SHE WOULD REMAIN UNTIL HER 18th BIRTHDAY!
A TOWER WITH NO STAIRS, DOORS, OR ACCESS...
SHE WAS STUCK UP THERE!
4

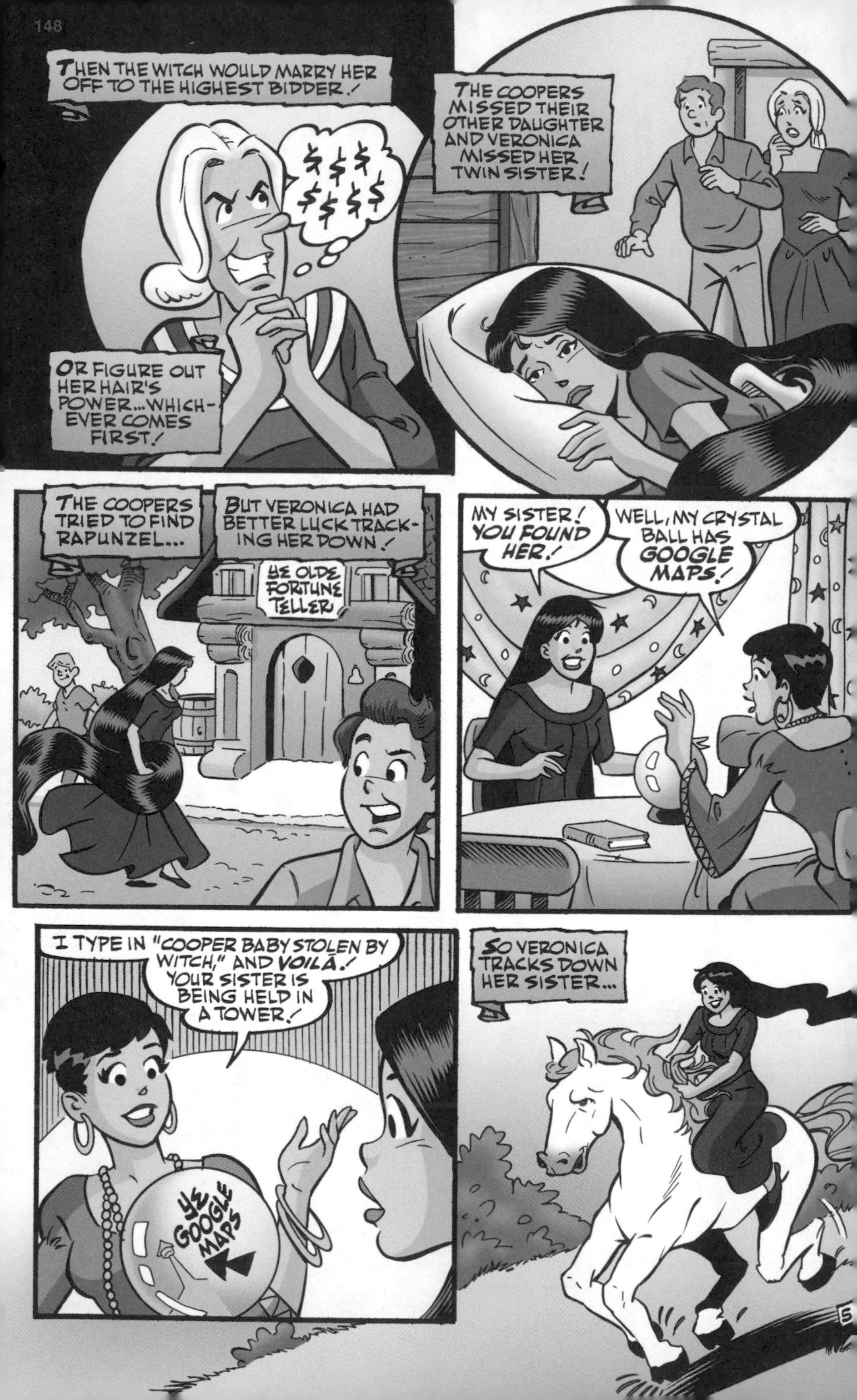
THEN THE WITCH WOULD MARRY HER OFF TO THE HIGHEST BIDDER!
$$$ $$$$
OR FIGURE OUT HER HAIR'S POWER...WHICHEVER COMES FIRST!
THE COOPERS MISSED THEIR OTHER DAUGHTER AND VERONICA MISSED HER TWIN SISTER!
THE COOPERS TRIED TO FIND RAPUNZEL...
BUT VERONICA HAD BETTER LUCK TRACKING HER DOWN!
YE OLDE FORTUNE TELLER
MY SISTER! YOU FOUND HER!
WELL, MY CRYSTAL BALL HAS GOOGLE MAPS!
I TYPE IN "COOPER BABY STOLEN BY WITCH," AND VOILÀ! YOUR SISTER IS BEING HELD IN A TOWER!
YE GOOGLE MAPS
SO VERONICA TRACKS DOWN HER SISTER...
5

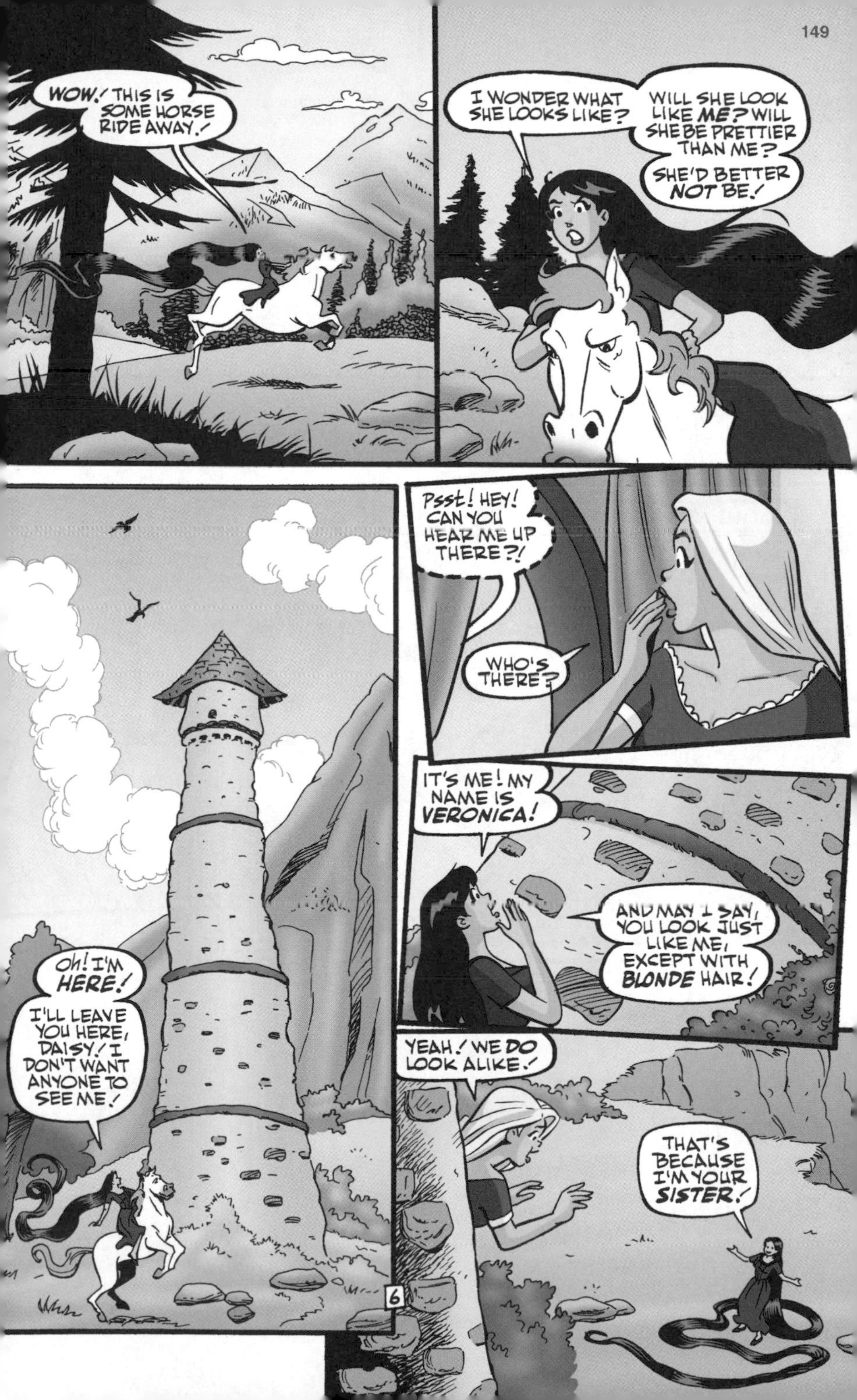
WOW! THIS IS SOME HORSE RIDE AWAY!
I WONDER WHAT SHE LOOKS LIKE?
WILL SHE LOOK LIKE ME? WILL SHE BE PRETTIER THAN ME?
SHE'D BETTER NOT BE!
Oh! I'M HERE!
I'LL LEAVE YOU HERE, DAISY! I DON'T WANT ANYONE TO SEE ME!
6
Psst! HEY! CAN YOU HEAR ME UP THERE?!
WHO'S THERE?
IT'S ME! MY NAME IS VERONICA!
AND MAY I SAY, YOU LOOK JUST LIKE ME, EXCEPT WITH BLONDE HAIR!
YEAH! WE DO LOOK ALIKE!
THAT'S BECAUSE I'M YOUR SISTER!

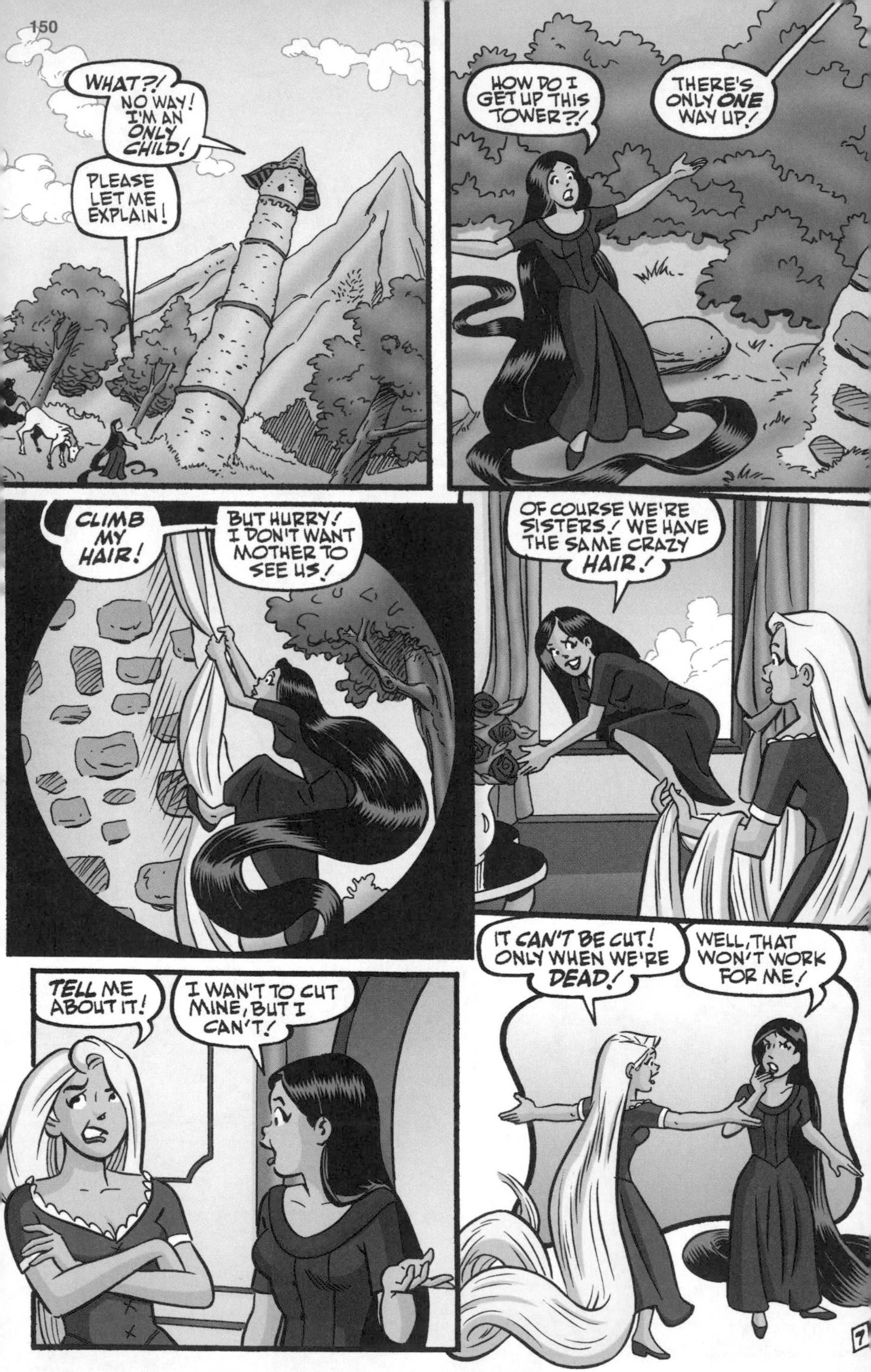
WHAT?! NO WAY! I'M AN ONLY CHILD!
PLEASE LET ME EXPLAIN!
HOW DO I GET UP THIS TOWER?!
THERE'S ONLY ONE WAY UP!
CLIMB MY HAIR!
BUT HURRY! I DON'T WANT MOTHER TO SEE US!
OF COURSE WE'RE SISTERS! WE HAVE THE SAME CRAZY HAIR!
TELL ME ABOUT IT!
I WAN'T TO CUT MINE, BUT I CAN'T!
IT CAN'T BE CUT! ONLY WHEN WE'RE DEAD!
WELL, THAT WON'T WORK FOR ME!
7

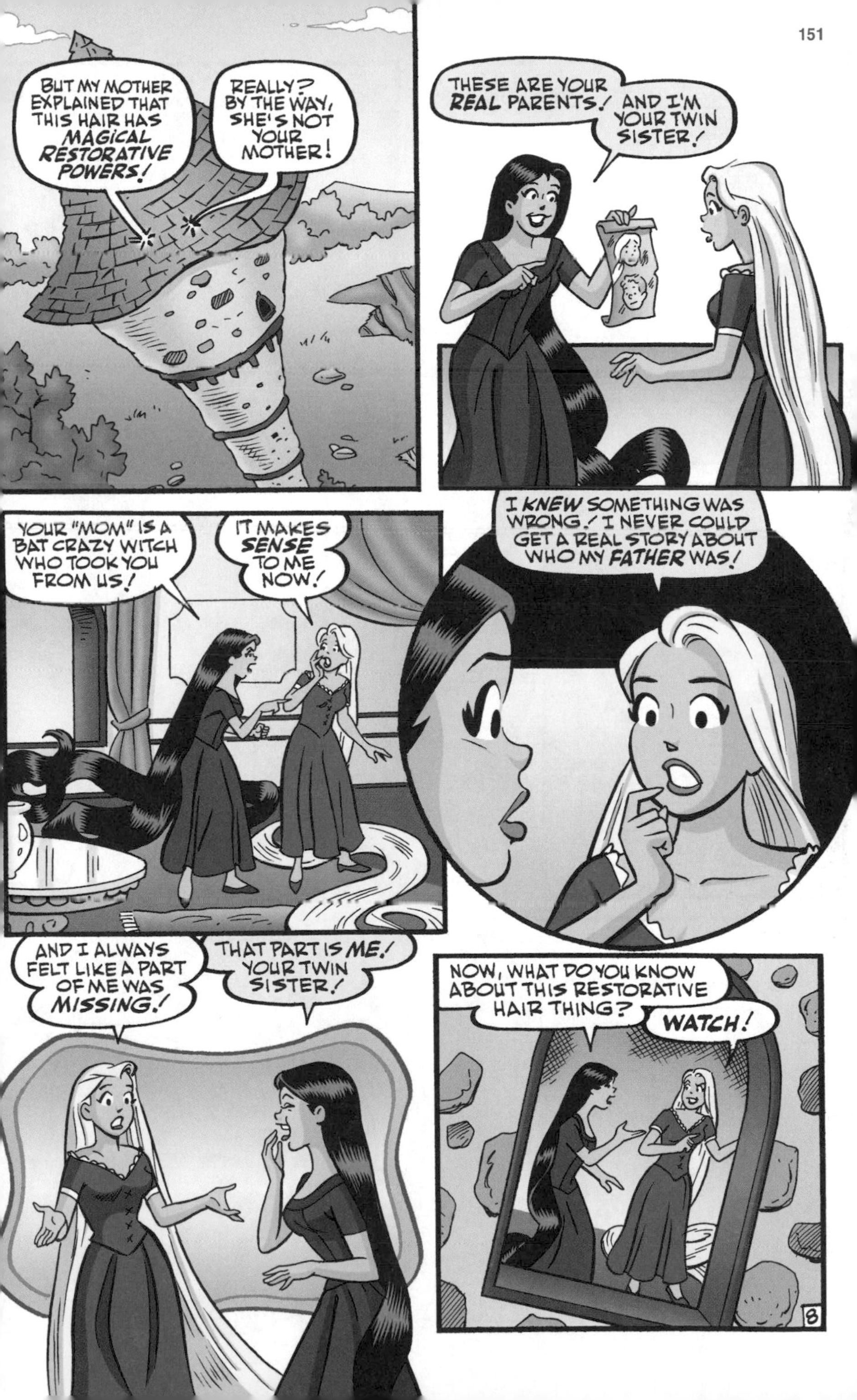
BUT MY MOTHER EXPLAINED THAT THIS HAIR HAS MAGICAL RESTORATIVE POWERS!
REALLY? BY THE WAY, SHE'S NOT YOUR MOTHER!
THESE ARE YOUR REAL PARENTS!
AND I'M YOUR TWIN SISTER!
YOUR "MOM" IS A BAT CRAZY WITCH WHO TOOK YOU FROM US!
IT MAKES SENSE TO ME NOW!
I KNEW SOMETHING WAS WRONG! I NEVER COULD GET A REAL STORY ABOUT WHO MY FATHER WAS!
AND I ALWAYS FELT LIKE A PART OF ME WAS MISSING!
THAT PART IS ME! YOUR TWIN SISTER!
NOW, WHAT DO YOU KNOW ABOUT THIS RESTORATIVE HAIR THING?
WATCH!
8

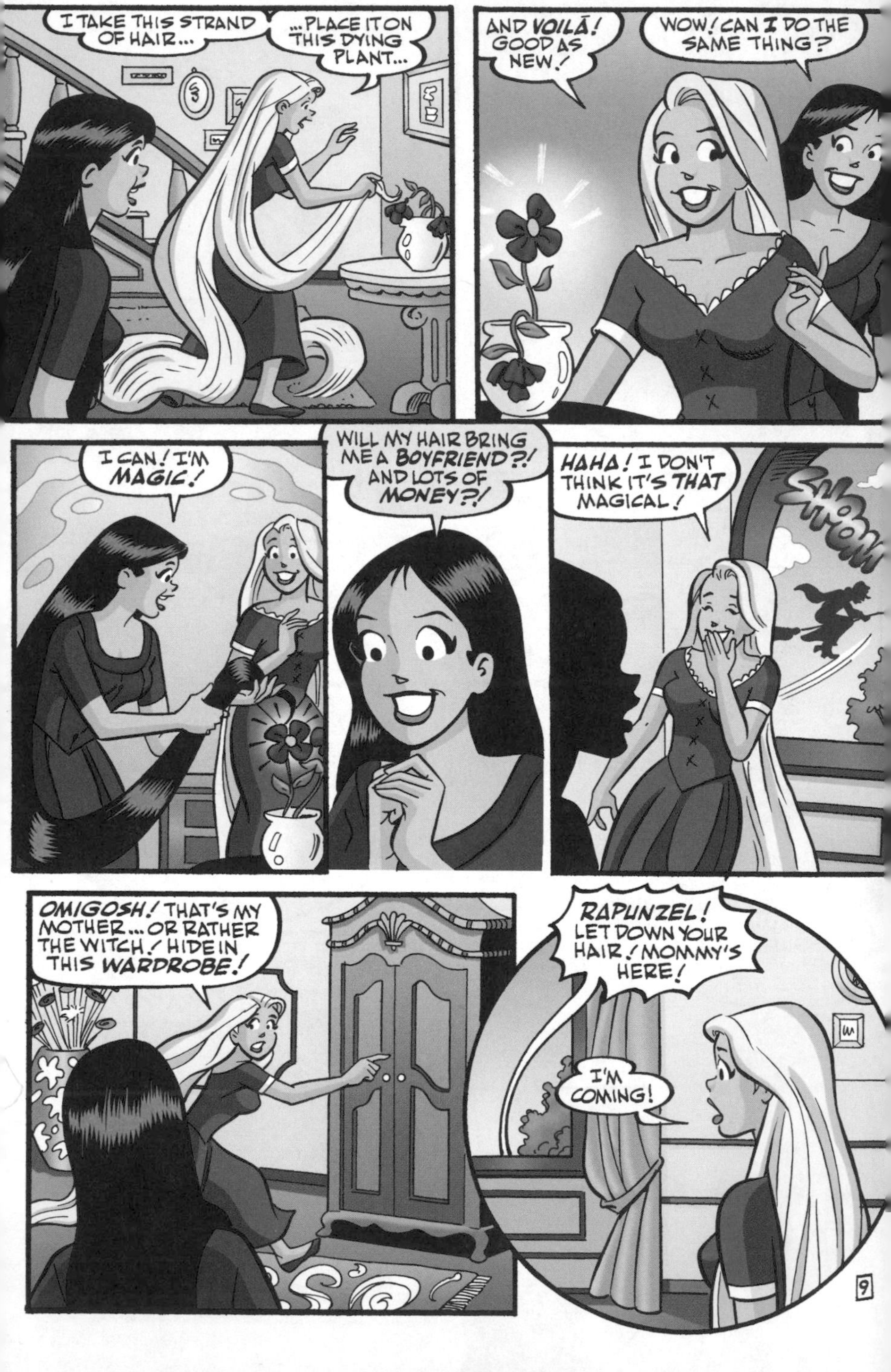
I TAKE THIS STRAND OF HAIR...
...PLACE IT ON THIS DYING PLANT...
AND VOILÀ! GOOD AS NEW!
WOW! CAN I DO THE SAME THING?
I CAN! I'M MAGIC!
WILL MY HAIR BRING ME A BOYFRIEND?! AND LOTS OF MONEY?!
HAHA! I DON'T THINK IT'S THAT MAGICAL!
SHOOM
OMIGOSH! THAT'S MY MOTHER... OR RATHER THE WITCH! HIDE IN THIS WARDROBE!
RAPUNZEL! LET DOWN YOUR HAIR! MOMMY'S HERE!
I'M COMING!
9

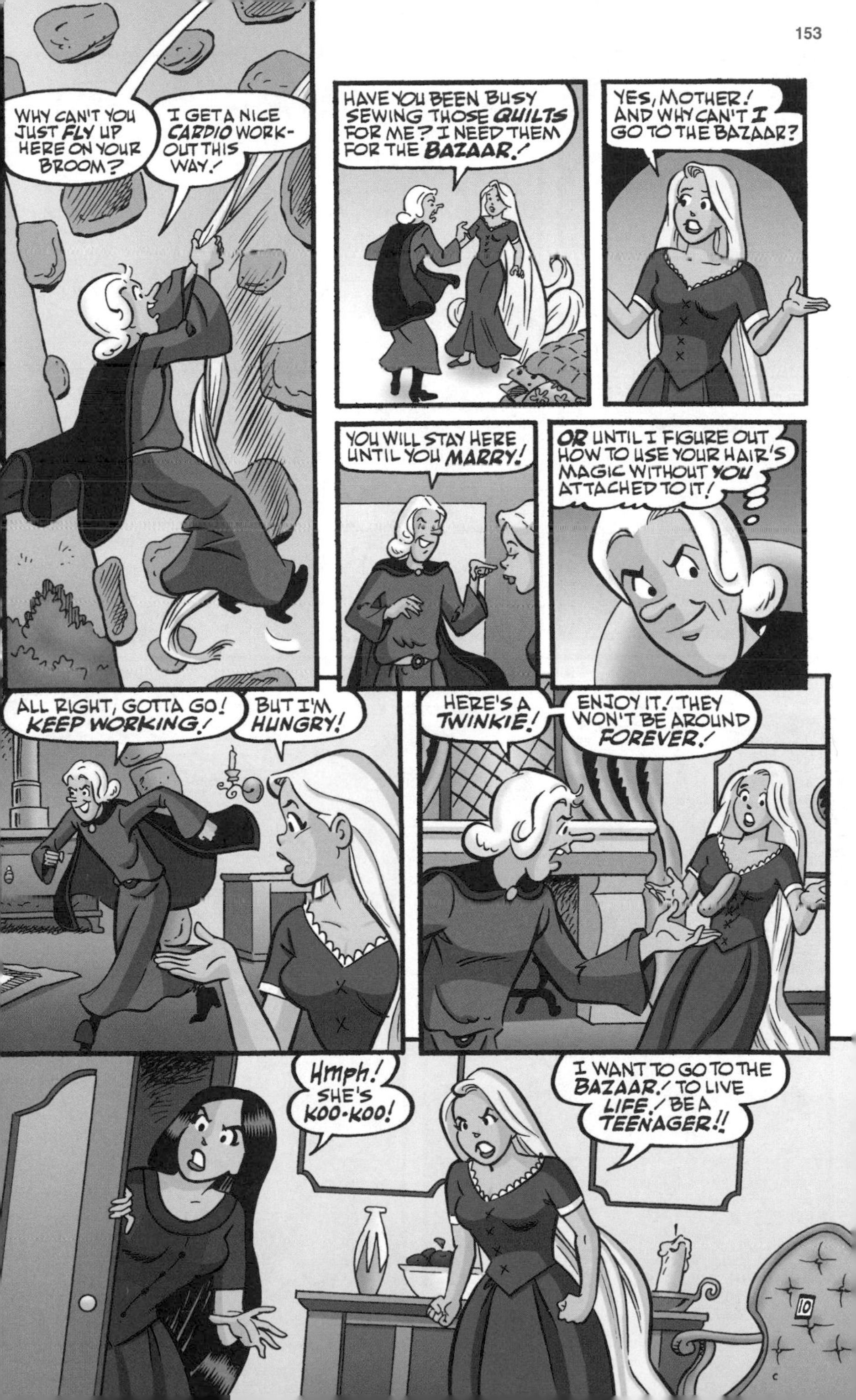
WHY CAN'T YOU JUST FLY UP HERE ON YOUR BROOM?
I GET A NICE CARDIO WORK-OUT THIS WAY!
HAVE YOU BEEN BUSY SEWING THOSE QUILTS FOR ME? I NEED THEM FOR THE BAZAAR!
YES, MOTHER! AND WHY CAN'T I GO TO THE BAZAAR?
YOU WILL STAY HERE UNTIL YOU MARRY!
OR UNTIL I FIGURE OUT HOW TO USE YOUR HAIR'S MAGIC WITHOUT YOU ATTACHED TO IT!
ALL RIGHT, GOTTA GO! KEEP WORKING!
BUT I'M HUNGRY!
HERE'S A TWINKIE!
ENJOY IT! THEY WON'T BE AROUND FOREVER!
Hmph! SHE'S KOO-KOO!
I WANT TO GO TO THE BAZAAR! TO LIVE LIFE! BE A TEENAGER!!
10

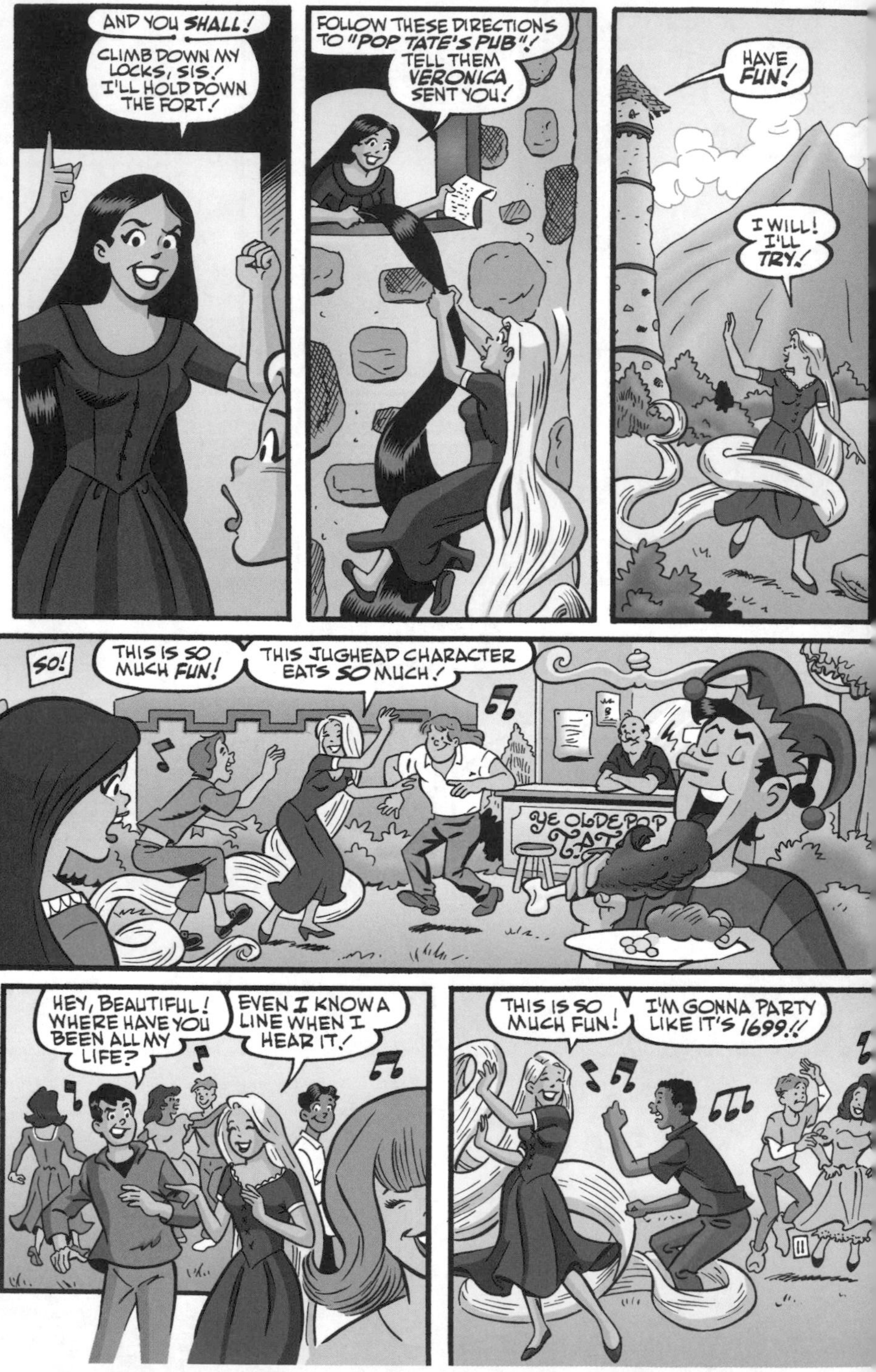
AND YOU SHALL!
CLIMB DOWN MY LOCKS, SIS! I'LL HOLD DOWN THE FORT!
FOLLOW THESE DIRECTIONS TO "POP TATE'S PUB"!
TELL THEM VERONICA SENT YOU!
HAVE FUN!
I WILL! I'LL TRY!
SO!
THIS IS SO MUCH FUN!
THIS JUGHEAD CHARACTER EATS SO MUCH!
YE OLDE POP TATE
HEY, BEAUTIFUL! WHERE HAVE YOU BEEN ALL MY LIFE?
EVEN I KNOW A LINE WHEN I HEAR IT!
THIS IS SO MUCH FUN!
I'M GONNA PARTY LIKE IT'S 1699!!

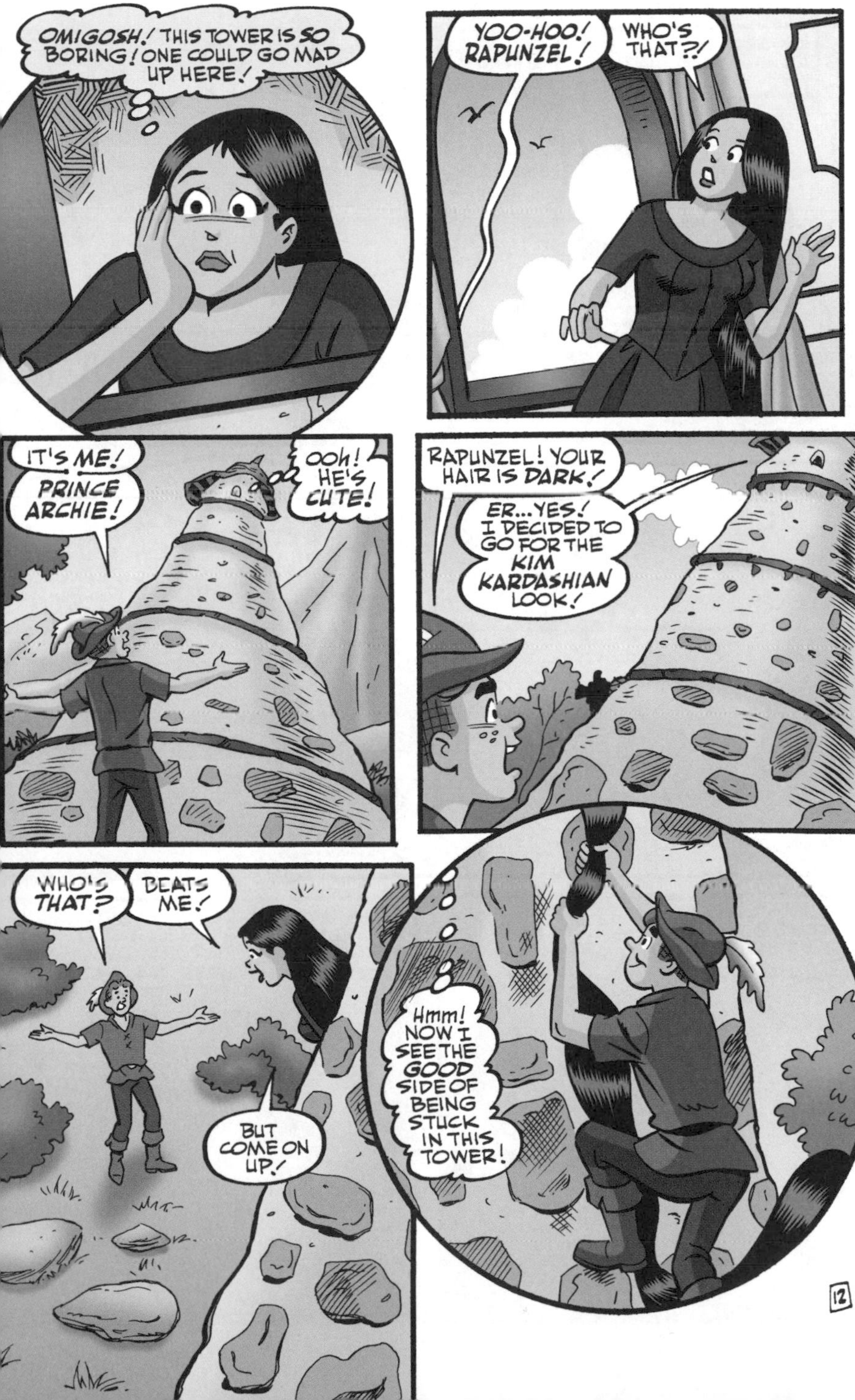
OMIGOSH! THIS TOWER IS SO BORING! ONE COULD GO MAD UP HERE!
YOO-HOO! RAPUNZEL!
WHO'S THAT?!
IT'S ME! PRINCE ARCHIE!
Ooh! HE'S CUTE!
RAPUNZEL! YOUR HAIR IS DARK!
ER...YES! I DECIDED TO GO FOR THE KIM KARDASHIAN LOOK!
WHO'S THAT?
BEATS ME!
BUT COME ON UP!
Hmm! NOW I SEE THE GOOD SIDE OF BEING STUCK IN THIS TOWER!
12

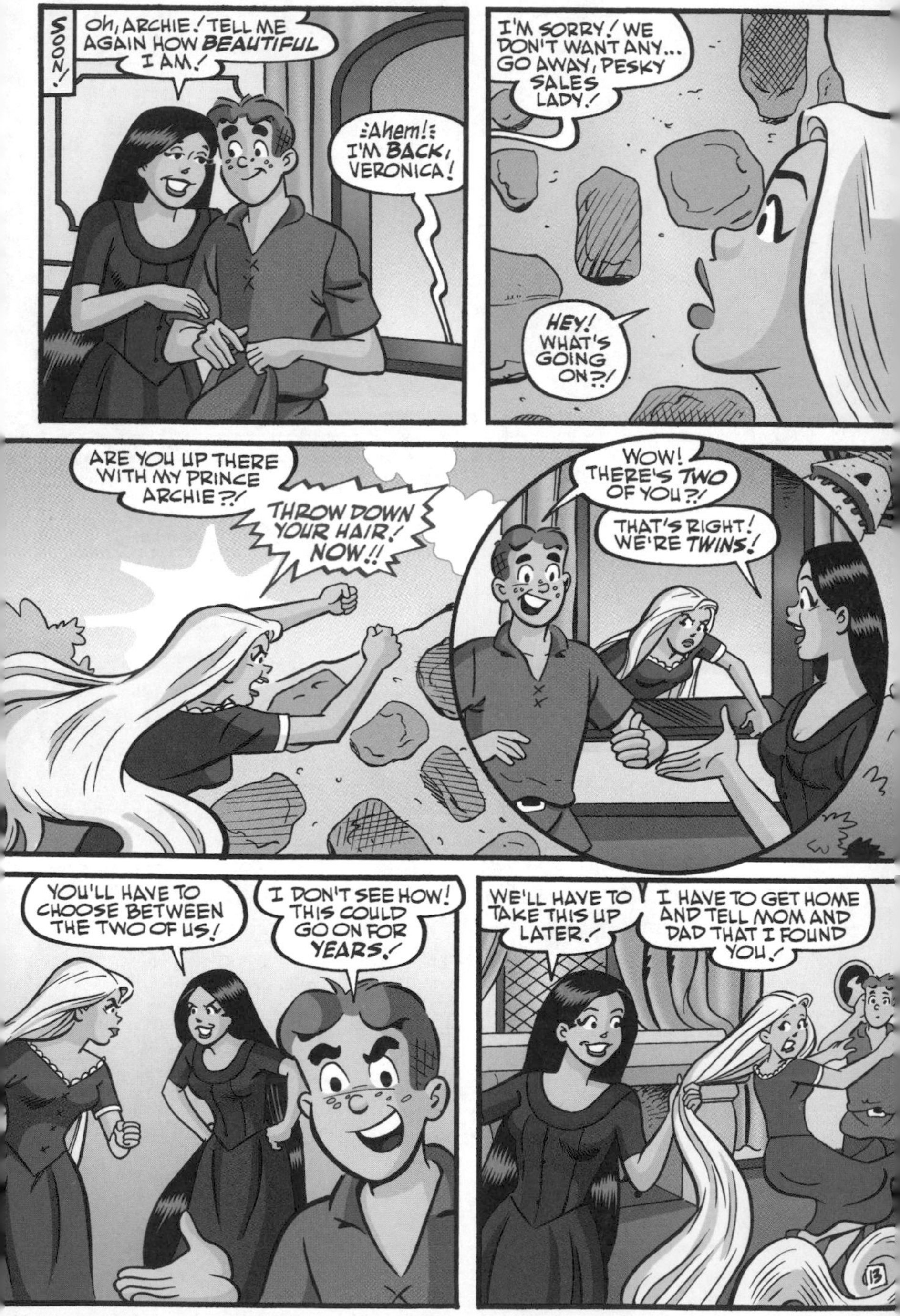
SOON!
OH, ARCHIE! TELL ME AGAIN HOW BEAUTIFUL I AM!
AHEM! I'M BACK, VERONICA!
I'M SORRY! WE DON'T WANT ANY... GO AWAY, PESKY SALES LADY!
HEY! WHAT'S GOING ON?!
ARE YOU UP THERE WITH MY PRINCE ARCHIE?!
THROW DOWN YOUR HAIR! NOW!!
WOW! THERE'S TWO OF YOU?!
THAT'S RIGHT! WE'RE TWINS!
YOU'LL HAVE TO CHOOSE BETWEEN THE TWO OF US!
I DON'T SEE HOW! THIS COULD GO ON FOR YEARS!
WE'LL HAVE TO TAKE THIS UP LATER!
I HAVE TO GET HOME AND TELL MOM AND DAD THAT I FOUND YOU!
13

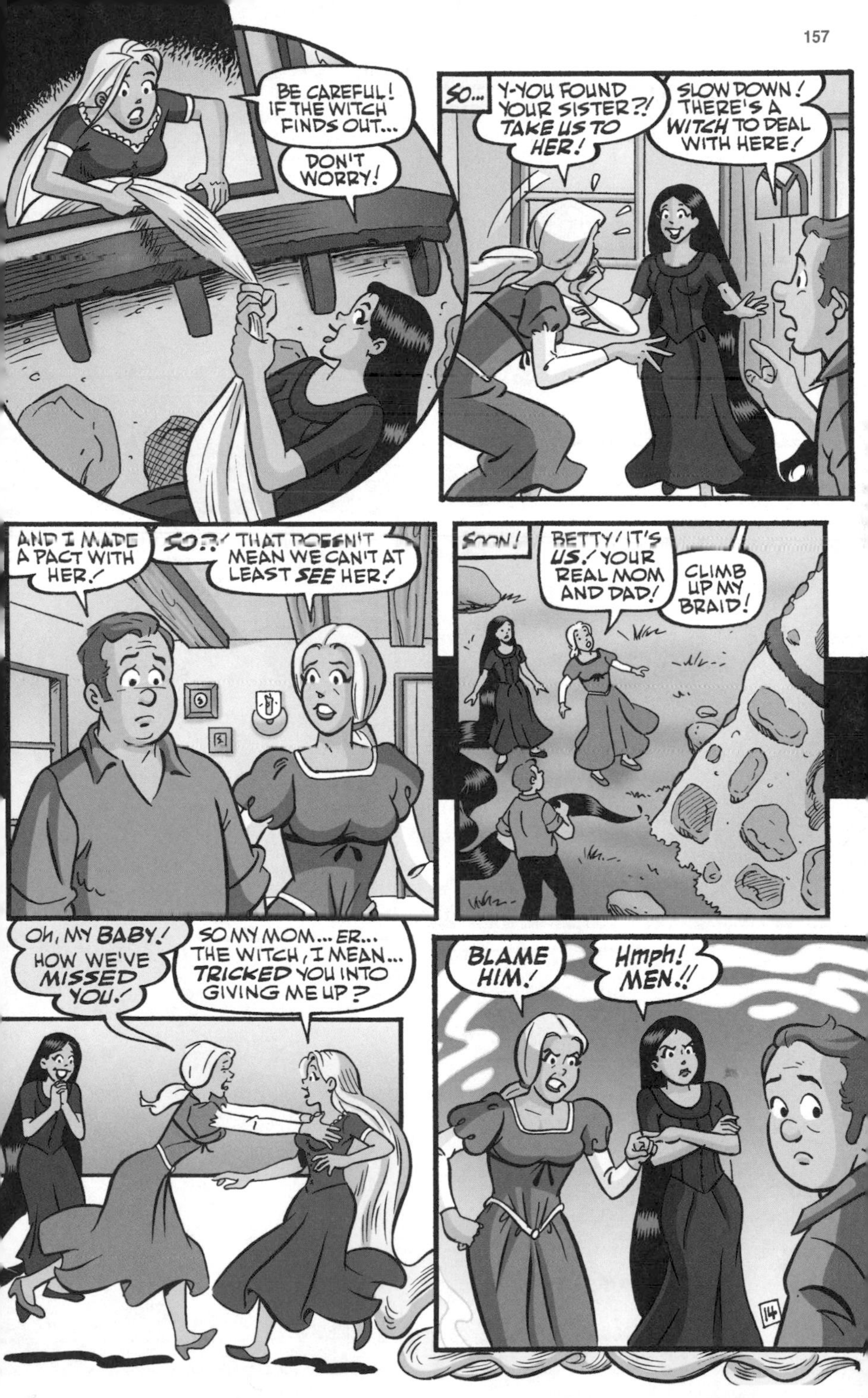
BE CAREFUL! IF THE WITCH FINDS OUT...
DON'T WORRY!
SO...
Y-YOU FOUND YOUR SISTER?! TAKE US TO HER!
SLOW DOWN! THERE'S A WITCH TO DEAL WITH HERE!
AND I MADE A PACT WITH HER!
SO?! THAT DOESN'T MEAN WE CAN'T AT LEAST SEE HER!
SOON!
BETTY! IT'S US! YOUR REAL MOM AND DAD!
CLIMB UP MY BRAID!
OH, MY BABY! HOW WE'VE MISSED YOU!
SO MY MOM... ER... THE WITCH, I MEAN... TRICKED YOU INTO GIVING ME UP?
BLAME HIM!
Hmph! MEN!!
14

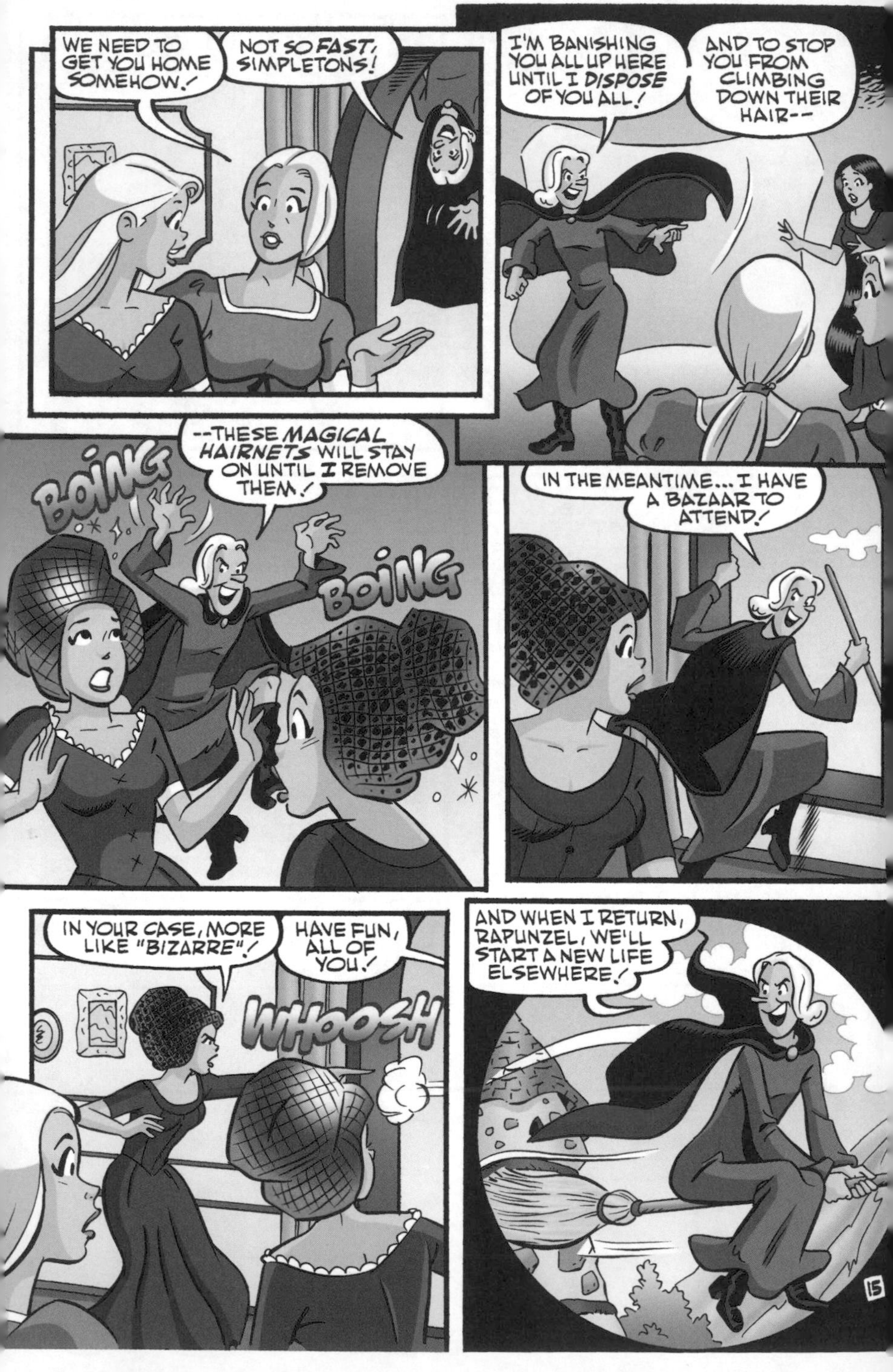
WE NEED TO GET YOU HOME SOMEHOW.!
NOT SO FAST, SIMPLETONS!
I'M BANISHING YOU ALL UP HERE UNTIL I DISPOSE OF YOU ALL!
AND TO STOP YOU FROM CLIMBING DOWN THEIR HAIR--
--THESE MAGICAL HAIRNETS WILL STAY ON UNTIL I REMOVE THEM!
BOING
BOING
IN THE MEANTIME... I HAVE A BAZAAR TO ATTEND!
IN YOUR CASE, MORE LIKE "BIZARRE"!
HAVE FUN, ALL OF YOU!
WHOOSH
AND WHEN I RETURN, RAPUNZEL, WE'LL START A NEW LIFE ELSEWHERE!
15

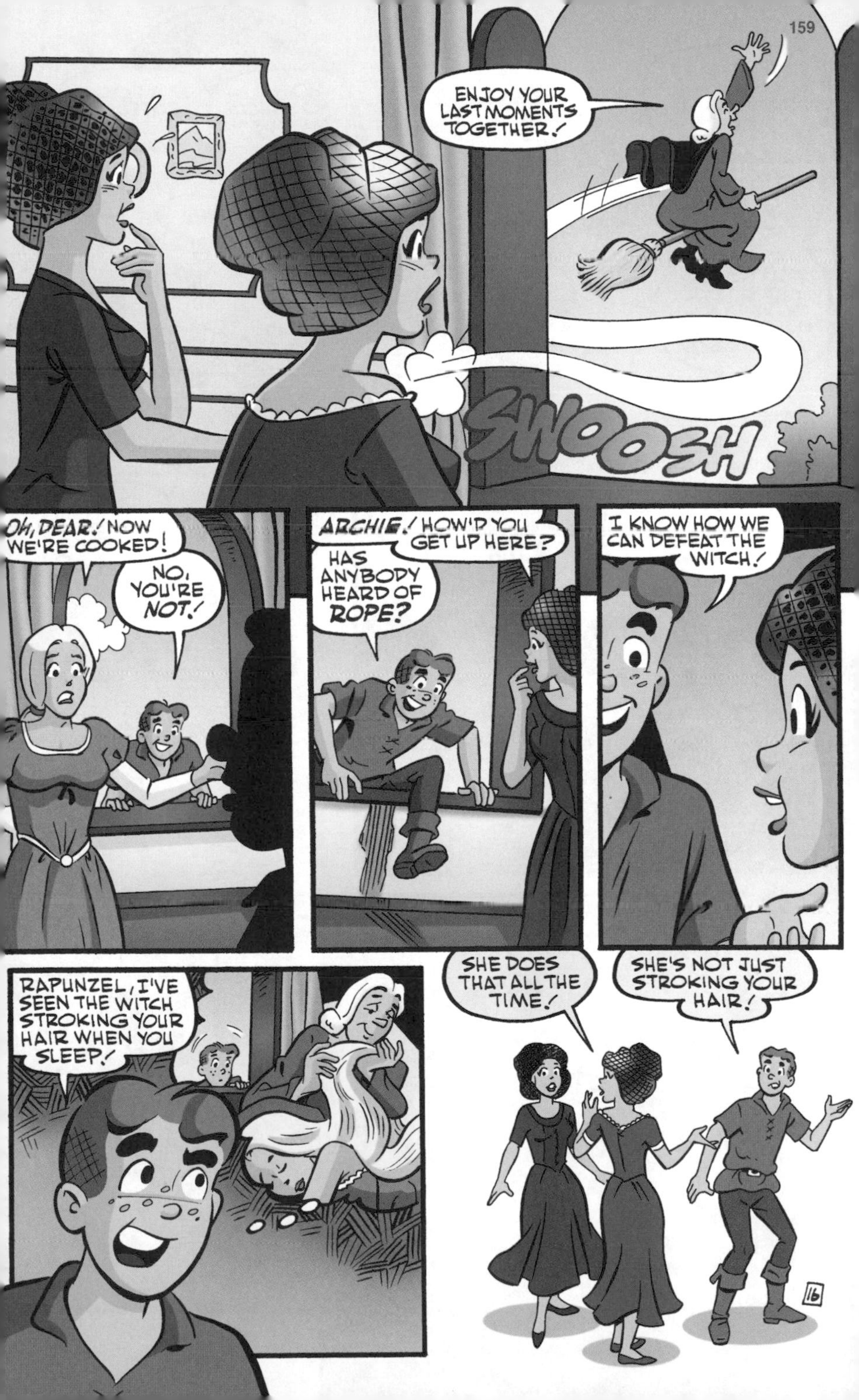
ENJOY YOUR LAST MOMENTS TOGETHER!
SWOOSH
OH, DEAR! NOW WE'RE COOKED!
NO, YOU'RE NOT!
ARCHIE! HOW'D YOU GET UP HERE?
HAS ANYBODY HEARD OF ROPE?
I KNOW HOW WE CAN DEFEAT THE WITCH!
RAPUNZEL, I'VE SEEN THE WITCH STROKING YOUR HAIR WHEN YOU SLEEP!
SHE DOES THAT ALL THE TIME!
SHE'S NOT JUST STROKING YOUR HAIR!
16

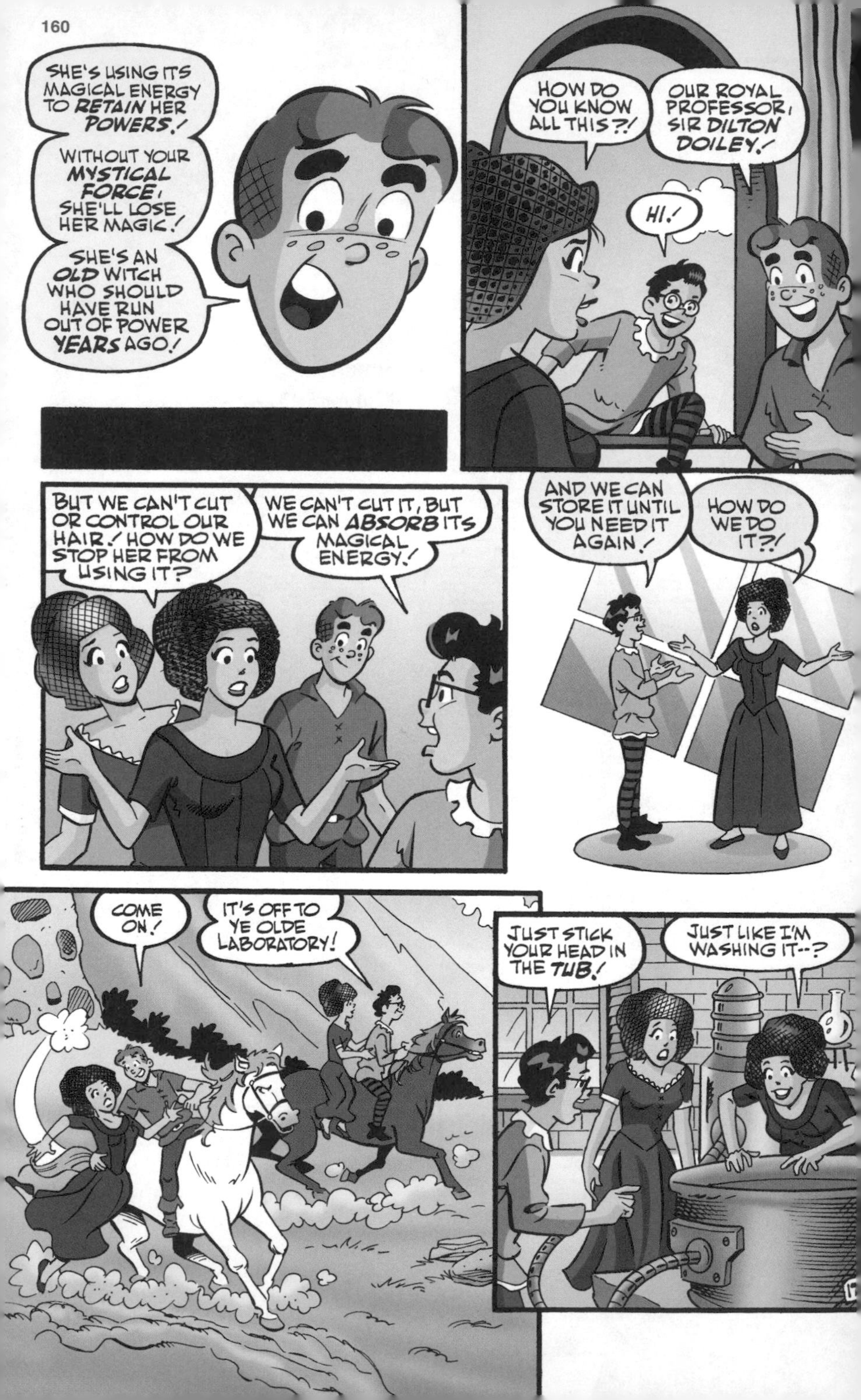
SHE'S USING ITS MAGICAL ENERGY TO RETAIN HER POWERS!
WITHOUT YOUR MYSTICAL FORCE, SHE'LL LOSE HER MAGIC!
SHE'S AN OLD WITCH WHO SHOULD HAVE RUN OUT OF POWER YEARS AGO!
[redacted]
HOW DO YOU KNOW ALL THIS?!
OUR ROYAL PROFESSOR, SIR DILTON DOILEY!
HI!
BUT WE CAN'T CUT OR CONTROL OUR HAIR! HOW DO WE STOP HER FROM USING IT?
WE CAN'T CUT IT, BUT WE CAN ABSORB ITS MAGICAL ENERGY!
AND WE CAN STORE IT UNTIL YOU NEED IT AGAIN!
HOW DO WE DO IT?!
COME ON!
IT'S OFF TO YE OLDE LABORATORY!
JUST STICK YOUR HEAD IN THE TUB!
JUST LIKE I'M WASHING IT--?

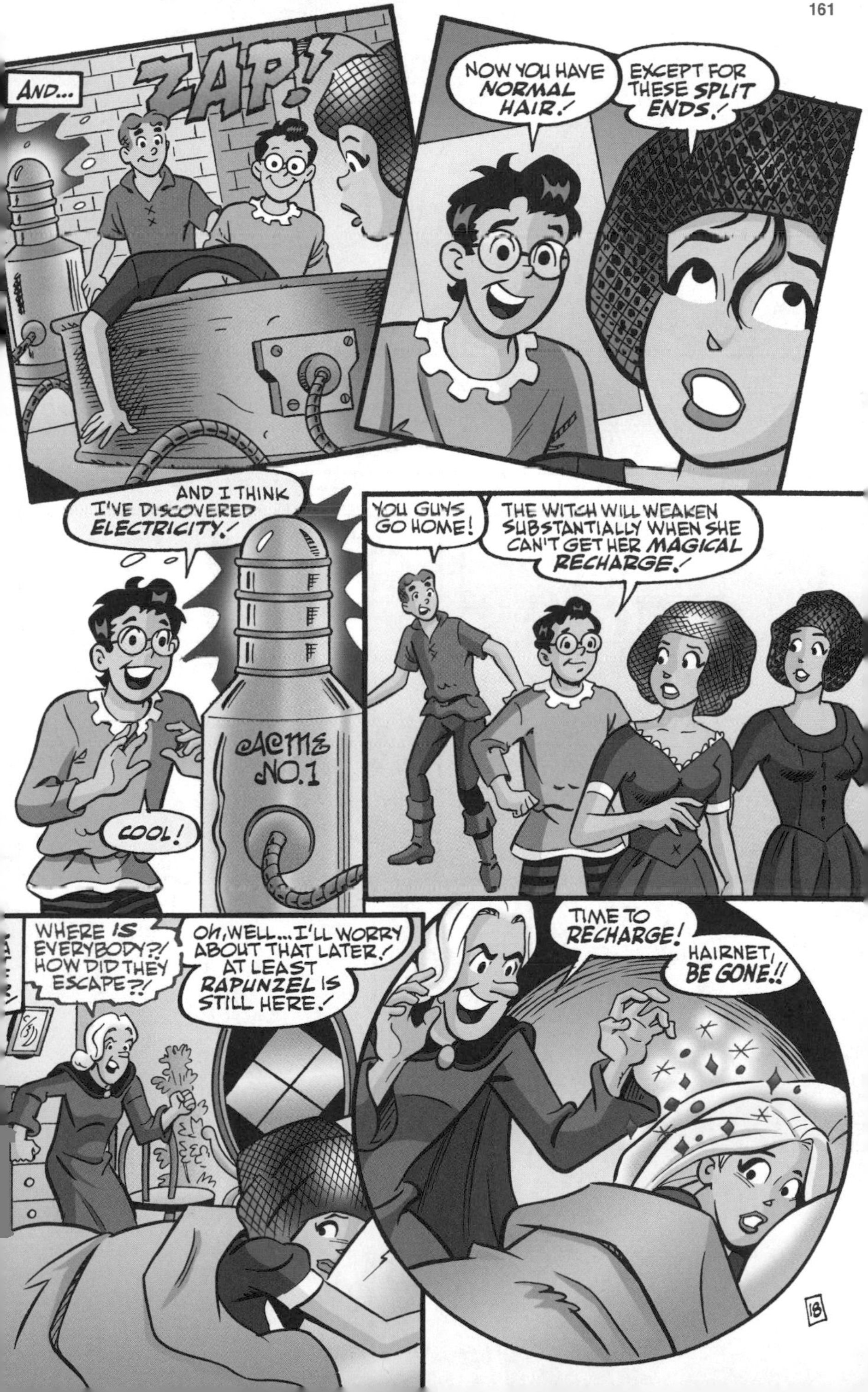
AND...
ZAP!
NOW YOU HAVE NORMAL HAIR!
EXCEPT FOR THESE SPLIT ENDS!
AND I THINK I'VE DISCOVERED ELECTRICITY!
COOL!
ACME NO.1
YOU GUYS GO HOME!
THE WITCH WILL WEAKEN SUBSTANTIALLY WHEN SHE CAN'T GET HER MAGICAL RECHARGE!
WHERE IS EVERYBODY?! HOW DID THEY ESCAPE?!
OH, WELL... I'LL WORRY ABOUT THAT LATER! AT LEAST RAPUNZEL IS STILL HERE!
TIME TO RECHARGE!
HAIRNET, BE GONE!!
18

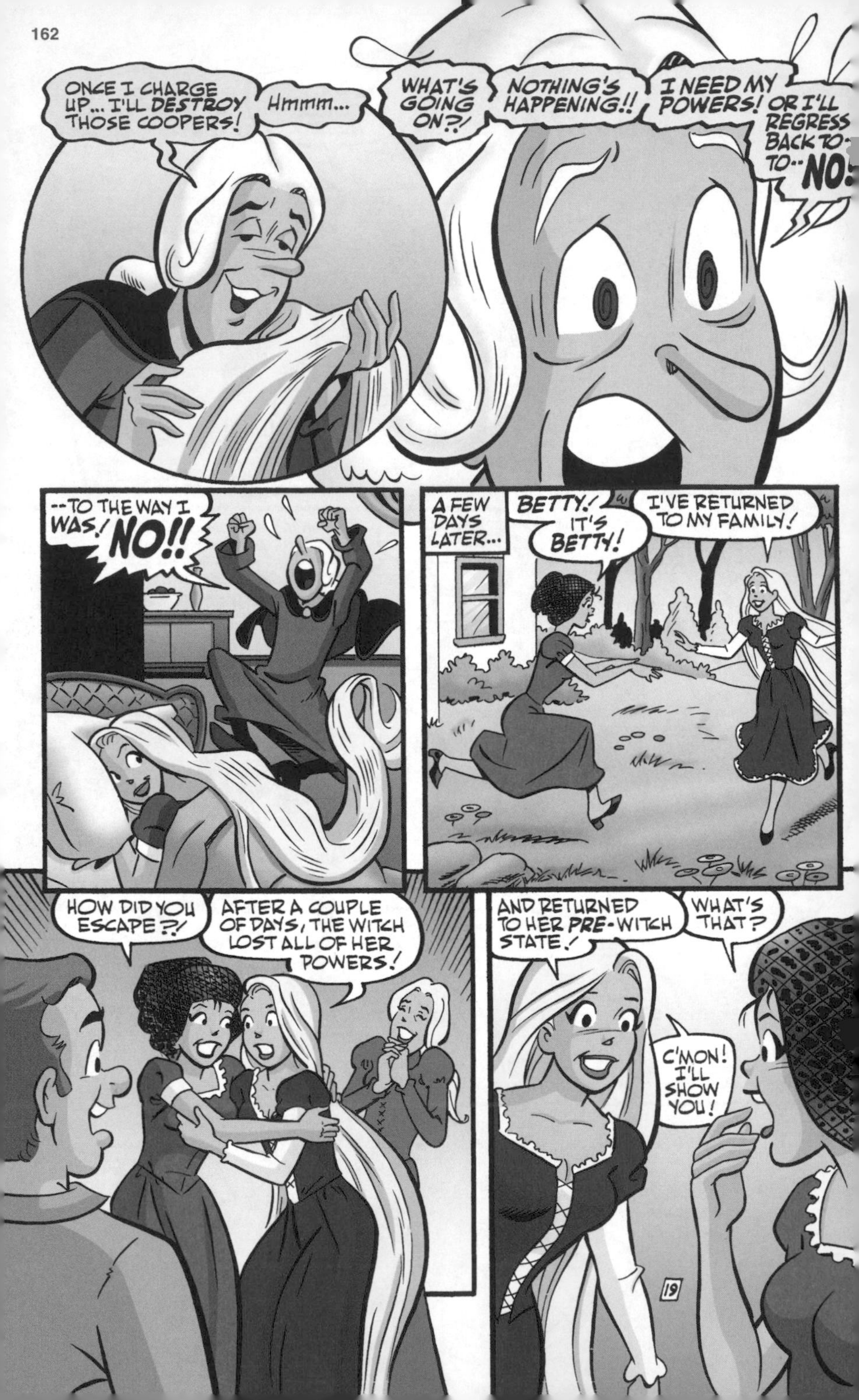
ONCE I CHARGE UP... I'LL DESTROY THOSE COOPERS!
Hmmm...
WHAT'S GOING ON?!
NOTHING'S HAPPENING!!
I NEED MY POWERS! OR I'LL REGRESS BACK TO-- TO-- NO!
--TO THE WAY I WAS! NO!!
A FEW DAYS LATER...
BETTY! IT'S BETTY!
I'VE RETURNED TO MY FAMILY!
HOW DID YOU ESCAPE?!
AFTER A COUPLE OF DAYS, THE WITCH LOST ALL OF HER POWERS!
AND RETURNED TO HER PRE-WITCH STATE!
WHAT'S THAT?
C'MON! I'LL SHOW YOU!
19

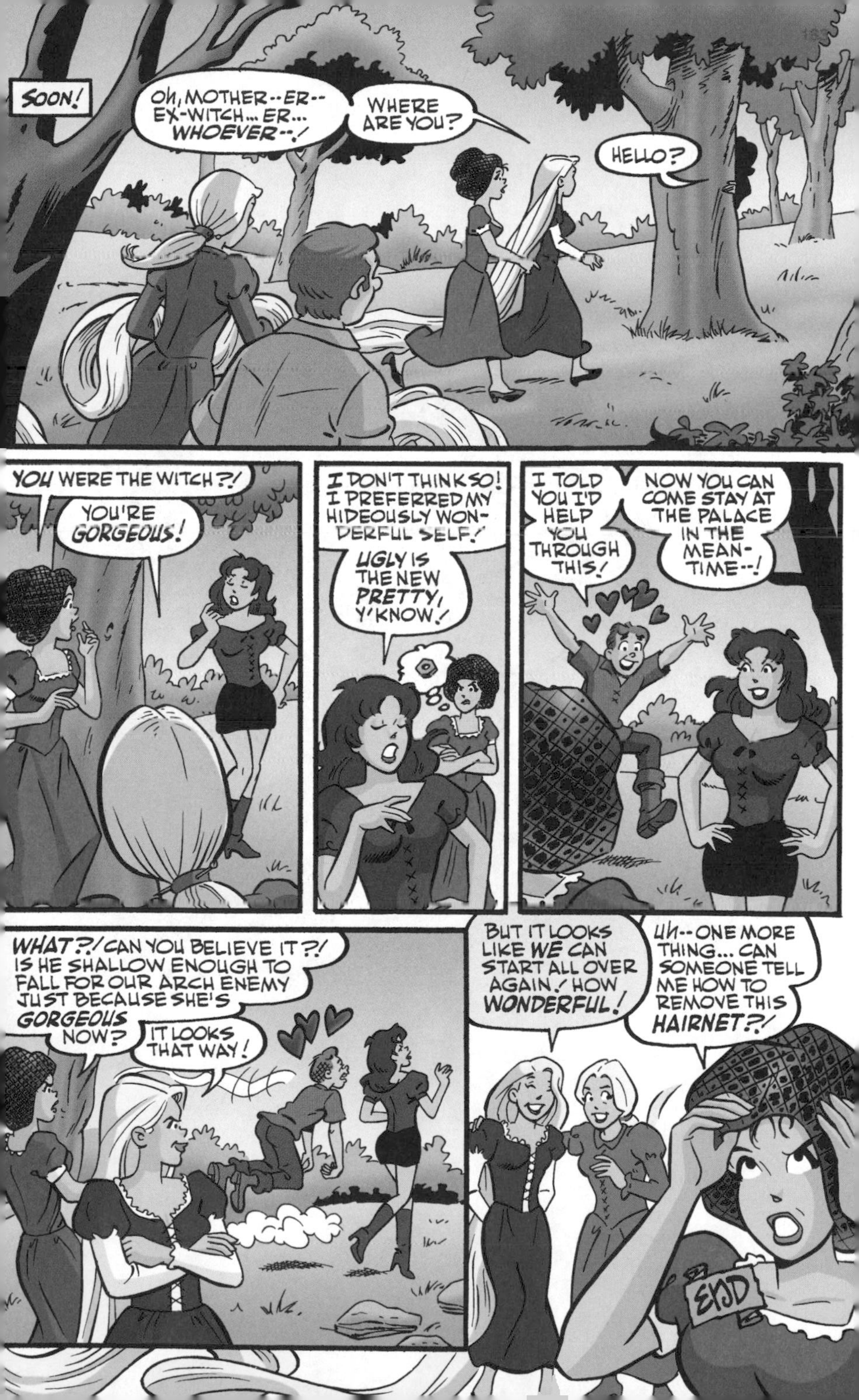
SOON!
OH, MOTHER--ER--EX-WITCH... ER... WHOEVER--!
WHERE ARE YOU?
HELLO?
YOU WERE THE WITCH?!
YOU'RE GORGEOUS!
I DON'T THINK SO! I PREFERRED MY HIDEOUSLY WONDERFUL SELF!
UGLY IS THE NEW PRETTY, Y'KNOW!
I TOLD YOU I'D HELP YOU THROUGH THIS!
NOW YOU CAN COME STAY AT THE PALACE IN THE MEANTIME--!
WHAT?! CAN YOU BELIEVE IT?! IS HE SHALLOW ENOUGH TO FALL FOR OUR ARCH ENEMY JUST BECAUSE SHE'S GORGEOUS NOW?
IT LOOKS THAT WAY!
BUT IT LOOKS LIKE WE CAN START ALL OVER AGAIN! HOW WONDERFUL!
UH--ONE MORE THING... CAN SOMEONE TELL ME HOW TO REMOVE THIS HAIRNET?!
END

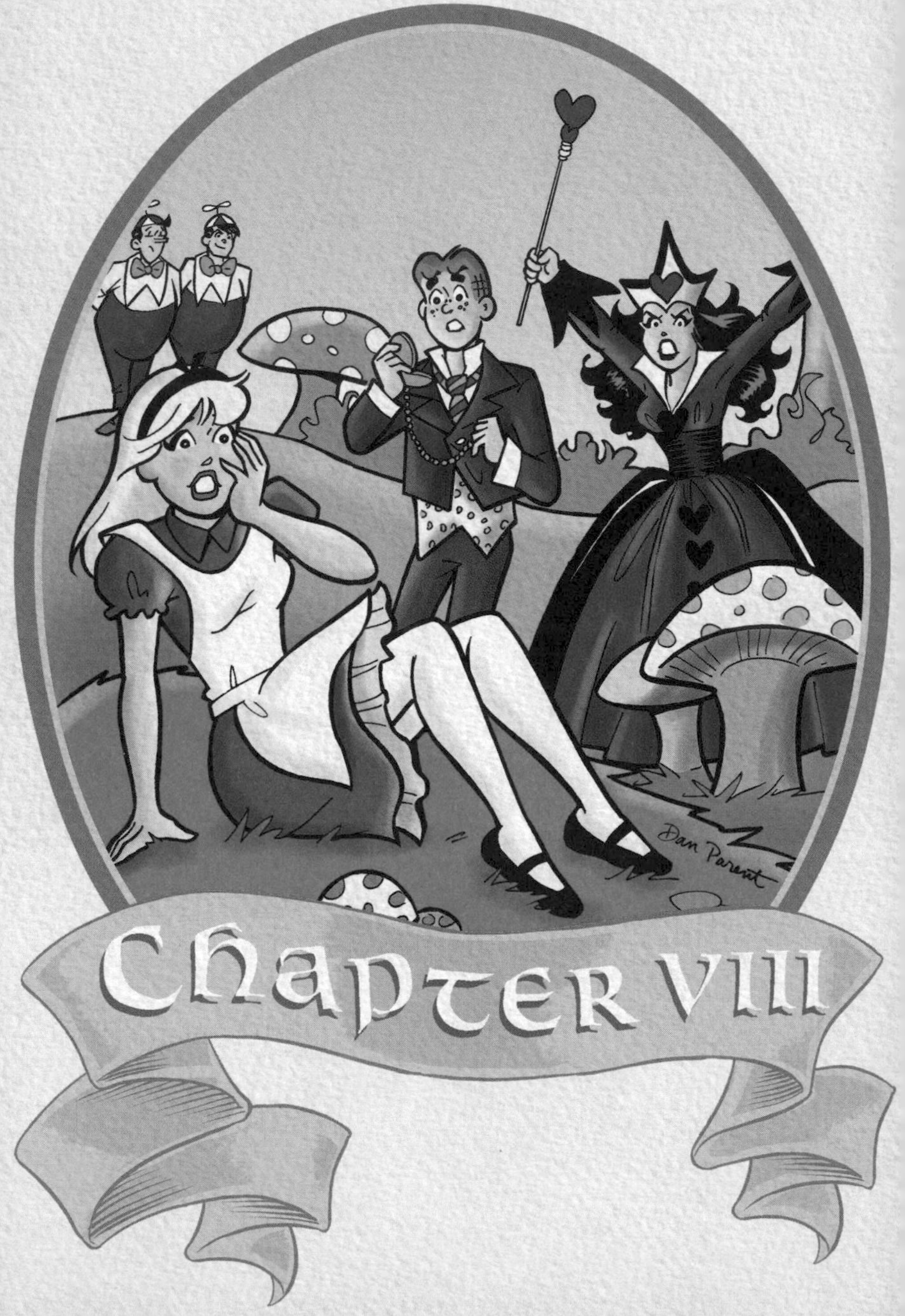
Dan Parent

Chapter VIII

 Betty in *** Wonderland

Riverdale becomes Wonderland when Betty slips through the looking glass while chasing after Archie in this modern twist on the classic tale.

The adventure unfolds as Betty encounters some interesting and rather familiar characters, including a bookish worm, Tweedle-Dee and Tweedle-Dum and a Cheshire…dog?

With the help of some magical and tasty products from Pop Tate's, Betty must find her way home, and away from the menacing yet beautiful Queen of Hearts, Veronica!

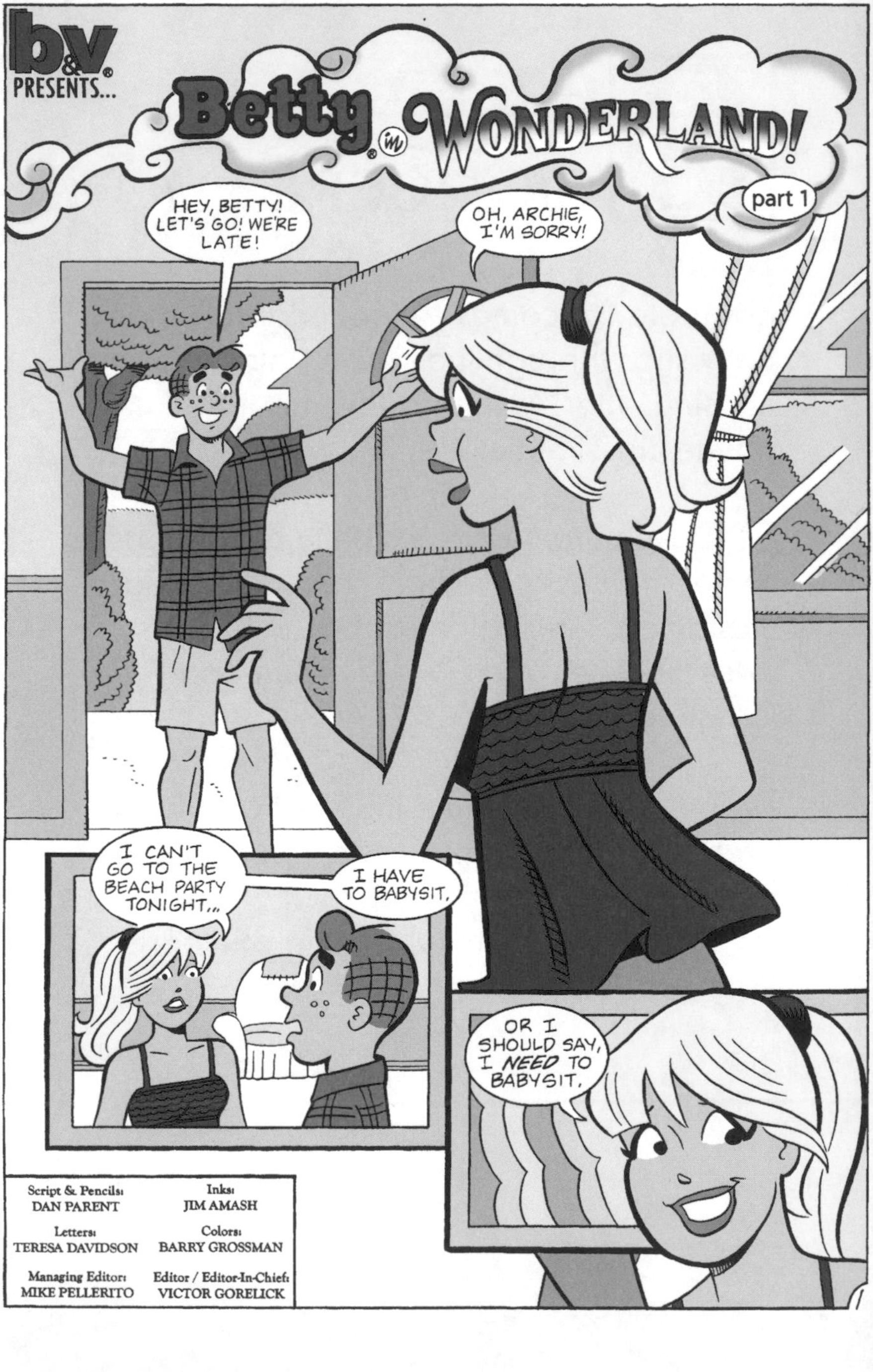
b&v PRESENTS...
Betty in WONDERLAND!
part 1
HEY, BETTY! LET'S GO! WE'RE LATE!
OH, ARCHIE, I'M SORRY!
I CAN'T GO TO THE BEACH PARTY TONIGHT...
I HAVE TO BABYSIT.
OR I SHOULD SAY, I *NEED* TO BABYSIT.
Script & Pencils: DAN PARENT
Inks: JIM AMASH
Letters: TERESA DAVIDSON
Colors: BARRY GROSSMAN
Managing Editor: MIKE PELLERITO
Editor / Editor-In-Chief: VICTOR GORELICK

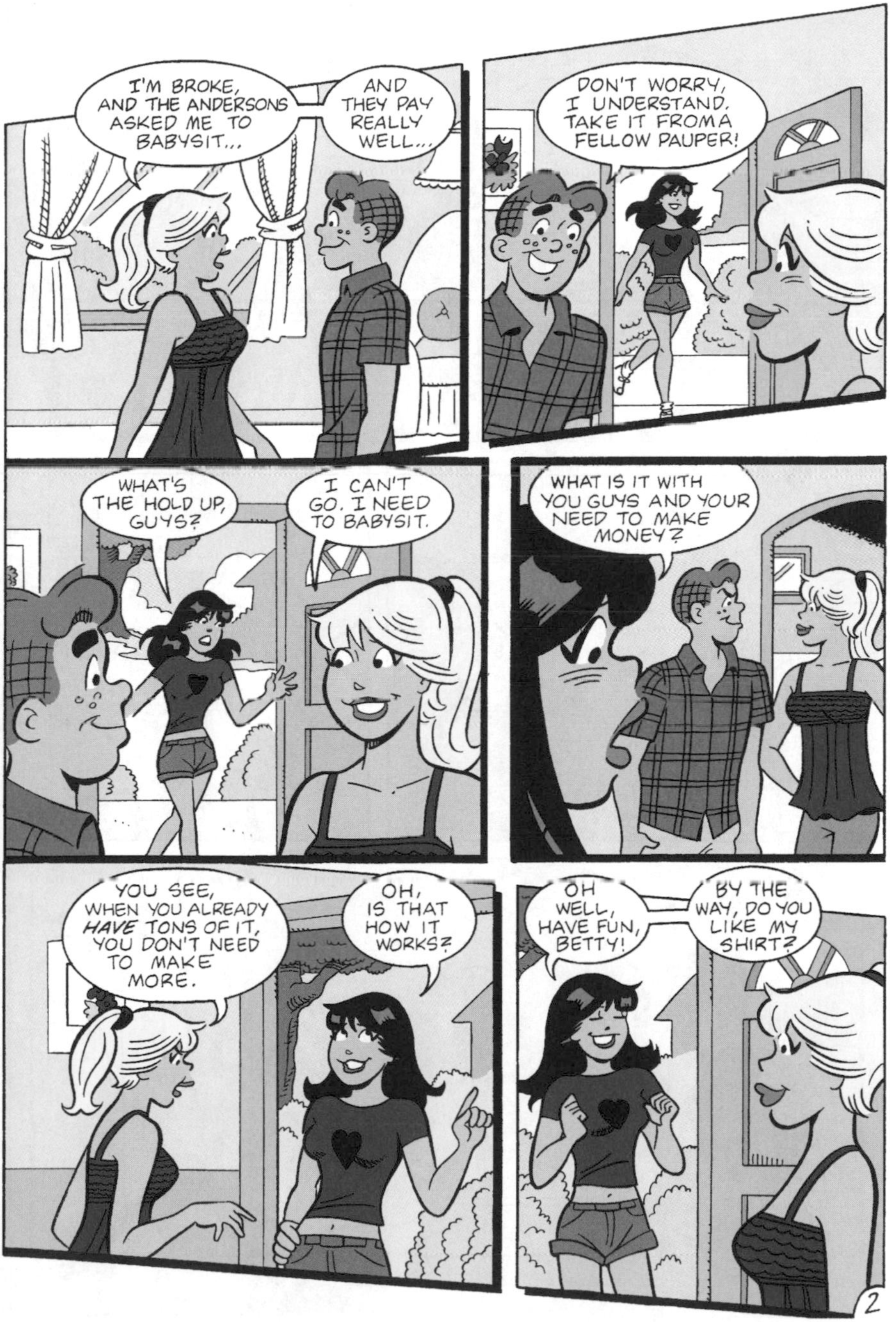
I'M BROKE, AND THE ANDERSONS ASKED ME TO BABYSIT...
AND THEY PAY REALLY WELL...
DON'T WORRY, I UNDERSTAND. TAKE IT FROM A FELLOW PAUPER!
WHAT'S THE HOLD UP, GUYS?
I CAN'T GO. I NEED TO BABYSIT.
WHAT IS IT WITH YOU GUYS AND YOUR NEED TO MAKE MONEY?
YOU SEE, WHEN YOU ALREADY *HAVE* TONS OF IT, YOU DON'T NEED TO MAKE MORE.
OH, IS THAT HOW IT WORKS?
OH WELL, HAVE FUN, BETTY!
BY THE WAY, DO YOU LIKE MY SHIRT?
2

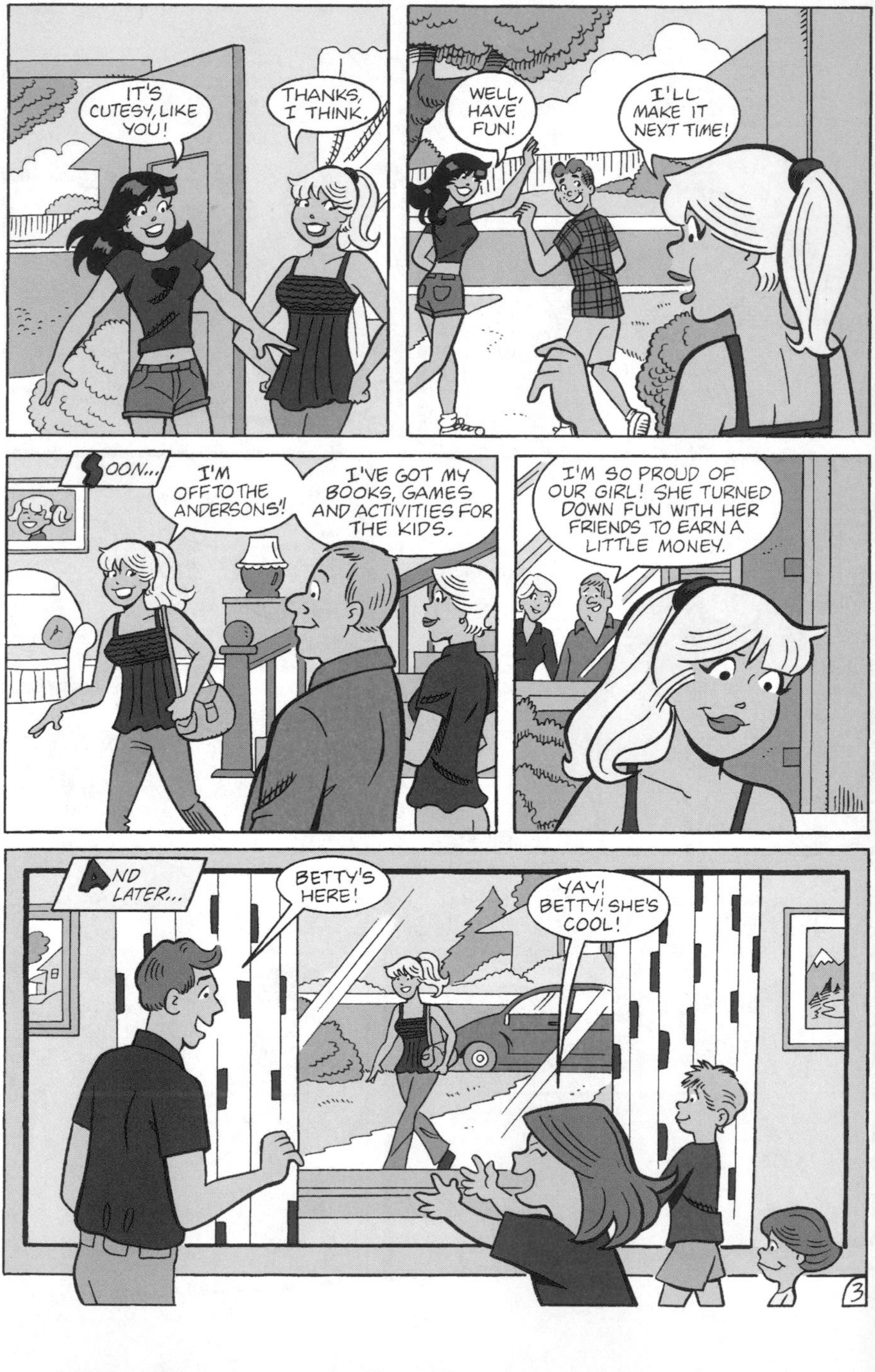
IT'S CUTESY, LIKE YOU!
THANKS, I THINK.
WELL, HAVE FUN!
I'LL MAKE IT NEXT TIME!
SOON...
I'M OFF TO THE ANDERSONS'!
I'VE GOT MY BOOKS, GAMES AND ACTIVITIES FOR THE KIDS.
I'M SO PROUD OF OUR GIRL! SHE TURNED DOWN FUN WITH HER FRIENDS TO EARN A LITTLE MONEY.
AND LATER...
BETTY'S HERE!
YAY! BETTY! SHE'S COOL!
3

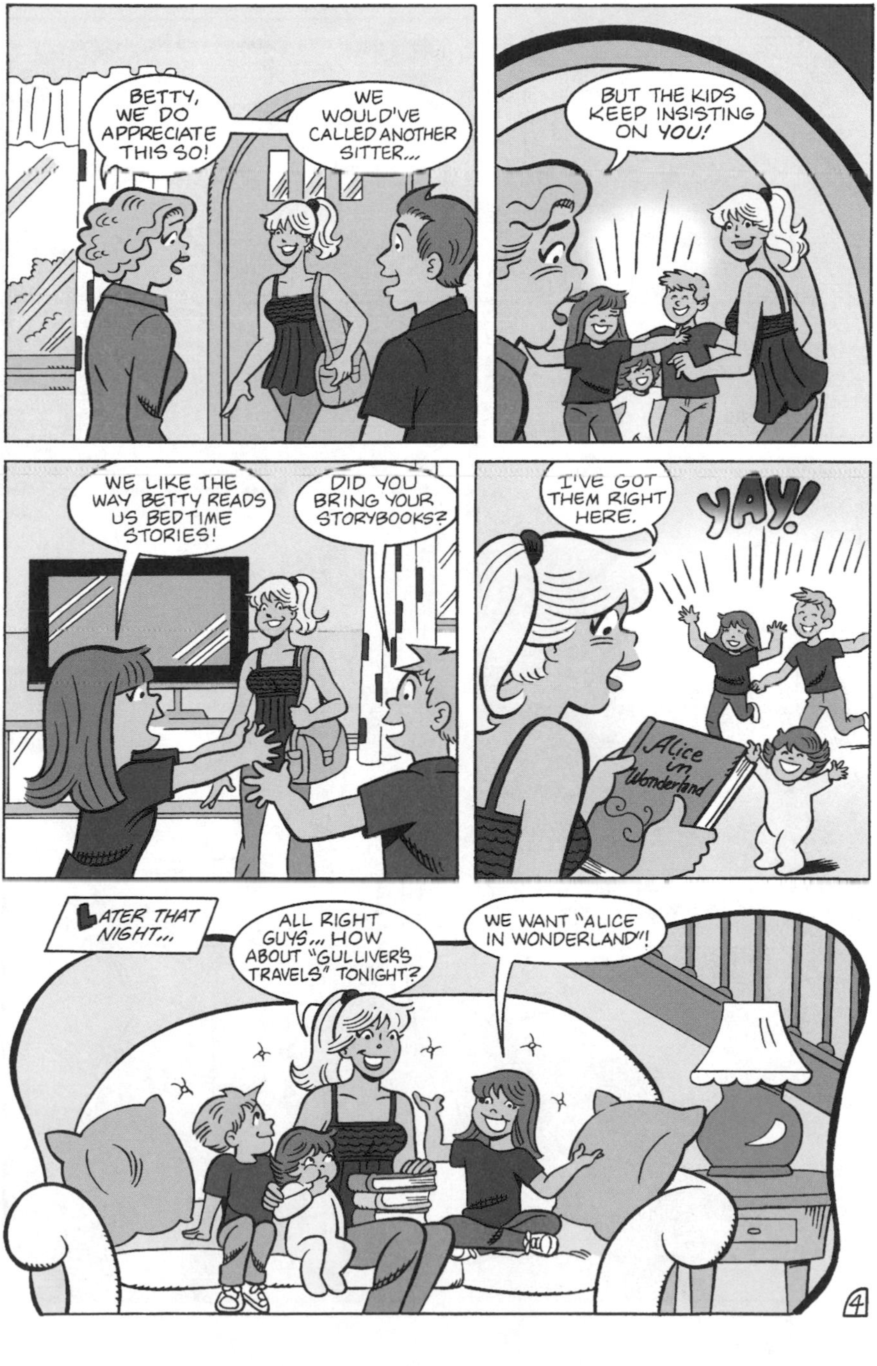
BETTY, WE DO APPRECIATE THIS SO!
WE WOULD'VE CALLED ANOTHER SITTER...
BUT THE KIDS KEEP INSISTING ON YOU!
WE LIKE THE WAY BETTY READS US BEDTIME STORIES!
DID YOU BRING YOUR STORYBOOKS?
I'VE GOT THEM RIGHT HERE.
YAY!
Alice in Wonderland
LATER THAT NIGHT...
ALL RIGHT GUYS... HOW ABOUT "GULLIVER'S TRAVELS" TONIGHT?
WE WANT "ALICE IN WONDERLAND"!
4

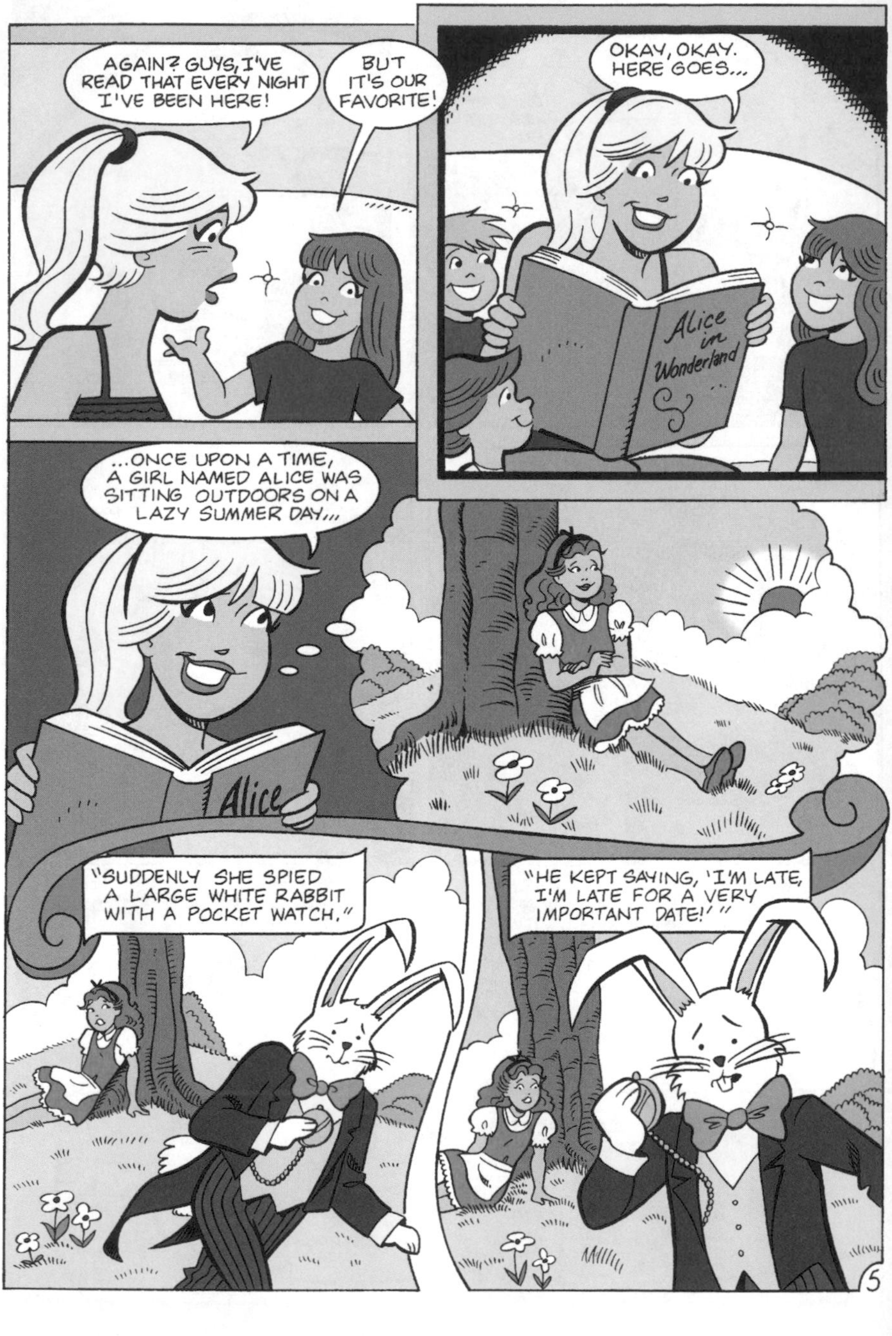
AGAIN? GUYS, I'VE READ THAT EVERY NIGHT I'VE BEEN HERE!
BUT IT'S OUR FAVORITE!
OKAY, OKAY. HERE GOES...
Alice in Wonderland
...ONCE UPON A TIME, A GIRL NAMED ALICE WAS SITTING OUTDOORS ON A LAZY SUMMER DAY...
Alice
"SUDDENLY SHE SPIED A LARGE WHITE RABBIT WITH A POCKET WATCH."
"HE KEPT SAYING, 'I'M LATE, I'M LATE FOR A VERY IMPORTANT DATE!'"
5

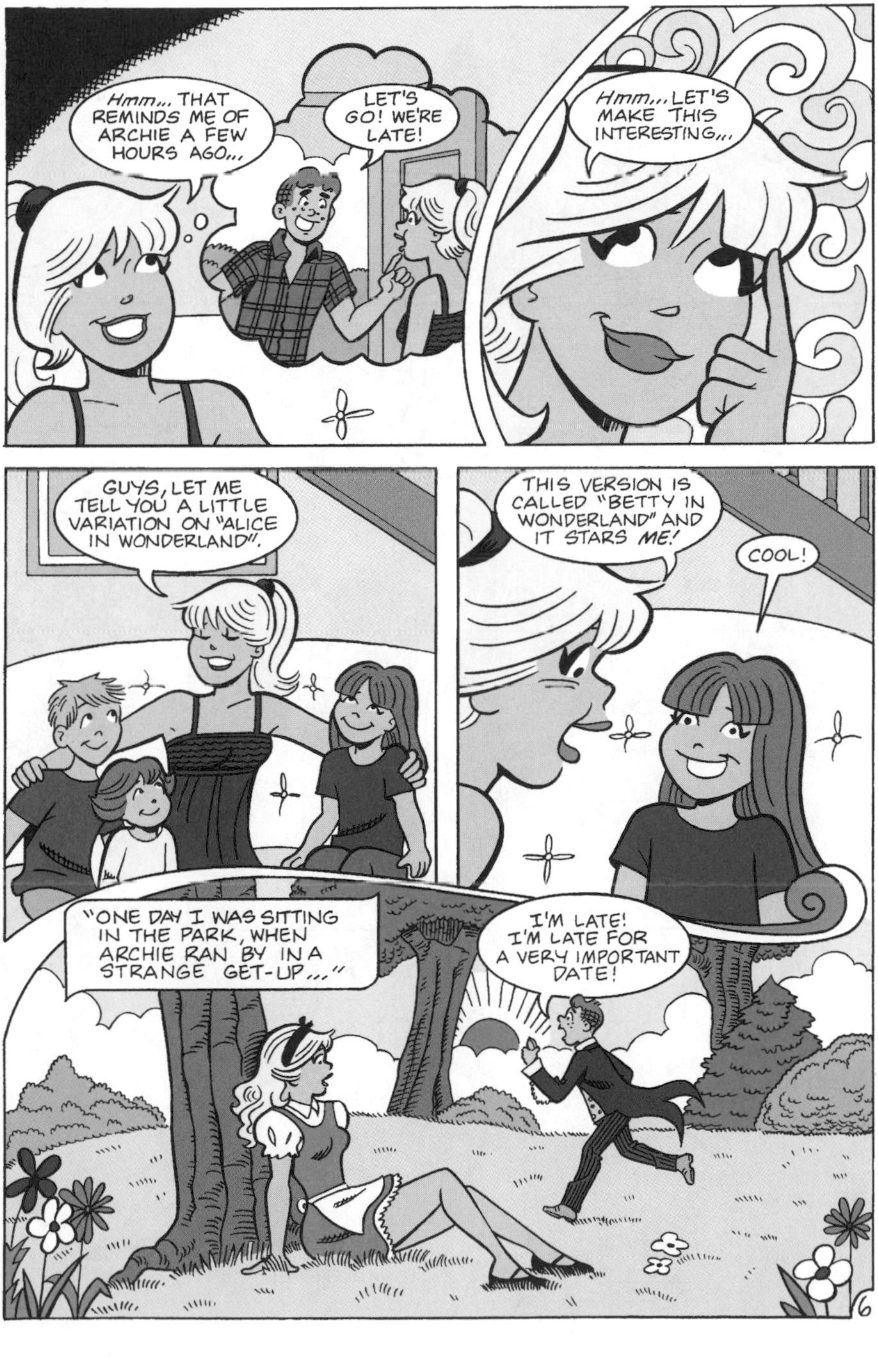
Hmm... THAT REMINDS ME OF ARCHIE A FEW HOURS AGO...
LET'S GO! WE'RE LATE!
Hmm... LET'S MAKE THIS INTERESTING...
GUYS, LET ME TELL YOU A LITTLE VARIATION ON "ALICE IN WONDERLAND".
THIS VERSION IS CALLED "BETTY IN WONDERLAND" AND IT STARS ME!
COOL!
"ONE DAY I WAS SITTING IN THE PARK, WHEN ARCHIE RAN BY IN A STRANGE GET-UP..."
I'M LATE! I'M LATE FOR A VERY IMPORTANT DATE!
6

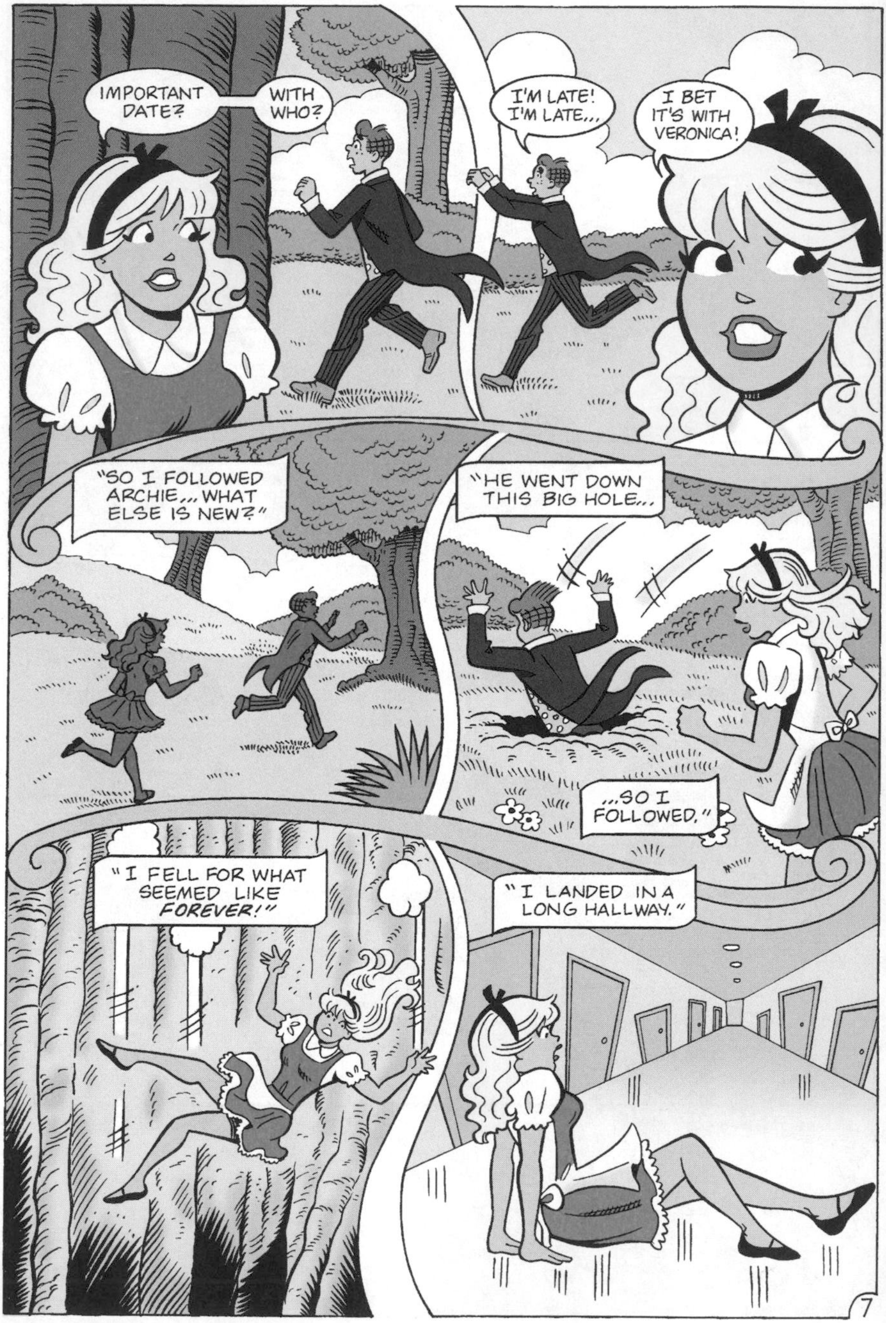
IMPORTANT DATE?
WITH WHO?
I'M LATE! I'M LATE...
I BET IT'S WITH VERONICA!
"SO I FOLLOWED ARCHIE... WHAT ELSE IS NEW?"
"HE WENT DOWN THIS BIG HOLE...
...SO I FOLLOWED."
"I FELL FOR WHAT SEEMED LIKE *FOREVER!*"
"I LANDED IN A LONG HALLWAY."
7

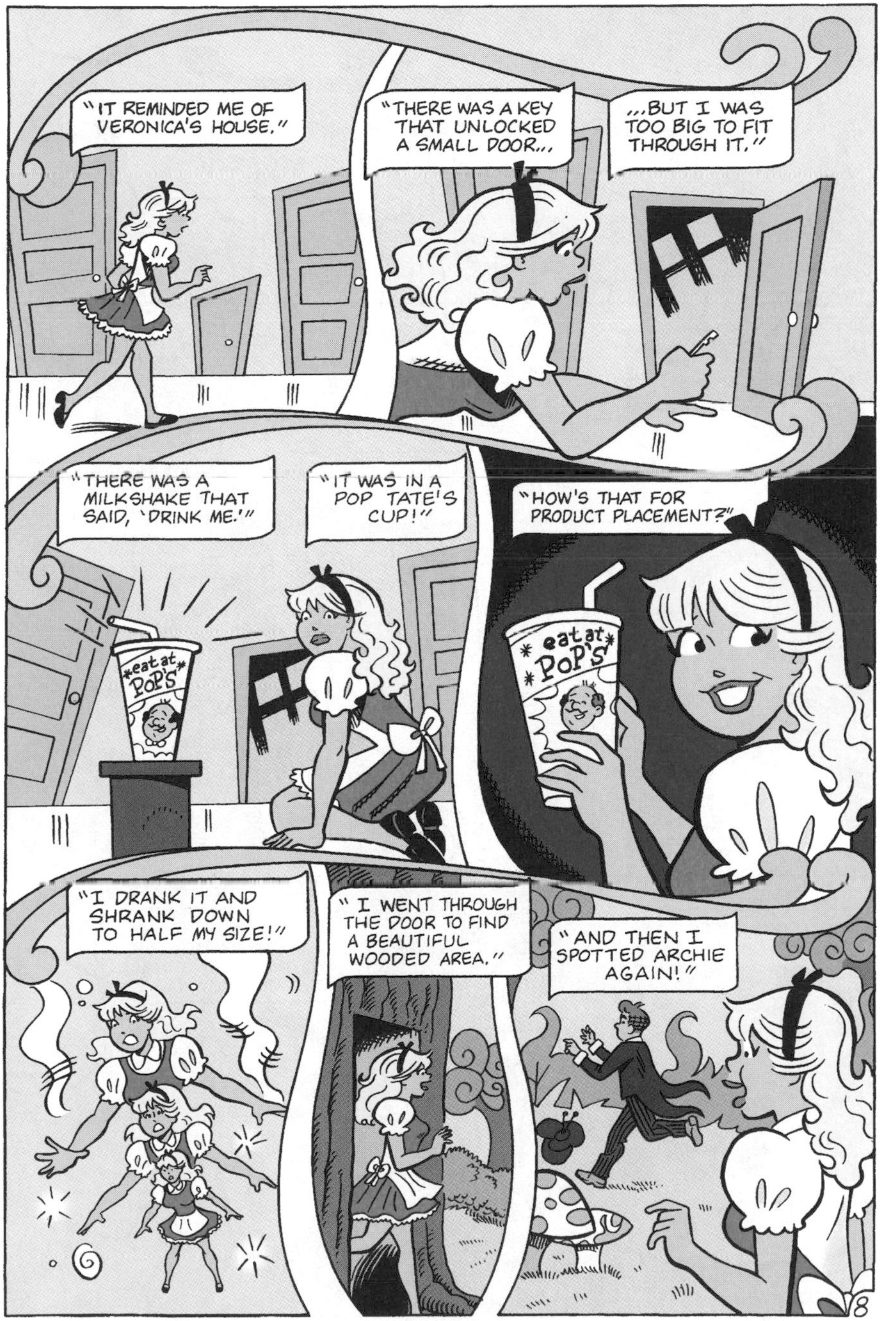
"IT REMINDED ME OF VERONICA'S HOUSE."
"THERE WAS A KEY THAT UNLOCKED A SMALL DOOR...
...BUT I WAS TOO BIG TO FIT THROUGH IT."
"THERE WAS A MILKSHAKE THAT SAID, 'DRINK ME.'"
"IT WAS IN A POP TATE'S CUP!"
eat at POP'S
"HOW'S THAT FOR PRODUCT PLACEMENT?"
eat at POP'S
"I DRANK IT AND SHRANK DOWN TO HALF MY SIZE!"
"I WENT THROUGH THE DOOR TO FIND A BEAUTIFUL WOODED AREA."
"AND THEN I SPOTTED ARCHIE AGAIN!"
8

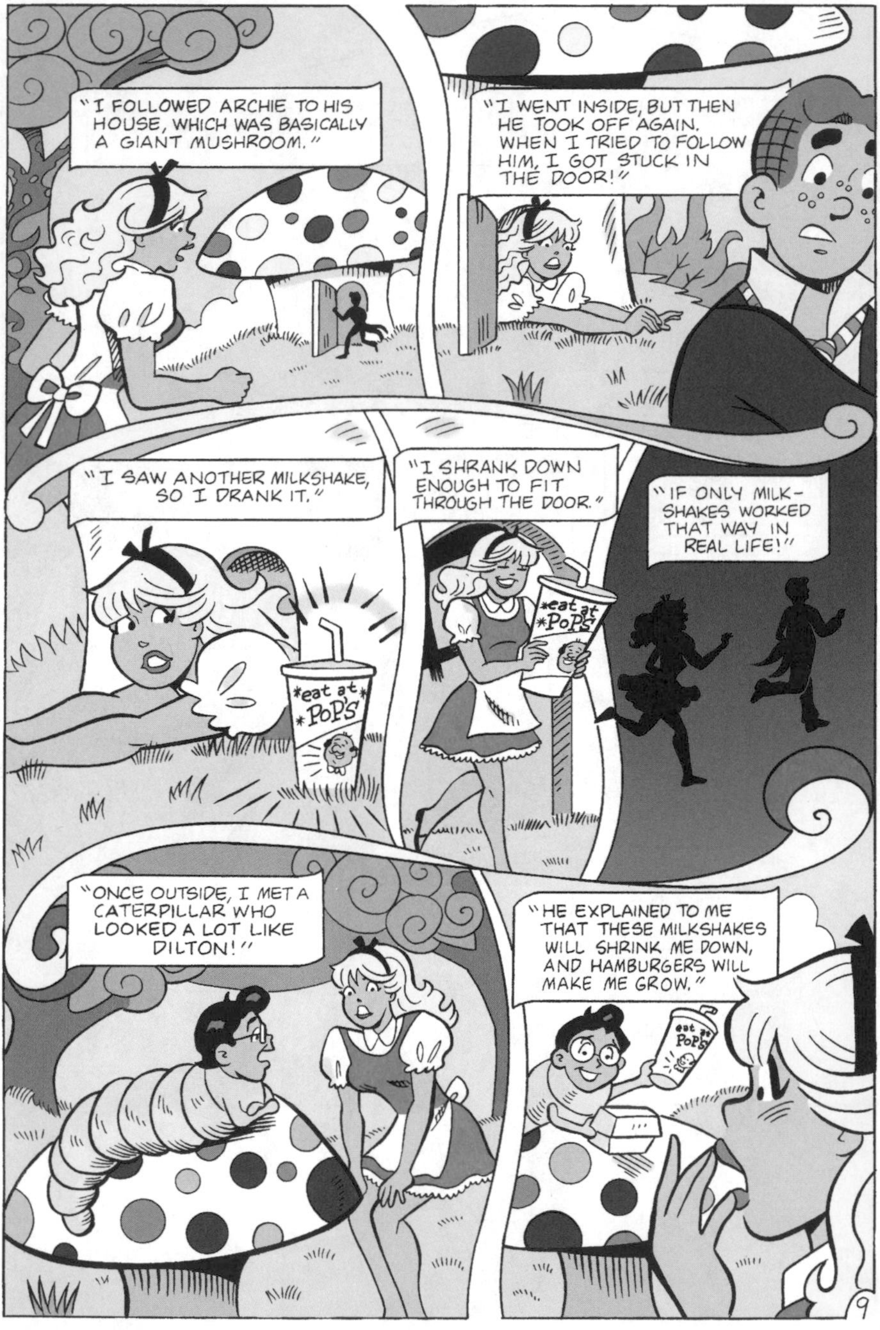
"I FOLLOWED ARCHIE TO HIS HOUSE, WHICH WAS BASICALLY A GIANT MUSHROOM."
"I WENT INSIDE, BUT THEN HE TOOK OFF AGAIN. WHEN I TRIED TO FOLLOW HIM, I GOT STUCK IN THE DOOR!"
"I SAW ANOTHER MILKSHAKE, SO I DRANK IT."
*eat at *POP'S
"I SHRANK DOWN ENOUGH TO FIT THROUGH THE DOOR."
*eat at *POP'S
"IF ONLY MILK-SHAKES WORKED THAT WAY IN REAL LIFE!"
"ONCE OUTSIDE, I MET A CATERPILLAR WHO LOOKED A LOT LIKE DILTON!"
"HE EXPLAINED TO ME THAT THESE MILKSHAKES WILL SHRINK ME DOWN, AND HAMBURGERS WILL MAKE ME GROW."
eat at POP'S
9

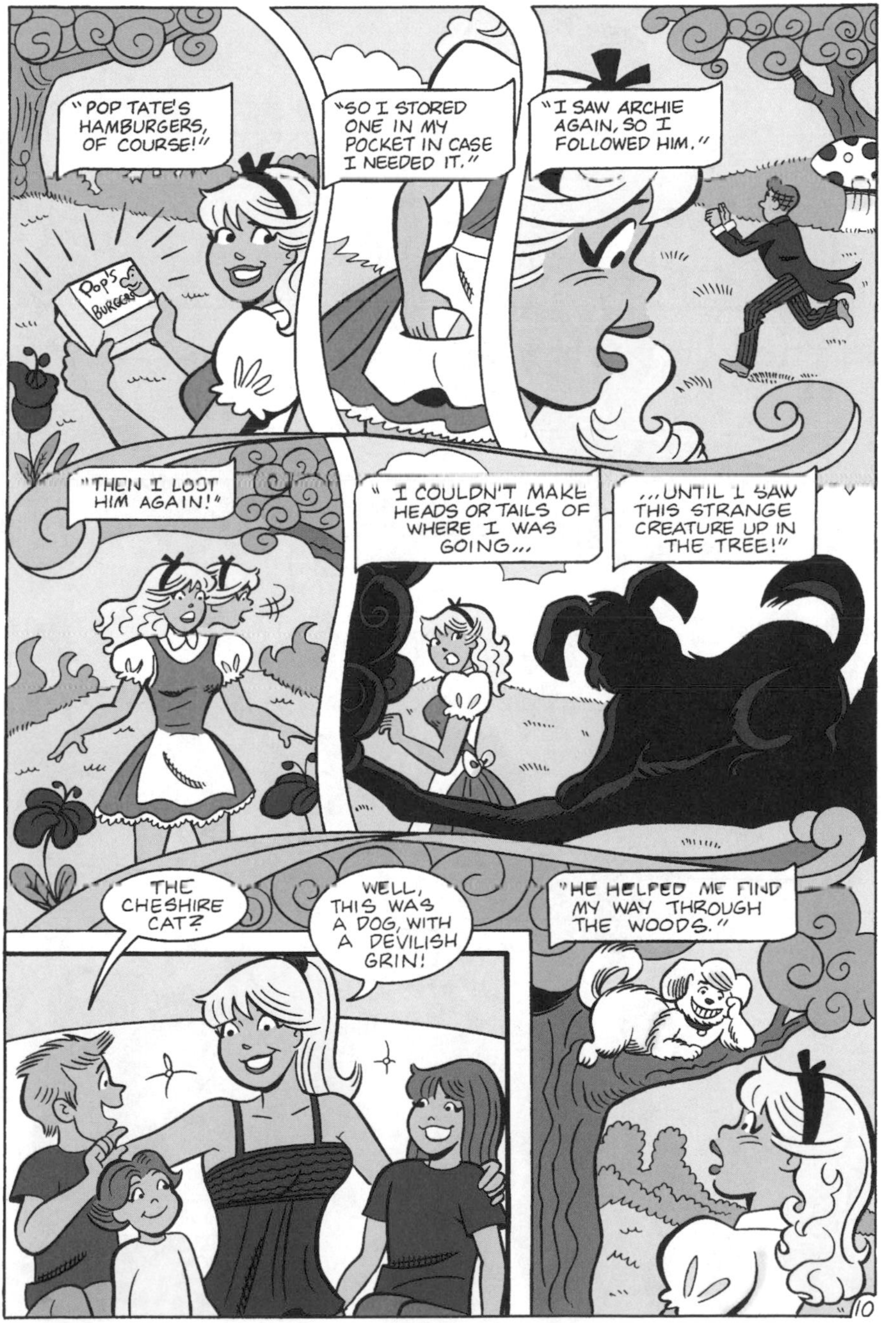
"POP TATE'S HAMBURGERS, OF COURSE!"
Pop's BURGERS
"SO I STORED ONE IN MY POCKET IN CASE I NEEDED IT."
"I SAW ARCHIE AGAIN, SO I FOLLOWED HIM."
"THEN I LOST HIM AGAIN!"
" I COULDN'T MAKE HEADS OR TAILS OF WHERE I WAS GOING...
...UNTIL I SAW THIS STRANGE CREATURE UP IN THE TREE!"
THE CHESHIRE CAT?
WELL, THIS WAS A DOG, WITH A DEVILISH GRIN!
"HE HELPED ME FIND MY WAY THROUGH THE WOODS."
10

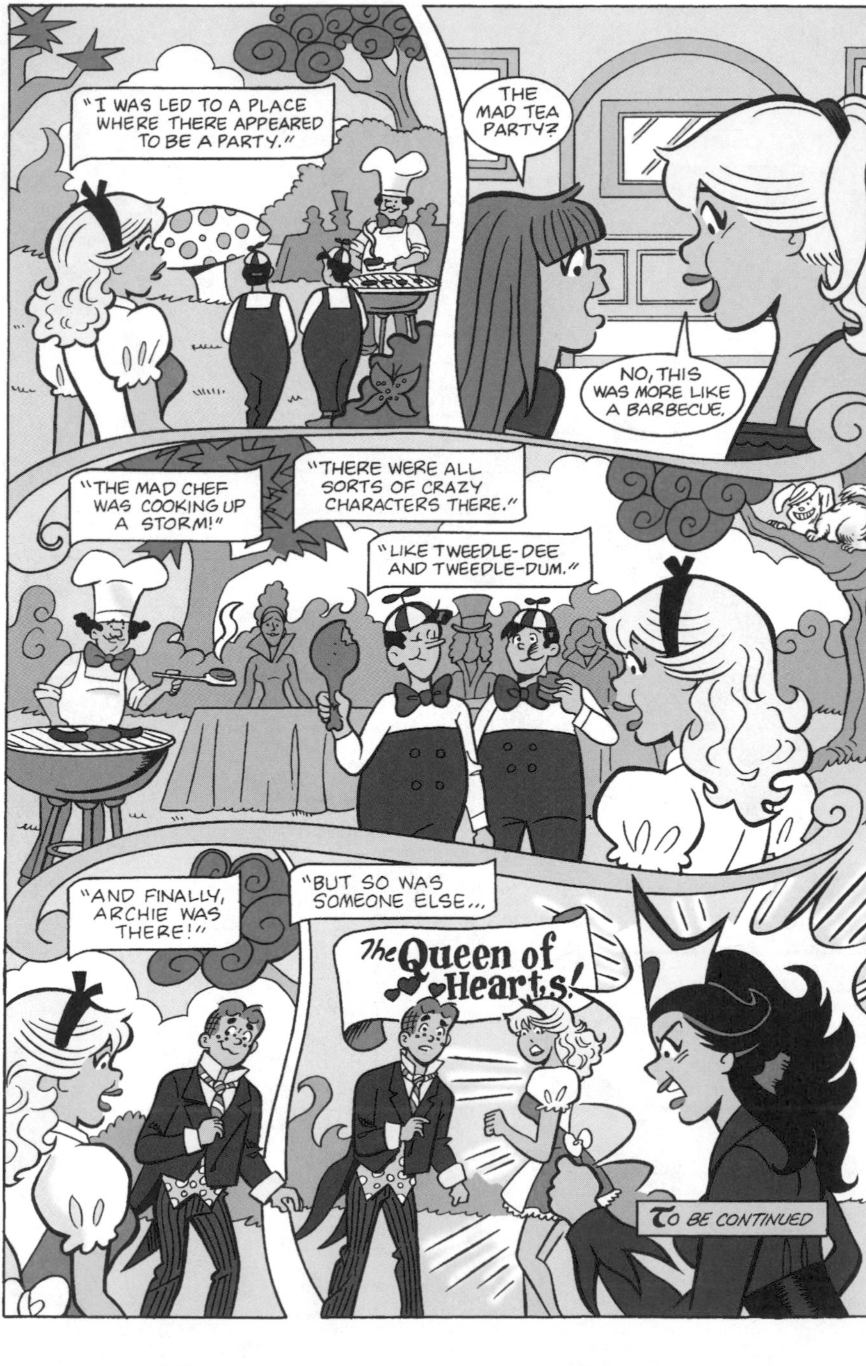
"I WAS LED TO A PLACE WHERE THERE APPEARED TO BE A PARTY."
THE MAD TEA PARTY?
NO, THIS WAS MORE LIKE A BARBECUE.
"THE MAD CHEF WAS COOKING UP A STORM!"
"THERE WERE ALL SORTS OF CRAZY CHARACTERS THERE."
"LIKE TWEEDLE-DEE AND TWEEDLE-DUM."
"AND FINALLY, ARCHIE WAS THERE!"
"BUT SO WAS SOMEONE ELSE...
The Queen of Hearts!
TO BE CONTINUED

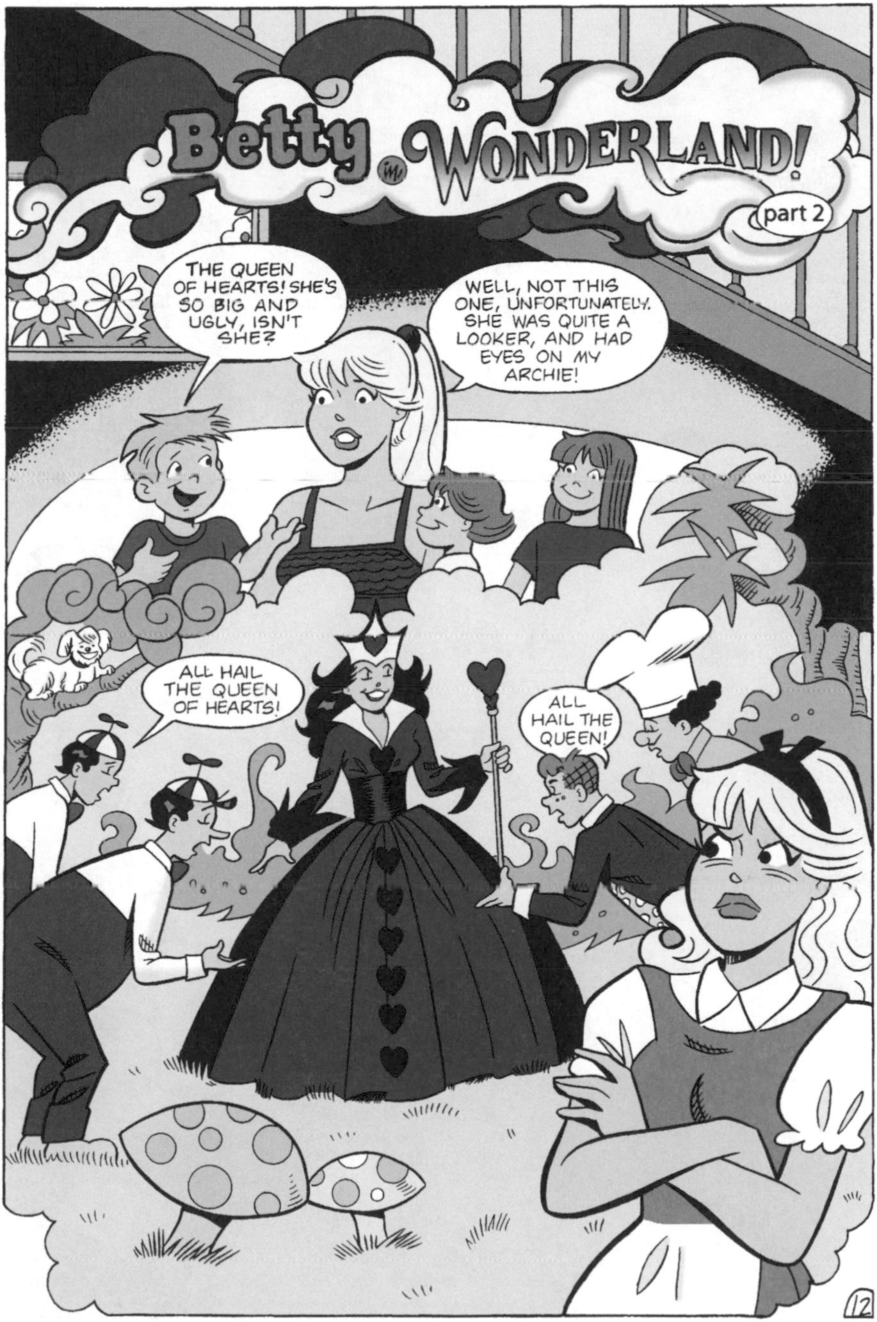
Betty in WONDERLAND!
part 2
THE QUEEN OF HEARTS! SHE'S SO BIG AND UGLY, ISN'T SHE?
WELL, NOT THIS ONE, UNFORTUNATELY. SHE WAS QUITE A LOOKER, AND HAD EYES ON MY ARCHIE!
ALL HAIL THE QUEEN OF HEARTS!
ALL HAIL THE QUEEN!
12

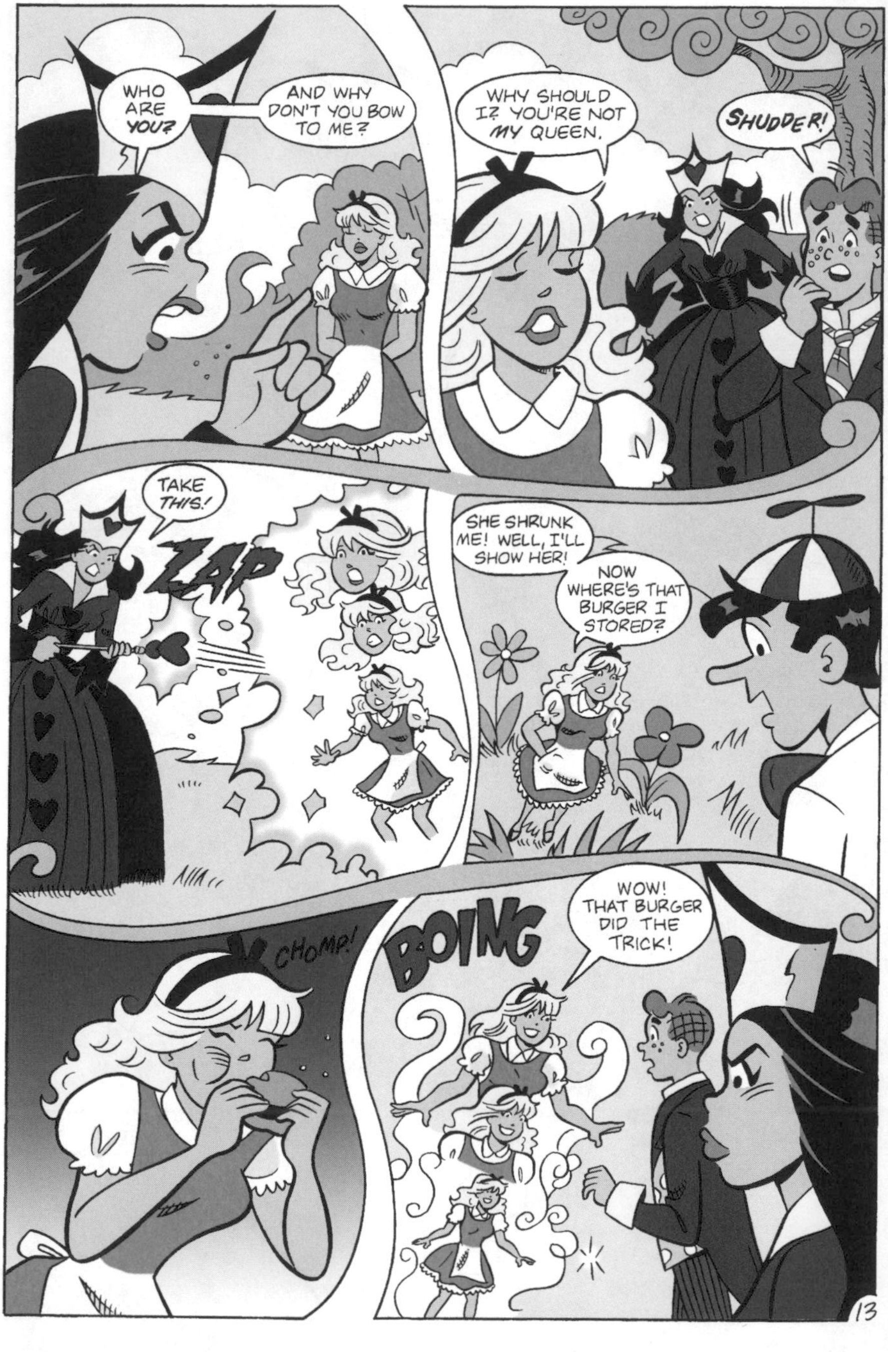
WHO ARE YOU?
AND WHY DON'T YOU BOW TO ME?
WHY SHOULD I? YOU'RE NOT MY QUEEN.
SHUDDER!
TAKE THIS!
ZAP
SHE SHRUNK ME! WELL, I'LL SHOW HER!
NOW WHERE'S THAT BURGER I STORED?
CHOMP!
BOING
WOW! THAT BURGER DID THE TRICK!
13

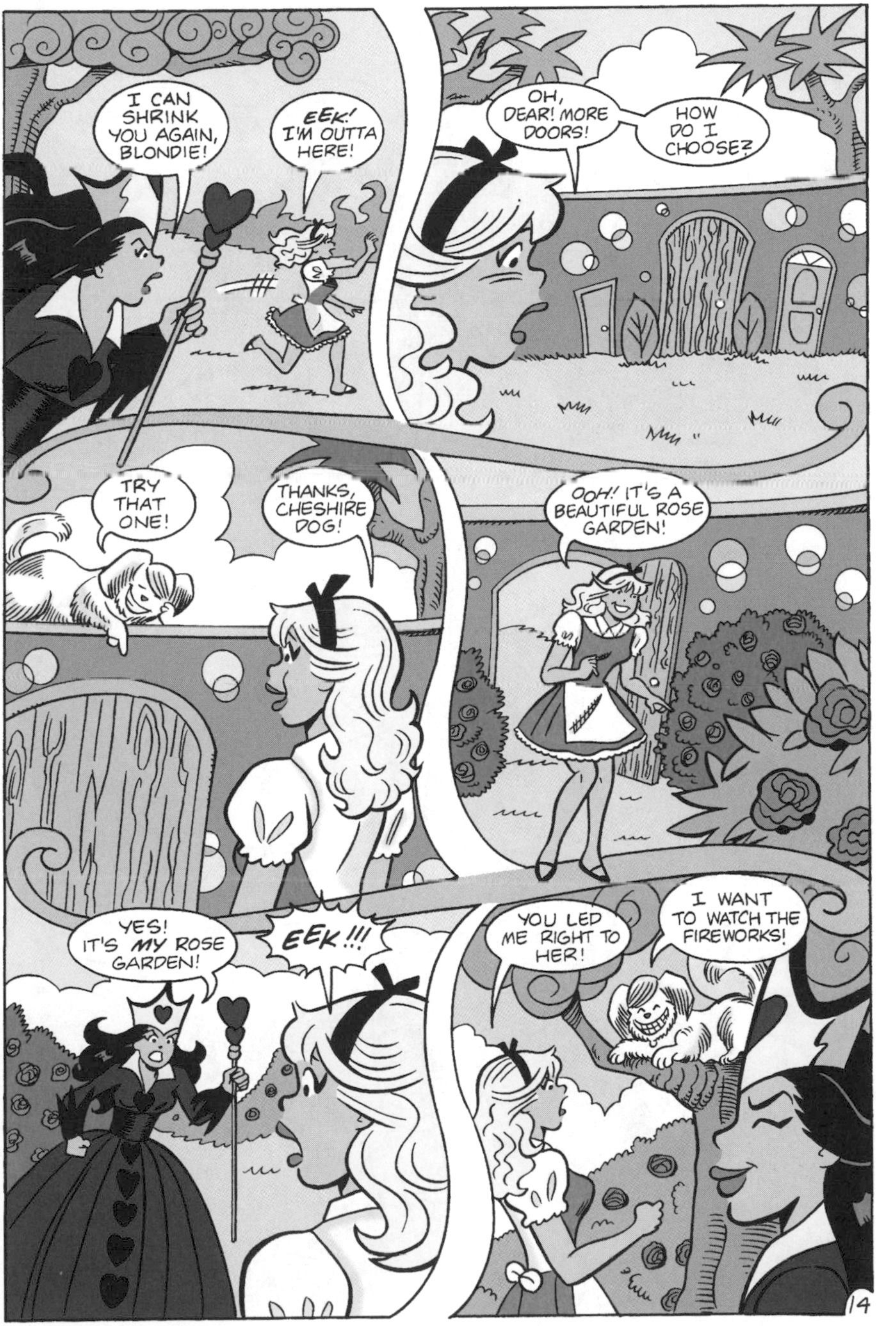
I CAN SHRINK YOU AGAIN, BLONDIE!
EEK! I'M OUTTA HERE!
OH, DEAR! MORE DOORS!
HOW DO I CHOOSE?
TRY THAT ONE!
THANKS, CHESHIRE DOG!
OOH! IT'S A BEAUTIFUL ROSE GARDEN!
YES! IT'S MY ROSE GARDEN!
EEK!!!
YOU LED ME RIGHT TO HER!
I WANT TO WATCH THE FIREWORKS!
14

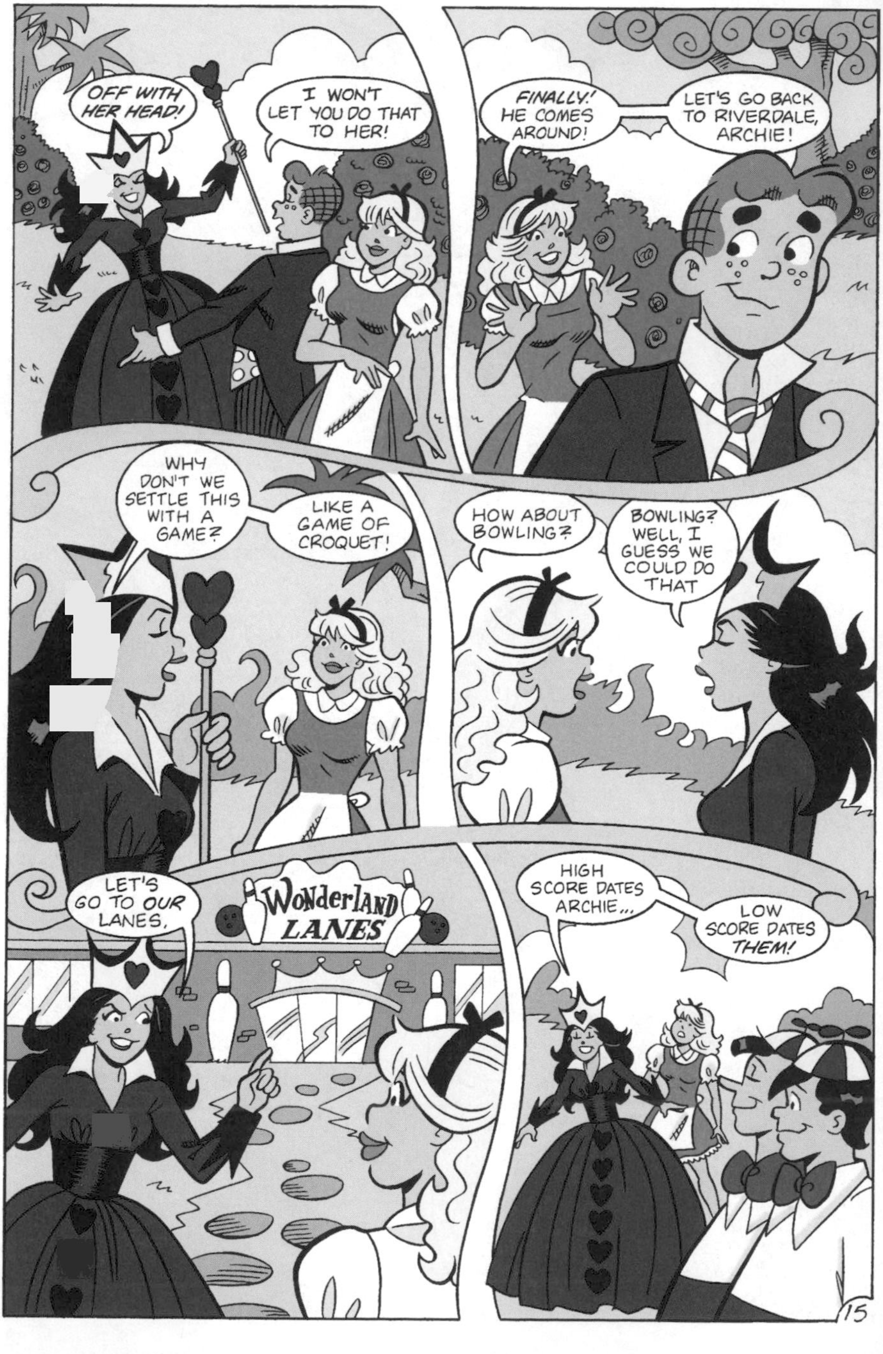
OFF WITH HER HEAD!
I WON'T LET YOU DO THAT TO HER!
FINALLY! HE COMES AROUND!
LET'S GO BACK TO RIVERDALE, ARCHIE!
WHY DON'T WE SETTLE THIS WITH A GAME?
LIKE A GAME OF CROQUET!
HOW ABOUT BOWLING?
BOWLING? WELL, I GUESS WE COULD DO THAT
LET'S GO TO OUR LANES.
WONDERLAND LANES
HIGH SCORE DATES ARCHIE...
LOW SCORE DATES THEM!
15

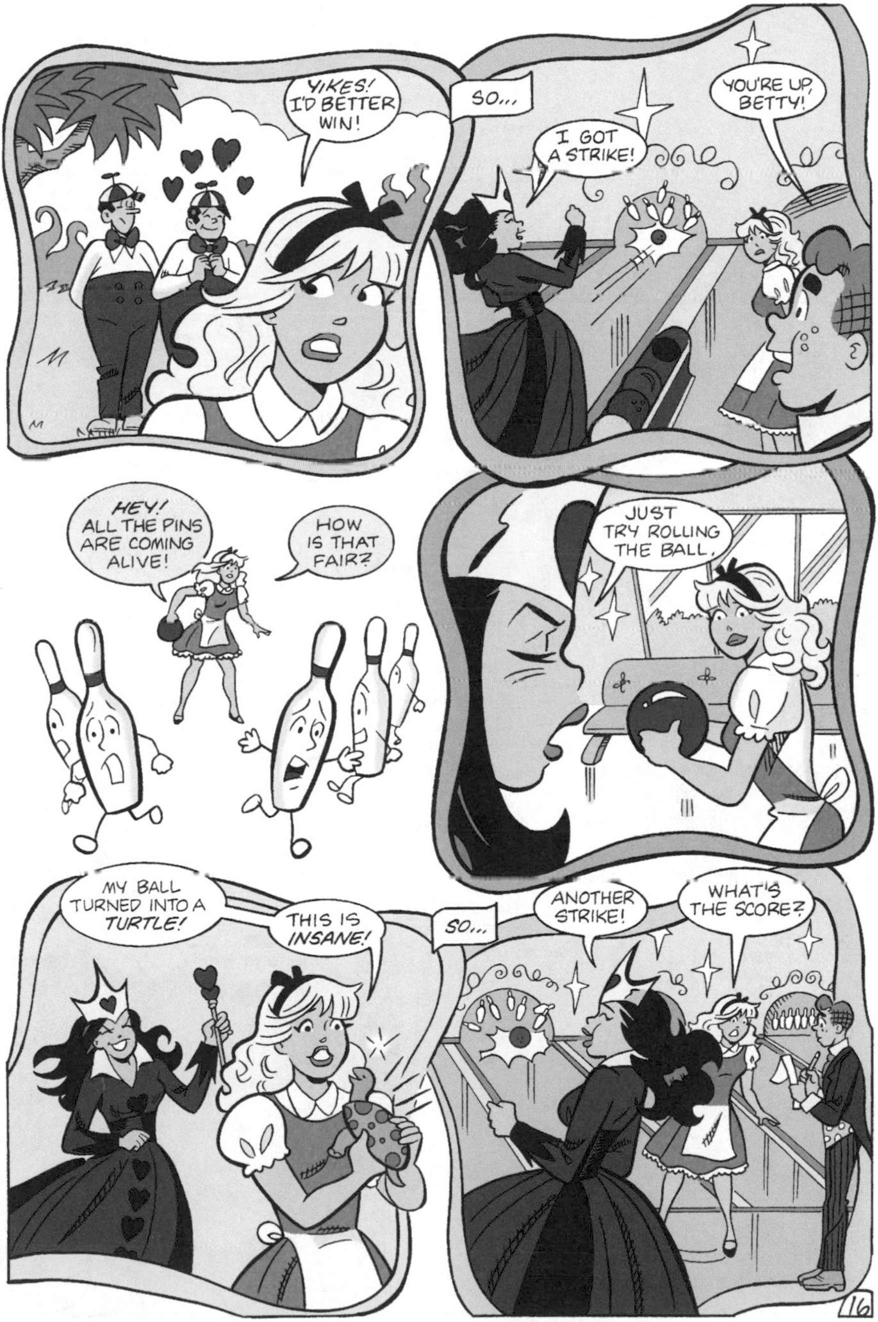
YIKES! I'D BETTER WIN!
SO...
I GOT A STRIKE!
YOU'RE UP, BETTY!
HEY! ALL THE PINS ARE COMING ALIVE!
HOW IS THAT FAIR?
JUST TRY ROLLING THE BALL.
MY BALL TURNED INTO A TURTLE!
THIS IS INSANE!
SO...
ANOTHER STRIKE!
WHAT'S THE SCORE?
16

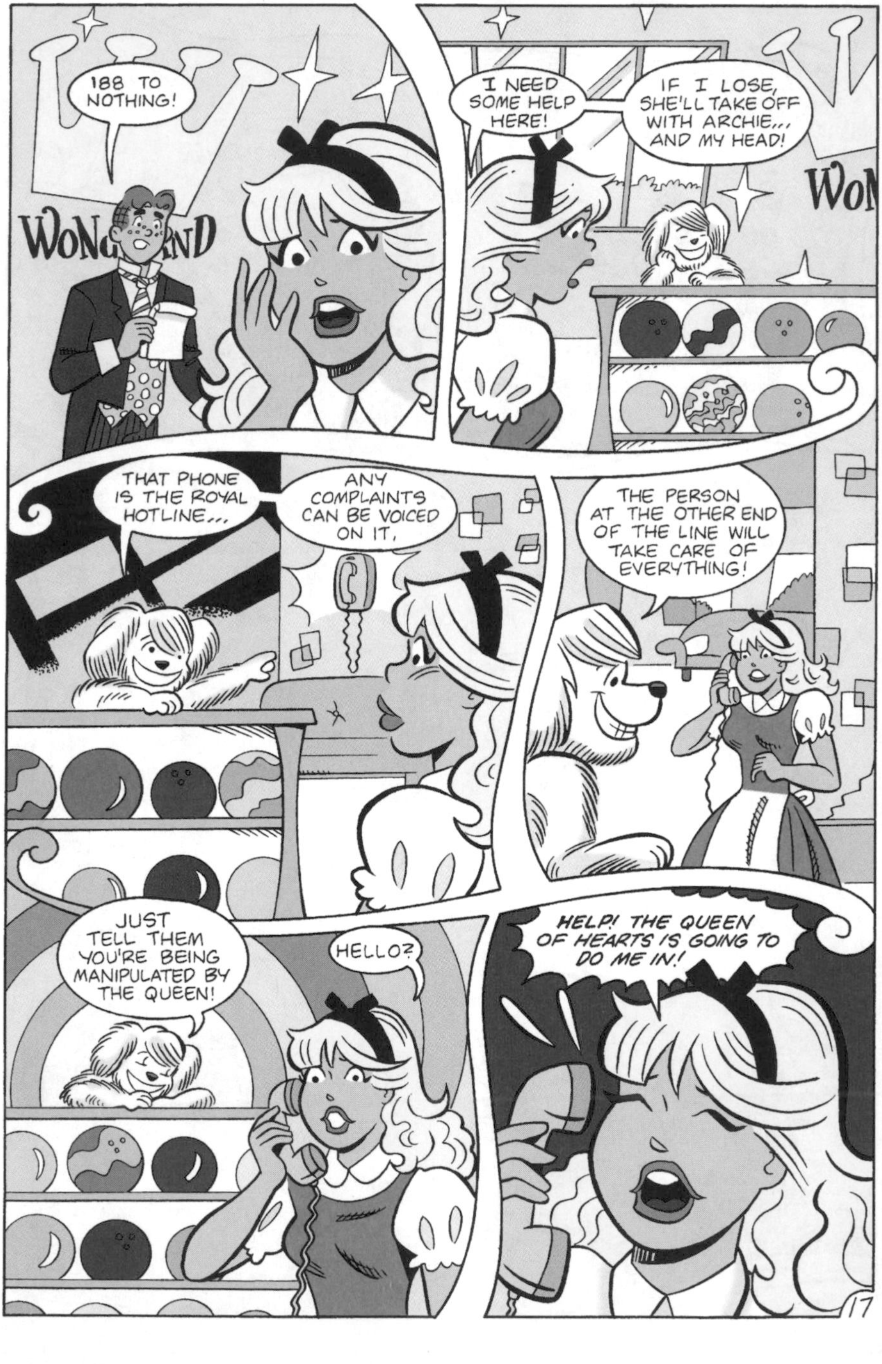
188 TO NOTHING!
WONDERLAND
I NEED SOME HELP HERE!
IF I LOSE, SHE'LL TAKE OFF WITH ARCHIE... AND MY HEAD!
THAT PHONE IS THE ROYAL HOTLINE...
ANY COMPLAINTS CAN BE VOICED ON IT.
THE PERSON AT THE OTHER END OF THE LINE WILL TAKE CARE OF EVERYTHING!
JUST TELL THEM YOU'RE BEING MANIPULATED BY THE QUEEN!
HELLO?
HELP! THE QUEEN OF HEARTS IS GOING TO DO ME IN!
17

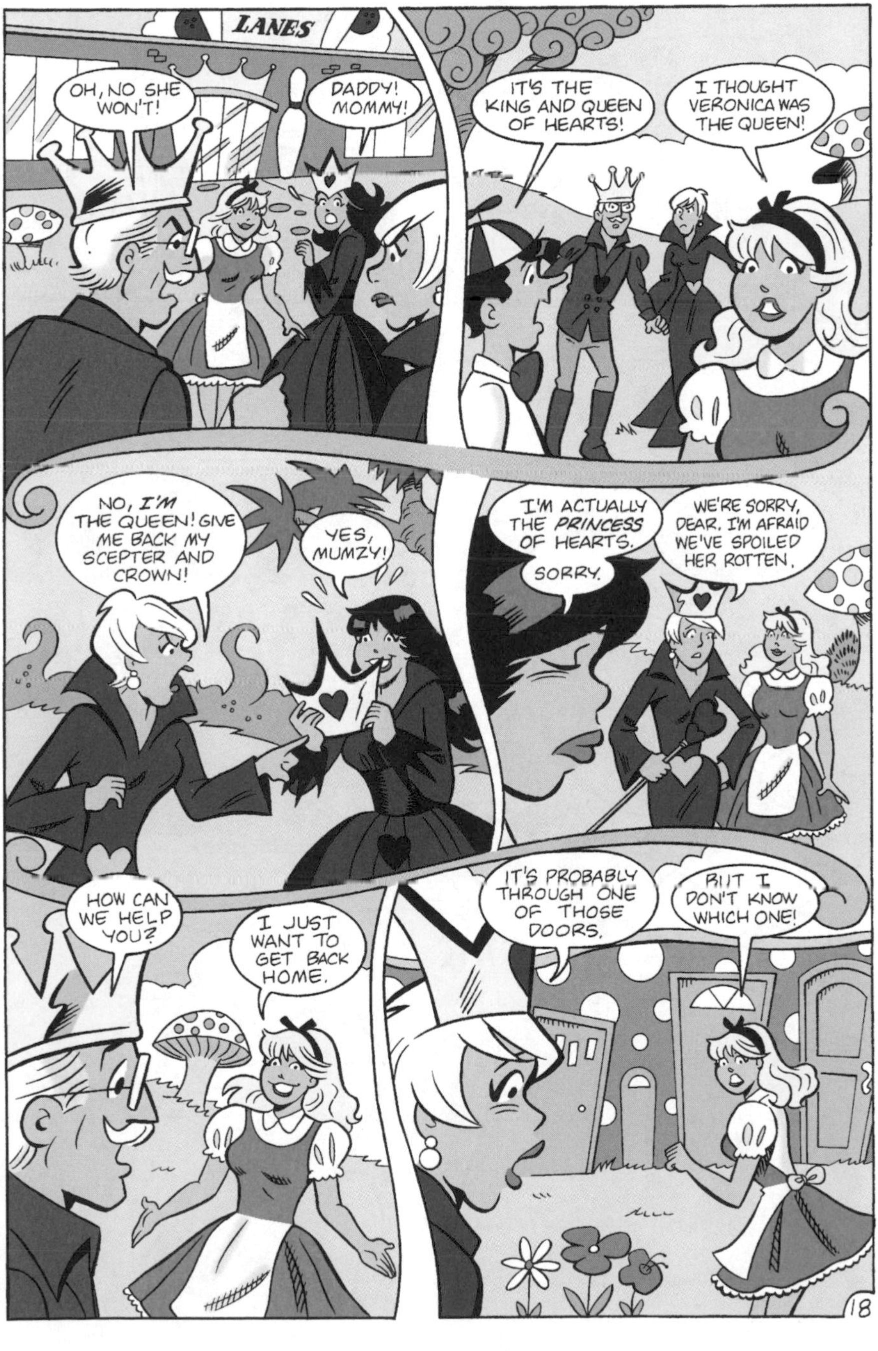
LANES
OH, NO SHE WON'T!
DADDY! MOMMY!
IT'S THE KING AND QUEEN OF HEARTS!
I THOUGHT VERONICA WAS THE QUEEN!
NO, I'M THE QUEEN! GIVE ME BACK MY SCEPTER AND CROWN!
YES, MUMZY!
I'M ACTUALLY THE PRINCESS OF HEARTS.
SORRY.
WE'RE SORRY, DEAR. I'M AFRAID WE'VE SPOILED HER ROTTEN.
HOW CAN WE HELP YOU?
I JUST WANT TO GET BACK HOME.
IT'S PROBABLY THROUGH ONE OF THOSE DOORS.
BUT I DON'T KNOW WHICH ONE!
18

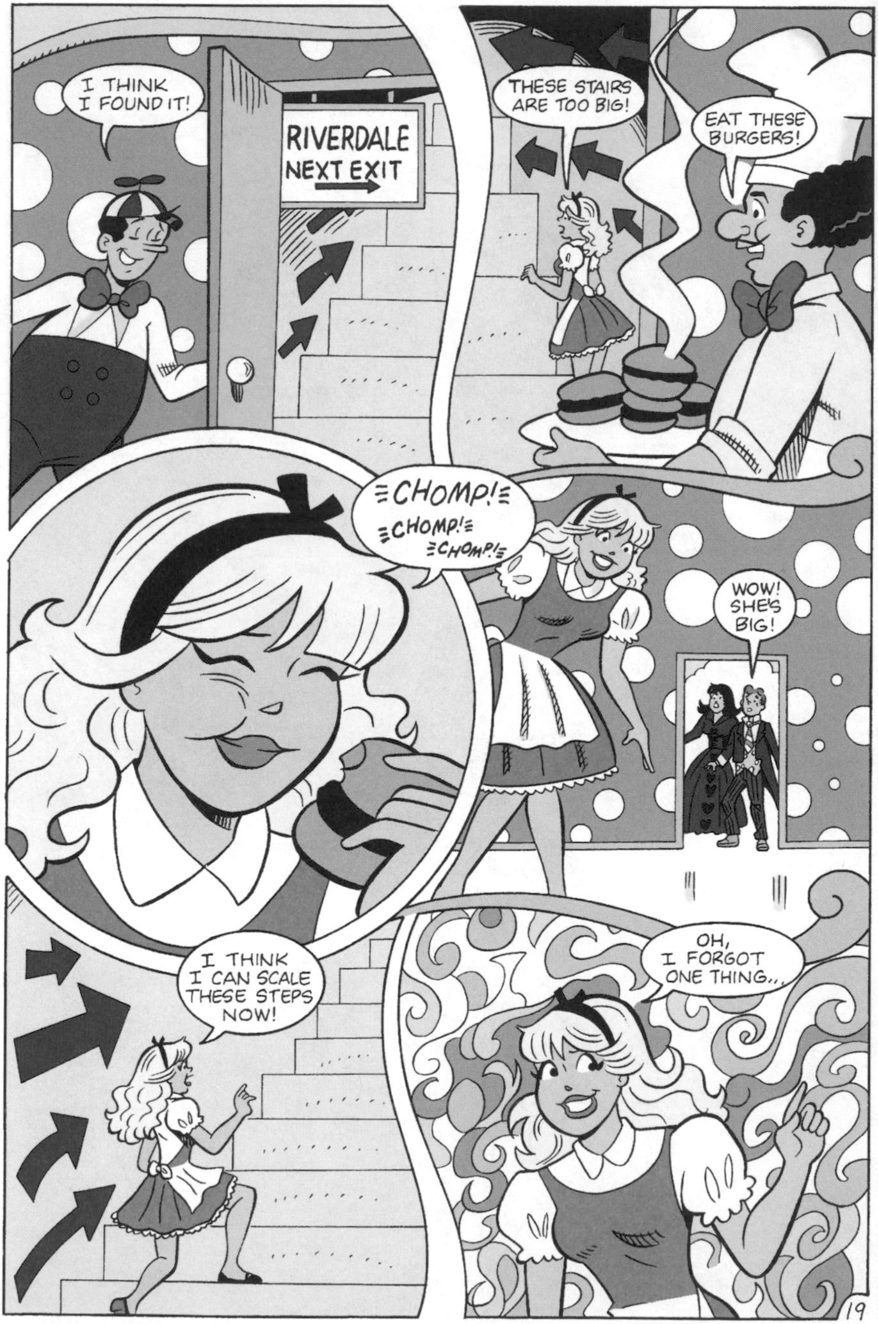
I THINK I FOUND IT!
RIVERDALE NEXT EXIT
THESE STAIRS ARE TOO BIG!
EAT THESE BURGERS!
CHOMP! CHOMP! CHOMP!
WOW! SHE'S BIG!
I THINK I CAN SCALE THESE STEPS NOW!
OH, I FORGOT ONE THING...
19

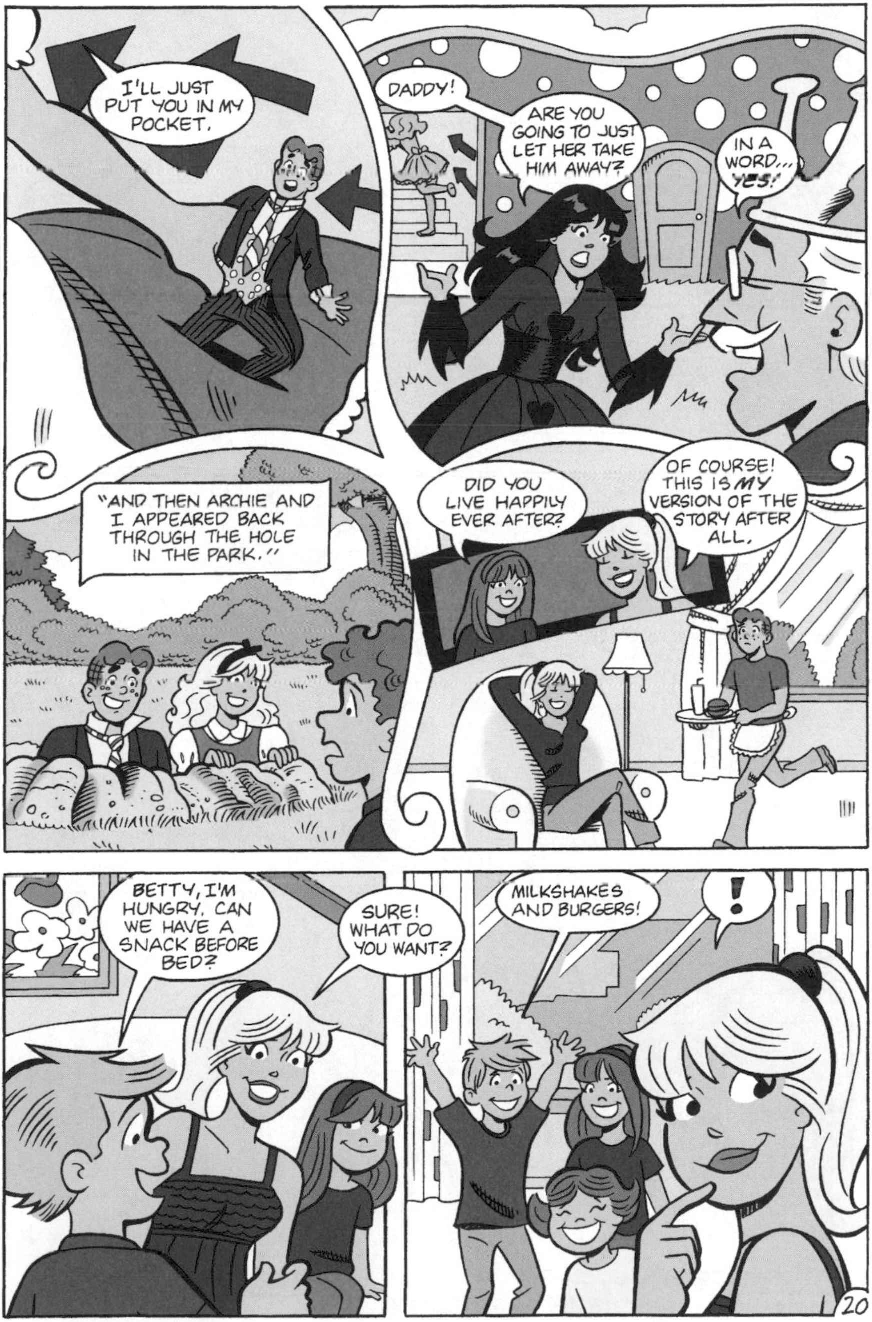
I'LL JUST PUT YOU IN MY POCKET.
DADDY!
ARE YOU GOING TO JUST LET HER TAKE HIM AWAY?
IN A WORD... YES!
"AND THEN ARCHIE AND I APPEARED BACK THROUGH THE HOLE IN THE PARK."
DID YOU LIVE HAPPILY EVER AFTER?
OF COURSE! THIS IS MY VERSION OF THE STORY AFTER ALL.
BETTY, I'M HUNGRY. CAN WE HAVE A SNACK BEFORE BED?
SURE! WHAT DO YOU WANT?
MILKSHAKES AND BURGERS!
!
20

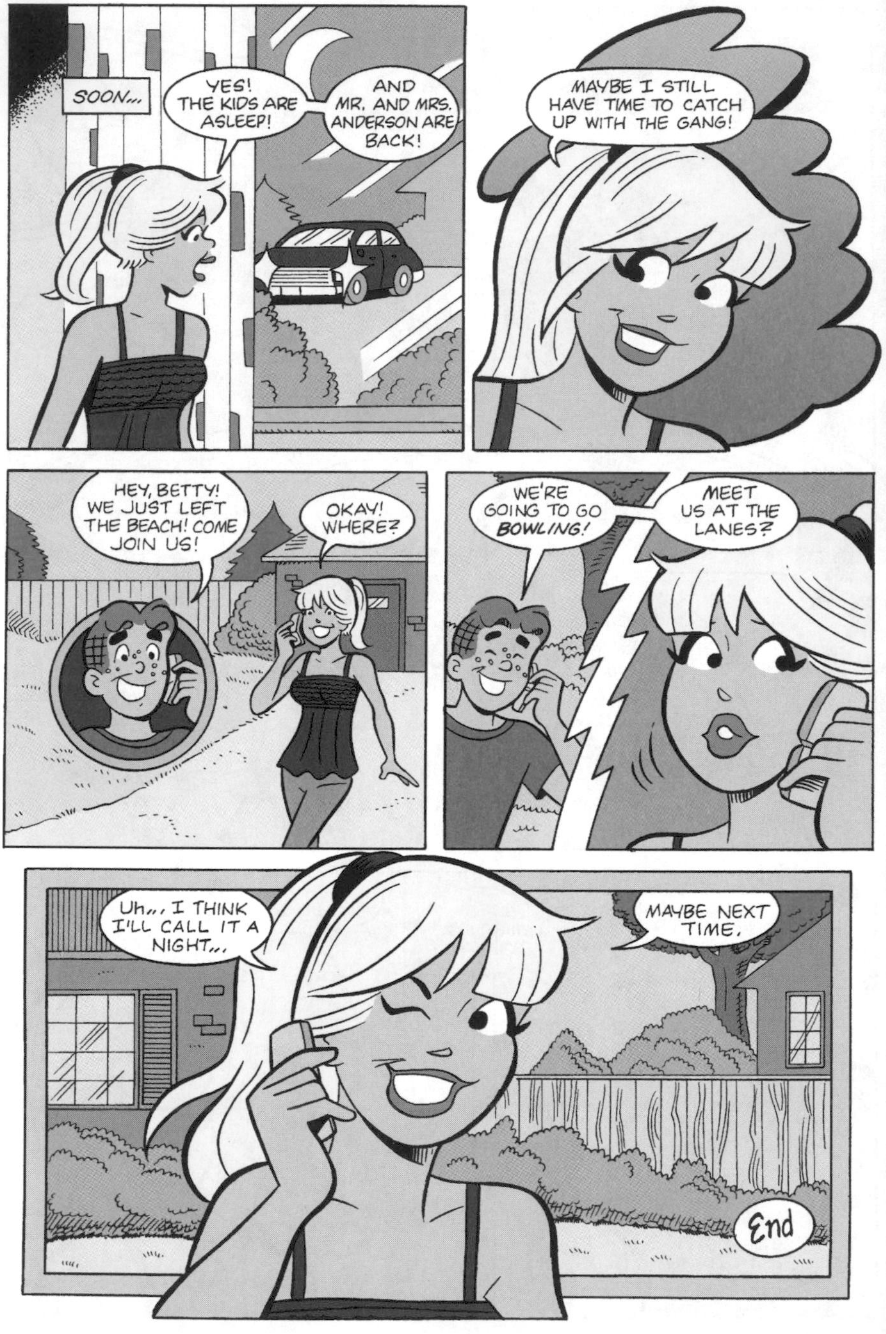
SOON...
YES! THE KIDS ARE ASLEEP!
AND MR. AND MRS. ANDERSON ARE BACK!
MAYBE I STILL HAVE TIME TO CATCH UP WITH THE GANG!
HEY, BETTY! WE JUST LEFT THE BEACH! COME JOIN US!
OKAY! WHERE?
WE'RE GOING TO GO BOWLING!
MEET US AT THE LANES?
Uh... I THINK I'LL CALL IT A NIGHT...
MAYBE NEXT TIME.
End

Bonus ** Pinup Page

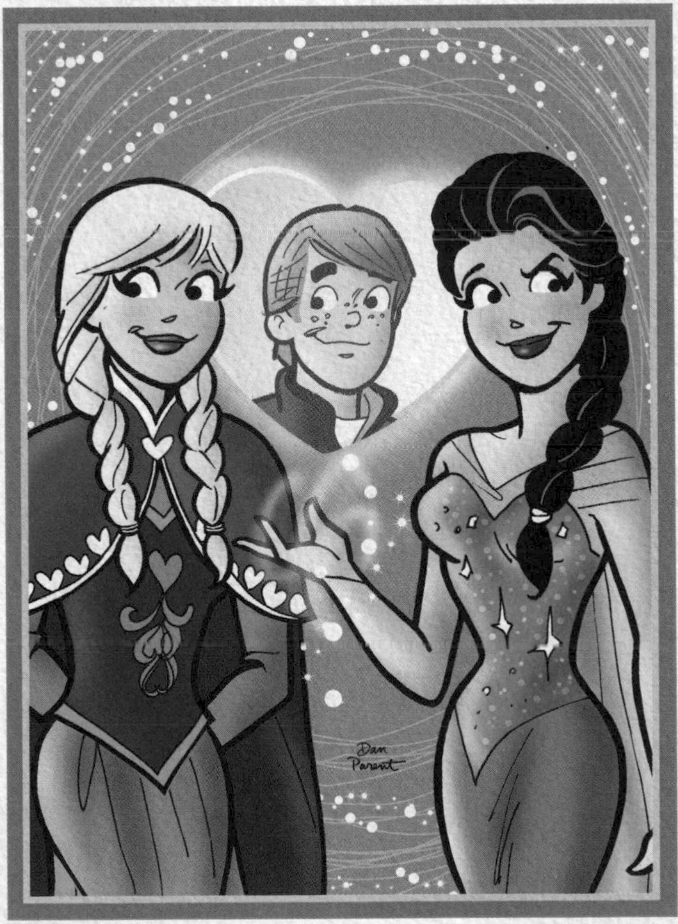
Dan Parent

B&V in "Chilled"

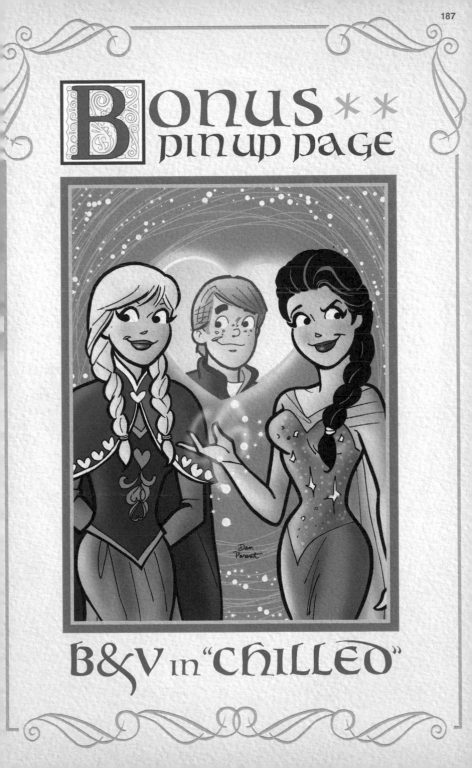

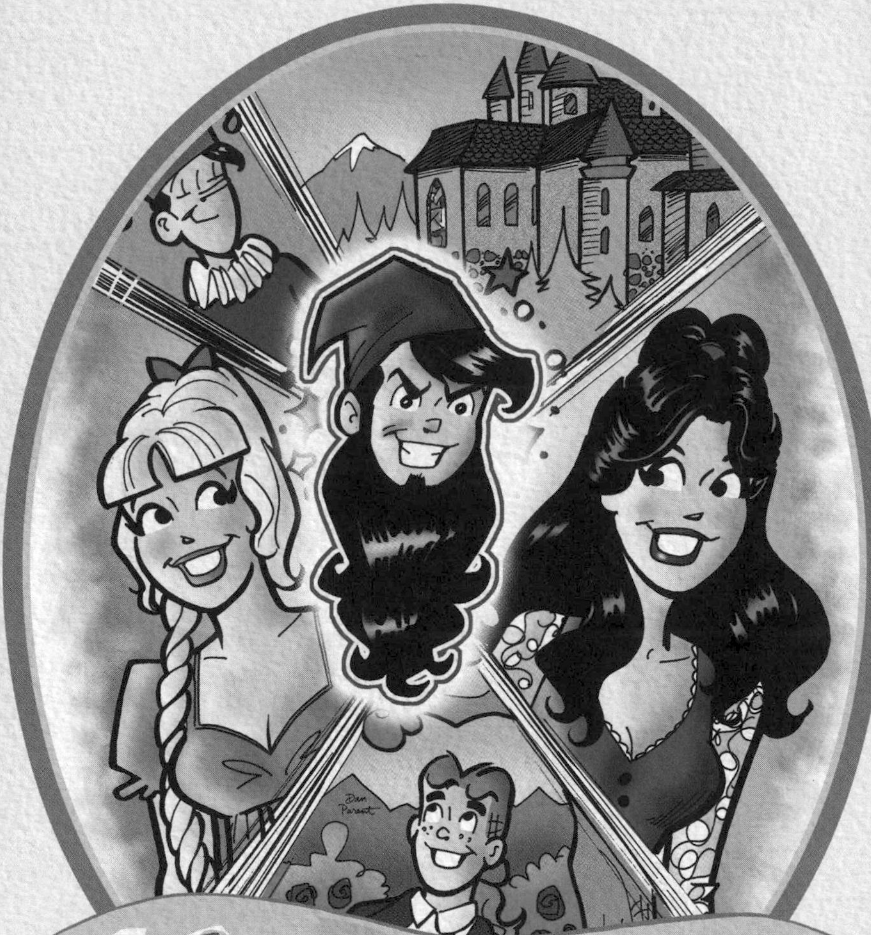
Dan Parent

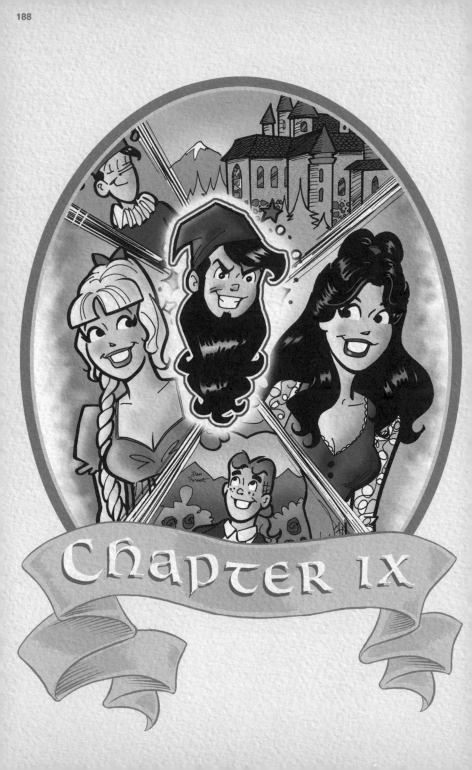

Chapter IX

 Reggiestiltskin

Betty and Veronica are two peasant girls who fall in love with a Prince named Archie—unfortunately Prince Archie is already betrothed to the evil princess, Cheryl!

When Cheryl finds out that Archie's eyes have wandered to the two lovely peasant girls, she imprisons them in her dungeon. The only way out? The girls need to spin straw into gold!

When an evil troll enters the mix, things go from dangerous to off-the-wall. Will the magical imp be friend or foe? The answer lies in this modern, Riverdale-style take on the classic fairy tale, "Rumplestiltskin!"

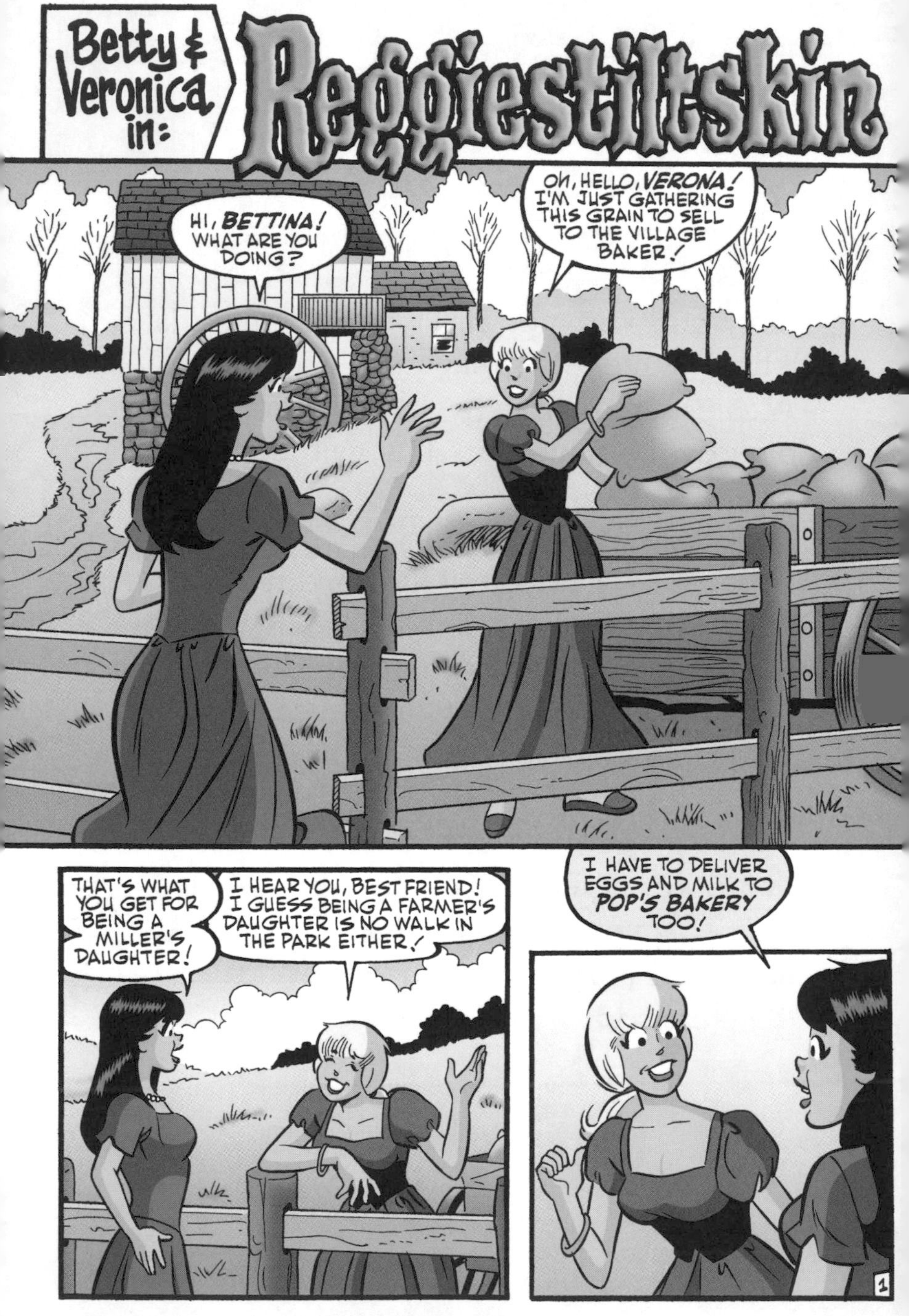
Betty & Veronica in:
Reggiestiltskin
HI, BETTINA! WHAT ARE YOU DOING?
OH, HELLO, VERONA! I'M JUST GATHERING THIS GRAIN TO SELL TO THE VILLAGE BAKER!
THAT'S WHAT YOU GET FOR BEING A MILLER'S DAUGHTER!
I HEAR YOU, BEST FRIEND! I GUESS BEING A FARMER'S DAUGHTER IS NO WALK IN THE PARK EITHER!
I HAVE TO DELIVER EGGS AND MILK TO POP'S BAKERY TOO!
1

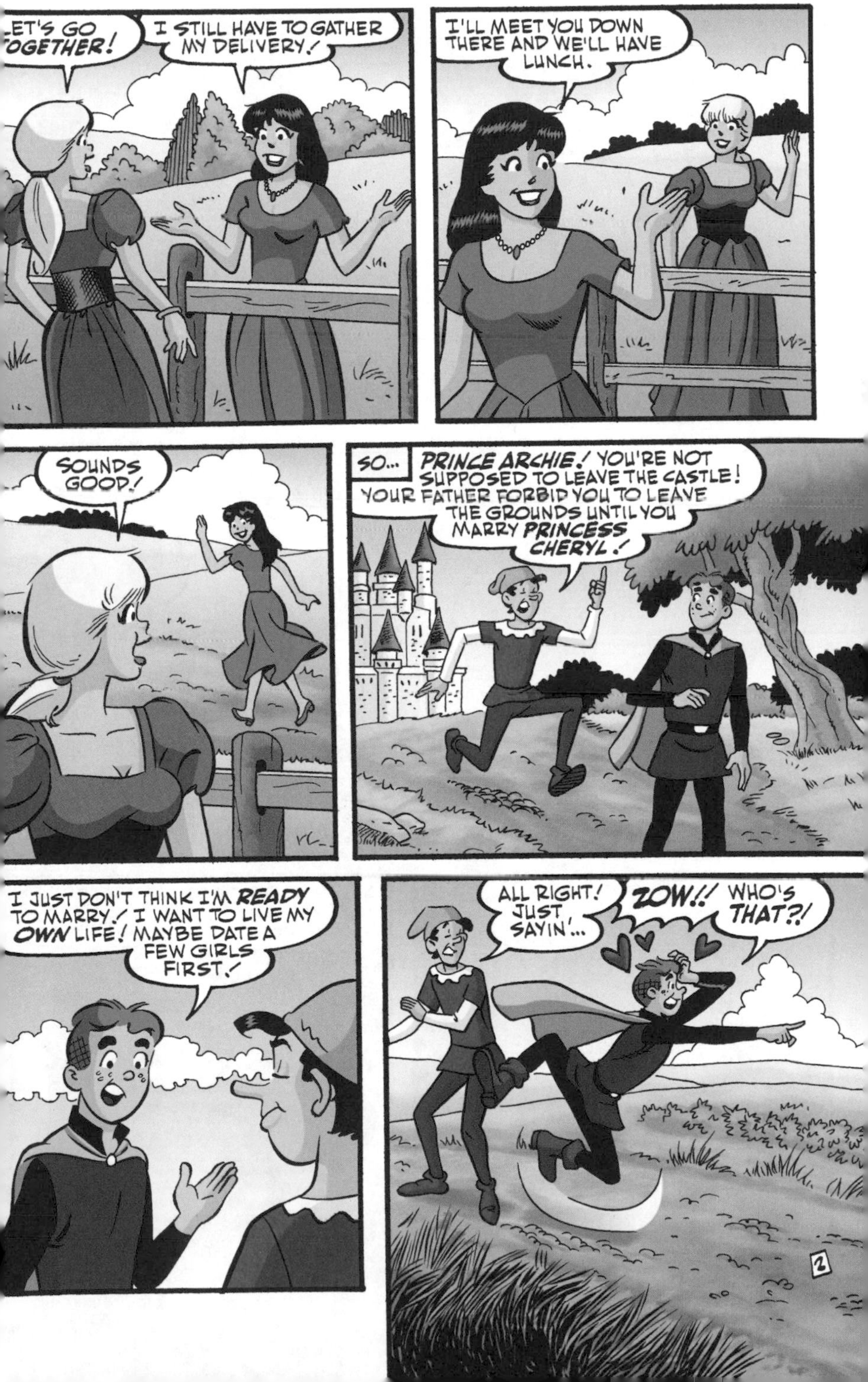
LET'S GO TOGETHER!
I STILL HAVE TO GATHER MY DELIVERY!
I'LL MEET YOU DOWN THERE AND WE'LL HAVE LUNCH.
SOUNDS GOOD!
SO...
PRINCE ARCHIE! YOU'RE NOT SUPPOSED TO LEAVE THE CASTLE! YOUR FATHER FORBID YOU TO LEAVE THE GROUNDS UNTIL YOU MARRY PRINCESS CHERYL!
I JUST DON'T THINK I'M READY TO MARRY! I WANT TO LIVE MY OWN LIFE! MAYBE DATE A FEW GIRLS FIRST!
ALL RIGHT! JUST SAYIN'...
ZOW!!
WHO'S THAT?!
2

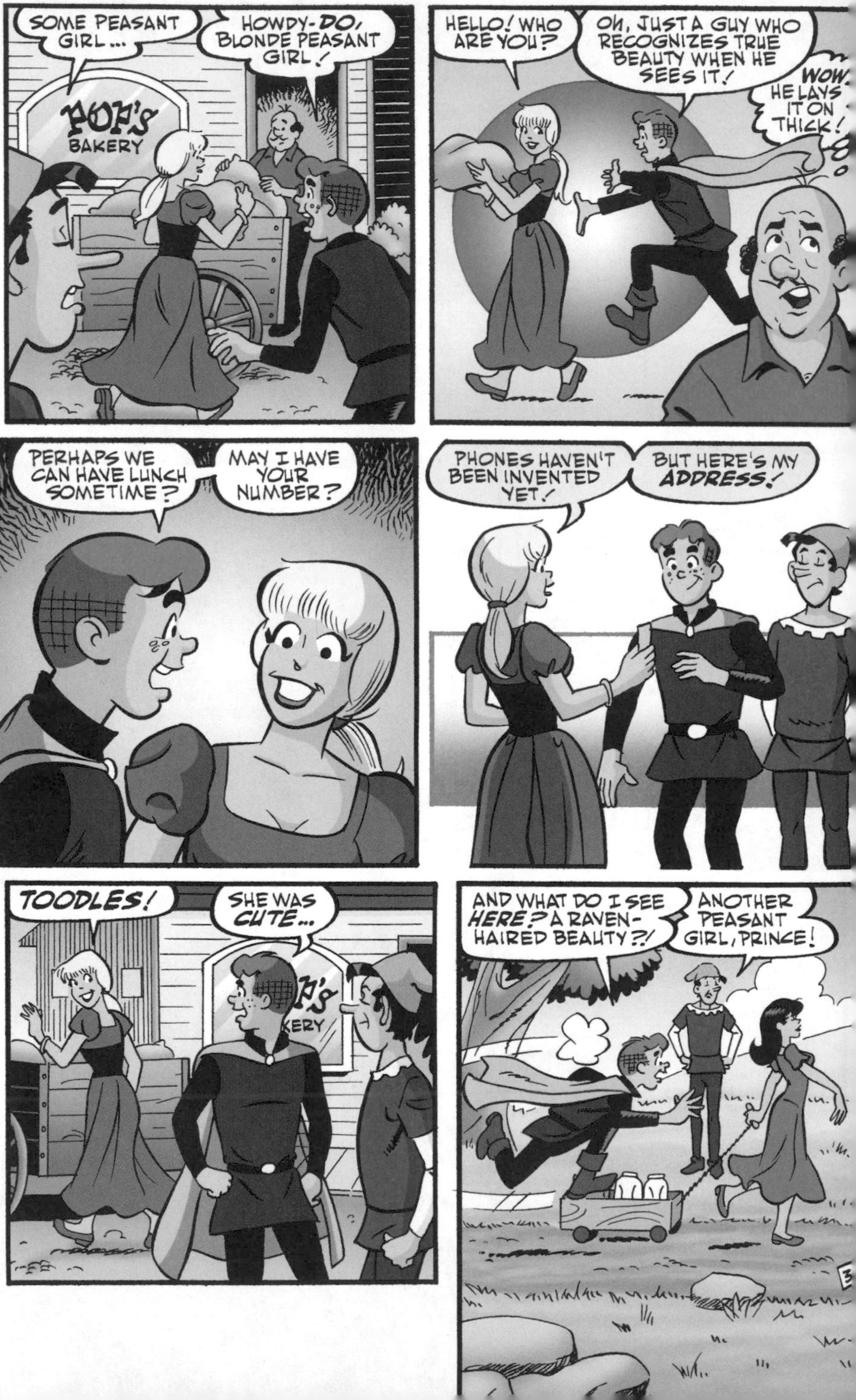
SOME PEASANT GIRL ...
HOWDY-DO, BLONDE PEASANT GIRL!
POP'S BAKERY
HELLO! WHO ARE YOU?
OH, JUST A GUY WHO RECOGNIZES TRUE BEAUTY WHEN HE SEES IT!
WOW. HE LAYS IT ON THICK!
PERHAPS WE CAN HAVE LUNCH SOMETIME?
MAY I HAVE YOUR NUMBER?
PHONES HAVEN'T BEEN INVENTED YET!
BUT HERE'S MY ADDRESS!
TOODLES!
SHE WAS CUTE...
AND WHAT DO I SEE HERE? A RAVEN-HAIRED BEAUTY?!
ANOTHER PEASANT GIRL, PRINCE!
3

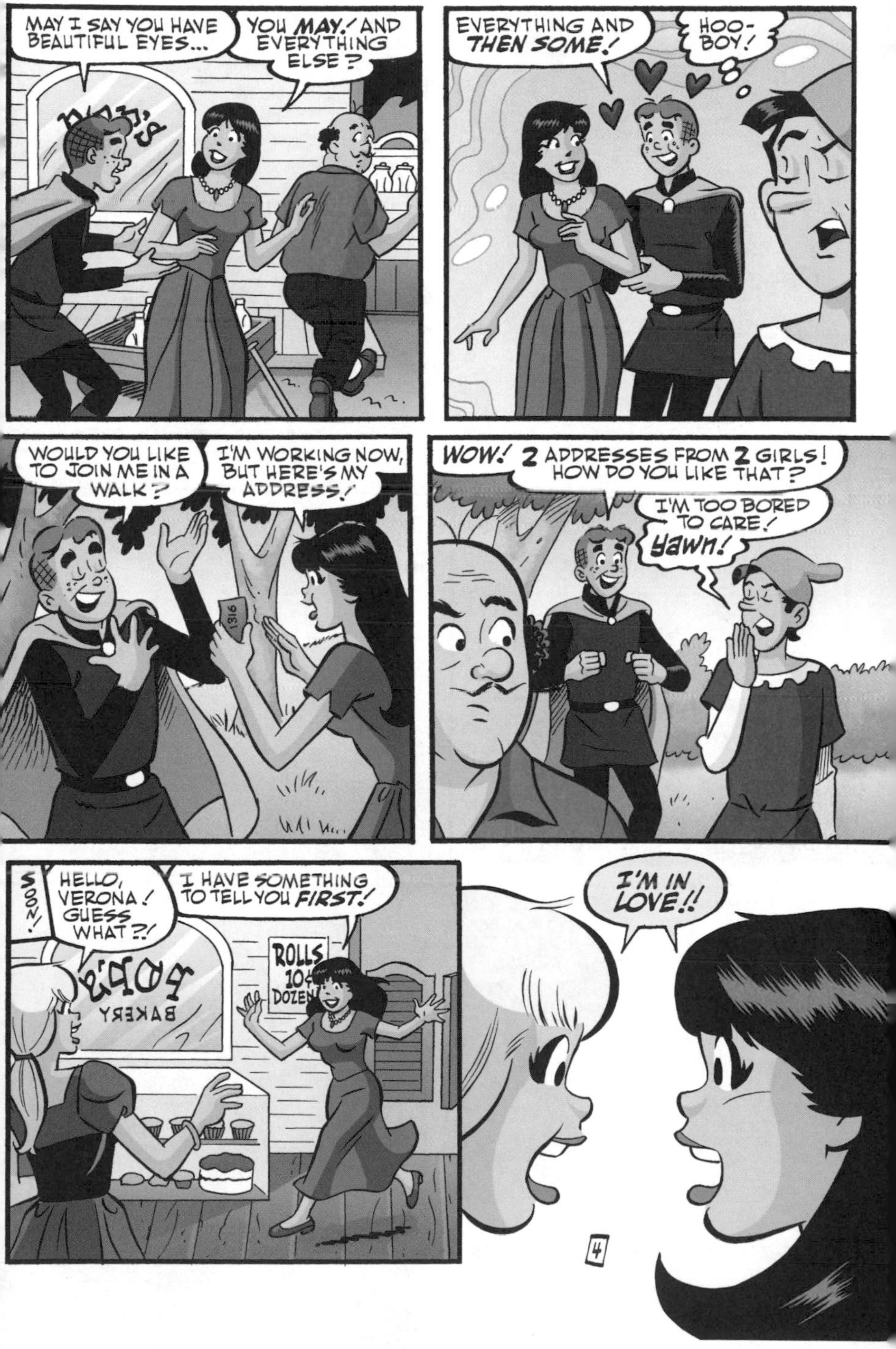
MAY I SAY YOU HAVE BEAUTIFUL EYES...
YOU MAY! AND EVERYTHING ELSE?
POP'S
EVERYTHING AND THEN SOME!
HOO-BOY!
WOULD YOU LIKE TO JOIN ME IN A WALK?
I'M WORKING NOW, BUT HERE'S MY ADDRESS!
1316
WOW! 2 ADDRESSES FROM 2 GIRLS! HOW DO YOU LIKE THAT?
I'M TOO BORED TO CARE! YAWN!
SOON!
HELLO, VERONA! GUESS WHAT?!
I HAVE SOMETHING TO TELL YOU FIRST!
POP'S BAKERY
ROLLS 10¢ DOZEN
I'M IN LOVE!!
4

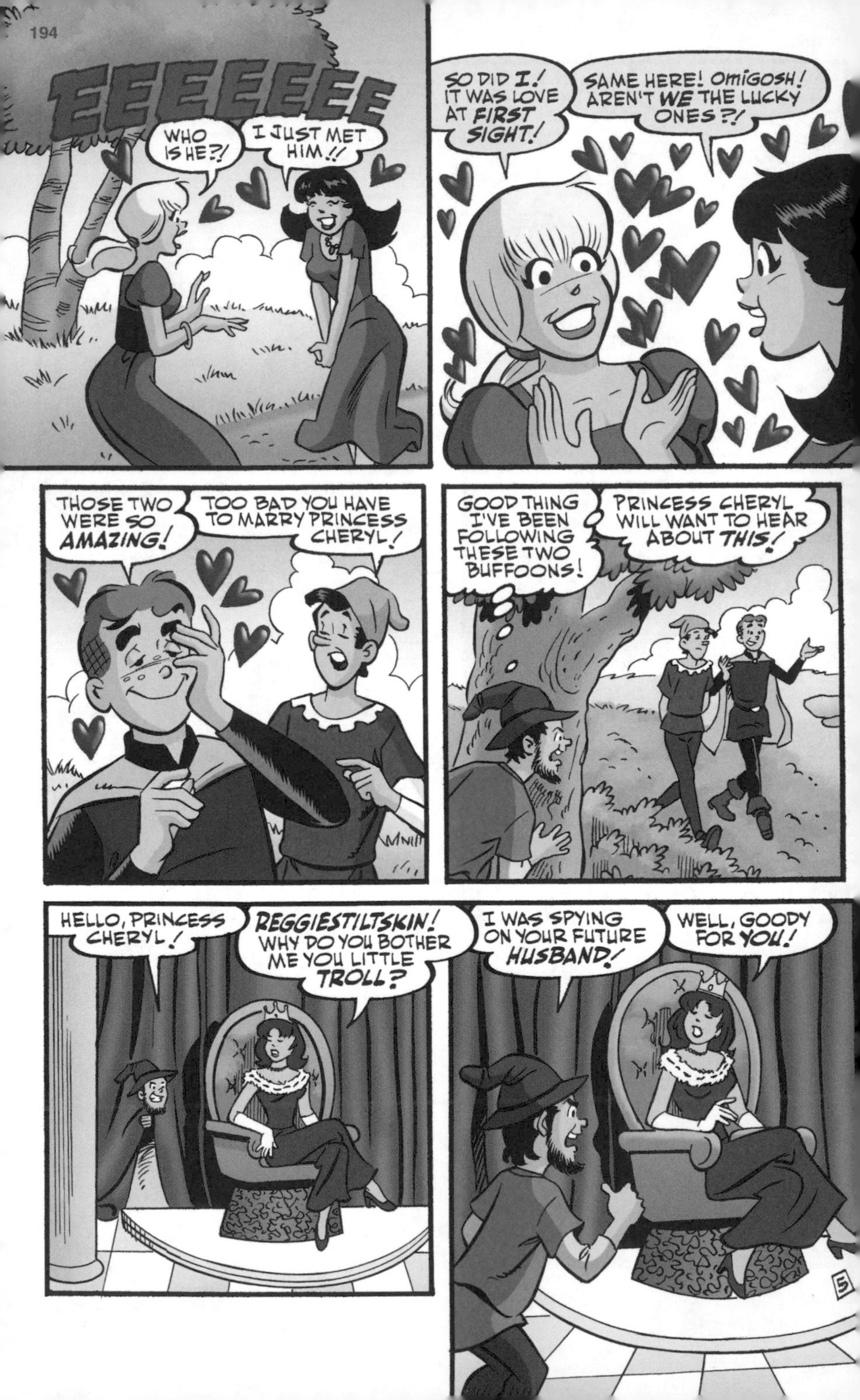
EEEEEEE
WHO IS HE?!
I JUST MET HIM!!
SO DID I! IT WAS LOVE AT FIRST SIGHT!
SAME HERE! OMIGOSH! AREN'T WE THE LUCKY ONES?!
THOSE TWO WERE SO AMAZING!
TOO BAD YOU HAVE TO MARRY PRINCESS CHERYL!
GOOD THING I'VE BEEN FOLLOWING THESE TWO BUFFOONS!
PRINCESS CHERYL WILL WANT TO HEAR ABOUT THIS!
HELLO, PRINCESS CHERYL!
REGGIESTILTSKIN! WHY DO YOU BOTHER ME YOU LITTLE TROLL?
I WAS SPYING ON YOUR FUTURE HUSBAND!
WELL, GOODY FOR YOU!
5

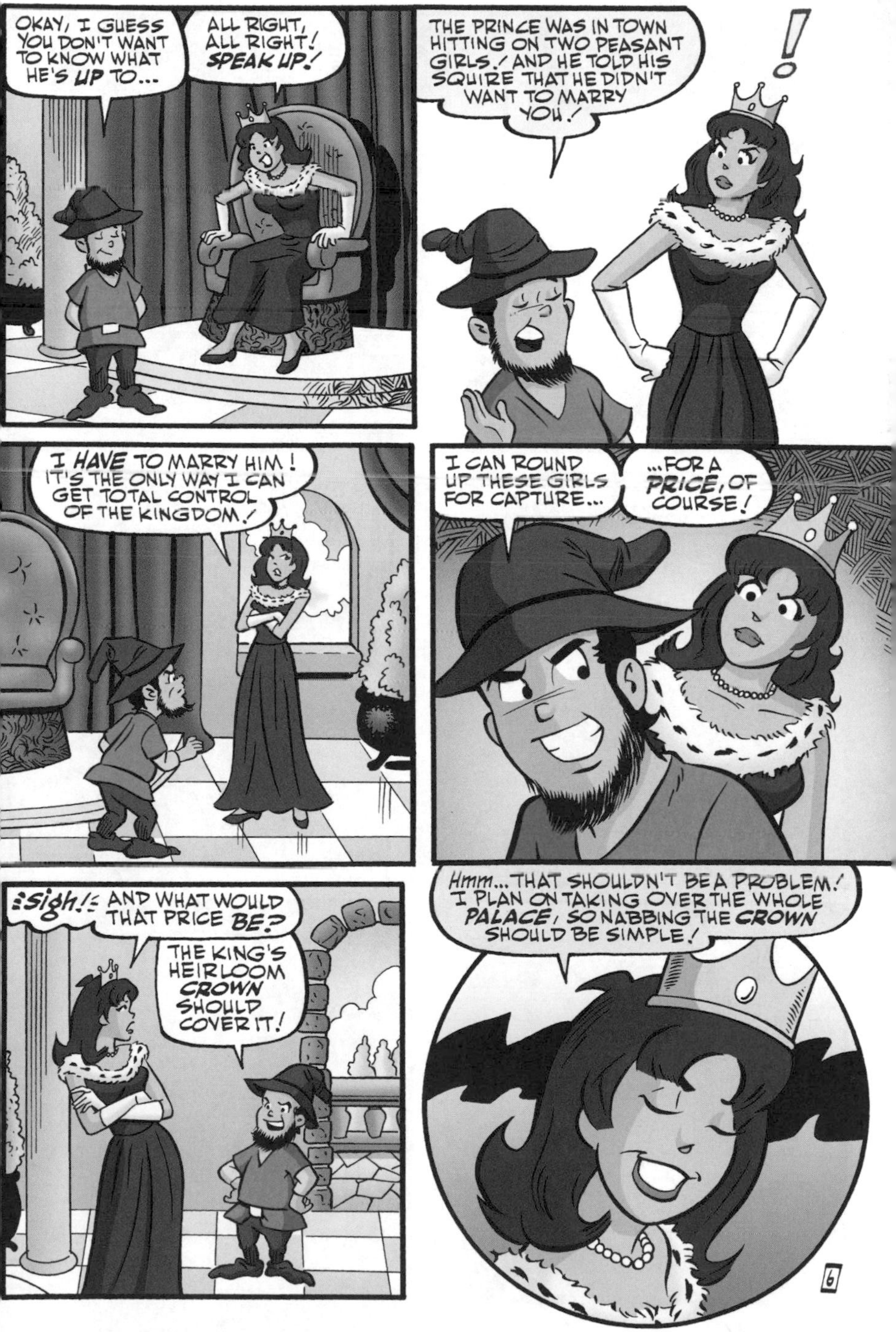
OKAY, I GUESS YOU DON'T WANT TO KNOW WHAT HE'S UP TO...
ALL RIGHT, ALL RIGHT! SPEAK UP!
THE PRINCE WAS IN TOWN HITTING ON TWO PEASANT GIRLS! AND HE TOLD HIS SQUIRE THAT HE DIDN'T WANT TO MARRY YOU!
!
I HAVE TO MARRY HIM! IT'S THE ONLY WAY I CAN GET TOTAL CONTROL OF THE KINGDOM!
I CAN ROUND UP THESE GIRLS FOR CAPTURE...
...FOR A PRICE, OF COURSE!
:SIGH!: AND WHAT WOULD THAT PRICE BE?
THE KING'S HEIRLOOM CROWN SHOULD COVER IT!
Hmm... THAT SHOULDN'T BE A PROBLEM! I PLAN ON TAKING OVER THE WHOLE PALACE, SO NABBING THE CROWN SHOULD BE SIMPLE!
6

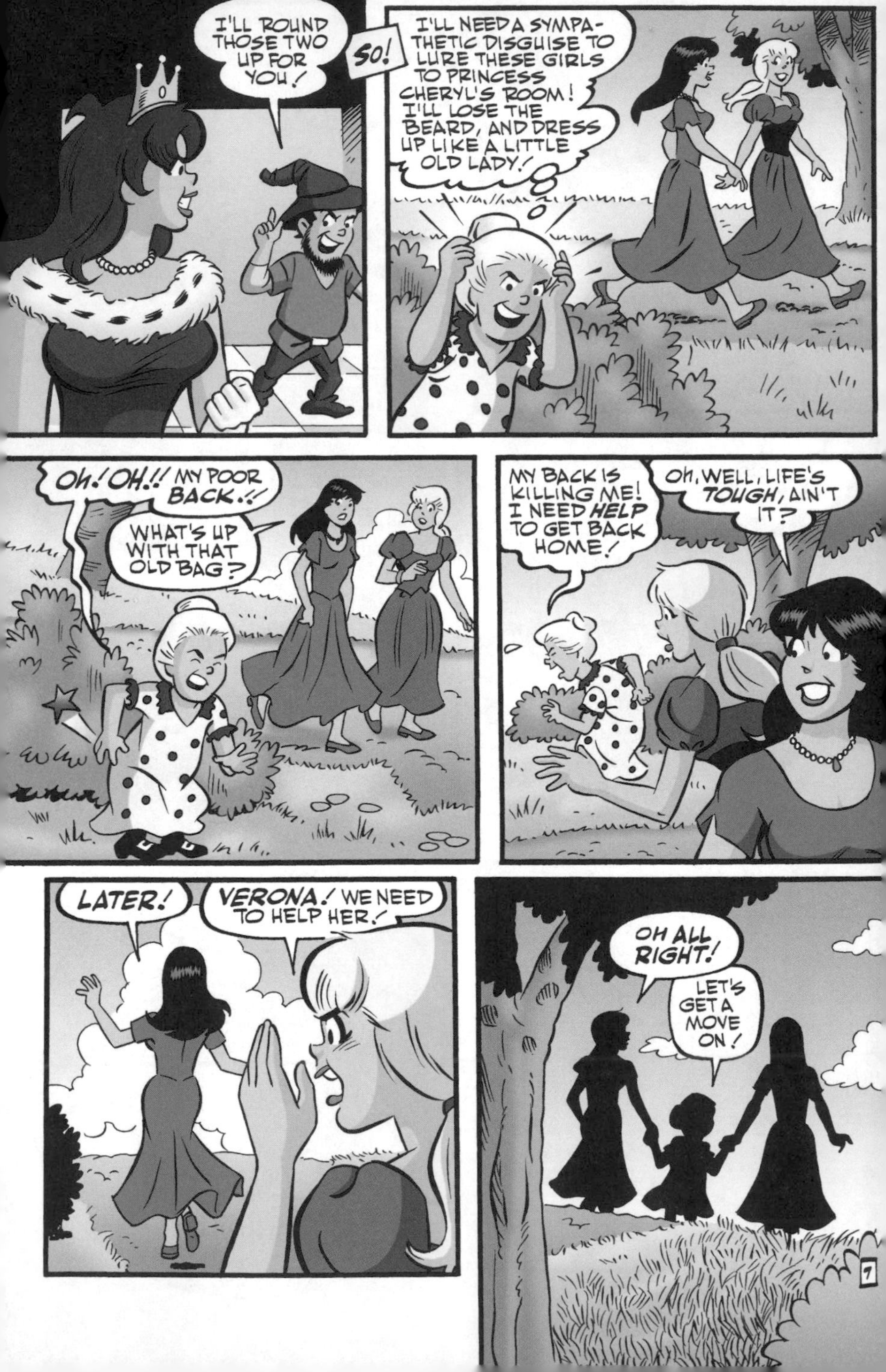
I'LL ROUND THOSE TWO UP FOR YOU!
SO!
I'LL NEED A SYMPATHETIC DISGUISE TO LURE THESE GIRLS TO PRINCESS CHERYL'S ROOM! I'LL LOSE THE BEARD, AND DRESS UP LIKE A LITTLE OLD LADY!
OH! OH!! MY POOR BACK.!!
WHAT'S UP WITH THAT OLD BAG?
MY BACK IS KILLING ME! I NEED HELP TO GET BACK HOME!
OH, WELL, LIFE'S TOUGH, AIN'T IT?
LATER!
VERONA! WE NEED TO HELP HER!
OH ALL RIGHT!
LET'S GET A MOVE ON!
7

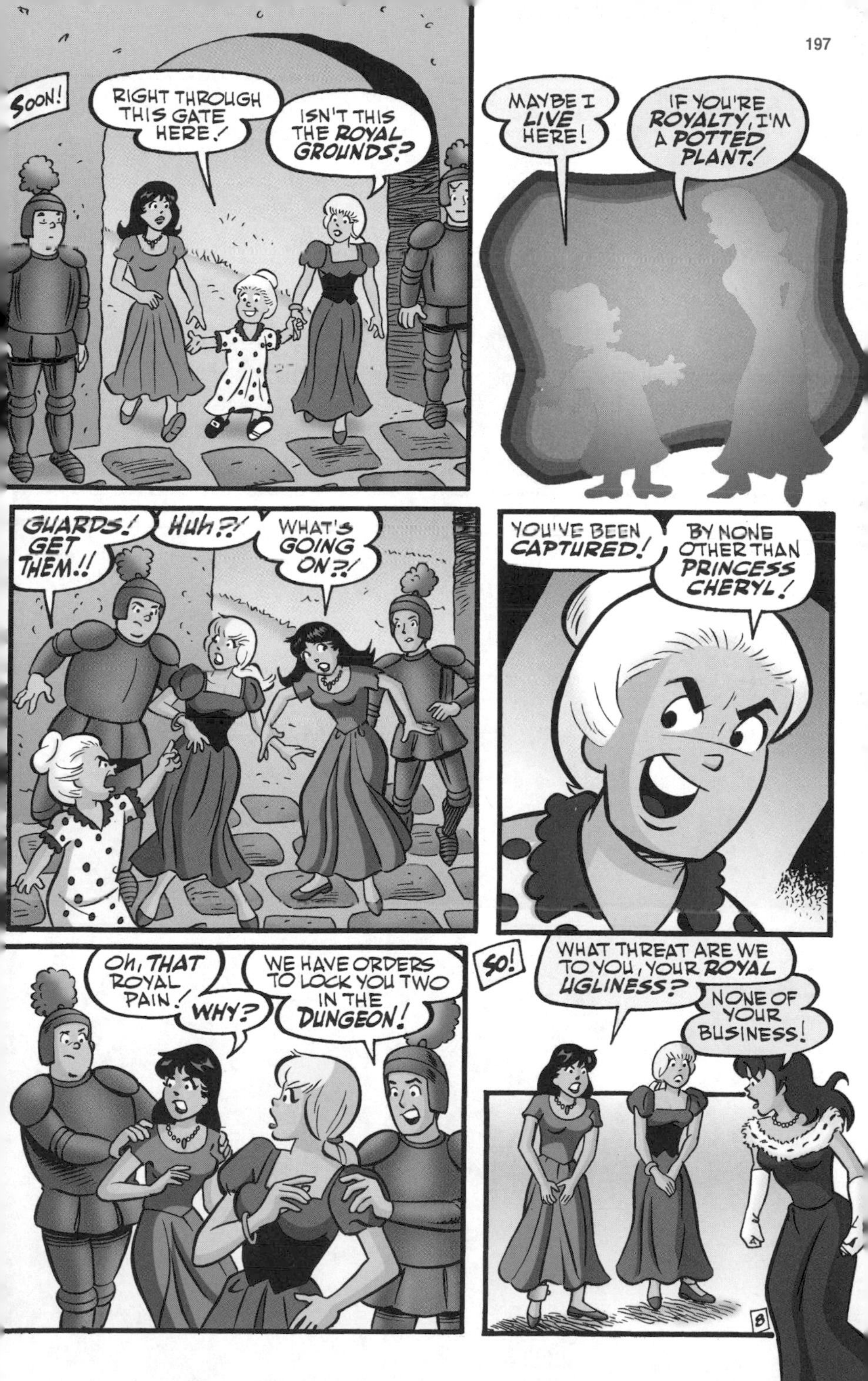
SOON!
RIGHT THROUGH THIS GATE HERE!
ISN'T THIS THE ROYAL GROUNDS?
MAYBE I LIVE HERE!
IF YOU'RE ROYALTY, I'M A POTTED PLANT!
GUARDS! GET THEM!!
HUH?!
WHAT'S GOING ON?!
YOU'VE BEEN CAPTURED!
BY NONE OTHER THAN PRINCESS CHERYL!
OH, THAT ROYAL PAIN!
WHY?
WE HAVE ORDERS TO LOCK YOU TWO IN THE DUNGEON!
SO!
WHAT THREAT ARE WE TO YOU, YOUR ROYAL UGLINESS?
NONE OF YOUR BUSINESS!
8

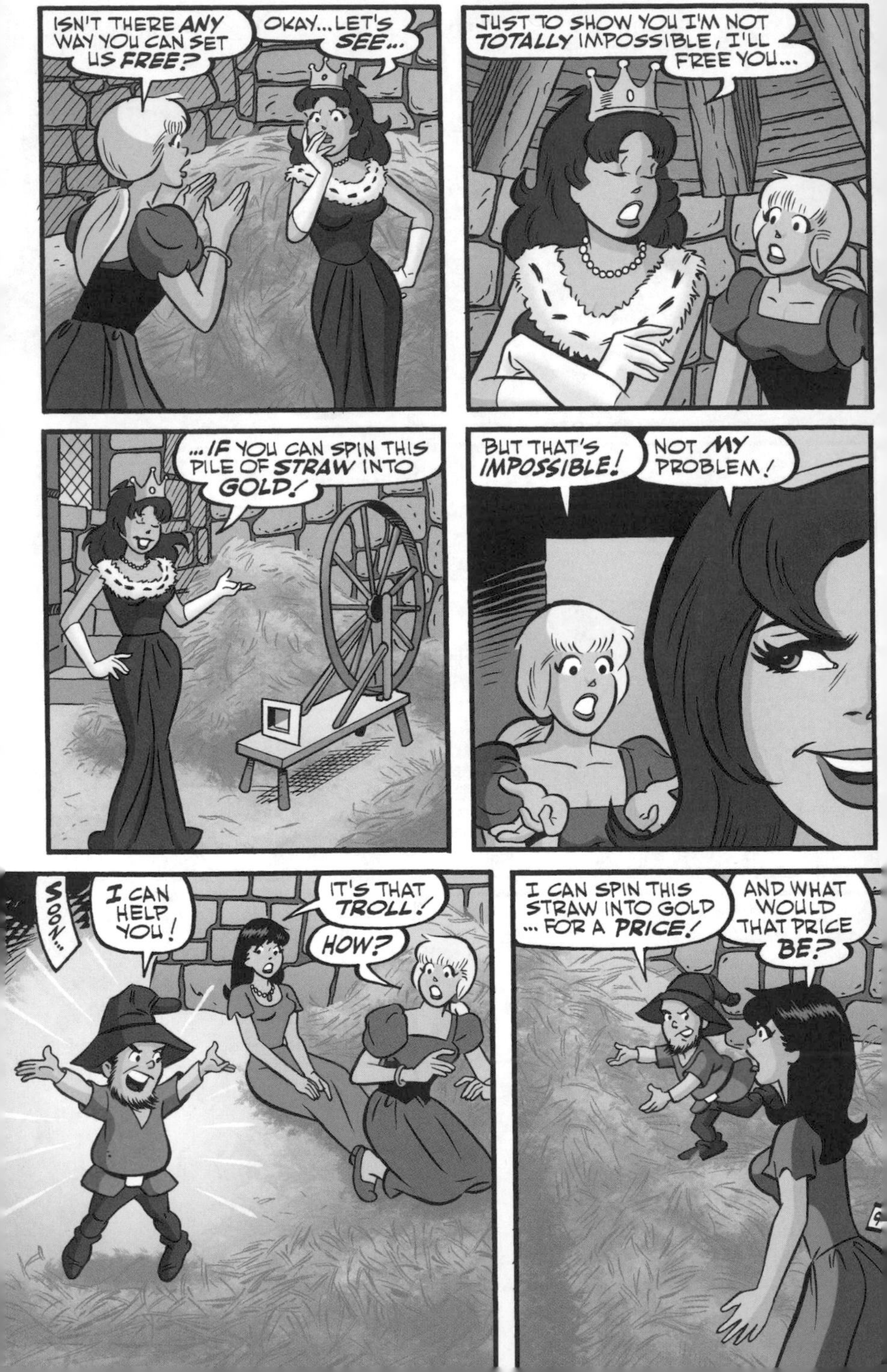
ISN'T THERE ANY WAY YOU CAN SET US FREE?
OKAY... LET'S SEE...
JUST TO SHOW YOU I'M NOT TOTALLY IMPOSSIBLE, I'LL FREE YOU...
...IF YOU CAN SPIN THIS PILE OF STRAW INTO GOLD!
BUT THAT'S IMPOSSIBLE!
NOT MY PROBLEM!
SOON...
I CAN HELP YOU!
IT'S THAT TROLL!
HOW?
I CAN SPIN THIS STRAW INTO GOLD ... FOR A PRICE!
AND WHAT WOULD THAT PRICE BE?
9

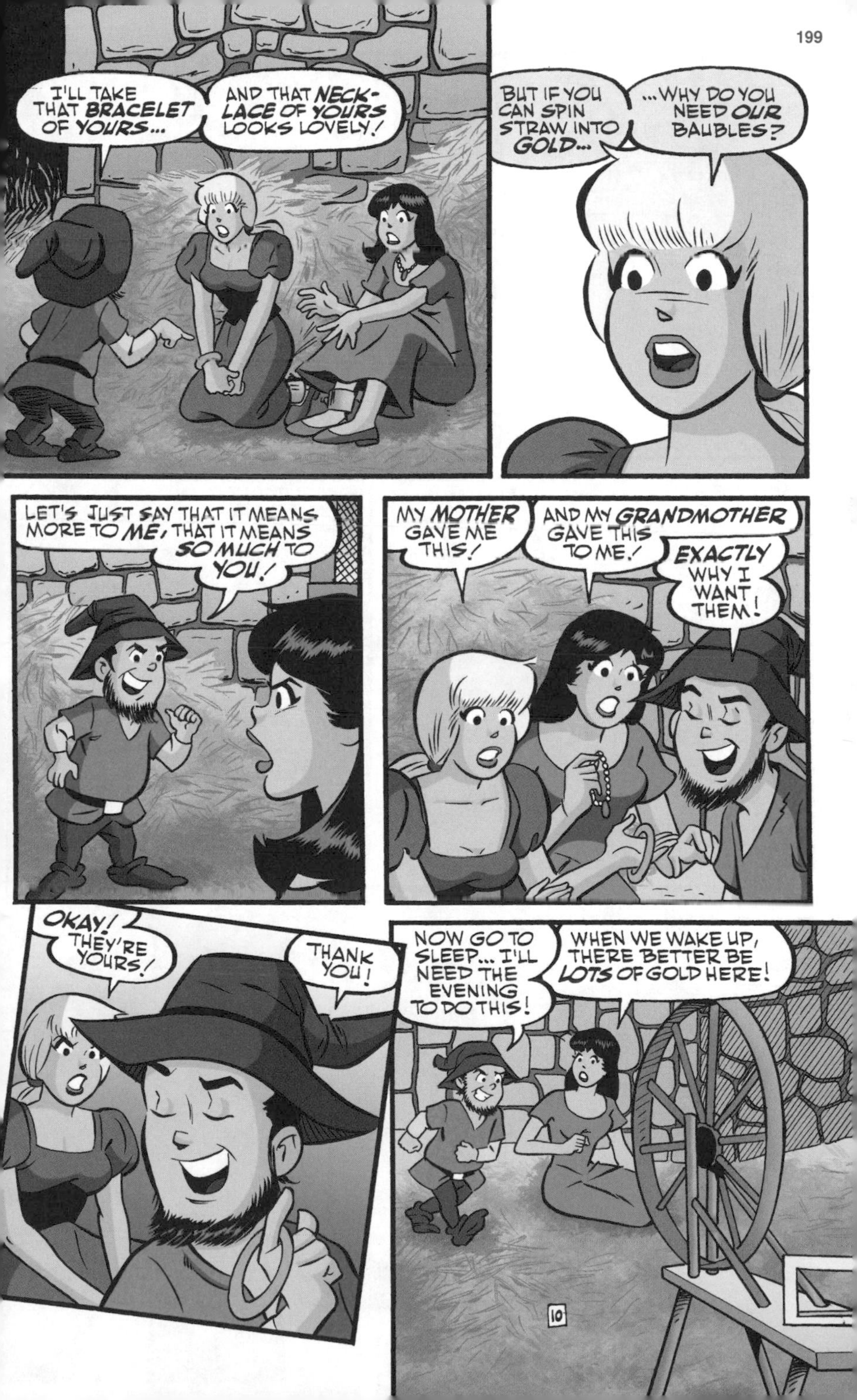
I'LL TAKE THAT BRACELET OF YOURS...
AND THAT NECKLACE OF YOURS LOOKS LOVELY!
BUT IF YOU CAN SPIN STRAW INTO GOLD...
...WHY DO YOU NEED OUR BAUBLES?
LET'S JUST SAY THAT IT MEANS MORE TO ME, THAT IT MEANS SO MUCH TO YOU!
MY MOTHER GAVE ME THIS!
AND MY GRANDMOTHER GAVE THIS TO ME!
EXACTLY WHY I WANT THEM!
OKAY! THEY'RE YOURS!
THANK YOU!
NOW GO TO SLEEP... I'LL NEED THE EVENING TO DO THIS!
WHEN WE WAKE UP, THERE BETTER BE LOTS OF GOLD HERE!
10

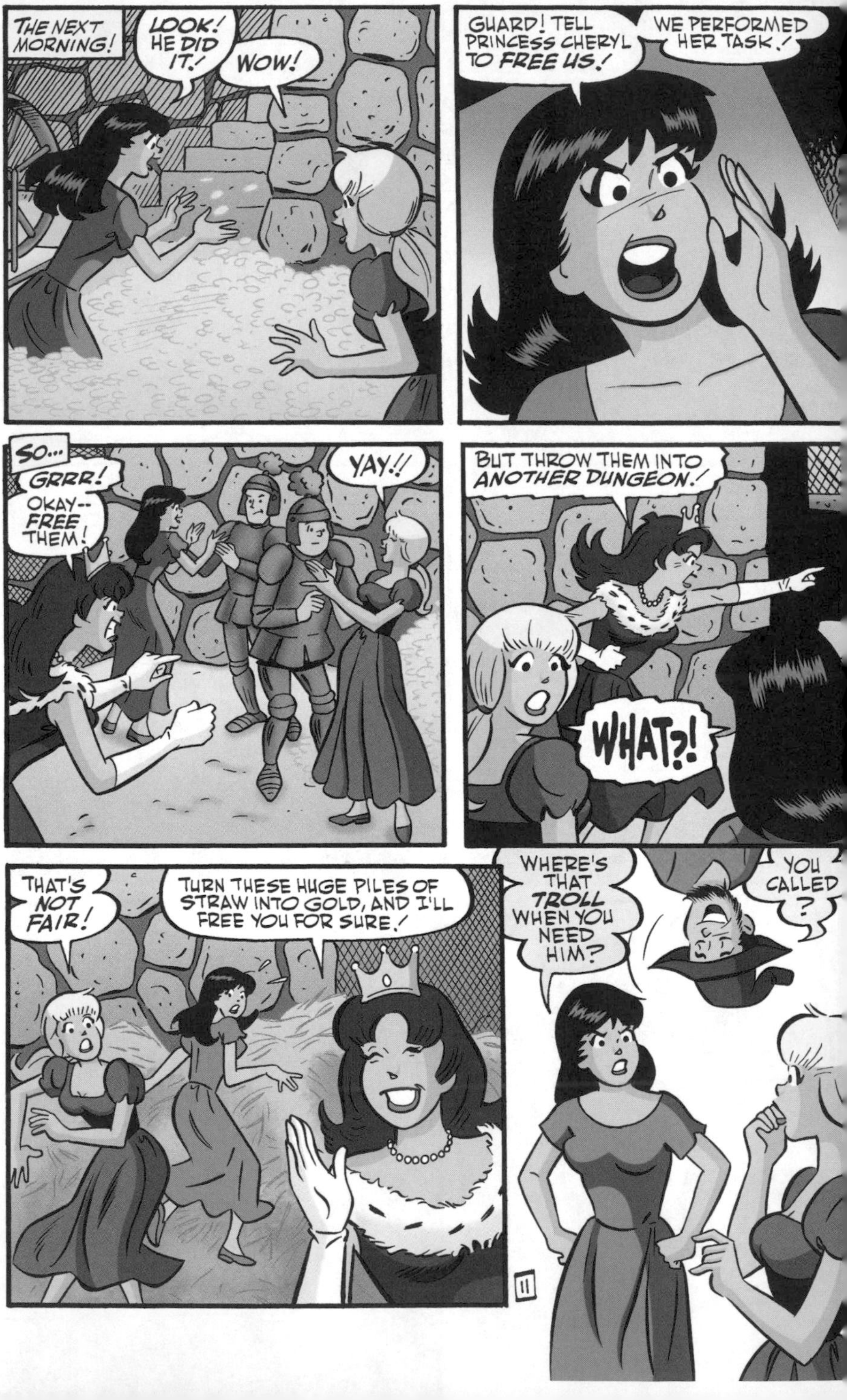
THE NEXT MORNING!
LOOK! HE DID IT!
WOW!
GUARD! TELL PRINCESS CHERYL TO FREE US!
WE PERFORMED HER TASK!
SO...
GRRR! OKAY-- FREE THEM!
YAY!!
BUT THROW THEM INTO ANOTHER DUNGEON!
WHAT?!
THAT'S NOT FAIR!
TURN THESE HUGE PILES OF STRAW INTO GOLD, AND I'LL FREE YOU FOR SURE!
WHERE'S THAT TROLL WHEN YOU NEED HIM?
YOU CALLED?
11

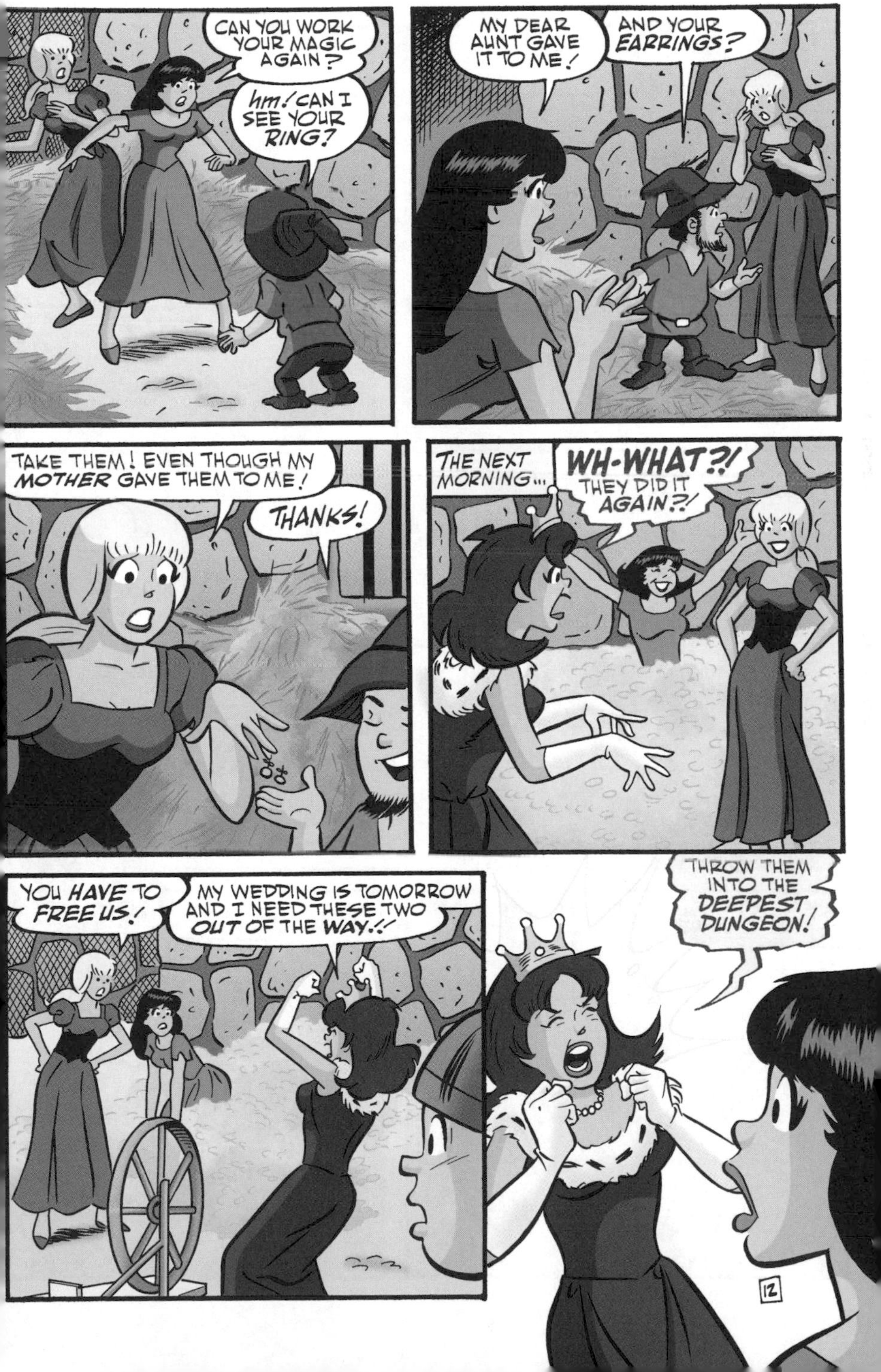
CAN YOU WORK YOUR MAGIC AGAIN?
hm! CAN I SEE YOUR RING?
MY DEAR AUNT GAVE IT TO ME!
AND YOUR EARRINGS?
TAKE THEM! EVEN THOUGH MY MOTHER GAVE THEM TO ME!
THANKS!
THE NEXT MORNING...
WH-WHAT?! THEY DID IT AGAIN?!
YOU HAVE TO FREE US!
MY WEDDING IS TOMORROW AND I NEED THESE TWO OUT OF THE WAY!!
THROW THEM INTO THE DEEPEST DUNGEON!
12

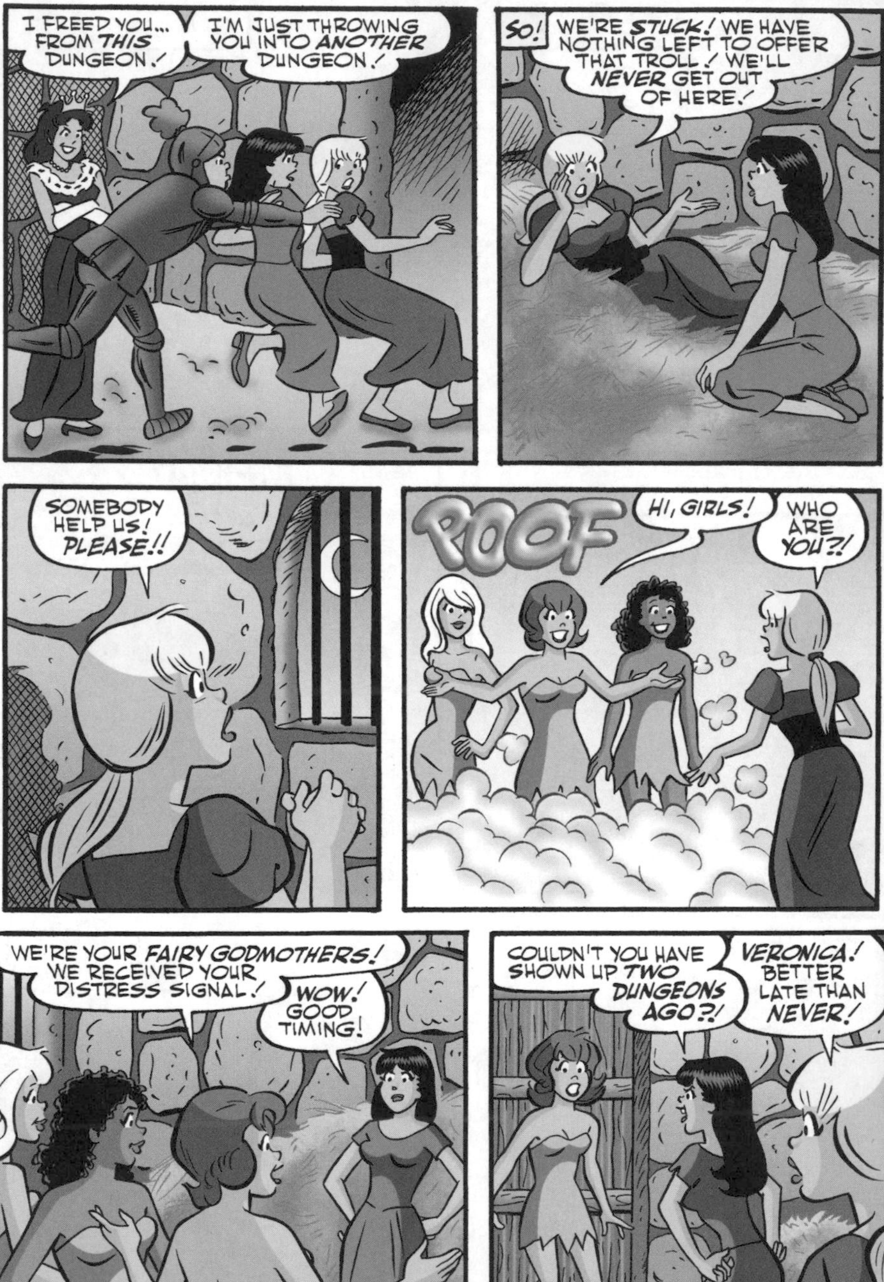
I FREED YOU... FROM THIS DUNGEON.!
I'M JUST THROWING YOU INTO ANOTHER DUNGEON.!
SO!
WE'RE STUCK! WE HAVE NOTHING LEFT TO OFFER THAT TROLL! WE'LL NEVER GET OUT OF HERE.!
SOMEBODY HELP US! PLEASE!!
POOF
HI, GIRLS!
WHO ARE YOU?!
WE'RE YOUR FAIRY GODMOTHERS! WE RECEIVED YOUR DISTRESS SIGNAL!
WOW! GOOD TIMING!
COULDN'T YOU HAVE SHOWN UP TWO DUNGEONS AGO?!
VERONICA! BETTER LATE THAN NEVER!
13

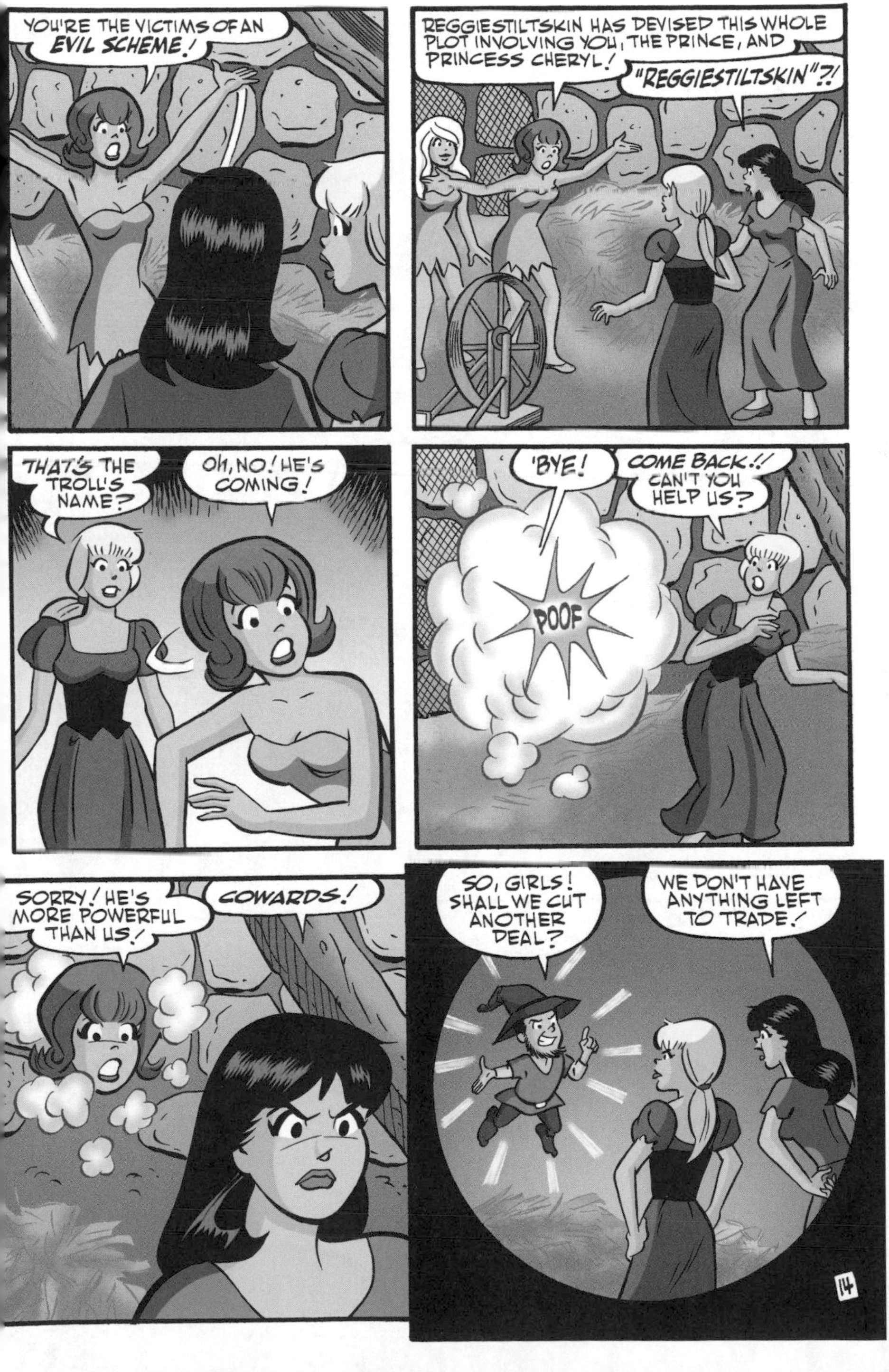
YOU'RE THE VICTIMS OF AN EVIL SCHEME!
REGGIESTILTSKIN HAS DEVISED THIS WHOLE PLOT INVOLVING YOU, THE PRINCE, AND PRINCESS CHERYL!
"REGGIESTILTSKIN"?!
THAT'S THE TROLL'S NAME?
OH, NO! HE'S COMING!
'BYE!
COME BACK!! CAN'T YOU HELP US?
POOF
SORRY! HE'S MORE POWERFUL THAN US!
COWARDS!
SO, GIRLS! SHALL WE CUT ANOTHER DEAL?
WE DON'T HAVE ANYTHING LEFT TO TRADE!
14

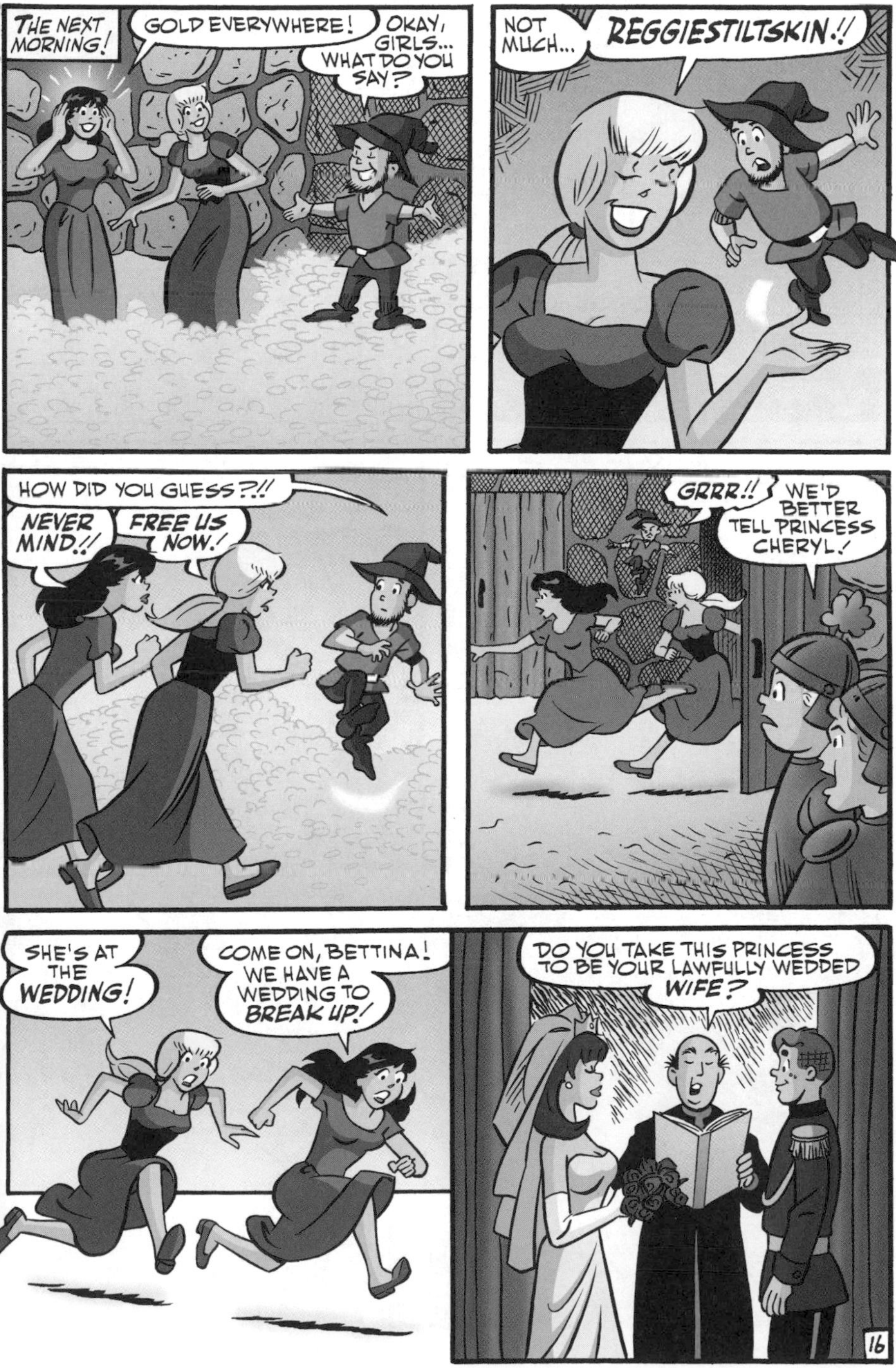
THE NEXT MORNING!
GOLD EVERYWHERE!
OKAY, GIRLS... WHAT DO YOU SAY?
NOT MUCH...
REGGIESTILTSKIN!!
HOW DID YOU GUESS?!!
NEVER MIND!!
FREE US NOW!
GRRR!!
WE'D BETTER TELL PRINCESS CHERYL!
SHE'S AT THE WEDDING!
COME ON, BETTINA! WE HAVE A WEDDING TO BREAK UP!
DO YOU TAKE THIS PRINCESS TO BE YOUR LAWFULLY WEDDED WIFE?
16

17

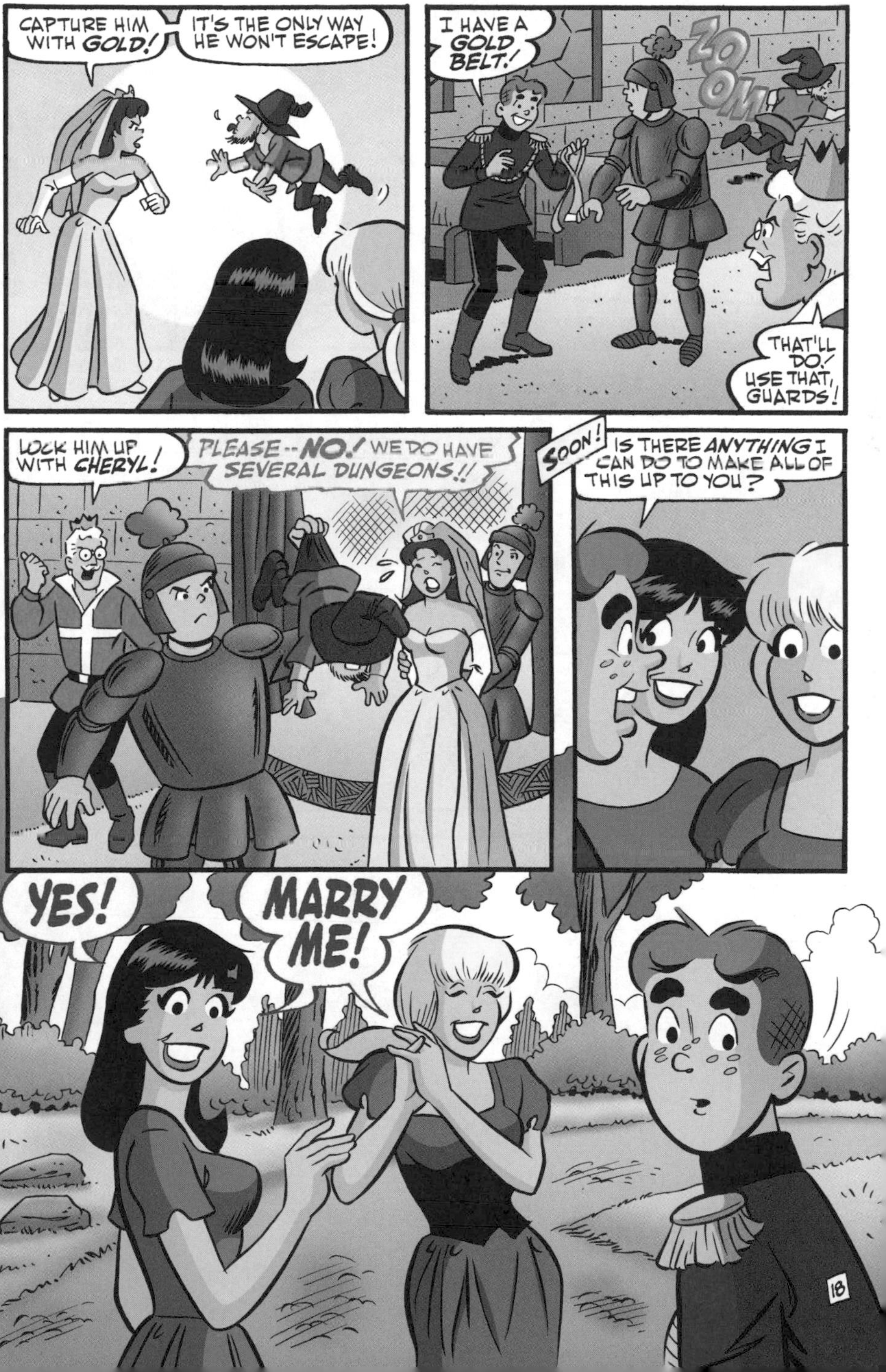
CAPTURE HIM WITH GOLD!
IT'S THE ONLY WAY HE WON'T ESCAPE!
I HAVE A GOLD BELT!
ZOOM
THAT'LL DO! USE THAT, GUARDS!
LOCK HIM UP WITH CHERYL!
PLEASE--NO! WE DO HAVE SEVERAL DUNGEONS!!
SOON!
IS THERE ANYTHING I CAN DO TO MAKE ALL OF THIS UP TO YOU?
YES!
MARRY ME!
18

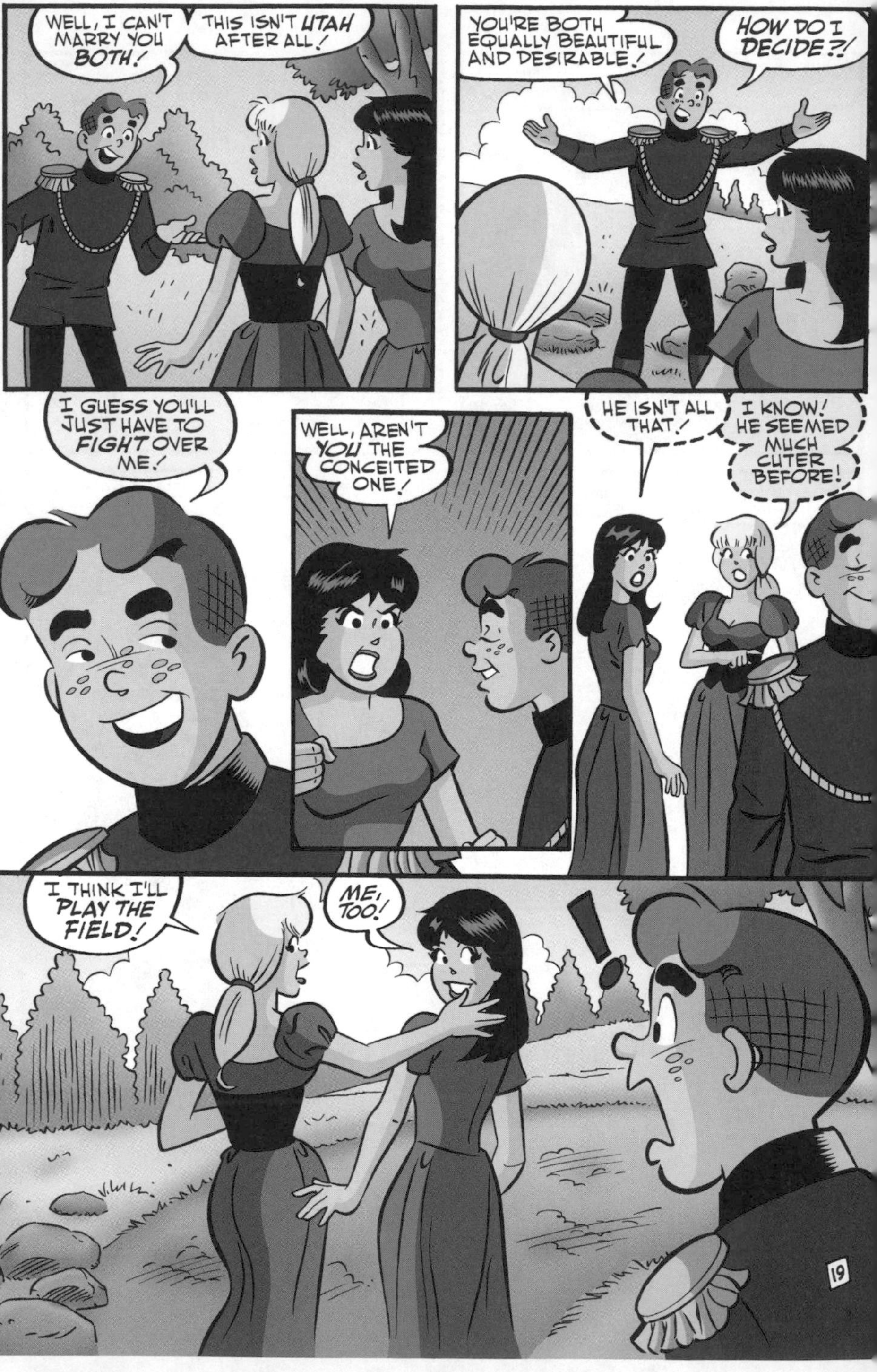
WELL, I CAN'T MARRY YOU BOTH!
THIS ISN'T UTAH AFTER ALL!
YOU'RE BOTH EQUALLY BEAUTIFUL AND DESIRABLE!
HOW DO I DECIDE?!
I GUESS YOU'LL JUST HAVE TO FIGHT OVER ME!
WELL, AREN'T YOU THE CONCEITED ONE!
HE ISN'T ALL THAT!
I KNOW! HE SEEMED MUCH CUTER BEFORE!
I THINK I'LL PLAY THE FIELD!
ME, TOO!
!
19

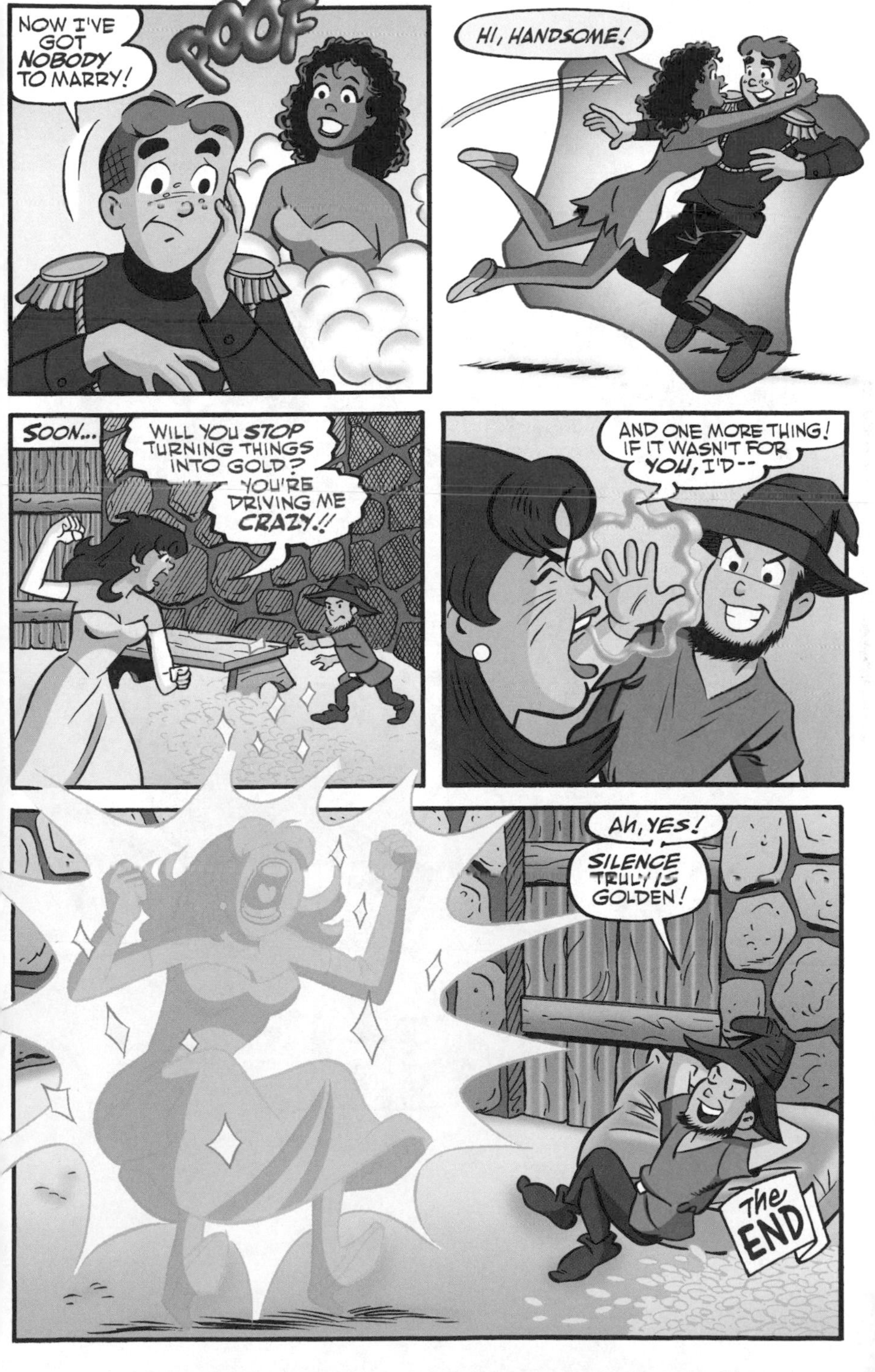
NOW I'VE GOT NOBODY TO MARRY!
POOF
HI, HANDSOME!
SOON...
WILL YOU STOP TURNING THINGS INTO GOLD?
YOU'RE DRIVING ME CRAZY!!
AND ONE MORE THING! IF IT WASN'T FOR YOU, I'D--
Ah, YES!
SILENCE TRULY IS GOLDEN!
The END

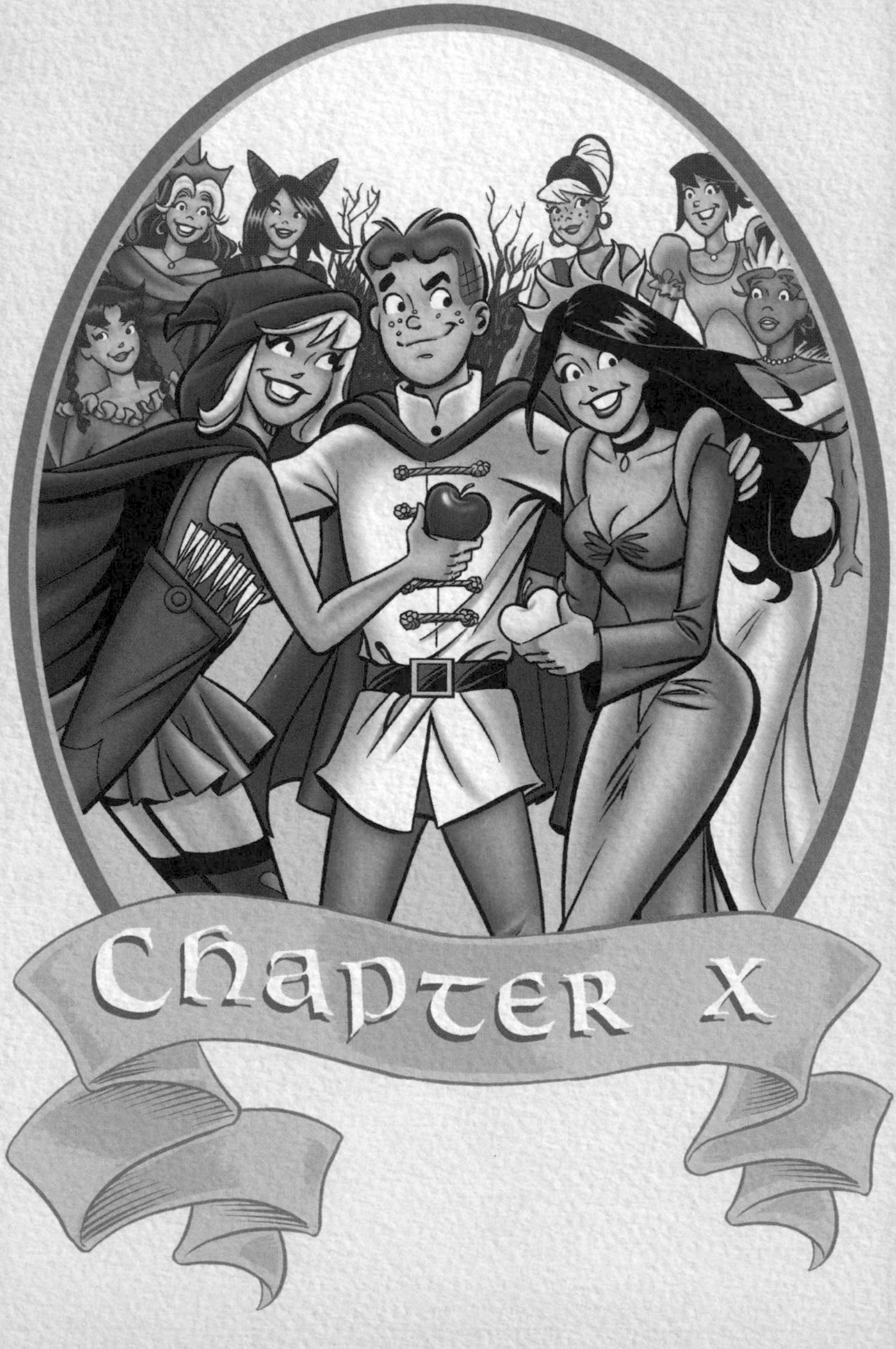
Chapter X

What's * * * * * The Story?

When Archie unleashes the hidden powers in an old statue in the woods, things get very strange in Riverdale. He wakes up as the prince in a fractured fairytale, with everybody and everything in Riverdale taking on the traits and characteristics of classic storybook characters. And he appears to be the only one who knows what's going on.

Well, except for Jughead, who seems to have the answers as Old King Cole. But Archie has to decide who's the fairest in the land, while saving Riverdale from the Queen of Hearts, and potential war from another dimension.

Just another typical day in Riverdale!

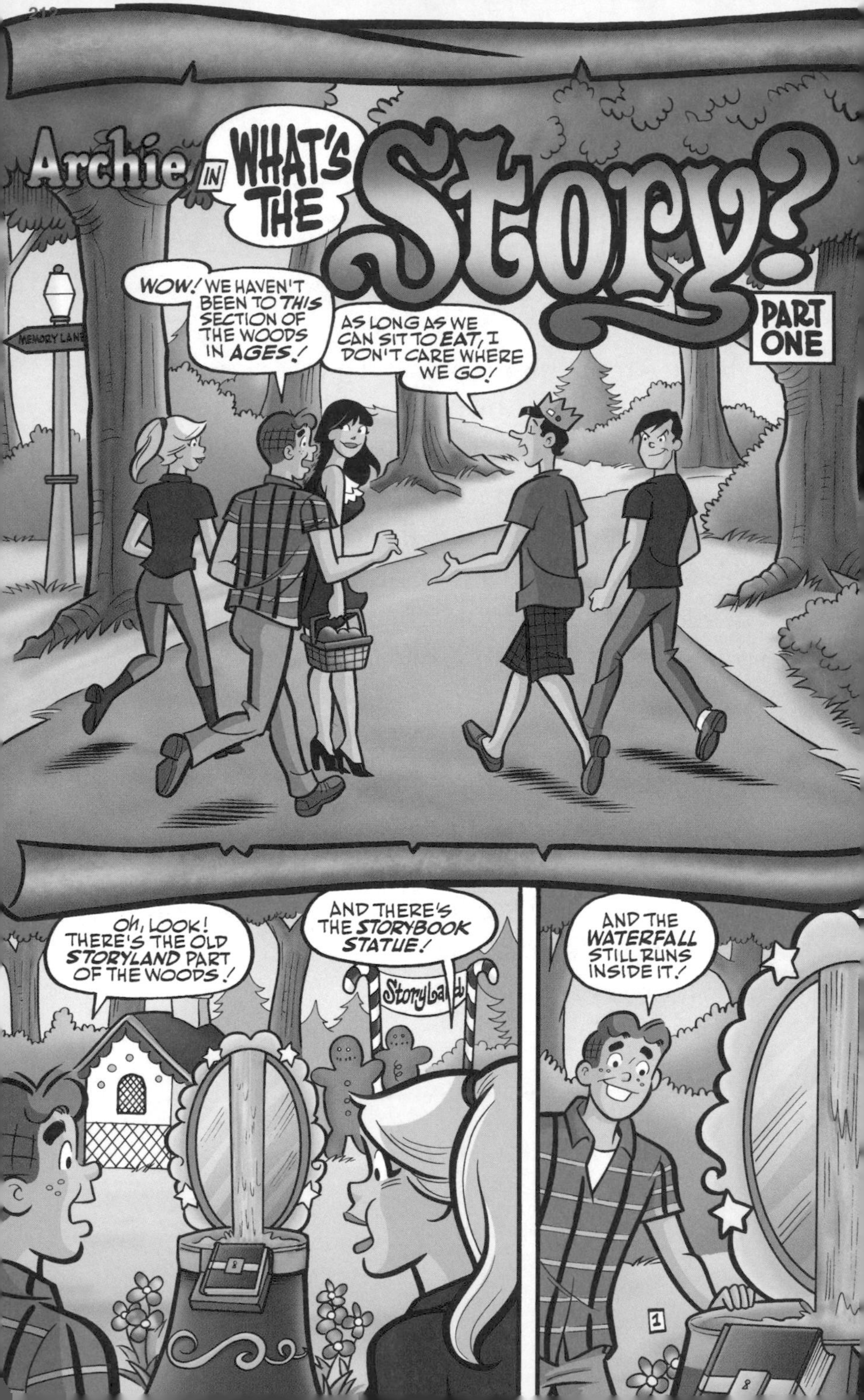
Archie IN WHAT'S THE Story? PART ONE
MEMORY LANE
WOW! WE HAVEN'T BEEN TO THIS SECTION OF THE WOODS IN AGES!
AS LONG AS WE CAN SIT TO EAT, I DON'T CARE WHERE WE GO!
OH, LOOK! THERE'S THE OLD STORYLAND PART OF THE WOODS!
AND THERE'S THE STORYBOOK STATUE!
StoryLand
AND THE WATERFALL STILL RUNS INSIDE IT!

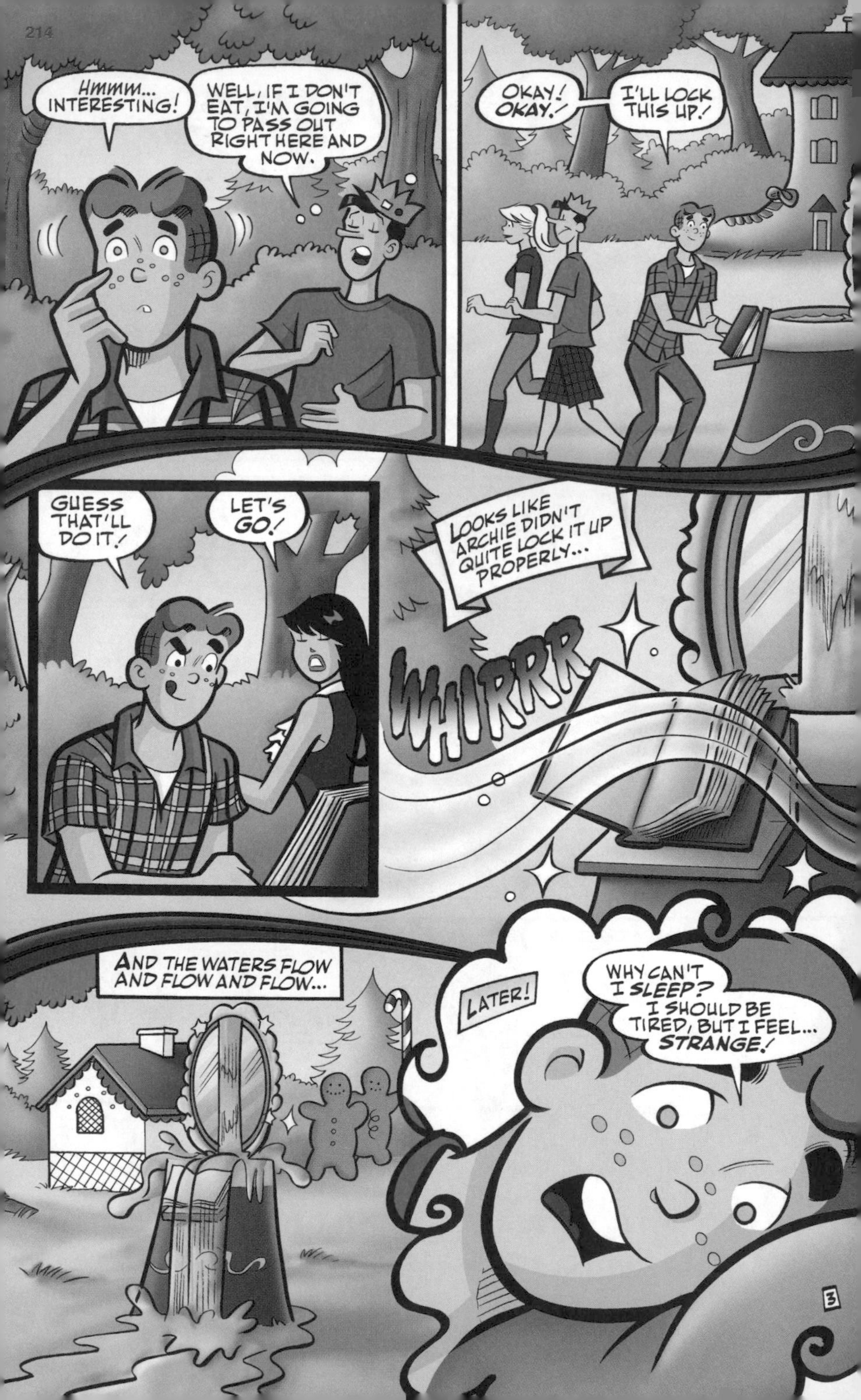
HMMM... INTERESTING!
WELL, IF I DON'T EAT, I'M GOING TO PASS OUT RIGHT HERE AND NOW.
OKAY! OKAY!
I'LL LOCK THIS UP!
GUESS THAT'LL DO IT!
LET'S GO!
LOOKS LIKE ARCHIE DIDN'T QUITE LOCK IT UP PROPERLY...
WHIRRR
AND THE WATERS FLOW AND FLOW AND FLOW...
LATER!
WHY CAN'T I SLEEP? I SHOULD BE TIRED, BUT I FEEL... STRANGE!
3

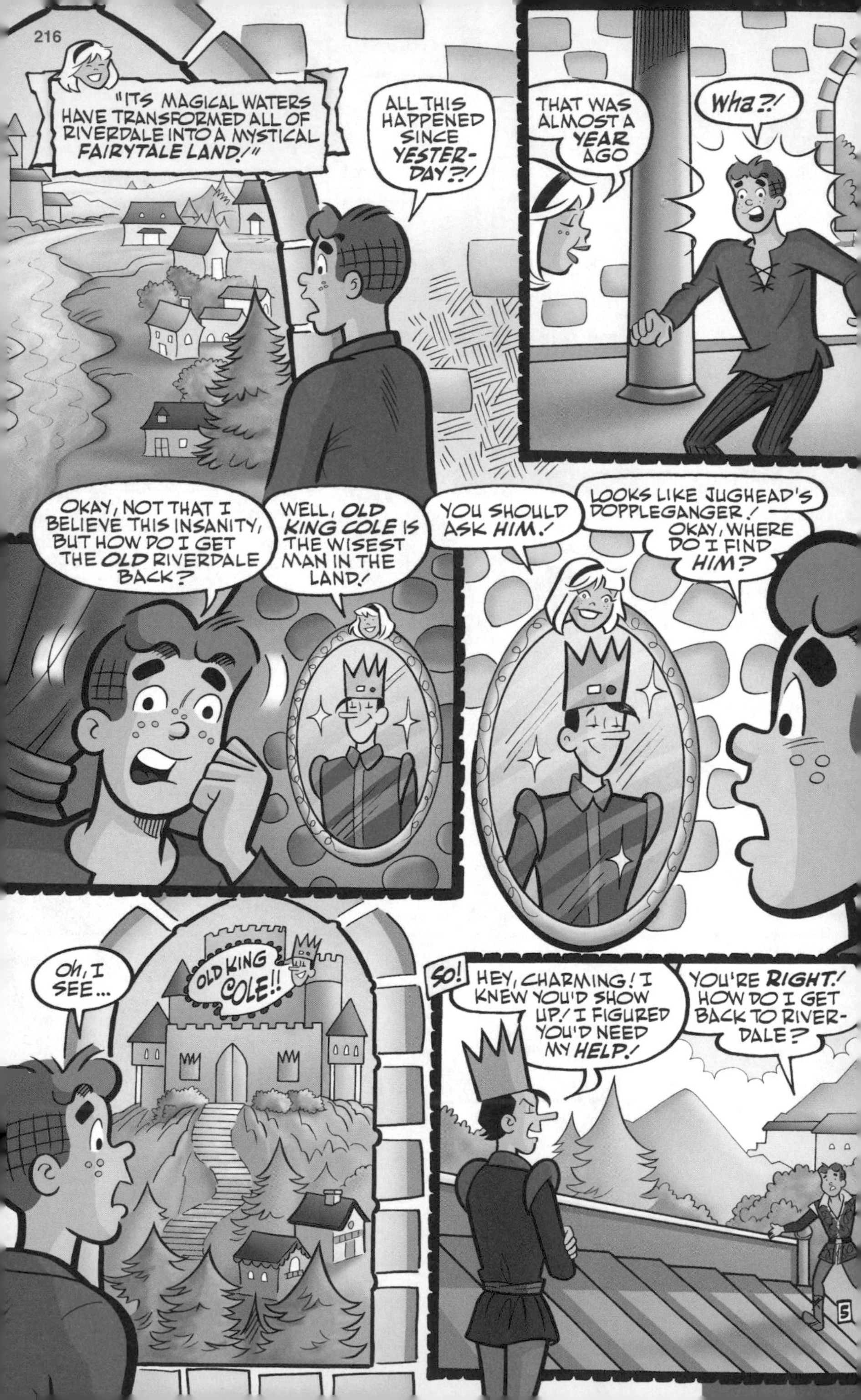
"ITS MAGICAL WATERS HAVE TRANSFORMED ALL OF RIVERDALE INTO A MYSTICAL FAIRYTALE LAND!"
ALL THIS HAPPENED SINCE YESTER-DAY?!
THAT WAS ALMOST A YEAR AGO
Wha?!
OKAY, NOT THAT I BELIEVE THIS INSANITY, BUT HOW DO I GET THE OLD RIVERDALE BACK?
WELL, OLD KING COLE IS THE WISEST MAN IN THE LAND!
YOU SHOULD ASK HIM!
LOOKS LIKE JUGHEAD'S DOPPLEGANGER! OKAY, WHERE DO I FIND HIM?
Oh, I SEE...
OLD KING COLE!!
SO!
HEY, CHARMING! I KNEW YOU'D SHOW UP! I FIGURED YOU'D NEED MY HELP!
YOU'RE RIGHT! HOW DO I GET BACK TO RIVER-DALE?
5

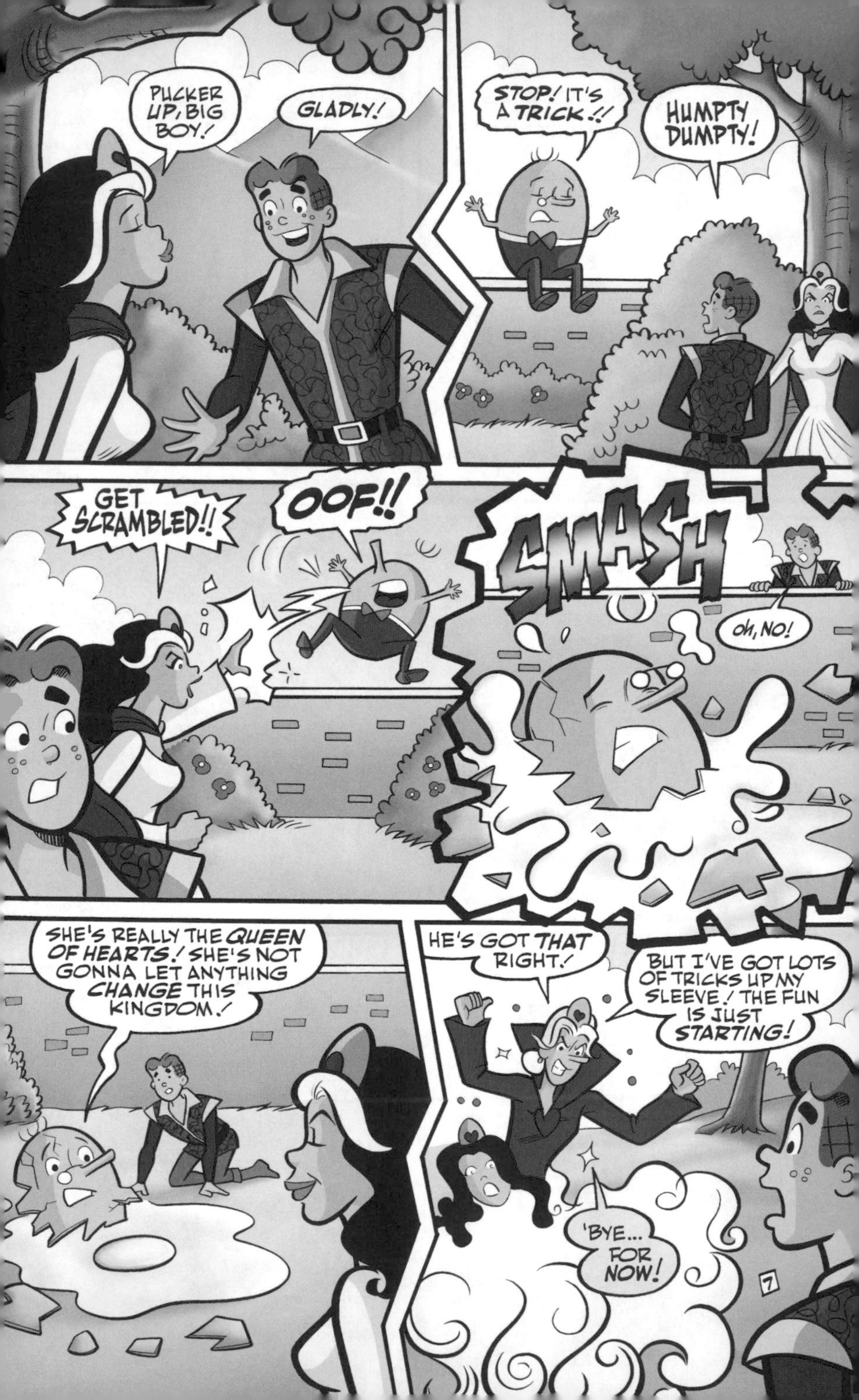
PUCKER UP, BIG BOY!
GLADLY!
STOP! IT'S A TRICK!!
HUMPTY DUMPTY!
GET SCRAMBLED!!
OOF!!
SMASH
OH, NO!
SHE'S REALLY THE QUEEN OF HEARTS! SHE'S NOT GONNA LET ANYTHING CHANGE THIS KINGDOM!
HE'S GOT THAT RIGHT!
BUT I'VE GOT LOTS OF TRICKS UP MY SLEEVE! THE FUN IS JUST STARTING!
'BYE... FOR NOW!
7

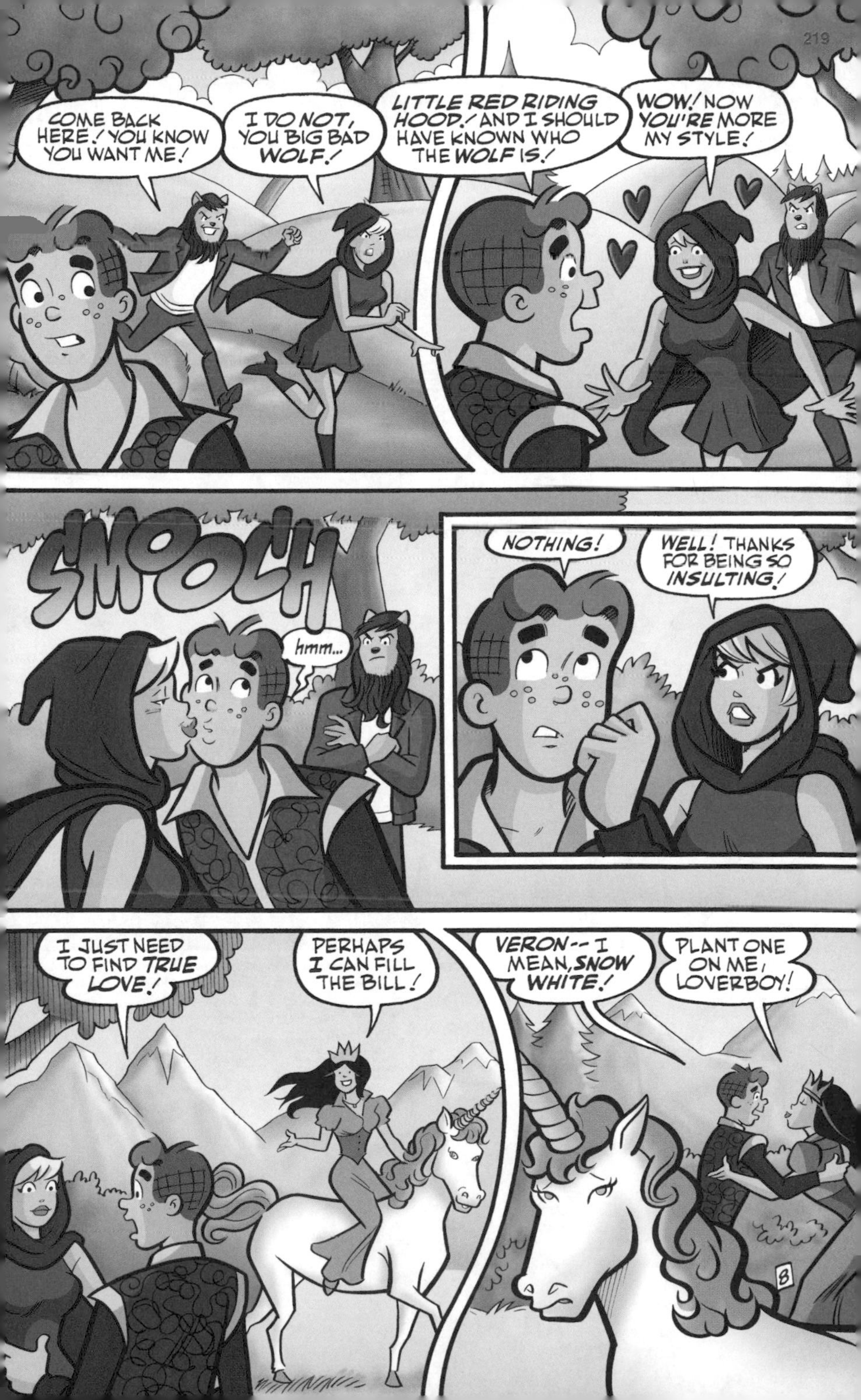
COME BACK HERE! YOU KNOW YOU WANT ME!
I DO NOT, YOU BIG BAD WOLF!
LITTLE RED RIDING HOOD! AND I SHOULD HAVE KNOWN WHO THE WOLF IS!
WOW! NOW YOU'RE MORE MY STYLE!
SMOOCH
hmm...
NOTHING!
WELL! THANKS FOR BEING SO INSULTING!
I JUST NEED TO FIND TRUE LOVE!
PERHAPS I CAN FILL THE BILL!
VERON-- I MEAN, SNOW WHITE!
PLANT ONE ON ME, LOVERBOY!
8

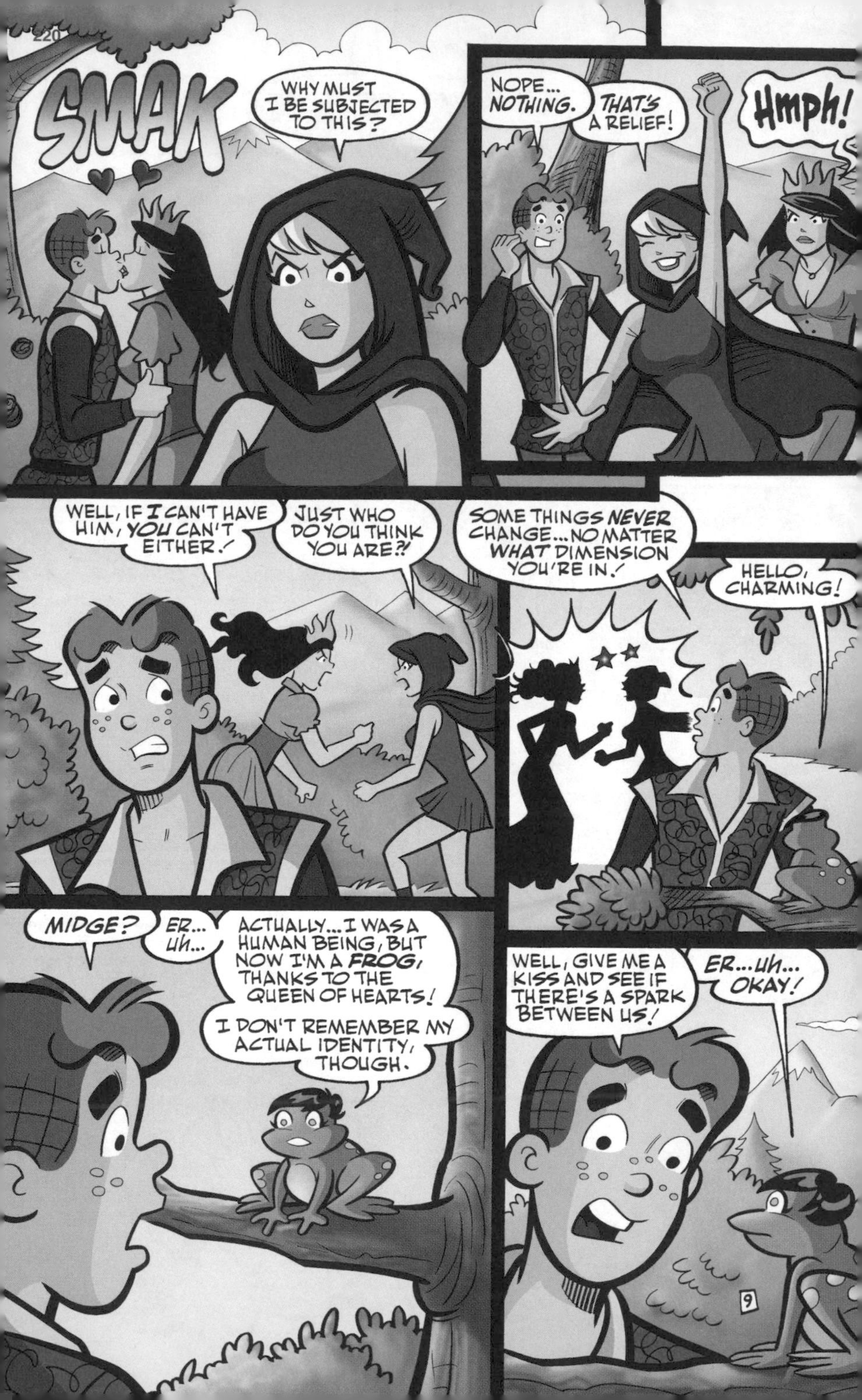
SMAK
WHY MUST I BE SUBJECTED TO THIS?
NOPE... NOTHING.
THAT'S A RELIEF!
Hmph!
WELL, IF I CAN'T HAVE HIM, YOU CAN'T EITHER.!
JUST WHO DO YOU THINK YOU ARE?!
SOME THINGS NEVER CHANGE... NO MATTER WHAT DIMENSION YOU'RE IN.!
HELLO, CHARMING!
MIDGE?
ER... UH...
ACTUALLY... I WAS A HUMAN BEING, BUT NOW I'M A FROG, THANKS TO THE QUEEN OF HEARTS!
I DON'T REMEMBER MY ACTUAL IDENTITY, THOUGH.
WELL, GIVE ME A KISS AND SEE IF THERE'S A SPARK BETWEEN US!
ER... UH... OKAY!
9

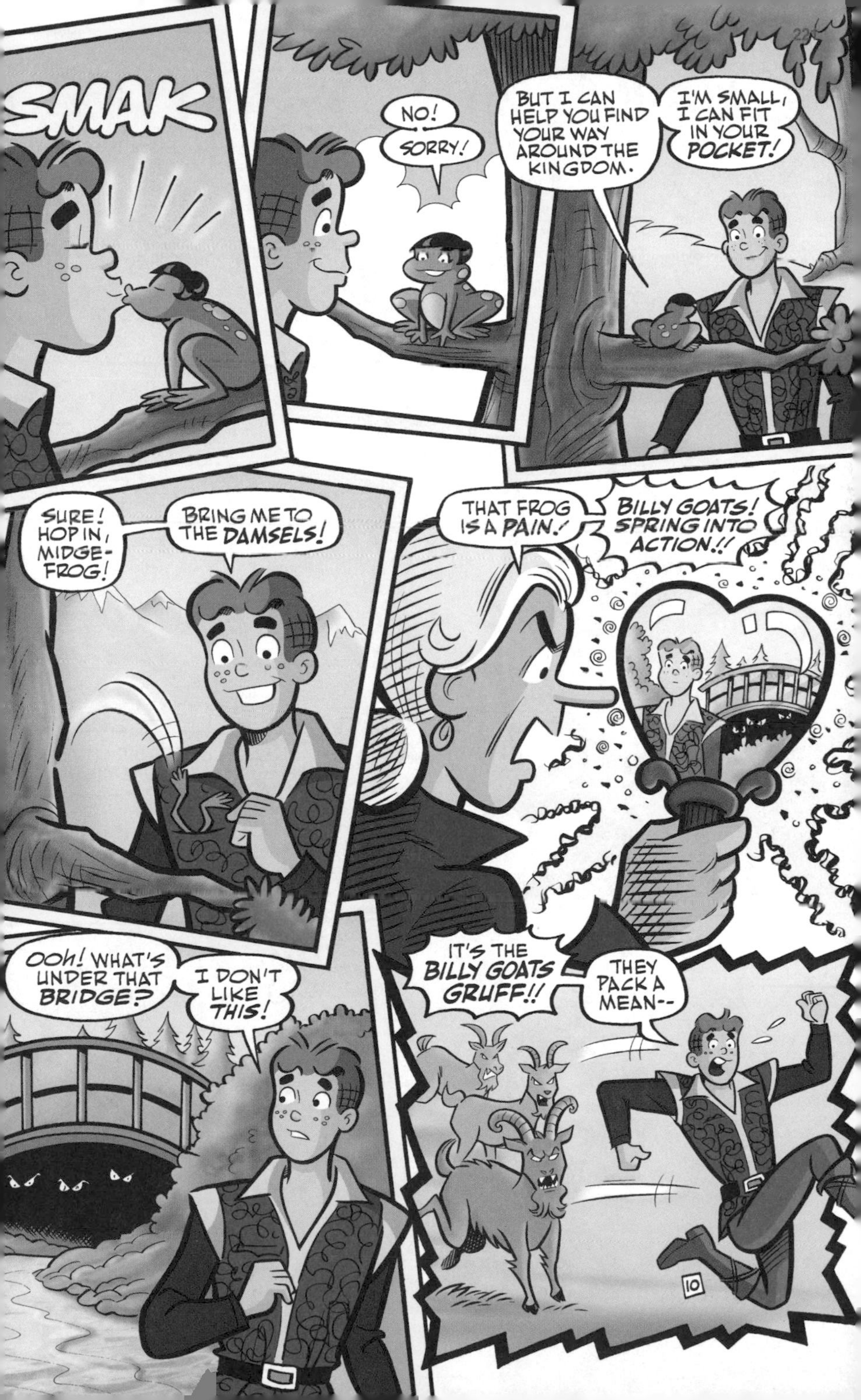
SMAK
NO!
SORRY!
BUT I CAN HELP YOU FIND YOUR WAY AROUND THE KINGDOM.
I'M SMALL, I CAN FIT IN YOUR POCKET!
SURE! HOP IN, MIDGE-FROG!
BRING ME TO THE DAMSELS!
THAT FROG IS A PAIN!
BILLY GOATS! SPRING INTO ACTION!!
OOH! WHAT'S UNDER THAT BRIDGE?
I DON'T LIKE THIS!
IT'S THE BILLY GOATS GRUFF!!
THEY PACK A MEAN--
10

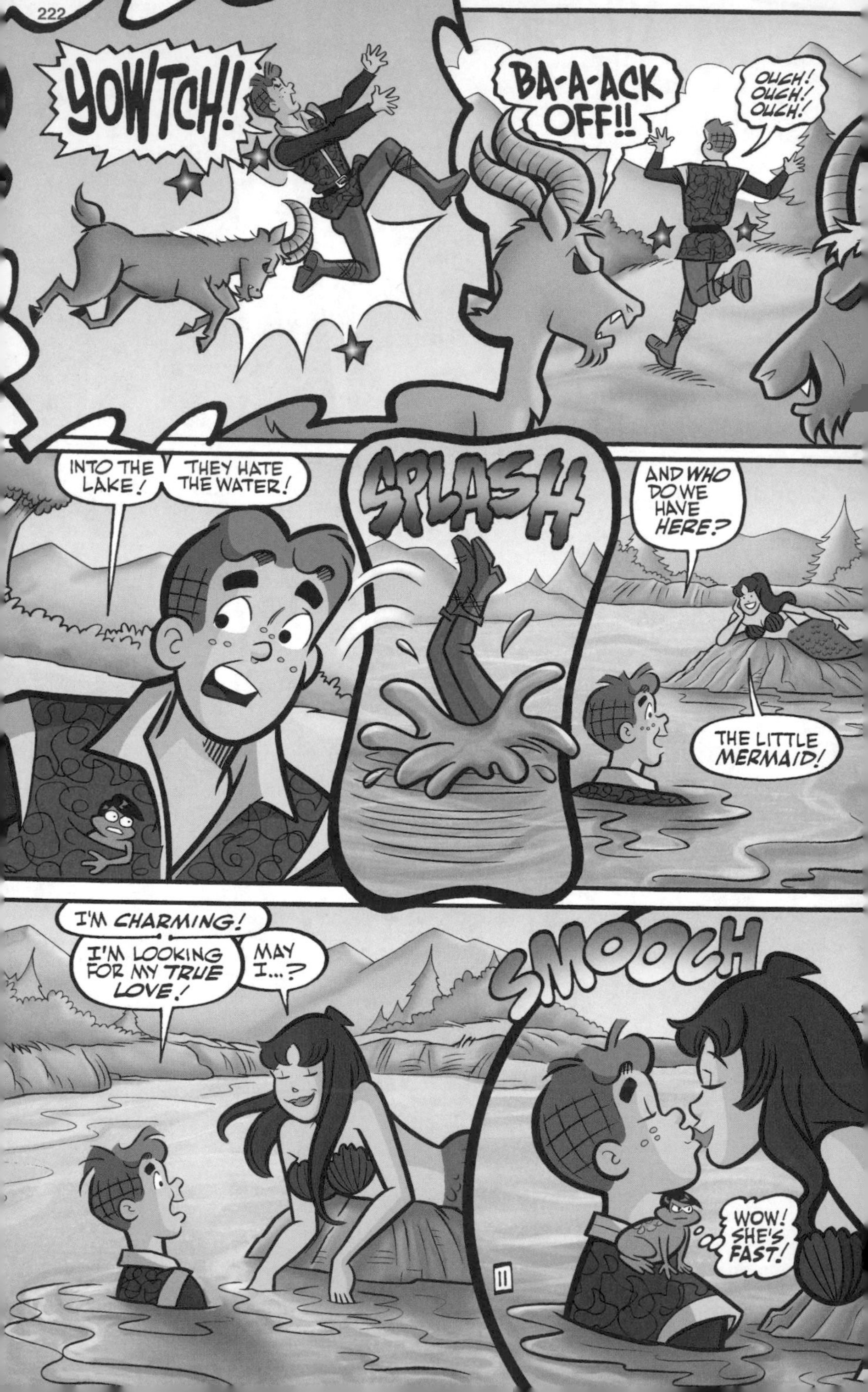
YOWTCH!
BA-A-ACK OFF!!
OUCH! OUCH! OUCH!
INTO THE LAKE!
THEY HATE THE WATER!
SPLASH
AND WHO DO WE HAVE HERE?
THE LITTLE MERMAID!
I'M CHARMING!
I'M LOOKING FOR MY TRUE LOVE!
MAY I...?
SMOOCH
WOW! SHE'S FAST!
11

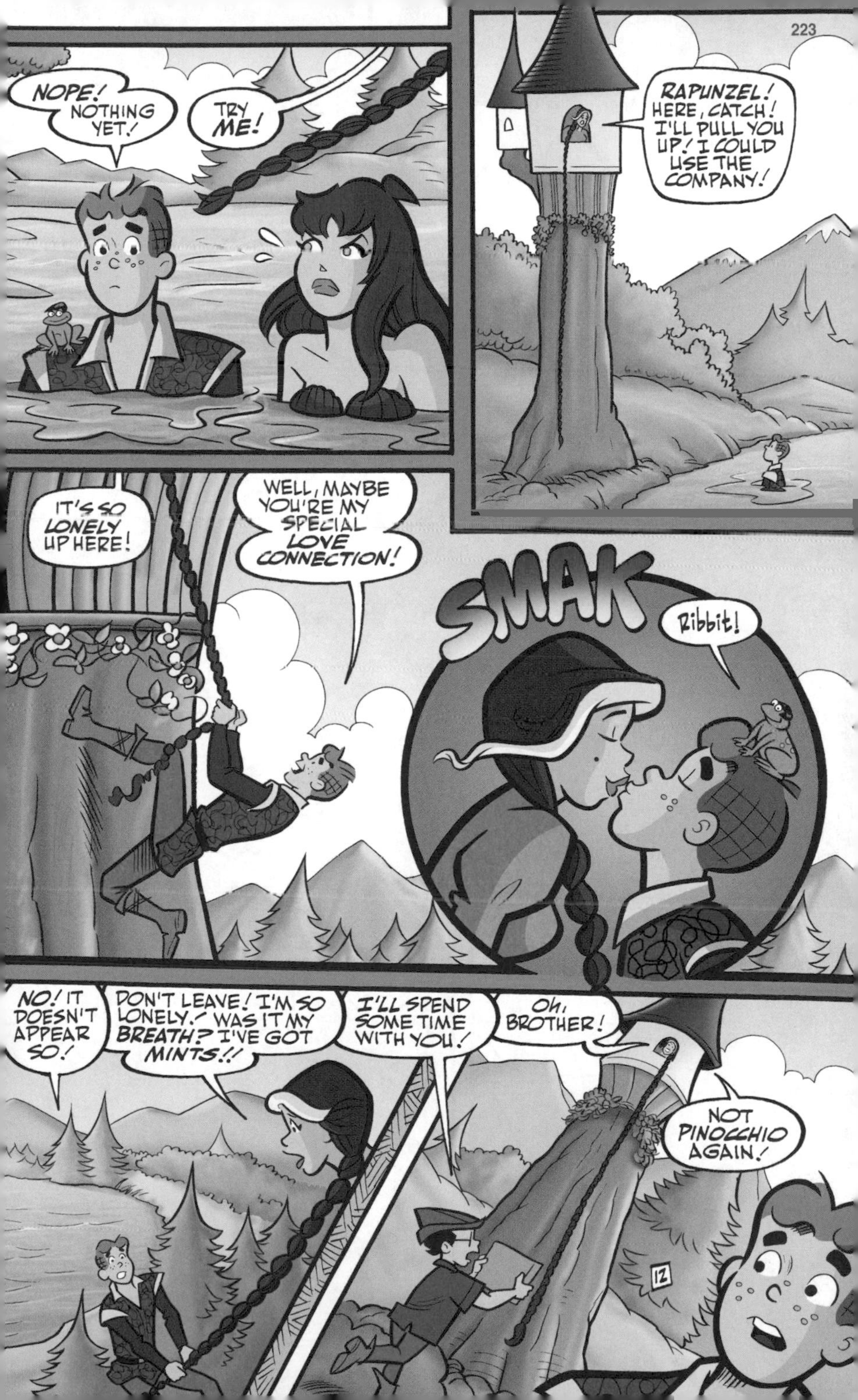
NOPE! NOTHING YET!
TRY ME!
RAPUNZEL! HERE, CATCH! I'LL PULL YOU UP! I COULD USE THE COMPANY!
IT'S SO LONELY UP HERE!
WELL, MAYBE YOU'RE MY SPECIAL LOVE CONNECTION!
SMAK
Ribbit!
NO! IT DOESN'T APPEAR SO!
DON'T LEAVE! I'M SO LONELY! WAS IT MY BREATH? I'VE GOT MINTS!!
I'LL SPEND SOME TIME WITH YOU!
Oh, BROTHER!
NOT PINOCCHIO AGAIN!
12

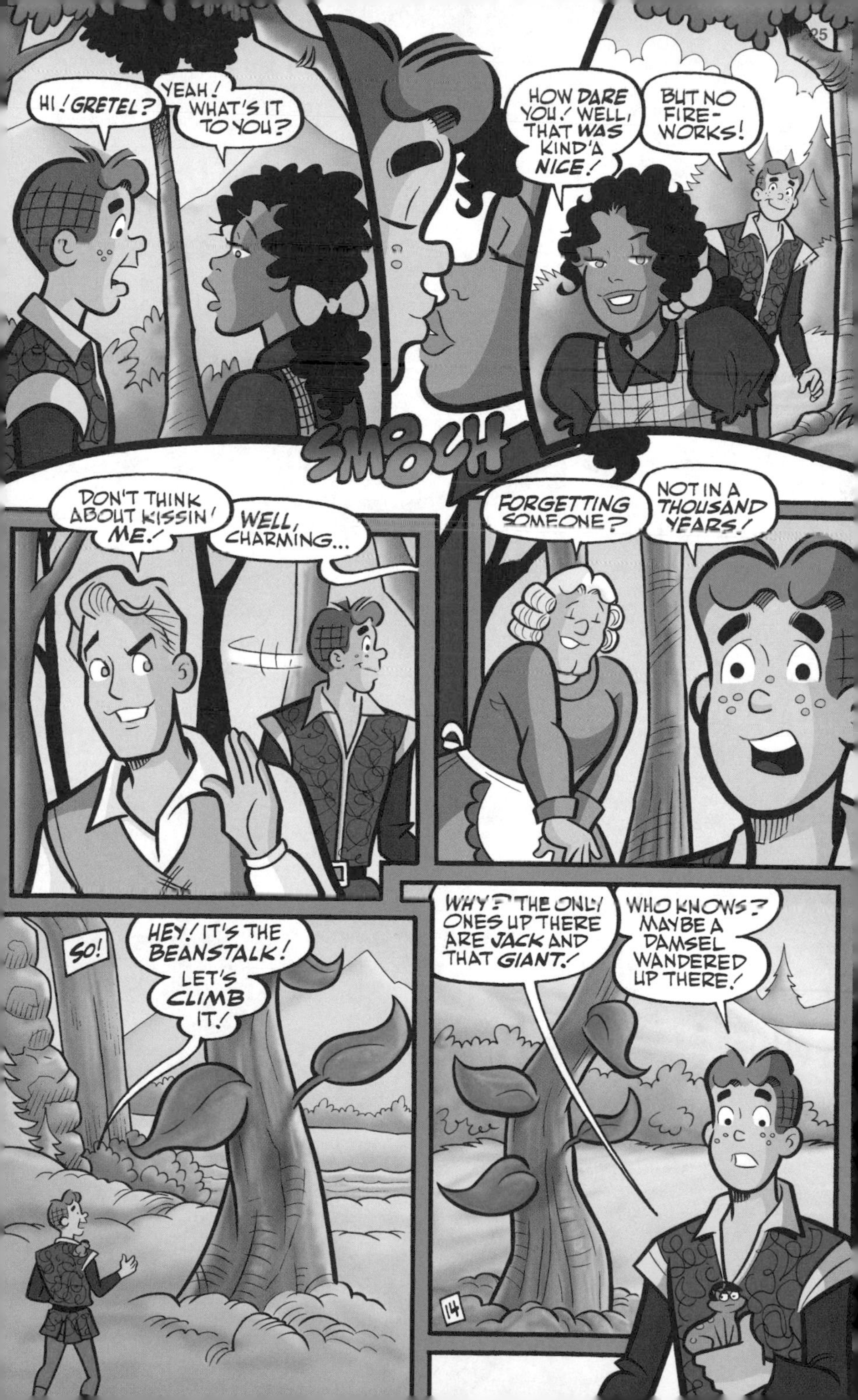
HI! GRETEL?
YEAH! WHAT'S IT TO YOU?
SMOOCH
HOW DARE YOU! WELL, THAT WAS KIND'A NICE!
BUT NO FIRE-WORKS!
DON'T THINK ABOUT KISSIN' ME!
WELL, CHARMING...
FORGETTING SOMEONE?
NOT IN A THOUSAND YEARS!
SO!
HEY! IT'S THE BEANSTALK! LET'S CLIMB IT!
WHY? THE ONLY ONES UP THERE ARE JACK AND THAT GIANT!
WHO KNOWS? MAYBE A DAMSEL WANDERED UP THERE!
14

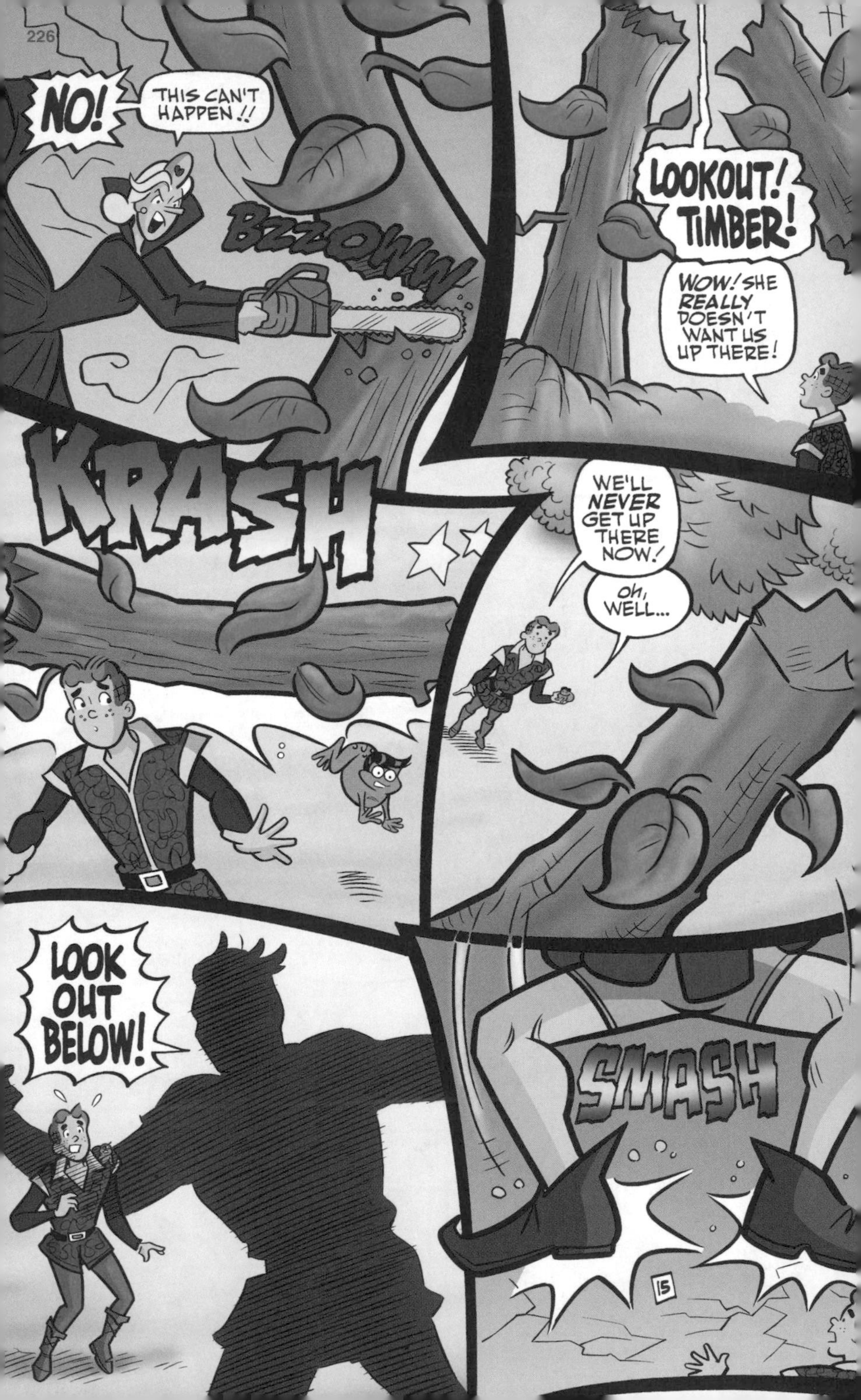
NO!
THIS CAN'T HAPPEN!!
BZZOWW
LOOKOUT! TIMBER!
WOW! SHE REALLY DOESN'T WANT US UP THERE!
KRASH
WE'LL NEVER GET UP THERE NOW!
oh, WELL...
LOOK OUT BELOW!
SMASH
15

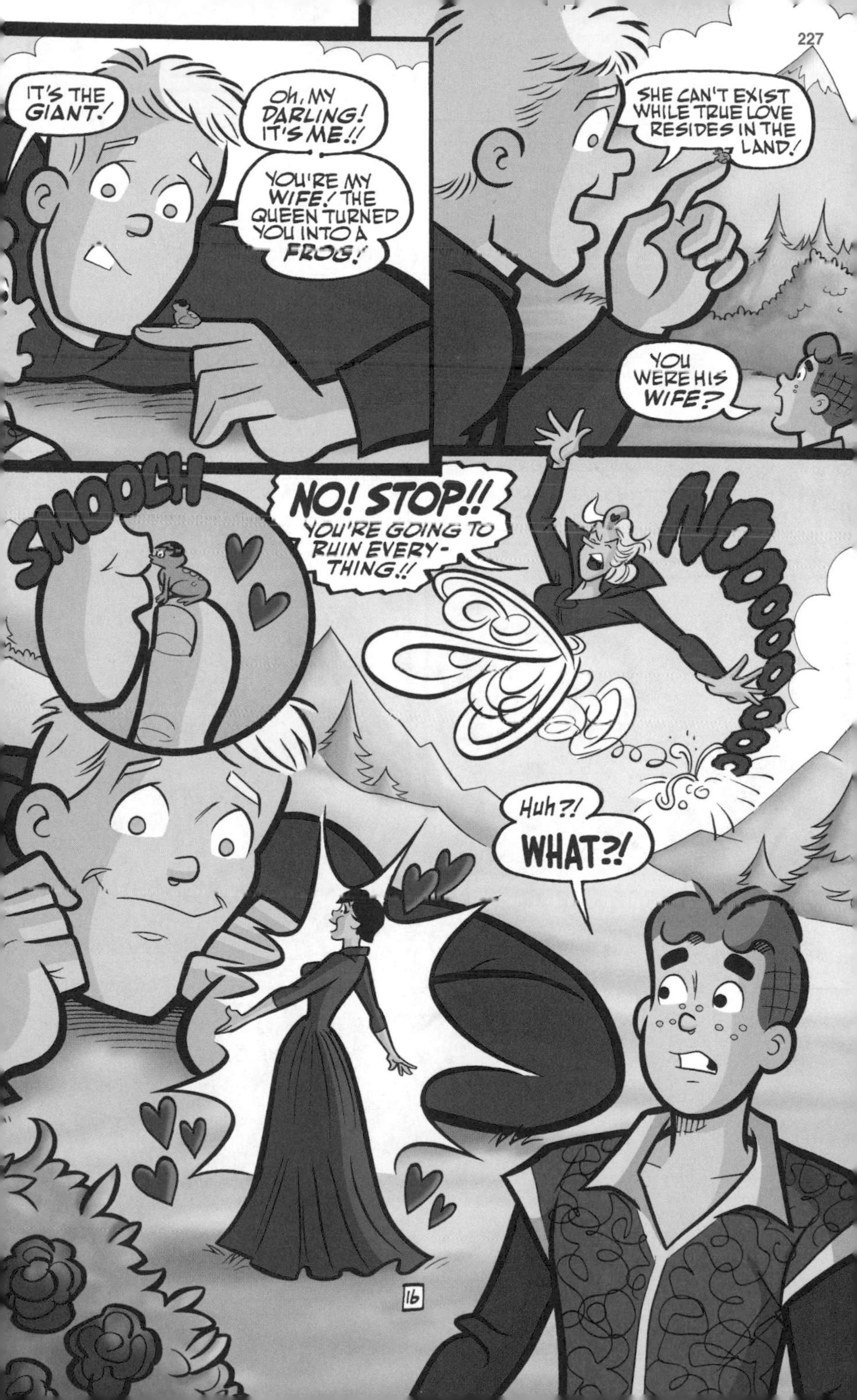
IT'S THE GIANT!
Oh, MY DARLING! IT'S ME!!
YOU'RE MY WIFE! THE QUEEN TURNED YOU INTO A FROG!
SHE CAN'T EXIST WHILE TRUE LOVE RESIDES IN THE LAND!
YOU WERE HIS WIFE?
SMOOCH
NO! STOP!! YOU'RE GOING TO RUIN EVERY-THING!!
NOOOOOOOOOOO
Huh?! WHAT?!
16

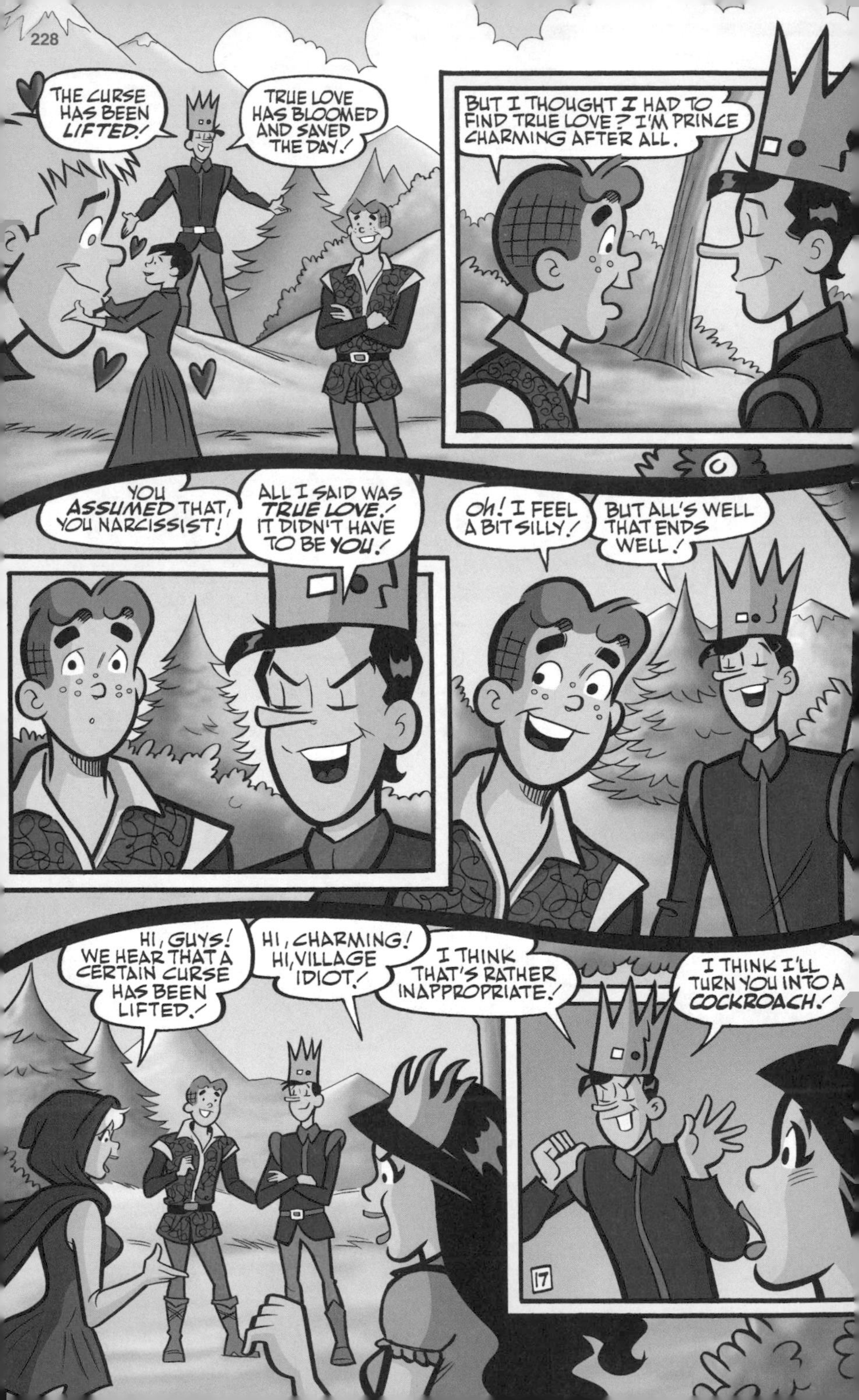
THE CURSE HAS BEEN LIFTED!
TRUE LOVE HAS BLOOMED AND SAVED THE DAY!
BUT I THOUGHT I HAD TO FIND TRUE LOVE? I'M PRINCE CHARMING AFTER ALL.
YOU ASSUMED THAT, YOU NARCISSIST!
ALL I SAID WAS TRUE LOVE! IT DIDN'T HAVE TO BE YOU!
Oh! I FEEL A BIT SILLY!
BUT ALL'S WELL THAT ENDS WELL!
HI, GUYS! WE HEAR THAT A CERTAIN CURSE HAS BEEN LIFTED!
HI, CHARMING! HI, VILLAGE IDIOT!
I THINK THAT'S RATHER INAPPROPRIATE!
I THINK I'LL TURN YOU INTO A COCKROACH!
17

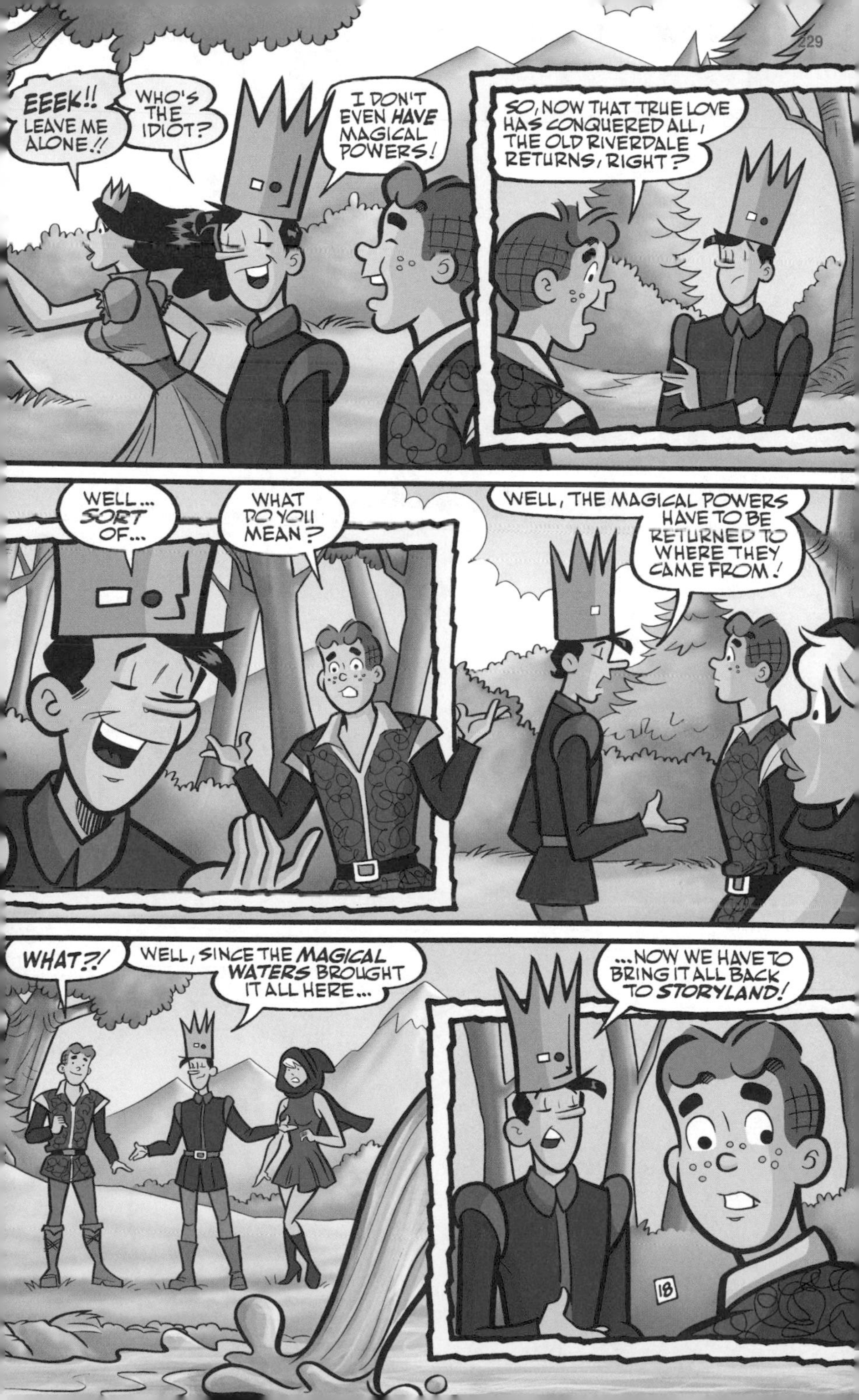
EEEK!! LEAVE ME ALONE!!
WHO'S THE IDIOT?
I DON'T EVEN HAVE MAGICAL POWERS!
SO, NOW THAT TRUE LOVE HAS CONQUERED ALL, THE OLD RIVERDALE RETURNS, RIGHT?
WELL... SORT OF...
WHAT DO YOU MEAN?
WELL, THE MAGICAL POWERS HAVE TO BE RETURNED TO WHERE THEY CAME FROM!
WHAT?!
WELL, SINCE THE MAGICAL WATERS BROUGHT IT ALL HERE...
...NOW WE HAVE TO BRING IT ALL BACK TO STORYLAND!
18

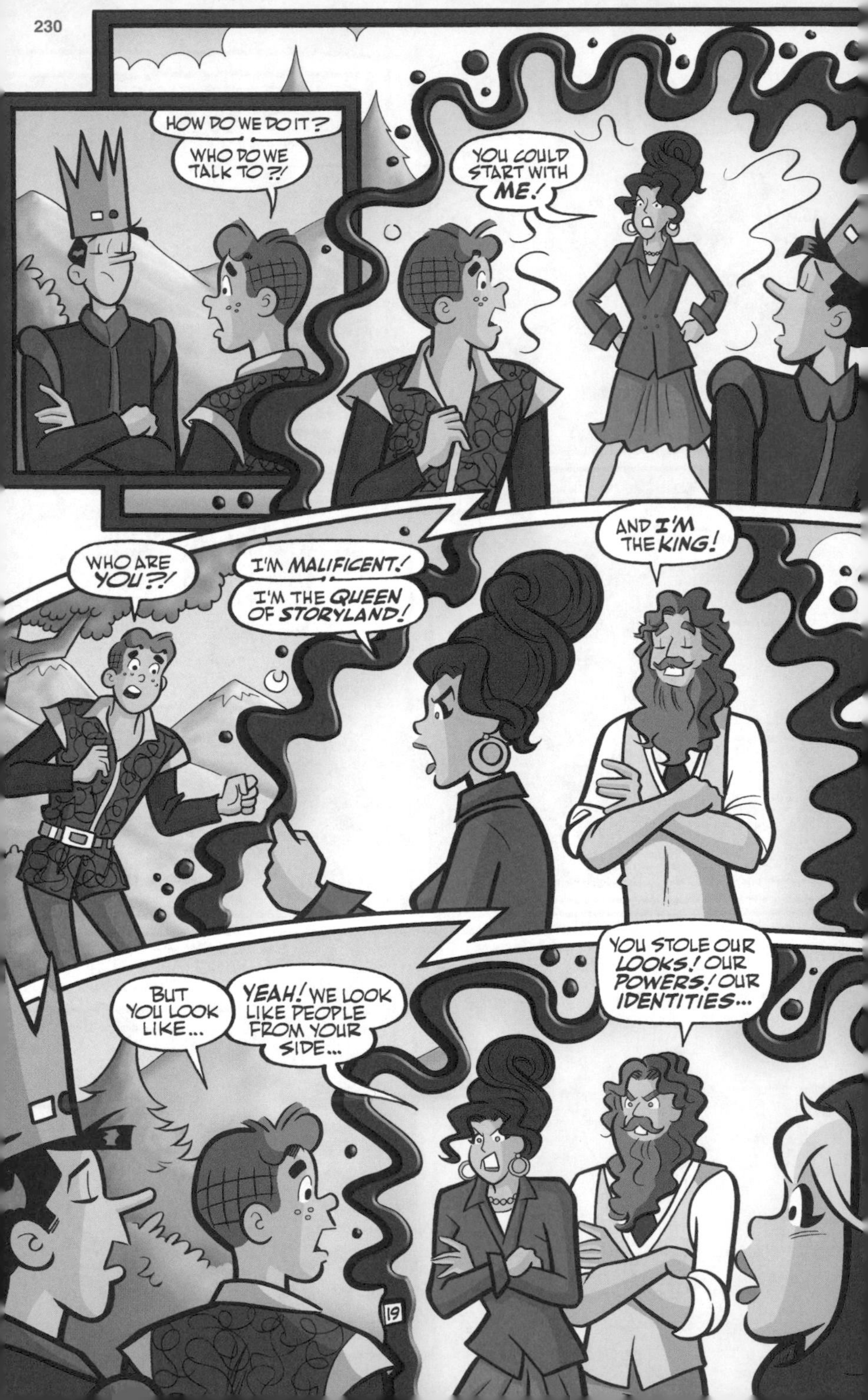
HOW DO WE DO IT?
WHO DO WE TALK TO?!
YOU COULD START WITH ME!
WHO ARE YOU?!
I'M MALIFICENT!
I'M THE QUEEN OF STORYLAND!
AND I'M THE KING!
BUT YOU LOOK LIKE...
YEAH! WE LOOK LIKE PEOPLE FROM YOUR SIDE...
YOU STOLE OUR LOOKS! OUR POWERS! OUR IDENTITIES...
19

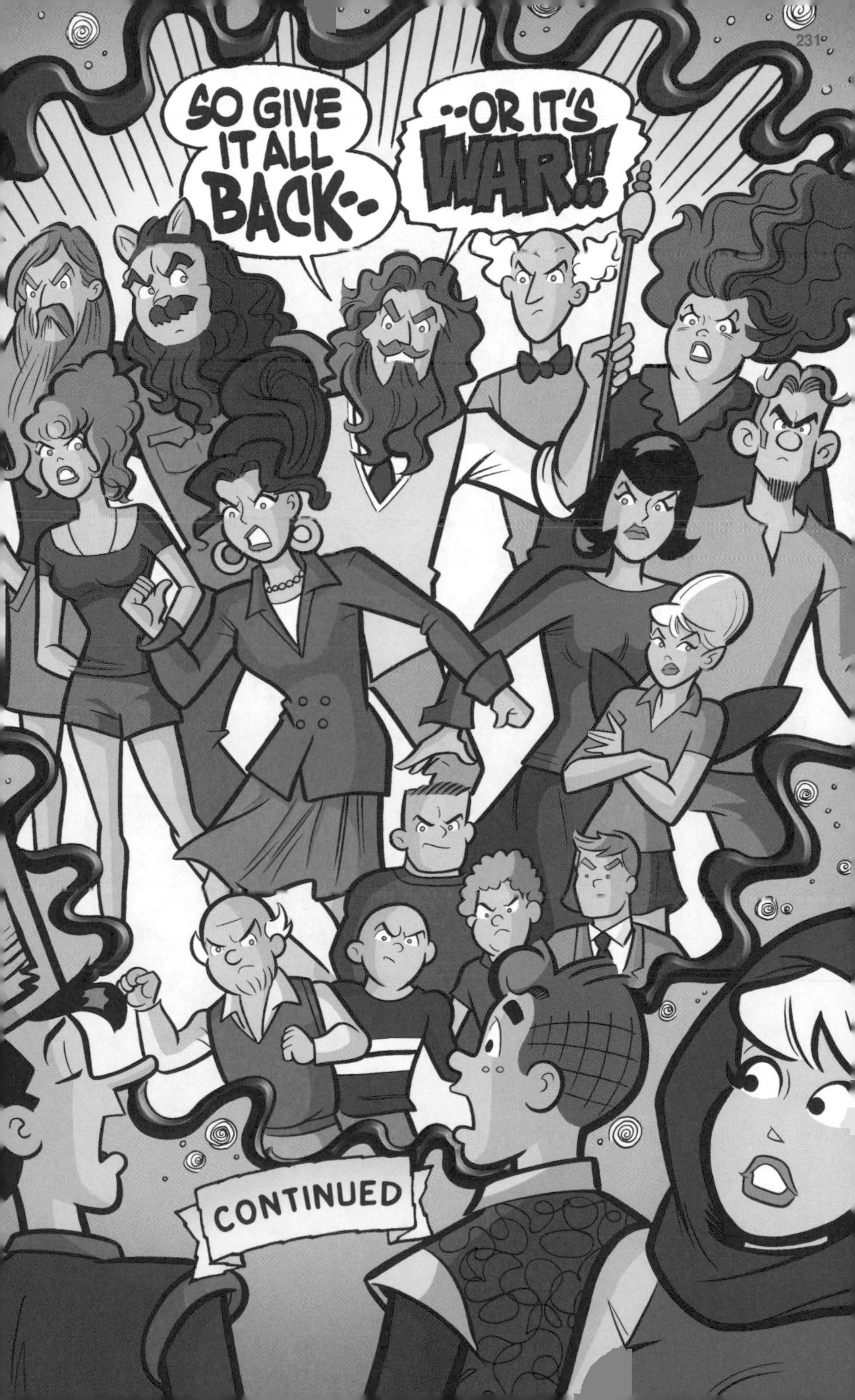
SO GIVE IT ALL BACK--
--OR IT'S WAR!!
CONTINUED

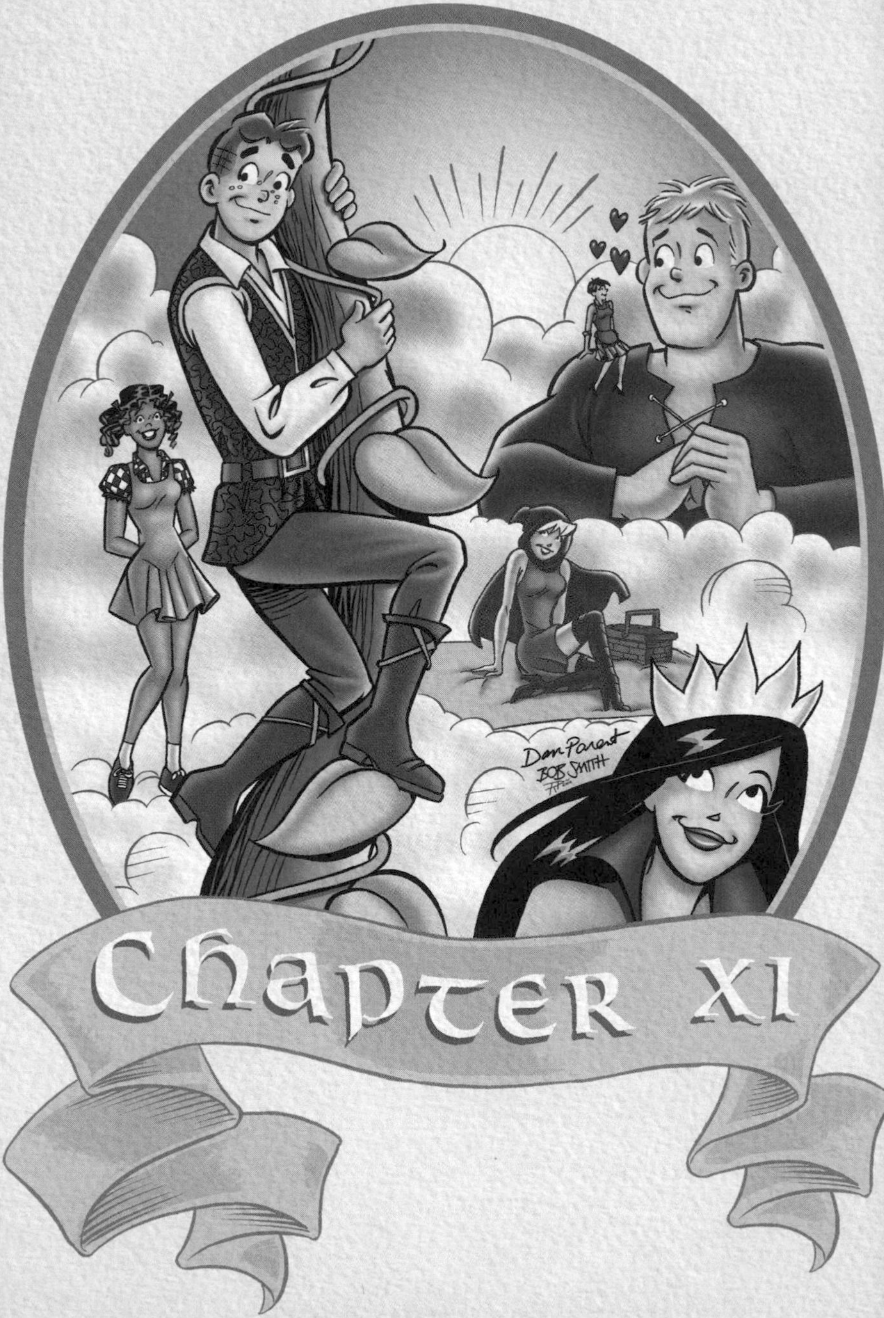
Dan Parent
Bob Smith

Chapter XI

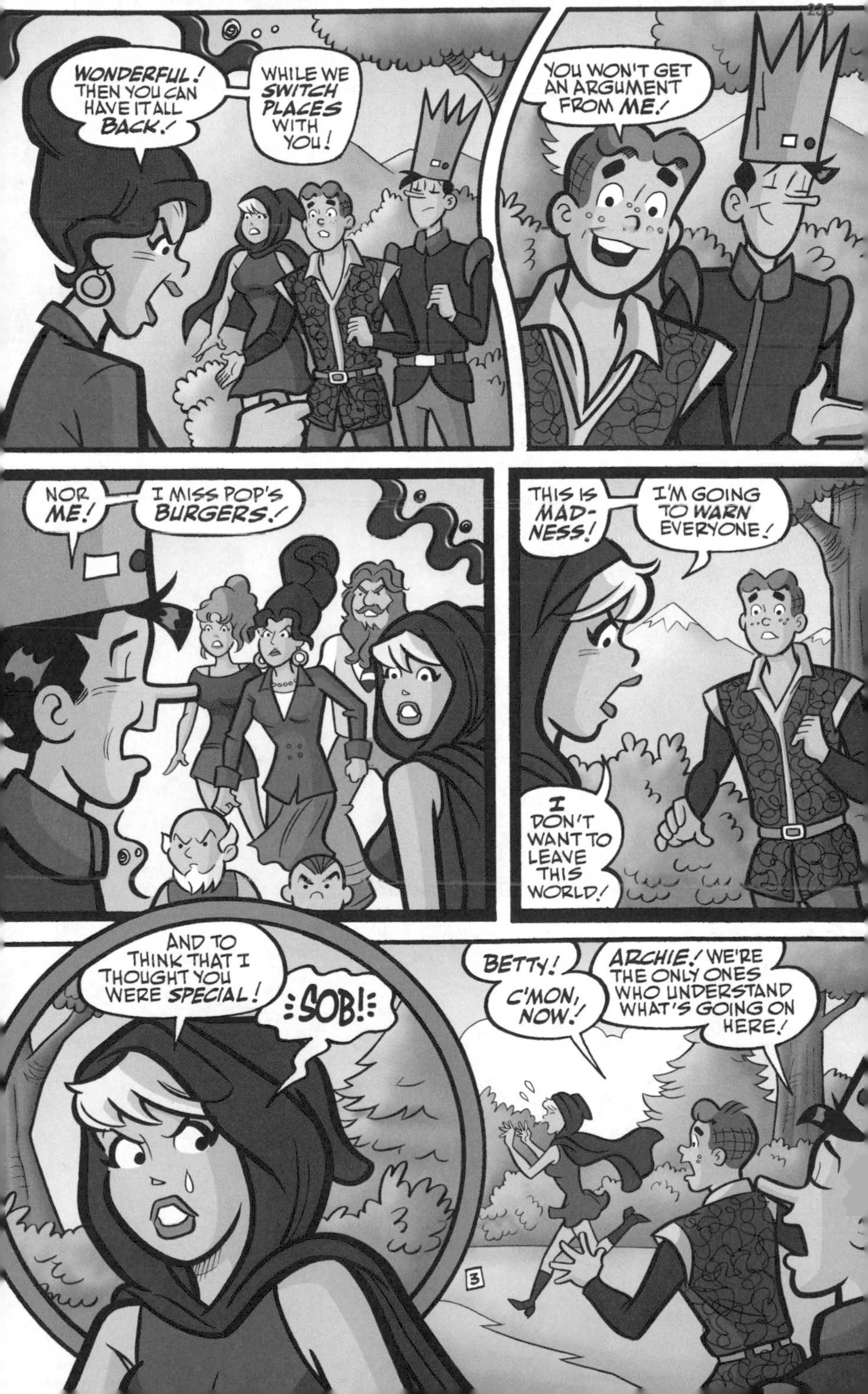
WONDERFUL! THEN YOU CAN HAVE IT ALL BACK!
WHILE WE SWITCH PLACES WITH YOU!
YOU WON'T GET AN ARGUMENT FROM ME!
NOR ME!
I MISS POP'S BURGERS!
THIS IS MADNESS!
I'M GOING TO WARN EVERYONE!
I DON'T WANT TO LEAVE THIS WORLD!
AND TO THINK THAT I THOUGHT YOU WERE SPECIAL!
SOB!
BETTY!
C'MON, NOW!
ARCHIE! WE'RE THE ONLY ONES WHO UNDERSTAND WHAT'S GOING ON HERE!
3

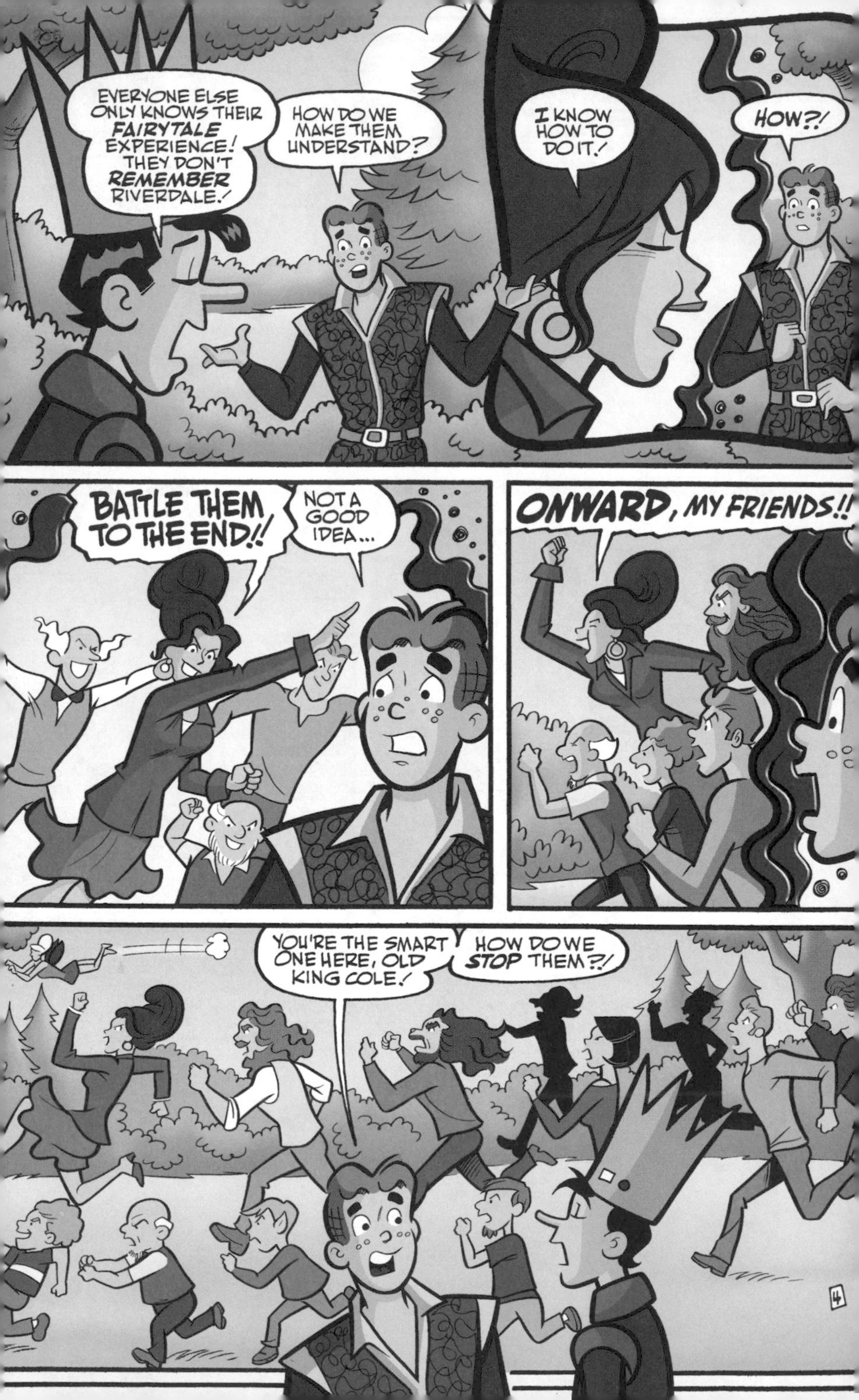
EVERYONE ELSE ONLY KNOWS THEIR **FAIRYTALE** EXPERIENCE! THEY DON'T **REMEMBER** RIVERDALE!
HOW DO WE MAKE THEM UNDERSTAND?
I KNOW HOW TO DO IT!
HOW?!
BATTLE THEM TO THE END!!
NOT A GOOD IDEA...
ONWARD, MY FRIENDS!!
YOU'RE THE SMART ONE HERE, OLD KING COLE!
HOW DO WE **STOP** THEM?!
4

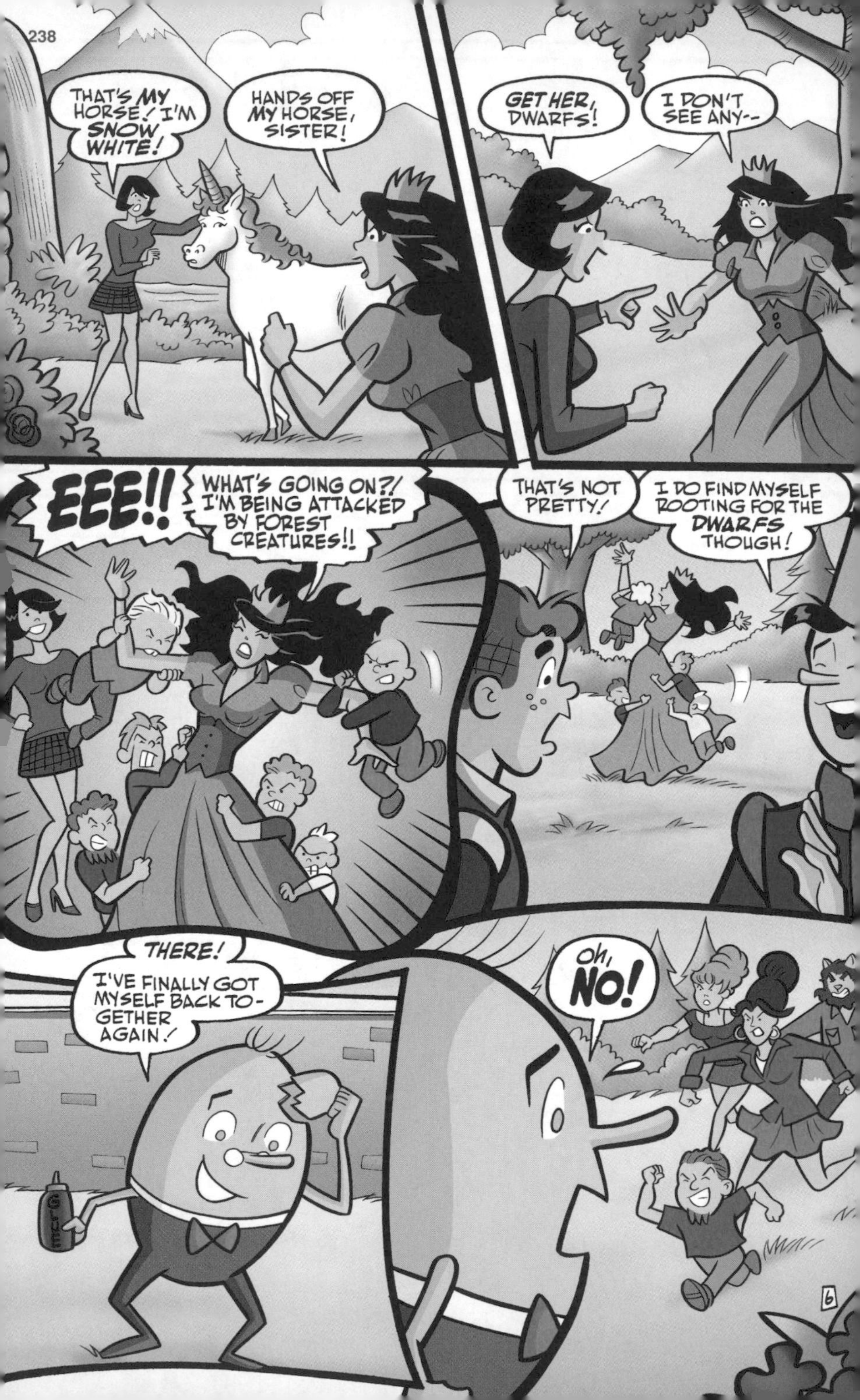
THAT'S MY HORSE! I'M SNOW WHITE!
HANDS OFF MY HORSE, SISTER!
GET HER, DWARFS!
I DON'T SEE ANY--
EEE!!
WHAT'S GOING ON?! I'M BEING ATTACKED BY FOREST CREATURES!!
THAT'S NOT PRETTY!
I DO FIND MYSELF ROOTING FOR THE DWARFS THOUGH!
THERE!
I'VE FINALLY GOT MYSELF BACK TO-GETHER AGAIN!
Oh, NO!
6

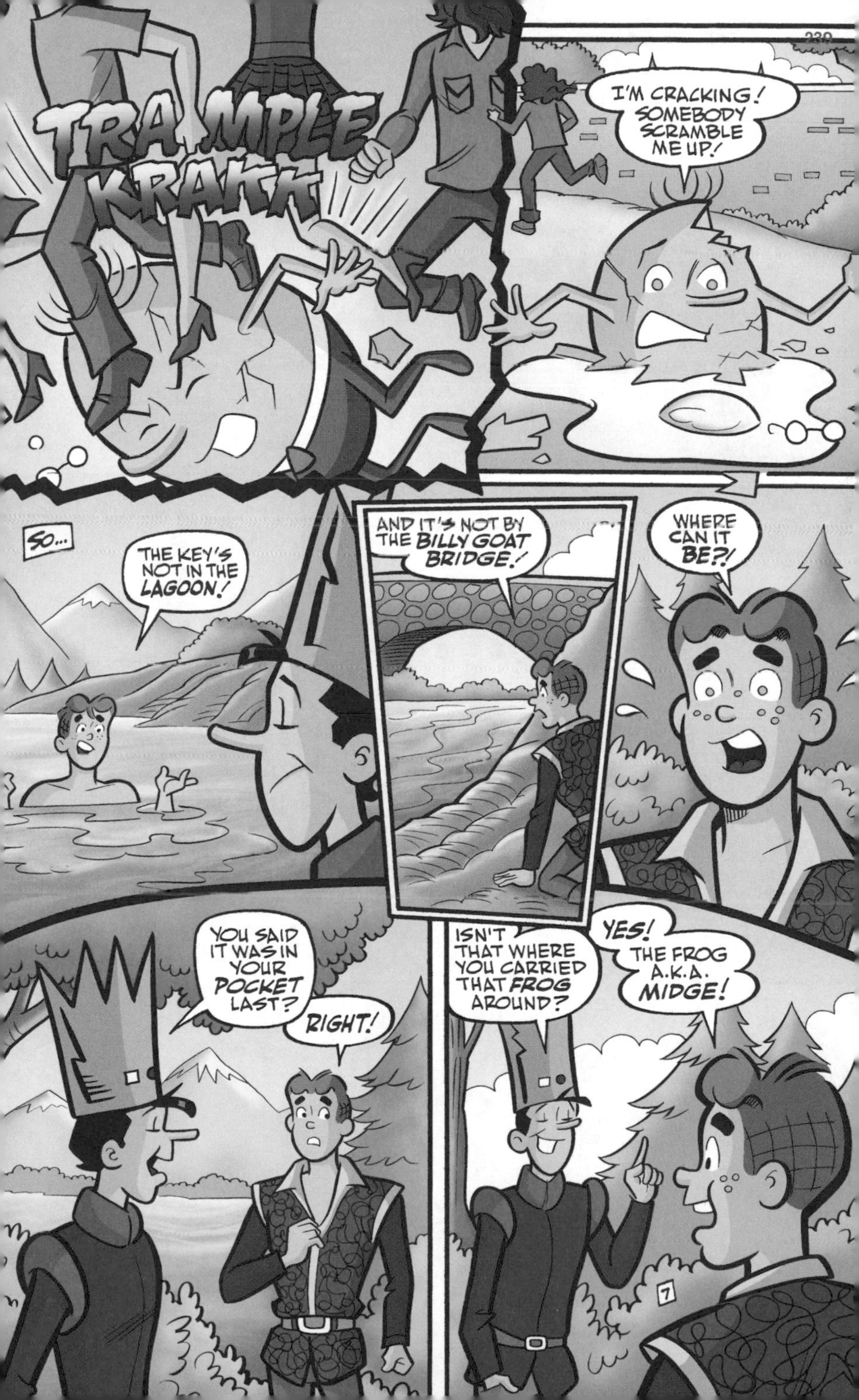
TRAMPLE
KRAKK
I'M CRACKING! SOMEBODY SCRAMBLE ME UP!
SO...
THE KEY'S NOT IN THE LAGOON!
AND IT'S NOT BY THE BILLY GOAT BRIDGE!
WHERE CAN IT BE?!
YOU SAID IT WAS IN YOUR POCKET LAST?
RIGHT!
ISN'T THAT WHERE YOU CARRIED THAT FROG AROUND?
YES! THE FROG A.K.A. MIDGE!
7

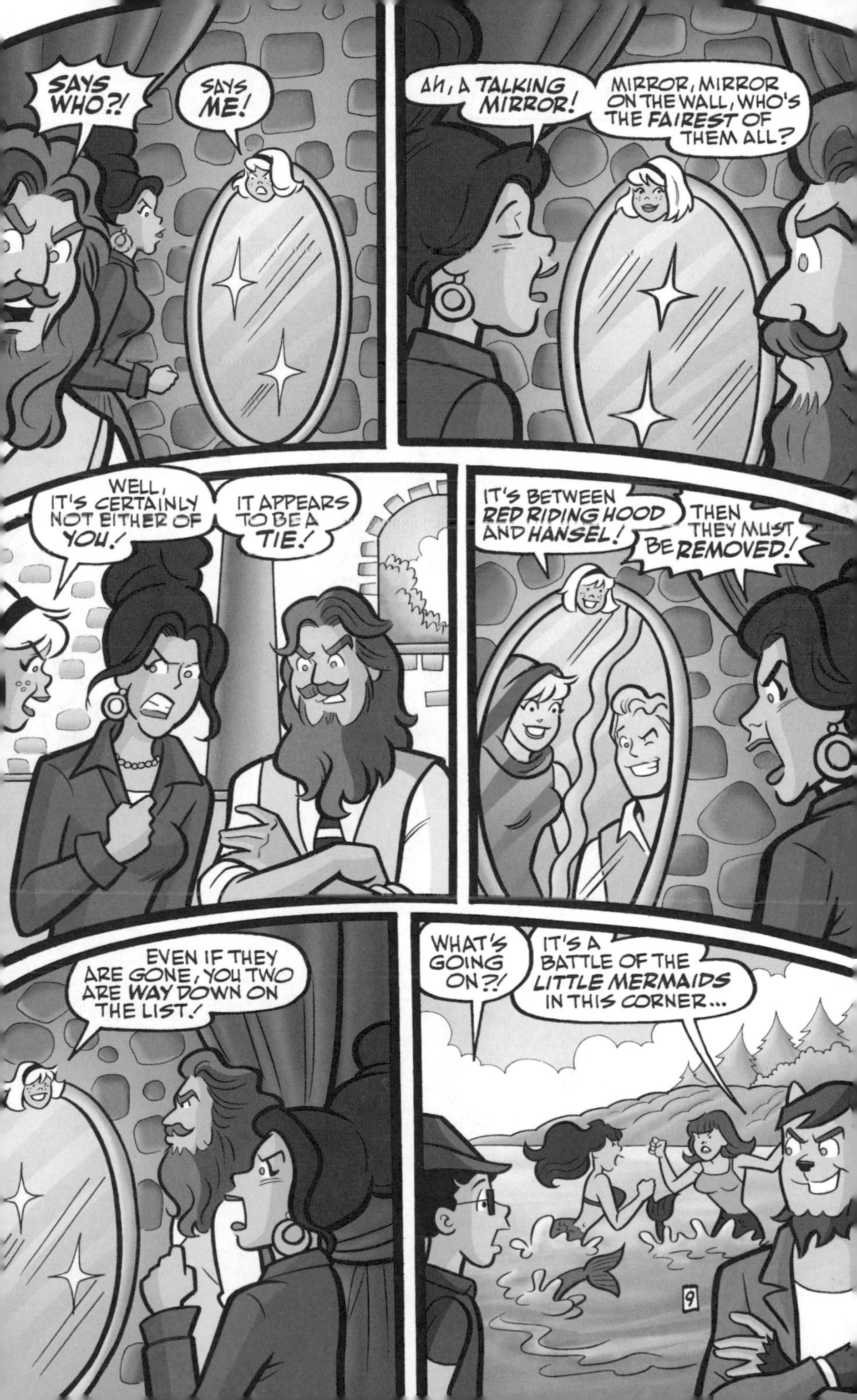
SAYS WHO?!
SAYS ME!
AH, A TALKING MIRROR!
MIRROR, MIRROR ON THE WALL, WHO'S THE FAIREST OF THEM ALL?
WELL, IT'S CERTAINLY NOT EITHER OF YOU!
IT APPEARS TO BE A TIE!
IT'S BETWEEN RED RIDING HOOD AND HANSEL!
THEN THEY MUST BE REMOVED!
EVEN IF THEY ARE GONE, YOU TWO ARE WAY DOWN ON THE LIST!
WHAT'S GOING ON?!
IT'S A BATTLE OF THE LITTLE MERMAIDS IN THIS CORNER...
9

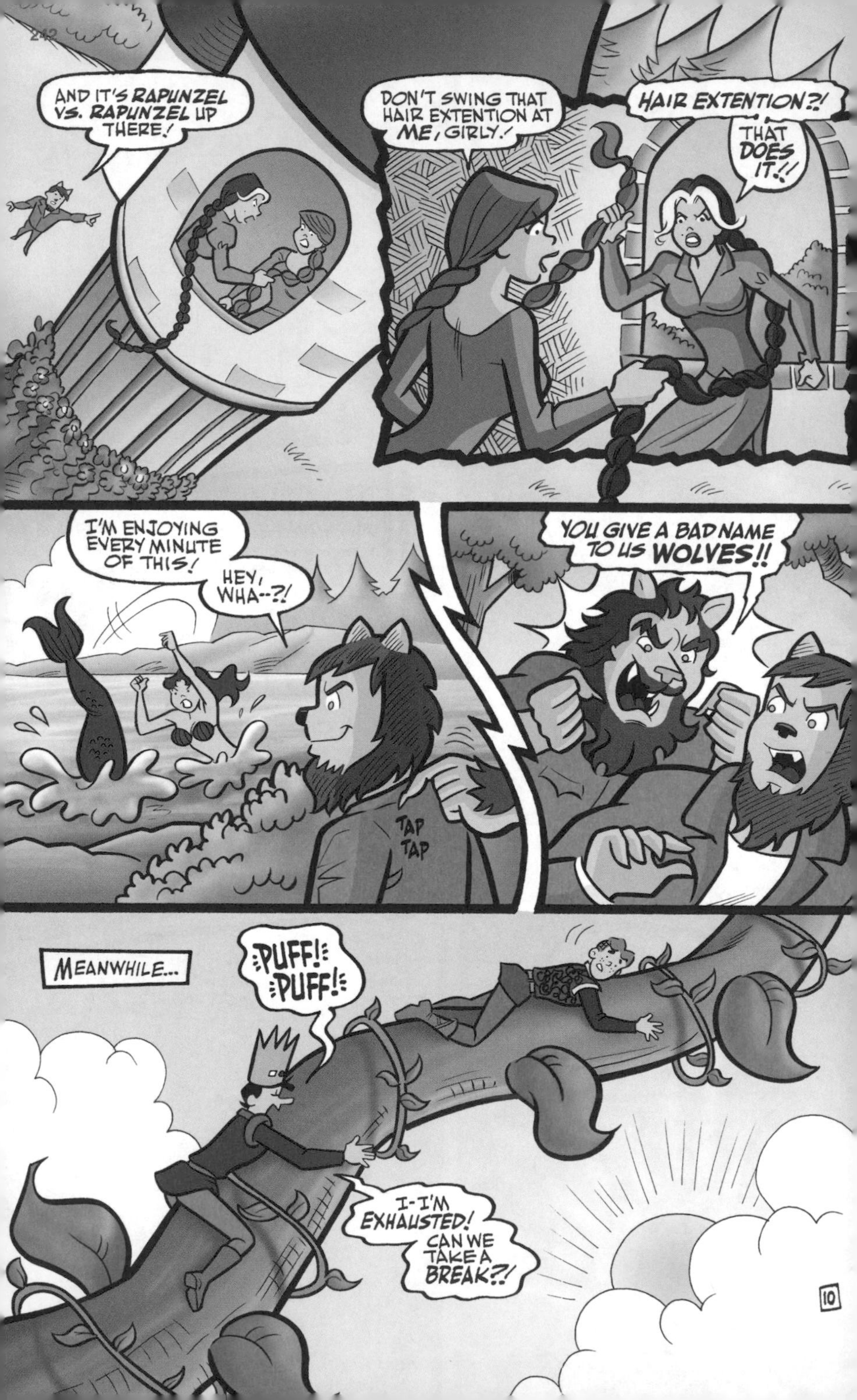
AND IT'S RAPUNZEL VS. RAPUNZEL UP THERE!
DON'T SWING THAT HAIR EXTENTION AT ME, GIRLY!
HAIR EXTENTION?!
THAT DOES IT!!
I'M ENJOYING EVERY MINUTE OF THIS!
HEY, WHA--?!
TAP TAP
YOU GIVE A BAD NAME TO US WOLVES!!
MEANWHILE...
PUFF! PUFF!
I-I'M EXHAUSTED! CAN WE TAKE A BREAK?!
10

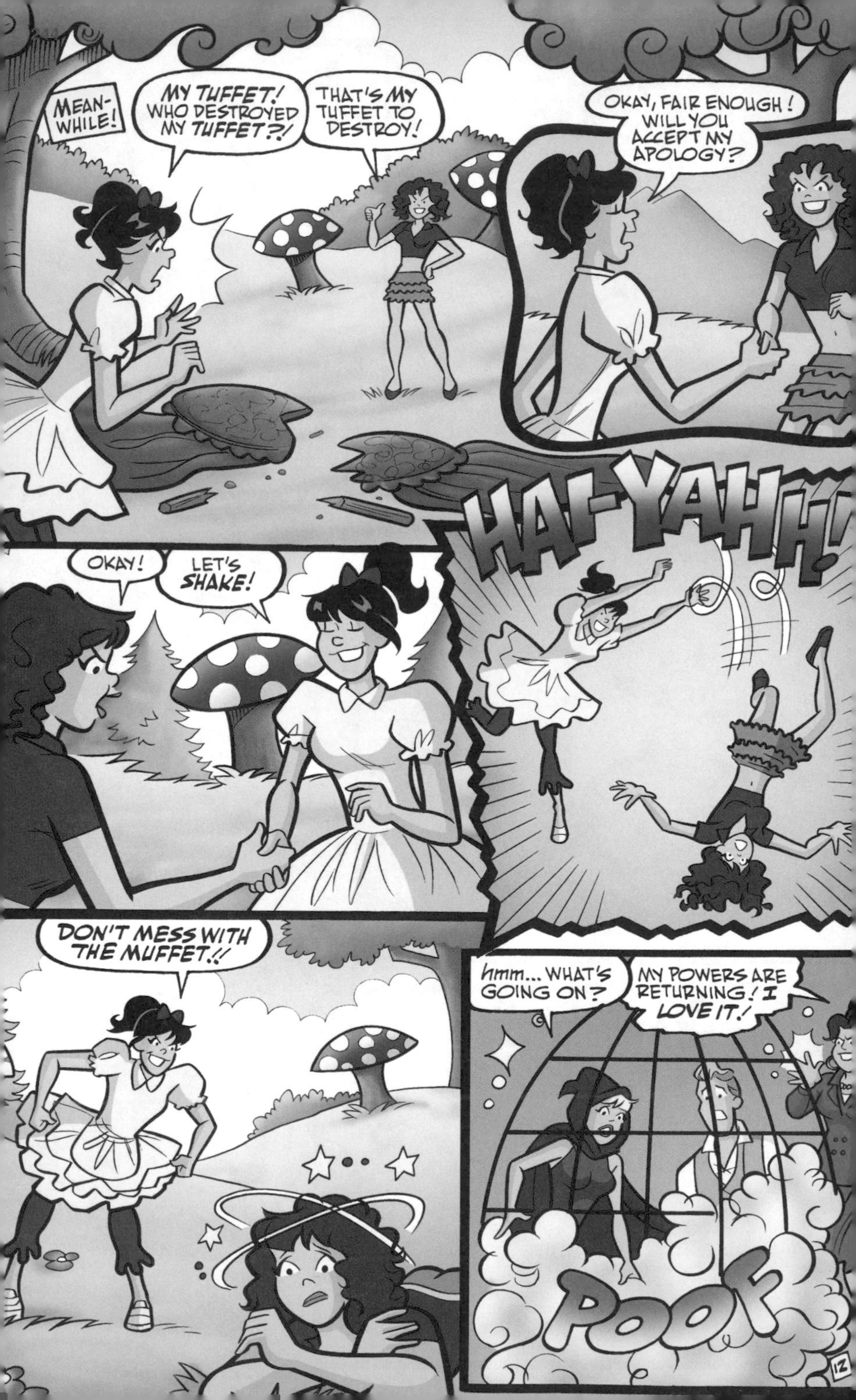
MEAN-WHILE!
MY TUFFET! WHO DESTROYED MY TUFFET?!
THAT'S MY TUFFET TO DESTROY!
OKAY, FAIR ENOUGH! WILL YOU ACCEPT MY APOLOGY?
OKAY!
LET'S SHAKE!
HAI-YAHH!
DON'T MESS WITH THE MUFFET!!
hmm... WHAT'S GOING ON?
MY POWERS ARE RETURNING! I LOVE IT!
POOF
12

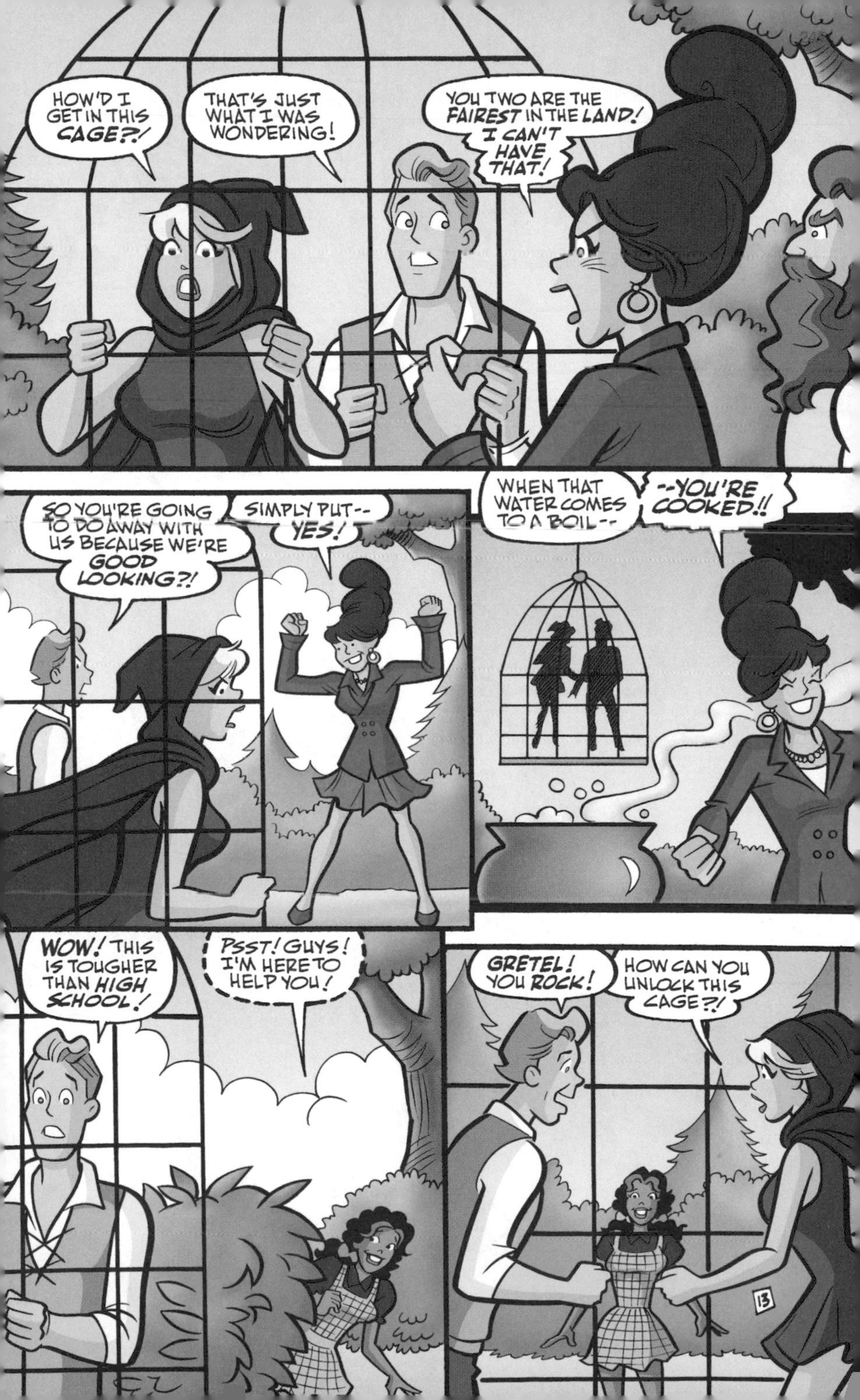
HOW'D I GET IN THIS CAGE?!
THAT'S JUST WHAT I WAS WONDERING!
YOU TWO ARE THE FAIREST IN THE LAND! I CAN'T HAVE THAT!
SO YOU'RE GOING TO DO AWAY WITH US BECAUSE WE'RE GOOD LOOKING?!
SIMPLY PUT-- YES!
WHEN THAT WATER COMES TO A BOIL--
--YOU'RE COOKED!!
WOW! THIS IS TOUGHER THAN HIGH SCHOOL!
PSST! GUYS! I'M HERE TO HELP YOU!
GRETEL! YOU ROCK!
HOW CAN YOU UNLOCK THIS CAGE?!
13

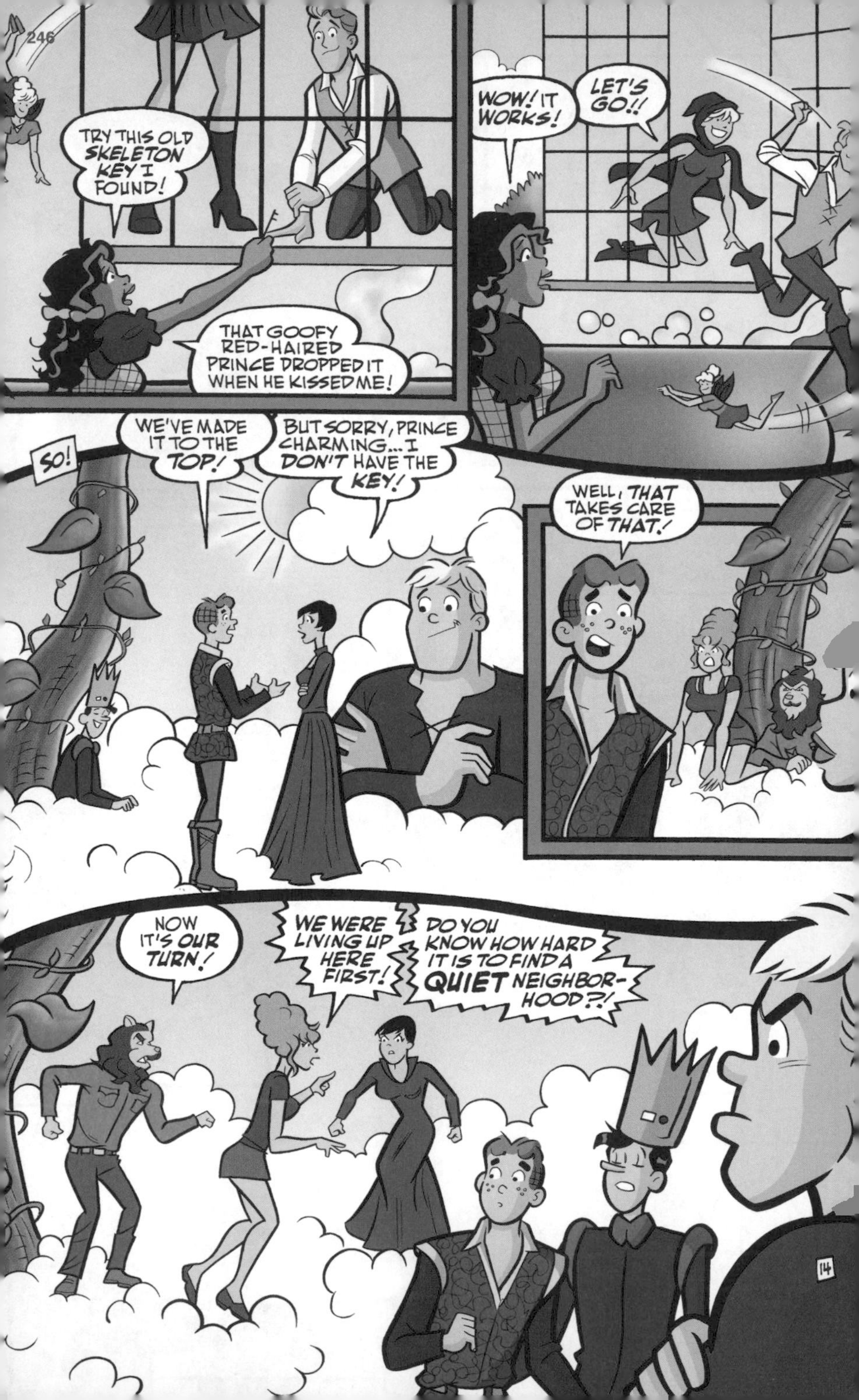
TRY THIS OLD SKELETON KEY I FOUND!
THAT GOOFY RED-HAIRED PRINCE DROPPED IT WHEN HE KISSED ME!
WOW! IT WORKS!
LET'S GO!!
SO!
WE'VE MADE IT TO THE TOP!
BUT SORRY, PRINCE CHARMING... I DON'T HAVE THE KEY!
WELL, THAT TAKES CARE OF THAT!
NOW IT'S OUR TURN!
WE WERE LIVING UP HERE FIRST!
DO YOU KNOW HOW HARD IT IS TO FIND A QUIET NEIGHBOR-HOOD?!
14

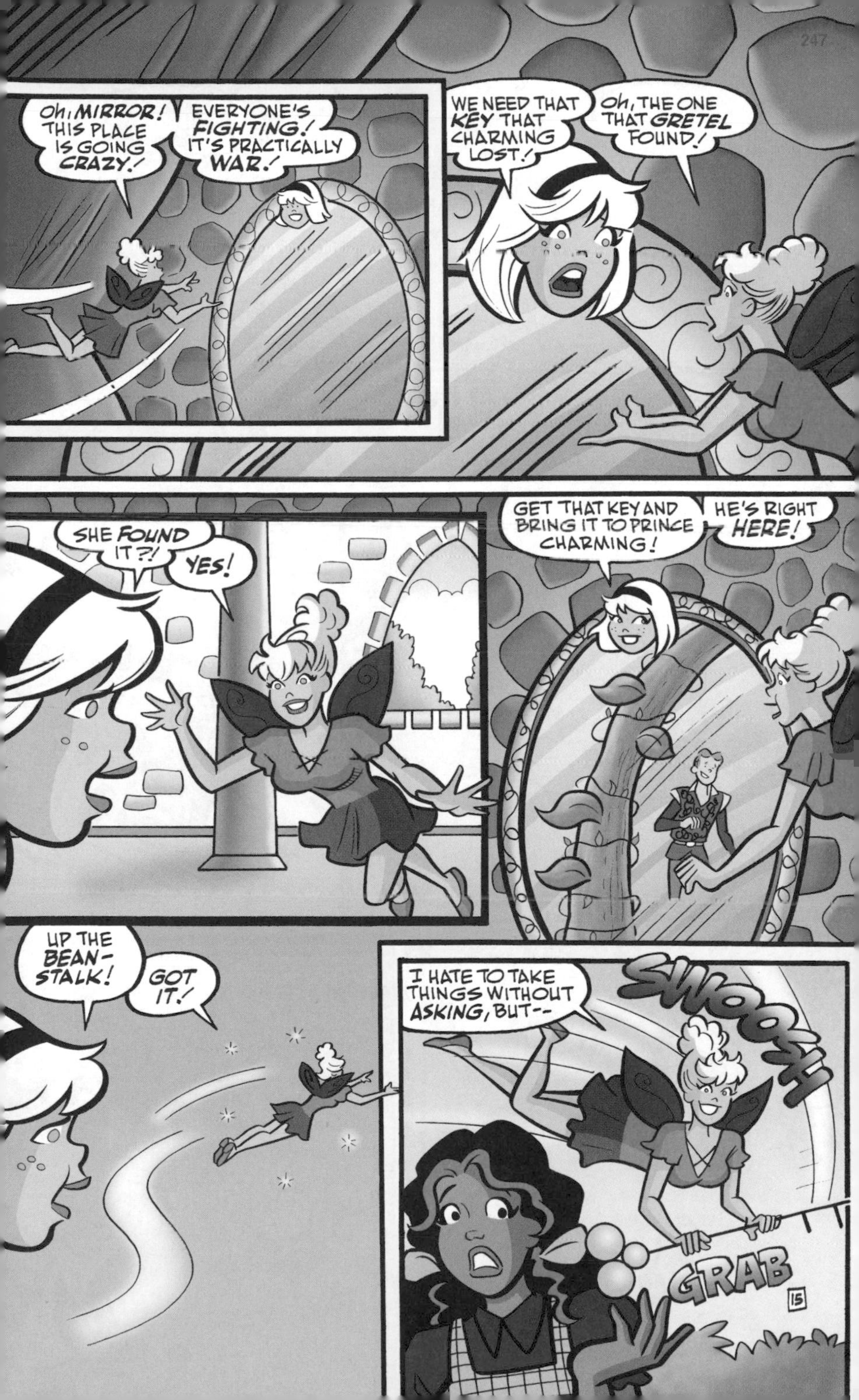
Oh, MIRROR! THIS PLACE IS GOING CRAZY!
EVERYONE'S FIGHTING! IT'S PRACTICALLY WAR!
WE NEED THAT KEY THAT CHARMING LOST!
Oh, THE ONE THAT GRETEL FOUND!
SHE FOUND IT?!
YES!
GET THAT KEY AND BRING IT TO PRINCE CHARMING!
HE'S RIGHT HERE!
UP THE BEAN-STALK!
GOT IT!
I HATE TO TAKE THINGS WITHOUT ASKING, BUT--
SWOOSH
GRAB
15

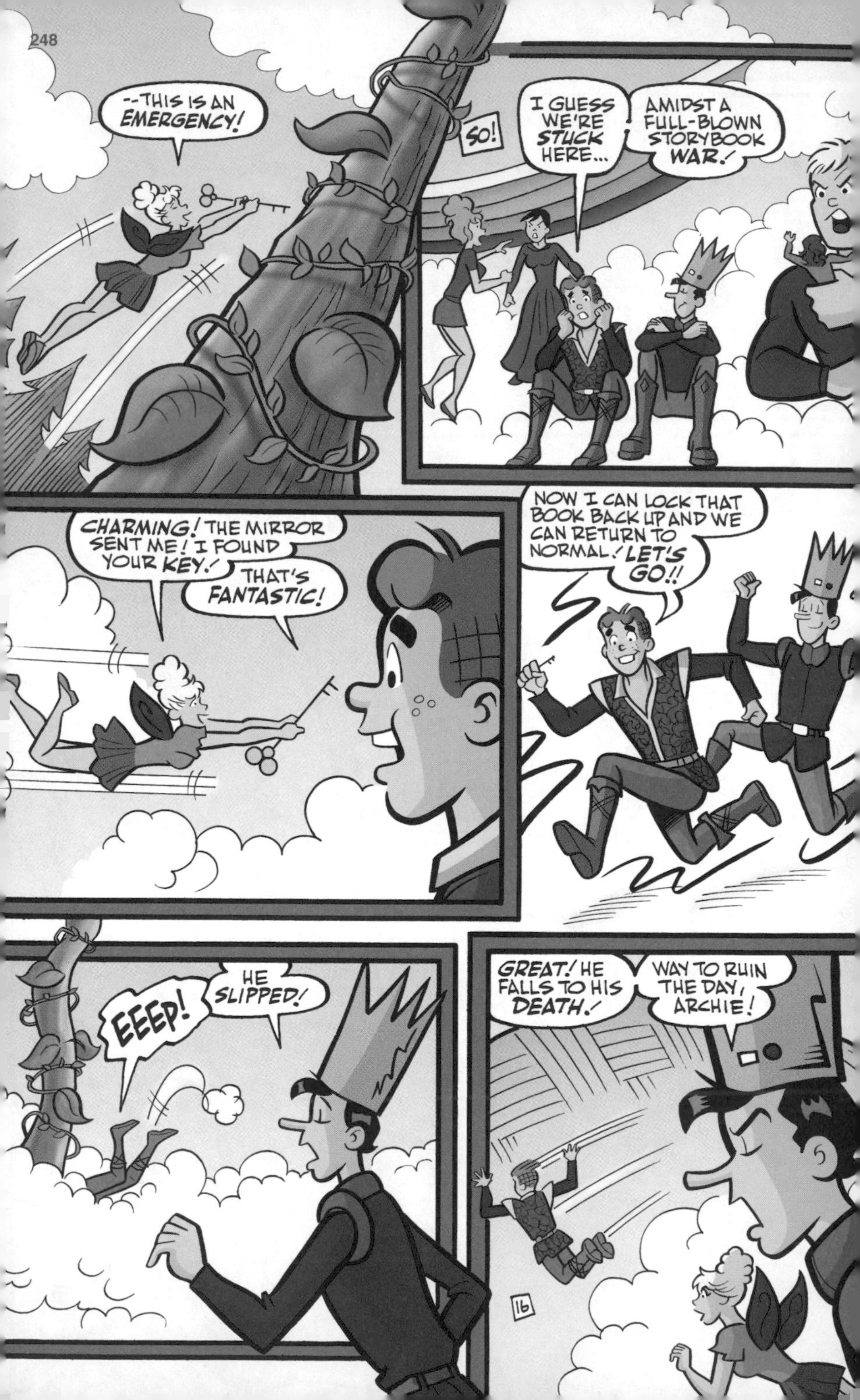
--THIS IS AN EMERGENCY!
SO!
I GUESS WE'RE STUCK HERE...
AMIDST A FULL-BLOWN STORYBOOK WAR!
CHARMING! THE MIRROR SENT ME! I FOUND YOUR KEY!
THAT'S FANTASTIC!
NOW I CAN LOCK THAT BOOK BACK UP AND WE CAN RETURN TO NORMAL! LET'S GO!!
EEEP!
HE SLIPPED!
GREAT! HE FALLS TO HIS DEATH!
WAY TO RUIN THE DAY, ARCHIE!
16

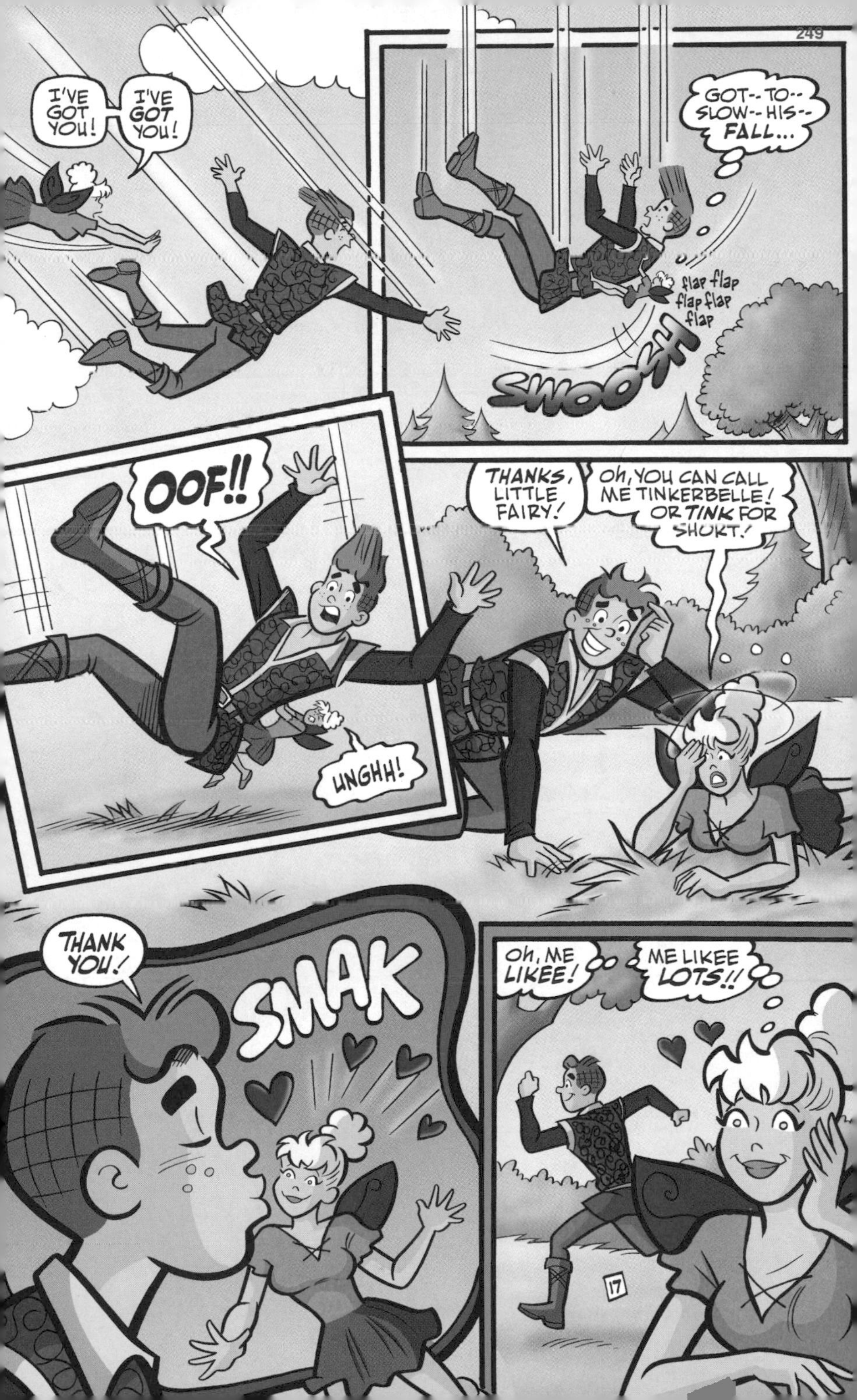
I'VE GOT YOU!
I'VE GOT YOU!
GOT-- TO-- SLOW-- HIS-- FALL...
flap flap flap flap flap
SWOOSH
OOF!!
UNGHH!
THANKS, LITTLE FAIRY!
Oh, YOU CAN CALL ME TINKERBELLE! OR TINK FOR SHORT!
THANK YOU!
SMAK
Oh, ME LIKEE!
ME LIKEE LOTS!!
17

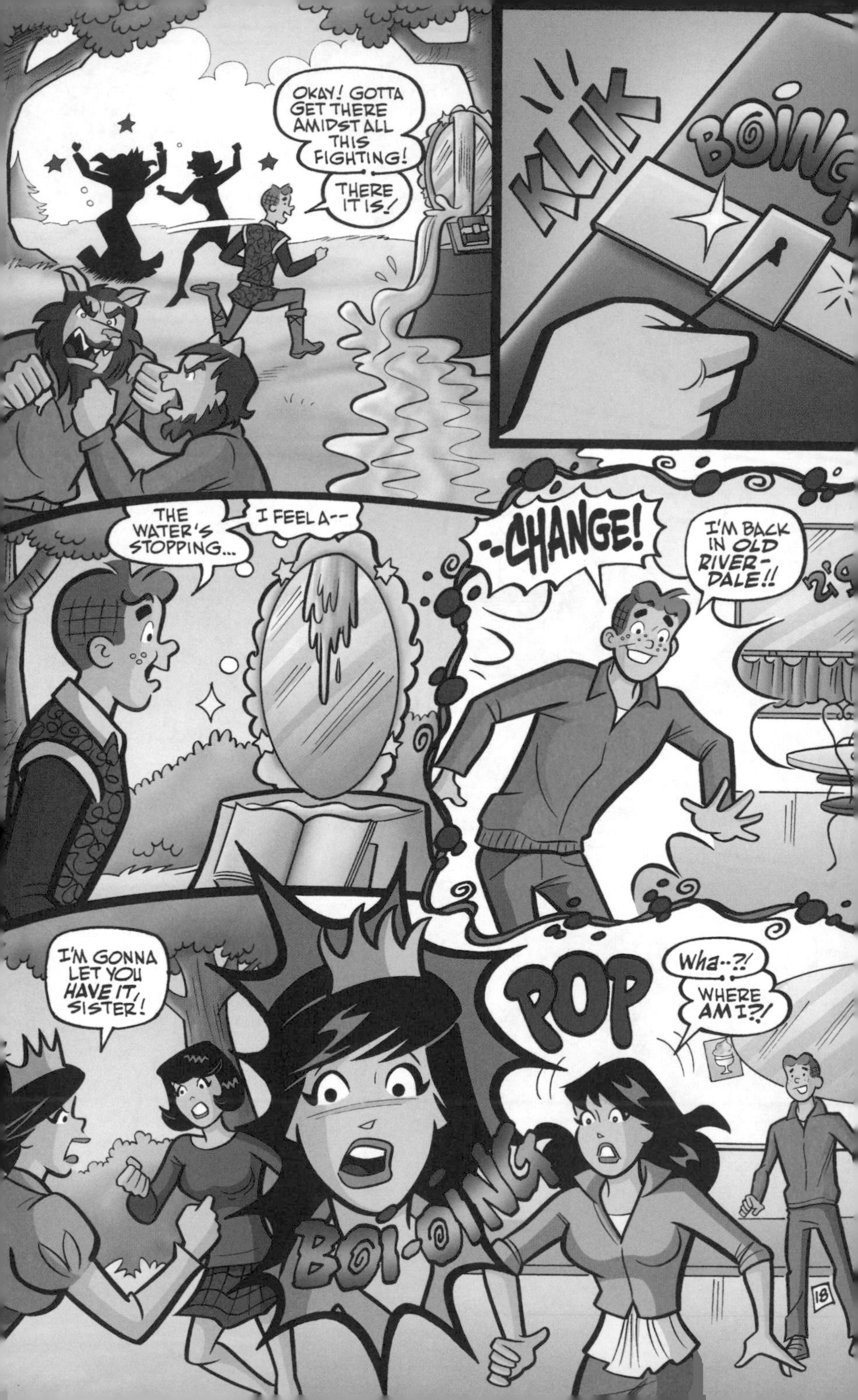
OKAY! GOTTA GET THERE AMIDST ALL THIS FIGHTING!
THERE IT IS!
KLIK
BOING
THE WATER'S STOPPING...
I FEEL A--
--CHANGE!
I'M BACK IN OLD RIVERDALE!!
I'M GONNA LET YOU HAVE IT, SISTER!
POP
Wha--?!
WHERE AM I?!
BOI-OING
18

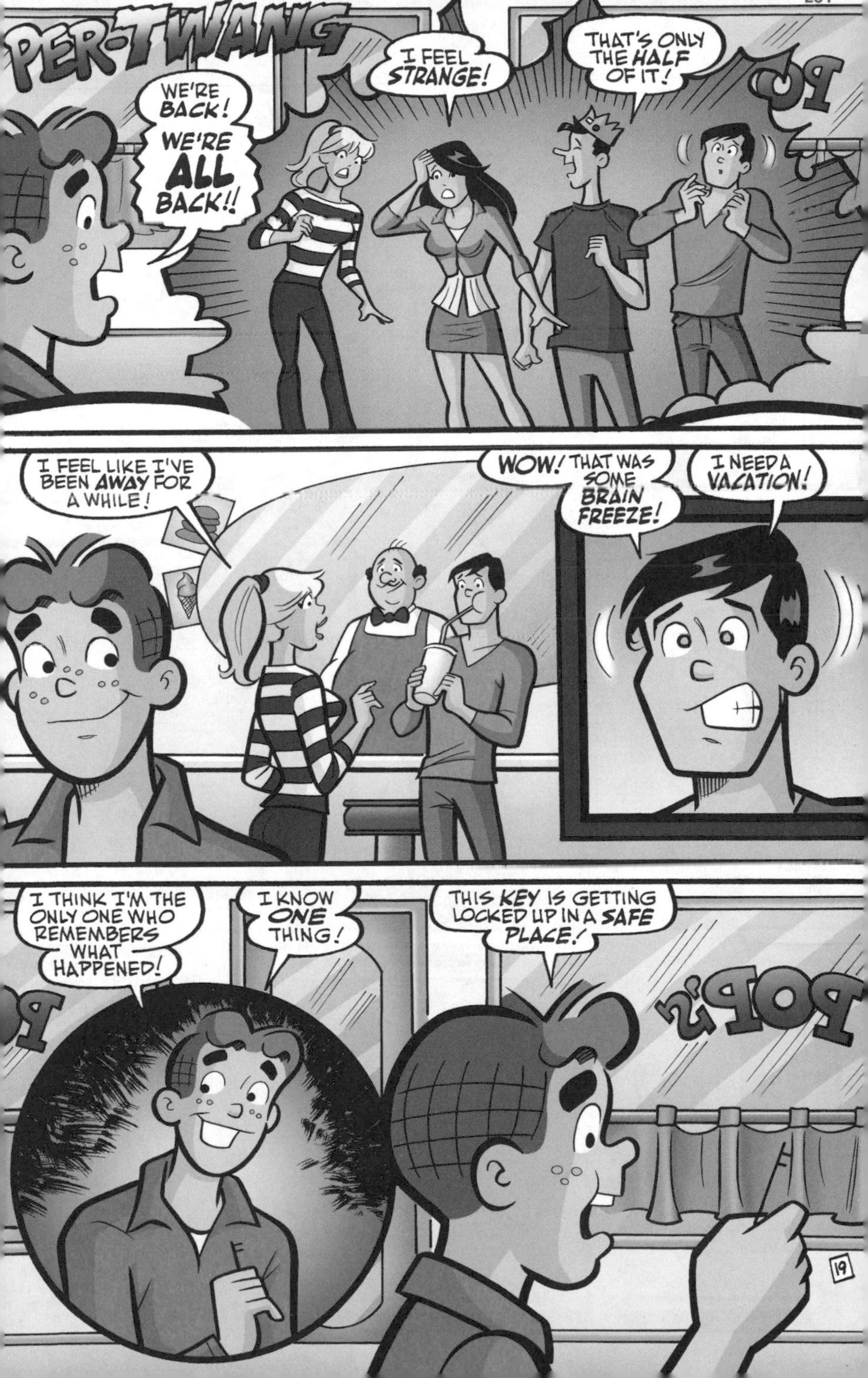
PER-TWANG
WE'RE BACK! WE'RE ALL BACK!!
I FEEL STRANGE!
THAT'S ONLY THE HALF OF IT!
I FEEL LIKE I'VE BEEN AWAY FOR A WHILE!
WOW! THAT WAS SOME BRAIN FREEZE!
I NEED A VACATION!
I THINK I'M THE ONLY ONE WHO REMEMBERS WHAT HAPPENED!
I KNOW ONE THING!
THIS KEY IS GETTING LOCKED UP IN A SAFE PLACE!
19

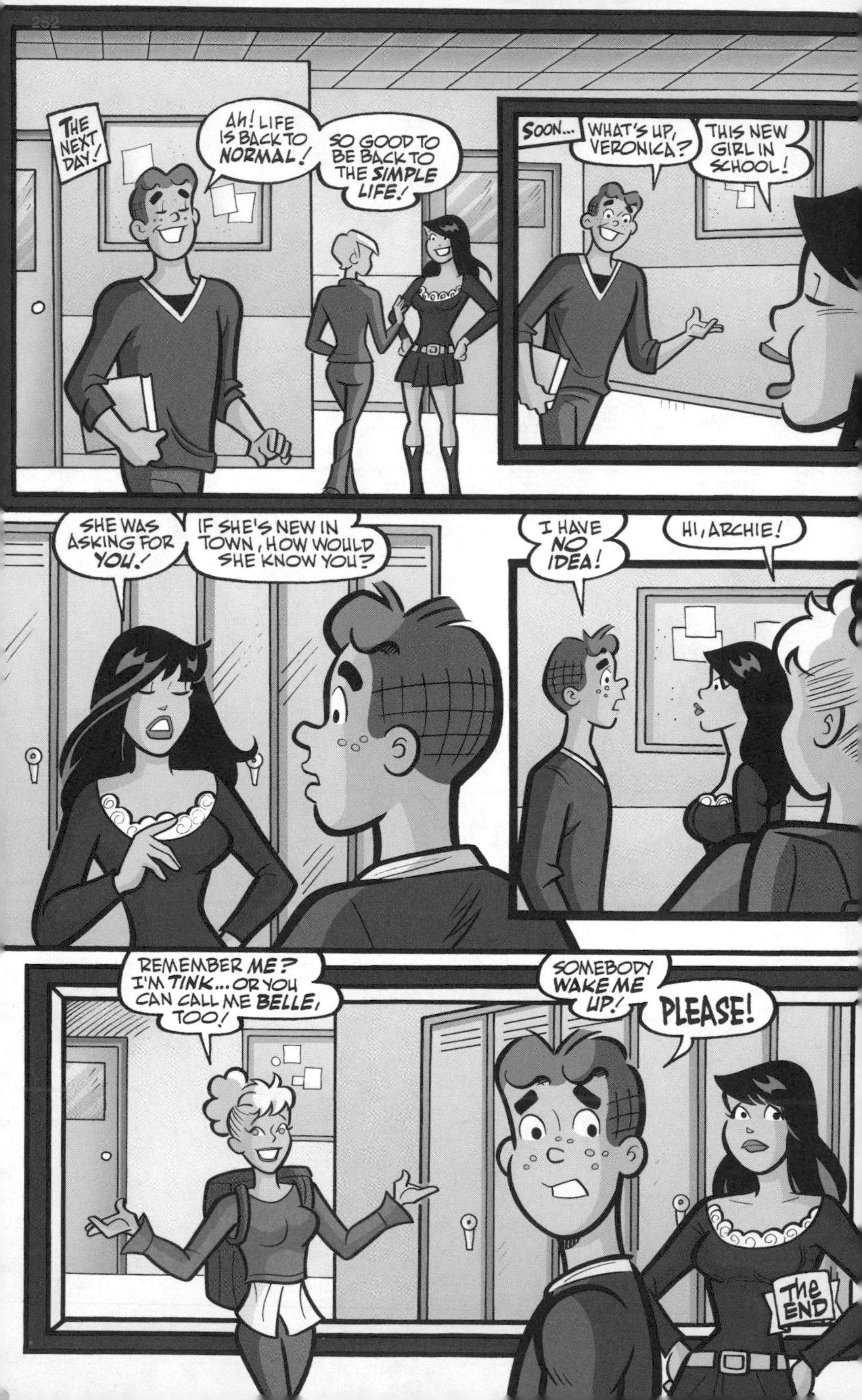
THE NEXT DAY!
Ah! LIFE IS BACK TO NORMAL!
SO GOOD TO BE BACK TO THE SIMPLE LIFE!
SOON...
WHAT'S UP, VERONICA?
THIS NEW GIRL IN SCHOOL!
SHE WAS ASKING FOR YOU!
IF SHE'S NEW IN TOWN, HOW WOULD SHE KNOW YOU?
I HAVE NO IDEA!
HI, ARCHIE!
REMEMBER ME? I'M TINK...OR YOU CAN CALL ME BELLE, TOO!
SOMEBODY WAKE ME UP!
PLEASE!
The END

 AFTERWORD
* BY DAN PARENT

I hope you enjoyed reading these classic tales, re-imagined with Archie, Jughead, Reggie, Betty & Veronica taking center stage as classic, literary characters.

It's so great that after all these years our fans keep coming back for more! I'd like to think it's because of the fantastic stories and art from myself and all of our amazing writers and artists, but we know the truth. It's the greatness of the Archie characters. And I should know. I'm still a big Archie fan. Before I started working here I was an Archie fan. And more than ever, I still am. That's why I still get excited writing and drawing these stories.

I only hope that we can continue to live up to your expectations and continue to bring you our very best and make you feel as if you are a part of Riverdale.

After all, Archie IS for everyone!

Variant Cover Gallery

See how some more amazing artists re-imagine these classic fairy tale stories with a Betty and Veronica spin!

Alitha Martinez takes on Rapunzel, Renae De Liz adapts Beauty and the Beast, Jill Thompson makes over Sleeping Beauty, Fiona Staples transforms The Little Mermaid and Stephanie Buscema reinvents Rumpelstiltskin!

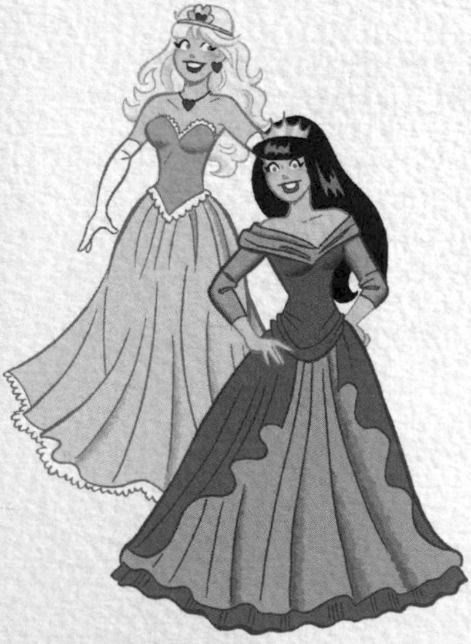

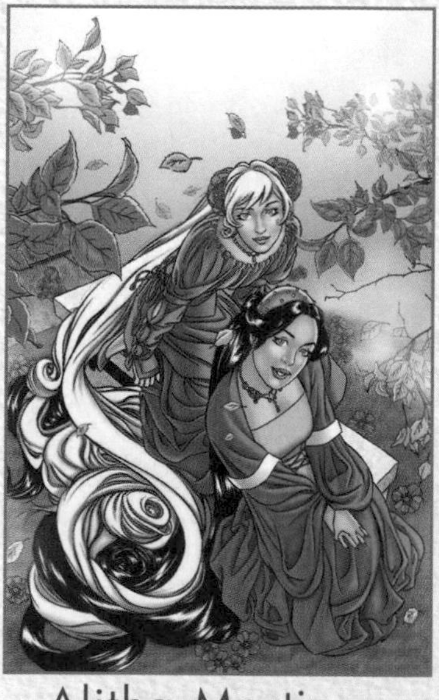

Alitha Martinez